I0819876

Thunder Road: Ice and Fire

Novels published by Midnight Fire Media

Your Own Fate
Night on Earth
Dreams Belong to the Night
ShadowWalk
Alarums of Reality
Afterglow Dust
Black Dragon
Falling

The Janus Clan series:

The Defenseless
The Slaves
Birds Flying in the Dark
At the End of the Rainbow

Poetry:

Amos Keppler: Complete Poems 1989 – 2003
Secrets - Descriptions of what cannot be described

(A few of the) novels to be published:

Afterglow Rain
Season of the Witch
Red Shadow
Lewis of Modern York
Fangs and Claws of the Earth
Forsaken

For a «complete» list of current and current future Amos Keppler and Midnight Fire Media projects see the Midnight Fire/Midnight Fire Media web pages.

Thunder Road:
Ice and Fire

By

Amos Keppler

MIDNIGHT FIRE MEDIA
2016

Midnight Fire Media

http://midnight-fire.net/mfm
For more about Thunder Road:
http://midnight-fire.net/tr

E-Mail:
Amos13@midnight-fire.net
manofhood@yahoo.com

Cover, text, design, premedia, art and photos Amos Keppler

ISBN 978-82-91693-21-7

STORYTELLER'S WORD - (1994)

During the preparations and the actual writing of this novel I had to, more than usual pick and choose between what should and shouldn't be included. The source material is so immense, the potential incidents so numerous that this could just as well have become a novel of a million words, instead of the approximately two hundred thousand. Some technical details had to be left out because of sheer necessity. The sum of the parts, the conclusion of everything, however, is still overwhelmingly obvious. There's more than enough literature and information, both official and alternative to find out what's going on. And you don't really need to read a single word for that, anyway. You just have to look around you, to look at the world as it is, not the way you're told it is.

I've chosen to emphasize the human factor and the prevalent changes we see today and will see tomorrow, no matter what humanity is or is not doing. To grow up in the stone desert's gray society, is like being constantly on a battlefield. Your senses are slowly, surely drugged and you're bleeding to death from a thousand small cuts. The current local, national and global society is a tailspin suicide run and it's not improving but worsening by the minute. It's getting progressively worse, not better. The world is not improving in any significant way. Humanity takes one step forward, ten leaps backwards.

There is no way this story can be told in a realistic manner. Reality will always, in every way, surpass imagination. The suffering, the violence, the river of blood, the total collapse of the horrible, artificial society we've constructed around ourselves, between us and the natural world, is an event without parallel in our history. There is no need to exaggerate the description of the coming decades. We can hardly imagine, far less admit to ourselves what's coming. This is the farthest I come from reality, without painting a way too rosy picture.

AMOS KEPPLER
Fire and Ice, Heaven and Hell, Thunder Road
April 1, 1994, July 7, 2004, October 13, 2011, June 20, 2016
(according to western, christian time-frame)
It is no April's Fool

This is a stand alone, independent continuation of the story told in Dreams Belong to the Night (1991, 2002, 2012).

PART ONE: ICE AND FIRE

«It's not only our fate
but our business to
lose innocence, and
once we have lost
that, it is futile to
attempt a picnic in Eden»

ELISABETH BOWEN

«It was like the Niagara Falls on flat ground»
Flood victim Risør, Norway 1996

RAGNARO'K

The end times described in Norse mythology.
The time when fire and ice meet, and the gods fall
and human civilization is collapsing under its own weight…

JOTUNHEIM

Steam rises from land heated by burning sun.
Huge drops of water flows from burning ice.
Jotun mountains covered in clouds of smoke and water.
Wet clouds release their heavy load.
Many a cloud pushed at the mountain.
Climbing, climbing, releasing its heavy load.
Flames from fires lit in secret place reach high.
Fire meets ice, half down, half up.
Ice is strengthened, fire is strengthened.
Ymir and Surtur's armies arrive simultaneously at the mountain farm.
All the nine worlds become one.
Heimdahl's bugle roared and no one could keep out its thunder.

The veil closing off humanity's vision from the unknown and hidden worlds was torn aside. In land and village, deep within the Stone Desert's tall spires.

Smoke rises from these spires only from ashes, and poisons the land and everything walking and breathing there.

Jotunheim, a disharmonic tone, followed by a whistle. Nine whistles sounding like one.

Nine hooded creatures meet at the mountain farm. Call them Jotun or Aesir or whatever you want. They have had many names.

Fires herald their arrival. The table is set: No food. No food is set. No one welcomes the guests. This place, Midgard has nothing more to give.

They have an ugly cough, all these nine and pull their cloaks tight around their skinny hides. So warm is the mountain, so warm is the wind and so frosty is still those who come from far away. Long and far have they ruled the nine and one worlds.

And their time has come to an end.

The Earth itself shakes. Not just in part, but in full. At a place in the immediate low land the world was blinded in a storm of elemental fire. The metal spires in one stone desert melted and transformed into glass.

– Other children of man will follow in our tracks here and seek the secrets of life, one said curtly. He sat so close to the fire that the rags surrounding his hide and bones were charred. – They have to, in order to rediscover what it means to be human.

– It's pretty funny, another acknowledged. – Damn hysterical, if you ask me. They have my sympathies.

Everybody sat still, in a moment's calm. It was so long since they had seen themselves as human beings.

– Hopefully and probably they will have a higher degree of success than we did, one

cried in despair.
– Shut thy ragged mouth, The Big One snarled.
They pulled away from him in a rush, but not so fast and so far they would once have done.
It was he who had called himself The One. Through trickery and brutality he had gained power over them all and ruled since. He had taken their discoveries of power and a living death ever further. Until Styx itself - the very river of death, knowledge and life - dried up.
Something worked itself up through his throat. The others looked attentive at him, raising their head.
He coughed a single time, fell on his side, and expired with a rattling sound. In the river of blood flowing from his mouth and onto the withered grass, crawled both worms and other creeps.
If this had happened earlier, perhaps they would have been able to take advantage of the fact that he was the first to slip into the nothingness. Now, it was too late. It could no longer be stopped. Nothing could. It had gone too far. The men and the women remained on their spot, desiccated statues without substance, life and fire.
Ragnarok is here. Human insanity has fucked with the earth for ten thousand years. The forces of nature finally gather for retaliation. The Midgard Serpent is crawling over the land. Surtur the fire demon burns the air, boils the sea and makes water pour from the sky. The Fenris Wolf is running, crushing dry skulls under its heavy paws. Its wide-open mouth is spitting fire.
Dust whirls in the air, showing no signs of descending. Rivers of blood become raging waterfalls. Tears drown in the vortex of red and black. Silence roars in endless space.
Silence rules in Aasgaard, near silence in Jotunheim. Only those traveling close to distant worlds hear the rush of Death. Every storm starts with quiet and breathless silence, until it starts blowing and without mercy ravaging everything and everyone in its wake. It lasts an eternity within an eternity.
The wind carried Death to all corners of the globe.

THE LIVING PLANET

The globe kept spinning, kept circling the sun, following the Galaxy on its journey through the Universe. Seen from Space nothing significant had changed. In the cold of Space one didn't notice the poison spreading to every nook and cranny down there. Spread your wings and strive to fly, and it paralyzes you.
Fly above factory pipes and between the stone desert's spires and the gray blinds you. Fly wild and free a single moment, and your glued eyes open… You sense everything they have taught you to forget.
The deserts are growing. You can see it, no matter how many telling you differently. The outskirts of Sahara have already reached Europe, in areas where life for a long while, now, has lived on scarce soil. At Greenland's southern point it's easy to tell that the lichen, the symbiosis of mushroom and moss, is withering across vast areas. As it is in Norwegian mountains. Along the edge of Antarctica, there is a huge hole in Earth's

protection against cosmic rays. In Chile sheep and their shepherds walk around with white, blind eyes under the Sun's ruthless radiation. What reaches them undiluted. In the cities, in the stone deserts, ever more people have trouble breathing. The air, the water, the ground, yes, even the fire is contaminated.

Mother's milk is choke-full of Dioxin, one of the most dangerous chemicals mankind has ever made.

We're constantly poisoned, from cradle to grave.

But forget for a moment the physical poison. You do that anyway, do your very best to forget it again and again and again.

The physiological breakdown is, after all, just another symptom of the horrible disease, the society of technology and the anti-nomad. What present society does with our will, our spirit, our humanity is what truly matters. We got stuck a long time ago. Hunters and nomads turned into farmers and city dwellers, and we lost our ancient contact with nature. Now, we're merely stumbling through our gray surroundings, a pale, broken figure, into the twilight. We're all so badly suited to the life we're born to live.

Your entire life you have seen things go from bad to worse to horrible. We're brainwashed from cradle to grave to be something we are not. You may try to fool yourself into believing it isn't that bad… but you know it is, at least if you want to be honest with yourself.

Humanity has lived so long out of touch with the living planet. We have hurt it - and ourselves - for so long. We look at it - and ourselves - as living (or dead) machines. We have lost patience with it. And ourselves. We claim to be its master. Our own masters. Push down the lid of a boiling kettle, and the pressure will only increase. The kettle doesn't need to have its own, conscious thoughts, but it will always behave like a boiling kettle.

The Mystery, joy-filled, ancient, numerous truths are rejected, and the suffering explodes. Suffering may be an inevitable part of life, but not a dominating part. The way the eager followers of technology and the singular path preach about. The ancient knowledge about the shadows and life's thunder, and what's hidden is rediscovered minute by minute every day, second by second every black night.

Ice is melting all over the planet. The sea is rising. The winds are increasing in strength and numbers. We human beings have lived ten thousand years in the gray shadow of our own insanity.

And our time has come.

CHAPTER ONE

Damon Terrill, the Storm Child, was born into the world in the morning on January 23, 1994 (western, christian time frame).

It was sudden, several days before he was due. He just slipped out, so easy that it was almost shocking. He made his first primal scream in a dirty attic in the coastal city of Bergen, in the western part of Norway, Northern Europe.

The wind increased tenfold outside. The first, abrupt labor pain began. The world welcomed Damon while the storm was at its strongest. Outside the small window broken glass, tiles, trees flew by… An entire roof crashed into the neighboring house. Emmet Terrill rushed to the window and stared out. He had never seen its like, not anything even resembling this. As he stared he witnessed how part of a chimney hit a parked car and buried itself in its hood.

– It's creepy out there, he mumbled.

That morning it was very dangerous to walk through the streets of Bergen. In addition to tiles and broken glass flying through the air like projectiles, signs and iron poles were twisted into unrecognizable works of art. Roads had to be closed because of all the fallen trees, broken like twigs. It was a small miracle that people were not killed already during the initial gusts.

Not long before 8.45 the hotel oilrig Polyconcord tore itself loose from «secure» berths at the Laksevåg Warf, and drifted at high speed towards the Puddefjord Bridge, one of the main access roads to central Bergen. Traffic was barred from the bridge around nine. Not long after that the oilrig crashed into it.

Elin collapsed exhausted and weary, surrounded in the blankets Emmet had tucked her. She tapped Damon on the back, and the first scream rose from him, choiring the enormous energy discharge outside. She took the boy into her arms, both jubilant and fearful. He didn't need milk the first few hours, but she pulled him tight, and patted and rubbed him. Rhythmic moves that calmed both mother and son. Suddenly everything seemed that much quieter. She closed her eyes and dozed off a bit, wondering if the wind had lulled just a little. She felt she had reason to be hopeful. It seemed like the noise wasn't that loud outside.

Another howl. A ghost in the night. The window quite simply vanished, vanished without a trace, from one microsecond to the next. The door to the room opened so hard that it crashed into the wall. The wind seemed to *fill* the room. The wind… and the Storm itself. Everything in the room suddenly levitated, as if gravity had just been suspended. The bed began shaking. Elin screamed.

– We need to go, Emmet cried, – go far, far away.

He realized what he had just said and shrunk in his tracks, turning small and weary.

But where do we go? Where is it safe?

Nowhere, the spirits of wind and death hissed, nowhere on Earth.

Emmet lifted his wife, and fled with her down the stairs. She clutched the baby in her arms. Emmet rushed down the stairs, seemingly without noticing his burden. The glass was gone in every single window. Elin's hair blew in his face and blocked his view. Sweat burned in his eyes. His forehead was wrinkled in concentration as he took the first steps on the floor below.

He kicked at the first door he reached, several times, until there was a reply.

– I c-can't open the d-door, they heard the insane voice from inside. – The wind will be let inside.

– My wife has just given birth, Emmet cried desperately. – God damn it, man!

– You can go to hell, the hysterical voice cried from inside. – I'm warning you. Don't make any attempt to get in. I'll fiiiiiiire.

They heard him cocking his gun.

– I'm not letting in the wind, they heard him mumble. – It carries the spirits of the dead, do you HEAR me

Emmet went desperately at all the doors. Either his knocking or shouting was ignored, or there was a brief, sulky rejection. Elin sat down with her back to a wall. Her wet hair, just as black as his, stuck to her body. The few pieces of cloth she wore were glued to moist skin. She was still sweating a lot, and this place was very cold, ice cold. He ran up to the attic again. The heart hammered in his chest in fear and rage. Everything floated in chaotic patterns up there, but he managed to grab a mattress and a few sheets and blankets. Later he would never quite understand how he had been able to carry everything through tight doorways and down steep, narrow stairs.

They pulled tight to each other on the floor and packed themselves in as thorough as they possibly could. The child had found a nipple and sucked energetically on it, filled with hunger. Emmet sensed how the unrest inside let up. He allowed himself to calm down, but never beyond a certain point. The unrest he had carried with him all his life didn't allow that, and it made him strangely relaxed.

Elin looked at him, touching him affectionately.

– Only fools forget the rule about always expecting the unexpected, he said. – If there is anything like one golden rule or rules at all, there is this, in this world of eternal thunder. If there is quiet for a while… what does it matter? Everybody knows this. Not everybody wants to acknowledge it, but they *know*.

Warmth surrounded them. They shared it joyfully and unconditionally, and it grew bigger than the sum of the parts.

– Perhaps they reacted to my accent? He joked.

– You don't have any, she responded dryly. – They are in the habit of reacting. Period!

– It's like this all over the present day world, he said empathically. – People are taught to discard the boiling in their blood, the thunder in their hearts.

– He won't. She kissed the child on the head. – Damon Terrill is born to challenge the Storm.

Emmet didn't say more. There was no need. They had always had an intense, intimate contact from the very first moment they met. They held hands and coddled tight. Somewhat convulsive, but they didn't care. While the storm raged on outside, and most other people shook fearfully in their homes, the two of them slept peacefully through the noise and the powerful, cold draft.

Cold wind from the south. Glaciers in a landscape of hot sand. Images and sensations chased him from his dream back to full consciousness. Emmet opened his eyes and lifted his head. He listened, wondering if the wind had quieted. At least its rage had faded a bit. He patted Elin on the nearest shoulder. Eyes met eyes. She nodded. He returned calmly to the attic and found some thick clothes. And necessities of whatever

may still be available.
– Let's get out of here, he said.
Out in the streets. Everybody passed so fast, so slowly for their eyes. They both sensed it, the paralyzing cold, the fire burning and warming. The frost clearing their thoughts. Focusing it enormously.
Is it possible? They thought.
Wondering if ice and fire could coexist like this, glimpsing it every time they blinked, so illogical, so beyond all reason. They clutched each other, silently taking in the confusion and the chaos they saw wherever they went.
A car had been flattened by a tree. A man took a photo of it with a sad look in his eyes. The two of them arrived at the bridge. The oilrig still pushed at it. A sandbank had softened the behemoth's speed, reducing the impact of the crash. There was no major damage, but it took time and effort before the behemoth had been removed. Traffic didn't start up again until the next morning, in spite of the congestion on the secondary roads. They heard about the kid that had been killed. A woman told them as she passed by. There was so much horror, like spikes of ice missing the heart, or spikes glowing, like the center of a sun.
– Time is quite… indistinct, isn't it? She said. – Ephemeral.
Since this morning everything had stretched and shrunk to nothing. Thunder and lighting rolled simultaneously and there was little beyond that.
– The way it has been today… is the way it has always been, he said slowly.
Emmet and Elin understood the moment their eyes met, the truth they had known for a long time. They watched, driven by curiosity as people gathered in the streets, but the smiles froze and in their deeper eyes the fear was unmistakable.
The couple heard the voice whispering in what might not be their ears.
This is so transitory, isn't it, all this? We're taught that a city is forever, but nothing is, and certainly not such a Stone Desert, such a rejection of the generous nature.
– This is a Stone Desert, she said abruptly.
He nodded with wide eyes.
They moved through the city, the ghost town. Elin hugged the baby, desperate to grant it whatever heat she could provide. People surrounding the couple and the tiny bundle resembled ghosts, people waiting for, expecting the next giant shoe to drop, knowing beyond knowing that there would be no rescue, no evacuation from this place of the dead.
– The storm has passed, a man said. – What was all the fuss about? It was just wind.
Elin heard the forced laughter following the outrageous statement.
– The denial has already started, she said. – In their despair they're rejecting the nightmare, the truth.
– But it will never fade completely, Emmet pointed out, – not even in their never awakened minds. There isn't really a sense of relief. It has hardly even *started* yet, and they know it.
They glimpsed, a vision shared tiny waves on a sunny beach, a horizon filled with seething dark clouds.
People gathered in smaller or bigger groups. Elin and Emmet passed them and heard snippets of what they were talking about. It was mostly about one thing and one thing only: The weather. It dominated the conversation and was no longer just a means to

keep an exchange of words without spark going. The sparks flew and gained further strength in the wind.

– Darn, they seem to be reporting about more harsh weather somewhere every day these days…

– They do and not even including everything. Storms that would have been big news ten years ago are hardly noticed, not worth mentioning anymore.

And on another spot:

– Storms, floods, droughts, when will it *end?*

Twisted, insane sculptures appeared wherever they looked, as if an artist in an ivory tower had succumbed to madness and ended up in the worst kind of hellish asylum. One working day and night, without breaks, from his stand beyond, sweating and cursing to make the garbage heap look different from a garbage heap.

Images and sensations kept assaulting the couple on their walk.

Elin hummed to the boy while he attempted to grab the big finger she poked in his chest. He looked at her with unexpected clear eyes, his night black eyes. She wondered if all newborns were like this, so confident and so certain of where they belonged, so curious. In the night sky threatening to drown her, she sensed all the world's wisdom, heaven and hell, ice and fire… the Thunder Road making a turn.

The eyes closed and he slept.

– He's big, isn't he? Emmet wondered. – I mean, *really* big?

– Bigger than big, she chuckled. – Both sides of his family are filled with big people, but he will probably become bigger than all of us.

– Good!

She looked up. What he implied with that single word, the tone in his voice sounded so unlike him.

Thunder from close and distant horizons spread soundlessly from shivering feet, to bodies shaking in the storm. Thoughts formed. They felt an insane rage rise within quickly conquered, for now. The thought had crossed their mind earlier, too. They had just not been able to speak it aloud, and didn't now either. It stuck in their throat, like a piece of coagulated blood.

What a hell for a child to be born into.

++++++++++++++++++++++++++++

They moved out of the city, to Elin's parents on Askøy. Damon grew up out there, a fairly long stretch north of the tight population center south on the island. The place was only about a twenty minutes' drive from central Bergen. In spite of this it could be mistaken for another world.

It wasn't.

Askøy seemed, in many ways like a Norway in miniature. There were mountains there, valleys, forests and skerries. There was room to roam, but no matter how deep into the forest people went, they always heard the disharmonic tone the four winds brought.

The house was ideally suited in a small forest glen, well protected from nature's whims, a fact making the neighbors grumble quite a bit. They had been forced to make a number of repairs on their homes in recent years.

– They don't know much, do they? Damon told his mother when the subject came up a day the two of them sat alone and watched the faraway tide in the horizon.

– They certainly don't, she replied, both somber and cheerful. – Your grandparents may not be that conscious concerning the world's woes, but they haven't cut all the trees around their house. They understand the fundamentals when it comes to humanity's place in nature. It's a symbiosis and it's better to work with it than against it.

East of the main road there was a much larger area of fairly untouched land. The kids called it the Bewitched Forest since they hardly could hear civilization's roar in there. There were some forest trails and lumber companies using them, but it didn't bother the kids too much in their secret tasks and they left it alone. The first few years, that is.

Childhood stretched out like a mist of memories. They always did, when he infrequently reached back with his thoughts.

Elin and Emmet were hired as consultants for the Ministry of the Environment in the Norwegian government after completing their university studies. They were quickly recognized internationally for their skills. But they also gained a reputation for excessive interpretation of available data (telling it straight up). In spite of this they kept their job for a while and enjoyed it… until the Ministry of the Environment was reorganized into the Norwegian Center for Sustainable Development. Their letter of resignation and the one from NCSD informing them they were fired crossed each other in the mail.

There was a lot of travel after that, as their new, independent consultation work took them all over the globe.

The ever larger dustbins around the Mediterranean illustrated what they saw everywhere. The desertification spread like wildfire on every continent, except Antarctica.

In Bangladesh people fought a hopeless battle against floods and the rising sea. In the Maldives they stopped fighting. The population quite simply jumped into their small and bigger boats and fled from there. Only a few reached land, and even fewer was granted asylum. Refugees remained drifters on the big oceans. Most of them died there.

But when the couple arrived in Mexico City, one of the world's most polluted cities, they truly gained a deeper insight of what awaited the world.

Flies swarmed in the damp, thick air. People attempted to breathe in the stench of thousands of garbage bags. Factories spat poison day and night. One could make heroic attempts at drying one's brow, keeping one's personal air free of smoke, in vain.

– Is this the world, Emmet? She asked him. – The world in fifteen years?

She spoke his name, a rare thing. He got goose bumps and she noticed.

People started dying «without obvious cause», as the government put it. What happened looked very similar to an AIDS-epidemic, except that people died much faster. Their immune system collapsed completely. The body virtually broke down into heaps of flesh. Doctors and scientists found no clear cause in the few victims they managed to study. A small infection could be sufficient. The victim died in a few days. And all the rotting bodies in houses and streets compounded the problem. Mexico was the first modern nation where everything, government, social structures, everything… broke.

– Rwanda and Burundi, the nation-wide chaos in China… small potatoes in comparison. Emmet spoke to a reporter from CNN in a bone-breaking queue at the airport. – Rudimentary structures remained somewhat intact there. Here? I don't know what's left, really, except rotting flesh.

Five policemen guarded the main entrance. They fired indiscriminately at the moving mass of desperate people. It was no use. People fell in droves, but they were simply stepped on and supplanted by the endless flow from behind. The policemen were torn apart. That was the last Elin saw before she ran towards the plane.

The Terrills succeeded by a hair's bread to escape the country in time. They practically held on to the plane's door as the metal bird rose and had to pull themselves inside. Both kept gasping in fright and shock for hours afterwards.

– A few minutes later...

She nodded. There was no need for him to elaborate.

No more planes left Mexico City.

They turned cautious, or at least more cautious, after that, even though they acknowledged willingly that no place was truly safe, or even approaching safe anymore.

The news from a country once called Mexico chased them everywhere they went. Television programs continued to probe the event for years.

– Mexico seemed like a fairly stable and secure society, the news anchor said, in a kind of editorial, – only hours before it exploded. Experts keep discussing its demise. Some say it's a one time incident... while others ask who's next...

– Experts! Elin snorted. – What do they know?

The brittle laughter was hardly audible.

They felt pretty down most of the time. All their efforts, their tiny victories didn't seem to make any difference. Every step forward was countered with ten leaps backwards.

But no matter how down they were, they were encouraged by the obvious fact that Damon loved traveling, loved each new place they visited. He didn't join them during all their international travels, only during holidays. They noticed, with a catching in their throat how his night black eyes caught everything, how they burned with curiosity and excitement and expectation of what life might grant.

Thoughts drifted, reached back to childhood's mist of memories. A few events stood out, events he knew to be self-experienced, what he knew he recalled without anyone having told him later.

One crystal-clear memory: He had been five. The news June 15, 1999 that two islands, Tebua Tarawa and Abanua in the Pacific had «sunk» in the ocean.

He had no personal memories of the millennium celebration, but recalled that he had seen video-footage of it a couple of years later, and seen how fake all of it was.

Spring lingered in the air this February evening. The Terrills had attended a festival arranged by the still existing Ministry of the Environment. The party speeches had been just that, bombastic words and phrases without substance, about how much was done to reduce the increase in pollution and how much better Norway was in this (and everything else) than other countries. Nothing seemed to disturb the peace until Elin took her stand. When she stepped down from the dais a few applauded and others expressed loudly their disapproval, but most of all her departure from politics was met with deafening silence.

The three of them left the meeting early. His parents walked so fast that Damon had to run to catch up. He looked at them with his curios eyes.

– «Things aren't good at all», Emmet imitated. – «In fact, they can hardly get any worse, except they will be, if today's lax attitudes prevail, unless the crucial work truly begins, not tomorrow, not today, but the day before yesterday».

Elin rewarded him with enthusiastic applause and passionate kissing. They chuckled together.

The city had been decorated for the celebration. Blinding streetlights hovered practically everywhere, concealing the shadows.

– People are told things are basically okay and they believe it, Elin sighed, – because they want to.

But if one looked carefully, there were signs of discontent. The police had combed the streets for expressions of rebellion in the days leading up to the meeting, but during the night people had put up posters and written and painted on the walls.

PROPAGANDA DOMINATES PUBLIC LIFE

And:

THE TYRANNY OF BOTH STATE AND CORPORATE POWER IS ONE OF MANY MEANS BY WHICH OUR ENSLAVEMENT IS DESTINED, OR RATHER DESIGNED TO CONTINUE

– That does make me feel a little better, Emmet sighed happily.

– The unsanctioned graffiti and tagging does comfort me, Elin said. – It's one of many signs that the human spirit is still alive, even though there are plenty of other signs of the opposite.

She squeezed Damon and held him close.

A man resembling a humpback walked restlessly up and down the street. He had done so several times just during the brief time they had watched. His movements were swift and almost energetic. His eyes revealed emptiness and death. He carried a placard on his front and back with the same message:

THE GODS ARE DEAD

Emmet caught a glimpse of worry in his son's eyes. He sat down on his hinges in front of Damon, while holding on to the boy's shoulders.

– You know what we think about gods, right? He said cautiously. – That they're something people have made up in order to more easily gain power over others.

Damon nodded eagerly, but wondering, surprised that his father stated such a given.

A man stopped distraught in front of them.

– What are you telling the child? He asked with a deep frown. – That our Great Father in Heaven doesn't *exist?* What parents…

– We're parents that aren't so stupid that we buy the garbage you and your likes are spouting, Elin interrupted him.

– We're great godless heathens, Emmet grinned.

Realizing he got nowhere with his usual tactics the man turned and spoke directly to the child.

– What… the man over there is *saying,* he said strict as a priest, – is that God has turned away from us in disgust because of our faithless and immoral lives. We deny the highly evolved civilization He has granted us and live and mate like BEASTS IN HEAT.

Damon started laughing, unafraid and free.

– What…

– You're so silly, the boy said in his direct and adult manner, – what you say doesn't make sense.

The man, frothing in anger turned back to Emmet.

– You're raising a Satan's spawn, he declared. – You're clearly deserving of each other and will all end up in HELL!

– That's enough, Elin said calmly. – Your very presence sickens us. Please leave!

He stamped off. After a while he turned abruptly and howled at them, completely beside himself.

– God will PUNISH you. We see the breakdown everywhere in today's society and your kind is responsible. You will all be CONDEMNED on Judgment Day.

– What you call breakdown is merely a natural longing for freedom, Elin shrugged. – But today's horrible society is mostly a result of what you and your fellow faithful have done. You've always sought to conquer everything and everybody. We've allowed you to do so for way too long.

– Everything has been wrong for so very long, she mumbled not long after.

– The world is wrong? Damon wondered, with worry in his eyes.

– It is today, honey. She patted him on the head. – With the beyond wrong and destructive society we bright creatures have created, we do our best to destroy the very planet giving us life.

– We'll fix it, his father assured him. – By working within society we'll change it.

+++

He had been bullied at school. It had seemed like a big thing then. When he looked back at it, it didn't mean that much. If it had influenced him in any way, it had made him stronger, better able to deal with the world, and the world to come. He disliked it there, disliked all of it. Everything was so correct, all the time. If anyone stepped outside the accepted boundaries of behavior the system reacted promptly and decisively. He hardly learned anything but what to him was plain garbage, garbage children were taught to know and accept, accept, period. He stayed there ever less. His parents helped him with that as he grew older. Officially they arranged private schooling for him. Unofficially they taught him themselves. The result of their teaching and his own independent learning and exploration of life and the world was that he was far more knowledgeable than his peers.

– But they don't understand me either, he told his friends. – My strange yearnings.

He paused a bit.

– I don't understand them myself.

The laughter warmed him.

They could sit for hours in the dark and warm and cozy cellar room and exchange thoughts and ideas, often heated and passionate, but never disrespectful.

– The important thing isn't to ask *why,* I guess, he eventually said. – Only *when*...

– And when is *now!* One of the others cried.

They looked at each other, they really did, in the pitch black surroundings, seeing each other's excited expression in beyond immaculate detail.

Six, they were six entering the forest, deep and far. They stayed there for many days and nights, living on fruit they had brought and whatever useful nourishment found in the bountiful nature. And for each new day and night they felt more and more like a part of the green world and learned better to survive there. And during the night, the Darkness... the visions assaulted them, dreams that brought even greater understanding.

– I see, a voice said, – I see so much...

He pictured it in his mind, the place in mist and smoke and twilight where the Thunder Road made a turn, saw himself as an adult, and he shivered and burned and grew.

And then… they were found, dragged kicking and screaming back to the modern chill of existence.

But the visions that he both dreaded and loved kept coming, as inevitable as the tides. Understanding kept eluding him, even as he glimpsed it, somewhere there, in the mist.

The water and the mist split. He stood on a mountaintop. Long hair and beard blew in the wind. Behind the adult features he recognized himself. Eagles danced in the air around him, the waves created by the flapping of their wings hitting him in ever harder strides. He found himself on the mountaintop, looking back at himself as a boy.

The night to November 1, he and his five forest dweller compatriots set fire to their school and danced in its yard free and uninhibited. He still felt the heat of the fire at his back, the chill of the night ahead.

Nobody ever found any evidence of their actions. None of the six were ever questioned. They lay low a few months, able to do so then. And then they returned to the forest. That spring the lumber industry experienced the first few accidents.

He remembered the fire, remembered it reaching for the heavens, remembered the summer his parents had brought him to Jotunheim, to the vast mountain area at the center of Norway, where, according to mythology ancients creatures resided. There was blinding light there, and deep shadows, and fresh air. He felt it all, just as he realized that his parents kept studying him with beyond curious eyes.

Another Journey, a world, as it was also pounding their joy, their wonder.

As early as 1988 the ocean devoured 250 000 square meters of Denmark's west coast each year. The entire coastline of brittle material slowly eroded, crushed by the waves, the rising tides. Almost twenty years later the situation had deteriorated further. The Terrills could observe it first hand, as they traveled down the coastline of Europe.

Their «Europe Tour» ended up with them on their backs to the wind by the enormous Ooster Schelde Dam in the Netherlands. Elin and Emmet discussed the rapport they had made with the head of the upcoming project, the next expansion of the Dam.

– But this system is designed to withstand everything weather and nature can throw at it within a time period of hundred thousand years.

The three looked at the woman, looking for signs that she was being ironic or was joking.

– You evidently don't understand how… uninformed, how insane such a statement is, Damon said, shaking his head in disbelief.

She ignored him, as she could do in her own mind because of his youth.

– Even during «normal» circumstances the studies you're referring to would be… doubtful, Elin explained to her with a strained composure. – And they certainly don't take the human created climate change into account. The sea is rising and the winds are increasing far beyond even the worst projections made by the IPCC. The impact of this new reality is growing bigger and graver as we speak. As a modest illustration I can tell you that to be reasonably protected you would have to build a hundred meter tall and very thick wall around your country, and still have to handle enormous amounts of rainwater…

It was quite evident. The woman and people employing her had wanted to be reassured, to have their fears for the untamable nature mitigated. She was scared to death to face the truth.

– Your report will be buried in a deep vault, Damon said to them on their walk back to the hotel, – or it would have been if you hadn't already published it on the Internet.

The newspapers, Dutch and others that had commented on the report, mostly low circulation papers and alternative sites on the Web had headlines resembling an obituary:

THE NETHERLANDS - THE NEW ATLANTIS

– I'm really happy we insist on ownership of our work, Emmet said. – I think we should keep doing so in the future, don't you. They can ignore it, but can't bury it.

– If only they would listen, Elin mumbled.

– Major parts of current human society are ignoring it, of course, the teenager kept at it with dark humor in his eyes. – Those living in all the low areas of the world, in all the cities close to the coastline…

– You don't need to stress it, Emmet said, doing his best to keep bottled inside his own worry, his own fears.

– Perhaps I do. Perhaps we all do.

Emmet looked like he wanted to say more, but he didn't. None of them did. Not then.

CHAPTER TWO

I can see him before my inner eye, unmoving in the Storm, proud, young and unbowed. Like all human beings squeezed between understanding and the wish for understanding, and those without it.

Spring arrived even earlier in 2008. Before the end of February the warm weather, with water and wind assaulted North Western Europe. Because of the warm winter extreme amounts of snow had fallen in the mountains, making the arrival of spring a very volatile and violent affair. Everything melted, over night. Big and small rivers flooded nearby land. Roads were flushed away. Basements were filled with dirty water. Houses were flushed away. City streets turned into rivers. Remains of houses followed the flood water to the sea. When the flood was at its worst people feared entire cities would go.

In and around Bergen the torrential rain kept going throughout March. Then, except for a shower on the evening of the eighteenth, in April it turned totally around, with not a single drop of rain, not on the entire west coast. At twilight on April thirtieth both the air and soil had become so dry that the floods a month earlier felt like a distant memory.

The clean up was still far from completed. Most people attempted to ignore the prevalent signs of destruction. They seemed to shrink in dread for every twisted sculpture in honor of nature's rage they passed.

Myriam Vallinger studied the people and the sculptures with equal interest. She walked through the city streets with a wily smile on her lips. The confident way she moved attracted a lot of attention. It wasn't just that she was stunningly attractive (she was). She had also dressed up for the evening. Lined pants, jacket, shirt and tie. She had done her hair today. It was short, with a little forelock, dark and shiny.

It was what was called a business look, one easily identified with a young, successful executive.

But people studying her quickly grew confused and haunted with a strange ambiguity and even apprehension.

There was something about the impression that didn't quite… fit, something that might have something to do with the strong colors of her clothes or her behavior, the powerful attitude of rebellion she conveyed or both. The outrageous pink slippers she wore were a dead giveaway. At least they were. The less ignorant among the ignorant realized why irritation riddled them: She wore a costume, a disguise.

Tove, her fair-haired companion was slightly less obvious, but still somewhat noticeable. Both females, as individuals and as a pair caught attention wherever they walked.

– The invitation said dank, dark and narrow passages, Tove swore under her breath. – There aren't that many left, you know.

– You're the expert, Myriam shrugged.

The conversation was in Norwegian. She hadn't been in Bergen that long, but her mother had grown up in the country, so Myriam spoke the language.

– The expert on Bergen's dark alleys, Tove snorted. – Thank you very much.

There was a scream from somewhere, from a direction impossible to pinpoint, a human howl that very much resembled that of a wolf.

More sirens filled the air, more screams from an enraged population.

– The entire city is set to blow, Tove mumbled. – The natives are restless, very restless.

– You're right, Myriam acknowledged. – I've rarely experienced anything like it, anywhere.

And she had been around.

The first spark had been struck a few nights ago, when a police patrol had evidently disliked the presence of a group of youths in a recreational area. The boys and girls had just chosen a bench to sit on, and done nothing discernibly wrong beside that. The police officers had brusquely asked them to «vacate the premises». The boys and girls had protested in what was clearly a good-humored manner, but started to slowly comply. That had evidently been sufficient for the patrol to act. They had started taking the «troublemakers» into custody immediately.

Observers had protested, pointing out that the youths had done nothing wrong. They had been warned by the officers to stay out of it, and had done so, but with lots of grumbling, while the police car with the youths had driven off. Lots of people had visited the police headquarters to lodge formal complaints that day. The police Chief's answer had been to warn everyone to stay away from the area in question.

People gathered there early this evening. They were still there when Tove and Myriam passed by.

The city exploded in a matter of minutes. The girls heard it well in advance of the first shot fired.

A boy, fairly stunned, but not really frightened joined them as they left what was the most affected part of town.

– It had to happen, he said, a shade of a grin in his excited face. – There has been lots of grumbling lately. I guess the police would have gotten away with it during what could be deemed normal circumstances, but nothing has been normal lately, has it…

A group of four cops was approached by a far larger group of citizens. There was a heated exchange of words, and then the first stones and pieces of garbage were thrown. Ten, fifteen seconds later the fight was on.

And this was outside the boiling kettle the inner parts of the city had become. A number of shots were fired somewhere, a gathering of cracks growing to a thunder, at the top of howls of pain and *rage* rising from the stone desert. There was no direction to it. It was just there, like a monster threatening to devour everything and everybody, a result of many lives with dammed emotions, caged passions.

– My Goddess, the boy cried. – My Goddess.

He speeded up and they followed him. The three of them finally reached the narrow alleys to the east, at the base of the mountain. They looked at him, studied him, while also being on the lookout for people they had sought the entire evening. He hesitated a bit.

– Are you, by any chance on your way to the Beltane celebration? He wondered.

– We are, they choired, suddenly excited. – We are!

– I happen to be on my way there, myself, he said, red-faced over the attention the adult women showed him. – It's up there, I know that much, up on the mountain.

He pointed, and the two wanted to embrace him.

They followed him as the terrain turned steep, and left behind the boiling kettle that

the city had become.
Out of breath they stopped now and then, and could observe the events below in relative safety.
– It's like New Year's Eve, he mumbled. – Lots of fireworks.
They followed the main road upwards, as it curved in the steep terrain. Walking in a more or less straight line, using the occasional stairs and trails, would have brought them faster to the top, but this didn't tire them as much as that would have done.
The entire mountainside was covered by houses, almost as tight as in the central parts of the city below. Myriam sensed eyes on her, as people stared at them behind curtains.
They walked up Fløyen, one of the seven (or rather nine) mountains surrounding the city, as it had been, with its old borders.
Myriam couldn't quite tell when she started frowning, when she felt something she startled realized she had felt for some time.
– What is it? Tove wondered.
– I feel… a pull.
Something unknown, known ahead, a *presence* practically embracing her in the dark slowly supplanting the twilight behind them.
– How did you gals found out about tonight? The boy wondered.
– On the Internet, Tove giggled. – That's irony for you. But we couldn't find out anything more specific, not find even a friend of a friend of anyone headed there. You are our savior.
She flirted shamelessly with him. Myriam wanted to chastise her for it, but practically her sole attention was directed forward, to what awaited them, *her* ahead.
– Steep, steep is the road to the dwelling of the gods, the boy cried. – The Mountain of Torches is our reward.
The name echoed within her, spoke to her in a way she couldn't name.
He increased his speed, like a horse pulling a carriage, spurred on by the reins. The girls followed him. Neither of them seemed to feel the burden of the hard path, but rather be inspired by it.
The city had spread out almost everywhere below, but not up here.
They climbed the Mountain of Torches, adding themselves to the others they met, others clearly headed in the same direction, towards the same goal. Eagerness made eyes glow. Hers certainly did.
The last few houses and stairs faded away in the slipstream of their path. They passed the old restaurant. The travelers had the opportunity to look back, at the city below. None did. They rushed into the awaiting forest.
It was a park of sorts, with broad roads, not trails going far ahead, in all directions, but they left them quickly, choosing the different and unknown pathway they glimpsed as they made their way into the bewitched forest.
Myriam smiled a little cynically when she spotted people dressed like elves pointing them in the right direction, but she could hardly conceal her excitement, her expectations.
Torches began appearing on both sides of them, flickering flames colder than the moon. Myriam wondered if they and the elusive elves were there at all.
She said something, something neither the others nor she could hear.
– What was that? Tove asked.

– It's been so long, Myriam repeated.
– What does that mean, girl? Tove grinned. – Don't go weird on me again, now, you hear…
Myriam struggled to speak, to explain what couldn't be explained.
They stepped out of the forest and stopped, stunned and a bit overwhelmed. Before them waited a small open stretch. The land descended a little towards the middle, and then rose again. Two rows of torches lit the trail through the swamp-like, steaming area. They followed the trail with their eyes to the other side. A man stood there. They saw him clearly, or as clearly as they possibly could in the flickering light, saw his long hair and beard, a towering shadow of delightful madness.
– Fight yourself through the valley of doom, he shouted, – to the Mountain of Torches.
They wondered where the thunder originated from. It wasn't like the gunfire they had heard before leaving the city. It wasn't quite like anything Myriam had ever heard. The small group started moving on the shaky ground. Birds howled in the night, from all the four corners of their new world. Smoke whirled in the air. It made tears flow from burning eyes. They looked anew at the place where the man had stood. He was no longer there, was no longer to be seen anywhere.
They heard the music then. She heard it, played on the most bewitched of flutes. They re-entered the forest. There was a dark passage, and at the other side the Shadowland. The forest released them, but didn't let go. Bonfires and torches lit the big open space. Myriam felt the smile on her lips and the flow of delight inside.
– We found it, she told Tove. – I found it, and when I, a stranger can do it, anybody can.
All the new arrivals looked at each other in wonder, as they took in the sights and sounds, the mood of the newfound place.
– It's a good thing the cops are *distracted* tonight, someone said, – or they would surely have found their way here…
The words and the way he said it encouraged everybody to let go further. One could actually see it, like something visible in their faces and stance.
Tove let herself be courted by the boy. Myriam shrugged and took the scenic tour alone, quickly losing herself in the dark surroundings, in the wild and untamed within and without. She spotted it wherever she looked and began shivering. It didn't let up, and didn't bother her any. On the contrary, it added to her already exalted and virulent mood.
A woman juggled five, no, six torches. A firebreather performed with her. His arms had to be incredibly long or his mouth had to match that in size or both. The flames stretched from his gap and hiiigh into the night air. The two of them were quite a pair.
Pieces of what happened on the various stages reached Myriam, reached her undiluted. People performed in a way, but it didn't seem *staged.*
A girl, considerably younger than Myriam called attention to herself with an aggressive stance on a stub. Her eyes sparked in feral resolve.
– … and none of humankind shall know any sort of calm or peace, she spat. – Our attempt to dominate what can't be dominated can be compared to the slow bending of a twig. It might take time until it breaks, and everything seems fine, but when it happens, everything comes crashing down. We're right by a *cemetery.* Look down and behold the

tombstones.

Those listening, Myriam among them did as she said and imagined that they really saw the local stone desert below, saw the buildings like the tombstones there were, row by row by row.

– Behold the tyrants' servants, the unformed bullies with their clubs and black guns. Smell the blood flowing in the gray death. See it become red in spite of it all, become an irresistible river…

Her voice changed into a whisper loud and just as intense.

– The city is so close, isn't it? No matter where we go, there it is, right there, with us, one of the many monuments in honor of the insanity we have built around ourselves.

Myriam threw herself into the dance of the more distant music for a moment, but she kept listening to the girl's intense speech.

– For thousands of years ours and the planet's frustrations have increased to the threshold of breaking. Now, it's finally happening. Now, the rotten tree, our house built on feet of clay falls. The sea can sweep everything away. There isn't enough water, enough food, enough of anything. The final days are here. This is a projection made on available facts, not a prophecy or a fever dream. Our casual observations reveal the truth, no matter where we look. We may close our eyes hard, and look back at previous disasters. No comparison is sufficient. Everything is happening simultaneously. Plague, famine, floods and storms will decimate the land and the poor creatures on it. We will all kill for the slightest nourishment. Tell yourself that you would share with a fellow man, one you love… When you've starved for many days and spot a breadcrumb on the ground there will be no mercy. Friends, enemies… just more stipulations without meaning. Whatever morals we've given ourselves… there has always been something empty about it, hasn't it?

Then it came, a shriek from the deepest pit rattling them all.

– *Sibling shall stand against sibling. No man will have mercy on another.*

Her voice changed, her appearance changed into something so vastly different that she didn't seem to be the same woman.

Myriam recognized a paraphrasing of the Völuspá, the Norse Poetic Edda and shuddered.

– She's out of her mind, a male whispered in Myriam's ears. – That's how it sounds and looks anyway.

– Yes, but perhaps that's the point? Myriam pointed out to him. – Perhaps she's illustrating a confrontation with the ultimate insanity?

He wasn't interested. She noticed that immediately, and made sure he noticed the expression of contempt before she moved on. He didn't attempt to keep up with her.

Impressions continued to assault her and she let them, with a brittle smile on her lips.

A boy experimented with the humoristic approach. He fingered in the air with a microphone that wasn't there and looked sheepishly at the audience.

– Two messages have dumped into our lap in the newsroom tonight. I'll read them in the order we received them: «There is no, I repeat no conclusive evidence that the human created climate change is real». And: «Tomorrow's weather: snow and cold weather. Good news for those of us that have invested in winter sports activities, of course. Winter must come soon… or what»?

He peered up from his non-existing glasses. They rewarded him with loud laughter.

The fool bowed more or less elegant as he accepted the accolades from a not so adoring public.

Myriam chuckled long after she had walked on. It felt good to laugh.

There were a few, brief plays happening on the large area. It felt like a festival of sorts, at least in size, a celebration of life, one immersed in night and fire.

She saw it displayed in brazen ways wherever she walked.

A tall, lean figure had climbed a tree. Myriam realized startled that he was hardly a teenager. He was taller than most present, but his cheeks were hairless. She knew, from the first sight of him that «brazen» didn't even begin to describe what she observed there in the tree.

He held up a big sword. Its shiny blade formed a stark contrast to the long dark hair. Her eyes were pulled to him, pulled tight to the fascinating face.

She watched how he practically danced on the shaky branch.

Two uniformed people stood under the tree pointing at him with rifles fitted with bloody bayonets. He cried out, unbowed:

– «Is life so dear, peace so sweet, as to be purchased at the price of chains and slavery? Forbid it, I say! I know not what course others may take; but as for me, *give me liberty or give me death!*»

There were several cracks, as the weapons were fired. The audience gasped. The large body in the tree shook, fell and hit the ground hard. It didn't move.

Goddess! Myriam swallowed hard. *What if there has been a mistake, what if…* Huge, large eyes seemed to penetrate her. Hard, like glass.

The body rose. The eyes were just as hard, staring.

– No chains, no slavery for me! The boy shouted.

The audience applauded. Myriam couldn't move.

– Sunset is here, he greeted all. – This is the Witching Hour. Enjoy yourselves!

Slowly, slowly Myriam's legs stopped shaking. She ended up smiling enigmatically. That was exactly what she intended to do.

She wondered once again how many people that had found their way here. It was hard to tell with all the movement, all swirling moves.

Well over fifty, she counted silently, closer to hundred, if one counted the elves lurking in the shadows.

Shadows, fire, it was all the same on this place.

She made sure to approach him the moment he no longer had any others swarming him. He stood alone between the campfire and the forest. She stopped before him and blinked. It hadn't been her imagination: His eyes were black.

– You meant it, didn't you? She asked softly.

– What do you think? He returned her question, not put off or threatened by her close proximity at all.

– My name is Myriam, she told him, her pulse quickening.

– That's a nice name…

He said.

– Thank you, she said coyly.

He didn't say anything.

A breath of heat struck them from the fire.

– And what's yours? She asked him.

– They call me Terrill.
– Is that your name? She asked, suddenly impatient.
– Name? He teased her.
– Oh, you're deep. She chuckled pleased and rubbed him playfully under his jaw, deliberately patronizing. He grabbed her wrist. – Such a strong little boy.
– Terrill, come here! A skinny girl waved to him from a group of more young teenagers.
The tightening grip let go. He pulled back, away from Myriam. She sighed in inevitable disappointment.
– He's cute, Tove said, suddenly back at her side.
– He's nothing but an overgrown boy, Myriam shrugged in contempt.
A brief turn towards Tove, and Terrill was gone. A prolonged glance searching for him, and Tove was gone. People and air and fire and shadows whirled around her, none of it solid or tangible. Everything and everyone seemed like ghosts and spirits to her.
She walked, crossed back and forth on the seemingly unlimited area of the celebration. Each time she had convinced herself that she had reached its boundary, she found yet another pocket of activity, one more arm reaching into the surrounding dark. She looked for Terrill, but didn't find him.
An adult male stopped before her, studied her with unadulterated interest.
– Hi, he greeted her.
He was tall and big. She felt the stirrings of interest as she met his eyes.
– I'm so glad to find a woman here, he said. – There are way too many kids present for my taste. They should be home in bed by now, the lot of them.
She frowned.
The two of them stood there for a while, exchanging a few words, before she left him, what little interest there had been gone with the wind.
She kept charging through the dark and misty surroundings, thinking about the seemingly attractive man she had had words with for what seemed like an eternity ago.
The dull man, as interesting as a rock. She forgot him.
Something stirred again. Something happened, not easily identified at first. She stopped at a minor rise in the terrain, overlooking the festivities.
A gathering of strangers heard the drums start up and quickly increase the beat. Suddenly, she found herself breathless. She heard feet hammer against the ground and realized startled that hers were among them. A trance-like state charged her, charged everybody she could see. Her eyes, filled with a dark haze, once more sought Terrill. Many present had long and dark hair. She identified him easily, among dozens of others. The dance and the night and the sight of him warmed her, and she sensed the heaviness of her hips as she shamelessly wriggled them in all directions. The nearest bonfire grew and displayed her moves on a tent wall, just before it was overwhelmed by one much bigger. At the edge, the blurring lines between the two dark fire spat and hissed.
Humming rose from the Earth and across the Shadowland. The two of them danced tight. She pulled close to him and didn't care if anyone saw her. He cast glances at his friends, the boys and girls giggling. Music flowed, seemingly from the air itself. She halted a bit in her tracks, clearly ill at ease. *She* was ill at ease.
The rhythm changed, turning harder, more accentuated. There was a catching in her throat. They separated. A thunder followed by a heartbeat rattled them. They moved

in accordance with each other, like mirror images. She blinked, listened, saw without seeing, listened without hearing. She sensed and felt… Her fingertips seemed to actually touch the dark. The arms of everybody dancing touched. Wings reached out like strands of fire and darkness.

The dance turned wild.

«Here is hard-tramped soil
Soft as swaying grass
Here is soft soil
Hard as shaking mountains»

Hair in the face, covering eyes. It didn't matter. They knew where to put their feet. Wriggling bodies knew. Consciousness seeking something they might never find.

«We've been drawn here
To this tall mountain
Pulled into the circle of the witch
This dance of ghostly fire»

A roaring drum solo ended the melody. Hearts and bodies were shaken to shreds. In a few, precious seconds the world opened up to them both. They saw far and deep. The sound of the drums faded. The flutes from another part of the forest turned quiet. The two of them stood there breathless and stared at each other with burning looks. She drew breath desperately. It seemed like she couldn't get enough air. She clapped her hands in boundless excitement. The happy laughter felt alien, both known and not in her ears.

– Midnight is approaching, he said, his voice penetrating deep within her. – The true night is about to begin.

A clock somewhere chimed twelve times, the signal for midnight used in present society, a warning about the darkest of times.

Someone struck what was clearly a different kind of drum, was a different drum, a deep, thunderous sound, and Myriam wondered if it was physical at all. Shadows kept reaching for them, kept spreading in the flickering light. A man stepped out from his hideout in there. She recognized the man with the long hair and beard, the guide. He placed himself behind a long table. Everything he needed of tools and props had been prepared for him and waited for him there.

– It is Midnight, he declared. – The next hour belongs to the dead. Styx - the river of death - is flowing nearby, and we will gain wisdom from its currents. We're here tonight to celebrate life, the planet we're a part of and that many of us are distancing ourselves from. We know that isn't truly possible, just like we can't live Life by rejecting Death.

The dark, coarse voice cut into them. It fit him. It, like him, like them belonged in this place.

He held up a skull, like the prince in Hamlet. Some gasped. The naked skull seemed strangely white, stark white in the soft glow of the fire. He had their complete attention.

– Is this so horrible? He cried. – Is it bad that we're part of an endless cycle of birth and death? YES, in today's society Death is something horrible and dirty, like the pale existence we suffer. Everything becomes *wrong* in the age of the stone desert and the anti-nomad. Everybody knows we can't build a foundation on feet of clay, but even such basic truths we, the people of technology and indifference keep rejecting today.

His words and passion surged through them all, bringing out what had been hiding inside.

– White wine, he indicated with his left hand. – Red wine.

He moved his right hand over the glass with the blood red fluid.

– Without the most important ingredient it will be no more than that. We will add that and drink To Life. I'll offer you the choice of doing just that.

– Added spices all of it, right? Myriam stated.

The sorcerer bowed to her. The subsequent shared free and loose laughter only served to deepen the mood further.

He picked one small knife in a long row before him and made a smooth incision on the meaty part of his left hand. The blade flashed in red. The blood flowed into one of the glasses. The white wine began boiling in red.

– On some nights the boundaries between the known and unknown world are no thicker than a hair's breadth. Tonight is such a night. We can reach out and touch the infinite and eternal…

He raised the glass, offering his salute to them all and then emptied the glass in one swallow. A minority followed his clue and cut themselves and drank bottoms up the mix of white wine and blood and spices. The majority drank the red wine. A few didn't drink from any of the glasses. They pulled back, fading away in the indistinct background.

Myriam and Terrill saluted each other. Their glasses met and parted. Fingers touched briefly. They drank. The blood, spices and wine burned in their throats stronger, far stronger than liquor, and then, not long thereafter, as they were staring at each other, the content exploded in their stomach. The drink filled them up.

– Say with me, he whispered in her ears, both her ears.

She did, and when it happened, it seemed so easy, like a second skin.

– I reach out my Shadow, he/she intoned, – beyond Time and Space.

The silent laughter when she looked at him with unbridled devotion enhanced her smile thrice over.

– I'm Damon, he told her. – Walk with me.

She found that a strange demand, since she was already doing that.

And he didn't really seem like a kid then. She felt the arm of the hand he held tingle to the shoulder and beyond.

He pulled something from the wide pocket in his jacket. She recognized the book, a Gideon's bible with a glance. He held it up and walked to the pentacle and the yet unlit heap of wood.

– I stole this, he cried to them all, – as the first part of a magickal act. Let its demise symbolize our final parting with christianity and all forms of religion, a bleak view on life that has brought us to the edge of self-destruction and beyond. During ten thousand years it has been a weapon in the hands of tyranny and its servants.

He put it on top of the heap with a movement both casual and deliberate. He signed for her to join him. With a rigid stare she did. She grabbed a torch from one of the poles stuck in the ground. Fire flickered in the wind.

She walked three, four, five steps forward and stopped by the pentacle, standing straight, shivering in anticipation. He had placed himself at its center. The wind wasn't blowing anymore. Myriam stared at Damon with eyes so wide that she feared they would burst. He signed for her to drop the torch. She did. It slipped from numb fingers. The circle and the five-pointed star flared. The fire spread to the heap and rose into the dark ceiling above, splitting the very night. Damon stood at the center of the pentacle, surrounded by flames, a sight to behold, smoke and fire, the phoenix of mist rising from the ashes. The inner five-sided figure had lots of room, but those watching him from the outside sent him many a worried look. The wind started blowing anew and the fire reached for him. It danced in the air and he was its partner. The circle had room for many more and many joined him there, both those who did and didn't know or suspected its secrets.

Myriam breathed the smoke and it felt like fresh air, like spices glowing in her mind. The night's colors haunted them, at one time out of reach, suddenly close enough to touch. The night surrounded them deep and mysterious, a friend they believed had left them and then they startled realized it hadn't. The Night Ravens called from Earth's distant corners. Myriam heard them, understood what they were saying. They chanted in strange voices to those dancing inside the ancient star of fire, those not burned by the searing heat licking their skin. The Mountain of Torches pulled close, pulled inside everyone present. The fire burned even stronger. The choir floated off in the night, in a tongue not a tongue.

The sleeper shall awaken.

We dance the eternal dance. We live the Dance of Life.

Everybody stumbled out of the circle of fire. There was little or no coughing, no adverse reaction to the massive inhaling of smoke.

The smoke affected her on a deeper level. Myriam knew that. It… roamed her, opened her up to new and different sensations.

She slipped down in Damon's lap. Her skin tingled. She put her arms around his neck and gave him lingering kisses on the lips. He had a visible color on his ears. Aside from that he had fairly good control over himself. He had a hardness inside she was unfamiliar with. It countered much of his inexperience.

– You guys have some setup here, she said cheerfully. – I was supposed to be present at another mountain tonight, but I'm pleased that I chose this.

– I am, too, he mumbled.

– The boy can give compliments, she grinned in acknowledgement, – compliments to melt a maiden's heart

She slipped down from his lap, but remained close.

– Let's go somewhere, she said, with promise in her voice and expression. – You know about places here, don't you, sweetie?

He rose to his full height and towered above her.

She didn't see him nod, didn't hear him speak. He held her hand and pulled her with him through the crowd. Then, in no time at all they had entered the forest and a quiet darkness surrounded them. She found herself listening to it, enjoying the loud noises in the silence. She took a considerable sip of wine and took her time to enjoy the taste on the tongue.

– It's weird, she said with a cracked voice, – I feel like I can finally breathe after a lifetime underwater.

– In a society without humanity we find ours.

His dark shadow overwhelmed hers.

– So young and so cynical. She pushed him in a clearly provocative gesture. – Such a

bleak view on the world.
– The world is bleak.
He slapped her on the butt. She gasped. It burned so pleasantly.
– But you're also a happy camper, she admitted, she stated after a moment or two of consideration, and then indignant: – Nothing is *right* with you, do you know that?
She was split between the seemingly contradictory aspects of his personality, striving to understand her fascination with it and him.
– That becomes more important the worse existence treats us, he said.
Trees cast infinite shadows from the flickering lights ahead. Smoke drifted between the trees and the shadows. They reached a clearing and stopped momentarily, briefly brought to silence.
Four torches tied to poles formed a spacious square, their glow filling this clearing that seemed to be such an integrated part of the forest. Someone had placed incense on the ground. The sweet, fresh scent lingered in the air. Tailspin smoke reached into and up in the thick, breathing dark mass staring at them from all sides. At the center there was a bed made of leaves and of many colors.
– You know how to treat a girl, she whispered in his ear.
The torches, whatever else was burning here had been lit recently. It couldn't have happened more than a few minutes before their arrival.
– Who has done this? She asked with a giggle.
– Why ask me? He replied and grinned. – I don't know…
– You can tell me…
She said seductively, breathing close to his cheek.
– We drew straws to decide who would be elves, he said red and sweaty.
– It's beautiful. You, their master deserve your just reward.
She pushed herself at him, took the final half-step close to his body.
– Your Patrick Henry monologue inspired me so, she whispered coquettishly.
– Get out of here, he said, clearly embarrassed.
– No way!
She registered like something insignificant and distant the increase in her pulse, the enchanted paralysis in his body that not even the fever-hot mind could break.
A sigh of release rose from her throat. She let her jacket slide down her arms, down her back. Her curves stood revealed, even more than before. She was unable to interpret his look, shyness mixed with those threads of night and fire.
– So young, so ancient.
She pulled impatiently in his shirt.
He grabbed her hard and demanding. Finally! When he kissed her he did so gasping for breath, clumsily, but so intense that she almost lost her marbles. He fumbled inside her blouse, so impatient that there was hardly any progression at all. A thread broke in the fabric and then one more. And another. She calmed him with a soft kiss and liberated herself with a sweet laughter. Without looking away she placed herself at the opposite side of the natural bed.
– I've grown quite fond of this little piece of cloth…
She started pulling in it, pulling it over her head. Nude skin appeared to him. He swallowed hard. The piece of cloth fell slowly to the ground. She stood there for a moment with her hands above her head, exposing fully heavy and firm breasts. The tie

tickled the cleaving as she moved, as her head moved back and forth in the dance. Arms lowered themselves slowly, slipping down along the body, with hands and skin hotter than she could ever recall. She pushed pants and panties down her thighs while the hips rotated, practically by themselves. *Shameless tramp!*

– Your turn, she said hoarsely.

He removed his shoes first. He remembered, wasn't completely gone. Then the socks. Movements seemed slow, hesitant, as if he was underwater. Then he increased the speed dramatically. It was like he couldn't become naked soon enough. He threw away the sweater and pulled in the belt. She swallowed and stared hard at the bulge in front of his pants. It seemed like the belt, the button, the zipper and the very pants slipped off in a single sliding move. Then he stood there, slightly crouched… with the biggest hard-on she had seen. He took one, two steps towards her, stopped abruptly and straightened, his muscles strained like tightened ropes. The semen flowed into the smoky air and wet the dry ground.

He reddened all over his body.

He does that a lot, she reflected.

– My Goddess! She gasped.

With both hands buried in her groin she collapsed on the bed. The orgasm overwhelmed her quickly, unwelcome and unstoppable. Of course it did. She hardly noticed that he hit the ground by her side.

They rested side by side, separated, in the ruthless silence of the forest. She couldn't hear him, couldn't hear herself breathe. She couldn't feel the cold, but it still grabbed her like an iron claw she couldn't see.

Ashamed, she thought. It razed through her mind like the dullest of blades.

They were both ashamed, ashamed by their own sexuality, paralyzed by the very notion of their natural, untamed passion.

She wanted to speak to him, explain herself, tell him that it was all right.

The lights shifted and the flame flickered. Myriam felt naked, vulnerable. She sought comfort in Terrill's eyes, but he wouldn't look at her.

They heard a sound, first so weak that they didn't hear it properly. It rose, in strength and depth. They listened and then they heard it. They turned and faced each other. A chime rose from the forest bed, rose all around them. With ears, without ears… they heard the owl howl.

– It is an owl, isn't it? She wondered stunned. – Not a wolf?

– There are no wolves around here, he said.

His voice, not his words brought meaning to his boiling insides.

– We are tamed, she said, she whimpered. – Even here the tyranny hostile to all life haunts us. We are crippled by a society destroying everything making life worth living.

She grabbed his shoulders and held on.

Three stone throws to the left they heard the howl shaking the Earth. The eagle spread its wings. They heard it, felt it, and glimpsed it, the wild beast displaying its fangs in the wilderness. Myriam once more pushed herself tight to Damon and whispered seductively to him, comforting the wounded beast.

– You should be *proud,* not embarrassed by your untamed passion, she told him softly, caressing him kindly, not just speaking to him, but to herself as well.

She gave him a dawdling kiss that slowly turned hungry and demanding.

He glanced at his limp cock, more shame in his eyes.
– Fear not, she comforted him, – you'll soon enough regain your power. Take your time, sweet one, enjoy it, and savor all its rewards.
He began returning her caresses, hesitating at first, but visibly gaining confidence and courage. She felt herself awaken, felt it happen to them both. He put a hand around one of her breasts, rubbing it, fondling it. She opened and closed her mouth, unable to utter the slightest sound, and now it wasn't shame that blocked her voice but rising desire. He climbed on top of her. Happiness and expectation assaulted her like a slow-moving lukewarm wave. His shadow, his many-faced shadow covered her, moved in the close flicker of the torches. She writhed under him, caressed him with her entire body, as she turned wet and warm below. Her smile, filled with joy revealed all its teeth.
– Soon… she moaned.
Stray thoughts, insignificant. In those Damon was busy considering his friends, dreading their presence, knowing that they sneaked around in the forest right now, wondering if they were merely a few steps away.
Let them. Let them *watch!*
Then he felt it, the hardening below, both so painful and so indispensable. His head fell down on the shaking breasts. He missed his first trust, and his second, and his third and he began panting in anxiety and growing terror. Hands touched him above and below, once more calming him down, soothing the troubled beast. They rubbed at each other some more. Now, she cried silently, do it now, sweet, beloved Damon. She spoke soft words in his ears and helped him find the spot, the spot embracing him and please him beyond measure.
After that he didn't feel anything anymore.
Felt nothing more, nothing less.

CHAPTER THREE

They woke up in a large bed in a spacey room with white-painted walls and ceiling. The night stood before them like a cluster of indistinct impressions and sensations. They re-experienced a nightly walk through a misty forest, to a strange, almost eerie house in the mountainside. That they now found themselves in a bright bedroom didn't convince them that everything they had dreamed had truly happened.

He stretched across the broad bed. His eyes opened and brought an insanely huge smile to his lips. He felt aware and energetic, alive beyond description. When he left the bed it was as if he effortlessly jumped out on the floor. When he walked to the window it was like his feet didn't touch the soft carpet. He pulled in air from the open window, unwilling to look at the sun, because that meant he would have to close his eyes. Five, ten seconds passed, before he sat course back towards the bed, and to her.

She rested on her belly. Head was raised and her attention was on him. She followed him with a speculative look. He rejoined her in bed. They greeted each other with hungry kisses. He felt the power rise again, abrupt, irresistible, further empowered by her reaction to it. A layer covered her already remote eyes. She clung to him. Lips kissing his chest sought down, down, down.

Then he pulled back a little. He kept her from following by grabbing her upper arms. She sent him an aggravated look. He rose unconcerned to his knees. Then he lifted her up and held her there. He studied her. She wasn't sure she wanted to stand for it. But he held almost her entire weight. His strength made her breathless. He seemed to be pondering something. When he turned her large body around, he clearly didn't strain himself at all. She couldn't see him anymore. Before she knew it he had pushed her forward and placed her on all fours.

– Hey, what are you…? She was unable to hold back the stunned cry-out, the burst of fear.

She made an attempt at getting away. He buried a hand in her hair and held on. The other hand he used to fondle a breast, hard and inconsiderate. He released the breast and led the hand backwards, below the belly, into her already steaming nest.

– Damon, NO!

He placed his hands on her tight, big butt and held on, handled her wriggling body with ease. There was a loud crack as his flat hand hit her butt. She turned her head and looked astounded at him. He slapped her again. She yelped in pain.

– Shut up! He growled. – Shut the fuck up!

His hand sought anew between her thighs and roamed with impunity. A loud, shocking moan rose from her throat and through her open mouth. He slapped her more, without holding her. She made no attempt at getting away. Her juices wet his roaming hand.

– Clever boy, she mumbled, – clever boy. You

He pushed himself into her, unskilled, hard, fast, full of wild, instinctive skill. Her words vanished in a loud snort. She resisted, attempted to pull away during his first, initial tryouts, but when he penetrated deep within her, when she felt him all the way up she was overwhelmed by an irresistible heat, one which like she had never before experienced. His hand, his glowing hot claws buried themselves equally deep in her skin, her very self. His breath… like a dragon roasting and devouring her.

– Snotty kid, she mumbled. – Snotty kid, SNOTTY KID! Don't stop, don't stop, you pathetic little worm, you swarming horny, yapping dog…

She threatened and begged in a long row of abusive language, all in vain. He kept going at his own pace, his own rhythm. She imagined a grin on his lips, as she surrendered to his moves, his desires. Through a red and gray mist he glimpsed the glowing body in front of him, its excessive demands, her pointed mocking and he doubled, redoubled his efforts. He reached forward and grabbed around her breasts, held around them. She lost all strength in her arms and when he let go of her, her head and shoulders fell down on the bed. Her upper half slid back and forth on the sheet as he pushed and pulled her. She panted desperately every time her mouth coincidentally had access to air. He grunted aloud and fell forward, on her. She turned her head around as far as she could and released a tiny yelp of joy when her lips found his. He pulled and pushed with his hips the two, three final times, and then briefly, an eternity, they became one creature. Before they once more separated and side by side hit the wet, warm and eventually chaotic sheet arrangements.

The sun disk burned their half closed eyes.

She slipped close to him with a smile on her lips.

– Mmmm, she hummed with a touch of mock terror. – Either you're extremely early in your development, or I dread your coming of age.

– You're the first girl I've met daring to show your inner fire, he said cautiously, petting her cheek.

– There is more than enough of it to go around…

She played with his pubic hairs before she put her head there, rubbing it against his cock. She faced him and worry touched her, as he studied her enigmatically.

– I know what you're thinking, he said cheerfully, with no sign of blushing. – But as you know I would have been seen as an adult in the pre-agriculture hunter/gatherer tribes.

– You would have indeed, she scoffed at him. – You would have hunted and protected beyond horny helpless and mindless females eager to obey your every impulse.

– Perhaps that wouldn't be so bad…

He raised her jaw and eyes with two fingers without encountering resistance.

– You scare me, she whimpered.

– You scare yourself, he shrugged.

– I do, don't I? She said softly.

He watched how she fought off her dread, and felt stark relief when the familiar coy smile once more lit her face.

– There is no need for us to shower, is there?

– No! He shook his head. – We should stink of body juices today, reminding us of the celebration of Life in the dark and deep Beltane night.

– That's poetry, she grinned startled.

She kissed him on the lips before leaving the bed. His and her combined body juices still flowed between her legs, joining the dry there from last night. She stood before the mirror, posing, performing for him, natural, not the slightest bit forced or even smacking of pretense. He looked down on himself, half expecting to be aroused yet again, but nothing happened. He began dressing and she did, too.

Their clothes were dirty, and even torn, marked by the hours of abuse throughout the night. Her slippers weren't pink in any way anymore, but dirty brown all over.

– I don't care, she shrugged. – This was supposed to be a one time use, anyway.

His clothes remained mostly black, but they were also ruined beyond salvage.

She didn't button her blouse or her jacket. Her breasts moved for each move she made, both concealed and openly. She refitted the tie. It looked just as weird on her as ever. He walked to her and grabbed it.

– Such a nice collar, he mused, pulling her close.

Her eyes turned hazy again.

– I know that the tie is the modern day version of the old slave collar, she said. – I'm wearing it in defiance of that fact.

She brushed a bit of dirt from the shoulder of his jacket.

– You like it, don't you, she snapped coyly, – and you would've loved seeing your woman kneeling before you in chains.

– It's an alluring thought, he declared.

– Oh, you fiend!

She struck him on the chest.

They left the room. Doing so felt weird. Doing that also felt weird.

He turned a bit, looking again at the glowing disk.

– Has it moved since the last time we looked? He wondered. – Moved at all?

They passed many rooms on their way down and to the living room, in the house without doors. They saw many others doing unrelenting fucking, like many must have seen them doing it.

The house looked different in daylight, but retained its unique qualities, its apprehensive disposition.

– What *is* this place? Myriam the night child asked.

– It has remained empty for decades, Damon replied. – We moved in last year, and no one has made any vocal protests.

– That's amazing. This isn't exactly a ruin and…

She held her tongue. The surroundings imposed themselves on them, unfolding before their eyes. They walked down a broad staircase and reached what was clearly the entrance hall, the first room people stepped into when they arrived.

– There are Norwegian historical objects here, she said stunned, – but also from the rest of the world. It's like a museum, but like nothing I've ever seen.

– Everything is like it was, he replied to the wonder in her eyes, her unvoiced question. – Somebody attempted to remove stuff the first few days after we moved in, but everything was back the morning after. There were no more attempts.

She studied his face, his expression carefully, listening to the ongoing basic anger in his voice, now laced with a sense of glee.

The hall expanded into the living room, a spacey place half-filled with revelers. Lots of glasses and bottles crowded the tables. There didn't seem to be any end to them. The numbers of unopened bottles seemed to stay that way, no matter how many were opened.

More people arrived during twilight, and as the dark night fell on the land once more. The intensity of the gathering increased further.

– Something happens with the onset of night, doesn't it? A girl said. – I mean, the day felt great and all, too, but this… this is… fffucking fffabuuulous.
Her voice and words shook the air. She took the second gulp of her drink, and the glass was almost empty.
– It is as if the place speaks to me, Myriam half whispered to Damon. – As if it speaks to me, *recognizes* me, speak to and recognizes us all. Does a place have a memory? Is it able to convey an event, a mood from the past, or is it the people making it that way, all these… ravens of the night tied… tied to Darkness?
Damon raised his glass to her, to all.
– To the nightravens, he cried.
– The nightravens, she replied, everybody replied silently and loud.
And they drank, breathing rising like wind, a hot, hot draft blowing through them all.
He heard the cry of eagles, felt them surrounding him, the wind from their flapping wings smothering him.
The prevalent mood snuggled close to everybody. Music flowed from speakers, from the house itself. Music with heathen chords, a few selected, clearly modern, and a selection of rebellious songs surviving the last two decades. One of the lyrics in particular gave them goose bumps:

«We found a fish on land
Gasping for breath
A human being kicking it
With a huge stick
Inside I felt the heat
From the kitchen
Turning me inside out

Steam rises from the campfire
On the rise behind our tail»

Myriam snuggled in Damon's arms. It was warm and cozy… and like standing under an ice-cold shower.
– I've never been taken from behind before, she whispered to him, with accusing voice and a diabolical look.
She stretched pleasantly, not caring that she displayed herself.
– As stated I should have been on another Witchnight, at that other mountain. She played with his long hair. – But under the costumes and skin they're pretty much nothing but normal, well-adapted people enjoying their vaunted position in society. I'm twice pleased that I chose this.
The mood from the Witchnight returned. Everybody felt it come with the darkness.
– I feel it, a boy whispered to a girl. – I can't explain it, but it's there, something I just can't express.
He tried, with acts, with all kind of pushy moves, and the girl giggled darkly and pleased.
They wolfed down the abundance of food and drink floating around, catching up with long hours of fasting. Food, drink and a selection of illegal substances seemed to flow everywhere. The feeding exceeded all rational volumes. Even those far gone, those existing more or less in their own, private world participated eagerly in the gluttony.

– Everything, feasting, celebration, drinking, feeding, fucking becomes wilder, ever more desperate these nights, a girl whispered hotly to a boy, seducing him with her beyond aggressive desire.

Everybody noticed it, in others, in themselves these days and nights, not only this night, in this place, but everywhere they directed their attention, the near past and fast approaching present. They shivered in delight.

The juggler and firebreather danced nude on a table. To those who had watched them or attempted in vain to do so it seemed like their clothes dissolved on their bodies. Some glanced at the floor to see if there were heaps of clothes there. There weren't. They blinked in confusion.

A crack, a thunder shook the premises.

– Fffloating, the juggler hummed, – fffloating across the molten sea. I am hovering above three caves, dddragon caves, choices of doooom. I fly on.

Blinking and strong lights, from nowhere, behind the eyelids. Some had been drinking and kept drinking a lot. Others had chosen to forsake alcohol… in favor of other things. And others were combining it. It didn't seem to matter, not tonight. The two on the table froze like puppets and intoned, in perfect choiring:

– Behold the organic machine! So fallible, so useless. We're all garbage like the heaps gathering in garbage valley, used and discarded by the self-appointed Elite!

– I've done similar stuff previously, Myriam whispered to Damon, – but it was so ritualized all of it, so damn boring. This is informal, without restraint.

– Release it within yourself, he bid her. – What you participated in was mere agricultural magic, a pale, washed up version of what's chasing through the blood of the hunter. Hold back no longer. *Let go!*

She heard him through what was a torrid steam, a boiling of blood. A thousand hopes and yearnings exploded in her simultaneously. The bonfire rose to the heavens, right there, at the center of the room. She imagined that she released a howl, a shriek of delight and flew away. The female cooed in Damon's lap and studied, incessantly fascinated his changing features. Her small wings grew large and powerful, and she fired herself like an arrow high above the mountains of the Earth. She drowned in the male's black eyes and shuddered. A fleeting thought didn't much upset or concern her. She suspected he was the reborn, not yet fully grown antichrist incarnated.

The night brought clarity, not dull confusion. They heard the sound of marching boots approaching. The sound of the sea drowned the noise of the boots, the seething sea the travelers rose through and from.

No more boundaries, no dammed waterfalls.

A boy stood up and spread his arms.

– The lion will never lie down with the lamb, he shouted and chuckled insanely.

– The human being's deep consciousness appears like an egg with many layers, peeling itself.

That voice came from everywhere and nowhere. Those listening swayed and nodded.

A girl danced to music only she could hear.

– Everything is so clear, she giggled. – Everything needed to see is two bigger pupils…

Shouts and cries kept echoing between the cave walls.

– I am I am. I AM

A primal scream sounded from below. Primal screams rose like rising and falling echoes, pain and joy. True!

Sweat poured from all over the body, on all the bodies present, extending into the mind, the overworked mind. Damon pushed the hair back, off his face, eyes and brow.

Thoughts whirled through his mind, so hard to catch.

– Wolf tribes, something… he strived. – *Yes,* that's it! The wolves were about to become extinct all over Europe, but in Spain they started living close to humans, unseen, untamed. The animal seemingly discarded its habits and characteristics. Eventually not even the animal researchers, the servoglobe's soldiers were able to catch them and put their radios in them. Wolves needed large areas to move and were so shy that they hardly approached humans at all. But now something has happened, a mutation, an adaptation. They're no longer at mankind's mercy.

People listened. They visualized his story. It turned real to them.

– I've heard that ever more dogs escape captivity and turn wild, the juggler said excitedly. – There is so much happening these days, these dark, dark nights.

More excited words, more burning visuals and scents and tastes and sensations surged through the wild human beings gathered under this roof tonight.

Each night powerful dreams visited him, rose from his depths. He rarely remembered much of them, except like what he experienced through flashes and mist, also when being awake.

Thunder rocked them, one they heard without ears, overwhelming the wall of sound stemming from the speakers. Everyone present looked at each other simultaneously and something dawned on them.

We're free, we can do what we want.

– Cuckoo, cuckoo, the cuckoo (not a human being resembling a cuckoo) sitting on the chair crowed.

Laughter made the ceiling rise and blow away and they saw the stars right above. The Milky Way dripped down on them and they easily found their way.

They wandered through a forest supposedly pitch black. The trail glowed in front of them. Embers pulsing in the air whispered to them, leading them forward, like threads of night and fire.

The sun's first rays reached them and they flew out of the night. Damon and Myriam penetrated even deeper into the mountain's fields. Everything appeared so clear to them. Every dot of mist, every blade of grass. The fresh mountain air. The ravages of the stone desert contradicted this in every way.

A few minutes later the field echoed with kicks, strikes and energy-demanding movements. Damon once again attacked Myriam, and once again she threw him on the ground. This time he made a somewhat better landing and didn't have that much air pushed from his lungs. After several throws and heavy landings they started sparring more with hands and feet. She taught him more initial moves.

– Aim beyond the target, she instructed him. – You knew this, even before we began. The trick is to listen to the rhythm of the body. The goal is to achieve an effortless flow between movements.

She blocked a cannonball of a fist, and gave him a light touch at the side of the jaw. Blood flowed from his mouth.

– We should stop, now, she said, clearly worried, – before your pretty face starts resembling a meatball too much. The progress you've made is more than sufficient for a first-time session.

– No! He shook his head to clear his mind. – I've never felt better than I do right *now*. I want to learn as much as possible before that is fading, like all good things do, like all things do. I want it to be hammered into my very consciousness.

His intensity felt inhuman, and frightened her.

– It's only two hours until I must show up for work. Even though there will be no sleep today, I should at least take the time to make myself presentable.

– You don't need to paint yourself to wrap your boss around the finger…

– Get out of here, she said, clearly uncomfortable.

– And you can just forget about work, he grinned. – You won't be able to sleep the first couple of hours, but then you'll grow so tired that you'll fall asleep at the first and best opportunity. Let's use our time in better ways. Come with me and I'll show you something that will never leave your fair eyes.

She turned mad by his first words. The last sentence made her feet and limbs and resolve weaken to nothing. She knew she would always crumble when he turned poetic, knew it, as she allowed him to take her hand and lead her into the thick mist.

They sought dark surfaces to focus on. The coming full daylight made already sensitive eyes flow with tears.

– We should have grabbed sunglasses on our way out, she mumbled, she grinned. – There was more than enough of that to go around, wasn't it…

It wasn't that important, though. They needed only to turn away from direct sunlight to see the landscape with wonderful clarity.

He got the remote look in his eyes again and she poked him.

– What is it?

– I wonder if I've walked this way before… ever. He shook his head. – I mean, I know I've walked here before, but even though a person walks through a terrain many times, it is never the same.

– I love it when you're deep…

Over a rise, down a hill, around a turn, he saw it. She noticed his smile and wondered, wondered again.

– What…

He placed himself behind her and pointed forward over her shoulder. One blink and he saw one setting, another and he saw one clearly different.

– What do you see?

She humored him, but also felt herself be pulled by something very invasive and powerful.

A deep ravine, a dried-out waterfall. Mighty wings cutting through air. A bird circling above what to her was a giant nest. The bird flew closer and she doubted no longer.

– Is that… She looked thunderstruck at him. – Aren't those *eagles?*

– Yes. A deep joy filled him. – After hundred years in exile, they've finally returned to the grass-covered mountains.

He closed and opened his eyes. He heard the flapping of wings very close. He saw dry sand blowing in the wind passing a derelict railway station. He saw the waterfall in its full power and shook. It didn't foam in white, but in red.

– W-where do they come from? She asked bewildered. – I thought they were practically extinct?

He mumbled something, she didn't hear what. She realized that he didn't hear her either. He stood there, his body rigid, listening to distant boiling. It was as if he wasn't even here anymore, and in one brief moment making her shake, she imagined that he truly faded away.

Concrete, steel, plastic and glass. Lots of synthetic material. Myriam met to work Friday. She met on time, dressed in formal attire of the most recent fashion, well done hair and thoroughly added makeup, as instructed. A pretty doll. She surveyed the bank's main offices and shuddered, over the surroundings and herself.

The second, top floor of the building was filled with other pretty dolls of both sexes. The biggest clients came up here, those with sufficient money and power to aspire to the higher levels of society. They expected a certain style. Myriam walked to her golden spot, the open office almost at the end of the hall. The climbers in this particular fish pond followed her with envious eyes.

She walked to her desk, ignoring the attention, treating it with the patronizing disregard it deserved.

The desk seemed like a total jumble before her. She grinned and chuckled and couldn't help herself.

– Snotty kid, she mumbled, – inexperienced snotty kid.

She sat down. It had an immediate effect on her, on her lower parts. The heat, the one that had never really gone away grew once again to what she feared would soon be a ravenous beast. She looked at herself in the mirror, at her flushed face, suddenly covered by a film of sweat.

– Miss Vallinger? As if in a dream her eyes focused on the man that briefly exited the big office at the end of the hall. – Would you step into my office for a moment?

His tone of voice, though pleasant as always carried his will, conveyed his wish in a subtle but undeniable manner. No inquiry, but rather an inquest, a direct, explicit order.

The buzz started immediately. Myriam spotted many a well concealed and expectant glee in the climbers' faces. She took her time before rising from the chair and gracefully straightening her tall and luscious body.

His office was totally closed off, with thick walls, dark windows and protected from the possible bothersome sound in the outer chambers. It had the latest in cooling systems, the latest fad in luxurious furniture and design.

– It's so quiet in here, Myriam said before she could stop herself.

She realized that the silence here had always bothered her.

Roar Høyland stood by the window, with his back to her for a while, longer than what was polite, before turning to her and sitting down behind the large and well-equipped desk.

– Sit down, he said graciously.

She sat down on the hot spot, not crossing her legs.

He leaned slightly forward from his position, a young, hungry potential mogul, the closest the established part of current human society came to a hunter. She had seen him go for blood numerous times.

– You were gone from work yesterday, Myriam. I would like to tell me why.

– I was ill, Roar, she replied softly.

– Is that all you have to say for yourself? His left eye closed slightly. – You won't tell me why you weren't at home or where you…

It boiled over in her. They had called, of course, and then gone to her apartment and checked, the usual procedure.

– That's enough! She cried so sharp that it cut him. – I have no intention of accepting any sort of bullying or dodgy personnel treatment. I'm fully aware of the fact that there is an official surveillance policy in this firm, but it isn't mine. Do you want my resignation, Roar?

– Certainly not, he coughed. – Aren't you overreacting a bit, now?

– Good for you. She sent him a patronizing smile. – Since we all know that there is no lack of companies valuing my services.

She often felt down, spending her days in this building. When she left what had become a damp office her mood had visibly improved.

The Golden Chair waited for her, an irresistible magnet in her path.

– You seem to have steered clear of much of the storm, Ingrid Tofte remarked. – Well done. You must have worked him pretty well, been pleasant as hell.

– I wasn't pleasant at all, Myriam said relaxed. – What purpose does that serve, when the bosses always expect you to crawl for them, anyway?

– Oh, I don't know, the other said, – It might give you an opening or two, if you choose your moment wisely.

Myriam, ignoring the last statement walked to the window, looking out at the city rain.

– Are you all right?

– Of course I am, Myriam replied lightly, turning towards the other with a surprised expression in her face. – Seeing Roar's red face always makes my day. He has never learned to deal with people not showing fear in his mighty presence, and I've never felt more right than the moment I left the office right now, right as rain, as undaunted as a cat before the mouse. You should try it, Ingrid. You might even like it.

Ingrid pulled back, leaving her alone.

The day passed in a way, like days were always passing. Myriam spent a considerable amount of her time studying the pattern on the wall to wall carpet, the black stripes on yellow. Rays from the afternoon sun shone through golden windows, shivering in the air and mixed with the pattern on the floor, an ever-changing shifting jumble giving her a headache.

She had slumbered in bed the day before, dozed off in a haze of gray and violet and a deep sleep, awake and aware, not woken up just to fall asleep, like here. Here, one was rocked gently to sleep.

Ingrid brought a young couple to her. Myriam recognized them instantly. Fredrik Blom and Anita Holt were rising stars within the fashion industry. They had recently married, and done so with all the elegance and bluster due the up and coming princes and princesses. Ingrid introduced them with just the right touch of awe and informal necessity.

Myriam shook their hands and welcomed them with her best smile, the best part of herself. She almost gagged. Only her experience in such matters made the vomit stay down and kept the bitter taint of her smile from revealing itself.

Later. She had sold the right package to the couple. The customers were pleased. The bank was pleased. Everybody was pleased. Later, in the restroom. Everything she had forced herself to stand returned to her with a vengeance. She crouched above the toilet bowl, pale and on shaky legs, and puked for the second time. Eventually she stumbled off on rubber legs, to the nearest mirror. She dried herself on and around the lips while staring at herself with burning red eyes.

– Stinking bitch wagging her tail, she mumbled in hateful spite.

She fell on her knees with hands rolled into fists.

Stinking world.

She kept it inside, as she crouched in fetal position on the floor. The pain scratched at her innards with claws drawing blood and silent howls. Slowly, slowly the darkness in her vision filled the room and she was enclosed in the horrible, empty black void.

++

Damon walked along Bryggen, the city of Bergen's internationally known street by the harbor, represented at the Disney exhibition in Orlando. The water splashed around his tall boots. He walked in the middle of the road without being plagued by cars. It was no sweat. The authorities had redirected traffic several hours ago. Quay areas all over town had been flooded by the rising sea. It had happened often the last few years and was about to become quite common. Damon pushed forward, quite determined. As he studied his surroundings this hot and humid afternoon quite the funny imagery emerged. The water reached high on the walls of all the houses to his right as he made his way north. The few stores that hadn't moved elsewhere lately were flooded… again. People walking on Bryggen tonight appeared to be walking on water (or just below it). It seemed incomprehensible that it was just a few hours ago that there had been a heavily trafficked road here, one that now served as seabed. The car owners and the store owners and business interests in general complained, as was their want. Who they directed their anger against was, as usual harder to fathom.

He often saw, as he closed his eyes a slow white flash behind his eyelids, one followed by impressions of surroundings in white, gray and black. There were glimpses of colors here and there, but rare and pale. They faded away every time he focused on them.

Nature and Youth, the youth organization of the national nature protection federation had called a meeting today, of all days. Damon left the Venice-like water edge and walked into the passageway between the old three houses. The so called conservationists had their offices on the ground floor and they hadn't yet moved. Their meetings were usually held upstairs, in the higher spheres, in the older generation's domain.

He walked through one luxurious room, and another and then one more, all very fashionable, containing the latest in design and technology. The major conservation organizations received more then enough financial support from the rich and powerful to maintain a certain (expensive) life style.

It was Friday night, and predictably there were even more empty chairs than usual. The board members knew there would be, of course. They wanted it like this, in order to hold the members on an even tighter leash.

One of Brian Adams' countless love songs played in the background. Pop music from the start of the nineties had once again grown in popularity. Damon studied the other people in the room and the temptation to leave right away grew almost overwhelming.

As usual small groups formed before the meeting was called to order, where the final pieces of the board's strategy were mapped out, and possible stragglers were reined in.

Tonight was a little different, though. Terrill realized startled that the rumors had run ahead of him, far ahead. Almost everybody in the room had their eyes on him. This particular evening might not turn out too bad, might become a little more interesting than what was usually the case.

– I heard that you guys had *some* party, man!

Roger Norlund put a hand on his shoulder and grinned in approval.

Roger wasn't among the worst. He had basically the same problem as many of Terrill's peripheral acquaintances: a resistance to letting go of the ties that bind. Quite a few of those present on the Witchnight had the same difficulty, at least with coming out of the closet, so to speak with the views they had no trouble expressing in the heat of the night, where only perceived outsiders heard them.

A sore spot inside Terrill grew a bit bigger.

– Terrill celebrated even harder than the others, a girl chuckled.

More chuckles followed, not unkind. Terrill joined in and managed to hide his embarrassment.

One potent moment he and the girl, Gerd looked into each other's eyes, until they both looked away in shame.

People found their chairs and the meeting started up, sort of.

Turid Indrehus placed herself behind the long desk at the end of the room, where the board members and most of the sycophants usually presided. They sat down and studied the motley gathering with an officious glare.

– I wish to welcome known and unknown people, members and nonmembers; we're quite simply delighted to have you all here.

Terrill imagined her as a future Prime Mini$ter and shuddered.

– We're gathered here to discuss ways to prevent oil drilling in vulnerable arctic areas and the preserves outside Lofoten. That's our main focus these days.

– Religious, Terrill commented to the unknown boy to his left.

The reward was an ugly stare.

– I've got a suggestion. A young slip of a boy brightened and raised his index finger high up. – Let's print *lots* of leaflets to better tell people what's going on.

– An excellent suggestion, Frode, Turid praised him.

Applause followed her praise.

– An excellent suggestion, Terrill repeated, pretty much mimicking Turid to perfection. – We give the paper producers more to do and we will also be quite busy. That's great, isn't it?

They did their best to ignore him, of course, nothing new there.

The children, from his age and up to about twenty-five continued yapping about oil drilling and everything under the sun, mostly about things that had little or nothing to do with environmental protection. And when Turid decided it was time to distract them she had it easy. She told, seemingly immersing herself in the story about her trip to Hardanger and her participation in the berry picking there. It definitely sounded to Damon like she was describing her ideal society.

And her audience stared devoutly at her.

He closed his eyes briefly. It was sufficient. In a vision after an eternity of darkness, a blinding white light he levitated, no flew above drying land. Prolonged drought made the ground crack. Former forests, plains and valleys were slowly covered by desert sand. A few withered trees showed in an endless dry sea.

He saw cars race on dusty roads, saw two mountaintops with icecaps and a thousand other images and sensations he knew he would never be able to make sense of.

Eyes slid open and nothing had changed. Once again he had confirmed to himself that he wouldn't be able to sleep through these meetings…

He closed his eyes again, and this time a blink was only a blink.

Nothing had changed since the last time he had dropped dead in this place, and it never would, no matter how many times he made a fool of himself believing in Santa Claus.

He yawned aloud and prolonged, reacting to something being said, unable to tell what. A howl pushed itself up from deep below. He felt it come and just then it was what he most of all wanted to do. The primal scream made the walls shake. He was breathing hard out in the street later, as if he had run many miles. When he listened he was able to hear the wind blow through his hair, to smell the exciting scent of pine needles… He growled like a beast and felt more human than ever.

– Yes, you wanted to say something, Terrill?

It dawned on him that Turid had spoken to him and that he was still inside. She strived to appear friendly. It meant so much to her to uphold the illusion of general participation. He found that hysterically funny.

– I wonder what we're truly doing here, he said, he challenged them all.

It turned absolutely quiet. Hearts skipped several beats.

– Why did you come here, Terrill? Why do you keep coming here?

It pleased him that she was unable to keep the open hostility from her voice and features.

– Gee, I don't know, he grinned, – I guess I didn't have anything else on my plate tonight.

The silence lingered, skipping more beats, and just as she was about to say something, to disregard him, he spoke again.

– And then I make the occasional visit to see if you guys have actually started doing anything, if you've got your act together, but as usual you're not even close.

– What are you saying? She exclaimed incredulous.

And yet again he had to ask himself if she really was this stupid, or if she was just playing at it.

– Like I clearly must repeat time and time again; there are certain facts you don't get or won't get, he drawled, completely relaxed. – I'm against the drilling, of course. Oil should never have been a part of human life in the first place. That is where you guys fail gloriously. You don't realize or won't realize what is truly at stake here. Why focus on such a tiny piece of land and sea when the entire world and all life on Earth are at risk?

He shrugged deliberately. It had the desired effect.

– That's a typical fatalistic attitude, a boy cried over the rising choir of voices.

– You must be kidding, Damon spat. – You guys refuse to see the bigger picture and play tea party, while the world is sucked into an irresistible, all-including vortex and you accuse others of being fatalistic?

– You speak about something that might happen in a far, far future.

– Do I? Damon looked at him with a pointed stare. – Have you taken a look outside today? Have you actually looked out the window for a change?

– There is a high tide, a girl snapped.

Damon's laughter was loud and noisy, because he wanted it to be, and because he

couldn't have held himself back.
– What's so damn funny? Roger wondered sourly.
– I'll tell you, Damon said, deliberately arrogant and patronizing. – You know, it's funny. My mother has told me that she had this very same «discussion» with passive creatures like you guys twenty years ago. Then there indeed had to be a high tide to reach the sea level we witness tonight. Is any of this reaching your dull-witted minds boys and girls?
Scowling and bewildered stares sought to silence him in the silence. They knew he was right, but weren't willing to admit it, not even to themselves.
High walls were erected, blinds glued to the eyes.
– No, he stated in a crushing blow, – fatalism is certainly not seeing the world as it is. Fatalism is to let everything slide, like almost everybody does today, like you do, your every waken hour, in fear and denial. Some of you may believe you do something good when you focus on a few minor details, I don't know, but you're wrong, of course. You help drawing attention away from what's truly important. We're told it's sufficient to clean up a little now and then, told that in due time more advanced technology will solve all problems. This is one of many gospels presented as an indisputable truth... all this while the quality of all life on the planet keeps deteriorating, while we all fall into an ever worse maelstrom of despair, disease and living death... No, people, this isn't the truth, but a *myth,* a myth created by those in charge, those wishing to hold into, come what may their hard won positions and aided by tea drinkers such as yourselves and others claiming to speak for the environment.
– Christ, how long are we supposed to sit here and listen to this crap? Roger cried enraged.
– It's indeed time to move on, Turid declared.
Most of the assembly applauded her words. But then Damon did as well, and they looked at him in more confusion and uncertainty.
Turid and her chorus line did their best to keep him out of the «discussion» after that, and no longer bothered hiding it. They never granted him permission to speak. But he didn't wait for permission, of course, didn't acknowledge their perceived power in any way. The loud quarrel started in earnest and the final illusion of peace ended.
– We can chain ourselves to the machines, if nothing else works, Roger mused reluctantly.
Most of those present accepted the halfhearted proposal. It excited only a few.
– If you truly want to stop oil drilling... all oil drilling... Damon felt the energy spread within. He wasn't bored anymore. – Traditional protests are no use and neither is helpless activism like chaining ourselves to machines. Look at what has happened the last twenty years. The various projects have hardly been delayed at all. Damn me, if not the protests have led to them being completed ahead of schedule. There has been no success in stopping anything and also scant success when it comes to spreading crucial information to people and make them take it to heart.
– There must be holistic thought and subsequent action. Are you guys willing to attack the very foundation of the modern society, the rotten fundament built on clay? Will you learn to be nomads and hunters, instead of city dwellers and rather support the collapse of civilization instead of attempting to prevent it? Nature, the planet itself will probably do most of the job, but it doesn't hurt to give the process a little help, a boost

now and then. We should join those blowing up stuff, really, giving them the support they deserve.

The cat was out of the bag. A number of unspoken names and events filled the buzzing air. A stunned but predictable silence followed his words.

– But… that's a criminal offense, Turid cried out in a hopeless mix of indignity and paralysis. – You're talking about a whole range of *criminal* activity here. The people you speak of are outlaws and practically anarchists, people paying no respect to the law at all.

She sounded like she was actually enlightening them about something. Damon grinned, a grin he knew infuriated her to no end.

– In the sense such a line of thought, such a terminology has any validity, any validity at all it is the criminals that are in charge, he stated, calmly facing the onslaught of all the accusing eyes. – The laws are made by the rich and powerful, to benefit the rich and powerful, against those who have little or nothing. Those supporting the rule of law are supporting the destruction of all life on the planet.

– You're completely nuts, Roger declared.

– Thank you. Damon smiled in something at least resembling pure joy. – Coming from you I take it as true praise.

He dominated the room. They realized that in their wet fear. In spite of him being alone, or perhaps because of it, he was the most powerful force among them.

– The Earth has fever, Gerd stated unexpectedly, in a startling development. – Humans are the bacteria that have become too numerous for the host body to handle. For the host to survive we have to return to a level where we once again can become an integrated part of the ecosystem.

Her colleagues on the board stared stunned at her. Damon looked outside, he looked at her. Outside faded quickly the harbor's light. In the girl's eyes he sought, and found the silver shadows of the moon.

The thought had crossed their mind before, but they hadn't dared express it. Now, someone had. One they had trusted not to pull the rug under their comforting illusions had betrayed them. Gerd returned their sore stares with a cheerful grin.

– Pacifism is like passivity, Damon said encouraged. – It's about time we stop allowing those in charge to give us anesthetics. Our healthy aggression is practically bred out of us. They've made us so dull-minded that we resemble walking dead, existing only as beings consumed by slow decay.

– I know where you're going with this, Turid spat, bitter and enraged, beside herself. – Warmonger.

Everybody knew where he was going with this. She just felt the need to stress it.

– Do you know that the Hellenistic war god Mars also was the god of agriculture? He grinned openly, now, couldn't hold himself back any longer. – Mars didn't exist before the destructive agriculture began.

Turid had turned red-faced and sweaty. The hair was still somewhat in order, but she was breathing hard. The veneer of sophisticated elegance was gone. Her eyes burned at him. She wanted to kill him, a desire, an urge she shared with quite a few in the room.

There had been far less shadow boxing than usual today, but to him it was way too much. Suddenly he had had enough. The rage and nausea stuck in his throat.

He stood up. They imagined he reached the ceiling and felt even more threatened. He knew he rocked their most fundamental convictions.

– Behold the tea party, he scorned them. Are we only playing here? Do we mean what say? How much more misery, disease and waste do we need before admitting that our way of life is just plain *wrong?* We, humanity have become the Sixth Great Extinction Event, become like a cosmic disaster for Goddess sake. You speak and act as if there is a choice, as if we haven't long since passed the point of any reasonable debate. Talk without action isn't just prattle, but also dangerous. One doesn't need a crystal ball to see the obvious.

He didn't, didn't need to look at them one more time. Even many of the youngest here were so busy with forging their future career that it was the only thing on their mind.

– Well, that was all for today, children, he said cheerfully. – I've enjoyed myself. At earlier «meetings» you've «listened» to what I have to say with your typical dull attention. Today, I can note with satisfaction that I've succeeded in tearing and pulling you out of that undesirable state of mind. Congratulations, you're human after all.

– Christ! Roger exploded and struck a fist at the table. – You can't seriously believe what you're saying? In the unlikely event that there should be a strong increase in temperature and sea-level, there will be visible signs well in advance and we can prepare for it.

– Do you ever listen to yourself, you pipsqueak? Damon responded instantly. – You guys couldn't wait to instigate the official politics of calming a potential restless population, could you?

There were those in the room that looked at each other with anxious glances.

He had turned to leave, but turned back for a moment and shook his head in bewilderment.

– What are we going to do with you, Roger?

The tall, black-haired troll counted on the fingers.

– Let's see, take a look at the current situation… What time would we have for instant preparations… with the warming already in the system, with the oceans growing inability to absorb CO2, if the next hurricane comes close to the previous, before clean up is completed and repairs are made? We have attempted to protect ourselves against the planet for ten thousand years and fortunately failed miserably. When the shit hits the fan it will be like a boiling kettle blowing up. Hell, it could happen over night and probably will. And that's just the Climate Change. *All* current human activity is ruining the ecosystem, the very foundation for our survival. This is the blatant truth you fail to accept, boys and girls.

The skewed smile turned even more skewed as he left them and walked out into the dank streets.

The sun hadn't set yet, but it was dark.

– Hey, Damon, wait for me.

Gerd rushed to catch up with him and the smile softened.

He stopped by the stairs. The water down there was cold and dark. He studied her bright hair. It was smooth and usually meticulously done and pushed back by the ears, but now the wind blew it astray. When she stopped in front of him she didn't fix it. Her mooneyes were almost on the same level as his black. She was, like him a well grown fourteen-year-old.

– The guys in there have made my stomach twist and turn for a while, but tonight they went too far. They don't deserve us.

He didn't voice a reply, didn't trust his voice.

They waded into Venice Street and continued wading to its end. The new name fit well and was used ever more often and the old ever less.

Outside the Narvesen Kiosk on Torgallmenningen they reached higher, dry ground and stopped for a while to let the water flow from the boots, boots now suddenly very inappropriate.

– It isn't difficult to see where we have been, she giggled.

There wasn't even a subtext of embarrassment in her voice. She no longer cared what others thought of her.

That pleased him.

They walked through the streets, through another world, one obviously attempting to isolate itself from the world. The spring fashions used bright colors and were quite heavy to wear, not very practical at all in the searing heat. It was more fake optimism to the point of denial and made him shake his head in dismay.

Around a corner a group of people, heavy, black clouds waited for them. All of them dressed in variations of black. They resembled shadows. Joy coursed through both Damon and the girl.

– Yo, Terrill, have you finally had enough of that shit?

Damon looked straight at he who had spoken, Yngve Greiger, a two-year older boy.

– Enough for a lifetime, he replied. – But as you can plainly see, the last effort wasn't completely in vain.

They acknowledged the girl with sudden brightness and happiness in their eyes.

– Those we left don't deserve us, Gerd said under the pointed stares and humming smiles.

Damon studied her as well, with eyes briefly narrowing. Those words seemed overly important to her, as if she had a chip on her shoulder.

He shrugged. Who hadn't?

They walked through Marken, towards the bus station, leaving the stone desert for the day.

– You waited for me, Damon said dryly. – You've earned my eternal gratitude.

– There's no need for you to turn sarcastic on us, Yngve said uncaring. – You didn't exactly make us wait that long, and that didn't come as a surprise to us either. We don't need a crystal ball to predict the obvious.

The wind was blowing and howling in the dank subway leading to the busses. Damon stood at the top of the stairs and waited for Gerd. She stopped and hesitated only briefly, before she went to him.

– Take me with you, she whispered, imagining she heard the echo forever, – to the Shadowland outside Time and Space.

CHAPTER FOUR

The old tree grew right at the edge between land, air and sea. The boy sat on a shaky branch reaching out on the frothing ocean.

The forest rustled behind him. The day was hot and dry, like the many days before this one. Black clouds raced across the sky, but they unloaded no rain. Yet another summer storm pulled and pushed. They had appeared with ever bigger strength and frequency throughout Damon's life.

Twilight filled the very air in his surroundings. It reached deep, into bone and marrow and soul. He saw more, not less. Reality expanded in his vision.

Waves rushed forward in front of him. The sea grew black, more so than he had ever seen it. Between white frothing waves he glimpsed the vast void shaking everything he was.

He fed on berries, fed on the entire forest embracing the shape of his body.

The night descended on the windy landscape. The clouds covering the sky made it blacker than ever. He imagined that the surrounding trees whispered to him, until he stopped and listened and realized that they all were, prompting images and sensations even more powerful than before. A landscape of mist and trees sticking up from water appeared to him briefly, but his senses told him it was true. Even as the moment faded it lingered. It was just a short walk on the trail through the woods. He caught himself in wishing it would go on forever. The house in the forest wasn't far away. All the lights had been switched off and silence dominated everywhere. Damon entered through the basement door and walked directly to his room. He switched on the computer and sat down in front of the screen. His face was lit by the characteristic glow.

He started cruising on the Internet, a technical innovation that had begun as a tiny ripple on the ocean surface fifteen years ago, but that had grown to become a world-wide, all encompassing wave, something that everybody with only basic understanding of current technology could access. It was, in short the biggest library in human history. Virtually any subject could be found and discussed, also the unpalatable and politically radical. He found his blog, his Twitter account and several other discussion forums and collections of radical articles.

Rough, moody music gave a sense of ancient times, of raw, unfettered nature and humans in it. He «met up» with what was clearly likeminded people and the very thought gave him a pleasant glow within.

«You can find anything on the World Web», stonefedup44 wrote, «even a gathering of techno-critical luddites».

«How great isn't it that people like us can meet like this», Damon (damon69) wrote. «It would most certainly not have happened by accident otherwise».

Barbarian Girl wrote: «Its use has spread from a tiny point to the entire world. Almost everybody is hooked up, one way or another. This is ultimately a bad thing, but right now it gives the rebels, the rogues and the immoral the chance to hook up. Anything goes… and it's such a thrill…»

«Come to Marseille», @trainingcamp wrote. «It has a great multicultural society, and working for me, you will be able to prepare for the upcoming deluge better than anywhere else».

It was easy, sitting here in the darkness, reading the words of other anti-civilization inclined to imagine barren mountains and vast wilderness and forests.

«The world has long since become a tragic comedy», Barbarian Girl wrote. «I've never cared much for those. They fit too well with the twenty-first century blindness».

He wondered if he would ever meet these people face to face, if it would be the same, the same great experience.

«It is funny when the people in charge find it virtually impossible to stop and even impede upon free exchange of thought and information», Sopping Wet Bitch wrote. «The Fourth, *supporting* Estate is losing its power, at least to a point. The wild growth of the Web was clearly unintentional. They know more than ever, now that control is an illusion».

She was clearly more, much more than her online name suggested. He grinned.

Damon took his time, participating in the most interesting conversations, reading the most crucial information, bookmarking what he filed away for later, very aware of the fact that he would probably never have time to read more than a tiny slice of it all.

«Natural disasters are picking up in number and strength again», stonefedup44 wrote. «I have a program that seeks out such and related news on the Web and its folder has lately become as bloated as a fifty-year old whore».

Everybody smiled grimly.

Damon knew they did. He knew them like he did himself. They knew each other like all kindred souls.

He had his own system of finding news about rebellion, natural disasters and the advanced breakdown of the modern society. The folder grew progressively bigger every day. He would have to add more hardware storage space soon.

Two men, two lawyers had made a film. They had incurable cancer. The start of the film showed how they swore loyalty and support to each other. They started doing what society perceived as misdeeds on a grand scale. One set fire to a police station while the other filmed it, and that was just the beginning of a long list of crimes they executed and documented, and posted on the Internet. It had taken quite a while and countless offences before the police had exposed them. The two men had been arrested… and then let go, free to continue their attacks on Law and Order. They had eventually been charged with countless felonies, but still managed to be released on modest bail before the upcoming trial.

They had enjoyed every second of what remained of their lives. The day before the court had set they had triggered a «bomb» inside a mall. It had released a vile stench making everybody flee the premises, and then the two had calmly waited for the police to arrive.

– I'm free, they had stated from the stand. – All webs chaining us have been cut. You have no power over us anymore.

The music, like everything else about the film and them and their final days and nights haunted everyone watching it. Damon knew it did.

They had died within days of each other, with a huge smile on their lips, well before the first judgment had been passed, after no more than ten days tops in custody.

It was a great story and it comforted him, comforted them all.

Other news… they flooded his mind like birds flying in the dark. Turkey had started the construction of huge dams keeping water from reaching the Middle East. Years of quarrel with Israel finally erupted into open warfare. Greece, after years of instability practically collapsed economically, but its army was still functioning well enough. They invaded Macedonia with all their remaining might. Serbia and Croatia went at each other's throat again. Spain fired at everybody, fired at the French and the Portuguese, and discreetly supported by their remaining European allies, at the ever higher number of people attempting to cross over from Africa.

Most of the stuff happening, the ever more distinct signs of the collapse were kept out of established media or given a less sinister form supporting the desired complacency, of course, but it was a useless effort, really. With the Internet and by gathering news from many sources the emerging picture was more than clear enough. The truth was undeniable. What Damon had seen with his own eyes everywhere he had visited in his young life was confirmed even in the strongest statement of denial. Chills of fascination and apprehension surged through him.

The harvest in the bread baskets in the United States and the Ukraine and elsewhere had failed for the third year in a row. Dust supplanted the once so fertile soil. And the Ukraine was so covered by radiation that it hardly mattered anyway. Its population fled in ever greater numbers, many of them already sick, dying, suffering and dying. The few remaining green spots in Africa became the sites for endless feuds, murders and genocide. Funny remarks had rechristened the entire continent *Sahara,* and that name grew increasingly common.

There was a classified, now very public report from a previous gagged professor in immunology about the beyond weakened immune defense system in humans, other animals and plants. Old, well known diseases grew increasingly lethal. Epidemics erupted anywhere, at any time. The new Streptococcus A, in popular language known as Streptococcus Death grew in strength and scope. Antibiotics failed big time. Tuberculosis or consumption once more became the scourge it once had been. New and previously unknown beyond viral diseases constantly found its way into the public eye. Malaria traveled north, with the heat.

Production and use of medicines reached new, insane heights, in vain. People finally began to look through Big Pharma's false and greedy reasoning.

And then, finally, news filed under *curiosities*. The Norwegian and Swedish parliaments had simultaneously and unanimously voted through a *total* immigration ban. The vote was merely a confirmation of what was already practical policy. Both governments stated this proudly, across the world. Ninety percent of the population in both countries supported the move, like they supported the ever more extensive powers given to the police and the army. The cheers pushed at Scandinavia's ever lower ceiling.

He printed out all of it and didn't know why he bothered.

Memories, clear, indistinct images… they flooded his inner eye almost like dreams, and just as precious.

Gerd spoke in a whirl of water and wind, fire and darkness:

– You were at the Witchnight, right? You're witches, aren't you? Am I to be initiated, now?

She looked roguishly at those present, at the people gathered around her. In the depths of the Askøy forests the warm bonfire reached for the night sky, mirrored in the dark water nearby.

– There's no need for that. Damon shook his head. – You're already one of us. You've always been.
– It's such a thrill, she said softly. – Thank you.
Something made him look even closer at her then, at the shadow at the edge of her eyes.
– So far from the tragic comedy the world has become, she said and met his eyes calmly, confirming his suspicions.
Startled, he suddenly knew with absolute certainty who Barbarian Girl was.
She walked to him, still a bit shy and kissed him on the lips. The others walked closer to them both. The young girl opened her eyes wide, not without apprehension.
Civilization was never far away. It couldn't be, in this day and age on such a fairly small island. They imagined they heard its sounds, spotted its gray lights. The bonfire lit only a tiny piece of land in the vast wilderness surrounding them, cutting them off from the wall of darkness smothering their senses. As far as they knew little or nothing existed or lived beyond that wall. They gathered in the borderland between night and fire, those who were ghosts and shadows.
Damon was vaguely distracted. Myriam was supposed to be here, but hadn't come. She didn't answer her phone.
The girl they called Kara, a tall, strange-looking blonde stepped forward with a glass and a bottle in her hands. She filled the glass with the pearly white wine. Her moves were quick and confident. Gerd glanced at Damon. He drew a shiny dagger from the boiling kettle. She couldn't tell when it had started boiling. He reached out a hand. She put hers in its palm. He pushed the edge of the blade at the soft flesh on the side of her hand. There was a quick incision, a sudden pain. The first seconds nothing seemed to be happening, as if nothing had been done. He placed the smaller female hand above the glass and squeezed. The blood flowed. There was still no pain. Drops of blood hit the surface of the wine, broke it and fell to the bottom, not really mixing with the transparent fluid.
– Stir it, he encouraged her.
She used a single finger and the fluid turned dark crimson, creating a stir of further excitement in her.
– We're the children of the Storm, Yngve cried loud but evenly, – riders of the Thunder Road, the force of life moving through the shadows of death…
Gerd raised her head. She heard the sound of a plane somewhere, shaking her head, ignoring it. She accepted the chalice Kara handed her.
The glass felt cold against her lips. She drank. The blood and the wine felt cold in her mouth and down her throat… until it reached the stomach.
Her face lit up like the glow it was.
– I feel it, she cried startled. – I *feel* it! I heard the sound of a plane earlier. They are everywhere, but not here, in the forest. Here, they will only *crash,* like the *wreckage* they are.
Such a strange taste. The heat spread. The blood returned to the system that spawned it, stronger, more potent than before, she felt it, how it changed and empowered her. She giggled, her body giggled, while she levitated up there, high above in the vast velvet night. The Gerd not giggling looked down on the bonfire during a timeless time span. She joined with the ghosts and the shadows of the world.

A female voice hummed in the forest, filling it, filling those walking it. With the voice, the humming turning to a chant, people near and far away heard music, heard the single voice turn into a choir, heard distant thunder with no lightning and no rain.

The wanderers in the wilderness, the riders of the storm felt it, felt it deep inside. Gerd felt it transfer from them to her, and then, in turn her experience reinforced theirs. The ghosts and shadows of the world joined with the forest, with the very air they breathed, rising into the night sky, imagining they could touch the stars.

The Terrill family relaxed, somewhat in the garden a hot afternoon. Damon sat on the low masonry and broke to pieces dead branches from a heap not far off. He threw the remains on the ground in abrupt, angry moves.

His thoughts reluctantly returned to a harder than usual workout he and Myriam had enjoyed. He had won an exchange, hit her and struck her to the ground. She had remained dazed on her back a few seconds, before she had regained her faculties and easily stood up.

– You've improved a lot, she acknowledged with a smile.

– I'm not so sure. He shook his head, clearly in doubt. – I fear that you lack the killer instinct, that I'm just taking advantage of it when you don't pay attention.

The smile vanished. She had looked at him with a strange, desolate expression in her eyes.

He heard her tiny voice the last time they had spoken. It had been over the phone and he had hardly recognized her. There had been nothing left of the spirited voice he vividly remembered.

Gerd had attempted in vain to comfort him at dawn, after the devastating phone call from Myriam. They had all been down, even more so, because the night had been so great.

– I feel asleep in a haze of gray and violet. She had subconsciously clutched the bandaged hand. – I dreamt about a place where there were lots of sun and lots of shade.

The words killer instinct returned to him, haunted him, without meaning or reason.

His mother and father wanted something. He knew their glances by now, like gnats that couldn't be dissuaded. A shrug stopped him from acting in any way. He made no effort to meet them halfway. They would get to whatever they were getting at sooner or later. They usually did.

– We received a phone call from Leif Indrehus today, his mother said casually, fooling no one. Damon closed his eyes demonstratively. – You know we're not exactly his greatest fans or anything. His claims made us worried, that's all.

– Scratch the hypocrisy and usual falsehood and he probably told something resembling the truth, Damon shrugged.

– I thought we had taught you respect for others' viewpoints…

– The viewpoints of those destroying all life? Don't make me laugh, father!

He strived to keep himself somewhat calm. To describe what was rising within him like a volcanic eruption seemed hopelessly inadequate.

A while later he started the bike in the garage and raced the few meters outside with screaming tires. He stopped for just a few seconds. When they heard him scream to them, down in the garden his voice sounded like thunder. It carried far away and the neighbors couldn't avoid hearing it.

– I'm looking forward to the collapse, do you hear me? I'm looking forward to it.

The screaming tires reminded of a banshee as he raced off.

A flow of memories chased his feverish thoughts, rushing towards him like the ground rising to meet his falling body.

Then they hardly seemed to move at all, like a miracle, a curse. He was able to savor them, to burn in their acid presence.

The day, the day's ugly light, and then the rain fell on what felt like an endless ride from the island to the mainland and the town slowly revealing itself.

He practically erupted from the dark mountain, the tunnel and raced across the bridge towards the city center. Through the tunnel, the bus only lane and he was there. The gray, dull and dead stone desert smothered him, pushed at him from all sides.

The City Park was hardly anything more than brown blades of grass and naked branches of something resembling trees. He turned right after the old, abandoned fire station and the fairly modern fortified police station towered over him. The abrupt halt made a giant cloud of dust rise in the air and surround machine and man. It didn't bother him. The echo of the whining tires didn't hurt his ears.

They strip-searched him, several times, as he passed through the various gates to the cellblock's inner sanctum, deliberately humiliating, until he finally reached his objective.

It felt strange, eerie how every detail appeared to him. The large room. The four guards, one in each corner. The one lamp hanging from the ceiling. The spider lurking in the gray twilight.

There were no windows, no ways to look outside, if one didn't imagine them.

The door behind him was locked with a sinister slam. He heard the key being turned in the lock and feet enclosed in heavy, polished shoes thundering against the floor. Everybody gathered at the center of the room, around the table under the lamp.

Myriam looked very pale, even in the weak, pale light. She wore the gray prisoner suit they had started using the year before, one clearly identifying, marking her as an inmate. They had chained her hands and feet. She could hardly lift her feet from the floor, hardly do anything but dragging them along.

Her subbing across the floor seemed to last forever.

– What have you *done* to her? He practically shouted to the guard.

– Be happy we let you in at all, boy, the guard spat.

The grown man's obvious distress sort of calmed the boy, kept him from losing his temper.

– Perhaps I should, he acknowledged. – Now, when you mention it, it does surprise me. Why *did* you let me in?

He had been surprised by such a relatively positive development, but no longer. Not when he thought it through. This was a scandal, one they had been totally unable to keep out of the papers and public discussion forums. It was also gross enough for Roar Høyland's less savory activities to be exposed. The fact that Myriam had been found cuffed had been extensively debated in unofficial media since the incident. They tried to manage the scandal, not extend it.

Høyland was the son in law of Tore Fosse, a leading man in international cosmetics and genetics' industry. They wanted to bury Myriam Vallinger, not charge and imprison her. Damon couldn't help but grin just a little.

They pushed him down on one chair, Myriam on another. The two sat on each their side of the table, unable to hold hands.

– How are you? He coughed.

He wanted to kick himself for asking such a stupid question, but he didn't feel particularly creative just then.

– I don't feel so bad.

She managed a smile. Eyes were hazy, as if covered by layers of shit and poison. The fire inside, if there was any of it left hardly burned at all.

It tore him apart to see her like this, and he was unable to hide it. She looked softly at him, as if she could see right through him, see all the rage and horror tearing him apart inside.

– The asshole will survive, he swore, – according to official and unofficial sources.

– A damn shame, she hissed. – I hit him and kept hitting him until I was so exhausted that I couldn't lift a hand anymore. I... lost it. After holding myself back for so long I lost it completely... and I'm glad.

He understood, deep inside. He didn't even have to try hard.

Everything was so silent in here, immutable. He stared at the walls, attempted to stare through them, to the world outside.

– Don't be stupid, she said to him. – Don't get any ideas.

He shrugged, deliberately, involuntarily. She understood. It was the same outside. There was not a single breath of wind, only the dirty, quiet rain, darkened in the day's foul light.

– There won't be any trial, not really, she said with the same muted voice. – You know that, right. I will do my best to embarrass them as much as possible, but let's not hope for more than that.

He rose abruptly after a while of insignificant conversation he recalled nothing about afterwards, backing away from her.

– Don't be a silly kid, were her last words to him. – Don't wait for me.

– I won't, he said with a raspy voice.

He was fourteen. He had to keep reminding himself he was an adult.

«Forget me», her dead eyes told him.

«Forget it»! The dull fire in his eyes replied.

The young boy stood straight on the branch reaching across the raging sea. He shouted at the waves and saw himself charge one by one by one, hardly ever managing to draw breath after beating one before the next struck him.

He jumped into the raging sea, charging all its mighty waves.

CHAPTER FIVE

Everything fell apart.

Lisbeth Kaspersen sipped the wine in her glass while staring at the Trondheim Fjord below. When she pulled the glass from her lips it rested in a slanted position between her fingers. The sea level was noticeably higher than what had been normal. There was no doubt about that. But she imagined that the sea suddenly rose so much that the fjord and the landscape were wiped out before her eyes and only the sea remained. She blinked, had to blink several times before the nightmare scenario faded away.

She was a guest at one of the older and distinct houses with a fairly close view to Munkholmen, the Monk's Islet. The noise from the city wasn't that close, but it still seemed that way to her. She stood on one of the house's many balconies, sipping her wine. Most of the noise actually originated from inside the building. She shook her head in irritation. The preparations for tonight's party had started. The decorators and carpenters made quite a fuss. Logic told her that the background noise from the city should have been submerged in that.

The sound of distant cars and conversation still reached her. She would swear that it did. The talk on avenues and streets and dank cellars hidden from public view whispered in her ears like a roar, making cold sweat appear on her brow.

An expectant smile changed the sour expression, as she returned to the assembly hall. Lasse, her aide waited dutifully for her right inside. He was an excellent aide, well trained and skilled, well versed in the labyrinths of modern politics.

– Everything is in order? She inquired casually.

– Everything is proceeding smoothly, Miss Kaspersen, he assured her.

– I've worked with this for a long time, she insisted, – worked hard to make this weekend a reality. Important people from all over Europe will come here. Nothing must go wrong. If anything does, heads will roll.

– Nothing will! He assured her.

Her worry faded once more, as she walked through the old manor. Everything did indeed seem to be in order, to proceed smoothly. This house was literally made for the purpose, for purposes like these. She bristled. It was happening, it really was.

A maid approached her, curtseying, waiting to be acknowledged.

Lisbeth did, nodding somewhat patient.

– Miss Hansen is here, My Lady. She's awaiting your pleasure in the library.

– Thank you, Mary, Lisbeth said preoccupied.

The news made her admire her surroundings, the expensive furniture just a little longer. She didn't delay too long before setting course for the library.

Annette Hansen was a tall, slightly plump woman about Lisbeth's age. Lisbeth embraced her and kissed her on the cheek.

– You made it, she greeted her guest, – and just in time for our own, private spa. I'm so happy.

– I'm happy to be here, Annette replied, clearly doing her best to convey enthusiasm.

– This is the place to be, you know, Lisbeth bristled. – It isn't quite ready yet, but that unfortunate state of affairs is passing with each approaching moment. Servants will roam the rooms tonight. The elite of the elite will arrive here in five hours and everything must be ready. We must be ready.

– We will be, Annette practically echoed.

Lisbeth looked pleased at her.

An entire team of maids waited for them in her thoroughly prepared salon. Among them were Mary and Renate, two dull-eyed Caucasians, but mostly colored girls. Lisbeth and Annette towered above them all, and the maids shrunk in their presence. Lisbeth noticed how that pleased Annette.

The maids undressed their betters fast and efficient. The big women, given subtle and humble directions were placed on tables and rolled into the luxurious bathroom. One of the girls spilled perfume on the floor, almost hitting Annette's arm.

– You clumsy slut, Annette snarled.

– Sorry, kind Miss, the girl whimpered, – Lisa is very sorry. She will strive to better herself. Please forgive her, kind Miss.

Annette mumbled something of a somewhat forgiving nature. The girl brightened in gratitude and stark relief.

Their skin was cleaned, washed softly with steamed cloths. It felt so pleasant and was done with such skill that Lisbeth hardly noticed the touch. She sighed content. They were eventually rolled into the next room. With a methodical, utmost care every single hair on their body was removed. The maids took care of their face, their nails and gave massage. Lisbeth noticed how she began feeling wondrously relaxed. For a while there, on the table she even imagined that the treatment would distract her from the thoughts grinding in her mind. It didn't. They rose unbidden to the surface, like they always did.

– I have to remind myself how effective these dolls are, she told Annette. – I know they will complete their work in time, no matter how I may fear they won't. The work can't be rushed.

– They are quite skilled, Annette mumbled drowsy.

– They are adequate, Lisbeth shrugged. – They know what will happen if they stray from their task.

Closed eyes flickered. Something kept stirring below.

– Damn! She practically shouted.

Both Annette and the girls shook, even though subtle awareness born of experience told them that this wasn't directed at them.

– I can't handle relaxation, she mumbled, – just can't.

– It's the nightmare again, isn't it? Annette said helpful, very helpful.

And Lisbeth kicked herself for the thousandth time, for having told her «friend» about it. And then she didn't care anymore.

Annette was her therapist. She was paid to listen to crap.

– I see giant seagulls, Lisbeth said. – I see them, even if I keep my eyes open. They have giant beaks and huge fangs. They fly past tall constructs, skeletons of floating steel, while the sunset is dripping huge tears of blood. Dead oilrigs, former mobile wreckage that is hardly more than scrap iron these days. They've been parked from Stavanger to Trondheim, awaiting a new future in the far north that will never come. I see tiny, tiny migration birds carrying with them microbes of invisible, sneaking DEATH. They drop their shit and people die like flies in their slipstream.

– You fear the future, Annette prompted, – the upcoming, uncertain times, what you can't control.

– I know that, Lisbeth sighed. – I don't need a crystal ball to see the obvious.

She enjoyed the hurt and bewildered expression in the other's eyes. She didn't have to actually watch it anymore to enjoy it.

The windows had been properly closed and locked. She sat in front of the three-way mirror, while the girls did her hair. The windows were closed, locked and bolted. It was no use. She still heard the wind. A conch had its labyrinth strapped to her ear. It didn't matter if she turned her head. She heard the howl of the wind and sometimes she imagined that she smelled it as well, smelled its wile stench, its spices and blood.

She heard the blowing of the wind around empty ski tracks. Every winter, now, it became more and more evident where the wind was blowing. She saw the green grass, heard the sound of lice chewing spruce needles, felt raven claws in the middle of winter. She woke up in a sweat, even while being wide awake.

– The world has gone off the hinges a bit lately, she stated firmly, – but that isn't necessarily bad, is it? There's nothing broken that can't be fixed by a good plumber or mechanic. A little bit of fine-tuning here and there, and everything will once again be what it's supposed to be.

– Please sit still, kind Miss, Mary said jittery. – Kind Miss is so big and strong that we can't keep her steady.

Lisbeth nodded, more to herself than to the girl.

– Your servants, both the males and females are so well behaved, Annette beamed. – It's hard to imagine that they've learned their… their place so well in just a few, short years. This is Norway, after all, the very home of the obnoxious youth.

– Times have changed. In the eleven years since…

Since absolute Chaos was released in the world.

– In the last eleven years times have changed and they know it, their parents know it, know that all pretense of equality between rich and poor, the powerful and the powerless have virtually disappeared. Teenagers today are much more receptive to the proper training regiments. After completing their thorough classes they still need to be reminded of their low standing now and then, but not very often. I used to pick my girls from Victor Russel's staff, but that isn't necessary anymore. We have our own schools by now, and they're filled with young boys and girls eager to learn the ropes of the new age.

After they had fitted her dress she made the final touches herself.

– Some things are quite simply too important to leave to the help, she told her companion. – Don't you agree?

– I most certainly do, Annette emphasized. – The dull-witted hens may be great for simple tasks, but fail completely when it comes to important details beyond menial work.

There was the sound of feet against the floor, of doors opening and closing. The two women of good standing were left alone. Lisbeth kind of missed the presence of warm flesh surrounding her, but steeled herself against the chill. She put on the final modest layer of makeup. There was no need for more. The rounding of the breasts was visible just above the edge of the dress. The split in the dress showed the modest part of her thighs. The girls had picked mostly low-heeled shoes to her, but she deliberately chose high-heeled. She noticed Annette's glance.

– I don't mind displaying my superiority, Lisbeth shrugged.

It pleased her to note the insecurity displayed in Annette's flickering eyes.

They had put the ice-blonde hair in a top. She shook it loose a bit.

The mirror image returned a smile.

She made a personal appearance before a gathering of the male and female servants well before the evening began, going through the details with them, stressing yet again the importance of the weekend.

– Remember, this is a formal party, but my hope is that there will also be… plenty of informality. The guests need to be shaken up a little, softened, so to speak before the crucial talks tomorrow. They must wake up in a good mood and open to new ideas. I trust you will take these instructions to heart.

She knew they would, knew there was no need to stress anything further. They showed their respect and fear and willingness to be an extension of her will in a thousand small ways.

The refurbishing and cleaning and polishing finished well in time. The shining, elegant halls opened up to her, as the sky turned red in the west. She walked through them and owned them, as more and more guests arrived and she greeted them and treated them to her charm. There was doubt in the shivering parts of her insides, but none of that was exposed. She noted pleased that also Annette played her part to perfection.

A string quartet played in one room, a jazz orchestra in another. Everything happening was very laidback and classy. The guests visibly relaxed and even showed signs of actually having a good time, which was close to unprecedented at these gatherings.

– They come here at my invitation, she said to Annette, speaking in a well-modulated voice, one that the other woman didn't have trouble hearing, but that didn't carry far. – We will make sure that they will be deeply grateful for that fact.

– Yes, we will, Annette, echoed her.

– That gratitude will certainly also extend to everyone in my circle, Lisbeth added graciously. – We all stand to gain tremendously from all this.

– Thank you, Lisbeth, Annette gasped in gathering ecstasy and shining eyes. – Thank you!

It was almost too much. Lisbeth considered acting on it, but decided against doing anything. Annette's and the others'… enthusiasm, if it wasn't way over the top could only add to a successful weekend.

Most of the guests were quite young, even amazingly so… if one didn't know the backdrop of the current state of affairs in European politics and enterprise, and recalled the unfortunate fate of the previous generation.

She quickly buried the sting of pain in the ground she had prepared for it.

They had grown up with rock and rap and new age music, but like the generations before them, they had quickly adapted to the art of power and the pleasant and undramatic sound of jazz and string quartets. Now, they took over an ever bigger part of the state administration and enterprise decision-making, like countless generations before them. The difference was that it happened much faster and more brutal compared to earlier. That was what happened when many flocked to fill a vacuum simultaneously.

The sun never set, or so it seemed. It hung blood red above the horizon forever, its rays' deadly lasers cutting her to shreds. The shiver inside almost broke loose and ran wild.

She was the host, even though Annette and a few others helped out. They came to her, as desired, and she received them and goaded them in the desired direction. She gave them all the same attention or at least the appearance of such. Behind the masks they spoke to her of their worries and fears and expectations and she listened to it all. She moved herself and her attention from person to person, group to group and room to room, giving everybody relief and hope for the future.

She did her duty with a cluster of prattling wives, giving them a reason for being.

– People become just more and more… rude these days, one complained with wavering eyes. – You can't get anywhere without people throwing insults at you.

– That's so true, Lisbeth told with a straight face. – The commoners are losing all respect.

It was quite evident to her that they reacted to that word, those words. They elicited the perfect response from her attentive audience.

– They need to be… dealt with… don't they? The woman stated with shivering lips, but with a rising anger in her eyes.

The host stopped by another crowd of wives and husbands from the construction industry.

– We will probably be starting on another mall next year, a proud wife said and winked to her rather nonplussed husband. – There is a high probability of us doing that.

Everybody here was very keen on telling Lisbeth about their newest construction project. She worked very hard on keeping a straight face through her boredom and impatience. These people had built their fortunes on the construction of such mammoths. She knew that.

– I've studied your conquests carefully, she told the crowd gathered around her. – Your experience will be invaluable in the coming years. Invaluable!

But they still loved to tell her about it time and time again. There was a new kind of restlessness hidden in the prattle and behind the wavering eyes before her… and something more.

A keen observer easily caught the nervous energy flourishing between these wet walls. The prevailing sense of boredom dominating these gatherings in bygone years was practically absent.

– Perhaps others don't quite get it, Lisbeth told Annette. – Not like I do.

– Lisbeth, dear, what in the world are you talking about?

Her friend's clueless response didn't exactly surprise Lisbeth.

– The talk, the celebration, everything, everywhere grows wilder, more desperate. She spoke more to herself than she did to woman by her side. – I sense it here, in every corner and room, in everybody present, in streets and alleys. It has gone too far and can't be stopped. In spite of my efforts I'm just as unable as anyone else to stop it. The old ways just don't *work* anymore.

And now she saw a glimmer of worry in Annette's impassive face.

– But I realized that quite some time ago, and I have a *plan*.

Calm, that was the thing. Allow reason to prevail every time the panic button became too tempting. If she lost control, here of all places everything would be lost.

Numbers and names of terror filled her consciousness, made her freeze like stone on her spot.

The new tuberculosis sanatoriums had yet to become public knowledge. People high and low whispered about them, but very few spoke aloud about them. They didn't dare.

The somewhat calm rehearsal of those numbers and names of terror did return reason to her frozen mind and mobility to her stiff limbs. It was a kind of exercise, a mantra.

AIDS: From July 1993 to July 1994 the number of registered global cases increased with sixty percent. From then on the number of cases had exploded. No one could make any reliable estimate about its propagation any more. The only useful surveys varied between hundred and two-hundred million infected. And there were ever more persistent rumors about the existence of a mutated strain, one infecting through air that had no need to spread from one moist piece of flesh to another.

Mexico City: There was no Mexico City anymore. There was no Mexico anymore. It had broken up in countless, uncountable factions.

And then there was Streptococci Death…

She discovered to her horror that her glass shook. No one had noticed. At least she didn't believe anyone had. It took all her inherent calm to put down the glass without first devouring all its content. There was a lot left. She had hardly tasted the pearly wine.

Control, precise control… That was the ticket.

The consuming of alcohol reached new heights around her. Others didn't show any of her restraint and she smiled in triumph.

The evening passed by faster than a breath of wind and night dawned. She fumbled and stumbled in the darkness and she felt it, the savagery beneath the surface. The frown deepened on her forehead.

Tore Fosse approached her. She noticed that her heart beat faster and it annoyed her.

– Dear Lisbeth, he began, – allow me to add to the praise you've already received for organizing this excellent gathering. It's safe to say to say that it would probably not have happened without you.

– Thank you, Tore, she replied.

He took her hand and she allowed him to lead her to the dance floor. Everything seemed to float and flow around them in ways she couldn't control.

He was in his late forties, but tall and well built, and she thought the graying hair by the temples fit him. She tried to do numbers in her mind again, but it didn't work.

– Some might say it was a mistake to make alcohol easily available, he grinned at her, – but I feel it is a necessity to loosen the mood. These people, with their iron hard control need to loosen up a little. Here, in this safe environment they use the opportunity… to go wild. There are exaggerations, but not worse than that your excellent and effective staff can handle it. I see nothing inappropriate here. Once again, my thanks for an excellent evening. I'm confident the entire weekend will prove to be both entertaining and useful. Your determination alone will certainly increase the changes for that. And they say preparation takes you half there.

–They say that, she said lightly.

She didn't hear the music. The surroundings faded away in an indistinct mass.

– And what do you say? He wondered.

It was a redundant question, and he knew that. The sudden inquiry in his eyes made her dizzy.

She met his eyes calmly and pointedly.

– Every step should be measured in advance. If the dark and unknown paths are brightened by a thousand lamps even unexplored land will be easier to walk. By careful planning and execution one will eventually achieve the control and safety one seeks.

She drowned in his smile.

– Let me again tell you how amazing you are. He shook his head. – The weekend has just started and everything is already far exceeding expectations. I must say I'm looking forward to what more you have to offer.

– Why wait? She heard herself say.

The roar rose violently in her ears. She was unable to stop it.

In the time and space the remains of the surroundings just faded completely away around her and she found herself and him in the building's abandoned dark hallways outside one of the empty bedrooms. He pulled her close and kissed her greedily on the neck and on swollen, sore lips. She released an involuntary moan. Her body pushed itself at his. He released a loud, triumphant cry, roaring like a beast. She closed her eyes in abandon. Her rationality, her hard won reason faded into something insignificant.

She relented, also in the remaining part of her somewhat calm mind. Okay, she shrugged, let it be. There was no stopping it. It was something that had to be done, like letting go of shit or taking a leak. He was married and she knew it wasn't the first time he took lovers. There would be just this one time. Then he would be gone from her life.

He picked her up and carried her into the bedroom, into the dim twilight. She had reason to be pleased. The evening had indeed been quite successful. Tomorrow she would show them even more, more of what she had to offer. It had been a promising first day, such an excellent foundation for the future. Everything would be okay then... if tomorrow would ever come.

++++++++++++++++++++++

The sharp, rotating blades spun above his head. Round and round and round.

Airports big and small blinded him with their grayness, the same everywhere.

The frozen wasteland stretched on endlessly to Emmet Terrill's eyes. He sat in a chopper flying across the North Pole. Below there was no continent, no land, only tons and tons of ice floating in the sea. If all of this melted, only sea would remain. He sat with a thick pile of paper in his lap. It struck him that he had been stuck for a long time like that.

There was so much to choose from, satellite images, graphic maps, population maps, surveys of plants, sea levels, changes in migration patterns and much more. The headache quickly asserted itself, as it always did these days.

It was more than sufficient to take a look at the photos of the Arctic from Space, though, those taken in the late summer the last five years. The last twenty years the ice had melted with between two and three percent each year, considerable perhaps, but not instantly alarming. In the latest picture one could actually *see* the changes. The last twelve months the loss of ice had taken a turn for the dramatic. There had been no need for him to go here to confirm that, but he wanted to see it with his own eyes.

– You've been around here before, I take it? The pilot more than suggested.

– I've been to this eternal ice that is no longer eternal quite a few times, Emmet nodded. – It has practically become a map in my head.

The markings for the ice's outer limits that he had drawn on his own maps had no validity anymore. The changes solely from his previous visit were beyond pronounced, really. What was revealed to him was more than a little disturbing.

The most prominent wasn't really the actual circumference reduction, but the ghastly holes and lines in the ice. They had, to a certain degree always been there, in the outer layers and drift ice. Now, the cracks reached all the way to the center of the rough, indistinct circle. Most of the ice was also new. There was almost no old ice left.

– You may stop here, he told the pilot in the casual manner he had adopted on such journeys.

– Is it safe? The man wondered. – I've never seen it like this before and I've been coming here the last thirty years.

– Safe? Terrill gave him one of his best grins. – You could probably have landed as well, but why risk it?

The virtually free-floating ice didn't look very inviting when he climbed down the solid rope ladder. It was huge, with a surface bigger than a soccer field. The surrounding black water seemed to pull closer every second.

Down on the ice he found the equipment from the sack. From then on he worked quickly and efficiently. He drilled a hole in the ice. The drill collected most of what had been in the hole. He worked feverishly and made all the tests he could come up with that was physically possible. He gathered the top snow in various containers and added a different set of chemicals for each. When he climbed back up the ladder with the samples in his sack, he easily felt how back-heavy he had become.

Ice gave way to ocean while it seethed and steamed in the transition. Emmet stared out of the window while the artificial bird flew south.

– It's fading away, he mumbled.

– Did you say anything?

The pilot looked up.

– The ice is fading away. Soon, there won't be anything up here, except the sea.

There was a noticeable break in the conversation. Emmet acknowledged it by smiling ironically.

– What were you doing down there, anyway? The pilot asked casually, very casually.

– I collected samples, Terrill replied with mischief in his eyes. – A number of tests in order to measure the ice's consistence, age, degree of pollution and stuff like that.

– But what's the… point?

An inborn stubbornness and, Emmet hoped an inborn mean streak made him keep up his perceived cruel treatment of the poor man.

– Well, as stated, the ice, all the ice is melting down there. Having confirmed that, the question is if it is melting before the human enhanced Global Warming, the human created climate change has started in earnest. In the larger scheme of things, it doesn't really matter much, but the question isn't completely uninteresting. Without the ice here in the north, the sun will heat up the ocean further, halting even more the ocean's ability to absorb CO2, adding to the rise of greenhouse gases in the atmosphere. If the Greenland ice melts fast and that sends lots of cold water into the ocean the exchange of water to and from polar areas may grind to a halt. The polar currents may disappear for a shorter or longer period, and that will certainly affect the globe longer south as well, affect the entire global conveyer belt. The Gulf Stream will stay away from northern waters, which may, in turn give us a local, temporary ice age, and that's just the start of it. All that will hardly give us more than a decade or two reprieve from the Global Warming and its cataclysmic effects, though.

– So what if there is a sea rise of one or two meters? The pilot practically snarled. – Will that have any significance, any at all?
– The one meter the last decade has given mankind major trouble, Emmet mused. – Eighty-four percent of the world's human population lives by the coast. Imagine, if you will what will happen if all of them have to move practically simultaneously. So far there isn't even a hint of any major, controlled migration. Because of the uncertainty about evaporation, for one thing it's hard to say how much the sea will rise. But if all ice on the planet melts modest estimates say sixty-four meters. Others say approximately three-hundred and fifty…
The man scowled at him. Emmet had long since admitted to himself that he occasionally lived for moments like this, when the red color of people's skin grew ascendant and showed above the collar. Lately, it had made him feel better than he had in years. He ended the conversation gleefully:
– How fast the average global temperature will increase depends pretty much on the ocean's ability to absorb CO2. No one knows what the threshold is, but ever more scientists claim that the sea is already saturated.
Green fields raced before his vision. People had started calling Svalbard the Green Island. It was an exaggeration, but he saw what it would one day become, and it wasn't hard at all.
The sun and the increasing heat melted snow everywhere, also in places where the ground had been covered by ice far longer than there had been human habitation.
Emmet was tired. The trip had tired him, inevitably. His son, the Storm Child appeared behind his closed eyelids, the rage he saw there helping in the task of savoring his own, the rage so necessary to move, to live so much stronger in the son than in the father.
The pilot talked with a crowd of anxious, even scared people. Terrill heard them without ears, saw them without eyes, and sensed without senses their insane rejection of Life. They stared at him with hatred in their wet eyes, as if he, the messenger of bad news was at fault for everything wrong with the world.
Thule, Greenland and beyond. The lichen withered and died. One saw it with the naked eye, saw large, dark areas, in Norwegian mountains, on the Siberian taiga.
The same everywhere. Variations. The same. Worse.
Norwegian forests, what remained of forests in Germany and Central Europe.
He rented a room close to Seven Dials, Covent Garden, London. There wasn't any name above the door or anywhere in the building, but he knew he had entered a Green Rose. He noticed a kind of familiarity in the people around him, the flickering eyes, the certainty they wore like a cloak: the fact that they were haunted. They, like him cast veiled glances at the dark coats they encountered on the streets.
The dark coats, an arm of the clandestine services, the hidden army of the power behind the power had shown an increasingly strong interest in him lately. He couldn't tell whether it was Norwegian, British Intelligence or yet another arm of ESF - the European Security Force. It wasn't important anyway. They were all the same.
Every state on the globe and also many of the multinational corporations had their own so called Intelligence services surveying the restless population and making sure they behaved. Those that didn't risked incarceration and worse, far worse.
The room was cast in darkness. Even the light from the street outside seemed dim. He

wondered if he had slept, if he was still asleep and was dreaming.

A dark shape stood over him on the floor and he remained still. It moved, in a flash of darkness. He caught a glimpse of the face, before the creature slipped into the shadows and vanished.

The next morning he found an extra pile of documents on the night table.

He recalled the night as red hot, feverish, confusing dreams. All doors and windows had been wide open and it hadn't eased the heat one bit. The draft, if there had been any had been practically unnoticeable.

Elin looked at him. He was willing to swear that she was there, in the room with him, and not a mirage.

– The room is the world, she said. – The smoldering inferno it has become.

He wanted to argue with her and couldn't tell whether or not he didn't because he agreed with her or because he realized how silly it was to argue with a mirage.

Sleep had touched him. It could even be said that he had slept well. Sweat steamed from his skin. He felt awake and aware and light on his feet when he drank the lukewarm water from the bottle and stumbled in a daze towards the bathroom.

He recalled only an indistinct face in the mirror afterwards.

When he approached the pile, he did so pensively, cautiously. Hands reached out and flipped the pages. He sat in the chair with a half-digested sandwich in his hand. Half an hour later the sandwich rested at the edge of the table, still not much more than half digested. Words and images burned behind his half closed eyelids, forming a somewhat cohesive whole. Abruptly he thirsted and hungered anew.

The material was extensive beyond words. Large droplets of sweat wet the paper and he didn't notice. Photos, journals, death-certificates, irrefutable evidence for the existence of the Tuberculosis-sanatoriums. Dates for ship calls, facts about pollution dumping and of oil dumped at open sea. Controllers' cover up about deficiencies in ships and factories all over Europe. Cover ups of the stark effect on nature and human beings. The latest research of the impact of air pollution on human beings. The Irish Sea, The Ruhr Valley, all industrial areas, the general health of all city people, the release of genetic manipulated animals and plants in nature... He had hardly seen anything like it (and he had seen a lot). Weak-kneed he attempted to stand up, but failed.

At the bottom of the pile there was a simple card. He turned it and read:

GAIA THEATRE

MIDNIGHT

That was all.

No more was needed.

+++++++++++++++++

Lisbeth had dressed strictly business-like for the day. Pressed silk pants, the latest fashion in jackets, conservative colored blouse with tie, dark shoes. The hair had been done so it fell down her shoulders from the neck.

She looked pleased at the gathering. Everything was as it was supposed to be. She beamed at them.

– The world has changed. She began with a loud but pleasant voice. – My Ladies, my Gentlemen, I thank you for your attendance. When I look at you, I see the *Elite*. I look at everybody that deserves to be here. Those not present today know nothing about our meeting, and this is also how it shall remain. I see before me the rightful Masters of the

Age to Come.

Loud applause, muted by soft carpets and thick walls accompanied her words.

– The Change is an ongoing, multi-faced event unparalleled in human history. The world is becoming bigger again. The international aspect of human life, in spite of the current, brief rise in global flights is decreasing in importance. Even the national is loosing favor to the local. Whether we like it or not the work force is becoming less mobile. The common factor for many of the most obvious changes is that they are currently beyond our control. Yes, Ladies and Gentlemen, there is a human enhanced increase in global temperature. The sea is rising rapidly and the winds are increasing dramatically in strength and numbers. Disease is very much present in all population groups. The deserts are spreading north and south. Inhabitable land becomes scarce. There's less *room* every day. Population growth goes through the roof, which in turn leads to more people seeking green pastures. More and more people speak about a nomadic life as natural and right. All these seemingly contradictory traits point in one, specific direction: The restless are increasing in numbers and grow more difficult to handle. The wild and desperate are impossible to keep contained within the old framework. In short: our old well-proven methods work less and less. Very soon they won't work at all.

She kept her eyes on the audience all the time, measuring their reactions, applying effortlessly what she had learned. They became even more open books to her. She studied their faces, their stance and body language while she spoke, like she had done since early childhood sitting in her father's lap. He had taught her about them, at meetings, at gatherings like these, taught her to see through their masks, to the indifference and condescending attitudes they hid beneath the surface. They had no desire to know the world beyond their narrow view on reality. She knew them as the back of her hand. If someone, anyone showed them a path that was more tempting than disgusting, they could be easily led. They weren't that different from the sheep they ruled. In her eyes she spotted everything useful to her. She saw it, how desperately they wanted someone to show them the way to cross their perceived insurmountable hurdles. Any way.

Hers!

Expectation rose within her. She had them, she knew she did.

After a while, after allowing expectation to rise in her audience she raised a hand towards one of the maps on the wall behind her.

– Siberia, the land of the taiga, the eternally frozen ground, no longer eternally frozen. All of it is thawing and enormous amounts of greenhouse gases are flowing into the atmosphere.

– Food production is going down all over the world. Food-producing soil turns dry and useless. Domestic animals are starving. Because of the previous insane over-production there isn't yet a lack of food in our part of the world. There will be. New production areas must be located and used. Analysis shows that major parts of northern Siberia are excellently suited to become the world's new and only breadbasket. Workers are easily available and easily persuaded to work hard. Russians have a long standing tradition of submitting to a strong and firm hand. Ladies and Gentlemen: Siberia is the future.

The slight, excited mumble in the assembly rose further in her ears.

– There are quite a few approaches to our quandary. We can choose to settle close to the production areas or create and maintain our own supply routes. Both choices inadvertently create their unique challenges. In the folders I've taken the liberty to supply to you, you will find several sketches for possible solutions. We all know well how explosive the situation remains in the former Soviet republics and also within the Russian federation. It is more important than ever to put our eggs in more than one basket. I will now present them all to you, in no specific order. When I'm done you will have the information necessary to make informed decisions about the future.

It was important to give them the impression that the decision was theirs to take.

– All the… baskets? A man in front row said lightly.

– Precisely, she grinned politely.

One of the other maps showed Mjøsa, Norway's large inland freshwater sea and a vast surrounding area. To its right was a giant, aerial photo of the same land. Lisbeth timed her response perfectly when a thin, transparent foil fell down in front of the photo. Clever lighting highlighted the map just before she pointed at it. A figure appeared, a structure so vast that it covered Mjøsa completely.

– Behold the Pyramid, she cried, with blushing cheeks, – our stone garden, where we will harvest everything we will ever need.

Silence met her words. She gave them her professional smile and kept on going.

– What you see is a closed, nearly self-sufficient system. Huge crop fields and pastures on all sides. The newest and best in technology, management systems on all levels and everything run from the top… by us. Perhaps our influence won't reach as far as before, but we will have absolute control. And with the airport and railroad under our command we may reach out across the new world in any way we wish.

She studied them from her dais, waiting both patiently and not.

– Why Mjøsa? A Swede asked. – It's because of the access to water, of course, but why not Vänern or Vättern, then?

He did sound almost insulted.

– They're too big. She permitted herself a soft smile. – Present or even future technology isn't even approaching the necessary level for us to cover any of those with any construction, far less one of our desired magnitude. Mjøsa's size, however, is damn near perfect for whatever purpose we may desire.

– We will need an enormous number of workers just to keep the wheels moving, another commented, exposing himself. – How do we assure recruitment?

– I assure you there are countless alternative methods, she replied calmly. – We control the vertical, the horizontal and the depth. After a while we will become time itself to them.

They studied her, there on her stage. The applause wasn't exactly a deluge. She smiled anyway. There was excitement there, in their laid back expression, if you knew what to look for.

And she did.

– They're not that different from their poor cousins and subjects, she told Annette later, with no idea how much later it was. – What they most of all want to hear is a confirmation of their own opinions and that life has meaning.

The dinner party started. Everything proceeded far more… civil than the night before. Many still retained an unhealthy green skin color after that excess. But they had still been present at the meeting. The slow, rising glow of pride swelled inside her.

Glasses met and parted. The life and fire she sensed spreading from her stomach flowed from bottles available all over the place. An older, not very tall fat man approached her. She forced herself to smile courteously.

– Excellent lecture, he grunted. – Convincing. Your father would have been proud.

They exchanged polite phrases for a while, before she pulled away. He believed she was touched by his praise. Let him.

Full moon. All the windows in the bedroom stood wide open. All possible doors all over the house as well. She leaned out of one of the windows. The heat remained irritating, suffocating. She exposed herself in a desperate bid to cool herself.

The noise from the distant streets cut into her ears. Howls of pain and rage rose from the mob as they clashed with the heavy police presence. The raffle renewed their attack on the outer ring of armored police officers and the first bullet of the evening was fired into the crowds. She feared the noise would make her ears bleed. The defenses held, barely. More police arrived, but also more protesters. People came from all over the country and even abroad to make their voice heard.

– Someone has blabbered, Lisbeth swore to Annette, not really sure anymore if Annette was truly there. – Everything has been done to assure the security and secrecy of this meeting. Everything! But there are obviously people unable to keep their mouth closed. If I ever find out whom, heads will roll.

The blood red moon kept leaking blood. She writhed on her back on the bed, fearing she was wide awake, fearing she was asleep… and the nightmare began.

A decade earlier the Nightravens, an independent cell of the terrorist organization the Green Rose had detonated a bomb right at the center of Oslo and removed the city from the face of the Earth. A considerable part of the world's elite had turned to dust that very moment. Leaders, politicians, industrial captains, leading, influential scientists, all members of the Norwegian royal family and several other clusters of people in charge.

Less than a month later, during a hasty planned meeting Paris had shared Oslo's fate. That had been the last time what remained of the world's leaders met openly, in large groups.

Enormous efforts had been made to protect the nations' integrity. United States, who had mostly stayed away from Europe during the nineties, now returned in force. Norway and France received unprecedented amounts of aid and funds to survive as nations. The generosity seemed boundless.

The French kept quarreling about the location of their new capital, if Paris should be rebuilt or not, eventually what other city qualified. Emotions ran high. Trondheim became Norway's new capital, a choice far more logical than the previous, since that city was much closer to the center of the country. There was a distant royal heir in South America somewhere. Plans *were* made to bring him to Norway, but the idea never caught on, not in the general population, not in the halls of power. Plans were shelved.

Nothing had been *right* in a very long time. The destruction of Oslo and Paris had left deep scars in people's mind. The physical structures of power were rebuilt fairly easy. But people's belief in authority had been considerably weakened. Monumental efforts had been made, at least the pretence of it to uphold Norway's artificial high standards of living and the pretence of people's participation in decision-making. It hadn't exactly failed, but hadn't worked either. People saw more easily through the illusions of those in charge and chose more often to make themselves and their distrust heard. The world had been changed, irrevocably.

As late as last week a maniac had fired four rockets against the White House in Washington DC before he was stopped. He was merely one of the countless independent operators that had risen across the world. Even the Chinese forgot theses of obedience and loyalty to nation and power.

Dawn, colors of rust and blood. Lisbeth Kaspersen imagined she heard drums from all sides, hating every beat, every single unstructured and disharmonic savage sound echoing in her ears. The headache returned, as unwanted as ever. She took a pill, swallowed it with lots of water. It was still as if it forced itself down her throat. The itching unrest persisted.

She imagined there was a creature down there, in the streets, not so far away. It carried a sack on its back and had many electrodes attached to its body. They had captured several of these fools the last ten years. Not all of them had prepared themselves properly against interruptions. Some were klutzes. Others didn't dare go through with their plan.

But there was no way they could stop them all, whether they carried ordinary bombs or a thermonuclear device. It was impossible to secure every city, every event, every time. They could never be *certain,* even if security was meticulously implemented. An idiot had suggested a ban on rucksacks and backpackers. The fact that the proposal had gained even partial support, showed how desperately some people screamed for solutions.

There were no simple solutions. Everything was connected, she knew that, as she rubbed, bugged, rubbed her forehead at the window frame. Everything she had learned during her childhood and adolescence, everything she had learned to appreciate was rotting from the inside.

Everything fell apart.

+++++++++++++++++

He imagined that he saw trees around him. England had once, in the mists of time been covered by forest. Mankind had chopped down the mystery and the shadows and the blood, supplanted it with exhausted soil, a confidence scheme leading to cities, highways, factories and massive destruction of nature and all life on Earth. He hadn't had this sense of ancient time in a very long time, not since the last time he had experienced the ruthlessness and generosity, the savagery of She Who Dances in the Forest. He had seen her with different masks, but he always recognized her.

Right here, at the street stage in Covent Garden she had danced Kacha, and he had danced, too, with her and many others. He had heard her voice and seen through her eyes.

There wasn't really any stage here. Everybody quite simply performed on the cobblestone. It mattered not. Sometimes, what was performed here was pure *magic.*

He walked a bit further and reached a staircase virtually hidden between the sidewalk and the wall. It was amazing how that could be. He hurried down the stairs and imagined he vanished below the ground. The door seemed like a black, impenetrable wall. It didn't open with his first, feeble attempt. But slid open without a glitch when he made an effort. Badly lit, crooked corridors revealed themselves to him. He had walked this path several times before. It looked different every time.

A harp played somewhere. Sensitive fingers played haunting, savage rhythm, mystical fantasy in the dark.

He recalled his last visit to this bewitched place. There had been many present then, an entire audience of people. They had filled up all the seats in the small hall and people had even been forced to sit on the floor. William Carter Lafayette had given one of his rare performances. Now, in the midnight hour there was no audience. If they knew, had known who resided here, there would have been a queue filling the entire dark labyrinth.

The enticing creature, a body painted in white with colored stripes in the face and other places danced across the entire deep stage. He recognized her. The sight didn't startle him, but drew him in, pulled him up there, on the stage with her.

The music, the heathen beat and chords, the Mystical Rock so popular recently brought him even further away. Anxiety and exaltation brought back the old awareness.

The first time he had seen her dance Kacha had been before she had led a pagan ceremony in the Jotunheim National Park in Norway around the turn of the century. Hundreds of Children of the Midnight Fire had been there, had gathered in a circle around her, around She Who Dances in the Forest.

His legs moved him towards the stage and on it. The force of nature there whirled towards him and stopped in front of him. She filled his vision, his being.

– Welcome, Son of the Midnight Fire.

– I would have recognized that voice everywhere, he said hoarsely. – I wasn't even a teenager when I heard it the first time. You played Gaia in a great, rewritten Shakespeare play. It was like you weren't of this Earth.

– I'm very much of the Earth, Terrill, she chuckled.

She turned and left for the backstage. He followed her through another labyrinth. Images, glimpses and sensations ravaged him every step of the way. They ended up in a fairly large room, one resembling a bar, with lots of tables and chairs.

The weak lighting didn't illuminate clearly more than a minor part of the furniture. In the blurring between light and shadow he spotted a few indistinct figures. He recognized a considerable number of those gathering around him and froze down his spine. Kurt Mørch, Jason Edwards, Lene Brevik, Susan Palmer…

– We're Nightravens, Lene stated. – We're birds flying in the night.

He looked closer at her, at the distinct face framed by the silver hair. She had just been a baby, newborn the first time he had seen her. Her hair had had the same color then.

She held up her hand so he could look and understand. The characteristic armband of rope flashed in green.

– It's just reasonable and right, she said. – You were there almost at the beginning, just like I was.

– I remember how he ran through the house all day, She Who Dances in the Forest said. – And contrary to his peers he hasn't quite forgotten.

forgotten the life, the joy that was a part of him.

What had happened? When had he… given up?

– Am I not too old for this kind of… initiation? He wondered hoarsely, fearing he was unsteady on his feet.

– More and more people turn around before they reach the Fat Forties, Kurt said cheerfully. – It's *music,* man. Age doesn't matter.

His voice sounded indeed like music in Terrill's ears.

– We will wait while you prepare him, Silverhair said.

He hardly noticed that they left. It happened that fast, that imperceptible.

The whole world knew Kurt Mørch as one of the founders of the Green Rose. Quite a few of the others had also been a public part of the movement for more than ten years and had survived to become infamous.

People knew about them, but not her. She was an enigma shrouded in mystery.

He watched her, unable to pull his eyes off the enigmatic figure. Contrary to many he knew her approximate age. Could this body belong to a fifty-year-old woman?

She pulled up her leg and revealed the mole. He nodded slowly.

– You had yours removed ten years ago. What it represents cannot be removed.

Two deep wells devoured him, transformed him, changing his perception of himself and the world. This ceiling, these walls were they real? The mountain walk under the icecap, wasn't that the true reality? And the impression that he found himself deep below the streets of a stone desert called London… the illusion?

– Our tribe is old, she hummed. – From an age before the first cities. We've always been persecuted, driven from our brief homes, but we have always returned, every time stronger than before. What you have, the Storm Child has in abundance.

He closed his eyes in anguish. So wrong he had been, about many things. And he had transferred his fear, ball and chain to his son. And he hadn't been the only one. Both the cow and the bull had forgotten they had been calves, like most cows and bulls did.

But now, in this place hotter than any forge he remembered, beyond remembering.

– I can feel it, he mumbled, – the ice and fire.

– Symbols change with time and place and identity, Emmet, she said softly. – They don't mean anything. Only the realities they're based on do that.

He nodded and let himself be led by She Who Dances in the Forest into the smoke and the lights in the air, in the mist and the flashes in it, into the forge of existence.

Through pain, through joy, a rift in the air and the sky.

The sharp blades rotated to his left and right, round and round and round. It was December, summer on the southern hemisphere, the eternal day of Antarctica. The old propeller plane floated more than it flew along the rand zone of the continent and the winds shook it hard. Through fear, through expectation fever-hot images and memories ravaged the brain of a body covered in cold sweat. A strange calm haunted him as he witnessed the incredible view below.

In the eternal day, in the blinding white light an armada of icebergs floated north. Wherever they flew, the Atlantic Ocean, the Pacific, the Indian Ocean the same images burned on the retina. Several established TV-stations had shown what happened at the start of the month, but had left out the best, the most revealing.

All in vain.

Such blatant attempts at hiding the obvious had worked before, but no longer.

The various recordings had exploded, «gone viral» all over the Internet.

Perceived experts had still stepped forward and supported the usual official calming down policy so successful at quelling unrest in times past. They claimed, in their stubborn persistence that the majority of the 4.8 kilometer deep ice mass covering the Antarctica mainland all in all was intact… which was true, as far as it went. In spite of countless large pools of water appearing like wounds in the ice all over the continent, the major melting process hadn't quite reached the inland yet. What the puppet scientists conveniently «forgot» to relate was the fact that the West Antarctic Ice Sheet showed clear signs of collapsing. That piece alone contained water enough to make the sea rise with at least seven meters all over the world.

They landed in Tierra del Fuego (Land of Fire) late at night. Among several striking facts Emmet noted people's extensive clothing and that everybody wore shades. Their shaky mental condition was far more pronounced, though. Fear far more extensive than the clothing coated them. Only a few dared stepping outside. Argentine and Chile had more blind people and cases of skin cancer than any other nation in the world.

There was still talk about moving up in the mountains, to relative safety, safety from the rising sea, into a few mountain valleys where one could live in shadow and protection from the dangerous sun.

– No horizon, no future, a woman cried out. – MADRE DIOS!

No places to hide, Terrill thought.

The krill had been «harvested» the last ten years, like most of the remaining naval food resources. Predatory harvesting was the rule, not the exception. It didn't stop, but on the contrary grew in both numbers and extent.

Terrill corrected his UV A and UV B sun glasses. The heat and the chill flowed through his blood. Everything fell apart.

The Planet

Imagine, if you will that Friday instead of Wednesday is the day after Tueday… sorry, *Tuesday*. Pretend, under the influence of consciousness-expanding compounds that December 21st is New Year's Eve. Be convincing when you tell people that your nation's flag will no longer sway on constitution day.

Perhaps you will be able to do this. Perhaps it won't even be that hard. You know, if you think it through that we're talking about fairly recent human created realities here. It has dawned on you that modern human society is an environment where most things may change at a diabolical speed. What one generation may hold sacred the next might end up holding in contempt.

Or it might end up holding itself in contempt.

It's certainly a strain. You've grown used to the finer things in life, an ordered existence, nine-to-five enslavement or nine-to-five idleness. There are regular meals there for you when you visit the grocery store. There's no need to kill anything that is already dead. But you still want to break someone's neck (your neighbor was a prick ass today). With the lack of imagination taught you by modern existence, you don't see how you can even make time crawl, far less walk.

What do you do when you're forced to look into the cracked mirror? The sun rises in the east (almost) every morning. Except for this small detail, very few things are what they are supposed to be. Criminals, outsiders and losers are dealt with more according to your wishes these days, but that doesn't seem that important anymore. You ask what has happened to the world. Your favorite quay from childhood is below the ocean surface. You and your spouse are now established after ten years of hard labor and ready to have children, but you don't succeed. What a drag! You own two cars, several color TV's, a fridge, a trip south every summer, two stereo players, countless computers and laptops, satellite download, the most recent technology and expensive furniture, but you lack 2.4 children. No healthy eggs, no fit sperm available. City life in a nutshell buddy.

Poisoned air, poisoned soil, acid rain, can you say hallelujah. What did you expect? What you do with nature, it returns hundredfold. Would you enjoy being poisoned, dug into with the most grotesque tools, do you know how radioactivity feels on the body, pal? You see tall waves and watch the fever rise. Yesterday is tomorrow. Tomorrow never comes. Where are you, Man? Where are you hiding?

Do you feel the wind in your face? Faced with insanity there is no other response than insanity. Ask a sad, sad question: Why wake up a creature that has no desire to wake up? Is there a choice with your back at the wall? In what hole have you hidden yourself, Man?

++++

A small group of humans surrounded by wind and grains of sand fought themselves forward step by step. They had the morning sun at their back, the horizon behind them. The horizon, as indistinct as it seemed had just recently released its hold on the burning disk and the temperature had already risen to an unbearable level.

The small town had been deserted a long time ago. Doors kept slamming in the constant wind. Something, both city and people had become unhinged here. Those coming here from far away found a few dead bodies, half rotten meat, half skeleton. Sand penetrated everywhere, in corners and hideouts, attic and basement, filling the well at the edge of town. The wanderers in rags stood still around the dry well for a long time. There were about twenty of them, twenty ghostly shapes, a myriad of cultures and races, joined by countless trials and circumstances. There had been far more of them, long ago.

Some of them had heard about a bigger oasis a night's march off. After a brief discussion the group agreed to continue. They slumbered and suffered during the day in the dead city, while the tiny supply they had left of the life-giving water dwindled further.

Twilight finally arrived and they continued their journey north.

The area they moved through resembled a desert, but the drought hadn't yet lasted long enough here. The soil hadn't dried up completely. It would soon, inevitably. Very soon giant heaps of sand would cover the land that not long ago had been green and fertile. They wondered if that was the reason they had postponed the departure, until the decision had been taken from them.

Many had traveled north before them, far more than the land could feed.

They died in droves. The land itself died, faded away to nothing, all around them.

Fever visions, memories, fantasies alternating in their consciousness didn't really haunt them. They had become used to them, like a natural, inevitable part of their life.

They wandered, had wandered, would wander at the edge of the desert. It hadn't been so bad. The laws of the desert were valid among those used to the dry, endless waste.

– The most important law of the desert: They shouted in despair at the men with guns chasing them away. – Never deny anyone water as long as you have enough yourself.

The men with the guns were deaf and blind.

This was the future, their future, that of everybody else's, this hellish march towards nowhere. They wondered if they felt anything any longer, anything at all, if they still had the right to call themselves human beings. The grains of sand rubbing against each other erased emotions like pity, compassion and even hatred, made it fade away into an ever larger emptiness.

There was no dawn, no reddening of the horizon. The sand erased it all and turned it gray and formless. The sound of the eternal wind submerged the travelers, submerged everyone and everything. They heard nothing except the sound of the grains of sand rubbing against each other and whispering to them. The road stretched out before them and they were amazed over how well they saw it. Even though it was occasionally covered, partly or completely by sand it seemed to stretch an infinite distance in front of them. They could never decide whether or not that was a bad or good thing.

The asphalt eroded. The road remained. Sometimes they felt gratitude because the sand protected them from the most dangerous sunshine. Sometimes they didn't.

They reached the water hole, the potential oasis just before the pale disk hovered above their heads. There was no water left. At least it was buried so deep below dust-dry soil and sand that they couldn't get to it. It didn't stand out from the rest of the landscape anymore. Sore eyes were drawn to all the human remains spread across the terrain. The sight of bare bones did something to them, like a fur-skinning knife against the skin.

– Useless, a man mumbled. – Nothing to eat or drink.

They moved on, always moved on. The tiny group shrunk with two more, but no more than that. Their number remained constant, as if they had become impervious to the storm they fought. For all they knew they might have wandered weeks and months since the last two succumbed to the harsh surroundings. They found water on their eternal walk, rare and precious, but always sufficient and often enough to keep them alive. They found dead people by the roadside, fairly fat bodies without visible marks that had seemingly just given up. They kept going and didn't feel weak or even weakened, and they wondered why not, wondered what was special about them. They wanted to surrender every time they put one foot in front of another. Many more steps later they kept holding their head high against the wind. They wondered why they kept striving, what they had to look forward to.

There was no horizon on their path, no end. Thought, sounds, words, senses faded. They fought on, from one hell to another, ever further north.

++

– Names mean so little, Xavier Thorgood told his neighbor in a clearly aggravated manner. – People have a tendency to name everything without any good reason. They piss me off, they do. I'm willing to bet that county officials put all these signs up just to piss me off. There are god damn signs wherever I look these days. I've made an effort to find out who's actually responsible for this travesty, but I'm getting nowhere.

They had placed one particular sign 200 feet and 7 inches from his present position.

POISONED WATER - ALL USE PROHIBITED

He left his neighbor without any parting words and returned to his house, to his kitchen. All attempts at staying away from the kitchen window proved futile. He returned after less than a minute holed up in the living room and stared at the dustbin of a former cornfield just outside the city of Mexico, west of St. Louis, in the state of Missouri, the United States.

Not that many years ago this land had been flooded with water. The two rivers Missouri and Mississippi had formed what former vice president Gore had called «the Sixth Great Lake». Now, the remains of the once mighty rivers evaporated before Thorgood's eyes.

The dry field was vast and still his eyes were drawn to the tiny pond and the damn sign.

Someone walked quietly through the door behind him. He turned his head half around. The doctor looked completely ridiculous when he virtually sneaked out of the bedroom.

Xavier kept staring out the window, at the damn sign.

– I'll get straight to the point, Mr. Thorgood, the doctor hesitated, clearly uncomfortable. – After conducting several tests reviewed by my colleagues I'm convinced that your wife suffers from something we call chronic fatigue syndrome. We've seen many of those the last few years, more for each year. No one quite knows what it is or why it is. Symptoms are extreme fatigue bordering on paralysis. We expect the cause to be a virus combined with psychological issues, but we don't know. Experience tells us that restitution will be hard and long. It is almost as if the patient has given up. No matter, she needs to be at the hospital as soon as possible.

Xavier grinned wickedly. They didn't have health insurance.

– Let's do a ditto titto, he cried darkly.

He stepped into the bedroom. A worried doctor followed on his heels.

The wife resembled a statue in her unmoving state on the bed. Eyes seemed strangely clear, but they didn't see much of anything about what was happening. Her husband grabbed the bedpost. He stared into her empty eyes and said in a casual manner:

– Listen to me. Your problem is that thick skull of yours. If you want to be well, you will be, it's that simple. Let's see, now, if you can get out of that bed, if you can do anything on your own, for once in your life.

– I can't bear even the thought, she whimpered.

Suddenly, she seemed even worse. Her eyes turned hazy and dull.

The news was on somewhere. It dawned on Xavier that he no longer knew where the damn machine stood. He didn't care, anyway. No matter the channel the square box showed nothing but draught, flood, draught, starvation, disease, draught, draught, draught. Chaos!

He took a stroll into an adjacent room, into the shed. There was so much to choose from in there, so many weapons of choice. There were hammers, drills, screws, but he took a shortcut to the shotgun. He loaded it. There were constant distractions. The doctor droned on with his nasal, irritating voice, a sigh, a wail of complaints from Gehenna.

– There are those who will claim we deserve this and everything subsequent. We're one of the most industrialized and polluted countries in the world. No one releases more CO2 than us. It's poetic justice at its best.

Xavier cocked his gun and strolled back to the bedroom. He fired a load of hails hitting the doc in his chest. The perforated body hit the wall and left a broad trail on its way to the floor.

The next second he had pointed the barrel at the woman on the bed.

– Now, you will get up promptly, or you'll stay there. Do you understand what I'm *saying?*

First there was incredulity, then laughter. The face cracked in an ugly sneer. He shot it to pieces.

He drank a jug of water before he left. The dust outside made his throat parched again in seconds. He sat down behind the wheel of his old pickup and drove off. The shotgun rested comfortably in his lap.

An irritating dustbin grew behind him on the road. He wondered what was wrong with people today. There was no rest from the idiots. Aware people easily spotted sand in the machinery everywhere. The word «disgust» didn't even come close to describe what he felt.

The patrol car reached him and the driver signaled him. Xavier stopped by the roadside.

The officer practically jumped from his seat and rushed forward with a huge grin painted on his mug.

– Hi, Xavier, he greeted the driver.

– Hello, Fred, Xavier replied.

– I was fairly certain it was you driving through the gate. Fred looked at him with the silly grin and his huge, childish eyes. – I figured that the doc was driving with you since no one answered when I rang the bell. You don't happen to know where he's headed, do you?

– TO HELL!

Xavier shot Fred in the face at close range. The officer didn't even manage to change expression before it was blown apart.

The driver moved on without delay. He had the means and he had the will.

– So much to do, he mumbled, – so little time doing it. Three down, nine to go. At the very least that many.

He imagined he heard the thunder roll across the cloudless sky and opened his skewed gap wide, laughing louder and louder, as he made his way towards the city of Mexico, Missouri.

– Nine, he cried, – ninety, nine hundred…

Thunder chased him down the road and he couldn't overwhelm it, no matter how loud he laughed. With a mighty roar that could just as well be the squeaking of a mouse, he pushed the gas pedal through the floor.

++++++++++++++++++++++++++++

Commander Rafael Guitierrez TY (the younger) in the royal Spanish army squinted his eyes and looked at the Gibraltar Strait. The tall tower he and his European chiefs of staff scouted from had been placed in the outskirts of the city of Tarifa. He had been told that people once had been able to see the coast of Africa from here, but that was long ago, long before the present day of polluted and poisonous air. Now, in the south, heaven and earth were indistinguishable, a misty soup of waste and countless nightmares.

Dawn's red and pale sunrays reached him from the left. The sun still rose in the east. Guitierrez couldn't quite tell what day it was. He had slept poorly lately. The activity was prevalent in the city below them. Activity was high every day these days, even on Sundays, where trade had been scarce in the past.

People roamed the streets on Sundays, too, and not just because of the trade.

– Madonna, he swore, – what has happened with the world?

It was a rhetorical question, and the others knew that. They didn't reply.

He squinted his eyes harder, glaring into the mist. Using binoculars was no use. The soup would just seem even thicker, even more impenetrable. Technology was, in general of little use. The air overflowed with metal particles and pockets of electromagnetism. He had asked the scientists to explain it, but they couldn't. He had ordered repairs, but it was no use. There was nothing to repair, really. No faults had been found, even after intense scrutiny. The advanced surveillance equipment just didn't work.

Some of the people in white coats had mumbled something about atmospheric saturation levels and Chaos Theory. It was obvious to everybody that they were struggling, were running blind in the mist like everybody else.

The flow of refugees had grown to become a *problem* a few years earlier. He had been in command of the Gibraltar area for some time now. He hadn't suffered major trouble at first. The refugees had arrived in an even flow, but their numbers could easily be handled and returned. Morocco had threatened to fire at the ships returning them. In an attempt to appease the Moroccan royal family Spain had made the unprecedented step of giving up its possessions in North Africa. They served no purpose anymore, anyway, and were nothing more than dustbins. It hadn't worked for long. Encouraged by their perceived prowess the African nation demanded further concessions. Then the Spanish government had threatened with war and with bombing the royal palaces, and *that* had worked.

Now Morocco had ceased existing as a nation and there were no more barriers on the other side of the Mediterranean Ocean.

The secretary of defense had asked him how many soldiers he needed and he had jokingly mentioned an improbable number, one he had no hope of having.

«Granted», the uniformed woman had replied.

Spanish beaches and coastlines swarmed with heavily armed soldiers with extensive powers and they were all under his command.

The irony (the commander had long since realized that life was filled with irony) was that almost the entire Pyrenean peninsula was almost as dry as North Africa. The dust and the sand surrounded them, even this high above the ground. The only remaining fertile areas were in the North West, where guerillas from both Spain and Portugal had had control for months. Elsewhere in the once fertile land, there hadn't been any rain to speak of the last five years. Huge crowds of Spanish citizens had already crossed the border to France to remain or to travel further north.

– Dirty mongrels, we should strike them down, every single one of them.

– Isn't that just a bit… hasty?

The commander turned towards she who had spoken, Madame Jeanne le Granier.

He sighed in relief when she was content with giving him her pointed look. The very act of exchanging words with her always made him ill at ease.

The insane look in those eyes disturbed his peace even further.

He scouted the sea of mist to the south. His eyes had been locked on to it for so long that he could no longer recall when his eyes had started to hurt. He wondered, for the tenth or hundredth time if there was any end to this nightmare, if there would ever be a time, a given point in the future where things would sort of normalize themselves. People he had spoken with about this had given him a strange glance he never could quite fathom or interpret properly.

It would be correct to say that he had been a soldier his entire adult life, used to follow orders and not ask questions. Now, he found himself with hundreds of them.

Ships patrolled the strait without cease, as many as they could spare with limited fuel supply. The patrols had picked up considerable numbers of illegal immigrants during the night, random convoys of smaller boats and practically sinking wrecks. Cautious assessments said it was teeming out there.

The surface looked like it had for a long time, gray and still. Garbage floated wherever the commander directed his attention. It didn't move, didn't twitch an arm or a hand.

There! Didn't he see… movement? He squinted his eyes hard, as hard as he possibly could and saw lines in the water, saw the front of a boat or the boat itself. There were more of them, more side by side and behind. They slipped forward like phantoms in the dark, and just as deadly. Sunlight highlighted them. He no longer had trouble spotting the crafts.

But… behind those behind… there was no more? The buzz lasted, ten, twenty seconds… No more crafts appeared.

Everybody glanced at each other. Le Granier snorted.

– Was *this* what all the noise was about?

The mist parted and the sky and the sea were once again divided. A wide and deep flotilla, an armada of various seafaring vessels appeared. A danger far more pronounced than a fleet of warships.

Rafael stood there with the communication device hanging from a slack arm and hand. The mouth opened and turned slowly into something resembling a slack snout, and he couldn't find the strength to speak a single syllable or utter the slightest sound.

– *Commandante?* He heard the voice from the speakers, far away. – Your orders, Commander?

– Fire, he said to the air, right before he raised the microphone to the mouth and shouted in panic. – FIRE! Shoot everything that moves and breathes. We have issued countless warnings. *Show no mercy.*

The crafts proceeded unimpeded another second, two… All of them were filled to the last spot. People held on to rails, to ropes, absolutely every available last ditch effort.

The first salvos struck the advancing vessels. Bodies, pieces of bodies rose into the air and fell into the water. The sunrays turned red anew. Every craft still floating kept advancing. If there was any deviation from the course, it was quickly corrected. Top modern cannons spat deadly salvos repeatedly. There was no lack of munitions in the Spanish army. Boats were hit. Boats sank. Boats sailed on. There didn't seem to be any end to them. Those gathered in the tower couldn't spot any, no matter how much they stared.

– They're everywhere, the panicked voice whined through the speakers. – There are reports coming in about armadas even bigger elsewhere, all along the coastline.

Rafael still strived to speak, even the shortest syllable.

– Where hides reason? He gasped. – Where does it rest?

He lost count on confirmed hits and kills early. Reports kept pouring in, piling up. No matter, there was no sign of any breach in the relentless onslaught.

They heard another unidentified voice break through the deafening buzz coming from the communication system.

– No one can stop them. They're the army of Death coming to fetch us to their Kingdom. FLEE!

They heard a single shot being fired and that was that. They didn't hear the sound of anyone hitting the floor. No explanation was forthcoming. They found themselves wondering, speculating in their mind, but found no explanation, no logic.

Distraction faded away, attention was locked. They realized they couldn't tear their attention from the astounding sight, the ever growing fleet.

Hundred meters from the shore, now… ninety, eighty, fifty… The first travelers threw themselves into the sea and started swimming. It was visible, now, all the wreckage, how few crafts remained. The machineguns started cracking. No song, no music. Just before hundreds, perhaps thousands of totally desperate people reached the end of the water and rushed onto the shore.

The wild hordes of Chaos penetrated Spanish soil with twisted, sick shouts of joy sounding in the Commander's ears. The soldiers began hitting each other. Some of them panicked and fired uncontrollably at their surroundings. Others quite simply threw away their guns and fled.

– Anarchy, Le Granier mumbled. The French woman was pale as a corpse in her black rage. – No Order. Law and Order must prevail, prevail, prevail!

She drew her gun and started exterminating every single deserter within reach. She hit her target every time, with an amazing, disturbing accuracy.

No mercy was shown, against anyone, anywhere. The refugees were persecuted far into the country. Everybody in a gun's sight was mowed down and many accidentally in the way as well. People stopped and stood frozen with their hands up. They were shot to pieces with the others. Perhaps humanity's fate was decided that day. Perhaps it was inevitable. The dry soil of Tarifa, languishing so long for lack of fluid received lots and lots of nourishment.

The blood flooded the land from the sea, the iron red sea. Blood flowed into the sea in fast-flowing streams, flowing from giant ponds. Life itself evaporated under a ruthless sun. Yes, the rivers… they were blood. And the rapids. And the waterfalls. And the dream of ice and fire filling the human being's every waken moment.

PART TWO: CHILDREN OF THE MIDNIGHT FIRE

«Loneliness isn't a need
for company, it is a longing
for kindred souls»

Marylyn French

CHAPTER SIX

The same everywhere. Blood flowing without boiling. Flesh and mind decaying and dying. Will asleep.

Asleep for a long time.

Trains raged on. No one entered and no one stepped off or wanted to step off. The dirty windows reflected only the passengers' dark thoughts back on themselves. No one looked outside if they could avoid it.

To Damon Terrill Marseille became an end station. He couldn't quite tell why. After having roamed Europe for several years he had ended up here. He had the Mediterranean, the growing Mediterranean ahead of him, a valid reason for sure.

Something pulled at him at the other side, the same irresistible something that had done so his entire life. The desolate, the vast, the endless, the eternal…

– You don't need to go anywhere to find the desert, the wilderness anymore, kid, Tom Rawlins told him from the empty air. – It will very soon find every single surviving human, no matter where they are.

Rawlins was very talkative in Damon's presence, even when he wasn't present.

Everybody looked out of the dirty window on the train these days. They fought, in their despair to avoid the dreary sight, in vain. Heads couldn't be moved from their frozen position. Eyes couldn't be closed. The body seemed stuck in one position. Nobody could turn their backs to anything anymore, no matter how much they wished to do so.

He sat on a decaying, practically collapsing bench at an upland part of a harbor. From his elevated position he had a «great» view of the lower pier, the one a meter below the surface. Artificial constructs no longer protected humanity's wonders from the rising and dirty sea. He stared at it, at the small and big items floating on the surface, a kind of mirror to all the tiny particles darkening the air. It had been quiet for some time. Suddenly the wind started blowing and the air cleared a bit. Gray water wet his feet. He ignored it for a while, before he rose abruptly and hurried away from there.

The wind vanished just as fast as it had come. That was pretty much like it went these days. It vanished and returned when one least expected it. The weather had turned even more unpredictable.

He spent some time checking out his secret hideouts, cautiously, from a fairly safe distance across the street, from busy sidewalks. There were a few of them, ready to be used in an emergency.

They looked okay, as safe as they could be. There were no obvious signs of intruders. When he walked on, he was pretty confident that they would be there, ready for use, the day or night he needed them.

He reached one of the newer parts of the city, close to Anse des Catalans. The stark contrast from the old city to here seemed just as abrupt and gigantic every time. Like with other stone deserts the modern Marseille was a tinsel town in glass and concrete, the amassing dirt well hidden in corners and shadows.

Marseille was, in good and bad ways a melting pot of cultures. Its population had been doubled in forty years, from something below a million, to «somewhere above two

millions». Most of the increase, the most rapid increase had been the last five years.
The need for services had increased equivalent to that and was also valued considerably higher than before.
He wore his street smarts. It didn't come harder to him than to put on his old, worn clothes. The evening and the lights glimmered. There were so few visible dark spots in this neighborhood. Neon lights flared. The only break from them was found in-between the flares. All encouraged people to buy, buy, buy. He saw that some of the signs advertised for the recently introduced genetic milk.

MANMADE AND BETTER

One sign stated proudly.
He had tasted enough of it to know that it tasted like the worst dishwater shit he could imagine.
Distractions, distractions were everywhere. He shook his head in an effort to clear it, to remove what could divert attention from the task ahead. It wasn't really that hard. He focused on his surroundings, while staying on course, the shortest possible route to his destination.
His hand reached inside his jacket and touched briefly the gun there, a Smith & Wesson Automatic. The ice-cold metal burned the skin of his fingertips.
His eyes moved constantly, catching everything that moved around him. He had, for some time been able to utilize the Street Gaze, an awareness, a prerequisite for survival in the concrete jungle.
He turned a corner and entered a roofed street, one turned into a mall, a dazzling setting feeling strangely and dizzying familiar to him. The surroundings didn't really change much, except in colors and shades and standards. Its populace remained mixed, an uneasy coexistence found all over the city. There were beggars and homeless in such great numbers that it was impossible to keep them off public areas. Refugees escaped from miserable conditions in «camps» somewhere on Europe's southern coast flooded any city or area where they saw even grim hopes of a better life.
Damon stopped in front of a building resembling a high tower and that clearly worked as a fortress. Even with his relative inexperience he easily caught the sight of a half dozen sentries added to those fairly obvious. He would guess there would be far more.
The entrance «hid» between two others, a longer, darker path from the broad street. It looked very much like the gauntlet it was meant to be. Damon didn't let himself be threatened by any of it. The feeling it impressed upon him, he had felt his entire life.
They let him walk through the outer doors and also a stretch inside, before stopping him in front of the reception desk.
– Is this the Montmartre Hotel? He asked casually.
As expected he received no vocal reply.
They allowed him to keep the revolver, probably because it was seen as a fairly harmless weapon compared to what was on the market these days.
He had never fired the gun against another human being.
Perhaps they knew that, perhaps not.
He continued alone through three sliding doors. The elevator door was open. Two guards, one of each sex waited for him inside. The elevator door closed behind him and they rose up into the tower like a pile driver. He quickly lost count on how many floors they passed on the way. Retardation was as soft as the acceleration had been. The door

slid open in the sky. Terrill didn't want to be blinded by the luxury he stepped into, fought against it with tight-woven lips. His heart increased its beat. The blood flowed faster through his veins. So fake this emotion could be, so deceptive.

Music flowed around him, a velvet touch hardly noticeable. He didn't actually see anyone at first, but heard splashes from a swimming pool, from the party spread out throughout the floor, on several floors, the signs of wealth assaulting him ever harder, as he walked on, as he approached his destination. The thick carpets, the lighting, the material used smothered him. Quite a few rare tree species had gone extinct here. The few luxurious «rags» people wore could hardly be measured in terms of wealth. A significant part of the world's scant resources had gone down the toilet because of acts taken by people such as these.

– You're the messenger?

He was met by a woman giving him an ice-cold stare.

Terrill didn't bother with a reply. They had long since confirmed his identity.

– Well then, Monsieur Terrill, she said kindly enough, – I represent the interest behind your mission. If I could have it right now, you can join the party immediately.

– Call me Terrill, he said laidback. – To speak plainly, Madame, I can't release what I bring to any representative. My employer insisted on *personal* delivery.

His lower lip shook a little, but he held her eyes.

– Please, follow me, the barracuda said, even more forthcoming.

He followed her at a safe distance. The male and female gorillas remained by the elevator.

She led him on a long walk, through corridors, hallways and parties. There was one secluded party for each new bigger room. He saw no windows. There weren't any, no one leading to the street and the night. He hadn't realized how wide the tower was, when he had seen it from the outside. It seemed narrow because it was so tall, a stone desert tower ripping the sky, one making it rain disease, the slow and agonizing death.

Rooms within rooms revealed themselves to him, yet another space filled with celebrating people. The decoration changed. Aside from that there was no notable difference between them. People fed and drank and some only drank. There were spared no expenses. People seemed to be having fun, in a desperate, downtrodden manner, the eyes behind the haze easily revealing their pain.

Then the mood changed, abruptly, violently. In a misty passage, from one moment to the next something appeared, an emotion, a shift, something hard, a brick wall, a fist in the face. The poison in the air in front of him led the way. The music whispered seductively to him, only to him. Carefully arranged lamps brightened the path. Nude men and women danced and displayed themselves within circles of light on the floor. Volatile moves made droplets of sweat jump from their bodies.

Everything looked distorted, twisted and corrupted. The sweet, intoxicating memories from the Witchnight at the Mountain of Torches felt even farther away than they had done lately. Only tiny snippets remained, and he couldn't even hold on to those.

The barracuda leading him on suddenly disappeared. He had a direct line of vision to the group somewhere ahead. They sat on large pillows coated by black velvet. All of them had hard eyes, not revealing any mercy. But even among these… these giants one stood out. The man was the biggest Damon had ever seen. Thick, fair hair flowed down the giant's shoulders, the beyond broad shoulders. Not all the baggy clothes in the world would have been able to hide much of the muscular body. Damon had seen him often during news reports on television and on the Internet. They hadn't done him justice. He was far more imposing in real life.

– So, you're the Storm Child, the man acknowledged the boy.

They had truly checked up on him. Damon's voice shook when he spoke and did his best to act confident and casual.

– So, you're Victor Russel…

The man's laughter shook the very room and everybody in it.

– Great men's reputation precedes them, Terrill. Welcome to my castle. Sit down, enjoy yourself, feel yourself at home.

There was no kindness or warmth in the rough voice, the broad smile, only ruthlessness, a snarl tearing apart and destroying everything in its wake.

Russel had a woman on his left side and a man on his right. They pushed themselves at him with a lazy, devoted expression in their face. They wore a collar and had a brand on their thigh.

Damon swallowed hard, unable to prevent it. When he sat down at the edge of a pillow he made an effort to not look to the side, but his eyes were drawn towards the boy and the girl - and Russel.

– You bring something that belongs to me, the first pages of my Black Book.

It was the correct phrase. Terrill pushed a hand inside his jacket and presented the envelope. Giant hands grabbed it. Russel, totally indifferent left it by his feet.

– The rest will follow by further negotiations, Terrill said, very officious.

A bright woman and a dark man brought refreshments. Russel seemed to be obsessed with *couples*. The boy felt awfully vulnerable right now. He wasn't stupid. In Russel's presence he felt very much like a boy.

– Blanche! Russel said casually.

One of the dancers rushed to him and knelt at his feet.

The giant's attention was directed directly at Damon.

– You like them big and strong. So do I! They still bare their neck to the strongest.

He appeared totally indifferent in his treatment of the girl, of the beautiful, beyond desirable animal making herself available to him.

– Blanche, entertain our guest!

Damon had studied her, hadn't been able to take his eyes off the captivating sight, the whirling dance of submission and still wasn't. Her eyes were constantly lowered. She had smooth, fair brown hair falling down on her right side from a ribbon at the top of her head. Shoulders were broad, her entire body broad and muscular, but still more than a little agile. And all her agility was geared towards… being looked at. Something convulsed and hurt within the boy.

– Look at her, Russel chuckled. – Her entire reality revolves around how others perceive her. You've seen something similar at school, haven't you, boy, how some obedient and attentive students make every effort to win the teacher's favor? The training of smiling dolls is very common in today's dead society. This is merely that taken to its logical conclusion. Most people aren't branded, but the brand is still there, invisible on their skin, very evident in their mind and behavior.

Damon didn't look at the doglike Blanche when she crawled to him and pushed herself at him, and started caressing him with playful fingers, eager and yearning. He made a

deliberate effort not to look at her, not to notice beyond a casual glance the soft body already shaking in need, the very evident thoughts showing through the hazy eyes how unconditionally grateful she would become by the first, slightest caress from him.
– Don't move, he commanded her very strict.
She smiled just as humble and sweet, but couldn't keep back a tiny whimper of disappointment, something she would undoubtedly pay for.
Confusion haunted him. He wondered how he would hurt her the least. By «rejecting» her, like he had done? Or if he had ravaged her with all the brutality he could muster, and thereby shown her how much he appreciated her? He had made a choice, the one everybody had to do every time in life and death; that what benefited himself and not others.
– How old do you think I am, boy?
Terrill realized slowly, waking from his slumber that Russel spoke to him, smiled to him behind the cold mask.
– I don't know… forty… fifty… somewhere between…
– Don't be silly. The smile turned hard. – You know perfectly well how old I am.
A rain of embers fell behind Damon's open eyes.
– You fathered your first child in 1958, fourteen year's old. You were born in Warsaw at the end of July 1944, just before the massacre there…
Damon faltered and couldn't keep going. He swallowed hard, once, twice.
– Yes, *you understand.* Russel whispered, not audible for anyone else in the room. Damon heard him. – I was conscious that early. I understood what the world was about, and I've seen it even more clearly since. I've waited for the Storm, the yearning, the Hunger to explode. The time is finally near, my friend.
He kept droning on and the boy listened breathlessly. Several other people in the room would have frightened the wits out of most people. Jean Luc Trevenniet sat only a few seats from Damon, Janet Lombard as well. Russel shadowed them all. They turned invisible in his presence.
– You see, most of my children have been deeply disappointing to me. Only a few have broken from my shadow. But those few have left powerful footprints of blood on Earth.
No sound, no other voices, only *his*. There was a buzz in Terrill's ears. He didn't know of what.
– By the way, don't you want Blanche? She is a well trained slave and not without certain skills. I can assure you she will be docile and obedient and eager to serve.
Terrill shook his head.
– I prefer independent people, actually, he replied, as if revealing a great secret.
He realized to his horror that he had forgotten that Blanche was there and that he had a giant, painful hard on that was impossible to hide.
Russel leaned closer, his eyes growing to giant pools of poison.
– But surely you hadn't stayed long in France's biggest city before you found out that everything is for sale here, that everything has a price? Rare and precious medicines, food in abundance and to inflated prices, clean water, bodyguards, rare animals, weapons in all categories… and humans, not the least humans.
– I've never cared much for popular opinion either, the boy clenched his teeth.
Russel cackled aloud.
– I will of course punish Blanche, he said, quite relaxed. – She has failed in the sole

task her master has charged her with: that of being a delightful, irresistible creature.

A giant hand landed on Terrill's shoulder and squeezed. Damon gritted his teeth and returned the stare.

– You have great potential, my young friend, I believe I will let you live.

It sounded like a threat and the boy believed it was.

– You have the eye of the eagle and you will use it, use it on all the obstacles you will encounter on your path. We will meet again, where the Thunder Road makes a turn.

He clapped his hands twice, signaling a change in the revelry. The light's intensity picked up, the dancing turned slow and tight. He pulled back, leaving his young guest shaken and stirred.

Damon couldn't keep his eyes off Blanche. No matter how much he desired to keep his stare on Russel. She remained in position, unmoving, completely submissive, just as irresistible. Her nipples rose hard and long. Her sex twinkled wet and swollen. She begged him with her entire body.

– Shame keeps you from embracing your lust, doesn't it boy? I have good news for you: you will leave that behind, like you will everything else.

The voice sounded far away, but it still invaded him like a cancer.

Slowly, as if in a nightmare he was distracted by a disturbance in the room outside, by loud shouts from panicked people. A man broke the heavy door and stumbled inside. It resembled a man. Electrical lights dispelled the murkiness, splintered the «peace» of the tower. In a moment stretching into seconds everyone froze like statues… until they fled to all sides in insane desperation.

– Holy shit, one cried out and released the utter and complete panic. – It's Streptococci Death

The figure resembling a man faltered and stopped. Smoke erupted from all over his body, but there was no fire. He fell on his knees. Or… did he merely… collapse? He tore off his shirt and started scratching his inflamed skin. The completely insane banshee scream echoed between the walls. Soft carpets on the walls didn't seem to soften it at all. His skin fell off in large pieces. The entire form broke apart. The scream turned to a gargle and then to a death rattle, before fading away. What just a short time ago had been a human being crumbled to a heap of clothes, bones, flesh and blood and puss.

The spectators exchanged glances, studied each other for seconds, perhaps minutes. There were no more dramatic events.

– The choice was taken from you. Don't you hate it when that happens?

Terrill opened and closed his eyes one single time.

– Look at this as a demonstration of life and death as it truly is. Russel kept paralyzing him with his presence. – There is decay and there is death. Everything else is just happening in the interface. Do you have any comments, pup?

– I would say your observations are correct. Damon scowled at him. – But that your conclusions are way off.

Russel slapped his thigh and chuckled well and loud.

He started giving orders. Two shaking servants with most of their bodies covered in plastic mopped the dust and the empty clothes on the floor. He followed them with his watchful eyes, also those fleeing like scared rabbits from the scene.

– Looks like the party is over. He shrugged and turned towards the boy with the same complete disregard and indifferent intensity. – Claire will give you the advance on the way out. I suggest you use the backstairs. Claire will show you the way.

What an honor. Terrill didn't say it aloud. He left the room without a word. The shark appeared before him and he followed her to an isolated, quiet part of the enormous apartment.

She unlocked a door and handed him an envelope. He put it in his pocket without checking it.

– I can order an escort for you, she mewed. – There are lots of dangers out there for youngsters without hair on their chest and cheeks.

– Thank you for your kind offer, but I'll manage.

He grinned at her.

She couldn't hide the flare of anger. He left without wasting more time on the empty shell.

– There is an elevator twenty floors down, she shouted to his back.

Stairs, step by step forever. He took the elevator just to spite her and to leave the castle as fast as he possibly could. The tiny box fell down, down, from one hell to one even worse. He knew he would, if necessary crawl from there.

Far away, out on the street he took a deep breath. The air actually tasted better. A still, overgrown pond, but outdoors. Up from the coal mine to the sandy, remote desert. He faced the wind, the wind playing with the long hair.

People passed him on all sides, brushing against him. Claustrophobia grabbed him by the balls and wouldn't let go. His surroundings… fell on him. One horrible second he imagined that air was kept from reaching him.

– It doesn't matter, does it? It has no bearing beyond the moment, beyond the fire moving you on, no matter the strife or annoyance or pesky idiots keeping you down.

He realized that Russel had supplanted Rawlins as the voice in his head.

A hand rolled into a fist inside the jacket. The other kept striking the brick wall. It hurt the first couple of times and then it didn't.

A sleazy man passed him close by and said something. Damon never could recall the content in the statement, but he exploded in anger.

– Can I help you with anything? He snarled. – Is there a point you want to make?

– Hey, chill, man.

The tall and muscular man turned visibly pale.

Just then another man rushed past them and interrupted it all.

– Another Strepto, he shouted. The fear mixed with the sensationalism in his eyes. – Streptococci DEATH.

Some fled. The majority of people in Damon's proximity rushed to the circle made by the gathering crowd. He followed them, helplessly drawn to the unfolding spectacle.

Just a small child this time. He couldn't tell if it was a boy or a girl. The sound and sight of hissing meat filled his being. He watched the father and the mother stand there frozen with arms extending towards the doomed offspring. His vision turned white and pale.

He had seen Streptococci Death in action the first time just after he had left Bergen four year's ago. Since then the bacteria, which ancestors had only brought wounds and sore throats had grown both in intensity and number of victims. In 1994, the first year its epidemic character had come to the attention of the public panicked rumors said it was actually feeding on tissue. That had been an exaggeration. At that time the «wicked» microorganism had been content with releasing poison and destroying skin. Now, it devoured everything it encountered. It destroyed the host body fast and furious… and thereby, if it didn't transfer to a new host brought its own destruction. One could never know for certain. It could be dormant for a long time and then engage in a feverish eruption. The medical profession, the few of them that did deal with it in public at all, spoke about an untraditional incubation period, explaining that it was constantly looking for weak spots in a given organism's immune defense system.

No one was so stupid that they even got near the already dead child. They had watched photos and videos and heard horror stories of what could happen then. Everybody relived those sensations now, knew well how volatile the disease was in its active form.

Damon Terrill felt sick to his core. When the gathering dissolved he felt exhausted, burned out.

– Did you see it?

A girl spoke to him. Her face skin glowed in excitement.

– Yes, he replied with a jarring voice.

– Shit, I missed it again, she cried exasperated.

And she spoke with focused indifference:

– Well, there will be more of it.

– You're absolutely correct.

He managed to keep his tone of voice casual, uncaring.

– I like you, she flirted. – Is there anywhere we can go together?

The look he sent her was so ugly that she instantly backed off. She was still running when he saw her vanish behind a corner fifty steps down the street. He wondered if he truly was this terrifying, also for people like her, those that had destroyed something so very valuable in themselves long ago.

– Disgusting, isn't she?

He turned around. She stood by the wall with her hands folded behind her back. He looked puzzled at her.

– Blanche?

– Close, she grinned. – I'm Yolanda, the prettier version. You have met her?

– Briefly, he replied hoarsely and ashamed.

– That's so her, returning to the city, probably weeks ago and not a word to me.

There were only minute differences, even when he studied her closer. Her hair had the suggestion of curls and a stronger touch of red. And the eyes displayed the fire her sister no longer possessed.

– I'm on my way to Phoenix Green Earth, she told him with a speculative smile. – They're always playing great Mystery Rock there.

There was something about her, something drawing him to her.

She got going and turned her head halfway back towards him. He hurried to catch up with her.

– What about you? She asked pointedly.

– I play badly, he admitted.

– Oh, you *fiend.*

She rewarded her companion with a big smile, a reproachful stare.

They had walked side by side for a while when she looked curiously at him.

– You had quite the volatile reaction to the silly goose's mindless and uncaring banter. It isn't your style to care so much about what happens to strangers… is it?

– It isn't. The fate of people I don't know doesn't concern me, but I don't enjoy others' misfortune either.

Their destination was in the old part of town by the old harbor, Vieux Port. Twenty years ago it would probably have been called shabby. These days it hardly stood out from the rest of the city, or the world at large. Twenty years ago a given trendsetter specialist would have called it *trendy*, because of its popularity, or quite simply because people felt good there…

The world had in desperate ways long since grown beyond such meaningless concepts.

After several alleys with steep streets and abrupt turns they noticed the vibrations in the air. Yolanda's wriggled her hips harder.

– I love the old parts of the city, Damon grinned. – I see it as a twisted piece of architecture in an insane artist's chaotic mind. Wicked!

The girl looked at the boy with admiration in her eyes.

A torch flickered. Pottery filled with fuel hung from the roof. They walked through a portal and turned a corner and they reached their destination, an old cellar wide and high under the ceiling. There were openings everywhere. They seemed to be both outside and inside simultaneously. A place that was many places seemed like a labyrinth to Damon, several brick walls in shades of gray.

The walls seemed almost unreal, just as much in the mind as a physical reality.

The place had electricity installed, but it paled compared to the wild embers between the people. The music, the savage mood… sneaked up on them, opening up everything within those present.

– I like you, Yolanda said softly.

And he knew she was sincere, at least in that moment in time.

Tonight was special, also compared to other nights he had visited the place. He felt something inside, a release valuable and wild.

A slide projector burned images on a white chalk wall. A man sat leaned back in a chair with partly closed eyes. The white chalk wall remained… white. The machine hummed when the first image, when no image was shown. Then colors and outlines started appearing, flying in the air. Voices called Damon's name, a hiss, a breath of death and life in his inner ear.

Yolanda sensed it, too. He didn't doubt that. She challenged him with every little move she made. They danced at the center of the circle making out the dance floor and were able to see everything. A timeless time later he was unable to measure she pushed him backwards at the wall and kissed him on the lips with cannibalistic fervor. He lifted her up and responded with equal force, devouring her flesh and her mind. He held her like that for a long time. She slipped breathless from his grip.

– Some place this. She rubbed a palm across his chest. – So hot, so deceptive…

She had worn her street smarts all the time. Now, big cracks showed in her armor, like in his. Her scent scathed his nostrils. He smiled knowingly, without really knowing why.

– You're a beast, she said with aggression in her voice and stance, – a wild creature in the forest.

– You, too, he returned to her.

They imagined that other people around them were also dancing tight and rough, but they weren't certain. In flashes, in more or less aware moments, they saw nothing but the two of them dancing alone together, circling a bonfire in a remote wilderness. They heard the wind race across the water, the waves rolling against the shore. Damon closed his eyes for a second. There was no sleep, not even anything resembling it, but raw, pulsating awareness and the fire of life following an existence in untouched nature, limitless freedom.

He held on to her in his Hunger and ravaged her with touches. She fought against it at first, but then she sighed and relented, and pushed herself at him in powerful, demanding moves. The roar, the winds of change running wild rose from the abyss. He felt hard nipples against his palms. Her hungry lips kept kissing him and her playful tongue kept teasing him.

– Down below, she whispered. – There are more than enough rooms there. Allow me to go first. I've got a surprise for you…

He wanted to ask her if she was shy, but didn't.

She left. Was he imagining it, or did he glimpse a touch of regret in her sweet face? He slowly grew aware of his surroundings. There were so many other wild and beautiful females present that he grew momentarily distracted from the sight of her flushed face. With that added thought was added more. He had just made a few, hesitating steps towards the stairs leading to the basement when he put a hand inside his jacket. His eyes narrowed to chinks and he rushed towards the entrance. Several grinning boys slowed him down, but made no real attempt at stopping him. There was no need for that.

He reached the entrance, stormed into the city night. His feverish, fast-working mind saw only one probable route away from here, and he sat out in that direction. At the top of a long row of stairs he reached a clearing. He spotted her far ahead. She rushed towards an approaching car. The envelope flashed in her hand when she waved to the driver. Damon drew the gun and pointed it at the happy girl. He had her in the sight virtually in an instant. Hitting her wouldn't be any problem. It was like standing on a shooting range and fire at a practically unmoving target. A light pull and the powerful gun with the big caliber bullets would blow her apart. She would fall and hit the ground and life would leave her. He lowered his arm and smiled curtly. The girl jumped into the car and it drove off.

He returned to Phoenix Green Earth and looked for those who had aided her, but didn't find them. It mattered not. They believed he wouldn't remember their faces, but were fatally wrong. He recalled them in crystal clear detail.

He walked down below, ran up to the attic, took a stroll back down. Something had changed in him. He didn't know if it had happened recently, the last few days or tonight, but it was there, poignant, potent and powerful. This place could be inspiring. Perhaps he would have enjoyed it here, five minutes ago. Something approached him, rising within, a Hunger he so far had only known while hovering above the Abyss in the deepest part of his self.

This place… he didn't belong here.

CHAPTER SEVEN

He stood before the open door. It felt a little strange after losing count of how many gates he had walked through the last half hour, in this dank, dreaded fortress. He was able to glimpse a few outlines in the room in front of him. It was pitch black there. The only light came from far away in the hallway where he had stopped.

– Enter, the rough, cold voice bid him. – Close the door.

The boy obeyed, stepping inside, pushing the massive door until it closed. Not a single bit of light penetrated the dark surrounding him, but he still saw, saw in the one, two, three seconds the room rested in eternal darkness.

A single click and light flooded the room. Soft light, resembling that found in an ordinary living room. The walls appeared, closing off what had seemed like infinite space. The room had two chairs, one sofa and a table and nothing more.

– Welcome, Terrill, Tom Rawlins greeted him. – My home is your home.

Damon didn't know, had no idea how to respond to that and kept his mouth shut.

A collection of smaller screens covered the entirety of one of the walls. Damon sat down in the sofa, facing that wall. It was very elaborate. He had a nice view of all the screens, which was no doubt the intention.

Rawlins sat in a solid, deep armchair. It had a control panel with pushbuttons on each side of the two armrests. The man's eyes seemed hollow in the strange, sunburned face, framed by the shoulder-length gray hair.

– Observe. Follow it and see where it leads.

The screen seemed to come to life, with sound, images and impressions so powerful that Terrill couldn't decide whether or not it was live or recordings. Sometimes the small screens combined into one single giant image. Several players clearly played simultaneously.

– I spared no expenses for this setup, Rawlins added. – It must be good for something.

The composite movie showed English-spoken language news from the turn of the century and to date. The selected material and the manner it was presented hit the unaware viewer hard and brutal, like a sledgehammer in the chest.

The Rhone-delta, as it had been, as it was or wasn't from several angles and levels. From the first signs of its decline had revealed themselves and to date, when the ocean had almost devoured it all. The Lion Gulf leading to Marseille… the lion had been skinned alive and reduced to cinder.

The focus shifted to ice, the inland ice on Greenland. The land there was shrinking by the coastline, like all land on the globe did these days. The inland changed color from white to green. All maps had to be redrawn, at least once a year. Glaciers and its arms all over the world grew the first few years of the increasing heat and then they shrunk dramatically. The sight of Antarctica in January was an amazing sight. A completely different continent revealed itself. Damon froze down his spine.

On Iceland, in northern Norway, by the Canadian coast the mood grew bitter and hateful. These people had been overfishing and had taxed the sea's riches beyond repair for decades. They had finally succeeded in the task of completely destroying their own livelihood. The ocean's food basket had shrunk to the point of being virtually empty.

There was no more profit to be made, not even sufficient food left to avoid starvation.

And they were screaming bloody murder, blaming everybody but themselves.

Gigantic factory trawlers... trawled the world in a desperate search for fish. Every country or group of countries guarded their representatives with swarms of warships. Powder was desert dry and exploded often.

In Siberia it blew up in earnest when a territorial war between autonomous Russian republics escalated into an exchange of available nuclear warheads. Major parts of northern Asia became uninhabitable, a radioactive wasteland suggesting how it would be if it happened on a global scale. India and Pakistan had led the way a few years earlier and the insanity showed no sign of even slowing down.

It didn't slow down the warming either, but speeded it up, with further release of the greenhouse gases trapped in the former frozen earth.

Little over a year ago most of the crew members on the American aircraft carrier USS Nimitz had refused to leave it. They had taken control and left the harbor again. They hadn't received supplies since. The carrier would usually have supplies for two years, but it was a long time since such normality had been present in the United States navy or anywhere. A group of officers and privates had quickly gained control of the onboard arsenal of thermonuclear rockets. After that everything had proceeded in the classic spirit of the cold war. The government in Washington DC had threatened to blow them up and the people on the carrier had threatened to blow up Washington DC. And the rings had immediately started spreading in the water. The United States, to that point seemingly a fairly stable nation crumbled at its seams, as people sided with one or two or ten of the parties involved, with militarism and pacifism, urban and rural, land and sea, cheese and milk. Conflicts kept in check for decades, centennials erupted everywhere. September 30, when their supplies were almost empty and they were surrounded by units from the United States' navy, those controlling USS Nimitz issued an ultimatum where they demanded immediate deliveries. Washington DC rejected their demands. The deadline passed. On the morning of October 2, many rockets crossed each other. USS Nimitz was reduced to dust. With it, into the nothing of existence they brought the carriers USS Reagan and USS North, and the cities Washington DC, New York and Boston. United States stopped existing as a nation at that very moment.

Not many days afterwards European authorities voted to close themselves off from the rest of the world. The final voices of moderation vanished with the United States. The American soldiers still there were either expelled, thrown in jail or executed, and the army equipment confiscated.

Some countries had center/left governments, others center/right. France and possibly Austria had turned fascist. All acted in solemn agreement. Orders were issued to deny non-Europeans access. A week later the No Access sign was extended to also include East Europeans. A new iron curtain was constructed, just a little further east than the previous.

The French and the Spanish took care of the Bask together, practically exterminating major parts of the Pyrenean population, men, women and children, without thinking twice about it. Most of it was recorded. No one could effectively deny the facts. Representatives from other countries spoke a few angry words and issued a few diplomatic protests. Some leaders spoke up, but no one used the word *genocide*. They had their own axes to grind.

The screens showed a man being hit by a hail of bullets. They had filmed him from four sides simultaneously and another broadcaster had also done so from above. Rawlins had it all. It seemed like an awesome display of the power of modern television.

Outside what had once been called Groningen in the Netherlands people burned their witch, a twelve-year boy that had enjoyed a good time with the police chief's wife the night before the flood.

In Stockholm *concerned* citizens hanged a group of nudists. No particular reason was given.

There had been many such incidents lately. It had been contained to rural areas, but not anymore.

Western Norway was hit by yet another hurricane. This time Stavanger was hit the worst, but Bergen also suffered considerable damage.

– Look at it, Rawlins commented cheerfully. – It's one of the few places in the world it's raining. Those not living there must think it's raining all the time. Perhaps it's one of the few places in the world it will be possible to live?

Terrill looked closer at him, but there was little or nothing to see in the phlegmatic face.

Unrest rose like a sore thumb, as tens of thousands of protesters marched and bled through European streets.

An empty, remote coastal landscape appeared. Athens resembled a ghost town. It was one. This summer the temperature had stayed over forty degrees Celsius in the shade. Traffic was banned early in the summer. There wasn't the slightest draft in the air in the ghost town revealing itself. Poisonous fumes gathered around the increasingly weathered acropolis. Ruins thousands of years old just crumbled to dust. People saw red. The Greeks had thrown the gauntlet and blamed everything and everyone.

Someone blew up the Aswan Dam. The Turks blamed Syria and Iraq, but their skirmish with the Greeks kept them from instant retaliation. Syria and Iraq, on the other hand used the opportunity to take action.

In Australia an inferno of fire and ash vanquished major parts of Sidney. Forest fires roamed ever more often the world. It turned increasingly drier almost everywhere. Ever more powerful dry storms brought more and more lightning strikes.

Hanover in Germany, the entire city had been closed off from the surrounding area and its population quarantined. Something unexplainable and unfathomable was happening there. People became ill and died in hours or lost all remnants of civilized behavior. A film recorded with a powerful lens showed a rather large group roasting the major, his associates and a number of police officers over open fire. The people in the group clearly had a healthy appetite. And all the time they had this eerie, wicked expression on their twisted faces.

Damon's face cracked in a smile. He couldn't help it. The entire scene seemed unreal, almost like a non-fiction feature film, an insane theater performance.

All of it, also what wasn't included in the presentation, a world that for so long had been out of balance, now tipping over churned through his head. To see it presented and suggested like this… overwhelming.

The North Sea, The Atlantic Ocean, The Pacific Ocean, The Indian Sea… an endless flow of icebergs made international shipping more than a risky affair. A film director with a love for gallows humor had called his latest film «The Invasion of the Invisible Icebergs». It dealt with the world's clandestine services and had, as it turned out indeed ended up as his last movie.

Images flickered before the boy's inner eye, from hospitals the world over, detention centers for the ill and infirm, and unexplainable wounds and diseases. People having grown up close to chemical plants were particularly at risk, but humanity as a species moved ever closer towards an epidemic state. There was an explosive increase in the number of childless people. They rushed to doctors, witch doctors and various health stations to get help. People living in cities were most disposed for environmental injuries, but the poison from civilization's final death rattle had spread everywhere on the planet by now. Humans and other animals that had lived far from cities their entire lives were found with genetic damage. Their ancestors had lived near factories for generations. The Ferryman no longer waited patiently for his due.

Shots were fired, and then more shots. Smoke kept rising, not falling. The Kingdom of Death rose from the depths and surrounded the entire globe. The mythological, fabled kingdom where all secrets were exposed, all illusions crushed. A gigantic, untamed figure rose from the heaps of ashes, a creature of fire and life, with face and body and soul and blood.

– The world is like a ruined Toyota, Rawlins said unexpectedly. – No one cares about saving any of it.

Damon shook his head, once again unsure how to respond.

The film ended with volcanoes erupting, with ice melting across the world. Steam descended from the very air itself, a hole in time and space, inverted geysers of blood.

Rawlins rose from the chair. Damon had heard that he hardly ever did that while others were present. The screen showed city images in daylight, what was happening in Marseille right now, showed it from the most unlikely angles and outlooks. It did indeed seem like Rawlins had grown roots here.

– Now, what's your impression of Russel?

His distinctive rusty voice turned even more pronounced. Rumors had it that it was a result of a knife-wound in South America many years ago.

– Why ask me?

– I am asking you.

The man's voice changed again, making Damon swallow hard and straighten.

– He… gets to you, moving inside you in ways that can't be properly described. He's no force of nature. He's way too damaged, twisted for that. But he resembles one.

The boy repeated his conversation with Russel word by word. It didn't feel hard, didn't feel hard at all.

Rawlins kept assessing him with his sticky eyes.

– You interest me, kid. You interest *him*. He let you live. It's a first, according to my sources.

A rough grin.

– And I pride myself of having reliable sources.

Damon felt anger then, felt it rise within and overwhelm the sneaking fear, the sense of being the victim of other people's whims.

– He's a *slave trader,* he cried. – How can you trade with him?

– I trade with everybody, Rawlins shrugged. – It's my strength. I'm uninhibited by hypocrisy and morality. Everybody knows what I am about.

– Oh, it's just business, right?

There was a bow, a light touch of irony.

One moment, a mere second he imagined that the older man was far away. When his eyes once again focused, it seemed even sharper than before. To Damon it looked like he was actually nodding to himself.

– You lost something that is mine, young man…

– I'll get it back, the boy replied, gritting his teeth.

Rawlins strolled to his large and well-equipped desk. He picked a cigar from a box.

– This quality is getting hard to obtain, he said, speaking from the corner of his mouth while he was lighting the monster. – The world's cigar production has gone downhill after the ocean drowned Castro and Cuba.

The arms dealer had been born almost fifteen years after Russel, but often looked older. Aside from the obvious signs like the hair color and the lines in the face, it revealed itself by the curving of the shoulders and the lack of agility.

But not now. The eyes resting on Damon and the slightly overweight body revealed the power of the sharp mind.

– There is something we must explore together, kid. The in spite of it all powerful body stepped out from the smokescreen. – You had the girl in your sight and chose not to pull the trigger.

«I've got a thousand eyes and ears, also in this city», the Storm Child had heard him say once.

– I've seen you shoot, kid. You're a natural and this was an easy target, even for a fairly untrained shooter. There was little or none potential bullet drift, and you knew that well, even before you took aim. You didn't have to aim, god damn it.

The heavyset man counted on his fingers every time another observation was pointed out. Terrill found it annoying as hell.

– You've never shot anyone before. That might have explained it, but I just don't believe it was a decisive factor in your case. At the time you were so embarrassed, so angry with yourself that you gladly would have executed an army of choirgirls.

– Is there a point you would like to make or do you just enjoy the sound of your own voice?

Damon jumped up from the couch in anger, very aware that he threw caution to the wind.

Rawlins covered the distance between them amazingly fast, grabbed him, lifted him high up and shook him like a rag doll. Once, twice… and no more.

He stood still when the big man placed him back on the floor. The arms dealer smiled in a very predatory way and kept speaking casually, as if nothing had happened.

– That's also valid when it comes to a certain satanic long-fingered courtesan. I know you're quite familiar with the coldness and hardness inside needed to do what's necessary. And here, I believe we're at the heart of the matter: Your levelheaded reasoning told you that the content of the envelope wasn't worth killing for.

Damon was breathing hard. He felt more than he sensed his asthma. Breathing turned practically convulsive and desperate, and his growing panic made it worse. He was visibly shaking, now, exposed and vulnerable.

– A view I happen to share. There was a shrug, but Damon knew that the charge was far from complete. – To a certain point.

– It's no problem for me, but we aren't talking about me, kid, but you. It falls back on you, really. You have to know the price for your neglect. It strikes people down all the time. It has always done that. In the years to come we all might have our light put out by trifles. You stayed your killer instinct because you split the hair between killing and murder. Very decent of you. A very civilized action. Your problem is that we don't live in a civilized society, and that such a beast has never existed and that it's pretty much a construct and a deception, anyway. You've come a long way already. I've seen major improvement on your part the last year. But you're still behind and need lots of incitement in order to catch up. Look at my lesson as a small contribution on the road you and everyone else must walk, and you might survive a while longer.

Tom Rawlins sat back down in his chair. A push of the button and the screens yet again showed a number of channels simultaneously. Damon wondered again how he could get anything from it all. The lights were dimmed. The audience was done. The door slid open. Terrill hesitated momentarily, before leaving tight-lipped.

They waited for him at the end of the hallway. He didn't consider the fact that there was no other way out, that he had left his gun in the apartment, he just continued forward.

Six sentries waited for him. He didn't really count them, but charged them, charged them hard. Perhaps they would have taken it easy on him if he had gone meekly to the gas chamber. He ignored *that* whispering voice as well.

His foot hit the closest adversary and he felt something give. One of the women collided with his fist and blood flowed from the cracked skin. He delivered more hits and kicks than he would have considered believable and even possible before the decisive blow hit him and he hit the floor.

The four still standing revealed a truly admirable patience and restraint when they carried him off, when two of them pushed him against an already bloody brick wall and the other two had fun with softening him up a while, a good while, before getting on with their work. He felt their skill on every point of his body. They worked him over from head to toe. It made him feel better, in a backwards kind of way.

He woke up in the streets, at the base of a staircase. A painful kick in the belly and he heard patronizing laughter. They left him, and the laughter no longer sounded too pervasive. He hadn't been out very long. The darkness still lingered in the Stone City. He looked up. The staircase was tall and steep.

– They didn't throw you down it, kid, but they told you, in not so many words that they could easily have done so.

Tom Rawlins had regained his spot as the loud voice in his head. That comforted the boy in a way.

The bloody figure stumbled upstairs, downstairs, humming a melody on the more or less familiar route to his apartment. A loud sound thundered in his ears, no matter how much he shook his head. The splitting headache took a turn for the worse. He almost fell and had to stop.

It dawned on him that he heard the sound of a waterfall. And at that precise moment the visions began assaulting him as well. He heard the flapping of wings and then he actually *saw* the waterfall and the eagles roaming the air around him.

Slowly, only slowly he managed to gain control of his fast breathing, the influx of oxygen to his brain. The stark impressions faded away.

Even as they lingered, as he covered the last remaining distance to his brief-home.

He took the last few steps inside the apartment and slammed the door behind him with the weight of his body. His eyes instantly drawn to the barrel of the gun sticking out from under the pillow, he wanted to rush across the room and grab it, to feel the cold steel in his hands. He resisted the almost overwhelming temptation.

A lone lamp burned in the room filled with shadows. He froze, noticing the… discrepancies almost immediately, the difference between the room, as he recalled it and how it was now. The creature, the anomaly, the woman had, in her mastery placed herself in the deepest darkness. She practically had become one with her surroundings. He recognized her with that one look. His mother looked at him with fond eyes.

She had changed. He noticed and sensed that instantly. She hardly even resembled the innocent wife he remembered. She seemed younger, almost young again. The way she moved reminded him of Rawlins' bodyguards, of people living a life of danger.

– It's been such a long time, she said softly. – But perhaps my visit is… inconvenient?

A flash of fangs, cheerfulness, amusement, not concern. It was all so bizarre that he fell back on old patterns, becoming defensive.

– I'm okay, mom, he shrugged.

Pain cut through him and he crouched, unable to keep the hurt from expressing itself. She walked to him and grabbed him cautiously.

– I don't think you're telling your mother the entire story here…

She led him to the bed and pushed him softly down on it.

– How did you find me? What are you doing here?

He tried, in vain to mask his bewilderment.

– I realized that each person is potentially many. She replied in a manner of speaking. – It led me to a startling, but eventually obvious conclusion.

She started pulling off his clothes. He drew the line when she reached the underwear.

Sensitive hands handled him fast and unceremoniously. He grimaced involuntarily several times. She continued her examination undaunted and resolutely.

– It seems like you have avoided major injuries, as unlikely as that is, she mused. – The giant tank that ran you over can't have wished you much ill. There are no broken bones and serious lacerations. They have even gone to great lengths to avoid loosening teeth. Considerate beyond words, if you ask me. Someone must have had your continued good health very much in mind.

Her gentle voice didn't really register in his conscious mind.

– But listen to your wise mother, now. You've been knocked around a lot. If you don't get any sort of treatment the skin will swell even worse than it already has and you will wake up stiff as timber tomorrow. I have an ointment that will help and you will sleep like a rock.

He squirmed in bed while she applied the cream-like substance on every inch of his skin. She practically massaged him and she was very good at it.

She sat on the edge of the bed. He rested on his back and looked at the brightening red sky in the east.

– I have to tell you something, she said quietly. He finally managed to catch her sky-blue eyes. – I should have done so long ago.

That made him pay attention.

– You are an adult, if that phrase or angle has any validity at all. You really were one well before you decided to venture into the larger world, more than capable of making your own decisions, your own mistakes. We, your father and I didn't want to realize that, since we would have been forced to take a long, hard look at ourselves and our lives then. Well, our reluctance was no good, even in that regard. When you left we did just that.

She smiled mischievously to the air, to herself, young again for one tiny moment, before smiling softly to him.

– We don't have much time, she said, clearly uneasy. – I've brought you something.

She pushed something into his hand. He stared incredulous at her and at the green rope armband.

– They're clever and smart, she said. – They contacted Emmett and me when we weren't together, so we wouldn't spoil it for each other. The band can be both useful and dangerous to you, but we felt strongly you should have one.

He pushed it up his arm, beyond the elbow. It fit perfectly.

– The Green Rose is becoming a major power in Europe and that's a good thing. Eyes twinkled like wells into his bottomless dark. – But the Rose will also fade away when the winds of change are blowing wild, vanish down the drain with everything else seen as important. And that is also a good thing.

Eyelids and limbs turned heavy. He heard the rumbling bass of distant thunder. The lightning flared behind the eyelids, that, too with increasing extent and intensity. The skin felt like it was stabbed with a thousand needles. He saw her wave, before fading before the door. There was something final over that gesture. She said goodbye.

She was gone and he didn't hear the sound of the door, leaving him to wonder if he would wake up in the morning and believe everything had been a dream. He clutched the arm and the band. The scent reminded him of ancient times, about us all, what we once had been.

– Life is a mystery, isn't it, kid? One we all need to live.

Eyes… dull eyes, not blinking, not shifting between day and night appeared to him. They bowed their heads, heads connected to bodies and thoughts sucked dry of juices and life. He watched while they walked off the cliff and he didn't, he held back, staying there on the precipice. Thunder rolled in his ears, no longer distant.

CHAPTER EIGHT

All the figures jumping from the shadows threatened everybody in the light. When Terrill in his daily exercise made his way through Tom Rawlins' sophisticated shooting range, he couldn't always tell what was real or not, if he was actually here or outside, in the streets of Marseille. This treacherous feeling didn't first and foremost come to him because of the virtual system, but from a nagging, unexplainable emotion.

All the figures were a potential threat, police officers, wives, gangsters, children… That was how the game worked. As long as they hadn't drawn guns or appeared threatening he would lose if he shot them. It worked like that most of the time. Sometimes he lost because he didn't shoot people standing far away in the back, or because he didn't fill a girl pushing a baby stroller with hot lead. She did that that to him when he turned his back to her or the stroller could be filled with explosives.

Everything, nuances of emotions and emotional expressions was conveyed, delivered to his tormented mind through his vision, hearing, taste, smell, through known and unknown senses. The glasses he wore and the sensors he had attached to his head made it all very clear, but also indistinct to him. There was no reason, no rhyme, no logic beyond the rudimentary.

He held a gun in his hand. That was real, he knew that much. The cold metal burned him. He moved through a spacey basement. Without the VR it would just have been impotent props. His subconscious, his ID pulled at his thoughts. He knew in his depths that he was just firing at cardboard disks and electronic images, but still saw how people were hit, how they fell and died. It seemed like a different kind of reality to him.

The somewhat fresh air outside, outside the confines of the enclosed hall hit him, right after he jumped through the narrow doorway. He had escaped the old, derelict building without being hit. Life and safety embraced him. He walked away, increasingly relieved. Fifty steps from the house he slowed down, started walking and relaxed. The virtual landscape dissolved around him. Then he heard the thunder from a gun and felt a tearing pain. He turned abruptly and managed to a see a woman stick a hand holding a gun up from an open manhole. Gunsmoke and fire flowed from the barrel. He registered that, just before the system sent him into the Void.

He tore off the equipment in one single, violent move. The room faded away and reappeared like a cellar filled with garbage.

– Technology is great, isn't it? He heard Rawlins' electronic voice from the control room.

– It is excellent training, Terrill admitted. – I learn to move without really using my eyes.

It gave him, and everyone using the equipment a headache, making them dizzy and nauseous.

His entire upper body hurt like hell. He rubbed his chest while throwing away the equipment and leaving the room. There was no blood, not on him or on any of the cardboard figures.

It was all right then.

The scenery shifted once again, turning indistinct again, turning real.

A splintering light filled the darkness, a surveillance chopper levitating above one of the newer parts of the city, one of the main streets, La Canebière, reminding people of who was in charge, at last above.
It didn't really illuminate anything in the chaotic and overpopulated streets. Every twenty-four hours, when the city lights overpowered the natural the street-activities turned even more keyed up. People hardly reacted when the chopper, with the newest in recording equipment flew away.
The heat clutched Marseille in its fist. Both the literal and the one concealed within raged with equal measure. Sweat flowed in filled-to-the-brim streets. In dark alleys people sought what happened away from neon lights and surveillance cameras. Groups of men and women, dancers in the forest and the night entertained in such places. The jungle telegraph, a rumor everyone and no one had known, had raged for days and nights that they would perform in Marseille and now they were here.
They didn't perform completely nude and had not covered themselves in the characteristic gray color, but they had painted their bodies. Heat grew stronger around them, in the blood of those watching them. There was no traditional stage. Everything happened in the midst of those watching/experiencing it all. In a manner of speaking, there were no spectators here, only participants.
This was the Nightravens, one of many active groups within the greater lattice that was the Green Rose. The dance was the outer expression, what could be seen without truly opening the eyes. The inner life of the dance led people far deeper, into the mists of time, back to forgotten times. It echoed pleasantly and wildly within everybody present. They sought eagerly and passionately the savagery and the fire they half recalled, half imagined in a misplaced place within themselves. The steam of the boiling kettle could no longer be kept contained, now, at the end of the year 2012.
According to western, Christian time-frame, Damon thought.
His attention was drawn to four of the dancers. They moved according to each other, totally immersed by their partners in a soft, aggressive and beyond sensual dance. He saw no shame, only pure, undiminished desire, so much easier to understand, now, compared to the last time he had witnessed it all, in Jotunheim as a child.
He shifted his attention slightly, and caught her in his eyes. Yolanda Durant laughed and joked with a rather large group of boys and girls. She clearly knew them well. They all distinguished themselves by their colors, by the fact that they didn't wear any. This was a rare group of independents that had banded together.
It had taken time and effort to trace her. She had stayed away from the most obvious places for a while. He had waited patiently, surveyed each new spot without surveying it, hidden in the shadows, until she, as expected had returned to her usual haunts.
They left the place with a collective laughter. He let himself drift with the flow in their slipstream. After less than a minute they found themselves on La Canebière, its hectic life surrounding them, swamping them, everything according to his plan.
Television sets had been switched on inside a store. Nobody watched them. They were all showing the same or practically the same. All channels broadcast the same: The Speak French Campaign, a support for the prohibition against all foreign, especially English influence. France had cheered when the American empire collapsed.
A strict, old-fashioned, very old-fashioned schoolmaster type of man stood straight and rigid in front of a blackboard with a pointer in his hand and a holier than thou

expression in his face. Everybody recognized Jordin, the French minister of the Interior. He had the power to enforce his phobia these days.

– Pay attention, now, boys and girls. His voice sounded weak and shaky, even electronically enhanced and modulated. – You don't say «walkman» or «IPod», but *Balladeur*. You don't say «disc jockey», but *Animateur*. You don't say «comeback», but *Reteur*...

Damon straightened the shades and pulled the cap down on the forehead. He slowly, meticulously unbuttoned the pale yellow coat, confident that he wouldn't make waves. The heat didn't keep people from dressing in the most insane clothing. French fashion houses prevailed.

He drew a large, ugly shotgun. His right hand closed around the handle. The index finger found the trigger. His left hand closed around the barrel. This was great. He could hardly believe his calm. The first salvo hit at the center of the giant window. People showed moderate interest, of course, but when the hails kept pulverizing machines and inventory their common sense and survival instinct overpowered the curiosity. They ran off in panic. Some threw themselves on the ground and crawled off. He emptied the shotgun without hitting anyone. His hands didn't shake. He could hardly fathom the calm and the drive and the unrest ravaging him.

Whirlwinds ensured that the final piece of the ruin collapsed. The dust didn't rest, but kept whirling in the air. He let go of the shotgun and left it and the place behind. Nobody cared about him, hard at work with fleeing the area, everybody being very aware of what the commotion implied. Few matters and events provoked the authorities more than disorder and insults against the state and its «integrity». The sounds of the police sirens were already notable. In just a few minutes the area would swarm with choppers and patrol cars.

Damon kept his attention locked on Yolanda. He discarded the gloves, the jacket, the cap and the shades while chasing her. The long, black hair flowed down his neck and whirled like dust in the wind. He followed Yolanda and her companions through dark alleys, through their twilight bordering the hidden world.

He reached out with his fingertips and touched it, the world that can't be seen, a hide he didn't have to wear. It was like he was born to roam the badly lit alleys. He observed while Yolanda and the gang without colors parted company, like they always did during times of casual, non-immediate danger. They spread out and turned unassailable.

Yolanda appeared exactly where he had counted on she would appear, and he waited for her. She passed right by where he stood behind a corner. He slipped close to her from behind and caught her in a hard and ruthless grip. A hand clutched around her mouth. He pushed her against the brick wall and struck her hard in the back. She stopped struggling and was hardly able to do anything except gasping for air. He tied her around the upper arms and wrists. She started struggling again. He struck her again. A hiss filled her ears. She turned completely limp in his grip. He tied her ankles, gagged her with duct tape and blindfolded her. She whimpered in fright. He put her on a shoulder and walked off. She struggled some more. He struck her hard in the belly. That was the last time she tried anything. Tears wet the blindfold. He felt how she started shaking and how she couldn't conceal the choking. She didn't know who, didn't know why. Voices reached him, reached her in the dark.

– Another headed for the slave pens.

She feared the worst, he knew that and it pleased him.

He moved light on his feet through the Stone Desert. There were more voices, more people observing the man with his catch. No one made any attempt at helping her in her plight. He brought her to one of his hideouts, the one by the railway station. It was below street level, an excellent place to bring his prey. He stumbled down steep stairs. There was no electricity anywhere in the building. He sensed the other rooms, the rest of the ruin, but saw no lights on his fairly long walk through the dark hallways.

Quite a while, something that felt like minutes but he suspected was only less than one brought him and his prey to a small room deep below. He opened the heavy door and walked inside. It slammed shut by itself. He lit a match and subsequently a candle. The lone flame illuminated what had been dark space.

The only furniture in the room consisted of a bed and a stool, and hardly anything more. He stood still for a moment, listening to a silence that had always attracted him. He put her down on the bed and lit two more candles. The three lights softened the shadows.

He found a can of hermetic fruit from a hatch in the floor and opened it without hurrying. The stool threatened to collapse when he sat down, but didn't. He started feeding. The fruit retained quite a bit of its original taste. He devoured it, taking his time, studying the helpless girl on the bed, her generous curves, the small signs of paralyzing fear.

She finally dared to move and was about to sit up. He found a stick and struck her butt in a stinging rap. She choked and from then on she didn't make a move, not the slightest attempt of one. He finished the fruit and put the can away. She worked hard to breathe through the nostrils, the narrow channels filling up with snot. Her heart began beating faster in anxiety. He climbed into the bed and lay down beside her. Suddenly, she hardly dared breathing. He touched her in thoroughly invasive ways, in every way he desired. Hands moved by themselves, pulling clothes aside, easily finding nude skin. It felt dank and cold. He made a fist, tightened his lips for a moment, before letting go. He untied her in pulls and pushes and snarls. She remained limp in his grip. He left the gag and the blindfold and sat down and waited.

She lay there unmoving. The ropes hadn't just been loosened, but removed. He studied her while she breathed like a terrified prey captured by a predator. A lot of time passed before she led shaking hands to her head and removed the blindfold. They pulled off the duct tape slowly, cautiously. She glanced at him as he studied her with a merciless glare. Wary eyes studied him. The mask staring back made her shake even more.

– So, it was a rotten thing to do, she begged for herself. – I'll make sure you get the money, ASAP, okay.

She attempted a smile. It faded fast.

– Come here, he snarled. – On your knees.

She obeyed in a rush, kneeling like a shaking leaf before him.

– Such a tasty fruit. He grabbed her around the jaw. – And mine to do with as I please.

He looked possessive at her. Such a stare wasn't unknown to her, only the total lack of compromise in it. She lowered her eyes.

– I don't give a shit about the fucking money.

She couldn't decide if he towered above her like a statue of ice or one seething with rage, and not what was worse. She shrunk further in his overwhelming presence.

– I will get them back and more when I sell you anyway.

She gasped and shook her head in denial.

– You wouldn't!

But fear and uncertainty revealed itself behind her cracked mask.

– You will probably end up at your dear sister's side, yet another sweet slave of your frequent employer.

She frowned, looking incredulous at him. His words didn't register at first, somehow, didn't reach her.

– So, you don't know that the man you work for has taken dear, sweet Blanche into his fold, his stable of pets?

– What are you saying? She shouted weakly, the final part of her facade crumbling. – That isn't true!

– I saw her… close up, he grinned, unable to resist twisting the blade one more time. – She has a mole under the left breast. I can tell you other details, too, if you want.

There was no visual response.

– Silly me, he kept pushing, – I would have saved myself lots of trouble if I had shared the bad news with you the moment we met.

– Please, Yolanda begged. – Where is she? In the Tower?

– She was there when he was, Terrill shrugged. – That doesn't mean any of them are there, now, of course.

He handed her a new can with hermetic fruit. She hesitated, scowling at him, cut open and vulnerable, but then accepted it and fed avariciously. She kept swallowing hard, while she kept fighting with herself. Tears formed and evaporated constantly in the eyes.

– Why did he do it? She finally gave voice to her sore inquisitiveness. – We've always strived to be loyal to him.

– Why not? Terrill shrugged again. – You know or should know that loyalty is rarely reciprocated. I think he enjoyed how easily he controlled you all. Blanche showed herself to be unruly and paid for it. But your most important lesson here is…

She warmed herself in his intense stare.

– … that no one and certainly not people like him need a reason. The world isn't separated into edible parts, but is hard and ruthless. Perhaps none of us realizes what that entails yet, but we will.

– Yes, she whispered. She jumped on her feet and grabbed his hands. – Yes!

The monotonous rhythm spat itself from giant speakers. They strived hard to stay in touch on the treacherous, crowded dance floor. At «Mont Blanc», one of Marseille's most well known discos contact wasn't merely desirable but mandatory. Sweaty youths pushed at each other both on the dance floor and elsewhere in the loud surroundings. Terrill curled his lips in very expressive ways. He felt Yolanda's hand in his, such an insignificant touch in the all-encompassing white light. The dark glasses they had purchases earlier that day revealed themselves to be invaluable here, in this desolate wasteland without mercy.

The two of them, dancing in a land of gray and grayish gray didn't stand out in visible ways from all the others youths. The dark glass hid the eyes never resting, the street children's guarded glances.

Damon, in a moment of overconfidence attempted to make room for them, a hopeless venture, of course. He relented and allowed himself to be devoured by the many-headed monster. Water surrounded him and he descended into an abyss of flesh and heat and moisture where he could hardly breathe.

– What is on your mind? She shouted, while studying him with wary but curious eyes.

He grinned, a snarl more than a smile.

– What strikes me most of all here is the over-the-top optimism, he shouted back. – Is there anything here that isn't fake, isn't this month's flavor?

– Nah, she snorted, – it's all part of the official and unofficial propaganda effort. They go to insane lengths to propagate mindless conduct.

The two of them heard each other just fine, in spite of all the hammering, even noise hitting them from all sides.

They danced in the whirl of flesh and heat moving with impunity between the walls covered by red tapestry. In glimpses even the furniture seemed to be covered by it, smothered in flashing crimson, in textiles resembling blood.

– I wonder if those running this are realizing what they actually have here, he grinned, – what ambiguity this place is projecting.

– There is something, she nodded slowly, – a hint of lightning and... thunder I can just about make out. It isn't just my imagination then? It isn't?

He pulled her close, pulled her tight. She gasped.

– They just don't get it, he beamed. – They don't get the world and not what's happening between these walls. Those in charge see this as a controlled environment. They're truly totally clueless, about everything.

Long hair fluttered in the whirlwind, in the ongoing draft surrounding the dancers. The illusion of complacency, of tradition was torn apart. Pacified youth touched the animal, even the wild animal within. The sea of faces revealed that, exposed that, inevitably and undeniably. Masks turned ugly, dilated, transforming into faces.

Damon and Yolanda found with audacity and force an available table. Eyes met eyes and didn't part.

She gave him a feather-light kiss on the cheek and spoke into his ear.

– Damon, Damon, she called, – why am I so attracted to you?

– That one is easy to answer. You fear me and we're all attracted to our fear.

He gave her a demanding kiss on her lips. She sighed and leaned hard on him.

– I'll take a short break. They heard Maxine Leary, the disc jockey, as if from afar. – In the meantime, please be entertained by The Rhythm of the Heart by Peter Gabriel.

Countless eyes followed her as she left the stage and her elaborate setup to a boy.

– Are they allowed to play that one? A girl sighed in expectation.

– They aren't, her boyfriend told her. – It has been banned for years.

A mood of expectation charged the air further.

Damon and Yolanda noticed it in ever more powerful ways as they pulled back, into the more distant spots of the place. The white light didn't seem to reach in there, a dark corner with visible dust on exposed parts.

The dust danced, too, and the very sight of it made it tingle in his frontal lobe.

– I feel so dizzy, she whispered.

He heard her easily, her seductive voice reaching him without impediment.

She leaned on a column. He pushed her at it and felt the firm and curvy body against his own. The smoldering uncertainty grew abruptly to uncontrolled Hunger. In a flash he realized he desired her and everything else turned insignificant.

He heard her breath, heard it above all the noise. Many were breathing and touching each other in the darkness. He kissed her again, potent and demanding.

– Not here, she protested shyly and breathless.

– Here, NOW!

The entire heavy and large body pushed against hers. She attempted to writhe out of his grip when he pushed an active hand against her groin. Two round eyes turned hazy and when she kept writhing, it was in burning lust. She kissed him hard on the lips and leaned backwards. With lazy movements she unbuttoned her blouse. She exposed her breasts fully and revealed a sight to behold, allowing him to peruse them as he saw fit.

– People are dead, she gasped. – They die day by day, little by little, like the world itself, but not you, not I.

He grabbed her bulbs and pulled her close. She began tearing and pulling in his pants with considerable strength, pulling them to his knees in one single move. Her own immediately followed suit in a combined effort of free hands. She clutched his liberated hardness in something that resembled a tight grip. He didn't feel even the slightest pain. One more pull and he had lifted her feet off the floor. A push and he found himself inside her. She made clumsy attempts at getting her legs free of the pants, in vain. She teased him and spurred him further on with arms, lips and her entire body, with sweet and engaging words and active and brutal action. She bit into his shoulder muscle. There was still no pain. He pushed himself as deep into her as he could possible come, emptying himself in what seemed like one, single ejaculation. She howled in delight through red and black hair.

It was over fast, so fast, like a dream perhaps lasting no longer than a second, one about the wilderness, endless green fields and deep forests, mist-covered mountains.

– Jeez, she whispered. They exchanged several sultry kisses, flames never fading to embers. – Jeez.

She slipped down his body. He put her back on the floor with a reluctant expression in his face.

They pulled up their pants. They didn't make haste, in any way. Everybody watching got that. There, in the shifting shadows they saw flickers of naked faces.

He spotted Maxine Leary bathed in the pervasive light and enjoyed every single move she made. She had long, dark and smooth hair, a tall and well-trained body, an innocent and sensual face both. He didn't find it strange that she scored high in all popularity contests. All his senses overwhelmed him at the sight of her catlike agility, the passion she could hide for herself, but not for him. He met her eyes.

– Hi, animateur, great music.

She blushed hard and pulled back. The laughter chased her. Damon laughed as well. Not because he had wished to ridicule her, but because it felt good to be alive.

The guards rushed forward with their wicked stare and pointy fingers. They found nothing to put their fingers on, but pushed and threatened people just for the heck of it, anyway. Nobody offered them more than hints and frustrations when they attempted to know what had happened. They pulled back mumbling and cursing, like watchdogs unable to sink their teeth into flesh.

– You showed great skill, boy, Yolanda said, back in the light.

There was no warmth in the hoarse voice.

– If you show more of that later tonight, know that Yolanda will know to please you…

The voice turned ingratiating, her touch intimate, practically abusive. Caresses didn't have to be benevolent, he was well aware of that.

– Don't you try…

He shook her off him.

They left the place, changed venue without their surroundings looking much different. Out in the street they were bathing in flicker, slivers of light and shadow. A surveillance chopper levitated high up in the air and cast its dirty rays at them. Damon shook in indignation. His mood didn't improve when they passed a store selling television sets. A giant image and a loud sound distracted those walking by.

The images and movie showed the city of Stavanger, Norway, where giant objects flew through the air and the torrential rain made the streets flood. A voice cried out:

– IS THIS ANYTHING TO LONG FOR, CITIZENS? ISN'T IT BETTER TO STAY AT HOME AND HELP BUILD THE COUNTRY? The world's leading experts strenuously object to the validity of temperature increase and so does the French government and loyal people. We are strong and we will resist this vile propaganda put forth by our enemies. They keep lying about us and claim that our way of life is fundamentally wrong…

Damon closed his ears to the voice and all of it. It was all too bombastic, too insane.

– Don't do anything, Yolanda warned him. – They're recording everything we do here.

He looked up at the church on the hill, at the high tower there with a hole at its center. The statue of Mary had been shot asunder. It calmed him down in a way. In thousand other ways it stimulated his inner fire.

– I wasn't planning on doing anything, he said cheerfully. – It amuses me that ever more people flee north in spite of the storms.

The glance she sent him was filled with irritation and interest, choke-full with ambiguity.

– Aside from that I must naturally, like the aware, living human being I am wonder how much the French government is subsidizing each television set…

– What did you SAY? She stopped and pulled in him so they stood face to face, chest to chest. – How can you JOKE about that? It's completely

– Completely, she attempted again, subdued.

She grabbed his collar with both hands and pulled him close. Her kiss, her beyond brutal kiss made blood flow from his lips.

– Here, she mumbled. – At this very spot!

She squeezed his cock. It hardened in an instant. From one flash to the next blood flooded his limb. Hands touched the other's body in beyond frantic, uncompromising moves. Breathing and moaning the two of them hit the hard and unpleasant asphalt. She put him on his back. He lay still and admired her untamed savagery. She sat on him and began rocking up and down. He had no recollection of any of them removing their pants. Fire flared around them in the forest glen at the end of the long field. The hard ground faded away and changed to soft forest bed. The dance in the forest and the darkness changed to a wind making the fire blow high and caressing soft skin. Strong hips squeezed him. Swelling breasts and sore lips smothered him. She didn't rock that much or that long, until the hips began jumping up and down. He pushed and pulled with her. The drums grew out of the forest and the sound spread with the four winds to all the giant, distant fields.

Everything swelled from within, in what felt like an instant. She turned rigid, and he did, too. The winds were blowing. She drew air into a wide open mouth, one single deep breath. She collapsed on him. The rhythm, the call of the wild and need for total satisfaction erupted from within, a contact not of this place but from everywhere, far from this and any stone desert. Slowly the world turned real or fake anew. The forest, the jungle, the wilderness shrank to yet another distant memory.

– The pigs are coming.

They turned their attention lazily to the hoarse voice. A kid in his late teens called to them from the nearest corner, before he vanished like a ghost.

They rose and pulled up their pants, before chuckling and setting out into the vast shadows. The floodlights and the chopper with the infrared system couldn't hold on to them, and they faded away into the night.

He studied her in the dark. The girl's skin had gained a fresh quality, one distinct departure from what it had been. The ever more dangerous sunlight made suntanned skin scarce and even unpopular. He sensed how his own boiling blood made his skin prickle, making it healthy and alive.

His hands exposed more of her skin, sniffing it, drawing in the scent of feral life.

– What? She asked curious.

– I just love the smell of you, he said darkly.

She chuckled pleased.

They stopped close to the hideout they had left earlier in the evening, standing there, listening with all their senses on alert. When no danger displayed itself they relaxed. Brief and relative silence embraced them and they moved on.

After a few minutes of casual walk they made a turn and returned to the disco district. A pull of rage and curiosity stronger than any fear led them back. They broke into an office building across the street. There were no alarms there, no strong security measures. Through one of the dirty windows on the second floor they had quite the useful view of the badly lit block. The tawdry pale, flickering neon sign hardly lit anything, except on the street right below.

– Look at them, Yolanda said excited. – How they move and relate to each other. They know that the shadows and the deep forest rule the streets, no matter what modern humans do to light them. The jungle has survived, though corrupted in the human heart.

She pushed her body against his, instantly eager and desirable again. Her words echoed within him. They rang true.

He liberated himself from her advances, caressing her cheek in the process. Something happened. Damon sensed how the body's muscles tensed. He couldn't instantly tell why, but it was there, real and true, unmistakable.

The first huge mass of youths migrated from Mansion Mont Blanc tonight. The night, the early part, approved by zealous authority ended.

– What yahoos, Yolanda hissed. – Most of them will go home early, so well behaved that they make me hurl. Only a few will seek out the smaller, dodgy places.

She knew something was off, too. He noticed it by a casual glance, saw how she frowned in puzzlement.

Maxine Leary stepped outside, into the darkened alley from the otherwise fairly well lit facade of the building. Very few recognized her or took notice. She had disguised herself, but Damon recognized her, did it in a thousand small ways.

– What is it? Yolanda inquired. – What does Damon see?

– The idol of thousands is hiding in plain sight to avoid howling admirers, he said.

And Yolanda understood then, realized what he was talking about.

Maxine crossed the street and started on the long walk away from Mansion Mont Blanc. A car lit its lights somewhere behind her. Damon couldn't tell if the engine was started then, too. The car painted in dark colors slowly caught up with the girl. Terrill had for some time felt a rising excitement inside. Now, it broke like a paralyzing cold sweat all over his body, an abyss of panic threatening to take away everything he had of vigor. He fought to breathe even, while seeking within. And then, suddenly everything fell into place, a calm not part of the grave but birth, in all its glory and horror. It felt like he had done something like this a thousand times before. He glimpsed the dark-clothed figures that unnoticed by most walked twenty steps in front of Maxine.

Two attackers jumped from the large, black car, just before it stopped with whining tires. Maxine shook. Damon caught a glimpse of her seemingly white face in the glare from the headlights. Everything happened so fast. They had surrounded her before he had even considered the possibility. She crouched slightly and kicked one of the attackers on the head. The man tried to deflect it, clearly prepared for her aggression, but he still failed and fell to the ground. Maxine jumped forward and struck a woman in the side with her elbow, cracking her ribs. The trap failed to close around her and then her path was free. In just a moment she had gained a five-step head-start.

– Help, she shouted. – HELP!

Several spectators clearly heard her and knew what was happening. No one came to her aid.

Terrill sat still, with eyes so open that they hurt.

Yolanda jumped on her feet. He caught her arm and pulled her back down.

– We must…

She gasped with eyes sparking in anger.

– No, he decided. – The predator can be patient. If necessary it can wait an eternity for its prey.

Figures approached Maxine from the gray haze and this time she didn't get away. They caught waving arms and kicking legs. The two observing it heard slaps on the cheeks and strikes in the ribs. The attackers beat the spirit out of her. She collapsed, turning limp in their ruthless grip. The spectators pulled close to the others around them, didn't even dare stand a step away from each other. The two in hiding followed her with hard stares while she was thrown into the backseat of the large car. It was done very casually, as if they got rid of old, well used goods.

Doors closed. The car cruised down the street, fading into the night.

– C'mon, he told Yolanda and charged forward.

A second, two passed, and then he heard her steps behind him.

The streetlight outside the entrance was broken. The darkness swallowed the weak sound when they opened and closed the door. They moved through this city and these streets as if all of it was an extension of their being. Those in the car took their time. The car didn't drive faster than the shadow creatures moved. The woman and the two men could easily keep up with their light run. Damon and Yolanda had no trouble hiding themselves by chasing the limo indirectly, by using shortcuts through dark alleys. The luxurious vehicle rolled through big turns, allowing everybody to witness its errand. Nausea almost overwhelmed Damon and he had to stop and crouch for a moment to sort of master it. Ugly and shrill laughter rose from his throat.

His steps sounded insanely loud in his ears. Intellectually he knew that they sounded far higher to him than anyone else nearby, but the unrest kept gnawing in him nonstop.

The shadows seemed to draw all the lights on and around the large, «open» area, the large-sized property of used cars and wrecks in front of them. Goosebumps erupted all over the boy's skin.

– I've heard about these assholes, Yolanda whispered with a shaky voice. – They're called The Three Shadows and are nuts like...

– Hush! He interrupted her.

He knew of them as well.

Everybody did. Even in high society, among the people placing themselves as far as possible from the rising ocean, they were whispered about.

The insanely long and broad luxurious vehicle drove through the gate and vanished quickly behind a heap of wreckage. Damon and Yolanda followed through a wide, well-used hole in the fence. They avoided being seen by a hair's breadth by the three shadow hunters closing the main gate.

An endless row of wrecks seemed to block their way. She forgot herself briefly and caressed the hood of a Citroen 2001. After a seemingly endless walk through the stone desert's most evident garbage, they reached an opening. The limo had been parked in front of an ugly-looking, square structure. They caught the sentries as they passed the rolling coffin and vanished into the building. They saw how they moved together, how they were obviously a trio, how they appeared with a kind of chilling aura bordering on the supernatural.

– They're too many for us, Yolanda whispered. – I can gather the gang in a couple of hours.

– We don't have time.

They moved forward on shaky legs. Very determined in spite of that, they advanced smoothly forward in a somewhat calm manner, moving from deep shadow to deep shadow, towards the target somewhere ahead. The behavior patterns they had gained on the street through most of their adolescence lingered in every movement they made. No one cried out, nothing happened when they briefly had to cross an area bathed in light. They reached the smooth, cold wall. The windows stood wide open. They heard faint voices. Both looked cautiously inside, at a large room. The floor was several meters below ground level and they had a nice view. Damon swallowed hard in fear and seething anger.

Four men and three women surrounded Maxine Leary and studied her with contempt in their eyes, like she was completely worthless, like she deserved what was coming. They had undressed her. She crouched on the floor, half sedated, half cowed and filled with despair.

– You can't fathom how they can do it, can you, how they can even consider molesting and ravaging that sweet and beautiful girl? Rawlins told him. – You have heard the saying that rape isn't about sex, but about power, but you don't get it.

He stared at her, at her dull fire and beauty and it still made a catching grow in his throat and caused a hard rise below.

– They have no interest in her inner fire, except for their desire to extinguish it, Rawlins shrugged.

The boy's heart hammered in his chest. He noted their faces, one by one, so he would never forget them.

– A perfect completion to the set, the only man in a suit stated pleased.

– We can call the auction, the biggest of the women chuckled, – with lots of time for preparations.

Damon glimpsed Yolanda's green eyes in the boundary between light and shadow. They seemed to mirror and enlarge himself and everybody inside to an insane degree. He touched his fingers. They felt numb. Something floated towards the surface, something dark, dangerous… necessary. But so slow and late. Visuals of faces drifted off in a soup of distorted reflections. Sweat poured from his suddenly wet and cold skin.

– Damon, Yolanda cried frightened.

Both he and the girl whirled around, way too late realizing that they hadn't spotted the female shadow hunter in the room. She, the enemy had already moved in on them.

He felt a fist hit him and heard the girl's scream of fear and rage. A horrible pain erupted in his scalp and he saw the wall fall towards him. He hit it hard and collapsed on the ground.

Through a vision, a film of blood he glimpsed several more feet surrounding them. Nothing worked and he muttered inarticulate curses to himself. His vision finally cleared and he counted eight pairs of feet. He saw blindly his own gun in the hands of one of the men.

– Big gun, small boy, the man chuckled spitefully.

The laughter assaulted the boy from all sides.

– He carries it as a compensation for his tiny dick, she who had dealt with the intruders stated, clearly proud.

– He isn't totally without potential, one of the other men pointed out. – I'm convinced that he will eventually bring us a good price.

– After the training.

– When we have given him the initial lessons he will quickly realize what it is all about.

Damon heard them spit the harsh and horrible comments at him without feeling much. When a foot pushed his head at the asphalt he felt little aside from the numbness spreading to all parts of his body and mind.

One of the men had put Maxine's limp body on his right shoulder. The biggest of the men held Yolanda in a crushing grip. Blood flowed from her slack mouth. She seemed helpless like a child in the giant's hands. It amazed him that there were no emotions, no passions, not even fear on the bright, dark spot he crouched. Life left him. He attempted to push himself up with his right hand. A brutal kick that almost broke his arm made him howl in misery and remain on the ground.

– That's it for now, he who held Yolanda said. – We take this downstairs and give them their first lesson. Join us when you're done playing.

– When the little boy is well done, another chuckled.

There were more grins and laughter, very funny all of it. Damon almost laughed as well.

The big man carried Yolanda away. When she struggled to free herself he struck her in the ribs. She gasped and turned limp. The man carrying Maxine and others also left. Like a cell the group split in two parts. Two men and two women remained to keep Damon company.

A pull and his scalp hurt. The brutal hand pulled his head up. Damon didn't see the man holding him, only she who stood directly in the line of his vision. She filled his entire being.

– You're merely a scabby stray dog, she spat. – You will become a docile doggie wagging your tail at every single command. There will be no freedom for you anywhere.

They narrowed his field of vision to practically nothing. He blinked with itching eyes. Through tears of flowing fire he twisted his head slightly and spotted the dirty window before him, a surface suddenly clean and transparent and full of life. During a harrowing moment he flew across the open, blue sky, before he once more was pulled back down into the abyss. He just about managed to draw breath there, a gasp of poor air, and he didn't suffocate.

Falling down. The elevator lights failed between two floors. Yolanda and Maxine shared glimpses of anguish before the light blinded them anew. Yolanda registered dully that every single piece of clothing was torn off her body. She had struggled, resisted, she had. The slaps and the numbing strikes made her unable to hold her head high. She and the other girl - what was her name again - were given collars. Their captors pulled them after the chains out of the elevator.

– Isn't he sweet?

The sickeningly sugary voice made Damon sick. He was still able to draw breath with the choking collar around his neck and felt something resembling doglike gratitude.

– Get up on all fours. He felt a stinging pain in his ribs. – That's it, that's a good dog...

They didn't want to harm him... physically. These people didn't want to either. It dawned on him slowly, painfully. He was «valuable».

– Why are you doing this? Maxine asked weakly. – I am at the top of the popularity lists. I do like I'm told... don't I?

– Your «popularity» fell with several points last week. You were already on your way down and will quickly become yesterday's news. That's a good thing. You've taken too many liberties lately. Your mother isn't French, anyway. It's your own fault you believed you belonged among true Frenchmen. But you shouldn't fret. In certain circuits you're still popular. Like any foreign parasite you will be useful in all ways we decide.

Yolanda wanted to say something, wanted to shout it, but she didn't dare, and she knew it wouldn't be of any use.

– You've got nothing to fear, any of you. You will both be immensely popular.

They pulled the two captives through a long, dark corridor, into a bright room with no shadows and no mercy. The two girls were thrown down on a giant, soft bed. They rocked up and down a few times, like in a horrible caricature of a sexploitation movie, before lying still.

– Smile! The big man commanded harshly.

Yolanda smiled and forced herself to move seductively.

– I've learned early in life what men want, she whispered coquettishly.

Maxine smiled, very cute and adorable, like a little princess.

– Gentlemen? The woman said ironically and elegantly. She held up a black, elaborate box. – Who will be first on these cuties?

A game, they saw this as a game.
Each of the three men pushed a hand into the box. Two of the marbles were white. The two lucky guys calmly undressed.
– Be my guests, Monsieurs, the women said.
Yolanda spread her legs and welcomed the man. Maxine fought and struck hysterically at her assailant. A few brutal strikes quickly pacified her. The end result didn't differ in any noticeable way.
The men penetrated them quickly, without foreplay and consideration.
– It hurts, Yolanda wailed, her ears filled with Maxine's sobbing and wailing.
The man slapped her around and struck her, making sure it hurt.
– You will both shut the fuck up, he snarled. – You will be trained and trained and trained, until you can think of nothing else but performing your only function in life.
He held her so hard that she quickly gained marks and bruises from his grip and he moved in brutal pushes and pulls, pushing her down so hard that she could hardly breathe. She tried, but only managed to gasp in something resembling a death rattle. He was so big and she so tiny and he smashed her to bits. When he was finally done the next in line took his place.
– I bet you believed in your independence and inner strength, he spat. – Rest assured you will soon be dissuaded from such silly notions.
They crushed her to dust. Their seed burned her and shrunk her to nothing. She descended, and kept descending into a deep, black hole.
The Storm Child saw the wind increase so bad that it made the images in the air seem indistinct. The transparent window showed him everything he wanted to see.
– When have you ever needed a crystal ball to see the obvious? Rawlins asked him.
Damon stood on all fours, soon kneeling like a palace slave before those hassling him. The hair hid much of his face. They didn't see his eyes, didn't see the Storm's mirrors. He saw something he had only glimpsed earlier in life.
The man in front of him played with his gun, waved it like bait, a longing. The four whirled before Damon, just like the Storm, the one he saw coming far ahead. Everything was whirling in that abrupt vision, blowing so hard that it caught everything and everybody.
A flat hand slapped Damon's cheek.
– Pay attention, brat!
The scornful, patronizing laughter rang out.
Damon laughed, too. Suddenly everything seemed so very, very funny and he lost all control of himself.
– That will do, the big woman snapped. – Remove his clothes.
– Yes, let's take a closer look at him, was the enthusiastic response.
Damon sensed, *saw* the Whirlwind approach and welcomed it. What began with a smile ended in a predatory grin.
The joker grabbed the long, black hair and pulled up the head.
Powerful lightning, seemingly appearing from nowhere split the sky behind them.
– What the hell…
The strong hand loosened and released its grip. The hair fell down, but not the head.
Will awakened. The heart beat faster. The blood flowed faster in the veins. And then the heart hammered in his chest and the blood boiled in his veins.

The boy hardly noticed the click. The long and deadly blade he had hidden in his right sleeve popped out, visible to all. He jumped up and forward. The blade penetrated the chest of the joker. Damon's left hand grabbed the hand clutching the gun, squeezed it hard and tore the gun from its weak grip. The man kept the silly, shocked expression far into death. Damon held him like a shield, easy, effortlessly. The three remaining turned back with slow motions. They had all had their attention on the lightning and strived to move, to act. Damon fired. The first bullet hit the oldest woman in the head, killing her instantly. He missed the second time. It passed the head of the other man. The man pulled the trigger and the bullet hit the chest of the still living shield. Damon fired for the third time and hit the other man in the chest. The force of the bullet pushed the man backwards. The gun slipped from his hand. The last of them, the young woman froze. It was the one who had surprised Damon and Yolanda. She stood there empty-handed, with her hands placed deliberately far from her body.

He pulled the hand back, and the body, without the blade stuck in it fell to the ground. The girl kept still. Her earlier pride had vanished completely. He read shock in her eyes, and also something else.

She fell on her knees fast, with lowered eyes and shivering lips.

– You took us out easy like *that,* she wailed, snapping her fingers. – You will vanquish the others as well. I don't want to die. Let me be your… your slave. I can p-please you. There isn't anything you can't do to me.

He held up the gun, but his attention never wavered from her or from the steaming bodies. Bottomless eyes followed two fingers sliding across the deadly weapon. He knew the flashes were visible in his eyes and it didn't bother him. The metal… it usually felt smooth and cold, but not… when it spat hot lead. The sun and the moon, ice and fire heated and chilled his vision.

So much had happened - and so fast. They were dead and he was alive. It felt so good to let go, so good to live.

He put the gun away and used the bloodied blade to push up her jaw. Empty eyes stared at nothing. She made no attempt at seducing him. Unconditional surrender and submission revealed itself in her pose. In her world you were either master or slave. There was nothing in-between.

He held on to his wrath. It was as if he could actually touch it, as if it was a tangible in his hands. He held on to it with all his might.

There was resistance to what he did. He ignored it. One step forward was sufficient. Lightning struck her chest. He pulled out his tiny sword and even more blood flowed on the bright metal. Cold eyes stared at the girl the few seconds it took her to die. He forced himself to watch her. The cold, hard place within had called him and he had replied. Only idiots let their enemies live.

He stabbed the man with bullets in his chest a few times, just to make sure.

The Storm raged towards him, towards everything and everyone. He sensed it, far out at sea, where sky and sea were one.

A pull and the collar was torn off. He threw it far away. Before he was conscious of the fact he had run into the building. He wasted several minutes looking for stairs. There weren't any. He pushed the elevator button. The enclosed box arrived and opened its doors in what only seemed like seconds to him. He jumped inside, and he fell, fell with the infernal machine at his disposal.

– There are no guards, right? Rawlins offered. – You're willing to bet your life on that assumption?

The enclosed air, heat and steaming moisture hit him as the doors slid open. Time crawled so slowly to him that he imagined it went backwards. He was still up there, fighting for his life against overwhelming odds, blinking sweat from his burning eyes. Feet denied him movement, backwards or forward and the gun turned heavy in his hand. He leaned against the wall. What had happened filed before his eyes. He shook his head in amazement and a lingering shock. The boy that had never before killed anyone, had showed amazing skills doing so. It had been such a familiar emotion, almost like a memory, something he had always known. He drew strength from that memory, that lethal certainty. Rage rose in him anew, so powerful that it almost hurt. He ran on.

He kept the blade in its visible position, advancing forwards and turning corners while holding the gun with both hands. Each corner made the heart beat that much harder in his chest. His throat turned dry and he could hardly swallow.

A labyrinth of corridors stretched out before him. He could practically see them. It wasn't hard, not hard at all. His vision reached far longer ahead than beyond the nearest corner, or at least he imagined it did. He heard… distinct sounds not far away. It dawned on him that he had heard them since he stepped out of the elevator.

As he appeared from the twilight and approached a bright-lit room, he couldn't keep himself from repeatedly swallowing hard.

They were busy beyond busy the four people handling their toys. Maxine stood on all fours. One took her from behind, while another forced himself into her mouth. The third man handled Yolanda alone. The woman whipped Maxine's back with a leather belt.

– So practical, the woman grinned. – She can't scream.

– I love it when they scream, the man on top of Yolanda stated pleased.

He squeezed her breasts while pumping her up and hurting her in a number of inventive and humiliating ways.

She looked at him with half-closed, dull eyes. He didn't allow her to do otherwise. Then he squeezed even harder her left breast, making her scream that much louder. Terrill closed his eyes, one tiny moment, a thousand years, but then he opened them. Wide. He saw how Yolanda was broken piece by piece and how she was made to «enjoy» it. With a savage howl he just about managed to keep contained inside, he walked into the room in a seemingly relaxed pace. At the edge of his vision he spotted the enemies' weapons among their clothes. He stepped forward and pushed the iron claw into the broad back moving up and down on Yolanda. The big body froze and croaked. The woman was closest to him. He shot her before she discovered he was there. One of the men was shot while his cock still moved inside Maxine. The other, at the opposite side, closest to Damon charged forward. The man hit Damon's body and pushed him backwards. The boy fell. A foot hit his arm and the gun dropped from his hand.

He managed to get up, but not to avoid a kick on the head sending him back down. His opponent avoided a wild swing with the blade, but had to jump backwards. It was sufficient. Damon jumped on his feet and could once again balance perfectly on his toes. They circled and measured each other. Terrill bared his fangs, slowly, deliberately. Anxiety showed in the other's eyes. He started maneuvering towards his clothes - and weapons. Damon charged him, but missed and managed only barely to avoid the counterattack. Damon attacked again and again, blocking the man's access to his guns, but he couldn't end this, in spite of the advantage the knife granted him.

Then he saw, at the edge of his vision Yolanda slip from the bed with a pillow in her hands. Another grin flashed across the boy's face. His heart suddenly beat even harder. A click. He feinted with his right hand. Yolanda threw the pillow. It hit the man in the side, heavy, big, not really unbalancing the big man, but clearly distracting him at a crucial moment. Another blade was revealed, as it jumped from its hiding in Damon's left sleeve. The enemy made a clumsy attempt at blocking the feint. The blade penetrated his arm and he was unable to stop the true attack. The shiny blade buried itself in his body and turned red, like its twin. Damon tore and twisted the blade as hard as he possibly could. Fearful eyes turned hazy and dull. The slaver choked in fear and slipped off the blade and down on the slippery floor, already dead.

Flashes filled Damon's vision. It lasted five seconds, ten… while he just stood there breathing, while the adrenaline stopped flowing into his veins. He fell on his knees, close to powerless. Every move he had to make to get back on his feet demanded an inhuman willpower. He stood, straightening slowly and painfully, turning towards the two women.

– You t-took them all out? Yolanda cried out with blushing cheeks. – They're all dead?

– Stone cold, he confirmed.

The sound of his own hoarse voice seemed to strengthen him, to empower him yet again.

The automag wasn't far away. He walked there and picked it up.

Yolanda began dressing up in the dead woman's clothes. They fit her somewhat.

Maxine crouched in fetal position. She looked dully at him when he stopped by her. He knew how he looked with his body sprayed with blood, but he didn't care.

– You can stay there and feel sorry for yourself, he noted casually, – or you can pull yourself together.

A fire appeared in the beautiful eyes. She crawled from the bed and placed herself in front of him without covering herself. The full sight of her made his throat turn desert dry.

– Come and have a look, Yolanda called.

They joined her, distracted and interested in spite of themselves.

Everybody stood there and looked cautiously at each other. Yolanda held up lots of different clothes.

– There's more in the drawers, variety and numbers in abundance.

– There are truly lots of clothes here. Maxine looked incredulous at Yolanda. – Heaps of different sizes and shapes, many not fitting any of… them.

She glanced at the bloody bodies.

It dawned slowly on the three, the suspicion turning to certainty.

– We should get out of here, Terrill said alarmed.

But they postponed it. They stayed. Something beyond fear tempted them to remain.

Terrill's eyes dwelled on the bodies. He had been both skilled and lucky, and focused on keeping those facts foremost in his consciousness. There were no regrets. He didn't have to ponder his own reactions to know that. They were dead and he was alive, and that was what counted. He felt the savage pleasure ride him. They had been slavers and slaves had been the only game they had been good at hunting.

Damon cleaned his claws with the clothes and sheathed them again, re-submerging them into his sleeves. It felt that way, hiding them from those who would do him and his companions harm.

All the spots didn't go away, but they were well concealed. He changed clothes, taking his time doing it. Maxine and Yolanda helped him, both shy and eager. It resulted in quite a bit of kissing and fondling, but not more than that. They made no effort to move beyond the pleasant low-level arousal.

He knew he still looked threatening, lethal. *Very good!* He studied the girls, how they held the weapons they collected. They seemed more than comfortable with them. The three of them appeared like a mean, confident unit.

They found the cages almost immediately. The second room was empty, but in the third they discovered two large cages filled with nude people. The teenage girls, highest in numbers had been imprisoned to the left and the boys to the right. A few of them might have turned twenty, but no one looked like it, young, dull and vulnerable like they all seemed.

Most of them had clearly been here a while, long enough for the captors to have dug their claws deep into them all. One saw that easily, with a casual glance. Eyes filled with emptiness revealed how worthless the prisoners felt. The sharp eyes of the three on the outside touched rows and rows of rigid, bloodless faces. There was no visible reaction from any of them. The prisoners didn't realize that they were being rescued.

– No keys. Yolanda nipped Damon on the shoulder. – Let's go look for them. Maxine will take care of things here, won't you dear?

– Trust me, Maxine assured them both.

She held a gun with both hands and looked truly dangerous.

They hadn't walked far beyond hearing range when Yolanda pulled the keys from her pocket.

– Behold, she grinned.

He waited for her to go on. She moved close to him. Playful fingers touched him.

– I'm positive you've considered what a fortune we have in there, she whispered. – It would be very simple for us to just take over the operation, don't you think?

– What about Maxine? He had a foul taste in his mouth.

– I see no problem there, the big girl replied with a shrug. – She's filled with this rage, what must be heeded, one way or another. With the right training she will be very useful to us, partner. We can point her at a target and she will perform splendidly and with boundless dedication.

– And your rage, what conduit do you give that?

– You understand. The fingers played with the skin on his neck. – That pleases me so much. And the answer is obvious concerning us both, isn't it? Any we desire.

He almost drowned in the promise of her sweet eyes.

– The slave wants to be a master, he forced himself to say. – What are you?

She figuratively backed off, but remained close to him physically, sending him a look filled with shame. He had never seen more expressive eyes.

– I'm sorry. She clung to him in horror. – Forgive me - me - me - me

The last of her word echoed in him many times the short walk back.

– We have killed them all, he said, he shouted at the poor buggers in the cages. –

Freedom is yours, if you desire it.
The doors opened. The openings weren't big enough for everybody to leave simultaneously, but it didn't matter. There was no rush.
The prisoners noted the blood in the hair and faces of their liberators and some of them began their first, robot-like movements, obviously fearing this was just one more vicious game staged by their captors.
– Get *moving,* Maxine snarled in contempt, – or I swear I'll close the doors again.
The stragglers hurried out of the confines.
– We've got something to show you, Damon called them. – Follow us.
They followed him, out of the room, out of sight from the cages.
– They're easy to lead, aren't they? Yolanda whispered in his ears.
The three brought them to the special «bedroom». Several hesitated by its entrance. Damon opened the doors wide and no one could avoid seeing what waited in there.
Steam rose from the bodies and formed dots of mist in the smoky air. Blood and guts and brains dried on the walls, floor and ceiling. They stood there staring, and time faded away slowly, like the red mist.
The spell didn't fade until a girl rushed forward and started kicking the body closest to her. She jumped up and down on it and made her very best attempt at disintegrating it.
– You're dead, she shouted. – Dead, dead, DEAD
Several others charged forward and joined her. Tears flowed and rage almost turned visible in the air.
The special mood, both unreal and tangible slowly eased. Frantic despair changed to something else. Sobbing and laughter stuck in the throat when they dressed. Like one person they directed their attention at those who had saved them.
– What has happened here? A boy choked. – How could something like this happen at all?
– You're mistaken if you believe anything in particular pointed to you, Damon said. – You're just part of the vulnerable and accessible crowd. It can happen to everyone.
– You're wearing my clothes, another boy sniffed. – I don't mind, since I plan on changing everything about my life.
Virtually without exception they all looked at the three with gratitude and devotion in their eyes. Damon didn't mind and had every intention of using it for all it was worth. The rage and momentum kept building within, to unknown levels.
– I felt we were done with this place, he said, – and that we should leave it, put it all behind us, but I've changed my mind. There is still unfinished business for us here.
They listened to his words, first with open eyes and fear, but then with a rising anger and determination and support. Only a few cringed before his burning resolve.
He gathered them before the elevator. They traveled up in three groups, back to the surface, to what some of them perceived as reason. Damon Terrill waited for them outside. Hope died in their eyes. The Storm Child stared at them and his fire froze them on their spot. The beast waited patiently. Several of them started backing off, step by step, towards the gate of the junkyard. When they felt a safe distance had been reached, they turned around and fled mindlessly in a useless attempt to escape their ongoing nightmare. They would never stop.
– Sooner or later, sooner instead of later they will all be recaptured, Yolanda said softly.
Flashes grew on the southern sky. There was no thunder, no rain, but an electrical

storm, until recently unlike anything else witnessed on Earth during human history. Damon had seen it on Tom Rawlins' screens, captured with extreme telephoto-lenses.

It moved slowly but surely towards them, like something alive and predatory, with eyes, blood and mind.

– You're all very lucky, he said aloud. – We are lucky. The slavers didn't need this foreplay. Breaking and brainwashing-techniques are so effective today that there's no need for the less sophisticated methods you suffered through. They took their time because they serve a special type of customers and because they enjoyed it, and they had allowed themselves to be fat and lazy in the belief that nobody would dare or bother attacking them. Those knowing their own good shouldn't even hope for such luck again.

They listened and got the message.

The bodies were dragged into the elevator and downstairs, to join the other slavers in a distant, closed off space.

– What about the… mess? Yolanda asked coyly.

She and Damon remained upstairs, visible to the world.

– Let it be, he grinned wickedly. – Let it serve as a warning.

– An excellent decision. She responded enthusiastically, very enthusiastically. – Excellent!

He caught her in his penetrating stare. She shivered imperceptibly and displayed herself to him, offering herself without a second thought.

They returned to the building. A moment of gravity caught her.

– Perhaps I should ask forgiveness of the world? She said, speaking hardly audible.

– Oh, why?

It was a rhetorical question. He knew the answer.

– I set you off, she said solemnly.

She grabbed his hand, her eyes ripe with untold promises.

They let themselves fall into the water of the midnight fire, down, down, down, in and out. The house that had belonged to their enemies devoured them.

++

What did he see in himself? What did the boys and girls see?

He stepped in front of a mirror and saw a bruised face and body. The sight didn't really impress itself on him, one way or another.

Figures danced in the darkness in front of him, and not just here, now. On some level there was the mirror. In another he stood by a water, looking at his mirror image, a riverside where the water whirled and whirled. Tall bonfires lit the landscape. Tired bodies danced and their spirits reached higher than the sky. They danced nude and no one seemed bothered by it. Humanity returned to the wilderness, to its roots, and it was good.

Solid shapes grew out of the shadows. Yolanda, Maxine and Renate sought him nude, filled with Hunger.

– O'Child of the Storm, Yolanda called softly, ironically, seductively.

She gasped when he grabbed her and pulled her close. Eyes widened in shock and expectation. Maxine and Renate pushed themselves at him from both sides. Maxine gave him a feather-light kiss on the earlobe.

– Let's go for a swim, she flirted, – enjoy ourselves in the pleasant water.

He grabbed her as well. With a thrilled, husky laughter she writhed out of his grip.

She rubbed her butt at his crotch and he turned hard in an instant. The girls noticed and their eyes turned hazy and wet, and he caught them easily. The three bodies froze, but softened quickly when he started touching them. He turned Yolanda around and placed her hands on the edge of the sink. They stood in front of the mirror and he had a great view of both her and the other two rubbing themselves at him. A kiss on the shoulder elicited a moan from her. He forced himself to bid his time, while the final hesitation and remaining anxiety faded in the girl's rising heat. Yolanda's nipples hadn't been touched yet, but rose long and hard. Her breasts swelled. He noticed how Maxine and Renate glanced down on him and was reminded of the irresistible pulse spreading from his pointing cock to his body. He kept holding back and gave each of the two a hard kiss. They clung to him with wet lips and unsteady legs. Yolanda turned half around with an annoyed expression in her sweaty face. He put her back in place again with a single push and pull. She submitted to his advances, more than eager, more than willing. He slipped a hand down below her hips, to where it flowed like a river. She moaned again, shaking in need. He rubbed her, rolling her button between his fingers, made her spread her legs so wide that it hurt… and then he pushed himself into her, as deep as he possibly reached. She gasped and snorted loud and pleased. Her smile lingered also when he pulled out after a while and turned to Maxine. She leaned against the wall and called him with her eyes. He stepped forward and grabbed her, and she squealed in delight. She climbed him. He helped her with his hands on her shaking hips. She squeezed him hard, tight and smooth, and he came before he had even started resisting her sly effort. She smiled in ecstasy and triumph. He felt like he drowned in hot water.

– You fake, little… Yolanda charged forward. – They taught you more than a pretty smile, huh?

– I had only heard about it. Maxine reddened. – I didn't know if it would work, but now we know, don't we…

She took one of Yolanda's nipples in her mouth and sucked on it. Yolanda put her head on the man's shoulder and licked her lips.

– No sweat, she mumbled. – What does it matter? This stud can easily serve us all.

They walked the few steps to the adjacent room and jumped into the swimming pool, slipping through the dark water, just below, just above the surface, shadows in the modest light. He glimpsed Renate's brown butt as she dived below the surface, as her feet first rose above the water and then pushed her deep under. He followed her. She waited for him at the bottom, trusting, filled with expectation. He grabbed her and pulled her with him back up. She chuckled. He placed her upper body on the edge of the pool and took her with hard thrusts. She screamed in joy. Yolanda practically attacked him, held on to him. He threw her off with a shrug. Maxine charged him from the opposite side. All the three females clung to the strong body. The brawl ended, somewhat in the shallow parts of the pool. Their experience of it was that they were pushed by soft waves at the shore a dark night, waves playing with their warm skin, making steam rise in the dark air. Movements slowed down, turning less violent, but the intensity remained. When Yolanda looked down on him, he imagined he spotted a kind of fondness in her eyes. They clung to each other, breathing each other's air while floating in the boundary between the shore and the water. They pushed tongues into the other's mouth. There was no air except what they shared. Not long afterwards he returned to Renate and then Maxine. They shared him and he had them all simultaneously.

All four rose, a timeless time later and waded to shore. And they weren't the only ones. Many shadows danced and lived between the tall bonfires.

– There will be more violence, he told them. – There always will be.

– Tomorrow, Maxine kissed him softly, – if tomorrow comes.

They rocked on the bed the four of them. He couldn't tell who he was inside of right then, only that he had taken them all many times. They danced around him and he rocked in concert with them all. What had happened in this bed earlier no longer mattered. The past was erased, the future didn't exist. They had changed sheets, but even that crucial information faded from feverish minds. In the twilight darkness and the mist of hunger they could only glimpse features and characteristics. They grunted and growled and moaned like beasts. The very memory of embarrassment and shame disappeared. Savagery rose within and filled them to the brim, and they embraced it.

Earlier tonight he hadn't felt tired in any way, but on the contrary felt incredibly awake and aware. Now, as morning probably approached he sensed that sleep was coming. They descended into this soft nest entangled in each other, tiny yawns and happy moans were exchanged with a deep and lasting silence.

Long ages passed, before something grew from that silence, a song, a beautiful and terrible song. He knew by now that he always heard it, no matter the place and circumstances. He just wasn't aware of that fact all the time.

Damon Terrill beheld She Who Dances in the Forest and the Darkness and he sensed a birdlike creature flapping its wings and dancing with her.

He slept and he was awake, glimpsing the tall mountains in spite of the darkness.

And he dreamed about Yggdrasil - The Tree of Life.

CHAPTER NINE

Two half moons encountered each other in front of the building at the center of the old junkyard. At the center of the full moon forming Damon Terrill and André Corbeau faced off.

Yolanda stood between them, between them all. The two half moons struck chains and sticks at the ground. The mood was tense, potentially explosive. The new night had already filled the air, so fast, compared to last time. During those twenty-four hours Yolanda had changed, changed visibly from the girl Damon had known briefly.

She turned towards Corbeau and her former friends.

– He exterminated The Three Shadows and their aides, she said loud and clear. – He practically *eradicated* them from the face of the Earth. Listen to him!

– We all agreed to attend this… meeting, little Yolanda, Corbeau said lightly. – The chosen venue in itself whetted our appetite, stirred out curiosity. By all means, my good man, make your play.

– With your permission… Damon bowed.

Rough laughter filled the air between them. He wasn't fooled by the other's pleasant exterior. The two of them had taken each other's measure right from the start.

He spoke to each and every one of them:

– What I have to say isn't original or strange, not anything you haven't heard before. We have given our surroundings and the world we were born into many names, many four-letter words, but these are all just one more word for *prison*. We're drowning in shit and poison and call civilization a good life. Most of us are «content» with existing within the bigger prison in order to avoid the smaller, obvious. Fortunately this method of stick and carrot is becoming less effective. Ask a simple question: ask why and the reply becomes evident. We're human beings, not the domestic animals they have raised us to be.

He waved a hand, a movement including everything around them.

– This city is *dead*. To me it's irrelevant whether or not the imminent electrical storm will grind all the buildings to dust. The place and the moment to claim our humanity isn't here.

The noise from the city faded. Everybody listened astonished. The image of tall and low buildings seemed to actually vanish, for just a moment, but enough, long enough for them to take notice and for it to vibrate within them. They stopped talking, stopped rattling chains. Harsh words were no longer shouted back and forth.

– So, that's the plan? You want us to join you on your journey… Where?

– Far north… everybody wanting to go and no one else.

– I'm not holding it against you that you want reinforcements, Corbeau grinned. – Those watching your back are the poor sods you liberated, right?

– What they might lack in experience, any of them, they gain in the seething wrath coursing through them. I wouldn't underestimate them if I were you.

A low murmur, a low frequency roar, a rumble in the earth and the sky tore into them.

– You've got a fascinating setup here, Corbeau stated pleased and filled with expectation. – I won't rule out that some of us would have been interested… in different circumstances. But you see, I've got my own plans and I see here a perfect opportunity to explore them. And I'm the leader. They do as I say.

– That's regrettable, Damon said kindly. – That means it's you I have to convince.

– Knives, sticks, guns? André cut right to the chase.

His voice might have turned slightly louder, but the change was hardly noticeable. The conversation reminded those listening of a friendly chat during a dinner party.

Silence suddenly dominated the stage. There was nothing of the loud shouting and noise usually following a challenge.

– Let's do it the old way, Damon suggested. – Nude as when we entered this world. Let's not use any other weapon aside from ourselves.

Yolanda rushed to André and spoke fast and low-keyed to him.

– Didn't you *hear* me? She attempted to catch his eyes, but it was locked on Terrill, on the imminent fight. – I've seen him change. Until last night he had never killed anyone, not a single person. Then he offs the feared Three Shadows and their aides, doing so single-handedly. We certainly didn't help him. And there is more, Andy. I've met never m-met anyone like him. He's way above you, now, but that is nothing compared to how far he will go. You've often spoken about us leaving this cemetery. Well, he can and will take us away.

– We shall see…

André ditched the shirt with a very determined stare at his opponent.

– I'm very much aware of the fact that you've killed a few poor sods, she said, still low-keyed. – There's no comparison.

Terrill removed the clothes on his upper body. When everybody present spotted the rope armband they released low mumbles and startled cries. Yolanda smiled triumphant to everyone in her surroundings. Terrill removed everything, also the knives attached to his arms. The bloody metals hit the ground with two twangs. Everything was removed, except the armband.

Damon stood there completely nude. André hesitated imperceptible before he pulled his underwear down his thighs.

– Perhaps we should postpone this a few days, he said with compassion in his voice. – You look like you've taken enough punishment for a while.

– You should have seen the others…

Terrill did notice the stiffness of his limbs, the bruises and cuts. He didn't ignore them. There was nothing to ignore.

– Until death does us apart… is that it?

– That's up to you, Damon replied. – I have no desire to waste you…

– He thinks you may prove useful, Andy, Yolanda chuckled.

Damn her! Damon gritted his teeth. She didn't exactly make this easier. He saw that she had chosen, and wondered if that made her a better or worse person, and he had no answer to give himself.

Then he didn't care anymore. Nothing mattered, except the sensations the limited, vulnerable shape in front of him created in the depths of his mind.

The two were even in size. The force moving them forward appeared to be the same when they danced barefoot on the shingle, circling each other.

Terrill hardly noticed the fear, except as a slight itch at the back of his mind. Excitement dominated his consciousness. He heard the low hum rising from the spectators, the beating of their hearts. It didn't distract him. Savagery within and without strengthened him. The first strikes and kicks back and forth hammered the fighters. Damon felt the salty taste of blood in his mouth. It strengthened muscles and spirit.

Pain blinded him when he deflected a kick with his right arm. He ignored it, it didn't weaken him. In pain and hot rage he struck André on the head, struck him so hard that he was practically pushed back. The French boy fell and didn't move. Damon strolled towards him. André kicked at him in an insidious, lethal attack. Damon easily avoided it. In an uncompromising move he grabbed the foot and twisted it, twisted it hard. He kicked back hard and buried his foot in the belly below. The body below him turned limp. He turned André over on his belly and seized his neck.

– One of two, Damon hissed. – Do you surrender?

– No, damn you, the other snarled, still full of life and rebellion.

But he didn't get anywhere, no matter how hard he struggled.

The ruthless pressure behind the ear hurt terribly. André screamed.

– I don't *want* to kill you, the dark voice thundered from the demon squeezing the life out of him.

– I give. I GIVE!

He wanted to live, not die now and not by *his* hand. He wanted to live.

Damon released him and rose. He reached out a hand and waited. André could just about lift a shaking hand. The living storm towering above him raised him up on unsteady legs.

– How do you know I won't stab you in the back at the first and best opportunity? He asked, astonished by how casual he sounded.

– I don't, Damon grinned with black lightning in his eyes.

Over so fast, done, like a snapping of fingers. Damon turned towards the new half moon, towards his warriors. They moved uneasy. Everything had happened so fast, so abruptly and in such a sovereign manner. They looked attentive at their new leader.

– Something has been liberated in me, he cried. – Call it Hunger or drive or something with no name, it doesn't matter. I know it, whatever it is, will never more fade.

They, all of them practically re-experienced the battle. Corbeau had been at his best and most lethal, and he had been trashed, been conquered beyond doubt.

– They tell us many things when we grow up, Damon cried, – lots of bullshit and words and phrases and statements without content, but the essence of it is at we're either masters or slaves. According to them, if we're not one, we're the other.

His voice stayed thick with rage and longing. They listened closely.

– That's rubbish, of course. He smiled. – They control us, keep us exactly where they want us with thousands of strands like that.

He hammered his words and philosophy into them.

– We have all escaped from something. It's time for us to start escaping to something. I'm heading north. You are free to join me or not. Those of you wishing to leave my leadership may do so now and not a single attempt will be done to stop you. From this moment on, we will all make our decisions freely and without force.

He and André stood there side by side, still nude. No one found it really strange or instantly amusing.

– I'm going with him, André said with his head held high. – Because he's right. Right now I want to blow his head off, of course, but I suspect that that urge will pass.

Then several of those assembled, one by one began to pull back, out of the moon circle. They backed off five, ten steps… until becoming fairly confident, and balking, vanishing into the distant cityscape.

– That was a mistake, André told Damon in a frank and open manner when they dressed.

– Letting people go that don't want to stay with us was a mistake? Damon asked rhetorically, cheerfully. – At best they would be a liability, at worst a clear and present ongoing danger. Besides, it's about time we start acting like we preach.

The two half moons dissolved and joined. The lost, the condemned, the outcasts, the wanderers seeking in darkness joined, in one more attempt at getting it right.

Damon imagined he noticed a slight draft. He stared north.

– Our Journey starts now, he cried. – Not to anything familiar, not for any of us, but towards something new and unknown. The ultimate destruction is behind us, chasing us. Hope and survival and a possible life await us ahead.

There was still unrest among them. One casual look was sufficient to confirm that.

– Money is still important… isn't it? Renate said hesitatingly. The dark skin was covered in sweat. – My guess is that we need lots of them wherever we go, and need them fast.

Terrill looked closer at her, at them all. The seething rage rolled back and forth among them like a living thing. Everybody present, not only those recently freed from cages needed an outlet, something to direct their anger at. He easily recognized that impossible to deny need.

– You need someone to kill, he said flatly, waiting a bit before continuing. – Don't worry, I feel the same way myself. Incidentally, it also fits my plans…

His words answered their silent prayers, curses.

– We will kill and die together, he told them quietly, intensely, – and those of surviving that bloody and horrible battle will be tied together like a warrior tribe without peer.

A silent thunder followed his words and echoed endlessly in the ensuing silence. They stepped forward as one person, joining him in the smaller circle, becoming his.

++

Yolanda sat in a chair in what was clearly an office, looking at Damon.

– The slave traders have left very detailed accounts, she reported. – It's clear that they were subordinates taking orders from people higher up, but aside from that they worked as a very independent unit, handling all potentially buyers from here.

The newly formed moon formulated a plan, one bold and without recourse.

– I think everybody knows what it is about, Yolanda commented. – You don't need to be concerned whether or not they support our course of action. They do! And perhaps the reason they do support it so wholeheartedly is that they do indeed know what it is about. Their eyes have been brutally opened and their view on the world and themselves has been changed irrevocably, and they have embraced the ensuing transformation.

Her hot stare burned him in a very pleasant manner.

The old landline phone rang. Yolanda answered its call.

– Voltaire Repair Shop, she chirped.

– *Is this x?* A woman said at the other end of the line.

– No. Yolanda turned inspired. – This is Y.
She waited breathlessly for the conversation to continue.
– I call for confirmation.
The deep female voice remained even.
– You've got it. The young girl started reciting her lines in a very indifferent voice. – Everything will go down at the usual place. The payment will be in cash only this time and in Euro. No deviation from this will be accepted.
– I get it, the other woman chuckled. *– You won't get any protests from me. It's wise to take into account what the weather may bring these days.*
A click. Yolanda sat there for quite a while with the receiver in her hand. The horrible conversation had ended on a happy tune.
++++++++++++++++++++++++++++++++
A long tunnel led from the subterranean «apartments» to the harbor, to a cave-like hall, almost to the ocean. The first the members of the new tribe noticed was the sets of chains attached to the floor on a giant podium, the first of many signs of the cruel insanity. They found movies and upon playing them their horizon was expanded more than they had ever wanted, and it made them sick to their stomach.
The recordings showed how young meat performed, how they offered themselves, seemingly filled with eagerness, with eyes empty like wells filled with sand.
And the shooting practice grew even more intense.
Yolanda heard the cracks of the guns from the wardrobe. She felt the pure killing rage.
She sat in front of the mirror applying makeup, preparing what was to come, listening to Damon's voice in her head.
– Your role isn't a massive killing of our enemies, but it's just as important, even crucial.
He sounded like an adult, a cruel and confident man. She shivered in acknowledgement, in delight and anxiety.
The suddenly much older woman studied herself critically, noting both the uneven face and the luscious body with the same calculated indifference.
– Pretty girl, she spat. – Ugly pretty girl!
She used the cruel expression of her face, now, as she tied her hair in a ponytail. By deliberate use of makeup and by focusing on the cold hatred swelling inside, she looked far older than she was. She dressed conservatively, hardly revealing any skin beyond the face. The black gloves completed the image, the disguise. She reveled in Maxine, Danielle, André and Robert's shocked expression when she posed for them with her dark glare. Damon's stunned features pleased her even more, even though he clearly approved.
Sometimes she feared him, both when she understood what moved him and not.
They joined their fellow warriors outside in the hall. It seemed empty. They sensed how it seethed and boiled everywhere. Damon stopped before everybody and called attention to himself, like he always did.
– It's once again close to midnight, he cried, – and its fire is lit, a fire creating shadows in the darkest night. The lot of us met and joined yesterday, but since that yesterday eternity has passed and passed again. We are the Children of the Midnight Fire. Our flame isn't visible. There's no need for that. It has no limit, no beginning or end.
Drums rumbled under their feet, in the walls and ceiling surrounding them.

– Only twenty-four hours, Damon shouted. – And our two half moons are already becoming one, inevitable and irreversible.

They didn't cry out or even speak, but they heard him, deep within.

The gallery surrounded the hall in an almost oval shape. The floor turned less crowded. People left it and headed for their designated positions. Armed to their teeth, filled with tense anticipation of the coming battle, tasting the blood in their mouth the Children of the Midnight Fire awaited the arrival of their enemies.

Some had extended experience with guns, others clearly hadn't. Everybody had the same visible determination in their eyes.

A group of ten and to remained on the floor, in full view of those who would soon arrive. André pushed a button at the center of a panel. More thunder shook the premises and a major part of the wall opened towards the outside world. They saw the ocean and the white froth spray from the waves hitting the shore. Burning eyes noticed the sleek boats setting course for the elaborately made quay stretching from one end of the artificial cave.

Damon recalled the conversation with Yolanda, her seductive pose and voice, how she had tempted both him and herself with power.

That power was here, very much present, something fundamentally seductive, if they hadn't been the people they were.

The twelve registered the froth spray created by the yachts and their powerful engines, white against the dark surface of the ocean, mirrors reflecting the flashes of lightning miles to the south.

– This is it, fellow warriors, Yolanda shouted. – The doomsday clock is ticking.

They felt their pulse just as strong as heartbeats. And their heartbeats thundered in the walls, ceiling, floor and air, at the core of their being.

The sound of nervous checking of guns kept haunting their ears, unavoidable and cruel. The most anxious bit their lips, bit their lips to shreds.

The boats parked along the quay, like spears covered in blood.

– Only half of the spots are filled, Yolanda bristled. – In the movies the place was packed. I guess even most of the worst kind of scoundrel stay away from Marseille these days.

She shrugged deliberately.

– Oh, well, there will be more than enough money anyway, and fewer assholes to kill, better for us, worse for them.

Her remorseless observations echoed within them all.

The buyers stepped ashore. They and those accompanying them stemmed from many nations and cultures. Terrill counted forty-two of them. He measured them in an inner haze. Rage moved him forward.

He had gathered his hair in a ponytail and wore dark glasses and a fake beard, a disguise sufficient to make him look like a completely different person to those that might recognize him.

A quick meditation brought a kind of calm. His hands remained dry. The fear stuck in his throat didn't cross over to physical realities.

– Welcome, Yolanda greeted the guests.

She took one step forward. Damon and André, dressed in traditional dark suits placed themselves by her sides.

– Please follow me, ladies and gentlemen.

She turned and walked off without waiting for a reaction, a masterful act of contempt. Her lips shivered. Damon and André stayed close to her like the bodyguards of the slavers stayed close to those they were supposed to protect.

The other nine carried trays with refreshments. They served the guests food and drink at the elegant table in very effective ways, and it didn't seem hasty in any way. Everything looked very professional and relaxed. The servants didn't pull back until Terrill had given them his discreet but visible nod.

– I see that a new *crew* has taken over again, the man sitting closest to Yolanda commented.

– We were… given the opportunity, she replied indifferent, but pleasant. – Things are… floating a bit right now. The operation is being moved away from Marseille.

– They get younger every year, a woman said, not too discreet to her companion.

– I recognized Maxine Leary among the waitresses, the man continued unabated.

His eyes rested unwavering on Yolanda.

– We recruited her not long ago, Yolanda told the man in confidence. – She was quite reluctant at first, but was quickly persuaded. People originally had different plans for her, but a decision was made to counter that and that makes us quite pleased. She's a natural when it comes to training the merchandize.

Is this me? Is this how I can be or how I am?

She couldn't decide and it bothered her, bothered her terribly.

Survival, she thought, Damon thought.

– I remain interested in purchasing her, the man insisted.

– Perhaps the opportunity will re-present itself later. Yolanda smiled tight and polite. – Will you excuse me?

– Certainly! He nodded in acknowledgement, showing that she had found mercy for his critical eye.

She rose. Larry and Joe, uh, André and Damon followed her as double shadows.

– Eat and drink to your heart's content, she suggested generously. – There won't be too long to wait.

The three pulled back, setting out to leave the room, not too fast, not to slow.

The stench of sweat tore at Terrill's nostrils. He met the eyes of one of the bodyguards, one of the women. She had one brown and one green eye. He nodded to her. She returned the nod. There weren't that many steps to the corner, between ten and fifteen to relative safety. The hall had two exits, where they were headed and the quay. It struck him again how easy it would be, if everything worked out to take out the enemy in a murderous crossfire. This was a death trap.

A whine started in his left ear. He managed to put a stop to it, but a moment or two later it started up again.

A fast glance back allowed him to map the entire setting, doing it once more to his satisfaction. He could do that, now, as a perceived bully in a suit. He didn't register any sudden moves, no open suspicion.

Only a few steps more.

He was very much aware of how those on one side of the gallery no longer could see them. Muttering under his breath he realized that he was praying, praying that they had the nerve to wait long enough. Wait

only a little longer
until
the joyride began.
– DIE, ASSHOLES, DIE D…

The insane shout from the gallery drowned in the machinegun fire. Damon and André grabbed Yolanda and jumped into hiding, as if they were really two gorillas hired to assure her safety.

Thunder and lightning rocked the ground and people's perception. Bullets filled the air. During one tiny second the first, angry death-cries overpowered the thunder. The doors opened behind the three. Three nasty-looking UZI's were thrown into their arms.

André glanced forward from behind the corner and fired his machinegun. Terrill stuck his head out the next second. What he saw during that moment, when he imagined he hardly noticed anything burned itself into his total recall forever.

Many shots went haywire, but people were still hit. The crossfire was so intense that those pulling the triggers couldn't avoid hitting the targets. Close to half of those gathered around the luxurious furniture died during just the first few seconds. Blood flowed from countless open wounds. Some managed to fire at the gallery, but not more than a few rounds before they went down in yet another rain of bullets. Others sought hideouts, but there was no place to hide.

The first on the gallery was hit and died. Bullets hit Yolanda's gun and it was wrested from her hands and a few bullets also hit her arm. Oliver took her place. In his anger and inexperience he exposed himself for too long and was hit by a shower of bullets.

Damon rolled on the floor. He fired at a black clad figure advancing towards them. The man was hit. Damon rolled back behind the relative safety of the corner. Pieces loosened from the corner like projectiles when bullets hit it. He had difficulty breathing and felt like he never got sufficient air.

One of the girls on the gallery screamed when she was hit. She fell and hit the floor below with a thud, broken and shot to pieces.

Several of those up there panicked and those turning to flee got hit in the back and collapsed.

The slyest and most cold-blooded from the enemy camp sat course directly at the harbor and the boats. Seemingly not in any way influenced by their surroundings they rushed off with suppler, unpredictable movements. Damon counted seven of them. He fired the machinegun at an indistinct figure and missed, emptying the clip making another attempt. He threw away the UZI and drew the revolver.

He took aim and pulled the trigger. A man in a white shirt was hit several times. Red roses grew on the broad chest.

Only three reached the quay. André and others fired their bazooka. Only one grenade hit something vital, but when one of the boats exploded it destroyed almost everything nearby. The explosion blasted the three runners and pushed them through the air. They landed on the floor, covered in blood, but kept firing, like invulnerable demons. All seemed downright inhuman as they kept the bullets coming. Terrill felt himself got hit. He turned dizzy for a moment, until he found himself pushed at the wall and the pain cleared his vision. The metal in his hand burned his skin. He raised his gun and kept firing, almost as relentless as the three enemy gunmen. By now there was so much smoke in the hall that he had to strain himself in order to see anything except indistinct shadows. He fired at anything moving down there. Through fire and water and white-glowing tongues of flame he spotted a woman firing two guns simultaneously while pulling back, each step bringing her closer to safety. She loosened, with a simple twist the moorings on one of the undamaged boats. André fired another grenade from the bazooka. He cursed when it passed harmlessly over the boats and vanished in the waves. Damon pulled the trigger again, and just as he knew that he had hit the target, he met the woman's eyes. She was pushed backwards. As incredible as that seemed, she managed to stay on her feet. She balanced on the edge of the quay when several more bullets hit her. Some of them went straight through flesh and body, while others met with harder resistance and was stopped. It looked like she was being hit by a giant sledgehammer. She landed in the water. Everybody expected to hear the splash, even in the prevailing inferno. There was nothing, nothing except the sight of her as she went straight under, one tiny wave among all the big.

The shooting from the gallery kept going for ten, twenty more seconds… until it dawned on them that no one returned the fire.

The smoke whirled in the wind and the air. Everything shifted and nothing was the same from one moment to the next. A draft could draw away the smoke and clear the air. Not long afterwards the smoke would return with a vengeance.

They fought themselves up on unsteady legs. The fabric of Terrill's jacket had been like glued to the wall when he pushed himself off it. He stood still and steady. The bullet had penetrated his side and the wall. Blood flowed from both holes.

– We did it! André exclaimed faint and incredulous. – I can't believe we did.

He wasn't hit.

A suitcase filled with money had opened. The bills kept whirling in the air, creating an impression that they would never fall. They made a pretty landing on the floor, where the bodies seemed to be stacked in heaps.

The illusion of timelessness eventually ended. Some finally began to put out the fires. They pumped seawater through hoses over the boat wrecks. The silence, when it came felt potent beyond potent. It was only broken by single shots when André and three others began killing off the few enemies still breathing. It didn't take long.

Damon removed his jacket and the other clothes on his upper body slowly and painfully. He didn't feel anything in particular. He felt lightheaded and he seemed to be floating, but aside from that everything felt amazingly ordinary. Maxine directed him to a chair and began patching him up. She did the job in a remarkably relaxed, quick and effective manner.

– Hey, you're good at this, he said stunned.

– As stated, they made me take classes, she said lightly, darkly. – They wanted me to become a nurse, wanted that added to my other capabilities.

She tightened the bandages, making sure they stayed in place.

– I can't help those with grave wounds. They saw no need to have a surgeon doll in their stable.

The bitterness in her voice was palatable. He raised a hand to comfort her, but she pulled away.

She looked down at him with those beyond cold and pretty eyes.

– I'm pretty confident, but not absolutely certain the bullet didn't penetrate vital parts. You should have the wound examined no later than tomorrow morning.

He shook his head.
– We have to get away from here as fast as possible.
Four of their own had been killed. Two more could die anytime. Seven more seemed as good as dead. The survivors gathered in a close circle in order to confirm and tighten their bonds. Yolanda sat down at Damon's side while Maxine did her job. She rubbed him in the neck with her strong hand. Cold and simple math roamed his thoughts like a razorblade. It had been a massacre. The enemy had walked unprepared into an ambush and had been annihilated. Almost everything had gone according to plan.
Vladek Kostov stood on the edge of the circle, looking very down and depressed, refusing to meet Damon's eyes.
– I know I… fucked up. I… lost my cool.
Damon didn't look at him when he spoke, but at them all.
– We had all the advantages on our side tonight, he said empathically. – We will probably never be this lucky again. That being said, I will claim that we were still testing ourselves. They stood with their backs to the wall and we bested them, many of us surviving and thriving. We did good! The next time we will do even better.
– Behold the child of the storm, Yolanda said softly and a little sad.
He would always be close to them, even if he should be far away. And he would always be far away, even when he was close.
Later. Departure drew near. Damon and André were the last to leave the lifeless, empty tomb. Damon bent down and picked some pieces of tiles from the floor.
– Mahogany, he grunted and let go of the remains again. – They spared no expenses here.
– A-men, André chanted ironically.
They walked fast through the tunnel to the elevator.
– Btw, I was impressed about how easily you changed from right to left hand and back again when firing and fighting, André said casually. – You must have trained hard for that.
– Not really. Damon shrugged. – Using both hands has always felt natural to me.
Maxine held open the elevator door for them. She had tied her hair in a braid and looked mean and tough, far removed from the cute doll, the idol of millions her former masters had attempted to mold her to become.
– Hey, are you okay? She wondered. She held a hand at his forehead. – You're not warm, not excessively so, but definitely breathing a little hard.
– It doesn't have anything to do with the wound, he said. – I have a weak form of asthma.
It had never really bothered him much. One of Rawlins' physicians had mentioned it to him a year ago, when he had patched him up after a quarrel. He had also told him that the disease never would have been noticeable at all, not even the weak variation if it hadn't been for the pollution.
The pollution had weakened mankind in so many ways.
The elevator door opened. The entrance door opened up towards the bad, but open air, the night, the eternity outside.
Something waited for him out there. Something would always wait everywhere. But something waited for him out there.
He met the eyes of his traveling companions and warmed himself in the heat of the

fire visible in their darkness. He stared at the wall, at the inferno of death and lightning now covering almost the entire southern horizon. It didn't resemble even remotely anything in his experience. If any human being had ever seen anything like it, it would surprise him. He met the sight without fear.

A long row of motorbikes and buses rolled out of the old industrial area, shaking and stirring all the surroundings they passed through, all of the flesh and metal and concrete and glass and plastic and shivering mind.

They left the lifeless stone desert at dawn.

CHAPTER TEN

He had a night out, drinking his guts to pieces. Aside from that he didn't recall much of anything or anyone. He knew there had been nothing special about the evening, nothing making the evening stand out, in any way.

The group sat around the table, sipping sour beer or rather classic Norwegian piss-water, engaging in a more or less meaningful conversation. He couldn't recall the name of the establishment, only that it was the fifth or sixth place they had visited that night.

The light from the candles burned in his eyes. He moved them to the neighborhood table. They still burned. It didn't make any difference that he sat with his back to them. A girl moved them back to their table. He shrugged. The meaningless conversation continued.

The night faded in his mind. It quite simply vanished down a deep abyss. The only thing he could recall, that truly stood out in his mind was the bitter taste of the beer.

He was easy to find. They picked him up early in the morning, while the darkness still clutched the city. He was pulled nude from his bed. When he attempted to resist they struck him hard in the ribs, pacifying him. They pulled his arms hard behind his back and cuffed him. The desire to scream grew to something resembling panic, but it was too late. He could hardly breathe, far less make loud noises.

They dragged him from the apartment in a series of brutal acts. People saw what happened. They had to. He knew they didn't sleep. The little sounds they made reached his ears somewhat. He saw no one, hardly saw anything, except his own legs stumbling forward.

Two police officers held him. Two walked in front and two behind him. They practically pushed him down the stairs. He strived to keep his balance, to hit the steps with his nude soles. Every time he fell more brutal strikes hit his already sore skin. He felt very much relieved when they threw him into the humid and overheated patrol van.

The van charged forward with a mighty roar. Two turns and he no longer saw his home through the tiny window. He crouched on the floor on the large humid and overheated van painted in red, white and blue, crouched there with five other nude people. He assumed the vehicle drove through the Bergen streets, but he couldn't quite convince himself of the validity of his assumption.

Both his immediate and more distant surroundings felt completely alien to him.

He was freezing, and to such a degree that his teeth clattered. The beyond deep chill he experienced clearly befell all the other prisoners as well. The crouching, shaking creatures hardly looked human at all. Everybody sat still in the icy space, filled with shame, and in their embarrassment they didn't share each other's heat and remained cold. A woman and a man held hands, but they didn't sit close either.

The newcomer didn't speak. No one did. The extensive bruises on the nude bodies and the blood on the officers' shoes and knuckles told them what would happen if anyone dared to stand up for themselves. The newcomer didn't know what to say anyway. He didn't know anyone here.

The drive didn't bring them to the police station. The van passed that ominous building and drove south, on the road closest to the mountains. Lack of understanding kept fogging his mind. He wanted to say it, to shout it, but he only worded it silently with his lips or in his befouled mind, unable to tell which.

I - DON'T - UNDERSTAND

He didn't realize that they were on their way to Haukeland, the local central hospital until they turned left off the main road just before the tunnel. And even as the realization hit him he kept protesting silently.

This place was big, he knew that, like a small city, with businesses and conveniences and everything. On some level, on what felt like vastly improved senses he felt it all like a machine, with interconnecting tiny wheels turning and turning.

On what he perceived as his consciousness everything had become mud.

«Their» van was revealed as just one of many, a long line of vans driving up the narrow road. They passed the main entrance, all the new buildings and moved on to the backstreet with tall fences and a large, heavy boom. Wasn't this… Sore eyes widened. He recognized this old building as the old animal testing laboratory that had been moved twenty years ago.

The door was kicked open. Blinding light flooded the prisoners' minds.

– OUT, OUT! The guardians spat and started using their clubs before anyone even had the opportunity to get up on their feet.

Many were pushed outside, landing hard on the asphalt. Under the blinding floodlights and hounded by more guardians holding rifles the prisoners were placed in lines and made to run, to jump up and down without the slightest forward progress.

– UP DOWN UP DOWN, that's it, that's GOOD!

They «ran» as ordered and quickly lost track of time. Only the growing, devastating pain in their legs felt real.

When they were made to stumble into the cold brick house, they welcomed that. Nobody raised their eyes or turned their head, no one that wasn't made to pay for it. They heard the sounds of cracks, beatings and screams, but no one was tempted to look, to see what was going on.

– WHAT HAVE I DONE?

Several complained and wailed. They were generously rewarded. Clubs hammered them and they were dragged off like rag dolls. Those lucky few avoiding that shrugged in stark relief.

He found himself in a cold cell, or rather a box. The «cell» was no more than two meters long, one meter wide and a height no more than half of that. The total darkness surrounding him felt like nails smothering him. He writhed and twisted his body and head as much as he possibly could, but there was no light anywhere. Time completely lost its meaning to him. They had removed his watch. No one had told him anything, no matter how much he had begged them. They hadn't told him what he was charged with, whether or not he had been charged with anything, what he had to do to be released, just treated him with the same, prolonged indifference every step of the way. Dull, panicked thoughts kept hammering his consciousness. He was unable to form a single coherent thought, wondering in his feverish mind what they were *doing* to him.

Somewhere in the flashes originating in his delirious psyche where nightmarish images rested he glimpsed impressions that couldn't possibly be true. They made him writhe and groan on the cold slab, and more or less convinced him that his wits had left him and never would return.

He kept wondering if he had truly spotted Gerd in one of the rows, chains of people being pulled and pushed into this terrifying place. There had been others he knew appearing in the same row, in several rows, among them Myriam Vallinger, the bank lady Terrill had screwed around with and *that* just couldn't be real. She was in prison. He choked. She wasn't supposed to be here. His reason, what he hung on to with the thinnest of threads convinced him that if she was here, they had displayed her to put the fear of God in the prisoners. Yes, that made sense. Come the morning they, all those not criminal would all be released with a slap on the wrist and that would be it.

He imagined he had seen her, and Gerd, and all the others, and that he was still home in his bed, dreaming sweet dreams.

But he wasn't certain.

He wasn't certain of anything.

wake up.

He had to…

WAKE UP

He knocked his head in the ceiling and couldn't move past the dizziness for minutes.

– LET ME OUT, he shouted. – I HAVEN'T DONE ANYTHING.

After a while, after many days, after two minutes he started sobbing like a little kid. He feared he would go completely insane and screamed himself hoarse. A thousand loud shrieks replied. For each of his screams ten thousand echoes hammered him. And he screamed even more and louder. And more echoes returned to him, until he no longer had any voice left and descended into the most horrible apathy.

Everything was spinning. He had been chained on a flat sacrificial stone. Priests and priestesses raised their sacrificial knives and stabbed him simultaneously, in unison agreement. He fell into the deepest, darkest abyss and paralysis spread to all his limbs. He died and couldn't move a muscle, couldn't resist the draft, the pull from the vast hole. HELP help help help help help

The hatch opened, had the hatch opened? Sensations almost overwhelmed him completely, as he imagined he smelled food. His foot, his big toe bumped into something. The sound of something of metal being pushed across the floor was unmistakable and he felt something wet on his skin. Suddenly sweat flowed down his forehead. Silent pleas flowed between his lips. He had to go deep within himself in order to calm down. It took forever to keep his right hand from shaking and he was able to stretch it as long as possible down his body. He had to twist his body hard, into what he would have just minutes ago considered an impossible position and every piece of him hurt. He felt the edge of the bowl and imagined that his fingertips turned wet, imagined that it took forever to pull the bowl towards his mouth. The fear that he would accidentally turn it and waste the food almost paralyzed him for real. He died of that a thousand times. Finally, there was no need for him to do the impossible anymore, no need for him to exercise his rock hard control over himself. He slurped the cold soup, the rotten meat.

And relapsed, returned to that horrible state of nothingness. The next time he was aware, he realized that he was just as hungry, that the tiny meal no longer helped him.

Food, give me food, he shouted silently.

– I will do anything you ask, he shouted. – ANYTHING

There was no reply, no sign of anyone hearing him at all.

– Satan spawns, he mumbled with his hands pushed at his lips.

He kicked the cell door repeatedly in a steady rhythm. His foot had turned numb a while ago. He kept it up without break.

After that he slept or was awake, he couldn't tell.

He couldn't tell at all.

A lamp was lit close to his face, right in front of his eyes, blinding him. Its close proximity burned his skin. He sat in a chair. He didn't think he was alone in the room, but he saw no one, not even the hand that had lit the lamp.

– Name?

A voice sneaked close to him from the dark, ingratiating, poisonous. He grabbed the opportunity with a need equal to a man that had died of thirst a thousand times.

– Roger Norlund, he replied, filled with gratitude.

He perceived more now, the faint image of a brick wall, a man in military uniform sitting behind a desk and taking notes.

– Born?

He was tempted to say yes, a joke that would fit well with his old life, one he knew wouldn't be appreciated by his current hosts. Fear flowed through him like an electric charge.

– December 4, 1994, he replied, so hoarse that he couldn't fathom how they could hear him at all.

There was a break while the man in uniform pretended to take notes.

– Why am I here? He blurted out, close to panic. – What the hell do you think I've done?

A hard fist struck him, struck him so hard that he fell off the chair. The fist, either left or right grabbed his hair and lifted him back on the chair.

– YOU WILL PAY ATTENTION, a loud, ghastly voice thundered in his ear. – YOU WILL ONLY SPEAK WHEN YOU ARE TOLD TO SPEAK

Roger wanted to assure them of his obedience, his undying loyalty, but failed to utter a single sound.

– Any immigrants in your family? The man behind the desk asked casually.

«Casually» didn't sound good, didn't sound good at all in Roger's ears.

– No, he assured them with as much sincerity he could muster.

– Any immigrants among your friends or acquaintances?

I enjoy the company of quite a few, he thought feverishly. Americans, Swedes, Danes, Englishmen, Egyptians, Serbs, Argentineans, Kenyans, Turks, Spaniards…

– Yes, he replied on autopilot.

After ten or more totally meaningless questions the voice and the words it spoke just blurred to him. The room itself and everything in it blurred into one single mass. He knew that he replied honestly to every question they asked him. He had long since convinced himself that they had access to his brain and could expose all attempts at lying.

When they dragged him from the interrogation room he had his jaw on his chest and snivel flowed from his slack jaw.

– What have I done? Please tell me, *please*…

He crawled back into his cell, actually helping out when they pushed him inside. Every time an interrogation ended, he looked forward to return to his tiny home.

Day, night didn't exist, just the cell and the interrogation room. No windows, no hallways or doors. He never saw anybody except the chief interrogator. He felt the man behind him. He heard horrible screams, never certain if it was other prisoners or himself, unable to tell whether or not he was completely alone at this place.

There were no thoughts, no will. They emptied him, like turning a garbage can on its head, and he welcomed the emptiness. There was nothing more there, nothing left to loose. He realized that he bit himself and sucked his own blood.

– Gods of Darkness and Horror, he called and cackled insane. – COME TO ME

But in his madness he found something tangible, something to hold on to.

Will… awoke. It felt so good. Suddenly he felt invincible.

– I want a lawyer, he said in an even voice.

Strikes followed strikes, followed by the familiar verbal and physical abuse, now bouncing off him without leaving any mark, any pain. It was like he was totally indifferent to it all. They couldn't reach him.

– I want a lawyer, he said in an even voice.

Time passed. They placed him in the interrogator chair again, showing off their tools. It didn't faze him.

– I want a lawyer, he repeated for God knows what time.

He had done so during two interrogations before this one. He grinned like a savage to the man behind the desk.

– You stubborn fool, she said softly.

It was a voice he hadn't heard before. He strived hard in an effort to see the woman behind the voice, but as before he saw only the desk, the man behind it, and the surrounding shadows.

– That certainly calls for a certain admiration on our part, doesn't it, ladies and gentlemen?

Lights were lit everywhere, white, sterile. His eyes were filled with tears. Aside from the chief interrogator there were two women and one more man in the room. He recognized Lisbeth Kaspersen instantly. He couldn't take his eyes off her. She smiled to him and the smile pulled him into an abyss of despair and hope. He knew she was employed in public service and understood why she was here. He didn't understand shit.

Big fists, the giant close by seemed indistinct, out of focus. He didn't really count here.

The man behind the desk rose with a very official, strict appearance.

– You, Roger Norlund, on February 24, this year 2013, at the new offices of Nature and Youth in Øvregaten 13 signed a declaration designed to undermine people's faith in our government, a declaration spreading obvious lies about the upcoming drilling of oil in the Barents Sea and outside the Lofoten archipelago.

He could hardly believe his ears. Relief flooded him.

– What are you *saying?* He chuckled. – Everybody signed that. What's the matter with you guys?

Not everybody, an unpleasant flashback reminded him. Not Turid, not Fredrik and Anita and their inner circle. The three of them had looked downright weird then, as if they shared a secret.

– The drilling is extremely important, even crucial to the defense of the realm, the tin soldier boasted.

It would have been easy to ridicule this man… if one saw him on TV, at a comforting distance.

– Last time I checked there was still freedom of express…

The human gorilla held him, struck him and kept striking him.

– There is no freedom for TRAITORS

A shower of saliva and bile mixed with the blood on Roger's skin.

The uniformed man picked up something that Roger knew was a whip, even though he couldn't quite believe it. The uniformed man straightened, seemingly completely relaxed, now, and started whipping Roger in a harsh and methodical manner. From the top down, from the low up. From side to side. At the already thoroughly battered body.

Hurt, it doesn't hurt anymore. Roger choked and choked during his continued bouts of hysterical laughter. Playful fingers massaged his neck. It gave him the creeps.

– C'mon, Roger, be a man, she chastised him, – show us you've got balls.

She grabbed his testicles and squeezed. His screams turned to howls, more from his heart than ever before. His body turned limp again. She held him to keep him from falling, but he still felt like he was doing that, falling. She rubbed his head tenderly. His sobbing rose to sore, choking sounds.

– You're all so obstinate, she said softly, her voice sounding so comforting, like a valve on a haunted soul. – But with just a tiny push in the right direction, a few minor encouragements you once more become diligent and useful, so eager to perform, to be at your very best.

He and the chair he sat on were pulled up, carried a few steps and placed in front of the desk. A sheet was placed before him, a pen in his hand. The words on the sheet faded before his eyes. He wrote his name on the dotted line. The words higher up had no significance to him anymore.

Kaspersen grabbed the sheet he had signed without reading it and held it in both hands.

She tore it to pieces, shrugging as she let them fall to the floor. Roger's face turned slack and dead. He collapsed in the chair.

– That's right, she said, totally indifferent. – We have no use for this, not anymore.

He was sobbing when they returned him to his cell and he kept sobbing. There was no more laughter, hysterical or not.

There was no change in his state of mind when they came and fetched him, when they dragged him to a large truck and threw him into a dark hole with lots of other unreasoning meat. Tears stopped flowing, but kept coming inside.

Very few moved as the truck moved. He wasn't sure it had in truth moved at all. The drive didn't seem to last very long, not even long enough for him to register it in his lofty mind.

They were all loaded on to a train, very much like meat ready for transport.

He crouched unmoving on the floor in a coach filled with other, miserable prisoners. No one spoke or even released a sound. The train started moving with a shake. No one reacted, not in any discernible way. They didn't breathe. At least their breathing wasn't audible or noticeable. Everybody stayed silent. The noise the train made racing away on the tracks muted any other minor sound anybody here might release. A female body leaned on his. He felt so little from that contact that it just as well could have been a dead body sitting there by his side. Neither time nor space existed for him.

His eyes kept staring at nothing. He began counting the rhythmic sounds from the tracks. Many rotations later it dawned on him that a dead body really sat by his side. Its limbs had stiffened and the skin turned cold. The realization brought neither grief nor any immediate, noticeable reaction. There was sufficient room for him to push it away. He waited with neither expectation nor dread. She wasn't pushed back towards him. He wondered briefly whether or not he or she on the other side of the body had also croaked. Roger's companion on the other side didn't seem to be breathing either. Perhaps they were all dead, and he was the only one breathing in the entire coach or even train.

Pain paralyzed him, convincing him that he, at least was indeed breathing. It did no more than gnaw, now, like a glow within. There was nothing else. This didn't ruin him like the cell had done. It ruined more. There were times, when the train charged through turns that lines of light revealed themselves on faces. Eyes staring at nothing revealed nothing but eyes staring at nothing, at copies in gray and pale. Those still breathing were given food and water. Flashes of light blinded them, waking them up a little. There was the occasional struggle over the nourishment, but it hardly seemed real, any of it. They fed, without thought, without will. The stench of piss, shit and death never went away. Pain paralyzed him, gnawing at his insides like a glow. There was nothing else.

The train stopped. At least he imagined that it did, imagined that they were transferred to cold barracks somewhere.

They ran in the mud and the rain, and slowly it dawned on them that they were no longer on the train, even though the dead were still with them. Soldiers with unmovable faces and big guns moved them forward and did so without anything even resembling mercy. The prisoners had no idea where they were, and didn't care. All going through their mind, the obsession filling them was to put one foot in front of the other and not fall. Never fall.

When someone did fall they hardly noticed. Those crouching in the mud were already dead. It felt downright silly when the soldiers wasted ammo on them.

Exhausted beyond exhausted they kept moving, kept obeying the snarling and the vile voices commanding their numb minds and bodies.

The mist floated in the collective showers. Cascades of water hit sore skin. Bars of soap slipped from weak hands. Those shaking hands reached for the elusive bar of soap. They washed and rubbed off all external dirt. Greasy hair became clean and shiny. With dreamy smiles and empty eyes they were led into a large hall filled with bright lights. Hairs in front of mirrors appeared in their narrow line of vision. They understood what was about to happen, but didn't really attach any significance to it. Everybody, both male and females got all the hair on their heads shaved off. They sat unmoving in the chairs while tufts of hair added to the already large heap on the floor. Roger couldn't recall seeing any of the tufts actually hitting the floor, only that he had seen the various nuances of color float in a sea of gray, dissolved, devoured, lost.

In the next room, in what felt like an empty eternity later they were placed on benches by long tables and fed. They devoured the content in smoking hot bowls without even considering the content. It was food, nourishment filling the vast emptiness within. Stomach was filled and a relaxed satisfaction bloated their mind. The snapping of whips roused them from their brief slumber. They were moved again and taken to a room resembling a horrible version of a wardrobe. They were presented with military uniforms and effects. After measures had been taken snapping voices told them to get on with it. No one protested or resisted in any way, visibly or in other ways. They dressed, or rather were dressed. The very distinct impression in their dulled minds made them imagine that it wasn't truly their arms and hands doing the dressing, but the invisible strings moving them.

Everybody stood there, changed, transformed by cruel forces outside their control. After being nude for so long the stiff, uncomfortable clothes felt strangely comfortable. The bull cap hid the shaven head, its shadow the shame in the eyes. Sharp commands pushed them on. They rushed forward. Defiance didn't even occur to them. They felt a powerful need to obey.

A dark, narrow corridor squeezed them, forced them tight together. They hurried through it, like mice through a laboratory maze. They pretty much felt exactly like that, and identified with lots of other, unpleasant names they called themselves in the waking nightmare their existence had become. The dark, narrow corridor expanded into a long hall. It could be a gym hall, but what it most of all reminded them of was a sports arena.

Three other groups, indistinguishable from theirs were herded like cattle from three other entrances. Perhaps if anyone in the four groups had spoken it would have dawned on the rest that that person had a different dialect and that he or she possibly came from another part of the country.

Roger didn't bother with exploring the thought, though, and he doubted that any others did either. Any thought came to him unbidden, now, hurt him, now. He obeyed the commands the guards barked without resistance. Like everyone else he followed the directions given. It seemed to him that he and the rest were indeed born to do this, to follow commands and obey. He realized that he had always been doing it, from early childhood and throughout adolescence. They had always been told and believed that true independence was the greatest of sins. If a person enjoyed a big cage he or she would also enjoy a small.

– Welcome, soldiers! Lisbeth Kaspersen greeted them with a huge smile. – Let me offer you my hearty congratulations. You've made it!

She stood like a mirage up there, above them on the platform. Both the men and the women stared at her with devoted eyes.

– You're now in a position many will see as enviable, she boasted. – You get a chance to correct your many earlier missteps. I trust you will show yourself worthy of this trust.

Missteps? The old Roger might have been curious, wondered what she meant, but the pliant creature he had become didn't care. There was a slight itch in him to look at those by his side, in order to find out if they displayed any visible reaction to the woman's words, but he let it be. There was no purpose to it. The sea of faces would certainly reveal the same as his: nothing.

A man with a hard expression, wearing an officer uniform replaced Kaspersen on the platform.

– You're basically two groups, he said harshly, without introduction. – You're either foreigners who have come to our land to plunder its riches, or you're Norwegians failing your privileges and duties. You will have many opportunities to pay your dues.

He just kept on ranting. He didn't seem insane, but *mighty*. Roger paid attention.

– At this place you will learn to listen and obey. It will be the only thing on your mind. From this moment on and during the rest of your miserable lives you will serve your betters. You start at the bottom. Seek consolation in this, in case you need comfort like small CHILDREN

Every word he spoke hammered them, impregnating their conscious and unconscious mind.

Kaspersen walked between the rows. She inspected the new troops with two giant Schaefer dogs in tow. The dogs growled and snarled. Froth flowed from their mouth. But when they started barking she pulled their chains, pulled them hard. That was all it took to make them whine in shame. Everybody watching, (and everybody did) shook down their spine and their lips shivered.

– Yes, she nodded, – this is you. You are savages hardly above the caveman, with so much misdirected energy and rage. You lack discipline, the proper teaching, a master to give your life meaning. This is our gift to you.

The inspection lasted well beyond the stage where it hurt, until it didn't hurt anymore. Time crawled for any soldier as she passed them. Sometimes she turned and came back. She studied them like she would a commodity, a machine in need of oil. Each and every one she left behind felt diminished, a little less human.

She checked their teeth, roamed their mouth with a glowed hand. Fingers dug into flesh, studied muscles and sinew. The commodity was measured and judged. A pointed stare read their minds. Nothing belonged to them anymore.

They believed she was done when she finally passed the last in the last row… when she started up again. She stopped in front of the first woman in the row.

– What's your name? She asked softly.

– Myriam.

The voice that Roger recalled as strong and deep was now weak and insecure.

– Look at me, Myriam. The wavering eyes were pulled towards the steady pair facing her. – That's good! You will now give me an honest answer, child. If you fail in this you will be *punished*. Do you understand?

– Yes, Mistress.

– Very good, Mistress said pleased. – Tell me, you're a sweet little child… Don't you think life has more to offer than this, what you see around you right now? Surely, there must be more?

– There isn't more, the child replied.

– Very good, my child.

Lisbeth applauded and then petted Myriam on the cheek.

A snap of the fingers and an aide stepped forward and saluted her. He presented a metal ring, a… collar? Myriam pulled one foot slightly back, but then she froze. A shivering passed through her and a film covered her eyes.

– Read aloud, soldier.

Lisbeth held up the ring in front of the pale face. There was an inscription on it.

– 2001, Myriam Vallinger read with a coarse voice.

– *This* is what you will be called, the way you will be identified from now on. You don't have a name, unless we choose to give you one. If you don't obey when your number is called you will be punished. If you, at any given time remember what we have taken from you, you will be punished. Do you understand, 2001?

– *Yes, Mistress.*

The ring was put around 2001's neck. There was a click and the collar was locked in place. The number was visible, even at a considerable distance. Everyone received one. Roger felt the cold metal snap around his own neck. After a while he hardly noticed it. He felt more and more that it belonged there, as a natural part of his skin.

– SOLDIEEERS, MMMARCH

The march, the eternal march began. Every left foot hit the ground exactly the same moment as every other left foot, every right foot the precise moment every other right foot did. They fell in line without thinking about it, as if they had always done so.

They were led to the barracks, to large, naked sleeping halls, where they slept on their mats, sleeping their apparent dreamless sleep.

2010 still writhed in his sleep, imagining he heard Lisbeth whisper «you're mine» in his ears. He kept hearing those very words, until they had faded from his consciousness and become an integrated part of his self.

The reveille woke them up before dawn the next morning. They were commanded outside. Their training started in earnest. They were aware of their surroundings at some level, convinced by the fact that they were in some sort of military camp, but they didn't know. They didn't know anything.

– I'm your sergeant. A tall and muscular woman appeared in their line of sight. They looked straight forward and couldn't tell if there were other people nearby. – You're in your early stage of imprint, where we will teach you everything. I will teach you to march. I will teach you to crawl and eventually to walk. I will teach you to eat and drink, shit and piss. Without me you're *nothing*. You're not dead. To be dead you must have been alive at some point. I'm the bitch that gave birth to you, the very soil you tread…

She emanated terror. 2010 recalled some sergeants he had watched in movies. She didn't resemble any of them. They had never had that kind of power, power over flesh and spirit, life and death.

She marched them, also to places where they witnessed and experienced unspeakable acts. They were never given a moment's respite. The commanding voice was always present. When they were finally given permission to sleep after days and nights of drilling and regimentation they kept hearing it.

The voice told them rules to live by, the tenet of their existence. They listened, wide open, both their minds and bodies being washed and rinsed, and transformed into what their masters desired. Blind obedience was hammered into their very core. They ran in the mud and the rain, and kept hearing the voice, striving in all ways to obey, serve and please.

Indoctrination continued relentlessly. And if they at some point expressed doubt, they were brutally reminded of their place, their spot in the scheme of things. They were told time and time again that this was right, that this was necessary, and they learned, learned to believe it with all their hearts. Everything turned indistinct. Everybody believed. No one could recall a time when they hadn't believed. They forgot their old lives. They forgot that they had ever had any other life. The camp had become their entire world… and… they no longer remembered their dreams.

PART THREE: THE ROAD NORTH

«A land without nomads is a land without freedom».
Ancient Bedouin proverb

CHAPTER ELEVEN

The rows of motorbikes raced through the slight turn without reducing speed. The bus at the center of the crowd of two-wheelers also kept it up without trouble.

A beach flashed before his eyes, sand, garbage and a campfire, the dance under the midnight sun.

Terrill rested at the back of the bus, covered in blankets. He raised his head, wondering if he had been freezing. The blankets had been soaked. He felt cool and calm, now, still sweaty, but aware, awake.

His body had been weakened, but periodically his thoughts had still soared higher than the eagles, touching the edge of the sun.

Maxine appeared in his line of vision, along with lots of other smiling mugs. She put a hand on his forehead, removing it with a relieved expression on her face. He sat up, feeling no more than a weak, distant pain.

– What happened? He wondered hoarsely.

Maxine pushed a glass to his lips and he emptied it of water, sucking it dry.

– Don't you remember? We drove past Nice, along the coastline, in order to get out of France as soon as possible.

– Remember…

Yolanda didn't have her arm in a sling anymore. He recalled bonfires on a beach, and smoke mixed with sand rising toward the sparking clouds.

Cautious eyes sought to his sides. Maeve rested on his left and Jerry to his right. Both had pale skin, but their fever was also gone.

The fourth mat was empty.

He felt sweat cover his skin. Insane eyes locked on to Maxine.

– Imogen is dead, she confirmed, totally unnecessary.

He fell back on the mattress with sticky eyes that never quite closed. The sand and the smoke and airy red hair whirled in the wind. He recalled her face and its defiant expression. She had been shot to pieces. It had been a small miracle that she had held out as long as she had. He had stayed up the entire day, felt healthy, fast and strong. She had expired at dusk, between light and darkness, just before they reached a dirty, poisoned shore. They had been driving far onto the beach and stopped there, in the deep sand.

Dreaming, while writhing on his back he still remembered every frozen moment in detail. The dry wood they had used to build her pyre. The unmoving body on the bed of that easily combustible wood. The flames returning her ashes to the air, the sea and the earth, into the anvil of Crom. Damon grinned in his dormancy. He enjoyed that image. It felt right.

They had danced there in the sand, until cramps grabbed them with both hands, until he felt the first pain. The wound had reopened and the blood had wet his hands. He remembered.

– You will never beat me, he had shouted at the gray waves.

He had challenged Death head on between the dirty dunes and it had replied.

The fever had returned and the feverish visions had begun.

– Where are we? He asked her.
– We're approaching the Turin suburbs, Yolanda replied. – We sent out scouts. The mood doesn't seem that agitated in there.
He sat up. A firm hand pulled the blanket off. He didn't have any clothes beneath. Hands touched the floor. He attempted to rise and failed. Hands rolled into fists and he fought himself up on shaky feet. The bus shook. He grabbed a seatback and stood without aid. They looked concerned at him, but didn't say anything. He removed the bandage. The wound was healing nicely. There was only a loose, external crust left. He pushed and squeezed on both sides and felt nothing but a slight stiffness.
– Don't get pissed. Yolanda held up a set of clean clothes. – You almost look good as new, but we all agree that you should relax a few more days.
– Thank you, he said good-humored. – Kind Yolanda.
She was blushing. She was actually blushing. It was a remarkable spectacle.
– Yola, she corrected him. – I'm Yola now… I have changed.
– We all have, he said lightly.
– Thanks to you, Jerry said from the floor.
– Thanks to us all, Terrill stated.
He looked outside. The commotion began when one spotted him and blew his horn long and loud. The bus responded and then the noise roared from every single motorbike in view.
For a moment they looked very much like horses to him. He heard hooves thundering against the ground.
A bike almost in front fell back in the line.
– André is coming, Dominic reported.
Damon nodded. He pulled on his t-shirt with certain difficulties. The stiffness in his limbs was notable.
– Switch with him, he told Dominic. – Take his place in front.
André slowed down until he was close to the bus. The driver, Stefan opened the door while the man on the bike maneuvered as close to the entrance as humanly possible. It seemed right away as a hazardous enterprise and even more so when Dominic prepared for the jump.
Dominic made the leap. A horrible, extended moment he seemed to float in the air between two objects at high speed. The next he sat behind on the bike with a solid grip around André's shoulders. The vehicle turned away from the danger. When they had switched places in masterful ways a few seconds later it returned to its position. André jumped into the bus. Perhaps he overreached himself a bit, since his hand slipped before he managed to get himself inside.
– I see that the late sleeper has awakened, he grinned, stopping a step from Damon. – About time. You looked a bit pale there, in my opinion.
They shook hands. André squeezed hard. Damon returned the gesture. André was clearly overdoing it when he shook what appeared to be a sore hand.
– It seems like I could have slept even longer, Damon replied in the same ironic manner. – We seem to be styling.
– We had a little trouble passing the Italian border, Robert injected cautiously.
– Somebody had blocked the road with wreckage, André explained casually. – But no one attempted to stop us when we cleared it.

Damon and Yolanda… Yola exchanged glances.
– What do you think? Has he changed as well?
– Yes. She stared straight at André. – He has learned the fine art of irony…
Damon sat in front of the bus and stared through the front window. He glimpsed his own mirror image in the light of the coming dusk. His eyes didn't move. He let his fingers touch the wolf skin in his lap. Hesitant, determined he put the «hat» on his head, like he had done on the beach. He had found it half concealed among all the other «treasures» in the dunes and picked it up without deliberate thought. It had been dirty, with a dull gloss, drowned in sand. Now, it was washed and cleaned, alive. They had glared at him, his travel companions. The howl he sent into the night made them hot and cold and every other sensation under the moon.
The snout moved close to the window and he heard a snarl. Then he heard a howl. He heard one first, then more, many replies to the first. They rose from the hills and deep between the stone desert's tombstones.
– It suits you. Yola slipped her hands over his shoulders and rubbed the fur. The green rope around his upper arm called her attention like nothing else. She touched it with something resembling awe. – And you never took this off.
She sat down astride his lap, allowing herself to be caught by the black stare.
– You've probably not had the opportunity to study the gang's reaction to it, but I have, in all nuances. My congratulations! Your plan works to perfection. Two half moons of a bunch of angry, obsessive individuals join into one, cohesive whole, now, when you've given them a purpose in life.
He felt them, felt them all, like he did his surroundings and more, on and off the bus, far off the bus.
She looked at him, tilting her head, aware of his awareness in amazing ways. He nodded. They both did.
– Can you hear the wolves? He wondered. – They follow humanity north. They walk in our tracks, like they according to myth did long ago.
– Perhaps they do, she nodded, – but they follow you as well.
Maxine was strumming a guitar. She played haunting, ghostly chords.
Turin's suburbs and then Turin's streets slipped past them. There wasn't much that hadn't changed since Terrill's last visit seventeen brief months earlier. Broad, straight streets hardly looked broad and straight anymore. They and the large, open squares had been the city's hallmarks. Random parked car wrecks, garbage cans, garbage heaps and oozing bonfires transformed the comprehensible to labyrinths of clutter and confusion.
They didn't see many people, but those they did see scurried off and stared at what they perceived as bikers with suspicion and fear.
– The natives don't see past our disguise, Dominic said pleased. – They see only predators on the prowl. Perception is everything these days and has been for a long time.
– They are wise, Yola flashed her fangs.
– I don't care shit about how they perceive us, Terrill snorted, – as long as they fear and respect us, increasing our chances of survival.
He walked in front of his pack with the wolf skin on his head, walked past large, abandoned areas, through blocks full of terrified and subdued human-like creatures. There was a kind of curiosity in those empty eyes, but twisted, sick.

– This is a dead city, André mused, – even more than Marseille, even more a cemetery.
The others easily spotted a shudder in his unusually expressive face.
Pale shadows played on walls covered by moss. Visions of another world revealed itself on dark surfaces. The pack glimpsed themselves there, in the dark mirrors, but sometimes those images seemed to change, and they saw other groups of people wandering through a desolate land, something resembling a desert. The movie playing in their heads looked thousands of years off, and they couldn't tell whether or not it was the distant past or the distant future.
The infinite wheel turned and turned.
Terrill had brought half of the tribe on the walkabout. Dominic took them on a guided tour on what had been his hometown.
– Nothing is familiar. He shook his head in distress. – At least everything has become so… muddled that I can't be sure I am where I think I am. Even the more or less famous landmarks don't look the same. And I used to play here as a kid. At least I think I did.
They passed an old cinema, or what might have been a cinema.
Just before midnight they returned to their point of origin, to their fellow tribe members, feeling a very distinct sense of relief. They joined them in guarding the bus, the bikes and the defense perimeter they had made with aggressive, restless moves and visible arms.
The full moon appeared again and the restlessness was curbed a bit, but they kept changing position. They sat and the next moment they were pacing back and forth from one side of the designated safe area to the other.
They waited patiently or at least they waited.
They kept the bonfires burning and did their utmost to not hide themselves, to not even appear to be hiding.
Palazzo Reale and the surrounding area remained as empty as most of the city.
They waited, but no one approached them.
– Perhaps we scared them shitless? Robert wondered half hearted.
– Nah, another rejected his diagnosis, – they're hassling us, softening us up to see what we're made of. We have guards on all tall key points. There's no way they can approach us without being seen and they know that. So they take our mettle in the only possible way.
They stayed in constant contact with the sentries, the first line of defense. Nothing happened.
– What happened here? Maxine said to the air, clutching her shoulders.
– It's hard to tell exactly, of course, Yola said, – but I would bet there has been a coup d'etat on a smaller scale, a very brutal version of it.
– But where are all the people… and the bodies?
Yola looked at Damon, suffering a loss of words.
– Hard to tell about those still breathing, he shrugged, not mincing words, – but the dead bodies are stored in freezers.
Maxine turned pale, and swayed, but didn't fall.
They had to wait until dawn, when rust and blood began painting the horizon in the east. The local pack arrived with that first stronger light, walking in the middle of the street, completely in the open. A woman with fair hair, dressed in white led the

considerable delegation. The two even-numbered groups faced each other, like broken mirrors. Damon and the woman split from their groups, met at center of each half moon. The space between them was about five steps.

– You're not from around here. She spoke with a voice not really resembling a voice. – What is your errand?

Damon spoke lousy Italian. Dominic translated.

– We're just passing through, Damon replied in English. He signed for Dominic not to translate. – If we can make a favorable trade, we will do that, though.

One behind the woman started translating his words. The woman stopped him with an irritated gesture.

– We have lots of stuff and goods available for trade, she continued in Italian, – if you can pay.

– We can make payment in several ways.

– Money is quite satisfactory, she stated. – If it is the right kind. So, what is your pleasure? Meat? We have lots of meat available…

The sick glow in her eyes and twisted smile told him that she knew that they knew what she was talking about.

– We're vegetarians, he said casually, very casually. – We would be very pleased if you have fruit and vegetables. And fuel. We definitely need fuel.

He couldn't keep up the pretense completely. His seething rage did show. The need for expressing that and the very necessary restraint warred within him. He watched her with vigilance and she watched him with an eerie expression in her eyes, as if she didn't really look at him at all.

She didn't really resemble her at all, being smaller, darker and more ordinary, but it dawned on Damon that she reminded him of Lisbeth Kaspersen.

– It looks like you've done okay for yourselves, she challenged him. – We can use people like you.

She suddenly spoke English, in a deliberately patronizing tone.

– We thank you so much for your kind offer, Terrill said kindly. – But like I said: we're only passing through.

– What keeps us from just take what we desire? She wondered, still with the dead voice.

Terrill didn't say anything. He waited and listened, scouting with his ears for unrest among his people. There wasn't any.

– I asked you a question, she flared.

– That one is easy to answer: *we* keep you.

The morning's ugly light fell over the assembly. The holes in streets and buildings, general damage turned distinct, glaring in everybody's eyes. The stone desert decay could no longer hide itself. The negotiations, stalled in the twilight of the night ended with agreement.

– They want to take us on, don't they? Renate whispered. – Want it as much as we want to take on them?

Replying was unnecessary. One look at the other group revealed the hunger, the bloodthirst in the pale woman and her followers.

– Both groups will lose if there is a confrontation, Renate kept pondering to herself, – but we still want to fight.

– Know that you've been given excellent terms, the pale woman stated eventually. – Perhaps we should have gathered the city against you and treated you like the trespassers you are?

– If you need to consult with your king or queen, that's your damn problem, Damon snarled at her. – We will wait until sunset, not a second longer.

She fumed and boiled, but kept herself in check. The completely insane expression in the watery eyes didn't turn into action. She turned abruptly and left. Her horde followed her. It didn't seem like they moved very fast, but it wasn't that long before the travelers imagined that the city had swallowed them.

Like it would swallow everybody staying too long.

The Children of the Midnight Fire couldn't rest. They slept in shifts. It was unusual for them to not sleep during the day. All sleep became turbulent. Damon couldn't sleep for a second. The nightmares about death and destruction returned and he experienced them every time he closed his eyes.

Every thought, every act, every drop or blood.

The others shared his turmoil, he knew that, somehow, and it comforted him somewhat.

– They will learn, Rawlins told him, – like you have, that uncontrollable, stormy emotions mirror those vibrating in the Earth itself.

That didn't quite sound like Rawlins, like his usual, sardonic voice. Damon shook his head in irritation.

– Our potential, brief trade partners don't make haste, Jerry said with a nervous twitch of his mouth.

It dragged on. The travelers became more and more edgy.

– Relax, Terrill told them. – Enjoy it!

And they stared incredulous at him.

– A devil-may-care attitude is always an advantage and joy, he stressed, – and even more so these nights.

They nodded to themselves, with a distinct, stronger clarity in their eyes.

– That makes sense, Vladek nodded. – It actually, definitely makes sense.

– Take to heart that we listen to your words, Yola told Damon, understanding him so well. – That we're not merely following the leader.

The local traders showed up well before sunset. The woman's «henchman» led the group, now. She didn't show herself at all.

– You're heading north? He spat casually.

– Isn't everybody these days?

Damon shrugged.

– Well, I would stay away from Switzerland, if I were you. The sick, fever-hot eyes didn't leave Damon. – According to our reports it is not a healthy place to visit. They know how to treat intruders there.

– Thanks for the info, Damon thanked him. – We appreciate it.

It came out garbled, as if he was choking on something.

They had no intention of passing through Switzerland, anyway, way too close to France as it was.

The trade ended quickly, accompanied by more snarls and ugly stares.

– It doesn't matter if he was telling the truth or not, right? Yola said.

It was a rhetorical question.

The trade ended. The other part pulled back, returned to the backstreets and alleys. The Children of the Midnight Fire remained, scouting for enemies at every turn.

– We're ready, André approached Terrill.

– Let's leave.

Damon turned and headed for the bus.

They didn't hurry, but didn't waste many seconds either. The bus engine started easily, its thunder drowning in the roar of all the bikes. The caravan continued on its crooked journey north. They left Turin towards the east. Never-resting eyes studied the surroundings. Muscles tightened inevitably for every new building, every new potential hideout they passed. Hands touched cold steel and handles. Finally, after lots of sweating and hammering hearts they reached the main road towards Milan and dared to relax somewhat.

Traffic moved smoothly, like it had done all the way from Marseille. There weren't that many vehicles on the road and no one cared about speed limits anymore. They encountered the occasional body or heaps of bodies. Bottlenecks of wrecks blocked their path now and then. It didn't delay them significantly.

But the darkness, when it came did. Working road lights had been scarce for some time. Now, they turned out to be non-existing. They stopped at a kind of guesthouse well before the light vanished completely. Sentries had been posted around the house and the parking lot. Both they and their shotguns were quite distinct.

– There's no peace, is there, Maxine said. – No matter where we go.

That was yet another rhetorical question. Her fellow travelers didn't reply to her and thereby they did.

The parking lot was practically free of vehicles. Perhaps that was why a smiling man that was probably the host welcomed them.

– So, how is business? André wondered casually. – It's probably a slow season, huh?

– Slow indeed, the host replied. – Most people choose motorbikes as transport these days and most people are leaving Italy and traveling north. I have relatives in Germany. We used to be Germans here, you know. Perhaps I will go north myself.

The employees acted nice. Everything seemed… safe. The travelers remained alert. It had become second nature to them by now.

Jerry, a part of an exploratory group consisting of one third of them returned from upstairs.

– They have real beds here, he said with a dreamy expression in his eyes. – How nice is that? How long is it since we have slept in real beds?

– Not long, Maeve said casually.

It just felt like it was.

– Three groups, Damon instructed them. – One third will sleep, another will guard the equipment outside and the rest will eat. At any time we will follow this method of conduct.

He spoke a little haltingly, his voice a little strange, as if he pulled something from memory, from the deepest possible memory.

They saw his frown, the certainty that not even this satisfied his safety concerns, his paranoia.

When one third sat down by the table to eat, one half of them waited while the other half tested the food, in order to see if it was *edible*. Half of the group set to sleep opened their windows wide. The other closed them tight. The group outside spread out and made it unlikely that they would be taken by surprise. There was constant contact between the groups.

– Paranoia is good, André said pleased. – The question, the way I see it is rather whether or not we're sufficiently paranoid, not if we're overdoing it.

– I don't know if I am really hungry much, Maxine said to Terrill.

– You are very much hungry, he stated with conviction.

She started eating, started feeding and devoured three helpings more than usual. The others looked bemused at her. She reddened.

– I recall my time at the diet *institute,* she giggled. – Wondering what my skinny «friends» there would think. I know that perfectly well, of course and I don't care!

She returned Damon's intense stare and a different kind of hunger rose within her.

Not even during the most extreme couplings then and later that night did the travelers on guard duty loose their focus. The loud sounds and moans did distract them, but didn't deter them.

Terrill shared his good mood with them all when they breathed the hot, but fresh morning air. There had been no incidents, no overt threats to their life and health. The dreams had haunted him this night as well. He had slept well, awake with closed eyes.

Maxine glowed that much stronger this morning. She jumped on the bike on his right, her eyes filled with mischief. They returned to the highway. She was the first speeding up. The roar from the engine and her savage, joy-filled howl mixed and sounded like one sound in the others' ears. Damon smiled and speeded up, joining her in front. Everybody replied to her howl with their own.

The sky had darkened behind them, on both sides and in front of the travelers. And when the sun, on rare occasions showed its pale face they made sure the shades covered their eyes. The eternal road stretched out ahead. They kept racing forward.

They passed Milan to the north, well outside its gates. They avoided cities as much as possible. Led by the Storm Child the children of the storm followed Italy's northern road east, passing Bergamo and Brescia to Verona, passing the sickening garbage heap once called Lake Garda.

By Verona they turned north. Everybody stopped by a sign saying INNSBRU. The two last letters of the sign had been *removed* by what was probably a hail of bullets. Terrill smiled in a way surpassing devil-may-care. They all saw it and joined him.

North? He struck out a hand. The engines of fifty-three bikes and one bus responded as one.

Something changed around them as they traveled further north. After Verona non-motorized movement changed from being the occasional to a common occurrence. People used bicycles, used their legs and wagons pulled by horses and bulls. Animals, wagons and people carried a heavy burden. No one moved south anymore. Both lanes on the dusty road were used for north-going traffic, on the rising terrain, towards the tall mountains, on the highway to Innsbruck. A caravan traveled north. Desperate people that had hardly experienced desperation before used any available method in their zeal to head north, fleeing from the seething, rising heat, the powerful storms. It headed slowly, hesitatingly north, a caravan unlike any other in human history.

++

The mountains towered above him but didn't weigh him down.
– Something is waiting for me up there, he said aloud, speaking to himself, not even to Rawlins.
The others didn't hear him, of course. He hardly heard himself in the infernal noise.
Impatience tore at him and only the common sense still prevalent kept him from attempting best speed, fully aware that the fuel and the engine would burn itself out quickly with such a brutal act.
The desert crawled north and mankind fled in its path, on the road with sharp turns and steep rise. The mountains, they looked majestic again, they seemed eternal again. The eyes his met confirmed that, if nothing else did.
He saw dull eyes, packs of people striving on, pulling heavy «assets» behind them, while staring at the world with confused gazes.
The tribe took a break at what had been a designated resting area, a small pocket on the right side of the road. They watched those still not letting go of their possessions with a bemusement that was hard to hold back.
– I wonder about them. Yola shook her head. – I wonder if they will ever understand anything, anything at all.
Then they were on the road again, the break experienced as brief and shallow.
The short, withered grass followed them upwards. The terrain changed, but the drought prevailed. The dust, seemingly, eerily lighter than air, whirled up from the dry soil far from any obvious influence and mixed with the exhaust. The Storm made itself felt, even when there was no wind.
Most of the houses along the road had long since been abandoned. Only a few still had old or new tenants. They had been excavated and emptied for valuables like old tombs countless times. All of them more than resembled ruins already. Both new and old tenants gawked at the world with fearful, distrustful eyes. Damon froze lightly down his spine in the white hot sunshine.
Something happened somewhere ahead. His attention was slowly drawn to it. Not long after that lots of people rushed towards them, in the *wrong* direction and it was visible, stark fear in the wild stares he caught. There was no need for him to give any kind of signal. All the motorbikes and the bus stopped just seconds after he had done so.
The wave of inverted refugees mostly stayed away from them. Anxious glances were cast in their direction.
– They can't tell if the greatest danger is behind or ahead of them, Maxine chuckled.
A man, fairly relaxed shouted two or three sentences as he rushed by.
– Two groups are firing at each other, Dominic translated, – And at anything else that moves.
Terrill nodded. He had understood the basics.
It wasn't that hard.
Everything was chaos and confusion as always. He didn't mind, but still strived to ignore it, to think and act past it.
– There is a part of me that do want to keep moving straight forward, he said, – to not give an inch, but that would be…
They looked at him with trust in their eyes, confident he would make the right decision.

– To be mixed up in that melee would be foolish, wouldn't it…
It was a rhetorical question, but he still asked for their opinion.
– There must be an alternative route somewhere, Yola said, – even if we have to drive offroad for a while.
– We don't know how extensive the fighting is, André said, clearly worried. – We lack crucial information. To go straight through might be easier, where we have the biggest chance of survival.
– Everything is exploding down here, Yola said, more anxious than Terrill had ever seen her. – We need to move on and we need to do it fast.
He remained unconvinced. While they stood there, considering their options, they spotted a woman approaching them, doing so deliberately, without the arbitrary movement of the others. They studied her like one creature, even as they never stopped moving their eyes back and forth in the terrain.
She knelt in the dust before Terrill. That told them something about her. They weren't certain of what.
Her head was bent forward, her eyes lowered. She waited patiently.
– We're neither masters nor slaves here, he snarled. – We've put that behind us.
The intensity in his voice surprised the others.
She rose. The eyes didn't focus. They couldn't decide whether or not she was breathing.
– I must be strong, she said hoarsely. – I know that.
Nobody spoke. They studied her and waited.
– My name is Irena and I have grown up here. This has been a place of unrest for quite some time. I know a place where people meet… a neutral place, where you can relax and have a nice time until morning. The night is unsafe in these parts, especially for strangers…
– And what do you want, Irena? Terrill asked softly.
– I want to get OUT of here, she exclaimed abruptly and fiercely. – Let me join you. I'm smart and cunning and will contribute to the tribe's survival. I will follow your laws, become one of you.
Terrill glanced casually at the others.
– I don't doubt her words, Yola said. – She has already found out what makes us tick. She is a sly bitch.
– She's a cutie, André shrugged.
Terrill saw no strong objections in the eyes he met.
– Sit behind me, he instructed the girl.
He sat down on the bike and she didn't hesitate to join him. On the contrary. She made a point of holding on to him, even before he had started driving.
They turned off from the main road, still on their way to the mountains, but taking an eastern detour. Irena quickly convinced them that she was on the level. She truly knew the area, perhaps too well. Damon signaled André, imposing on him the importance of being on guard. The Frenchman sent him an indignant look.
She stopped distracting him, evidently sensing how riled up he was, showing her worth without showing it, so to speak. The sly bitch, like everybody present had learned early what life was about.
Very good.
She did indeed belong with them.

Withered forest turned slightly green. Dusty tarmac turned to gravel. The noise led them to the right place. Somehow it overwhelmed the roar of the bikes in their mind. They glimpsed electric light between the trees. The alley of the deciduous forest broadened to a tarmac-covered half-full parking lot. A large building towered over the parked vehicles. There were no signs of guards anywhere. The people staying outdoors basically ignored the newcomers. Through a large window that by a miracle was still undamaged, they could watch the dance and the drinking and the life inside, all of it quite formidable.

They parked between the building and the withered woods. The roar of the engines faded slowly. Everybody stepped off the bikes and left the bus.

– Looks like a school, Vladek remarked.

– It used to be one, Irena willingly explained. – They use it for better things, now.

– The road seems kind of incomplete…

– You can follow the remains of the old road past the turn over there, she said sweet and sour. – It vanishes into a giant *hole*.

Only sixteen remained by the bikes and bus. Fifty entered the building, fifty more to make the temperature rise further in the already beyond scorching hall. Damon noticed that body heat had made steam cover some open windows. The moment they stepped inside the heat seemed to rise a hundredfold.

– Everything is… hot here, Maxine said, not really whispering, as that would have made it impossible for the others to hear her. – I'm not only talking about the physical heat, even if that is tangible as well, but… more. This place… everything has been… discarded here, in both and good ways.

Sweat kept flowing. It didn't matter whether or not they stood still or moved.

Her words made them nod, giving them a good feeling inside.

The electricity supply, far from being even or in any way reliable, disappeared and reappeared in an impossible-to-discern pattern. All lamps glowed with reduced effect. Sometimes they blinked and it could last for seconds. It generated a ghastly and ghostly mood in the hall.

The speakers spat indistinct, unidentifiable noise. Nobody listened to it, but danced to music only they could hear.

The bar reached almost along one wall. Somebody had put up a black blanket on that wall. Damon imagined there was nothing behind it, that eternity began right there.

The mood encroached itself on them, or from them to their surroundings. Damon studied Yola, Maxine, Irena and André in turn and the fire seemed to become something tangible, something to touch, more, something touching them, here, now, tonight, at one of civilization's last stands before it was discontinued. Damon smiled energetically to Maxine and she returned it with a radiant glow.

On a sign above the bar it said in English:

HELLHOLE BAR

ALL LIQUOR IS GUARANTEED THREE DAYS OLD

– A bold statement, Robert remarked. – And most certainly a blatant lie…

He walked to the bar and had his first of many drinks that night. They watched as it hit him, as it seemed to shake him apart. Damon and Maxine's grin turned even more pronounced.

Somebody kicked the already derelict stereo-equipment. What happened then was practically a living miracle. The speakers started producing great sound.

And that was the start of it, the moment they later easily identified when everything started *ungluing*.

Maxine started dancing. She began dancing. What she did afterwards nobody could quite explain or categorize. Terrill closed his eyes and envisioned an opening flower. He walked to her, spreading his wings. Irena followed them both and the three of them began dancing tight and intimate.

– Yes, you made the right decision joining us. Maxine kissed her fast and hard on the lips. – With us you will find everything you will ever desire.

She waved to the others.

– C'mon, all of you, she cried, – let's have fun, enjoy ourselves so much that flesh falls off the bones.

Her crazy laughter echoed between them.

– She didn't specify which bones, Robert noted and then he joined her, and joined in on the laughter.

They all did, all of them and also others drawn to her like the moth to the light… or the fire.

She danced so well that no one managed to keep up with her, so most just gave it up. They stood there and enjoyed the view, the both fiery and «angelic» display - humanity's contradictions in one creature.

– I've never seen anyone dance Kacha like that before, one whispered.

Damon had, in Jotunheim many years ago.

– I saw her in Marseille, Vladek said with wonder in his voice, – but it looked nothing like this.

– We started dancing it when the oppression turned beyond cruel and inhuman, Irena said. – They could never stop that, stop nature itself from expressing itself.

It was as if many of those watching the girl and the dance couldn't even stand watching, but had to avert their eyes.

Kasha and its accompanying music had been banned in major parts of the world, to no avail.

Maxine Leary liberated herself from the chains she had allowed others to put on her, and thereby, by her very presence she also liberated many others. They reached for their dignity, their humanity and here, at the frontier of human experience they found their first, bigger pieces.

Everybody… was letting go. That was more evident tonight than on any previous night. There was a tangible quality in the air those present couldn't help but notice.

Damon and Irena and lots and lots of others joined dance incarnated there on the slippery floor.

André followed his friend and the many strangers with his eyes while they danced and clapped their hands, as they stretched their hands above their head and reached for the ceiling, the very sky above. He sat down on one of the many available barstools.

– Quiet night? He said to one of the bartenders.

– The wildest so far. The man shook his head. – Everything will blow up soon in these parts, mark my words.
– I see what you mean. André nodded to himself.
– I'm considering moving north, the man said, suddenly very talkative. – Get my own place. It isn't like it was here or anywhere. There is no place here one can settle down and expect to be left in peace.
He visibly brightened.
– I love it! Damn it if I don't enjoy my ass off. It's the first time I can remember that I look forward to waking up in the morning.
He shook his head again, evidently very much aware of the apparent contradictions in his own statements.
– Nights are wild here?
– They most certainly are, and getting wilder. I was convinced it had reached a boiling point last night. That didn't happen, so I guess there is statistic evidence to claim that it won't happen tonight either.
André took the hint and gave him a glance.
– That is correct. I worked and strived at an opinion poll institute. It was nothing more than a dead turkey at the end. Eventually there was no one interested in what we had to offer. I was pretty depressed for a while, but suddenly, from one boring moment to the next I realized that this was the best that had ever happened to me. After that I changed. I no longer let things happen to me. I make them happen!
It trickled and flowed inside André, as he nodded to himself. That had been his self-imposed problem as well. He had allowed things to happen to him, fallen asleep and needed a rather brutal wake up call. Never again!
He let his eyes move back and forth in the hall, seeing many colors and cultures, all ages.
– People throw old rules out the window, the talkative bartender kept going. – One here, many there. The lid on the boiling kettle has been pushed down for so long. The explosion has to be violent.
A large, muscular man from another clan put a hand on Maxine's shoulder and said something. She smiled and shook her head. He insisted and turned intrusive. She crouched slightly and struck him down. He did everything he could to stop her, but was helpless to prevent her onslaught. She moved much faster than he did and with far more skill.
– You were smiling, he said, actually sounding offended through the mouth filled with blood.
– You mean one can't say no in a nice way? She wondered, a little hurt.
She helped him up. The others had stopped dancing, but did nothing to interfere. He mumbled something and walked away. None of the Children of the Midnight Fire laughed. Not even Irena. She did what they did. Even though she had to push a hand at the mouth she kept it inside.
Others didn't show such restraint. Some spectators laughed very loud. But in spite of some poisonous comments the situation didn't deteriorate then. Everybody stayed with their group and a kind of calm settled in the hall.
– We had so much fun all of us, Irena said with disappointment in her voice.
– Let it go, Damon shrugged. – The night is still young.

André waited ten, fifteen minutes before pulling Yola and Vladek aside.
– Listen up, he told them. – I want you to seek out everybody. Be discreet. Tell them that the trouble will begin shortly. Make sure they're ready.
Yola looked like she wanted to protest, but then she nodded.
Maxine leaned her head against Damon's shoulder while they danced, while they turned round and round. Quieter music shivered in the air, now. She saw only indistinct spots of color as they moved.
– There is something I can't grasp, she said frustrated. – Sometimes I feel like I have it right in front of me, but every time I reach for it, it slips away.
– That is frustrating, he agreed.
He stared above her, at a distant point far beyond this place.
The sound turned muddy again. Another kick. The stereo equipment groaned and gritted its teeth in protest, before turning completely silent. There was no longer any sound at all. The woman who had done the previous kicking tried again. She started breaking the black box in front of her apart, not taking no for an answer. She kept attacking the dead thing, until it resembled nothing but a heap of junk.
A man approached her with a hopeful grin. She kicked the crap out of him with a pleased chuckle.
It took only a few more kicks before he stopped moving. She walked to a table and joined her friends there.
– That was all? A giant of a man complained aloud. – I kind of expected more, you know, more active participation.
– People are too busy watching the entertainment to fight, his friend comforted him.
– Too fucking hot!
The giant waved a hand the size of a bear paw in front of his face.
Hot! Maxine thought feverishly.
Everything had been opened wide, every possible window and opening.
– O'Pluto, dance with me again.
She made a pirouette and stopped before Damon, displaying herself to him.
– It's funny, isn't it? She understood when he smiled that he understood what she meant, what stirred her thoughts. – Human civilization has for millennia spoken about a mythic Kingdom of Death and then we've always been born into it. It's everywhere around us.
– The biblical Hell got nothing on this heat, she groaned. – It should have been paralyzing, but sweet, little me feels such a great vitality, one making me downright dizzy.
He grabbed her and pulled her close, kissing her hard, almost brutally. She released a happy sound, a howl of savage delight and returned as much as she received. Nails, fingers bent like claws rubbed the wolf skin. She felt how sweat spread from the spot on her back, from the cleft between her breasts. With a teasing smile she began unbuttoning her shirt all the way to the belly button. Then she leaned backwards, allowing him and everybody else close enough to enjoy the sight.
They were dancing, front to front, cheek to cheek, isolating themselves from their surroundings.
– Do I enjoy displaying myself? She wondered. – Am I ready to accept possibly consequences of that?

He didn't respond, but just studied her. The mere sight of her, of her closeness threatened to overwhelm him.

– Of course I enjoy it, she answered her own query. – But that's not the true main issue. The freedom, the devil-may-care, the natural desires ruling us all is what's important… if I should bother to label something so self-evident… so precious.

The thrill of the moment rushed through him.

A whisper, a draft in the air, where nothing such existed distracted them.

A group of approximately twenty men and women walked through the open doors. With the exception of each of them wearing a loincloth everybody roamed around nude.

– They call themselves quite simply «The Wolves», André's old friend the bartender informed him. – Their arrival will do it for sure.

He removed his apron and sat course for the stairs.

– Where are you going? André asked and held up his empty glass.

– I'm packing. It just became clear to me that the remaining lifespan of this place has become frighteningly short.

– There's no rush, is there? André said relaxed. – Give me another drink at least.

It didn't take long, not long at all before the wolf pack sniffed its way to Damon. He watched as the play, with its inevitable result unfolded. They would have circled him, terrorized him with patronizing stares and small, teasing pushes and a thousand small movements, if he, as if by magick hadn't been surrounded by his fellow tribe members.

He waved them aside, standing face to face with the female and male leading the wolf pack.

– We have unsettled matters?

They kept staring at him. He noticed stains of blood on their skin. But they had clearly cleaned themselves recently, an unusual act in an area where most of the usable water was consumed.

– You're wearing a wolf's clothing, but you're not a wolf.

He perceived her words as a snarl from a well-formed snout.

The female wolf had hair past her shoulders, and yellowish, shimmering eyes. She was half a head taller than her mate, almost as tall as Damon himself. A large scar dominated her face, but Damon found her immensely attractive and didn't hide his interest in any way.

– The truth is that I found it, he said casually. – I felt that it fit me, that it was *me*. I still do. If I should give you a piece of my mind, and I have the habit of doing that, I would never kill a wolf, not for the skin or any other reason… unless it attacked me first.

He didn't use the same challenging tone she had used, but he didn't give an inch. And she didn't fail to notice that.

– Perhaps you're the right person to wear it, she snorted. – We shall see.

She spoke English with a strange, humming accent. He couldn't place it. She had clearly not grown up in Italy.

– I'm Gwendolyn.

She stared into his black eyes and he noted that she shook lightly.

– I'm Damon.

She nodded to herself and pulled the lead wolf away. He sent Terrill a cold stare, but didn't seem jealous. They and the rest of the pack spread across the hall and turned into a part of the general background. He imagined that they were fading away before his eyes. They seemed far more dangerous than their four-legged brethren. Damon chuckled pleased and with his devil-may-care attitude.

– So wild and so beautiful, Maxine whispered with admiration in her voice. – Caution is clearly mandated in their presence.

He laughed aloud.

– We would have to be quite stupid to not show caution.

– I realize now what I didn't earlier, she said. – We're the Children of the Midnight Fire. We've waited for midnight to come like the salmon swimming up the river to spawn. We're on our way home.

For just a moment there her words sounded like an unpleasant echo of Victor Russel's in his ears. He let it go.

She was right.

– That sounds quite reasonable, he declared.

She kissed him and bravely pushed her tongue into his mouth, playing with his tongue.

A man threw himself from the banister on the second floor. People chuckled and made an effort to avoid being hit by the falling body. Only pure luck or a string of coincidences placed his pals close enough so they could catch him.

The mood in the hall, in the building, in the house of the Earth exploded. Several events happening more or less simultaneously made it that more potent.

The wolves harassed the man that Maxine had rejected. They didn't threaten him openly in a healthy respect for his very present clan, but they teased him ruthlessly. Terrill made Maxine aware of what was happening. Irena pulled closer to them both.

– They seek their prey in sly and ruthless ways, she mused with a look both cold and hot. – It doesn't have to be the most obvious target.

– Wait always the unexpected, Damon told her. – That has always been one of the rules I live by. One coming for you is always lurking in the shadows. Lightning can strike from a blue sky.

– That's deep and fundamentally brutal. She glanced at him with lowered eyelashes. – I love it!

André put down his empty glass. He observed how the bartender, several of the bartenders pulled back towards the stairs before he turned his full attention at the stage unfolding before him.

Nothing was heard, nothing was seen, but fast movements all over the hall whirled the air. She who had crushed the stereo smashed a chair on the head of a random man walking past her. No one reacted or even paid attention much. A man poured liquor on the bar and set it on fire. His wicked stare discouraged everyone set to involve themselves. The smoke spread. The dim lighting turned even more pronounced.

– Everybody outside has armed themselves. Vladek slid up discreetly behind André. – We're ready!

– Excellent! André smirked. – Let's relax and enjoy life then.

The two of them and everybody in the tribe present in the hall hurried to Damon's side, doing so just in time.

A delegation approached the Children of the Midnight Fire, very serious-minded, very

grim.
– My friend wishes to have a dance with you, the spokesman said to Maxine.
– Piss off! Maxine responded promptly.
– I don't see your friend, André added with potent sarcasm.
– Only one dance, the man said, polite beyond words.
– Fetch your friend and I will be happy to give him my personal response, Maxine challenged.
– This isn't just about him anymore. The leader gestured, including all the between fifty and sixty bloodthirsty companions behind him. – His honor has been sullied and that reflects badly on us all.
– Honor? André chuckled darkly. – That's ridiculous!
The man reddened.
– There's no need to throw insults here, he said, still somewhat calm. – We're all adults here, right?
– Let's be adults then, Damon Terrill raged at him. – There's no way in hell we'll stand for any type of infantile gang mentality. The sooner you get that beaten into your thick skull the better.
And before anybody could act or react he had struck the man in front of him to the ground. He jumped and kicked the woman by the man's side on the jaw. She dropped to the floor as well. The others stared shocked at him.
– C'mon, let's kick their ass, he shouted, waving to his fellow tribe members with badly concealed expectation.
A fist struck his forehead, just as he charged forward. He shook it off and struck down his third opponent. The two groups that afterwards would be unable to explain their disagreement collided like two immutable forces with wild howls and brutal joy. The fight started with them, but spread quickly to the entire hall, and also outside, becoming an all against all melee. It spread everywhere, to the deepest basement, the tallest tower.
The giant who had complained so loud was struck several times while having a drink. He scratched his jaw and brightened. The next in line charging him was given a brutal swing and sent straight into the mirror. The world broke in a thousand pieces.
Terrill could taste the blood in his mouth. He couldn't recall being struck, but the taste of dawn and dusk swelled within. An indistinct figure aimed for him with a broken table leg. A jaw entered his focus for a tiny moment. He struck it, felt the abrupt contact, and it vanished. A memory of a twisted, swollen face burned itself on his retina.
He never saw it coming, the fist from behind. His vision cleared. He saw a female wolf. She cut the throat of an opponent. The deep-red sludge decorated the floor and all the figures near the dead man. Crouched between a whirl of feet he glimpsed the alpha male wolf. There was a snarl, a challenge and the big man attacked his crouching opponent. Damon kicked out with his foot. A stiff sole hit something hard, something soft. The snarling creature rose in the air and disappeared. Damon fought himself back on his feet, striking out with his wings. It hurt when his fists hit mouths and jaws and heads and every other body part. He grinned pleased.
Suddenly he and André froze face to face. They suppressed the urge to strike at the other, at anyone close by.
– It's time for us to end our part in this carnival, Damon shouted as loud as he possibly

could. – Give the signal.

André fired the signal gun. Its projectile hit the ceiling and exploded in violet light.

Just in the nick of time. They were pushed down and away from each other in a row of cursing and swearing fighters. Damon caught the sight of Yola and her thumbs up as she made her way to the exit right before the tidal wave pulled him away. He glimpsed Irena just as she was struck down. Vladek and several other unfortunate warriors decorated the floor with flesh and blood. They had to get out soon, before there would be too many to carry, before there were any dead bodies.

Fear overwhelmed him briefly, before the exuberance returned. He laughed insanely while assaulting two big bruisers. They pulled back and he struck them down easily enough.

Suddenly, before he knew it, he was first in line of those facing the giant. The enormous man opened another bottle. He seemed totally unfazed by the spectacle surrounding him. Damon bet everything he had on a solid kick and hit the rock exactly where he was supposed to, on the side of the head. There was no visible reaction, except a giant fist chasing Damon's head. He avoided it with a margin call that only made him see sparks.

When he shook his head he added double vision to his woes.

The retreat was blocked by enraged combatants. The road forward was definitely blocked. There was no easy way to any of the sides. Without making a conscious decision he threw himself down on the bloodstained, slippery floor and slid past the unmoving rock. He felt the wind of another giant hand aiming for him that narrowly missed.

His head groaned THUD THUD THUD somewhere close to his ears, but he gained time to think and consider his options. Irena remained where she had fallen. She moaned in pain when he grabbed her and lifted her up, placing her on his shoulder. She didn't wake up. He drew his gun and fired at the ceiling. Vladek, stumbling, carried Robert. Others also carried one unmoving figure each. They pulled close and rushed outside through a narrow, transitory opening, one closing in seconds.

– Is this everybody? Damon asked with a piercing shout. – I mean absolutely every single one?

He received eager nods and assurances from those around him.

It made him feel good, better than good. He was laughing all the way to the bus and the bikes, and the others, those still conscious joined in.

People flowed out of the burning building. Flames surrounded the entirety of it as they watched. They had to leave one bike behind, since there was no one able to ride it. The bikes roared and started rolling across the parking lot. The bus began moving while the door was still open. A man jumped aboard in the nick of time. They recognized one of the bartenders.

– My name is Paolo, he grinned, exposing his rows of white teeth. – I would appreciate it if I could catch a ride… for a while.

Maxine sat in a chair with a cloth pressed at her head. Except for Dominic at the wheel, she was the only one on the bus more or less unscathed and fully conscious. She nodded graciously.

The nomadic tribe traveled further north.

CHAPTER TWELVE

Flames surrounded them long before they emerged from the forest. Dry wood everywhere dissolved in fire in a matter of minutes. Other people also riding their machines escaped the inferno right before or after those calling themselves Children of the Midnight Fire. It seemed as if something… broke, and it was nothing like a dam, but a natural, unnatural barrier.

– What a blast! Vladek shouted.

He rode the bike standing, with both hands raised above his head. The others didn't hear him above the inferno of noise and deafening silence, of course. On a different level, independent of physical realities he knew they heard him.

The fire spread so fast that those fleeing from it feared it reached for them, and that it never would give up its chase. They fought on, beyond determination and willpower. Tongues of flame reached across the road behind them. A few embers hit the bushes on the opposite side… a few sparks and everything exploded in an ocean of energy. They saw houses catch fire and burn like tiny models made of matches.

The inferno devoured the valley, meter by meter, second by second. Those not aided by motorized vehicles succumbed quickly to the brutal forces chasing their tail.

They were once more alone, now, those that had started together from Marseille. The tribe stopped briefly and cast their attention back at the valley. Even from such a vast distance the flames seemed to threaten them, to hiss right by their ears.

Other groups had moved on quickly, not looking back for a second, but they did, facing head-on the past on a collision course with the present.

– Nature's detergent, Yola mumbled.

– Yes, but there won't be much more than ashes stemming from this, Terrill said. – It won't rain here in a long time.

After roars and confusion weren't peace, but an ominous silence, a strife of the soul threatening to consume them.

– Kali Yuga.

André didn't realize he had said it aloud until he noticed the others' reaction.

– What did you say? Yola blinked stunned.

– Kali Yuga, interpreted *loosely* by that particular author as the Age of Man, when the world ends in a storm of ice and fire. I read it in a book once. It fits!

– You… read a book?

– In a moment of weakness, he admitted.

– Something is happening aside from the obvious, Damon said, – a slow, abrupt change, fish and bird, flesh and spirit.

He blinked and shook his head, in an effort to clear it. It didn't work.

The waken nightmares almost overwhelmed him, now. Keeping himself from closing his eyes was no use anymore.

The dead didn't stay dead, not to him. He saw them. They hissed at him. The loud whispers filled his ears and mind. Yola rubbed his back. It failed to comfort him.

– Every thought, every action, every single drop of blood.

He muttered to himself, unable to decide whether or not he spoke aloud.

Maxine examined him. He couldn't hide his pained expression. She didn't exactly behave like a professional nurse and normally that would have distracted him, dominated his thoughts and actions, but not now.

– The wound hasn't reopened, she reported in a sobering voice. – I would say you have recovered completely. You are clearly healthier and… more vital.

She blushed deeply.

– Your head injuries are superficial. She pulled herself together. – That is by the way true about all of us. The only danger is that we will run out of bandages if we do this often.

– So, what's wrong with me? He asked straightforward.

– I don't believe there's anything «wrong» with you, she replied promptly. – I'm not a medical doctor, but I don't think such an animal would have had a clue about what's happening with you either, not if he or she wanted to be honest.

Her words echoed within him, cast from wall to wall in his mind. The mountains fell behind them, rose in front of them. Damon's mood fell and rose with them.

Somewhere in the Alps there was something attracting and repulsing him, a presence, a sense of something close. Not farther away than a veil. The visions assaulted him with increasing frequency.

They saw more fires, hungry monsters feeding off the dry landscape. No one made an effort at putting them out. Some they experienced close up and personal. They fought themselves past them, from inferno to inferno, and struggled with the certainty that the Inferno would follow them wherever they went.

The road turned ever more inaccessible. Old wreckage and vehicles were fairly easy to remove, but the long queue grew ever longer the closer they came to the Austrian border.

At a turn where half of the road was gone Damon attacked the wreckage. He practically attacked it. The other tribe-members made no effort at stopping him, but let him rage on. He kept sweating profusely afterwards, when every obstacle had been removed, almost more than he had done during the hard work, not able to decide whether or not he felt more or less exhausted.

– I don't know what's happening to me, he mumbled. – If I'm cracking up or worse, if it can be any worse than it already is.

Maxine rubbed his cheek, comforting him as much as she was able.

The bus remained a problem. While the bikes easily bypassed every obstacle, the big and bulky bus met with ever bigger difficulties as they passed ever more abandoned buses and trucks. They realized the futility in holding on to it and abandoned it early one morning, packing what little they could on the bikes and moved on. The only stuff they kept that could be said to not be very useful was an old radio. They put completely new batteries in it and used it as their link to the world they moved through. More and more stations stopped broadcasting and those remaining turned more and more agitated as time raged by.

Traffic slowed down even more as they closed in on the Austrian border. There was only one direction, like it had been for a long time. Large vehicles blocked the road well before the entry to the Brenner Pass. Only bikes and people could go on. People began abandoning their vehicles and started walking with heavy burdens on their back. Some of them just sat down and remained there. A number of them put barrels in their mouths and pulled the trigger. It no longer visibly shocked the travelers. There was no visible reaction, except for people rushing forward and tearing guns from dead hands. Some bodies had been dead for so long that rigor mortis had set in. Axes and sharp blades were used to liberate weapons from pale skin.

They reached thirteen-hundred meters above sea level. Engine roars were dulled by the dots in the ears brought on by the high elevation. The Brenner Valley greeted them with white, blinding sunshine. They had to blink behind the shades, blink away salt and water and sun. Snow-free mountains surrounded them. There was no snow as far as their eyes could see, not even smack in the middle of what had been called winter. Temperature had probably fallen with a few degrees with the thousand meter elevation, they wouldn't rule that out, but hardly noticed any difference. The water they had stored in big tanks faded away fast. Envious eyes stared at the life-giving fluid making its way from the bottles to parched throats. All of them carried guns, now, even Irena and Paulo and others that had never fired anything. The village Brenner, or Brennero on the Italian side hardly seemed like a place where people lived anymore, but more like a gate to eternity ruled by hatred and intolerance.

The border station on the Italian side had been unmanned for a long time. No one had any interest in traveling south anymore. The Austrian nation, however still guarded its borders.

The special bridges leading major parts of the traffic above ground seemed to reach an infinite stretch forward. Several of the interconnecting points looked more than frail. The haze covering the valley made it look much bigger than it was.

Until a few weeks ago Austria had been ruled by a fascist government seeing itself as more than powerful enough to guard the nation against scum (and Italians) from the south, an assumption that had been more or less correct, until the nation and those ruling it had been devoured by their own ashes.

The soldiers, the few of them still guarding the station stood still and stared with hatred at the long line of people passing them. They were content to stop the destitute and the helpless, letting them feel the brunt of their anger.

Damon almost blacked out. Everybody stopped when he stopped. A man perished while howling on the ground. Damon bit his lip and blood covered his jaw. A portable DVD-player nearby started whining so loud that they had to cover their ears. He had no idea how many hours, how many days and nights they had spent on the road since the community house mass fighting. They had passed several cities of a certain size since then. At least he believed they had. It was all just a blur in his mind. He knew he was «safe». The others guarded him when he got his seizures. They did it right now.

The guards ignored him, pulled back into the shadows by the sheer sight of the Riders of the Thunder Road. They instead entertained themselves with a couple and their two children. The man crouched on the ground with blood flowing from a wound on his forehead. The woman was pushed at a wall while they pulled off her clothes. The guards were caught in Damon's staring, sticking eyes. They hesitated and backed off. The man, the woman and the children suddenly realized that they stood alone in front of the low toll building. Filled with uncertainly they steered their steps towards the bikers, until they, too, met Damon's eyes. They froze and turned, starting on the long, endless road ahead of them.

– I'm not sure why I cared. He shrugged. – The four will probably die soon anyway.

I'm not even sure if I cared.
His friends looked at him with sympathy in their eyes.
– You've given them yet another chance at survival, Dominic said. – That will have to be enough.
Damon waved, waved to his friends and fellow travelers. With loud shouts, faithful to the role they had chosen for themselves they raced into Austria.
The landscape didn't change much, not in the eyes of those traveling through it, but in truth the Austrian province Tyrol departed significantly from the low country of northern Italy. This land suffered from draught as well, more so day by day, hour by hour, but it was still fairly green. Forest had covered about forty percent of Austria around the turn of the century. Now, this percentage had grown to over fifty, close to sixty percent. Young trees grew ever higher on the mountainside. Damon, and also several of the others had traveled through here only a few years ago, and there was a significant, visible difference. Land higher up turned more fertile. Ever more of the valleys and the lower land suffered from draught. This was the Alps, and there was no winter to speak of anywhere.
Around a fire in the forest glen the flames danced in Damon Terrill's vision. He felt stronger in many ways, but his eyes turned swollen. His surroundings quite simply vanished around him, and he was unable to sleep. Or, as he suspected: he slept all the time, even if he moved and communicated normally.
– What do you see? A voice whispered close to him. – Tell Yola everything.
– I'm not certain I can express it in words…
– Make an effort! She insisted with admiration in her eyes.
– Smoke and dust… dance in the air before me. I look back and it doesn't resemble anything but ordinary smoke and dust. I blink to clear my vision, and for each new blink more and more of the road ahead of me disappears. Not in air and sand, but in a mist hidden in blood.
– Very poetic, André remarked.
– A brick isn't a brick, Yola declared. – What in daily speech is called subconscious is a mirror, everybody knows that.
She appeared to be slipping away, supplanted by Irena in his vision. He saw almost no movement just then, only strange, frozen images.
– You must teach me to shoot, Irena begged him. – You must!
He grabbed her, like a snake with its long fangs. It had to hurt the way he squeezed her arm. She made no effort at freeing herself but twisted her body closer to his.
– You guys are practicing at every opportunity…
– No, you must teach me. You!
She exposed her heavy breasts, offered herself to him, kissed him on the lips, pushed herself at the fire. He accepted her offering and devoured her. She changed to Maxine sometimes, Maxine that also wanted to be taught. He burned her, burned everybody. In his worst fever visions he imagined he saw Myriam… and Gerd… striving, suffering and dying.
In one of his few moments of clarity he sensed their journey the last few miles before Innsbruck. He saw the boiling river Inn, now and two, three and five years from now, mighty torrents reduced to tiny ponds. The bruise blackened on Irena's arm, while she smiled apologetically and died inch by inch in front of him. Two long rows of human

rivers, from the Brenner Pass in the south and the Arlberg Pass in the East became one, endless stream. To his inner eye this river shrunk as well.

– You seek the Strega, the wandering witch? The voice came to him from nowhere, in a tavern in Innsbruck. Paolo conversed with a colleague. – It is said she is hard to find, but not to those truly seeking her. It is said that she is traveling with a Circus and if I'm not very much mistaken, there is one such north of the city right now.

Outside the tavern a man and a woman had attacked them with fire-spitting guns. Several of them had been hit before the couple had been blown away in a hail of bullets.

– Was there a reason this time? One tribe member bitterly complained. – Is there rhyme or reason anywhere?

They never found out why the couple attacked them. No explanation ever presented itself.

That was all Damon remembered from Innsbruck.

– Impressive way of committing suicide. Vladek sat by the wayside with a bloody arm, while Dominic made yet another effort at bandaging his wound. – What stupid assholes!

A number of refugees pretty much remained in the large city, tired and broken, as the travelers moved on.

– Look at them, Irena said with contempt. – They don't realize that there's no long stop anywhere anymore.

Damon had stopped the tribe here without knowing why, but it was hardly for more than sniffing the air and take stock. He looked strong as he dismounted the bike, but the beyond pale skin and the swollen eyes told their own story. That was his last clear memory for a while. Everything just went away, down a maelstrom of fever visions and broken thoughts.

A woman sat by a fire and smiled to him. A vision, a mirage he knew the others couldn't see or sense. She sat around many fires, on many plains, in many forests. He started running towards her, but for every step, every jump he made she seemed farther away. She sat in the forest glen, but then she rose and walked inside the forest, deep within the vast cluster of swaying trees and chilly darkness. He broke branches and trees like matches in his hunt. The madness grew to a crescendo. He heard the worried cries of his friends. It mattered not at all compared to what waited ahead.

Death, death surrounded him.

There was a loud crack and the world turned upside down. He fell on his back, more than suspecting that his head had collided with a thick branch. He laughed insane while drifting into a darkness of pain and suffering.

– I can see the DEAD, he mumbled in despair, – like strains of night and fire.

His back pushed at a soft cushion. He writhed and turned in his unrest, practically striking out at everybody daring to approach, so exhausted that he was unable to stand. His fingers, his claws of night and fire scratched a hole in the very air. The thin veil of time and space was for a brief moment pushed aside. Demons reached for him. A young two-legged animal of his own species stood crouched over a warm, steaming body. A wail rose from his wide open mouth.

– A wave will always remain a wave, the soft female voice stated. – A river will always reach the sea. Natural streams can be delayed, not stopped.

So many streams had been delayed. Now, they were all joining into an ear-cracking roar. The Twilight Storm had come.

All windows had been opened wide. The heat could neither be stopped nor softened. And the cold? That would always be there as well.

Wide open eyes almost cracked the skull. A body braced itself and fell backwards. A mind descended into an uneasy sleep, one granting a break from the storm, but no rest.

++

He fell. He rose. He floated in an unending stream, one of life and death. Understanding came to him in flashes, quickly fading, only bits and pieces making sense at all.

Soft hands put a cup to his lips and he drank. He saw known and unknown people dancing. He felt the rhythm in the ground below his back. On misty heaths between the mountains, the two mountains with icecaps he was a spectator to the fight between the wolf and the eagle. Two mountains, truly one and the same. The eagle and the wolf joined and became one. He was no longer a spectator.

He rested on his back with open eyes and stared at the sky, at the stars. Two women, almost identical in appearance smiled down at him. Both wore sleeveless shirts. He noticed the green rope band they wore on their upper arm.

– Anya, he greeted one of them, before he knew what he would say.

– Do you guys know each other? The young girl said stunned.

– We know each other of old, the other said.

She who looked like an older sister of the other looked at him with a strange gleam on her face.

– I've never seen her before, Damon said, not confused like he was supposed to be.

– Nice to meet you, Damon. Anya took his hand. – This is Claire, my oldest daughter.

Claire, not that much older than him, nodded with a rigid expression in her face. So similar and not, mother and daughter kept studying him. Whatever Anya had that made her special, so very, very special revealed itself only as an echo in Claire, though.

The black hair framed the extraordinary face. She wore big, golden earrings. She dressed like a gypsy, but was clearly more than that limited description.

– You look like a fortuneteller, he stated stunned.

She chuckled. She had a beautiful laughter. He imagined he glimpsed tears in her eyes.

– Strega, she stressed. – I'm the witch you've traveled half around Europe to find.

She pulled up her right pant, revealing a remarkable mole, formed like a half moon. She pulled up his right pant and revealed the practically identical mole.

– We're born with the mark of the witch, she said. He swallowed hard. – We're few, but more than people realize. In another world, another reality there might be far more of us and we're probably significantly more powerful.

He studied her and the sense of familiarity grew stronger.

– No matter, she mused. – We must make do with what and who we are.

Her words… he didn't understand them on a conscious level, but they calmed him down and pleased him in a way that couldn't be denied.

The surroundings appeared to him. He was really resting on a bed in a tent. There were other beds with wounded and the recently dead. They hadn't been covered or anything, but he still knew.

– Welcome back to the physical world, she greeted him. – The Shadow World is very interesting and all, but it isn't a «place» you would want to stay.

He looked curious at her.
– Humans have, in good and bad ways created a shadow world beyond the one we can see and hear, she casually explained, as if she was telling him something he already knew. – Where we go when we dream and don't dream. We've given it countless names throughout time, thousands of labels, the same origin. It's more distant than the end of the world, closer than thought. It is there for all searchers. Most of today's humans ignore, deny its existence, just like we deny nature and our ancient contact with it. And we become hardly more than empty shells, walking dead unable to find our way. We suffer and don't realize, refuse to realize that we torture ourselves to death.
Her words kept soothing him.
A younger boy, also a child of the witch, slightly younger than Damon stuck his head into the tenth.
– They're getting impatient out there, he informed her.
– That's okay, Josh, she said gently. – Tell everybody that everything is alright.
Damon rested some more, alone, listening to the peace and vitality outside, until he, without effort rose to his full height. His limbs seemed a little stiff this time. His head was throbbing. But he felt fine.
Someone played the flute. Maxine joined in on guitar. He didn't doubt that he heard her play. She treated the strings completely different from any other he knew of. Her playing, the ghostly chords haunted you. He stepped out of the tent, into the forest, the night and knew that also haunted those finding themselves there.
He spotted familiar faces and also faces that seemed just as familiar, and it confused him, since it didn't make sense or immediate sense. In the glow from hungry and soft flames he imagined he saw beyond the general illusion of life, at what was or appeared hidden. A jolt rattled him.
It dawned on him that he felt… at home here. Not here, not this random place or time. But among the faces, the people surrounding him. He recalled a silver-haired woman dancing on a stage, at a place crowded with dust, dirt and decayed beams, and wondered if his father hadn't told him about such a place, an ancient, derelict house demolished many years before his birth.
– Silverhair? He said hoarsely.
She stood before him, probably a bit younger than Emmet, but more marked by life and death. Then she smiled and the entire face seemed to transform.
– I'm Lene, I'm Silverhair. She clutched his arm above the rope band. He automatically did the same with her arm. – It pleases us that you're feeling better, Terrill.
She stared strangely at him. He stared into eyes just as black as his own.
– I'm Damon, he stated.
Lene Brevik. Her warrant was shown on television, the «news», in the papers and every time one visited official Internet sites. They had hunted her for fifteen years and she remained at large, alive and free, more alive than ever.
More faces from warrants smiled at him. Kurt Mørch, Susan Palmer, Ilse Frost, Vidar Tofte, Colleen Bell… That was those he recognized, but he counted more than twenty wearing the green armband openly. Kurt and Susan were the only ones that had participated in the fabled battle of Gothenburg still alive. Kurt was one of the fifteen original members, but he always stayed more in the background compared to Lene and Susan.

Damon didn't spot his parents, but two others he didn't know that still made him react in a way. Two boys reminding him in unpleasant ways of Victor Russel stood behind Lene. Both were clearly his descendants. One of them was slightly older than Damon, with oriental features. And then there was a younger teenager that would certainly tower above most people in a few years time. Lene smiled deviously to Damon.

– These are William and Magnus, she presented.

He greeted them with an undefined sensation raging through him. Magnus had the same characteristic silver hair as his mother, but his eyes had an eerie greenish taint, one that removed him from Lene's calm and brought him closer to Victor Russel.

But it was William that first and foremost gave Damon Terrill a sense of both joy and sorrow. He didn't know why, but right now he didn't see it as very important either. The most important was the sense of belonging he felt with so many of those present. He found himself among likeminded people, among kindred souls. He wasn't alone anymore.

She they called Strega waited at the end of the line.

– You are She Who Dances in the Forest, he said startled.

She just smiled to him.

– My name is Anya Kerien, she said. – I'm one of the original fifteen, but for some reason or another I've never been put on warrants or in public records.

– She's our shadow-walker, Lene said lightly. – There is a reason for us naming her Strega.

– How come I knew your name? He asked Anya.

The surroundings seemed to fade away, even as they still stayed with the others. She and he found themselves alone in a misty landscape.

– Some things you just know, right? There was a flash in her earring, in the jewel in her eyes. – All know more than they believe they do. Some people are more aware of their knowledge... because you are also a shadow-walker. We have both traveled far without encountering each other, but now we have.

– What did I tell you? Lene chuckled.

The others turned real around them again.

– Some bunch you're traveling with, Magnus said rigidly and very direct.

– A great bunch of nomads, Damon said and stared down the kid.

– They are half moons joined, Anya said. – As are we.

– «A tribe from all tribes», Kurt quoted, – «until the end of time».

That made a trickle flow down Terrill's spine.

++++++++++++++++++++++++++++++++++++

The traveling circus broke camp at dawn. On its Journey followed about hundred people of vastly different origins, a true confusion of styles and convictions. Everybody enthusiastically took part in its slow, unsteady forward movement.

– What circus have we stumbled upon here, old boy? André wondered slightly ironic.

– A... threshold. Terrill didn't need to ponder the issue. – A portal to another world, or at least a less dangerous way of traveling north.

They had realized it the moment they met his eyes in the night, between the strands of night and fire that he was calmer, more relaxed. They saw the eye of the storm, instead of its eternal circle.

They saved gas by letting the bikes stand in the trucks, even though it didn't mattered much in their present situation. The Green Rose seemed to have sufficient fuel. The two-wheelers were used for reconnaissance and only that, and the half moon from Marseille enjoyed the pleasant pace.

The days seemed to pass in a kind of dreamy haze. And when the night once again greeted them, the dreams turned real and true.

In the mountain and forest ever further to the north nature pushed itself at them, even stronger than before. Traffic lessened, turned bearable, at least for a while. The gray band hardly felt like a road at all, as the miles faded away in their mind.

The circus set up camp a dark night, yet one more time, several evenings after the last. They didn't unpack more than they needed, sufficient for a meal and protection from the rain. The climate was like a spring day much further north, cooling down after darkness had fallen. Progress was considerably slower than it would have been on bikes and they hadn't removed themselves from Innsbruck as much as they would have wished. But there was no lack of remote places they could camp.

– People receive us fairly well, William told Terrill. – We remind them, in a backwards kind of way, in spite of our exotic ways that things are still normal. We remain on guard, but our reputation precedes us and gives us a certain protection. Everybody knows we can defend ourselves and that we are downright dangerous if provoked.

Campfires burned between tall rocks, giant rocks stuck in the ground that had fallen from the mountainside and formed an oval shape that in a way isolated the hundred people or so from whatever happened outside. The Shadowland shimmered and moved as if it was alive.

– The Larsen C ice-shelf may collapse at any time, now, Claire stated calmly. – Then, not long after that momentous event, the West Antarctic Sheet will break off from the mainland and all of it will slide into the sea, and the total collapse of civilization will begin in earnest. We need to be dangerous, need to be everything we can be.

Her words sent hot and cold shivers of apprehension and expectation through them all.

They were training, learning many different techniques, among others what they called the language of the deaf, which was basic and basically sign language.

– This is hard, Maeve groaned. – This is really hard.

She and Jerry was one of many groups exercising their new skills, both around the campfires and other, more hard-striking skills between the shadows and the fires. They still followed the exchange of words easily enough.

A few stood guard. Most of the others gathered in and around a large circle. When one spoke no one attempted to interrupt him or her. There were occasions when people spoke simultaneously, but they stopped that quickly and left the word to one single voice. Even the locals seeking here stayed calm and relaxed. Many were content with just sitting there and listening in. Damon listened, a feat unusual for him. He saw no reason to add much to the conversation. In his eyes others said everything that needed to be said. He could allow himself to relax – and dream.

– It's strange, Vladek said, clearly embarrassed. – I've wanted to visit Venice my entire life. Images, tales from that city have captivated me since childhood. I'm assuming it was a kind of fascination, a form of substitute for everything else missing in my life. Now, when I had the chance, my last chance it suddenly didn't seem so important anymore. That a considerable part of the population is already moving to the upper floors in their flooded houses also helps demystifying my dream.

– Travel is victory, a man with Arabic features stated. – It's a proverb from my homeland. Travel is a victory in itself. The important is the journey, not the destination.

He held back. They heard such pain in his voice, so much that they could hardly fathom it. So much sorrow revealed itself in the smiling face. No one spoke, but waited for him to continue.

– I don't know how many we were before we started our walk, but we quickly turned many, more than we are now.

He spoke passable English. It was evident that it wasn't his native tongue, but every syllable was still close to technically correct, as if he obsessed over each and every one.

– We were killed, we died, we starved and our thirst lasted beyond death. But when there were no more than eighteen of us left and we feared we would all be gone soon, something happened. We… stopped dying. We were shot at, attacked, we starved, we burned with thirst, but we survived. We couldn't die. Life had already left us. For days and weeks we saw nothing but skeletons and carcasses. We were dead, but kept moving, moving, moving.

His vivid tale became true to them. They imagined it easily, didn't even have to close their eyes.

– We reached the Spanish possessions in Morocco. There were no Spaniards left there, no authorities, nothing except thousands of ghosts like ourselves pretending to be alive. The looting had been going on for weeks, but we still found more than enough food to fill our belly many times. We believed in our exhilaration that we had reached the end of the journey. Two of us died of binge eating the first night and more turned ill. Days passed. We and our enemies, our countless fellow competing travelers realized that time worked against us there as well, that we needed to move on after all. A kind of «cease fire»… old clichés turn ridiculous these days, right…? We, all the wandering tribes reached an understanding. From then on we stopped seeing our large number as a threat… An enormous fleet set out across the strait and the Mediterranean itself. We knew that the Spaniards patrolled the Gibraltar Strait and that they were waiting for us at the other side, at the promised shores. Warships kept returning refugees to Africa. Some of them just lay down in the sand and died. Others started the crossing again by swimming immediately. We convinced others to try our way. The Spaniards had limited resources and perhaps everything was merely a matter of waiting, of holding out. If we just could have waited…

The images, sensations burned into them with his voice, his intense tale.

He was good at this, good at telling, perhaps because he was also driven by grief and pronounced sadness.

– It isn't that long ago. It just feels that way. We crossed the strait at night. A thick fog, an electric storm I have never before encountered hid us from the radar or satellites or any other equipment. We took it as a sign from Allah, from Yahweh, from some god or another. Most of the fleet broke out of the fog no more than a short swim from land in and near the city of Tarifa.

He practically collapsed as they watched. Tears pushed at claw-like hands pushed at his face. Everything locked up inside him flowed from him like the puss from a wound.

Perhaps it is to his advantage, Damon pondered, that he's still capable of crying.

– I was at Tarifa, the traveler stated with determination in his voice. – I will bear witness to the events there.

Time passed. Time did not pass. A loud drum echoed in their ears. They did not hear the drum.

– They killed indiscriminately. If anyone attempted to return to the water, they shot them. If they raised their hands above their heads in surrender they shot them. They kept firing. The only thing we could do was to flee, to run for our very lives, and fervently pray that the bony hand of fate didn't touch us. I can swear that blood flowed from the very air that day. A feverish mirage, a waterfall, we all saw it and almost all of us froze in terror and awe, also the soldiers. I ran, I ran until I crawled on the ground in a world of my own. I survived as the sole member of my wandering, piecemeal tribe. Later, while I traveled the shadows north I heard about other survivors, a handful of the many thousands seeking a foreign beach that morning. Spain was almost as dry as Sahara, making our effort an even bigger joke. I never felt safe there. I will never more feel safe anywhere.

Those listening intensely to his tale heard the waterfall and the rise of a thousand voices.

Strega appeared, representing them all.

– Thank you, Jaiwad, she said. – You have a rare gift. Upon hearing your story we experience it in vivid detail, and it is important that we and others do that, so that it will never be forgotten.

She walked to him and touched his shoulder, a soft, rough touch.

– And it also pleases me that you're here. In spite of the bad things you've experienced, or perhaps because of them I'm happy for you. You survived the impossible and that increases your changes of surviving the years ahead and your contribution will also increase our changes of survival. You're the human being incarnated and it pleases me beyond anything that you're one of us, one of the Children of the Midnight Fire.

The fire grew, reached far and high and deep. She walked behind one of the outer bonfires. It brightened and darkened her features simultaneously. She spoke and her voice was that of the night surrounding them.

– The downfall of civilization has come too far, she stated casually, without even a taint of regret in her voice. – It cannot be stopped. Perhaps it never could. And to say that that is a blessing in disguise is to not go far enough. We've waited so long for it to happen that our anticipation has turned to despair, our hopes to dust, but now Ragnarok is finally here. The true transformation of humanity has begun.

The gathering felt it, felt the joy nip at their buds and their very self.

– All the poisons, both of spirit and flesh humanity has made or exposed are something very negative… but the growing quantity of CO2 and increasingly Methane in the atmosphere, what makes temperature rise on Earth… is humanity's salvation.

Cries of agreement filled the already heated air. Emotion ran high and hands were rolled into fists. Many, including Terrill and Jaiwad shook hard.

– We've brought it on ourselves, she said sad and happy. – We've committed collective suicide for so long. For ten thousand years we've been bathing in the poison of our own insanity. Be happy that it's over. Tyranny has ruled us and the Earth for so long. Now, retaliation is coming. What's happening will bring out the best and the worst in us all, will bring out an honesty that may be cruel, but true.

– Those in charge are done for and they know it. They've treated the rest of us like undesirables, like servants, like slaves. That ends now. All artificial selection ends now. Fascism and worse ruled before the final days. That will also fade away like the nightmare it is. Fighting civilization was like fighting a feverish mirage. In truth that was all it ever was. We can never properly imagine Ragnarok, except like a pale reflection of what it will be. We will have an advantage because we've realized the essence of what's happening, but luck and random coincidences will still determine much of who will live and die through what's coming. But no matter what happens we'll be free and once more have the moon, the sun, the stars and all the world's joy to play with. That's worth dying for, isn't it? Life is often hard and cruel. That won't change. The change is that all masks will fall, one by one by one, until they no longer dominate life on Earth, but only are a tiny bit of the multitude. Yggdrasil, the tree of life was withering. Now, it's once more healthy and strong. We will once more become what we're born to be.

Terrill felt the tree's branches, felt them grow and sprout. Thunder shook the ground and the Tree of Life grew and thrived.

Everyone present felt a kind of wild peace and a joy they had searched long and hard for, a unity with the surroundings and each other.

The day returned, it always did, but the days were short and the nights were long in the time they journeyed with the travelers, with the Tivoli, with the circus, with its roses and thorns. The ship sailed in smooth water, with the storm, a caravan on its way to the distant north.

Outside Linz they once more raised the larger tenths. Innsbruck already felt like a distant memory.

Also in this place people sought into the wilderness to experience its nomads.

And She Who Danced in it.

She danced with many other nude and painted bodies on the shadowy stage. Damon recognized her like he had always recognized her. She stood out even among other Dancers.

The rhythm rose slowly in the air and flesh and concrete and wood, the very bones of everyone there. The speed of the movement increased. The music seemed to be rising from the Earth, from an abyss, a savagery, a joy not to be denied, a rollercoaster ride not in any way inferior to what Damon had experienced by her side these brief last few days.

He chased Anya across green plains, through deep woods, up steep mountains. He crouched with aching limbs and hard breathing, while she teased and pushed him.

– C'mon, you're not tired, are you, a big and strong boy like you?

He made an effort at keeping up with her. She easily kept him from succeeding, light on her feet like a deer or a cougar. He gritted his teeth and kept going, going, going.

What's gotten into you? Rawlins asked him, speaking up for the first time in a long while.

The boy ignored him.

Ah, you're not merely chasing the enigmatic woman, but also the riddle of your life, the one you're convinced is waiting for you somewhere ahead, the one you've sought since early childhood.

Time and time again he fought himself on his feet and forward. Time and time again he had been convinced he couldn't go on. Lightning struck ground somewhere ahead, but there was no thunder. The lightning seemed eerie, ethereal, as if he imagined it, even though he knew it was real. It struck his bones, his mind, his blood. Something strange happened, was happening beyond all fatigue, all will he had believed he possessed. He blinked and blinked again. The haze in his vision… cleared. He didn't know anymore whether or not he was too tired to keep on running or if it mattered at all anymore. He ran, and kept running without break, and he felt the strength fill his body and mind, and at that very moment nothing else mattered.

The sole campfire rose on the naked rock. He sat on one side and she on the other. It was night, but between them it was bright as day.

– You will never know the complete truth about yourself, she told him softly. – There isn't any. It's the same with me. I know far more about myself than most people know about themselves, but to quote a famed philosopher: that has only convinced me how little I know.

– What I know is that if the past has been dark, then the years ahead will be even darker. Acknowledge that fact and thrive on its truth, Damon Terrill. Everything once born must end in ashes. This is the first part of a simple truth. The second is: Everything ending in ashes will be revived from it. Have you heard the legend of Phoenix?

– Yes, Terrill replied uncertain. – Wasn't that a heron, a bird worshiped by the Egyptians?

– That's one representation, she said distant, close. – Perhaps there was a heron the Egyptian called the Phoenix, but so what? Like all «rational» explanations it's insufficient, incomplete. The reason, Damon, why they worshiped a bird making their nests of ashes was that they knew a piece of the truth, an essential piece of it. *We* are Phoenix. We will, as both species and individual always rise from our own ashes.

The dream visions not dream visions returned to him, stronger than they had been, images, sensations showing him dry plains, snow-covered peaks.

– You see dry plains and snow-covered peaks reaching high above that pale land, she enlightened him, startling him yet again. – One of them, with the flat peak is Kilimanjaro in Africa many thousands of years ago. The land turned dry then as well, though on a smaller scale. The other mountain is Glitretind in the Norwegian Jotunheim. Now, like then the fertile green land below the ice will be mankind's salvation.

He had so many questions. One burned at his tongue.

– You say I'm a Shadowwalker like you… But that, if I understand it correctly is something that also has physical, active side… So, what's mine? Why can't I *access* it? What is hidden pushing itself to the surface and what's keeping it locked down?

He couldn't help feeling both stupid and relieved.

– You lock yourself in, she replied dryly. – But don't worry, it won't stay down much longer. I'll teach you a little, the first few steps on your further path, but there is in truth no need. There's nothing I can teach you that you don't already know.

knowknowknowknowknowknow…

The whispers rose in his ears and in glimpses he understood what they were saying. His dark eyes darkened further. An owl hooted, a wolf growled in the eternal mountains.

The night was the most beautiful of nights. The full moon shone from a sky brightened by small, pale clouds. At a mountaintop, in a valley surrounded by dark peaks, bathed in the moon's silver light, in the campfires' golden glow Lene Silverhair stepped forward. By her side in that small hollow in the ground stood Anya and Kurt, the timeless shadow-walker, the aging warrior. Damon Terrill sat in front of them, relaxed, seething with expectation. In circles above them, in a natural amphitheater several hundred excited participators and spectators sat as witnesses.

Two ravens landed on a branch of a nearby tree. They squeaked, but he didn't hear them. He saw their dance, but there was no sound. The others noticed them, too, he knew they did, and it made them breathe faster.

Lene held up an oblong object wrapped in canvas. She unwrapped it slowly, deliberately. A long, shiny sword appeared. A collective gasp echoed in the night and fire. Lene pushed it into the ground between two rocks.

– Reach out and touch it, she encouraged them.

Everybody sat too far away to touch it. They hesitated, but still reached out with their hands.

– Can you feel it at your skin?

The wonder in their eyes grew, as they seemed to squeeze something invisible in front of them.

– This sword is old, ancient even. Slightly breathless she held her breath. A film covered her eyes. – It has been known to me for so very long. It isn't the first time it has been used for an occasion such as this.

He was breathing, feeling each breath in a way he had never before felt.

– Blood unites us. Silverhair turned to Damon. – The sword unites us. I've had it in my possession for a while, and so did my mother and many more before us… But in more ways than one, I believe it has always «belonged» to you.

Damon pushed his left wrist at the edge of the blade. He knew what to do. He had done it a thousand times before.

– We had a far more stressful initiation in the old days, Kurt said lightly, – but these days it's hardly necessary. You've already walked a far harder path than most. You're already initiated.

Damon pushed harder. A light, added pressure and he cut his vein. Blood flowed down the blade, and ended up between the rocks, mixing with the soil. Anya bandaged the wound with a dirty-looking bandage smelling like spices and herbs. It turned instantly red, but felt cold and pleasant.

– It's soaked in an antiseptic compound making wounds close faster, Anya said. – I learned to make it long ago.

Damon rose to full height and grabbed the hilt of the sword with his right hand. He strived a bit before he managed to pull the blade out of the rock and the ground, but then he could raise the sword into the air. It shone in silver, twinkled in a golden light, while tearing a hole in the air itself. He had taught himself the value of show, of thunder and lightning in this world early. This time he felt no need for such. It felt completely natural when he raised the sword above his head, when he received the applause from the Travelers, those seeing like him, listening like him, feeling like him.

– DREAMS BELONG TO THE NIGHT, he shouted, the last word drowning in a roar.

An orgy of pain and expectation.

The words themselves made everything real to him.

CHAPTER THIRTEEN

Lene drove the truck. Terrill sat with her in front.

During many later moments he would ponder the days and nights spent in the nightravens' company and not quite believe everything that had happened. Then he pulled the sword from its sheath and raised it high. He trained with it, felt its balance, the truth in every movement.

– As they say, Lene mused, – our ways will soon part, but will eventually meet anew.

– Why? He asked hoarsely, not really needing an answer.

– We have unfinished business nearby, she replied brightly. – Very unfinished and dangerous. The changes of making it will not significantly improve if you guys join in. But I will ask you for a favor… If you can take William, Magnus, Claire, Josh and other youths with you. It isn't their fight *this*. If you can take those four as a special favor to me, Anya and Kurt.

He nodded slowly. Just a couple of days ago he would have considered it a strange request. William and Claire were after all four to five years older than he was. He no longer did. It seemed… right.

Everything raced through his inner eye. Events and glimpses of events flashed before him. They rattled him, but also intrigued him.

Closing his eyes, keeping them wide open made no difference. The images, sensations didn't change.

The sun fell fast below tall mountains. It didn't make the light fade that much, and it wouldn't for hours yet. The sky remained bright, even though the valley below had been cast in shadow.

He straightened in his seat, registering astonished how his facial muscles froze one by one.

– Is anything wrong? Lene wondered.

– I'm not certain.

An almost automatic head shake followed his words.

– Remember where you are, she said. – And who you are with. We are not strangers, but a gathering of strangers. We have lived with She Who Dances in the Forest for many years. We're used to «hunches».

– Stop the truck, he said. – Stop everyone.

The truck in front, the entire caravan stopped slowly where the road made a turn, at the edge of the valley. Terrill opened the door and slipped down on the ground on unsteady feet, a ground feeling unusually soft, gelatinous. Several of his traveling companions joined him. He knew their heat, their cold.

The puzzled, frozen look stayed on his face, as seconds trailed to a minute. Some of his companions had drawn their guns. He hadn't. Anya hadn't either. He sensed her close proximity even before she stepped forward to his side.

They both walked a few more steps. Then they saw it, saw one single skull clean of flesh decorating a natural shelf on the rock ahead. One more step and they spotted another skull. This one was of a goat. Both had its top covered by feathers resembling hair. There was a cabin not far away, derelict and decorated with death and feathers as well. Someone had painted ancient runes with blood that had only recently dried on the wall.

He and everybody else with him quickly retreated behind the turn again. They began spreading out in the terrain well before he gave the signal, finding cover, moving like the silent death they had learned to do. Four began moving in on the cabin, cautiously, but not slow at all. It felt like a thousand barrels pointed at the walls visible to them.

Kurt and Jason hit the wall with their bodies, cautiously, fast like lightning glancing into the cabin through the windows. There was no glass there or even remains of glass. They crawled inside. Others rushed in through the door. Damon could see them in there. Nothing happened. The all-clear sign was given.

Damon, Yola, Lene and Anya joined those inside. The others remained in hiding.

– I guess someone is saying hello, Yola said pointedly.

– There's no immediate danger, Anya shrugged.

Terrill noticed the nuances in her wording, even as he took in the mood of the cabin.

– I don't feel immediately threatened, he acknowledged her ambiguity, – but it, all this still makes me anxious.

– That's normal, Yola stated solemnly, – normal for you.

She studied him and the room with equally penetrating eyes.

But there was nothing, nothing to grab hold of, nothing they could point at directed at them.

They walked back outside. Damon's anxiety didn't let up. He cast his attention at the valley below. His vision seemed to split, turning hazy, as reality changed irrevocably in front of him.

Everybody could sense it, now, like a river, a waterfall, a storm

Then they could actually see it as well, see a hole in the very air. What was inside it, they couldn't possibly properly describe, even if they were able to observe what they perceived as alienation incarnated for quite some time. It faded slowly, until they could once again see only the background, the ordinary clear sky and air against the backdrop of the valley ahead of them.

– Was that all? Vladek wondered, visibly disappointed.

They spotted no shimmering anywhere, nothing similar to the northern lights they had seen the last few nights. The warm wind blew from the north.

Something hit Irena on the head, light as a feather. It stuck in her hair. She brushed it off without looking at it. It fell harmlessly to the ground.

They felt the light pressure, like rain against the hair, and believed they recognized it. But what hit them was no fluid. They spotted tiny bones fall to the ground and jump back into the air.

– Bones, William cried, – skeleton bones.

The sky remained blue and clear. A scream attempted in vain to overwhelm the sound of tiny skeleton parts drumming ever harder at the ground.

A large bone hit the ground only a few steps off, clearly as dry as the rest.

– I guess their owners died a long time ago, Josh said. – Even though the bones themselves show no major signs of decay.

– More answers without question, Claire nodded, – no rhyme, no reason, no rules, except this one confirming there are none.

From the space above the shadowy valley lots of human skeletons fell to the Earth, breaking the moment they hit the ground, jumping back up in an insane dance. And then…

The blood flowed. It hit the lower valley land and splashed everywhere, also on those standing in relative safety high above it. Thousands of microscopic drops penetrated fabric, hair and skin. They heard screams from the valley, from people drowning in the fluid, in the insanity.

– It is the dead, Damon stated with a frozen voice, as if in trance. – All the dead, the energy from those that has died recently, from those dying now… the countless numbers that will die.

It was an excellent testament to those standing by his side that the event didn't frighten them more than it did, and a testament to how much they, and the world had changed.

The blood from Tarifa flowed in the Austrian mountain valley, like it would many other places, from all the places the Earth and mankind withered and died.

Anya spoke in wrath and sadness.

– For so long, now, we've squeezed ourselves like a sponge, removing everything making life worth living.

She put a hand on Damon's shaking shoulder.

– Death has touched you. That's a good thing. You know what it is.

He nodded, welcoming what she offered, what he had to offer himself.

– Let's get going, he said.

They did. Their wheels kept rolling. They expected the blood, the bones to vanish, to fade away, but it didn't.

– Such stuff… manifestations usually vanish quickly, don't they? Stefan wondered in one of the trucks, – since they have no material reality, I mean…

– They usually do, the way I've heard it, André pondered, – but that doesn't comply anymore either. This has substance, solid form. No one can any longer pretend it isn't real.

– Though some people will always deny what their eyes tell them, Yola snorted.

– This is a part of the new world awaiting us, Vladek agreed, – the new, old world.

Skulls practically floated in the road, grinning at them. They saw bodies, rotting bodies as well, hardly cold corpses that had expired in this valley. Some had clearly died of pure fright, others of reasons those studying them didn't want to ponder too much. In yet another segment of the diseased population the cause of death was more obvious. A girl had been penetrated by a bone. It was stuck in her chest, an alien object that had become a part of her. The stench of acid vomit spread among the travelers. They shrugged it off, didn't ask themselves what made this particular sight twist their guts, when they had kept the horror at an enduring distance for so long.

– It will never end, will it? Paolo said in a low voice. – Never!

The others didn't nod or acknowledge his word in any visible manner.

But they knew there would be no end to it.

+++++++++++++++++++++++++++++++++++

The caravan left Linz, Austria. Two mixed half moons parted ways.

– You should definitely stay away from Munich and the entire southern Germany, Kurt admonished them. – It isn't safe there, isn't safe there at all. Like Einstein implied: the shortest distance between two points isn't always a straight line.

– What if you followed your own advice? Terrill said with a catching in his throat.

– We will! Anya said. – Any day, now.
++++++++++++++++++++++++++++++

Any day, now.

The clock struck twelve. It wasn't really twelve, but closer to twelve thirty. It was late.

Kurfurstendam in sunburned Berlin boiled like a kettle ready to explode. Its stench reached all corners of the town.

The old church, with the large hole high up still stood. The hole was a relic from the Second World War, a result of the allied bombing, yet another symbol of human irrationality and stupidity.

Soldiers in heavy armament surrounded the open square. A huge crowd threw rocks against windows. The modern shopping mall on the square's east side was looted and cleaned for anything even resembling value.

Quite some time ago, no one could tell exactly how long it had stopped raining in eastern Germany and the sky above Berlin stayed blue, blue, blue. The sun burned the land and cast Berlin's unprotected streets in its deadly rays.

The soldiers, with their protective goggles, their helmets and reinforced uniforms moved around like a constant formless mass. They wore the latest in gasmasks. It had become a necessity to those staying outdoors much of the day. And the soldiers patrolled the streets day and night.

They struck ruthlessly at the thieves, the protesters, the rebels, terms that had become synonymous. Only the privileged had the means and the influence to shop in the exotic stores in the luxurious area around Kurfurstendam, Kur'dam, and the unrest had gained momentum across months and years.

– Let's go, Terrill said. – If they aren't distracted by now, they never will be.

In the ruin-like, ever more extensive slum around Bahnhof Zoo the black market flourished. People with their illegal street stands packed their goods and fled from the unrest. Damon and those by his side, and those guarding their backs, on their way through Kantstrasse heard the noise well, heard it in front of them as well as behind.

They had heard it when they were stuck in Prague.

Now, they were stuck in Berlin.

Hot and deadly streets surrounded them. The brutal death squadrons usually stayed on their heels every night and day they ventured outside their hideout to forage essential supplies, but right now those squadrons were very busy. The stuck travelers kept looking out for other, not so obvious dangers.

There were no cars. Unauthorized driving had been outlawed for quite some time in Berlin.

Terrill and his companions crossed the street with utmost caution. Constantly moving eyes caught nothing, no suspicious motion anywhere. Everything kept flowing around them, as they kept flowing through what they suspected to be an invisible labyrinth.

A crack shook their ears and itching trigger finger. A singing bullet stopped singing. Francine was hit. She fell and died while they watched. The bullet had broken her neck. They surveyed every possible and impossible hideout, striving to determine from which point in the urban terrain the bullet had been fired. Sweaty hands slipped on the metal they clutched. Everybody gritted their teeth in their helplessness. They knew there were snipers everywhere.

The group circled back to the zoo, avoiding the heavily guarded and fortified railway

station.
– No one leaves Berlin, André snarled. – The best surveillance money and power can buy makes certain of that. We should have stayed away. It isn't just one big prison, but a cemetery.
There was no recrimination in his voice, no direction to his statement, only steam that had to find an outlet.
The Zoo had long since ceased being a zoo. There were no green spots left. Only a few withered trees bore witness to what had been.
– It's such a truly dismal place, Yola shuddered. – The poor cheered when they slaughtered all the animals, when gene-spliced milk was introduced and when the government started selling water only on bottles, eagerly participating in their own oppression.
– We are the Children of the Midnight Fire, Damon said. – We may find ourselves here at the moment, but we will never become a part of this dead place.
His words burned them and cheered them up.
One more step, and then another. Left foot, right foot. It felt like a military march, worse, a ballet, a death dance where the slightest misstep meant certain death, or worse.
Vladek Kostov, by sheer coincidence spotted a moving manhole cover. He directed his grenade launcher at it. The manhole cover was quickly put back in place.
They felt like they walked alone at night, tense, unable to stop eyes from wavering, from looking up, behind, to the sides and at every possible angle. They turned abruptly and saw nobody, but they knew the enemy, whoever he or she was, was there, always doubting, until they heard the crack again, and someone died, and blood flooded the street, and colored the dirt red, and the shit turned the blood gray.
They had walked through that kind of gauntlet, at least since Prague, and had died one by one, little by little on that long, long stretch of gray.
They had to wait it out between heaps of garbage, among ruins and derelict sheds.
Creatures dangerous like them, dirty like them, skinny like them slipped from hideouts, paying a certain respect to the lethal travelers. Damon observed how they spread out in the terrain, how they constantly attempted to surround their guests of honor. He registered pleased how the travelers' perimeter guard, led by André kept them from doing so.
Weapons were drawn. It clicked when both sides cocked their guns. No words had been uttered, no hostilities exchanged. Potential confrontation was imminent.
But there was very little actual anxiety. Everybody held their tools of death in a light grip and appeared like professional gunmen.
Except for Yola. She suddenly appeared jittery and unusually anxious. He noticed it with a glance the moment the strangers had shown themselves. She wouldn't look at him.
Something happened, something adding to the already tense situation. From the corner of his eye he spotted a third group to their left.
And then his neck hair rose in earnest.
– Damon, Dominic nipped him in the sleeve.
From the corner of the right eye he spotted a fourth group. All four paths to the open square surrounded by garbage and sheds had been taken. He didn't turn his head, but sent Yola to check out their retreat. She did so before he had given her the sign.

The four groups stood there, facing each other. Damon frowned. Everyone seemed to stand on a bed of nails. A thousands needles stabbed their skin. Imminent violence threatened to explode.

Yola returned. She confirmed his suspicion. The retreat was not blocked. The gallows humor bubbled in his throat a few seconds before dark laughter echoed across the place. Everybody stared astounded at him. Several people almost fired their weapons without wanting to.

– Two meetings, agreed upon separately happen simultaneously, he said aloud.

Everybody present heard him, sharing both the sense of incredulity and amusement.

Yola spoke to him without moving her lips:

– The pearl chain the leader opposite us carries around his neck… Blanche wore it, just before she disappeared.

Suddenly he had major trouble swallowing. Spittle flooded the cavity of his mouth. No matter how much he swallowed, it kept doing so, like the adrenaline setting fire to his veins. His limbs turned soft. His muscles tensed slightly. His fighter instincts awoke further.

Two pair of groups stared at each other with mutual distrust and hostility. Everybody present moved nervously.

– Looks like we have a situation here, Terrill called out to them. – My suggestion is that all of us pull back for now and return to our possible dealings at a later time.

– Sounds like a reasonable suggestion, he heard from his right.

No one said much, but they nodded to themselves and their companions.

Damon stared intently at the man wearing the pearl necklace. The man looked familiar, but he couldn't place him. The spite, he had no trouble identifying. He strived to keep his calm, to not be provoked.

All the four groups pulled back slowly, guarding each other zealously. The situation remained tense.

– «Ich habe eine nachricht für Sie», the man with the special necklace cried. Damon froze instantly, well aware of the fact that the message was for him and who was really sending it. – I have a message for you. It is as follows: YOU HAVE DONE WELL, STORM CHILD. I'M PLEASED WITH YOU. SO PLEASED THAT I WILL GIVE YOU AN ADVICE. I'M INVOLVED IN DELICATE OPERATIONS IN THIS CITY. MAKE NO BIG WAVES HERE. FOLLOW MY KIND ADVICE AND WE DON'T HAVE TO MEET YET.

The man had an insane, empty expression in his eyes. There was something there, but clearly mixed with something imposed from the outside. Someone had taken this human being, thrown it into a pot, added his own ingredients and stirred it until little remained of the original personality.

He reminded her of Blanche.

– What was that about? André wondered, more than suspecting the truth.

All his traveling companions stared intently at him as they pulled back. They needed, deserved to know the truth.

– Russel, Damon replied quietly.

Everybody mumbled to themselves. William froze in eyes and body.

They retreated in a flow of motion, even more alert than usual, attempting, failing in looking in all directions simultaneously. The noise, turning a notch higher cut into their ears. Feet drummed against the ground. Just as they reached the next corner a group mixed with them. They recognized several people from one of the groups they had encountered not that long ago, and they were recognized in turn.

– They chose the same escape route we did, Maxine said baffled. – Damn! *Damn!*

People in the other group nodded in agreement with her words. There was little aggression there, only a baffling anxiety shared by both groups. The mixed crowd crossed a street, and suddenly yet another stricken group crossed their path.

That group of disorganized, hysterical people was fleeing with the riot police hot on their heels.

Everybody ran, ran in pretty much the same direction. But two steps or ten after that they were all suddenly immersed in the same, smothering tight crowding. It turned from bad to worse to intolerable in seconds. People bumped into others and fell, and started striking each other. It was impossible to keep any kind of track of people.

Then the riot police caught up with them. It turned vicious fast, quickly removing itself from anything resembling the bar fight Damon and the others had experienced in Italy. It was…

It was a killing ground.

Two held Jerry. A third gutted him from hip to throat. Damon threw himself at them. He kicked one in the head, smashed it against a wall already decorated by blood and guts.

Everything happened so fast. Bones broke, blood flowed. Damon was separated from his companions. He tried to break through the living wall surrounding him, but he was quickly devoured by it. He took a hit on the head, then another. Perhaps yet another. A knife flashed in his vision. He received one more hit on the head and fell unconscious to the ground.

+++++++++

He woke up in a crowded cell. His hazy vision slowly cleared. Bloodied and bruised faces surrounded him everywhere. He had to push people off parts of his body. Many stayed unconscious. Those awake glanced at each other with anxious eyes. He recognized no one.

Moans of suffering and fear rose from sore throats. Time stretched on in the semi-darkness, as if everything was slow. All moves felt like an effort, like being suspended in quicksand. People spoke, but Damon felt only the pain of his aching head. Now and then there were commotion and loud screams from the outside, then more silence. Existence in the tiny world stretched on.

One discovery cheered him up to something resembling euphoria. When he touched his lower arms, he felt the hard metal still in place there. They had not searched him well enough. Triumph flowed through him. He strived to not show his good mood, to resemble just another sheep driven to the slaughter.

He drifted off again. Sounds and sensations kept imposing themselves on him. In one way the noise drifted in and out of his consciousness. In another it never let up at all.

Eyes opened abruptly. The sound of marching boots and the screams and wails had suddenly become that much closer. The door opened.

He was happy to be awake when the guards rushed inside and started emptying the cell, and saw how they treated those unable to move. Those not reacting after several kicks and strikes were just dragged across the uneven floor. Terrill rubbed his head and focused on staying on his feet. He looked for his tribe members, but could not see anyone.

They were driven off with sticks, hands and feet. Those still unconscious were dragged down the stairs. Bones broke. The sound was more than loud enough. They were heading down, down, down. He lost count of the number of stairs they had walked. Ever fewer light bulbs lit the ever murkier hallways.

The prisoners were pushed brutally into a room he imagined to be huge, to be infinite. He could glimpse the walls on the other side in the weak, weak shine of the source of light coming from an indefinite angle, but he still got his usual strange feeling of unreality.

More prisoners joined them, as the guards showed up with more shabby groups. Damon saw how those that had been here a while were forced at the walls, at solid walls.

Waken nightmares kept haunting Terrill, kept shaking him to pieces.

He heard a sound, one he initially failed to identify. A screeching sound everybody heard turned loud and unmistakable. He saw it, too, then.

A part of the floor slid aside at the center of the room. A hole deep and dark appeared to them all. Wails rose from the depths, from the throats of the poor souls captured down there.

The guards, grinning and cackling began pushing and throwing people into it, into the deeper darkness. They fell and screamed, and then their wails joined those from below.

– It's THE KINGDOM OF DEATH, a man screamed terrified.

He tried running off, but the guards caught him easily and dragged him to the hole and dropped him off.

Terrill frowned. He heard and imagined he saw what happened down there and turned cold or colder. There was a sound, a humming behind the screams… one of… expectation and hunger. Suddenly, he understood.

It wasn't hard, wasn't hard at all. Fear, deep, hard fear did more than touch him. It grabbed him by the balls and wouldn't let go.

When the guards came and fetched him he let himself be taken, be carried off towards the hole. He turned limp and focused on remaining loose and soft in the body.

They threw him into the black, black abyss. He floated through a vast darkness where there were no fixed points, attempting to keep his feet down, without any certainty of success.

He landed on his feet, on a smooth and hard floor. It hurt in his left ankle, but he managed to stay upright. Several of those had been thrown down with him writhed on the bloodied floor and cried out in pain. One had broken his leg. Damon could see the bone sticking out. One was dead. He had no marks on him.

Terrill glanced around him, and kept doing it, a quick, flashing look. In a wide circle around the newly arrived waited those who were hardly more than hungry maws. Damon waited as well, very aware of changes in the very air surrounding him. Everything happened in intervals, cycles. The ferrymen and inhabitants had, like he had more than expected developed a symmetry. The human rain eventually ended… and the expected feast began. All the hungry maws rushed forward simultaneously. He made no attempt at getting away. He waited patiently, jittery until the moment when they started colliding and began fighting each other. Then he attacked one section with a savage howl. He kicked out at them, threw them away, broke their neck, broke fingers, arms and legs, cut open hearts and throats. Blood flowed from the pointed swords sticking out from his sleeves. They avoided him, filled with reverence. He howled his challenge at them and they shrunk in terror. They quickly picked other, easier victims.

The different groups grabbed whatever they could and pulled back. More blood floated on the already slick floor, what wasn't licked by fast tongues. Terrill was sick and nauseas after just a few seconds, a sensation only growing as he kept observing the various patterns, here on this excellent representation of Styx - the River of knowledge, life and death. He gained knowledge - of life and death.

Some groups let their catches live, absorbing them in various ways into the tribe. Others tore them apart and began devouring the remains without delay. A group of females with eyes showing total lack of reason spared the female prisoners, but grilled the males over open fire and fed with obvious pleasure in vacant eyes. They devoured absolutely everything, including the grilled brain.

He stood alone. It didn't feel too bad. It wasn't new to him. He had been alone most of his life, also in the company of others, the closest friends. That thought brought both strength and weakness to his waxing and waning consciousness.

There was no lack of space down here. Both groups and the individuals standing alone had more than enough room. The catacombs reached seemingly forever in all directions. There were no walls, no one close he could spot, only retreats of columns and similar that could sort of shield his back.

He wasn't the only individual that had survived the frenzied feeding, but they became fewer as the hours passed. He quickly lost count over how many. In the time following the feeding, the groups quickly organized and took care of most of the stragglers.

They came for him. He attacked them, charged them as a madman again, with raw and brutal violence, and it impressed them. He still had to defend himself five times before they left him alone.

He stayed by the pillar close to the drop, staying alert and ready. There was a time it rained meat and not people, and he was one of the first serving himself. No one challenged him. If they saw it as a weakness that he wouldn't serve himself human flesh, they were quickly deterred of that misunderstanding.

He fed, unable to know for sure whether or not this meat (raw meat) was from humans. He filed it away at the back of his mind with many other unpleasant thoughts.

The meal made him drowsy. He couldn't avoid the inevitable lethargy brought on by a full stomach. This was even at an early stage of what he knew would be the challenging task of staying awake. He was unable to hide the worried frown on his brow.

When many hours had passed and people approached him, testing him and his resolve and ability his dull expression changed into a snarl, and it invigorated him… for a while, but increasingly less so.

He dozed off, inevitably. It happened once, twice, thrice… until he could no longer tell how many times it had happened, and he wondered how long it was since he had slept, since he had enjoyed that good, deep sleep.

One single sound within his self-defined territory and he woke up abruptly. They had fun with approaching him, but not come close. His wrath couldn't reach them at a distance. He resisted time and time again the temptation to chase them. They wore him down, confident that he would eventually become theirs.

In the eternal twilight down here there was no day or night, only strength and brutality. Everything flowed from that. In this eternity of mist and shadow he no longer thought much about his former life, except when he had to pull himself up from the mire of consciousness in order to retain his sanity. It brought pain, sweet pain. He embraced it and endured.

The material of the pillar seemed to burrow into his back. He rubbed against it in an effort to get rid of the itch somewhere between the neck and his butt. Lacking a more comforting and secure wall the pillar granted him fairly good protection. One quickly learned to sense with all senses down here. The pillar was sufficiently narrow for him to be able to listen in stereo and catch movement behind it. The trick was to properly judge how close the steps really were. One always heard the sound of steps down here.

He woke up again. He fell asleep again. The sound of steps shook him in his dreams. When they, after many a dream and a night awake registered in his consciousness without shaking him, he turned worried, and suffered bouts of anxiety. He combed dusty and greasy hair back on his head with his hands. Words, dancing words and images formed inside and outside his head.

His constantly moving eyes (even in dreams) caught shadows on the wall (the non-existing wall), devil may care laughter during what resembled a spirit hunt. *We will always cast Shadow,* Carla spoke in his head. *But what, in your opinion is the shadow and what is casting the shadow?*

He frowned. Another voice he hardly recalled butted in.

In Voodoo the words shadow and soul are the same, have the same meaning, and significance.

Damon's thoughts took flight. It happened without him willing it, or consciously willing it. They probed unusual and unheard directions. It took minutes, seconds, an eternity until he realized that he was dreaming.

A bird, a giant bird flapped its wings. The experience brought joy, but also more anxiety. Anya spoke more. He knew it was her, even though her features had changed.

You know, know we're talking about the Phoenix, the bird of fire and life. The sun itself cannot overwhelm it. A true Shadow always cast bigger twilight than the tiny spot on the ground.

More words and information came to him, coming from his inner self.

Phoenix had such a great wingspan that no one could keep it from flying. No one, nothing, whether it was flesh, storm or rain could halt its flight, because it was all those things and also those not mentioned. But it lived so hard, burned so fast that it was doomed to fall to the ground, to crash in flames and smoke. A time passed, while its ashes spread and traveled all the four corners of the world and beyond, until it rose from its own ashes to fly once more.

Anya's words, so beyond clear now:

– *Have you heard the legend of the Phoenix?*

Of course, who hasn't?

His own words repeated, so much more eloquent, here, in the Hidden World. He saw, in glimpses lasting forever Phoenix constructing its nest of ashes.

– *We* are Phoenix, Damon. Like Icarus we fly too close to the fire and crash, surrounded by flame and smoke. Phoenix will always rise from its own ashes, transformed, but the same.

He imagined, as he opened his eyes that he actually heard her voice.
Damon.
DAMON
The gates leading to the Kingdom of Death awaited him. He couldn't tell if he walked out or in.
Then wide open eyes saw everything around him. A creature sneaked up on him on what seemed like wolf paws. One moment he saw it only in silhouette against the twilight behind it. Then he had no trouble at all seeing it.
– Gwendolyn, he said with a coarse voice, practically speaking from his throat.
She posed for him, scar and all, allowing him to study her in her stunning entirety.
Two rushed him from behind. He crouched, stood on his shoulders and kicked them in the face. They practically flew through the darkness, hitting the floor far away. More closed in on him from all sides. He stood straight and waited for them. Gwendolyn growled, but not at him. She sent a message to the others: back off.
He waited calmly.
– You're so beautiful, she marveled. – We had convinced ourselves that you would be too tired to offer effective resistance by now, but we should evidently have waited a few more nights.
She said a lot without saying it, and what she didn't say wasn't exactly pleasant.
– What do you want? He asked her casually, pretending to be curious, pretending to not be.
– You're funny, she grinned darkly. – You're always so funny. I love that about you, that, too.
She smiled sweetly to him.
– I want you, she said softly, a hiss added to her sweet smile. – We invite you to join us. Come with us, become us.
– And what happens if I decline, if I like this spot and don't want to move?
– What can happen to a big, bad beast like you? She shrugged innocently. – We can still be friends…
He visualized in his mind how they came for him again a few nights from now, saw them overwhelm him and drag him off, making him theirs.
– I accept, he declared.
They pulled back, pulled away. He pulled himself with them, even deeper into the wolf's forest. Gwendolyn and also the others, filled with pride kept themselves at a respectful distance. They greeted him, welcomed him to the pack in a thousand different ways, by thousand small subconscious, conscious and instinctive moves. He focused on keeping himself in check, guarding himself. Their cave close to a wall, with good possibilities for defense at all sides awaited them. He nodded to himself. She noticed and smiled pleased, filled with expectation.
– They relieved you of the nice coat, she said. – What a pity!
– It was nothing but an old, mothballed skin, he spat.
– You're correct. Suddenly she stood close to him and caressed his hair. – Your true coat beneath is so much prettier.
Everybody sat down on their heels. He joined them. Everybody looked attentive at him. Gwendolyn offered him smoked meat. He didn't attempt to hide his suspicion while examining it with hands, smell and eventually taste. He was relieved when he

started feeding. The relief filled him, both weakening and strengthening him.

She related willingly her story, without any sort of coercion from him. Honesty, in all forms was part of her basic nature.

– We had crossed the German border. She spoke in a low voice, with visible enthusiasm. Her story became a living, breathing thing to him. – In our arrogance we had left our old hunting ground without getting to know the new. That cost us. We were ambushed in our brief camp in the middle of the day. My mate and many others were killed, and the rest of us, in our shame taken away in chains. They brought us here, threw us away like garbage. We fought for our place here, just like you did. With you we can do so much more.

– My take on this place differs slightly from yours, he said. – I don't think they threw us down here just to forget about us. If so, they wouldn't have bothered with feeding us any extra meat. I think they're watching us, studying us for some kind of twisted purpose.

– I think you're correct, she agreed. – They're still looking to use us for some kind of big or small purpose.

Her eyes, yellow and big shimmered at him.

One of the others, a big and muscular man rose with something resembling a beastly snarl accompanied by a hateful stare. Damon nodded to himself, not really surprised at all.

– This is my prince, she said softly. – I'm afraid he doesn't like you much. The fact is that he wants to break every bone in your body and then stamp on them.

– He wants to take my measure, Damon said cheerfully. – He fears he will lose your favor if I stay.

Her eyes twinkled. Her prospective mate growled. Damon nodded slowly.

He rose to his full height. There was no hurry to his movements, but no hesitation either. He tore off the remains of his clothes and dumped the claws tied to his arms. The wolf pack mumbled between themselves. Soon he was just as nude as any of them. They had ornaments on their bodies, like he had, but the sight of his green armband still made them mumble. They stared at it, stared hard. They formed a circle around the two combatants reminding him of the one in Marseille, though it was considerably smaller. He shrugged.

Those making out the ring struck hands at pillars, walls and floor. Those acts shouldn't have shaken the solid material, but Terrill sensed the thunder flowing at him, sensed the floor shake with every strike. Cold, clinical awareness and conviction shook him.

The prince attacked first, as expected. Damon had to take some hits before he struck his first punch at the fast-on-his-feet man. The wolf shook his head a few times, but stayed on his feet. He kept circling, clearly more cautious. Damon felt his pulse race, felt the berserker rage rise within, and he allowed it, welcomed it. He attacked. The doe tried evading him. Damon quite simply grabbed the man's hair with both hands and knocked his head at his. The rabbit used his strong feet, kicked at the opponent. Terrill jumped back in the last moment. There was no break. Both jumped back at each other simultaneously. Immutable forces met and one pushed the other backwards. The enemy's savagery paled compared to Damon's own. He tore the other down and landed on top of him, struck repeatedly the body beneath. He received a kick sending him backwards, until his back hit the ring, the circle of flesh, a creature reacting like one being, returning him to sender like a sack of flour. A kick made him go down. He was back up in a second.

They circled each other, snarling and spitting. Damon struck. The other struck. Damon struck him so hard and hit so well that his enemy practically flew through the air and hit the circle of flesh surrounding them. They returned him instantly. The two kept going. Terrill's red hot rage made him feel the pain only as glowing signals to the brain. It faded to insignificance. The only thing on his mind was defeating the man in front of him. They clinched. He broke the finger of his deadly enemy. The wolf struck back and backed away. Terrill followed him into another clinch. This time he broke the wolf's arm. A howl resembling a whine rose at the ceiling. He went for the kill and became a tad too eager, and was almost struck down when a vicious elbow strike touched his temple. He threw himself backwards, in a desperate act to defend himself from the wolf's next move, his body and feet floating well above the floor. The wolf did charge, doing so fast as death, a hazy mist in Terrill's imperiled vision. A rigid sole hit an exposed jaw. There was the sound of something breaking. The kick sent a deadly wounded body into the circle. The circle returned it once more, but this time the body didn't have any independent movement. It just collapsed on the floor, and died, even as it made the final few attempts at breathing. Damon was breathing hard, but landed on his feet and managed to remain standing.

The low, mumbling of approval rose to a roar. Gwendolyn approached him with a sensuous smile. She congratulated him with a hungry kiss.

She sensed his reluctance and pulled back a little, leaving him room.

– We didn't really have any reason to fight, he said reluctantly. – Only circumstances made us enemies. It was either him or me.

– Isn't that how it always is? She asked rhetorically. – You knew with a predator's slyness what you needed to do and did it without holding back, without giving your enemy an undue advantage. I was not wrong about you.

He gave her a wicked stare.

– How does it feel to be the hunter's prize?

– It feels good to be your prize, she mumbled, while drying his tears.

She tried caressing him. He turned away from her. She showed her strength and turned him back again, and kissed him on the lips, making blood flow.

– I need you, she breathed. – Release your beast.

– I like my beast just fine, he said with a sore smile. – We are indeed beasts, animals, no better or worse than others, and we shouldn't be ashamed of it.

– I like your words, she said passionately. – They stir me to no end. Now, let's act on it.

– Performing like animals in cages, he said inflamed. – Like circus animals in fear of the whip? *Never!*

She literally backed off; paralyzed and stunned by the obvious truth he had spat at her.

He sat by the wall alone later, when she returned to him.

– You're right, she whimpered. – We've been down here so long. I couldn't see it, just couldn't see it. Come to bed. You need sleep.

Sleep? He looked at her with distrust in his eyes, but knowing he would soon have trouble keeping his eyes open.

The pack gathered on a large low «bed» made of countless pieces of fabric, a thin cover so much better than the bare concrete floor. He joined them and lay down with her. The obvious hard-on didn't bother him. He turned his back to her in a deliberately relaxed fashion. She began rubbing his sore and bruised skin and limbs, comforting him while he stared straight forward with wide-open eyes. Another female, visibly horny wanted to join them. Gwendolyn waved her off, decisively, but not unfriendly. The she-wolf kept rubbing the male until he eventually closed his eyes, and not long after that slept hard.

He woke up startled, frowning. It took him a few seconds to get his bearings. Stiff limbs gave him a bit of trouble, but she had done a great job of softening his potential pain to a point where he could easily handle it.

She sat on her hinges by his shoulder. A bowl of fluid was pushed at his lips. He devoured it. She handed him a piece of meat. He practically swallowed it without chewing. She handed him a juicy orange. He chewed it without being haunted by disruptive thoughts.

– I wasn't certain that it would be smart to sleep…

– Don't be silly, she brushed off his concern, a little irritated, but keeping her sweet smile. – You know better than that. You know that I know much better than that, know that you are of much more use to us, now. That Damon Terrill has joined the pack voluntarily, instead of being forced to do so, increases the pack's chances of survival considerably.

– Cut the crap! He snarled. – Praise doesn't go far with me.

She smiled seductively to him, her praise and admiration delivered with glowing passion and a body language to match, making herself into an irresistible creature.

He began working out. She joined him, aiding and supporting him in any possible way. It was like a dance between them. It was a dance. A casual glance showed him how excited, how turned on she was, showing him in every way that she was available, that she was his.

Even her patronizing smile, her deliberately challenging stare told him that.

She showed him around, showing equal eagerness in that task. He suspected she would do that no matter what she was doing. They had six of her most trusted people on their heels. He had to admit to himself that it felt strangely comforting. He had witnessed firsthand how dangerous they could be.

They would have to be, in order to survive the upcoming Kingdom of Death, what was now only a gate or two away from manifesting.

They stood below the hatch, staring at the distant ceiling.

– I assume we, in theory could escape that way, she remarked subdued. – We could have built several human trapezes and surprised them and then overcome all the other guards on our way to the surface…

– Looks like you've considered the matter well and from all angles, he joked, earning a grateful smile.

She presented from a distance the various factions and groups in their big, small world. There were all kinds, from naturalists to skinheads, even a bunch of office rats, or at least resembling that kind dressed in suits and ties with only a few spots and stains. He shook his head in amazement.

– In there, we have most of the cannibals, she said, and now there was a distinct disgust in her voice. – Their numbers don't change much, but stay at the same level. One would presume there would be more of them because they… they have better access to food, but that hasn't happened.

He was surprised, after all to hear the shaking in the she wolf's voice.
– It might be that those from the outside are recruiting the most members from their group, Terrill said. – I wouldn't rule that out.
They exchanged glances, and in that moment they understood each other perfectly.
– We tried exterminating them, she said, more than subdued. – We never could.
At the end of the scenic tour, she brought him to a long, naked wall. He got it in an instant. There were no people there. Rats and bugs were all over the area, but no people.
– They come through here, she said with a loud and challenging voice. – They're always well armed and protected. They come and go as they please, picking up whomever they choose. I became… disheartened, no longer believing we could overpower or trick them, even if all of us down here joined a concentrated effort at escaping.
She sent him a fiery look.
– But now you're here…
He pulled back with her to their territory. They moved constantly on the edge between the open, free-for-all area and sudden confrontation.
Then he saw something… someone, a sight that made it impossible for him to not react in some way. He had no chance of hiding his interest to her.
– That's The Fishermen, the damn She Wolf enlightened him. – We've had quite a few *disagreements* with them.
He swallowed a bitter taste in his mouth and turned his full attention on his companion.
He knew that he no longer had any choice.
Among the whirling shapes in the twilight, in a cluster of heat and desire, he had spotted a familiar face, a pain, a wound that had never closed.
He had recognized Blanche.
++++++++++++++++++++++
Wahnzee rested like an old mirror by the old manor. The entire vast estate was guarded by a heavily armed militia. Here, the Nazis had planned «Die Endløsung» during World War 2, over seventy years ago.
Maxine and William were stopped at the gate.
– We have an appointment, she declared with patronizing flair, and showed the guards her note.
They were let through and started on the fairly long walk to the manor by the lake. Eyes moved constantly back and forth. It had long since become instinct, a constant part of their existence. Their surroundings left them stunned. This seemed like a Garden of Eden compared to the world outside. The grass and the plants were dry here as well, but not dead or dying. The water level in the lake was sinking, but there was still water.
– Such a well-groomed cemetery, she snorted.
They didn't talk much, didn't really communicate verbally. Their body language spoke much louder than words.
A guard grinned at them, pointing at them with his rifle, voicing a silent «bang, bang» with his lips. She grabbed William in the arm closest to her when he froze, and she felt his gathering rage.
– I know, I know, he assured her. – «Stay your rage. You will soon enough get the opportunity to express it».

William, she decided was a seriously troubled young man. It didn't bother her, but found an echo within herself. The same could be said about all of them, anyone in their circle of travelers.

In front of and around the big house, they saw the biggest private collection of arms they had ever witnessed. The presence of manned cannons, surface to air missile launchers, assault rifles and giant antennas seemed beyond excessive to them, no matter how concerned they were with their own security.

– I have heard it be claimed that our host is obsessed with monitor watching, she grinned. – That rumor does undoubtedly have a basis in fact...

The sentries at the entrance searched them, making the process as uncomfortable as possible. It didn't bother her that much, no matter how much she writhed under their cruel touch. She wasn't here, anyway. Her thoughts kept drifting, even though she never let go of the rock hard focus so necessary for survival.

On the first door down the hallway, they spotted a withered sign:

CENTER OF SUSTAINED DEVELOPMENT

– No one buys the propaganda anymore, she stated brightly, in a wry, sarcastic voice. – That is progress!

A little further down, the last door before they stepped into a dark gray nothing of hallways there was another door, slightly ajar with another sign, one even more withered.

EUROPEAN SECURITY FORCE

They saw no activity in there. Dust coated all surfaces. Everything had been abandoned. The ESF had been ridiculed and had lost all credibility and momentum after the incidents in Gothenburg and Oslo many years ago.

They walked downstairs, level by level, stairs by stairs. They encountered no guards.

At the last door, the final destination, they did. Ten gigantic men and women, some of them even taller than William, blocked their path. They did so as one being.

– Only one may enter. One of the men stepped forward. – The oversized gook will wait here.

William took one step forward and struck him down with one blow. The man hit the floor and didn't move.

– I hate Americans...

– Will the master please wait outside? One of the women said politely, but with expectation glowing in voice and eyes. – Only one may enter.

They stared at William with cold, snake-like eyes. Maxine glanced anxiously at him.

– Go! He told her.

They heard a click. The door slid open, the opening reminding her of a bottomless pit. She jumped into its jaw. The knight that might have slain the dragon remained outside. The access to the cave closed with a loud crack. All her senses ignored the countless, confusing images on the wall and focused calmly on the man in the chair.

– Your companion is not without interest to me, Tom Rawlins said with regret, – but I never accept more than one visitor at a given moment. Never!

– We need your help, Maxine said feverishly, the fever of the soul mirrored in her eyes, in her entire, rigid body.

– So, what boon may the emperor grant his loyal subject?

– The Storm Child was captured by the security police during an altercation in the city. We stumbled unaware into it all… into a completely insane situation. One moment we found ourselves in a quiet street, the next at the center of a nightmare. He vanished! There was nothing we could do. We quickly got word of where he had ended up. There isn't that many places in the city to choose from, is there? We realized quickly how futile a liberation attempt would be. After discussing hundreds of alternatives, the others decided to make an attempt, anyway. I convinced them to delay it, to try another solution first…

She could no longer hide her desperation, the catching in her throat.

– He's a prisoner in the Giant Bottomless Pit, she choked. – You're our only hope.

– And what will the Princess of Marseille do, if King Tom should have the power she thinks he has, in order to prove her loyalty and show her infinite gratitude?

– She's aware that he isn't the only power in this palace, she said hoarsely, – but that he's one of several with the necessary clout to grant her desire.

– I'm sick and tired of the game, he spat at her. – Remove your rags this instant, horny bitch.

She obeyed. It didn't prove difficult to her. She had dressed light, very light, wearing just a few garments. It happened fast, but not too fast, sufficiently slow to make him enjoy it. She turned slowly, displaying herself the irresistibly way she had learned in the classy cutthroat clubs in Marseille.

– You've been taught well, he grunted. – Perhaps you didn't understand how well before this very moment?

She didn't reply, but continued to perform for him, playing up her sensuality in every move she made.

– I have two demands. He seemed totally unfazed. – I want you completely, without you holding back anything. I desire your total, unreserved participation. Do you comply, bitch?

– I do! She lowered her gaze. – I will comply with the Emperor's wishes in all things.

– The other I will discuss with the kid when the time is right.

– He's no kid anymore.

– You will not say a word, he snarled. – The only reason for you to open your mouth is to release sweet, girly moans.

He was deliberately condescending, spitting on her with every word he spoke and every move he made. She didn't speak, but kept performing as if he hadn't spoken at all. He pushed a button on his well-equipped chair, and a bed seemed to flow from the wall, to part from it in one, fluid movement. The large, fleshy, muscular body revealed itself when he undressed with fast, casual moves, and wagged towards the bed. Maxine walked close behind his back. He turned and grabbed her, pulled her into his crushing embrace. He kissed her lips to shreds with his stinking gap and deadly fangs. She jumped up and embraced the barrel-shaped body with both her legs and arms. She returned the kisses and cut deep in his flesh with her long nails. He put her down on the bed and rested his full weight on her, pushed down her arms, pushed her down. She writhed beneath him, very active, giving as good as she got. He penetrated her callously, without showing anything even resembling compassion, without caring about her or her reaction in any way. She moaned and screamed every time he pushed and pulled. He finished up, hardly showing anything but a terrifying indifference. When he rose and dressed again, he seemed totally unmoved.

– You did not fake it, he said pleased. – You're such a good bitch!

She remained unmoving on the bed for some time afterwards. Only the eyes moved in the serene, doll-like face, following closely his every move.

– You're a fascinating man, she said with an insane smile. – Allow me to thank you. You've given me yet another reason to hate.

– That pleases me, he grunted. – It will give you greater odds at survival.

He sat down in his chair and pushed the button to activate the multi-screen. The wall to wall, composite image showed the hall outside. William Otterman had made mincemeat of eight of his opponents and started on the ninth. He didn't exactly look good, but the others looked totally trashed in comparison.

– You see my problem in a nutshell? The Emperor sighed. – All my people are overpaid.

+++++++

Light flickered in his vision and slipped into shades of gray. He woke up and opened his eyes with a distinct sense of unpleasantness. She approached him with a towel in her hands. He looked down on himself. It was wet and still hot down there. She sat down on her hinges and started drying him, showing great skill while doing so. It didn't really turn him on at all.

– This will happen, you know, when a man with strong desires denies himself the pleasures coming his way… What is repressed must be expressed. Steam will blow the lid of a steaming kettle.

He grabbed her firm flesh, held on to it and whispered into her ear.

– I do wish to suppress it, making it grow stronger, in order to enjoy it even more when we do get out of here, on our own terms.

Her eyes grew big. The whisper sounded like thunder in her ears. Anxiety faded and excitement took its place.

He wasn't certain he could actually smell her excitement, or if he rather sensed it, doing so through a series of sensations. The way she crouched. The higher breathing frequency. The tiny change in skin color. He knew he reached out his thoughts, that he had the ability to do that and more. Death pushed hard at you down here. That didn't harm him either, but strengthened him, reminding him that he was alive.

She brought him breakfast, displayed herself in a way he couldn't avoid noticing. There was no reservation there. She demanded his attention, but didn't submit in any way.

A man sat with his back to a pillar a considerable distance away, but Damon still saw him, sensed and felt him. Damon had seen him in the streets above as well, a demonic face, an insane grin creating unrest and fear wherever it appeared.

The man sat there alone. No one, not even the perceived tough guys among them dared approach him. There were no teeth in the steaming gap. The eyes looked like two deep holes. The face appeared dissolved, though it was still the face people noticed on the beyond skinny skeleton body. The grinning skull glowed in the dark and no one escaped its sick gleam.

– Can… you… hear… them? The voice not a voice whispered. – I can! I've heard them in ungodly Sahara. When I walked north to escape their ruthless whine, they walked with me. You hear them as well, I know you do… You convince yourselves that it is a million grains of sand rubbing against each other, but know in your hearts that you lie to yourselves. Everyone KNOWS it is the souls of the dead we hear, screaming at us, condemning us…

Gwendolyn pulled close to Damon and he noticed that she was shaking.

– Does he frighten you? He asked her curtly. – Or are you pretending? Tell me the truth!

– He does frighten me, she whimpered. – He frightens everybody out of their wits.

– Why? Damon asked casually.

– He's a spirit of the Abyss and is here to take us with him, she said subdued. – He isn't h-human!

Damon knew the Abyss. He suspected he had always known it, even been intimately familiar with it.

He started laughing.

– So, what you're telling me is that everyone down here is scared to death by a scarecrow, that you're scared of your own shadow? I had expected more of you.

She stared resentful, ashamed at him.

– Superstition has ruled mankind like a mare for thousands of years, he said enraged. – It must end, now!

She looked like she wanted to say something, but she bit her lip and stared at him with eyes filled with hatred. A sly expression returned to her features.

– I realized right from the start that you were not worthy of me, he said, clearly condescending, pouring it on, making her shrink in his presence. – You don't have more courage than what you reveal on the outside, a wall against the world dissolving the moment you touch it.

He started touching her, and she turned instantly soft in his arms. He saw surrender and submission in her wet eyes.

When he let go of her, she didn't move, or strayed, in any way from the position he had placed her.

– I would have talked like that, acted like that, if I had been who you believed me to be, and you would have been left like a wet rag on the ground, a doormat I could step on.

He rose. She remained on her knees. He studied her with casual indifference. She fought herself on her feet, clinging desperately to him.

– Thank you, she said hatefully, passionately. – I will thank you, be certain of that. You're callous beast, and I will help you realize that.

He didn't reply, but practically ignored her, just like she expected him to do.

– Come with me. Only you!

She obeyed with shiny eyes. The others remained unmoving. There was no longer any doubt about who was making the decisions, and the transference of power had happened so easily, so very easy.

He took a stroll and she walked behind him, like a good squaw. Sometimes, he grew worried on his own behalf, and this was one of those times. He had smelled blood the moment he had sensed her weakness, and like everyone else that had had the taste of it, he wanted more. He used that, used the intoxication to move him forward.

Damon Terrill walked straight to the Skeleton Man and sensed thousand eyes studying him. When he knelt down in front of the wreck of a human being, he had all his senses peaked.

– I have a message for you, man, he said gently, or seemingly gently, – and I don't want to repeat myself: You're ruining people's sleep. That may not be the worst you can do in a given situation in all situations in life, but in this place it definitely is. We don't need anyone to burden us unnecessarily, if you get my drift.

Terrill stared into the two deep wells with his dark fire. There was nothing, no discernible reaction, no one present in there.

– Are you one of… the condemned? The skull queried.

The grin of a mouth moved. The peculiar voice penetrated Terrill, like it did everyone else hearing it.

Damon kicked the man in the chest. Air wheezed from the squeezed lungs. A blow hit the side of the head. The thoroughly relaxed body was pushed to the side. Damon kicked him several more times. A stunned expression appeared in the inhuman face. There was someone home. Damon grabbed the unmoving body by the collar. Seemingly worn fabric didn't rupture.

Whitish eyes opened. Terrill noticed a change, a show of interest. His own fears stared back at him.

With a powerful show of force, he threw the other man at the pillar. The skeleton-like body slid down the rough surface and collapsed in a heap on the floor.

They walked on. The glowing rage reflected in the she wolf's eyes pushed him further on the path glowing in front of him. She frowned and looked around her as they walked, measuring directions and their place in the terrain, the space they moved through.

– We *are* heading for The Fishermen and their Camp of the Dead, now, right?

She spotted the snarl in the corner of his mouth.

– Of course we are, she grinned.

Her entire attitude changed and she speeded up, catching up with him, walking proud by his side.

– Uh, Randall, *King* Duncan isn't exactly the usual pushover, she enlightened him.

– I know! He shrugged.

– Of course you do, she mumbled.

Unrest kept charging through the Bottomless Pit, including the Camp of the Dead, but that paled compared to what happened when they crossed the invisible demarcation line marking its territory.

Duncan Randall, the king and singular ruler of The Fishermen «community» sat on his throne in a makeshift hall at the center of a large area framed by carpets and blankets. A straw hut, evidently the king's residence towered behind the throne. The stage would have seemed totally ridiculous in any other situation.

Two zealous sentries rushed forward and assaulted them the moment they approached. Gwendolyn struck them down without visibly exerting herself. She faced four others ready to join in. The man on the throne waved them off, and they froze. Terrill directed his complete attention at him, confident that the she wolf had his back.

Randall was young, hardly much older than Damon. He looked quite ordinary, not one able to command the respect he seemed to enjoy. That made him even more dangerous in Damon's eyes. Damon had sensed something like this, something hidden for quite some time. He felt it like a wet blanket around his body, talons of fear at the back of his head.

The two measured each other intensively, without visibly doing so. Damon spoke first.

– We're getting out of here, all of us. We will stop with our internal rivalry. When the moment comes, we will be one united force conquering everything in our path.

Everyone listened, listened hard, everyone in every single corner of the wasteland making out the giant basement. He had contact with them all, and could determine that with striking accuracy. His body… was glowing. He found himself outside himself and saw how a bluish aura stretched and twisted at all possible angles. Hearing the breath of the she wolf was child's play.

– They're indeed slick those who have placed us here, at the bottom of the artificial pyramid. They have for so long, for so many ages made us buy into the myth of the hierarchy so prevalent in modern society. That, that, too, will end, will end yesterday.

Randall rested his jaw on his fingertips, pretending to consider the other's words.

– There's truth in your words, he said noncommittally. – I presume you've given this enterprise some thought… who is supposed to lead it?

– I don't give a shit about that! Terrill said curtly. – I care about its implementation.

– I will consider your proposal, the man on the throne said carefully. – Is there anything more I can do for you?

– Give me her! Damon, tired of the game pointed at the woman, at Blanche kneeling two steps left of the throne.

– Her? Randall cackled incredulous. – She's only a slave.

– Exactly! The Storm Child shrugged. – Call it a modest sign of good will.

A snap of fingers, a signal and Blanche rushed forward and knelt before her new master.

He didn't look at her, didn't touch her, but turned and walked away. She waited until Gwendolyn had joined him before she followed in his steps, exactly in his steps. His feet didn't make any visible tracks, but she still knew exactly where to walk. Yet another hot chill passed down his spine. By a force of will, he brought forth a bit more of his slumbering rage, and he glowed even stronger.

Gwendolyn stared at him, visibly turned on.

– He fears you! She stated hotly, her voice and stance coarse with desire. – One snap of the fingers from him, and we would have been dead, but he was more interested in the mole on your leg.

– He was? I didn't notice.

– He was, I saw it, she insisted. – I think it was the first time in his life he encountered another of his kind, another… walking the shadows.

– Don't go weak-kneed on me, now, he admonished her. – That will make you useless to me, and I need you, little sister.

– I know that, and rest assured I will live up to your expectations, she said. – I know exactly what you need.

They walked a few steps in silence. She leaned her head on his shoulder. He waited patiently.

– You like her. I can see that with half an eye. It doesn't matter. I don't mind sharing you. Even the two of us combined are probably not enough for you. You're so cold, hotter than the flames of Hell.

She touched the skin of his neck with her fingertips cautiously, as if she feared she would burn herself. He shook his head. That had to be bullshit. She wasn't afraid of anything.

Or perhaps she was. She, after all was also a product of the society of her birth.
He stopped and penetrated her with his cold stare. She shrunk in her tracks, but didn't back down, kept stubbornly returning his stare.
– You *are* wrong about me, she stated, resting her eyes on him. – You're exactly like I imagined. I feared you wouldn't live up to my high expectation of you, but you do, and I rejoice.
He focused deliberately on Blanche. She was a welcomed distraction. He watched her as she looked around her in confusion.
– Everyone is nude here? She whimpered, fearing the sound of her own voice.
– We love being nude, honey, Gwendolyn said, not unkind. – And no one will treat you bad anymore, at least not if you become a wolf among wolves.
Blanche could hardly look at them. Gwendolyn grabbed her jaw and pushed her head up.
– You do need to claim your place in the world, you know.
Damon forced himself to look at her. Every time he met the wounds her eyes had become, he was cast back to the time in Marseille, the insane scene at the high tower and all his almost forgotten insecurities and painful memories rose from the hideouts.
They reached the wolf territory. He sat down with the others, but a dark, dark shadow grabbed him and held him in his grip. He had trouble sleeping, or even with getting tired. The glow within faded to embers. He faded. Rage went away, and despair took its place. It was as if he didn't notice the two pleasant and eager creatures by his side.
– I remember you, Blanche said cautiously, anxiously. – You do remember me, don't you? You… want me?
She could reason, could think beyond the mire her existence had been for so long. That encouraged him a little, just a little. He didn't voice a reply, but did sort of respond, sufficient to comfort her, somewhat.
The two girls fell asleep. Everyone slept around him, but he sat there, hardly even there at all.
He woke up the next «morning», or the morning after that. The periods of sleep and not mixed in his mind and were increasingly hard to separate.
Something happened at a given moment one day, several given moments he could not distinguish from each other.
A pack of wild-eyed two-legged animals dressed in rags appeared to him. He saw easily that they came from several different groups or territories down here. The man in front held up a green armband. They were all drawn to Damon, paying allegiance to him, coming from all deep forests, all mountain peaks penetrating the sky.
Some of them stayed. Others left, but returned from time to time. They pushed forward and pulled back at an uneven flow.
He sat there, with his head between his knees. Blanche groomed him.
– You don't have to do that, he told her. – You are not my slave or my servant.
– I want to, she mumbled. – Please, Damon!
The very act of saying his name seemed to rattle her, and she pulled back in distress.
But he felt her hands on his skin, noticed how she combed his hair with her hands.
– She's fragile at this point, practically fearing the dark, Gwendolyn said. – You're doing the right thing being cautious.
There were occasions, conversations such as these, moments of a certain clarity, but

time tended to slip through his fingers, and the floor beneath and his surroundings just seemed to slide away into nothing.

The next «days», the upcoming centuries he imagined a heavy mist wherever he turned. He forgot more than he remembered. There were lucid thoughts now and then, he knew that, but nothing stayed solid for long in the unending, indistinct flow his existence had become.

Females, Blanche, Gwendolyn and others offered themselves to him. The sound of mating grew louder and louder in his ears.

The two of them displayed themselves to him one day, like they did every day, did all the time. He grabbed them both, and warm and willing flesh melted into his arms, releasing a cry of joy when they realized what was about to happen.

– What about Those Watching? Gwendolyn breathed in his ear.

– I want to break them in thousand pieces. He shrugged. – Aside from that… they mean nothing to me.

He remembered grabbing Blanche's hips and lifting them from the floor, remembered pushing himself deep into her, and later the wolf bitch writhing under him. Thoughts went away, and his recall worked only from moment to moment. Time and space faded, and only sensations, flesh and blood, fear and rage were real. Everything vanished into the Bottomless Pit, until only the twilight storm within was left.

++

A blinding light struck him. Outlines slowly turned sharper and distinct.

Maxine stopped in front of him. He saw, felt and sensed her concern.

He had changed. She noticed instantly the remote look in his eyes. It didn't take away any of his intensity.

She and Rawlins stood side by side. They were quite the odd pair. She pulled away from the big man, as if she suddenly remembered something. The Storm Child and the woman grabbed each other hands.

– I'm so happy to see you, she choked.

– You're a sight for sore eyes, he replied. – All of you!

– It's fitting that we meet here, like this, Rawlins said. – In the storm and whirlwind of the world.

– In the anvil of Crom, André joked.

Everyone chuckled, but stayed solemn.

Terrill embraced her, so hard that he almost crushed her. She practically melted in his arms.

Surrounding them were the wolves, The Green Rose, the Children of the Midnight Fire… and Rawlins' band of cutthroats, a formidable army each and every one on its own. The sum of the parts made them a force to be reckoned with.

Damon studied their surroundings thoroughly. They stood in a refurbished part of the sewer system. The distance to the streets was about fifty meters.

– That's Blanche! Yola exclaimed. – Isn't it, Blanche?

– I… found her, Damon said dully.

Yola approached her sister on unsteady legs.

– You're… Yolanda?

– I am! Yola laughed happily. – And you're Blanche. You are Blanche!

Damon scouted the exit. He spotted military vehicles on both sides of the giant sewer pipe. He saw no people nearby, either with or without uniform. The sun kept casting a white light. Even here, in the pale shadows, the shades Maxine had given him didn't work very well. That didn't bother him much. The sun had always caused him pain.

– We haven't much time, Rawlins pointed out, finally giving voice to his obvious restlessness. – Not here, not anywhere near the city. I have it from a well-informed source that Berlin will cease to exist within a few days.

– Oh, which source is that? Maxine asked, not hiding her suspicion.

– The best possible, Rawlins grinned. – Myself.

– Do I understand you correctly if I say you want to travel with us, Tom? Terrill wondered with curiosity in his voice and expression. – May I ask why?

– You're by far the best traveling companions in town, Rawlins spat. – One cannot be too picky these days.

– Why should we drag with us such deadweight? Maxine spoke up instantly. – He needs us, we don't need him.

– A very astute statement, André shrugged when Damon glanced at him. – He's no more than a burned out wreck. We have no use for him.

– What is use? Damon asked rhetorically.

He dressed. A look from him and the wolves dressed as well. There were more than sufficient amounts of clothes - and guns. He felt the pressure of the revolver inside his jacket.

– It doesn't matter, another cried out. – We will never get out of here, anyway. Berlin is a closed-off plague pit without exits.

Damon Terrill smiled then, in a moment of «godly inspiration».

– How long have I been a guest at this place? He asked them.

– Uh, fifteen days and nights, William replied. – Why?

– It's Friday today, right?

– Yes, it is, but what…

He got it, and several others did as well and started smiling, smiles changing to cruel grins.

– Clean the entire Pit for rats, lice and people, Damon commanded. – There is sufficient time?

– More than enough!

André cocked his shotgun.

It didn't take that much time, less than half an hour, until everyone had been chased like sheep from the overgrown basement, including those resisting being set free. Terrill caught a glimpse of Duncan Randall in the stampeding herd. A few exchanges of glances and they were enemies, confirming the impression from their first meeting. It didn't pain Terrill as much as it once would have done.

The completely unruly flock rushed into the streets, filled to the brim with berserker rage and with murder on their mind.

Dawn, the color of rust and blood persisted. Damon breathed stubbornly the polluted air. A gathering ecstasy overwhelmed the unavoidable anxiety they all felt. Maxine took his hand and squeezed it gently.

– You're free! She declared. – You will never be captured by anyone, ever again.

– I knew I would get out of there sooner or later, he said, – but it would clearly have been much later, with far more sacrifices if you guys hadn't come.

The feeling of shame and inadequacy didn't let go.

– You're one of us, Yola stated as the most obvious thing in the world, and it warmed him. – Of course we came!

He wondered if he could turn that deep-felt shame stemming from his perceived sense of failure around, into something constructive, something that would help them prevail, survive.

– We will never again be taken unprepared, he stated, he declared with a passion burning them all.

– You believe that, Maxine said startled. – You truly believe that!

Her doubt, if doubt there was, didn't bother him. His unrest stemmed from another source of insecurity… from the certainty he shared with her, the female by his side… that he had started on the…

Road to Power.

CHAPTER FOURTEEN

The breakout from Berlin started on the old, honorable Olympic Stadium.

The stands were filled to the breaking point with howling people. The transparent dome protected them from at least some of the poisonous air and lethal levels of sun radiation outside. Enormous machines filtrated and cleaned the air. The machinery made a beyond horrible noise, but no one heard it. The war on the stands and on the pitch was set to begin. The upcoming, inevitable explosion seemed very close in time and space. Very few heard the man screaming through the speakers. Very few heard the people near them or caught any sound most places under the dome, except the insane roar constantly rising from the spectators.

Both how the game of football was played and the manner it was hosted had changed significantly in recent years. One such notable change was the decline of the old masters in Germany and in Europe as a whole. Bayern Munchen, Milan, Manchester United, Barcelona and several others had been reduced to insignificance or were downright *gone.* Previously unimportant teams like Hertha Berlin were now met with insane roars by its numerous supporters. The away team, Hamburg, one of the few remaining of the old champions, was bombarded with profanities, pieces of paper and wood, *and* bottles. The teams walked around the entire pitch, giving the spectators a change to display their disgust. The HSV-supporters, having been transported here from Hamburg, had been placed in the usual closed-off section behind one of the goals. They were allowed to vent their frustration against the home team in full, and the frustration among the Berliners rose to a dangerously high level.

The match started on time. The cleaning of the pitch was included in the schedule and it was cleared of bottles, wood, paper and tons of other elements well before the match was supposed to begin. Overzealous home team supporters attempted to climb over the fence to reach the enemy camp, but were quickly handled by numerous soldiers, police officers and uniformed guards. Everything seemed very well organized.

Damon and members of his tribe from many tribes wore headsets and miniature microphones, as they approached the gate.

– Check! He said.

Everyone on his team confirmed that they had heard him.

All of them had the proof of their Berlin citizenship checked, before being let inside and allowed to join the home team supporters. They didn't rush forward as close as possible to the fence by the burned grass like everyone else, but pulled close to the solid fence dividing the Berliners and the away team supporters. The soldiers, guards and police officers had lined up like living walls on each side of the fence.

– We are in the right spot, Paolo remarked, – right between the gates of hell and with a short distance to the exit.

Gwendolyn's close proximity and the sight of her kept distracting Terrill. It felt strange to see her fully clothed. She hadn't grown any less desirable.

– I haven't changed that much, have I? She asked him shyly, uncharacteristically so.

– You're exactly the same! He assured her and shrugged.

She rewarded him with a rich, throaty chuckle.

He had picked ten to accompany him. Gwendolyn (for obvious reasons), but also others had the perfect mindset for something like this, the same devil-may-care, bubbling mood he, himself hardly was able to contain.
Some of the others had been concerned for him, had attempted to discourage him from participating in the operation. Others again had suggested that everyone should participate. He had rejected both proposals.
– You are correct. He heard Rawlins' voice again for the first time in a while. – This is our best chance of survival, as a group and individuals.
Damon had stood before them, all the children of the moon.
– We won't all get out of this alive, he cried to them. – We may be separated, here, or later on our Long Walk. Let's prepare for that.
He had showed them on the map and described the surroundings and circumstances concerning the current end of their journey, told them about Bergen, on the western coast of Norway.
– They say it will always rain there, right? Rawlins said.
– If I reach it, you won't have any trouble finding me, Damon told them. – If I don't make it, you shouldn't have too much trouble surviving there, and decide for yourself what to do as circumstances change.
The roar filling Olympic Stadium demanded his attention anew. The explosion was imminent.
Claire believed firmly she studied him without him noticing. She didn't possess his skill at studying people without being obvious about it. She resembled her mother physically, but didn't possess the same intense presence, what made a human being stand out among thousands.
He would guess that it wasn't easy growing up in Strega's shadow and that might be the reason or one reason why Anya had sent her away, in order for her to find her own path.
– Everything set? He asked her lightly.
– Very much so! She said, painfully shy and opened her bag.
He looked down at the slithering mass. One thing was certain. She had inherited her mother's skills with snakes. He grinned, more than a little put off. She returned the grin.
The match started. A strange emotion grabbed Terrill as he witnessed the event on the pitch and the increasing hostility in the stalls. He felt brought back to an ancient Roman gladiator arena. It wasn't a new feeling. Every single sports event gave him that impression. But the various games had become even more bread and circuses recently.
Those in charge were on their last legs. False promises didn't work anymore. Threats and brutality turned out to be increasingly useless. But there were still places where people could direct their stored aggression and thereby be distracted.
But everything was slipping, both on Olympic Stadium and in Berlin as a whole. One strike of a match and everything would blow sky high…
Like Tom Rawlins so rightly had pointed out: no one was in control anymore.
Damon felt it come, felt it arise within, a need, a savagery stronger than any artificial stimuli, in himself, in people all over the place… and its energy flooded him and strengthened him.
He laughed aloud, a wild and hearty laughter, with a hint of madness encouraging his companions.
The referee blew his whistle and started the game again after a brutal duel at the mid-

circle. Hamburg's number ten, Hessler kicked the ball. The moves, the passes convinced Damon he had seen everything before.

Hessler received the ball again twenty meters from the goal. He was kicked down. The referee waved it all off. Enraged shouts rose from the Hamburg section. Hertha won the ball. An insane roar of anticipation rose from the home team supporters.

Hertha's number 24 ran with the ball on the left side of the pitch. Rackhof was seen as an immigrant by the fans and was not among the most popular on the team, but now he received a loud roar of support. It rose to a downright agonizing level when he outpaced his opponent. Rackhof passed the ball to number 7, Altman, in a three-way game, and got it back at the edge of the penalty area. He tricked one man, two men and suddenly only had the goalkeeper in front of him.

Then, Albert «Bonebreaker» Vosburg charged him and tripped him with his left foot. Rackhof fell and the goalkeeper caught the ball easily. The referee waved it off.

An insane roar of adrenalin and rage rose from the spectators. Rackhof rushed the referee in front of at least twenty enraged Hertha players. The manager and all the substitutes joined the delegation. In the meantime Hamburg's number five ran relaxed all over the pitch and kicked the ball into the empty cage. The referee blew his whistle, signifying goal. The security guard rushed forward and surrounded him. The mere sight of the towering hulks discouraged those having a strong desire to discourage the good referee. Rackhof was shown the red card and was carried off the pitch accompanied by wild celebration and sarcastic shouts from the Hamburg section. **Hertha 0 HSV 1** blinked on the result board accompanied by ear-shattering booing from the beyond chauvinistic local spectators.

No more than five minutes into the match the mood had already passed beyond explosive. The glass dome shook and threatened to break.

The match proceeded, more or less uninterrupted, another solid documentation of German efficiency. Damon and all his companions smiled, even those without any understanding of football. Terrill, with something resembling German diligence, had explained it to them two hours before the match.

– All of it is an excellent staged event. The winner has been decided before the start of the season. Hertha will probably end up winning 7-6 or 8-7. The point with the spectacle is to make people so emotionally drained that they have no more aggression left to fight against the daily injustice. The supporters transfer all their ambitions and frustrations into hopes of success for their hero athletes. They can celebrate with them when they win and lose without risk. The home team usually has one player sent off early on. It has become such a common, transparent ploy in any given game, long since becoming completely ridiculous. Number 24 Rackhof isn't seen as a true Berliner. He belongs to a pool of four to five performers playing the *prugelknabe,* a pawn that can be sacrificed without risk. At the end of the game, when the celebration starts very few will feel sorry for poor Rackhof. It is bread and circuses, ladies and gentlemen, a genius system in play and dishonor since the Roman Empire. It works insanely well… as long as those staging the game remain in control. As we all know: in a witches brew, no one knows which spice it may contain.

They still recalled his speech vividly and with immaculate fondness…

A startling, uncanny silence had descended on the arena. It was actually possible to hear people breathe.

– Why are you guys smiling? The man standing by Gwendolyn's side asked very suspicious. – We have started the match disastrously bad. The referee is rotten and we will play with ten men for the rest of the match. Our hopes of winning are just dismal.

Damon and Gwendolyn exchanged glances, despairing slightly because of the man's naiveté.

– If you ponder the issue, you will easily see that we can easily overcome such miniscule hurdles, Gwendolyn said, clearly condescending. – We're strong, and opposition just makes us stronger, though opponents like these are more like an insult to our great players.

She overdid it, but the bewitched man didn't get it. He looked at her with an almost religious expression.

– Speaking about the referee… *Ein schweinhund* like him will always receive his just reward, *nicht war?*

Damon's grin widened. Her performance just made him gloriously happy…

A casual glance at the ten tribe members surrounding him brought further joy. He saw many colors, many creeds, such a great variety of skills and personalities.

Ten minutes into the match there was more perceived decisive action. The Polish player, Janowsky climbed the back of a defender and headed in 2 - 0. The Hamburg supporters jumped and danced in joy behind the secure fences and the guards. A sour stench spread on the arena. The referee started sweating in earnest. The sweat was easy to spot on the shiny forehead.

Terrill nodded to Gwendolyn. She went to work without delay.

– I wonder about the guys over there, she told her doglike admirer. – Don't you agree they look suspiciously slack and generally speaking show little interest in the game?

– You don't say? He said astonished, but caught himself and eager to impress the girl, he made a strategic turnaround. – Yes, now, when you say so…

Those guys stood a little by themselves, and didn't really act up or anything. Damon suspected they belonged to an endangered species: those genuinely interested in the game.

– I overheard them when they walked past us earlier, she said, seemingly very agitated. – I swear they were speaking with a Hamburg accent.

– Spies, huh? He said with a thick, triumphant voice. – Sneaking around where they have no business. We shall see if their courage is just as yellow as their gut. You wait here!

He rushed over to his buddies and started talking fast and furious to them, pointing and gesticulated as if his life depended on it.

Maxine, with tears in her eyes, stumbled the last few steps towards a group of soldiers. Large, blonde skewed-eyed William supported her, clearly reluctant.

– What's wrong with her? The sergeant asked curtly.

– She sought my help, William said. – I don't know her and have never even seen her before.

– My husband beat me, Maxine sniffed, not hiding her French accent. – I didn't want to be a part of what he and his pals were planning and he b-beat me.

– This is on you, the sergeant snorted to William, – You must take care of her.

– Out of the question, William snorted equally condescending.

The sergeant sent him an angry look, but focused on the woman.

– This sounds like a police matter, he told her. – We can't do anything about it... at this time. I must ask you both to leave. There's a risk you will keep us from doing important work.

Damon chuckled. He couldn't help it.

– T-there's one thing I must ask you first...

– I must once again ask you to leave...

– My husband and his good friends have come here all the way from Hamburg, Listen to me, please.

– From... Hamburg, you say?

The sergeant strived to conceal the sudden eagerness in his voice.

– That's right, the despairing, loyal *hausfrau* said. – I told him, but he didn't listen to my well meant advice. I assure you my intention was honorable. I...

– What did you come here to tell us, woman?

The sergeant asked with a very visible impatience.

– I objected, objected to it all, I assure you I did. (Here the sergeant directed his eyes at the sky as if seeking aid from a higher power). – I did my best to convince him that this wasn't the right time of the year for fireworks. I *did!*

– Answer me, you silly goose. The sergeant shook her. – Only Berliners are allowed in this section. How did you get inside?

– Don't get mad! She said sourly. – I told him, I assure you. I had heard it was illegal to make your own passes, but did that idiot listen to me? Oh, no!

– Where are your husband and his comrades? The sergeant said, doing so in such a nice manner that even the silly goose had to give him a suspicious look.

– Over there. She hesitated a bit, but then she pointed. – By the main stalls.

The sergeant had already left his post and brought with him ninety percent of his people. The fence keeping the two supporter teams from each other's throat was now practically unguarded. Maxine and Will went ahead with their task without further delay.

– HAMBURG SUPPORTERS ARE FAT AND SHIT THROUGH THEIR MOUTH, they choired.

The two remaining guards frowned, but didn't take action.

People at the other side of the fence heard only pieces of it, but after several repetitions they got it. Other Berliners eagerly joined the choir and raging replies rose from the colony in the seething mirror image. People from both sides climbed easily the, oh, so ineffective fence. The two that had lit the fuse pulled back, to relative safety.

Gwendolyn's admirer, with friends had started beating up their intended victims. They gave as good as they got.

– DAMN HARBOR RATS, they screamed at each other.

Damon pushed the button on his phone and sent the signal.

Claire, fairly relaxed, started pulling the snakes from her bag and throwing them in all directions. Not long after that, the first, panicked scream rose from the masses.

– There are SNAKES here!

The man's howl was repeated by many a hysterical voice.

Claire threw two snakes at the pitch as well for good measure.

Less than a minute after a relative stability had dominated the arena, the unrest spread amazingly fast across the various stall sections. It exploded completely not long after that again. Contrary to during other recent football riots, the response from the security forces was not up to par. This time they seemed to be in the wrong place in the wrong time. They seemed disorganized and just didn't reach the rioters. A wall, a fluid mass of flesh prevented them from doing that. They tried pushing through the unruly mass, striking at everyone blocking their path, but this time that strategy failed completely. It didn't take long until the uniformed thugs had become a part of the show, an integrated part of the tournament of fear raging on.

Terrill and the others took no chances this time and pulled back towards the exit without delay. In spite of that, they were almost drawn into the melee. They had almost reached the streets when the first rockets hit the top of the dome and blew large holes in it. Glass and metal rained down on people filling the pitch, and the many still on the stalls. To this point panic and rage had been two distinct phenomena at Olympic Stadium. From that moment, they became one and the same.

People emerged into the streets with them, like they did from every exit of the arena. The eleven had taken only a few hits, some bruises, no more. Adrenaline surged through their veins. Euphoria rode them in beyond powerful ways. The fighting continued outside, and expanded in circles through streets, roads and even buildings.

– SUCCESS, Claire shouted with a grin so wide that it hurt.

She looked somberly at her fellow tribe members.

– We hoped for something like this, right? But this is almost too much.

– Almost, Damon agreed.

A warm trickle hammered his spine.

– KILL ALL HAMBURG RATS!

A man shouted while firing a gun at everyone close to him. People fell in pools of blood.

A crowd was chased down the street. It was hard to say what made them different from those chasing them. One unarmed group fled in nameless fear. The other, armed to their teeth chased them and killed them without mercy.

Everyone ran, ran flat out. Throats and muscles burned. The eleven ran until they felt the taste of blood, the taste of sweet, sour blood in their mouth. They ran in a more or less straight line towards their destination. The panic was present, lurking in their consciousness the entire time. The fear and the rage granted them what seemed like unlimited strength.

They climbed tall fences as if they weren't there, jumped down from high rises without trouble or injuries. Damon landed slightly wrong once and felt pain in his left thigh. He ran on. The pain only cleared the mind, sharpening the instincts and kept thoughts from drifting in unpleasant directions. They ran into the railway area behind Bahnhof Zoo, heaving for breath. The inferno of fire, blind, unreasoned hatred and destruction ruled there as well. It had already caught up with them, seemingly spread through the very air far faster than they had been running. Who attacked who and the reason for it, remained completely incomprehensible. It vanished in the event itself.

The travelers registered that, at the back of their one-track minds, just like they heard the scream from an inhuman creature pointing at them. Be prepared, their inner voice admonished them. Be *ready!*

HAMBURGER RATS, a banshee cry shook their ears, or perhaps only their minds. They shrunk a bit, unable to keep themselves from doing so. They straightened stubbornly, raising weary heads.

They found themselves alone between massive transport train coaches. Everyone glanced and kept glancing around as they ran, rapidly and constantly moving their eyes back and forth, up and down, back and front. They heard sounds of steps in the shingle. There were distinct forewarnings. Suddenly those sounds or those making the sounds were so much closer.

Three people rushed them from the right, seemingly appearing out of nowhere, armed with chains, axes and sledgehammers. The woman struck out with her axe. Its flat side graced Terrill's forehead. He saw sparks and existence made a tupsy turvy when he landed with his head in the single. The big, snarling woman was struck down by one of William's sledgehammers, his mighty fists. The three attackers were dealt with in a rush of fiery moves. Terrill fought himself up in standing position. More people rushed them, like bloodhounds chasing prey. Damon started laughing, a fiery laughter, a gallows humor stopping the attackers in their tracks.

The roar of bikes filled the air. The proud Berliners froze when the Riders of the Thunder Road charged them. The bikes and their riders pulled to an abrupt halt. The city natives stared sullenly at the foreigners. Even though superior in numbers, they pulled backwards with hateful eyes and faded away in the indistinct background of the area.

– We're not all Berliners, Damon taunted them. – Crawl back into your holes and stay there. We're leaving and we won't return.

Yola stopped in front of him and handed him clothes and driving gear. They dressed without haste.

Eleven bikes were rolled out of a smaller truck. They left it behind. They started the engines, and rode their mounts along the railway tracks. Wearing helmets and protective goggles they followed the pale, deadly sun west.

They rode into the dark tunnel, emerging from it without incident or having any notable experience of the time involved.

– WARNING, YOU'RE NOT CLEARED! A loud, metallic voice shouted from enormous speakers. I REPEAT: YOU'RE NOT AUTHORIZED TO USE THE GATE. UNLESS YOU STOP IMMEDIATELY, WE WILL BE FORCED TO USE DRASTIC MEANS.

The tribe gathered from many half moons started grinning after just a few seconds, long before they were actually convinced that there would be no immediate attack.

Dust whirled around them. The Thunder Road riders disappeared in that thick, thick cloud, unable to see more than a few meters ahead.

They looked for the chopper or something similar, but still didn't spot it until bullets whipped up shingle between them. Blood flowed in a straight line from those who were hit, mixing with the dust and the poisonous air. They looked up and discovered the bird of prey hovering above them. No one stopped, no one slowed down. André drove up by Terrill's side. In several seemingly easygoing moves, he loosened the bazooka from his bike, keeping a hand on the handlebar, while stepping up on the seat. Terrill and Renate grabbed one handle each, and steered the bike. The moment the bird of prey turned ahead of them, to attack anew, André fired and sent two heat-seeking rockets at it. The chopper was blown to smithereens. Its remains hit the ground fairly close to them as they passed, but nothing hit any of the travelers.

André threw away the weapon and sat back down. They waited hard and long for another chopper to appear. None did.

They reached open land. The German flat terrain stretched out before them. They drove on at an insane speed on the uneven surface. Some of them almost lost control in the shingle, but managed to remain on two wheels. They reached the highway and speeded up further.

Hours passed by, feeling like seconds, feeling like days, like the longest nights. They drove, as if possessed through what the Berliners called the Wasteland. They kept waiting for and expected another attack. There wasn't any, as seconds turned into minutes and eventually hours.

They eventually stopped at dusk, finally stopped looking back, but still jittery, on the edge.

The many half moons sat down close to each other around the fire in the shadows and the gathering darkness. The dead stayed with them. They saw, time and time again dear friends be hit by a hail of bullets. The images and sensations kept repeating themselves in their minds and acute senses. There was no end to it.

The wasteland of Berlin and Eastern Germany kept haunting them, slowly ripping them apart, never truly leaving them, joining the countless sensations of their age-old experiences already lurking within.

– It's so amazing, really, Vladek said, – when you think about it. Most of us are teenagers or not that much over twenty, and we have experienced more than most people do in a lifetime.

– It feels so great, Maxine said, – so beyond great!

They felt it, the glow within, and they nodded and acknowledged, accepted the spoken words, rocking, swaying as they sought even closer together in the circle of flesh surrounding the giant dark flames at its center.

Around yet another fire a few days later, outside Hamburg, they once more heard the wolves. The animals and the howls became common to the travelers, something they hardly gave any conscious thought anymore, though Gwendolyn and others visibly enjoyed themselves.

– Don't you want to walk into the darkness and run with them?

She spoke with longing in her voice.

– I hope you don't consider doing anything stupid, Irena said, seemingly very concerned on her behalf.

– It's a relevant question, André said condescending.

– Pompous ass! Yola told him.

She sat by the side of her still timid and despondent sister, happy and wild.

– You have a point. Gwendolyn shrugged, with her strange mix of exuberance and soberness. – They do belong to another pack.

Laughter, shaky and wild filled the empty spaces between them, pushing into the night. There was melancholy, but most of all fire, the triumph of survival and its ongoing presence.

– You did a great job, Terrill, Rawlins said. – You got us out of that hellhole of a city, and in less than a day to boot. I salute you!

Everyone did. Terrill felt the heat of their support.

The wasteland stayed with the travelers, no matter how many houses surrounded them. More and more ruins appeared left and right of their trail. They took and had taken lots of downright necessary detours. People kept leaving the wasteland and sought the few remaining functioning cities.

– Current humanity as a whole is drawn to the cities, Gwendolyn mused, not concealing her contempt. – I've always believed that most ants and sheep are silly beasts, but this confirms it.

– We're pulled to the stone desert, most of us, Josh stated abruptly. – It looks more and more like lemmings crossing a roaring river, as if we, in our stubborn, insistent mindlessness need to experience civilization's final days.

– We're heading for a city, right? Rawlins cheered, raising his glass once again.

Damon looked closer at him. Something bothered the old man, something making him jittery and unreasonable.

– I'm afraid you're correct, Terrill said with regret. – The few contacts I have left… at home tell me that the mountains are crawling with military personnel. There is the island where we can be fairly comfortable and «safe», though.

The visuals connected with the place he had grown up re-emerged in his mind. They brought no strong emotions, one way or another.

– So, there's no utopia where sweet Damon is taking us either, Claire giggled.

She was drunk. Restraint dissolved. The black depths rose to the surface.

– No - such - beast - exists!

Everybody looked astounded at Blanche. She had gotten up on her feet and stood there with shaking fists.

– This is what your almighty Master, Victor Russel told you? Rawlins snarled, and in turn had all astounded eyes directed at *him*.

– You bitter, old man, Yola returned his snarl, standing by her sister's side. – Isn't it about time you stop blaming others for your ruined life?

– Hey, watch it! Ralph, one of the bodyguards spoke up, rose as well.

– He s-showed me, Blanche choked. – He told me with meticulous thoroughness what counts in the world and how right he was. He, in his generosity granted me irrefutable evidence.

– It's mostly correct, all of it, Rawlins stated, with a short, rancid laughter. – You're more than correct. And what's worse; it's the very search for utopia that for so long has made existence that much worse. The defense attorney withdraws in dishonor. There's no reason for the jury to deliberate. The case is closed.

He emptied his glass in a few swallows and filled it up again without pause.

Blanche collapsed on the ground, dissolved in tears. Finally the tears came, followed by choking, heartbreaking sobs. It liberated, redeemed to a point, but didn't heal. It made no one feel any better.

The campfires burned down and at dawn only small embers remained.

++

Hamburg hadn't changed much, had changed far less than most cities. The mood in the streets seemed fairly light, open, peaceful. There was no lack of double bad here either. They saw people cough, crawl in the streets and men and women in armor-like uniform rush forward and brush them away. People got hurt if they broke the current imposed rules.

But all in all, compared to what the traveling tribe was used to… peace ruled.

The peace of the grave. A creepy, treacherous peace. Anxiety crawled like ants through burning veins. They were inevitably affected by the relative, fake tranquility.

People stared at them. They were used to that, and as they always did, they did their best to slip into a given environment, but they stood out without trying.

– Why are we hiding? Maxine wondered. – When did we start doing that?

They remembered vaguely a time they hadn't hid themselves, as if they were ashamed of themselves.

Sheds stood on a row on Reperbahn, selling fruit, textiles and meat (all kinds of meat, both dead and still breathing). Tall buildings still towered high above street level also in this stone desert, but in more ways than one, disregarding its size, it reminded the nomads of a medieval village. The river of time flowed upwards, towards the enormous waterfall awaiting them around the next turn.

What rested behind the obvious dominated, as always, what could be seen with the naked eye.

Fear lurked in the natives' eyes.

– Do we have everything? Damon asked.

– What we don't have, we can get easily enough, André replied.

Hamburg was a bottleneck to everyone looking for a way out of the bottle. Everyone traveling north on land had to pass through it.

A girl stared at them from the other side of the street. Fear and loathing mixed in her eyes. She was scared of them, scared for them. She feared what was awaiting them would also consume her.

She looked so cowed. Damon was sickened by the very sight of her.

– It's too damn quiet here, he swore. – Let's get moving.

The air whirled around them, almost visible, like a restless spirit attracted by blood. They knew this feeling well. The red already filled their mouth. They could taste it, bittersweet, pervasive, overwhelming their senses. Only Rawlins seemed to retain complete, fatalistic calm.

The old fox.

The children of the moon hurried towards their bikes, their two-wheeled horses, blinded by the dirty sunshine.

The roars from the engines sounded strangely diminished in the quiet street. Nerves nipped their skin. There were no uniformed people. The nomads continued on their way north, all the way to the German/Danish border.

The road appeared small. Everything seemed so narrow. The surroundings smothered the travelers. They turned their heads and looked behind them, and when they did, the once so familiar path was no longer there.

The border control boots tall as buildings grew from the ground ahead. These were brand new. They hadn't been there a few years ago. Such arrangements emerged everywhere these days, not just between former peaceful countries, but between cities and districts.

Terrill analyzed the terrain, its hills and mounts, a place where it was easy to hide, but no one was hiding there. The place crawled with soldiers armed to their teeth. Both light and heavy armament was rolled forward. Damon looked around him. There was no retreat. The road forward seemed open in comparison. Only two fairly small buildings and approximately thirty soldiers defended the gate, small potatoes compared

to the «lurkers» in all the other directions.
Roaring bikes pulled to a stop, but kept roaring. Minds worked overtime and kept looking for solutions to their desperate situation. Sweat covered many a frowning forehead.
– It's me he wants, Tom Rawlins shouted.
Damon heard him well above the roar of the engines.
– He will settle for that for now. He isn't done with you yet.
The words cut into the boy, cut deep. He felt the pain. No anesthetics could soothe that.
Pain is a good teacher, Rawlins' voice said in his head.
He imagined the tall, white beast standing in the window to the left. It faded in and out of his vision, through a thick, red haze.
He wondered how it was possible to hate a human being like that, one he had only met for a short time, «talked» with for a few minutes such a long time ago. He shook his head in an effort to clear it, in vain.
– I will only ask one thing from you, kid, the arms dealer stressed. – I want you to think about survival. I have often, in my adventurous life seen my... customers give in to the blood rush and fatalism. I guess their actions felt right at the time, perhaps even were right, but this time, in your case, it isn't. There might be situations where reason and emotions will get the best of you, and you must ponder hard what will serve you, not those that might be your enemies. I don't really need to paint a picture here, kid. You know, know well what I'm talking about. We don't live either in our reason or emotions, but in both, somewhere at the edge and even outside of both.
– I hadn't pondered it this hard, Terrill said. – You've made everything clearer to me. Thank you!
– What's going on here? Ralph asked with a catching in his voice.
A strange loyalty revealed itself in his voice and expression.
Cynicism and passion fought for dominance and reason won. In this instance, reason had to win.
When pain charged through Damon as he looked at Tom Rawlins, the human being, he knew he would never wish to be without it.
– They will let us through, Damon, having difficulty speaking, told his charges. – They know that there will be an insane bloodbath otherwise. They are not that afraid of their masters or even their Master, or so obsessed with winning that they want to die.
– Let him go, Maxine said. – He isn't exactly one of us, is he? He's to blame. Let him carry the burden.
– The burden isn't mine, my dear, Rawlins grinned, – but yours.
That was correct. No matter how one looked at it, it was those living on that would suffer. Peace was for the grave.
The two men, the young boy and the old man nodded to each other. Damon saw or imagined he saw a flash of the moon in the weary eyes.
They saw him wave once, before vanishing into the building with whatever he had to declare.
Damon drove the bike forward, to the excessive forces blocking their freedom.
– Open the gates! He shouted.
There was no discernible reaction, no change of expression in the sea of rigid features

in front of him. They merely stared at the threat facing them and clutched the weapons in their hands.

They heard the shots clearly, first one salvo, then another, the sound of four or five guns simultaneously. Everyone shook. No one moved, but fingers did twitch around the firing pin.

– Open the gates, NOW!

First nothing happened. The nomads steeled themselves.

A nod from the sergeant and everyone present relaxed, or relaxed as much as they possibly could. One of the gates slid open. Right after that, the next followed. Damon drove through as the first. The others followed mere moments later. The sight of the soldiers made them shiver in disgust. The uniformed women and men hardly seemed like human beings at all, but like wheels in a machinery.

They passed the gates on the Danish side. The considerable force present there made no attempt at stopping them either. They seemed much more concerned with the presence of the German soldiers outnumbering them five to one. Alert beyond alertness the nomads rode off, slowly at first, then faster and faster and faster until they moved with best speed through the vast alien landscape appearing in a vision filled with clarity.

The sun hung low in the west. The travelers removed themselves from it, as they moved ever more north/north-east. Dark glasses were put away. The world cleared even more. The added light made them feel the pain in the eyes even harder. Everything happened so fast, so slow. Years flowed like seconds. Seconds crawled like centuries. He imagined that he moved through a timeless world, a constantly shifting reality.

Tom Rawlins' voice fell silent in Damon Terrill's mind forever.

He felt like he recognized Copenhagen, even though he had never set foot there. He had traveled through Hirtshals on the northern Danish coast on his way south.

They stood still at the center of the windy Rådhuspladsen. Images, flashes of history appeared behind his eyelids. Twenty-five years earlier people had fought and died here.

– I was born here, William said low-keyed. – Mother sent me with Anya to Ireland when I was only a few months old.

– Your mother and father… were Kimberly Russel and Willhelm Otterman? Damon heard himself ask.

– Yes, with Judith Breen and Ole Sivert Olsen assisting, William replied dryly. – It's a well known story. I feel strange every time I think about it. Isn't that…

– Strange, Damon agreed, unable to confirm to himself whether or not he was speaking aloud.

The wind no longer blew ice-cold from the east, like it according to legend (and witnesses) once had done. Numb, he felt numb. He felt like they had crossed the German/Danish border only seconds ago. Now, they were set to cross the Øresund Bridge between Denmark and Sweden.

– We need to shake loose a little, just a little, Yola said to him. – It's practically a matter of life and death.

This time he knew he didn't voice a reply.

On the noisy, boxed-in disco they did shake loose. He watched as Yola and Blanche enjoyed themselves, laughed together. Everyone pulled a smile without conscious effort.

– This is such a dismal place, isn't it? André said offhand. – We must indeed be desperate in order to enjoy ourselves here.

The smile stayed on his sweaty face.

Later that night the twenty that had visited the disco returned to the tribe's temporary home, an abandoned office building by the main road to Kastrup Airport. All the other bikes had been parked just inside the large gate. Damon spotted Irena. She waved.

The attack began abruptly, without warning. Strands of night and fire, day and ashes reached for them, tore at them, and tore them apart. Tongues of fire from a thousand explosions rose into the air simultaneously. Bikes and people were pushed at the ground.

He stared at something he didn't want to remember. Irena was blown to pieces. He imagined he became every little detail of it, every single piece flowing through the air from a single point. He saw Death everywhere, and knew that it was no illusion.

It happened abruptly, before he could react properly. He crashed into the already considerable wreckage, and flew through the air. The landing rocked him hard, but he managed to land on his feet.

Everyone strived to adjust to the chaos growing to an inferno around them.

– They caught us with our pants down, André growled.

Terrill heard him, heard every single sound surrounding him. The survival instinct, refined for so long, took over, making them fight back. Two places, Terrill thought. The crossfire originated from two different hideouts within what had already been an urban disaster area. He signed, the language of the deaf never working so well for him as it did during this very moment.

They fucked up! He signed. They didn't plan it very well, not against us and our way above able mobility.

Members of his tribe had already climbed the bikes and started the counterattack. Pride and triumph glowed in his veins. The enormous dust devil raged across the field and road. The Riders of the Thunder Road split up, first in two, then in four groups. The shelling quickly revealed the attackers' anxiety, their growing *panic*. They had mostly bet on heavier arms, so ineffective against a rapidly moving target.

Explosions rocked the buildings where the enemy hid. Bricks and mortar collapsed in dust and blood. The fight was short and brutal. Damon watched it from afar with a certain detached interest. Survivors that had been a part of the previously superior force were mowed down without mercy and delay. Those very few able to run fled in terror towards Copenhagen.

Damon waited with uncanny patience for the riders to return. The savage pride and triumph were almost too much to endure.

They walked among cooling bodies and remains of what had been their friends. Not many had died. They shook their heads in bewilderment and relief.

– Amazing. Maxine shook her head. – They focused on taking out the bikes.

– It makes sense in a twisted way, Damon said. – Their main objective was to delay us.

Slowly but surely they all fought themselves back on their feet, not only in order to stand, but to walk and rush through the nightmare scenario visible everywhere they cast their attention. Dust and blood and remains covered them from head to toe.

André stopped his bike in front of Damon.

– Looks like we have a problem here, the Frenchman said, – but one easily solved.

– Go! Damon said aloud. – All of you with bikes. Go as fast as possible. Get out of the country, as far as possible before dawn.

Everyone, especially those with bikes looked stunned at him.

– There's no need to rush things, is there? André frowned. – We chased off the yellow bastards. No one will take us on for a while after this. The mere sight of us gives most potential enemies the shakes.
– You know as well as I do that this is just the modest vanguard, Terrill said. – We must all move on, as fast as we can, and not wait for the slackers.
He was deliberately patronizing. It seemed to make the point, get it through.
– Then you take my bike, André said. – I'll be alright.
– No, I will be! Damon replied. – I reject your offer. We'll see you guys when we see you. The Thunder Road will always turn. Go!
– I can't find Blanche. Yola stared at him. – Not among the dead, not anywhere. I must stay. Don't attempt to stop me. If you don't want to use my bike, you can sit behind me later.
He nodded, with a catching in his throat.
André waved as he drove off. Maxine blew him a kiss. Those with bikes faded away in the distance. The smaller group stood still for a moment or two, a little lost.
– Blanche has just run away, fled from the fighting, Maxine mused. – It won't take long to locate her.
They nodded, to her, to themselves.
– There are more than enough old buses here, Dominic thought aloud. – Sufficient wrecks with sufficient amounts of petrol. I'll have one up and running in less than an hour.
– Get someone to help you, Terrill nodded. – The rest of us will look for Blanche.
They started looking, in an ever wider circle. Worry turned to anxiety.
– We're so close, now, aren't we, Yola cried, – not that many days from our destination?
Damon nodded to her, not trusting his voice.
Dominic needed three buses and forty-five minutes in order to make a fairly drivable bus. They still searched for Blanche then. They called her name, coaxing her, speaking to empty spaces. She didn't respond and they didn't find her or any trace of her. They walked through a landscape of burned-out craters and what seemed like lasting fires. Wreckages of cars, houses and even boats had been unevenly redistributed around them.
– This is some place, isn't it? Yola said subdued. – Urban artwork worthy of the darkest age.
They nodded to themselves, confirming the truth of her statement.
The sudden sound of running feet made them turn with their weapons ready to fire. They relaxed somewhat when they spotted Magnus as he rushed towards them, but anxiety returned when they saw the expression on his face and noted his wheezing breath. They had never seen him… seen him this… down.
He stopped before them, unable to meet their eyes.
– We… found her, he whispered.
They caught the hoarseness even in his whisper.
They followed him into the building ahead, unable to quite decide how they had reached it. Some of them had searched here before, at least on the ground and upper floor, but not in the basement. Blanche had been afraid of the dark.
What resembled water was dripping from old water pipes. If that was actually any kind of fluid, or if the drops contained pure rust was hard to decide.
– We don't need torches? Yola asked with similar rust in her voice.

– There's only a short stretch, Gwendolyn replied, uncharacteristically meek.
– We heard death cries from down here, Magnus said enraged. – He begged us to protect him from the spirits of the dead before he breathed his last, that asshole.
They had dragged her all the way down here, confident that they would be able to work without being disturbed.
Two dead crouched on the floor. One of them had had his skull broken. She had defended herself well.
They had nailed her to the wall. Huge parts of the room resembled an altar. Torches on the wall made sure everyone saw everything. They had beaten giant nails through her arms and legs, until finally sticking a meat knife in her chest. There was no writing on the wall, no message, no additional message. Damon didn't take his eyes off the horrible sight, as if to commit it to memory, knowing beyond knowing that he would never forget it.
++++++
He stood there for something resembling an eternity, until Yola nipped him in the arm.
– I know what's burning within you, she said. – I feel it equally hard. Remember what Rawlins told us. We both know that it concerned something like this. It's good advice. The man… responsible for this has not caught up with us yet, but he will if we dawdle. This isn't the time or the place, but the time and the place will one day or night come.
She spoke wisdom or something similar, calming him down. He nodded slowly, so very slowly, before he finally exhaled.
Damon Terrill returned to Norway in the «fall» of 2014. The only physical things he brought with him, in addition to the two revolvers inside his jacket, were a few items packed in the sail cloth on his back.
The passengers had to change trains on the Swedish/Norwegian border. The soldiers picked a few of them, mostly those traveling alone, and pulled them out of the long queue. It didn't lead to that much trouble. Happy to not be one of those chosen, the row of cowed and desperate people walked on.
Fourteen hours later, in the middle of the night the train finally continued its interrupted journey. Exhaustion had long since claimed most of them then.
The next day, or perhaps only the next morning the train speeded up. It had moved slowly forward since the border crossing. The rail-tracks covering the last stretch to Gardermoen Airport had recently been significantly upgraded. Damon woke up after a restless night. The wind filled the compartment through all the open windows and refreshed him and everyone still traveling with him, Yola, Vladek, Gwendolyn and a few more.
He looked out of the window, at the dry, desert-like terrain. Twenty years earlier there had been a flood here. There were no signs left of that.
– Six months of drought, Vladek mused, – and this is the result.
– So far, Gwendolyn said. – It will grow far worse fast.
Trees already resembled ghostlike creatures. Damon saw them like that, like faded revenants from times gone. He imagined how all of it would look ten years from now.
He once again saw, through his inner eye the derelict building where a door slammed in the wind, and he saw the road, the asphalt road turning into a dusty, sand-covered surface. It… bothered him. Everything about it felt incredibly important, but he could

not make sense of it. Sometimes, like now, he would have loved his visions to have a manual.

The train stopped by the airport. Only a few left it. Not many wealthy and powerful people bothered with using the train anymore.

Damon and the others studied them. They seemed nervous and in a hurry, as if they had a goal.

– The railroad used to go further south, right? Maxine mused. – Where it used to be a city.

– Yes, Oslo, Damon said, a bit distracted. – Lene's mom blew it up with an atom bomb considerably more powerful than the bombs used on Hiroshima and Nagasaki.

– That's so wicked, Gwendolyn grinned. – I wish I had met her.

The others glanced at her. She didn't back down.

– It was the beginning of the end, she stressed, – the beginning of the end of civilization, and we should all be eternally grateful to her and the Green Rose. She, they started it. They did what everyone should have done, but no one else did. The collapse takes its time, like this slow train, but it is getting there.

– The funny thing, of course, Vladek said, – is that those set on adapting to and be in the forefront of the inevitable change are persecuted, as usual.

– You're a sensible young man, Yola joked.

– People are pushed into the cities and contained there, Damon snorted, – now, more than ever.

He was listening, half interested, half distracted to a conversation a few seats further down the coach. A friend attempted in vain to calm down a visibly neurotic man.

– I want to speak about it. I WANT TO! It took the train sixteen hours to reach Bergen last month. I'm willing to BET that it will take much more this time. Three days? Okay, let's say three days, seventy-two hours. Are you willing to bet against it?

Before half an hour had passed, well before the neurotic man began distrusting himself and his judgment… the train pulled to a stop. There was more ruckus as people rushed forward in order to see what was going on.

– It's just a dead cadaver on the tracks. The message was passed along the line. – Nothing but a dead animal.

He sounded almost disappointed.

Entertainment had always been lacking on Norwegian railroads.

The train started again only fifteen minutes after the stop. Fresh air once again blew between the open windows.

It lasted an hour, until the train stopped at yet one more abandoned station.

The commotion, the *trouble* began not long afterwards.

There was swift movement stemming from the coach at the opposite side of where they sat. Doors opened and closed.

– I didn't SAY anything. They heard the same man shout hysterically. – I was just complaining about the horrible lack of *comfort*.

– He pulls out a pistol, Josh, sticking his head just above the seat conveyed. – Three conductors do as well. They stare at each other with ugly glares. Fingers close around the firing pins. It doesn't look good…

Quite a few shots were fired. A bullet hit the conductor, another the impatient crazy-head. More people drew their guns.

– Let's get some fresh air, Terrill said anxiously.
The moment they stumbled out on the platform, they heard the first of several new bursts of fire. The military unit stationed here boarded the train with drawn machineguns. It lasted a good while, but the cracks of the guns eventually ended. Bodies were carried outside for all to see. Half-hearted attempts to clean the train of blood stopped halfway. When the few remaining passengers in coach three returned, the seats had been covered with plastic sheets. The train chugged on. The conversation in the coach resumed.
The children of the moon glanced uneasily at each other.
– He didn't really do much, Maxine said subdued, – except defending his dignity. He was fed up.
They felt the shame burn low but distinct in their gut when it dawned on them what they might need to do in order to follow the advice Tom Rawlins had given them.
The events from Gothenburg revisited their chilling thoughts. They had been forced to give up their heavy arms. They relived the countless humiliations they had been submitted to within the city, and thousand other incidents on their way here.
– Yes, he was fed up, Maxine said. – We must all ask ourselves how much we can take before we've had *enough*.
No one accepted the challenge she posed to them. The sick feeling in their gut intensified.
The train stopped, stood still for a while, before moving on. They approached Gol. Damon opened his eyes. The train stopped and stood still. They felt like they were withering in the campy coach. A dusty, acid wind touched their faces, touched Damon's skin. He imagined he heard the grains of sand rub against each other.
He put the sword on his back and hurried outside, practically ran to the other side of the railway station building. He heard the door slam in the wind. The building facade looked very familiar to him. It didn't really resemble what he had seen in his vision, being in far better shape, but… it was the same place. He could say that with absolute certainty by the shape of the other buildings and the mountains. He stopped doubting himself.
Nightmarish images came to him. Chained prisoners were brutally pulled and pushed from a derelict train, a freight coach with holes in its walls as numerous as Swiss cheese. He knew it didn't happen here and now. The human beings, prisoners and guards alike looked like ghosts to him.
He spotted a girl, worn down and miserable. She didn't seem as unreal as the rest of them. She had… to him she had *substance,* face, eyes, soul and blood. He froze. She saw him. He realized that when he met the almond-shaped black, now so murky eyes.
– What do you see, Samhain? Gwendolyn asked filled with curiosity.
The visions faded. He shook his head.
Something in the shadows caught his attention, a big woman of flesh and blood, just before she stepped into the bright sunlight.
She approached them with a casual stroll. Her hips and her breasts rocked up and down beneath the loose clothes. She didn't seem old, in any way, but certainly mature compared to her obvious youth.
Abruptly mature, he suddenly realized.
– Kara! He cried astonished. – Little Kara!

She rushed into his arms and gave him a hungry kiss on the lips. Her body felt completely different compared to the skinny girlish body he remembered. She gave him a teasing smile.

– Join me inside all of you, she said. – There are water and cooler shadows.

Her voice made him frown. There was something there, and in her expression unnerving him.

– Someone walked on your grave, Gwendolyn said. – I'm right, am I not?

He looked astounded at her and nodded curtly.

The inside of the building seemed, if possible, even hotter than outside. But there were water taps and water in the taps. It was lukewarm, but somewhat clean. It did visibly refresh them. They were among the first there, and could sate their thirst in the peace and quiet of the place. Only a few minutes later, the queue grew significantly longer.

They hurried back to the train and froze. The travelers and all other passengers stood still, watching while soldiers, submitted to ruthless abuse by snarling superiors, entered and filled all the coaches in a fast, efficient manner. A few stumbled, but was quickly back on their feet, whipped without mercy by the superiors. It didn't take long before all the sorry wretches were in place, and even less time after that, before the train left the station.

– I wonder where they are deployed, a voice said a few steps off, – and who they will slaughter this time.

Both he and others looked anxiously around them, but there was no danger, at least no one attacking them outright.

– I heard about unrest a few days ago, Kara told them a few minutes later, – at the new construction sites by Mjøsa.

Mjøsa was Norway's biggest lake, still a freshwater reservoir, a giant oasis in the rapidly growing desert.

– They seemed pretty puny to me, Gwendolyn said. – Poor creeps!

Anxious and enraged people sought answers and the people they believed had the answers, but even the uniformed employees in the main hall of the railway station seemed to have vanished into thin air. All potential passengers flocked to the desk of the ticket booth.

– Is there a train or isn't there? A guy asked, his voice and appearance more than revealing that he had reached the limits of his patience.

The man in the booth had reached beyond the limits of ordinary anxiety.

– The line is closed in both directions, he replied, sweating profusely. – There will be no train arriving or leaving until well into the night.

People growled and pretty much expressed their frustration in any way they could, or any way they could without attracting undue attention. They knew very well that if the frustration turned into violence, it wouldn't take long before peacemakers would come and take care of the disruptive elements, and most likely anyone nearby.

It ended up with everyone seeking a spot with shade. It wasn't that hard, with empty houses lined up all over town. There was even tap water in most of them, and the nomads could fill their once more almost empty bottles.

They sat there sweating and suffering, sweating and suffering some more, until they couldn't stand it anymore. Damon and Kara, almost like total strangers, like close friends sat there and strived to know each other anew. They stared into each other's eyes and saw the same… a hill, a dusty road and shadowy shapes riding on it. Like one person they turned and looked out of the window, up at the hill, the same hill. He rose.

– Where are we going? She asked anxiously.

– Don't you know?

– You've grown immensely since we last saw each other, she said with solemn cheerfulness and admiration. – You see far clearer than me, now.

– We're here, now, he said. – There's something I need to see, with my eyes.

Everyone joined them. They hadn't anything else to do in the afternoon heat, anyway.

They followed the road, until they reached the crossroads where Highway 51 led east. Some bicycle wrecks had been placed against a trashed wall not far away. They jumped on them and rode up the road, the entire road up. The plains stretched out before them, a gray, desolate stretch without end. Damon Terrill felt with everything he was what was happening, what time concealed. He felt Death. Death didn't harm him. It strengthened him. Suffering, dominating and vile hammered and picked his skin, his very self.

He said something to the air.

– What did you say? Yola was on him like a worn, excited she-devil on steroids. – You said *Thunder Road.* It's here, right?

– It's here and any other place, he said just as subdued. – It's' nowhere, nothing tangible, except like a fist in the belly. It's a state of mind present at humanity's beginning and one that will be there beyond the mists of existence itself. Where life, death and time may end, it will still be. It's tied to our existence and we to its.

He shook his head in bewilderment, not really understanding what he was saying.

– Don't look for meaning, he told them. – There isn't any.

They heard the train's whistle from miles away.

– Everything we do is fundamentally meaningless. It's when we realize this, we realize the meaning of everything.

– Deep, she grinned.

– We realize our own worth. He kept speaking, as if she hadn't spoken. – What's driving us, making us tick. These are thoughts strengthening me from the first moment I was aware of them.

The flow of words ended. The flow of thoughts didn't.

The vision of the Thunder Road, the spot where it made a turn brought him further away, to the outer limits of his imagination, the border of everything, where there was no rational thought. A dark wall grew, becoming three, no, many-dimensional. Silver letters burned on a blackboard of mist. He read them, and in glimpses he could even understand them.

Kara suddenly grabbed his shoulders. He looked at her with misty eyes only slowly fading into clarity. The echo of her fast, stumbling speech followed him into dusk.

– I came here for you on behalf of André. He's expecting you, but also because…

She stared at him with desperate, insane eyes.

– I saw myself die, she whispered and he felt what she felt. – I saw a black bird born of fire and ashes… dive down on me *and tear me apart.*

There was something deeply disturbing about those words, not only the words themselves, but also, especially the reaction they created in his consciousness, an indefinite place within.

The two places… they were the same.
The night approached them with its chill. They warmed themselves in its embrace. Their thirst didn't lessen. A skirmish started between two groups over a water tap. The Hallingdal River practically ran dry. This was one of the taps with a tank yet not empty. The temperature, amazingly, fell close to a freezing level. Abandoned houses without water was torn down and used to sustain many a tall fire. By one such a huge man sat and babbled somewhat coherently. He babbled and many listened.
– I recall us passing by here in the spring of '96. We stopped and watched the moon eclipse and the comet Hyakutake. It was visible up the Hallingdal road, but vanished behind Satan's clouds before we reached the top of the hill and could take a closer look, could expose it for what it was. I *knew* what it was, what it prophesized, the very first time I saw it on the sky. Everything started at that moment, all the crap. Nothing has been right since, nothing! An age-old presence visited Earth and a disaster was imminent.
The man enjoyed a not insignificant crowd of listeners. He spoke aloud and even those sitting two campfires away easily heard his compelling voice. What had started as an irritating grumble in Terrill's head grew quickly to proportions he had trouble handling. He didn't fight it, but allowed it to fester and grow.
– Oh, shut the fuck up! He snarled at the fairly distant campfire.
Everything turned… yes, «deadly quiet» seemed more than the correct phrase here.
– Everyone using their wits even the slightest knows comets have nothing to do with disasters. The foundation for the upcoming Ragnarok was also made long before the most recent return of Hyakutake.
– What's your name, friend?
A large frown appeared on the big man's forehead, as he rose to his full height. He looked very impressive and imposing.
– Damon Terrill, the boy said unafraid, and took the necessary steps forward, confronting the other man.
Damon, very tall and big himself, hardly reached the giant to his jaw.
– I've heard about you…
They stood there facing each other. Damon stared at him with unflinching eyes. The other's eyes flickered visibly. Damon saw fear there, and hatred and a hunger rivaling his own. The image of Victor Russel flashed before his eyes.
– I've heard that you have more than earned the right to have your own opinions.
There was an implicit threat in the powerful voice. Damon ignored it and turned his back to the man towering above him. He returned to his campfire, his turf.
– That's Frank Moldhaug, a shaken man sitting by another campfire cried out to him. – He's a great prophet. How can you speak like that to a voice of God?
Yola made a very telling gesture in front of her forehead.
– That's very simple question to answer, Damon replied generously. – The good prophet quite simply doesn't deserve the reputation given to him by sycophants like you. He's perfect for you guys, but a *disaster* for the rest of us.
A wicked grin followed the words. The citizen fearing God (and his possible prophets) turned very pale.
– The man's words are just as ridiculous as his name, Kara cried boldly.
Damon's grin grew even wider. Sometimes it was great to be alive.

His laughter made people shrink in their tracks and move closer to the fires, so close that it burned the hairs on their skin.

– His name… what does it mean? Vladek wondered.

– It means «soil heap», Damon chuckled, – but let's call him Dung Heap from now on.

He raised his voice several levels, and saw that Moldhaug crouched in anger.

The train arrived at dawn and moved on not long afterwards. A few lucky stiffs had succeeded in getting seats, and they guarded zealously their luck, didn't move from their position. It didn't take many hours before the stench of urine filled the train.

– We could have taken him out, Vladek said, – Dung Heap, I mean.

He held on to a pole in the hallway with many others Traveling with him.

– What would have been the point? Damon shrugged. – Those stupid enough to be led by him, would quickly have found themselves a new master. Crap like that will only go away when people like that go away. Then people like Dung Heap will also fade from the surface of the earth.

Vladek and the others nodded and then nodded some more. The rapidly growing heat and humidity didn't exactly encourage excessive movement. Everyone stood there swaying, approaching the first stages of exhaustion before the continued journey had properly begun. The degree of satisfaction changed quickly from unbearable to something even worse.

Vladek's eyes sought the hatch in the ceiling, once, twice. The third time he raised the arms above his head and reached for its handle. He made a concerted effort and managed to grab hold up there. A push, and it opened wide. Fresh air flooded what had felt like a greenhouse.

– It's quite amazing isn't it, that no one just didn't just go ahead and did this earlier?

It helped a bit, postponing the suffering for a while, but only for a few minutes and then it felt just as bad as before. A growing dissatisfaction made them exchange impatient glances.

Gwendolyn jumped, grabbing the edge of the roof and pulled her supple body up through the hatch. She waved eagerly, encouraging the others to join her. They needed no further prompting, hurrying after her, helping each other up the fastest they were able. It started with a cautious laughter, but grew to something like a full-blown euphoria when they stood on the roof and breathed the downright life-giving air.

The Children of the Midnight Fire were the first up there, but were quickly joined by many other groups and individuals. The stunning fresh atmosphere blew straight in their faces, as the train rushed through curves and across open stretches. They had to sit with their back to the morning sun and its dangerous rays, with sunglasses and bull caps and thick clothing covering their bodies, but they could breathe.

Damon wrung the long black hair. It had become so greasy that it was actually dripping. He slowly felt better as the minutes stretched on and approached the hour. They found a certain comfort in the normality of the sun rising in the east, not really confident that it would last.

The forest, green and fresh, grew around them, invigorating them further. Gwendolyn stood up and cried out, shouted in defiance, her voice echoing throughout the valley.

– The wind is BLOWING!

The train climbed slowly. Often it didn't seem to be moving at all, but they knew it did. They passed Geilo and continued into the mountains, penetrating further into the high country. Barb wire, tall and unpleasant covered both sides of the parallel tracks. They found no comfort, no rest and what had always been there with them kept haunting them, their souls scowling at the world.

No places to hide!

The train continued westward.

CHAPTER FIFTEEN

She found herself in the mountains. It was winter. She knew that. In spite of the fact that the small amount of snow was no more than slush. Feet couldn't quite connect with the ground in what resembled an unappetizing soup, one making the surface slippery and traitorous.

The man in front of her attacked her, doing so with a contempt and a ruthlessness she did her best to outdo. She knew he despised her and wished her dead or maimed, like she wished him dead or maimed. The knowledge, the certainty of that had been hammered into her, through ears, eyes, scent, taste and skin. It didn't bother her.

The warm wind turned to a chill through the thin uniform, depleting further the already emaciated skin. Thoughts came to her unbidden. She rejected them. Thoughts and emotions were both death, the big final one, without suffering. Something indefinite within made her keep fighting the final fate. A thick log of an arm, a sledgehammer with claws shot forward. It squeezed her neck briefly. Her teaching emerged, hard and ruthless, without passion. She broke the arm in one mighty impossible move. 2021 jumped backwards in a desperate attempt to avoid her hot embrace. She spotted resignation in his eyes and despised him. Only fools and weaklings ever retreated from combat.

She broke through his ridiculous defense. A hard, light hand broke his glass jaw. A knee smashed his rib cage. 2021 crouched on the ground, and the water and shit and death gained a red glow. He was still alive. She looked dispassionately down on him, and turned her attention to her leader ten steps off. He nodded. She shouted, a shout without anger, moving fast and deadly. Hands like claws tore apart the enemy's throat.

He died. She watched him as it happened, not really affected one way or another.

She straightened. Filled with pride she placed herself before her commanding officer. The cheers from the row of soldiers behind her warmed and burned.

She rejected distractions. Distractions were shame, dishonor. Those in Charge would punish her and rightly so. She, the disobedient, ungrateful worm would deserve every single hateful caress.

– Congratulations! The Lieutenant said. – Sergeant…

A warm, warm trickle filled her. He had just promoted her, had done so with a single word.

– Thank you, Lieutenant!

She saluted him, like she had been trained to do.

– Your squad is awaiting your command, he said with his forceful voice and stance. – Lead them to the reception area. A new load of recruits will arrive in two hours. By then your squad is expected to perform flawlessly, *flawlessly*. Do you understand, worthless little tramp?

– Yes, Lieutenant!

She noticed the light tremble on her lower lip, until the training and the hatred filled her and aided her, helped her prevail.

She saluted him again, and he dismissed her.

The sergeant hardly noticed his departure, how he dissolved in the air behind her, where he would always be. She stared at her minions with condescending eyes.

– You're a sorry lot, she spat. – You're my sorry lot! Your ass is mine!

– YES, SERGEANT!

Her power had been augmented many times, from one snap of the fingers to another. They did belong to her, were hers to do with as she pleased. They feared her now.

The train arrived. The squad drilled by the newly promoted sergeant performed flawlessly in front of dignitaries and superior officers.

It was an old train, panting in pain, with extensive ventilation. About one fifth of the poor sods thrown out of the coaches hadn't survived the transport. Several more was stamped to death in the tumultuous departure from the train. The sergeant nodded pleased.

Grabbed by an inspiration, she ordered her subordinates to carry the dead bodies to the ovens and to run the cattle there as well.

– You will taste it, she cried. – The stench will never fade from your nostrils.

The stench filled the air. Several of the wretches choked, confirming to themselves the cruel truth of the sergeant's words. The stench of shit, piss and death didn't fade, but settled in the deepest part of their self. Pain gnawed like a hissing glow. She held on to it, nurtured it. She had nothing else.

She studied the skinny bodies in the shower room through the one way mirror. In not such a long time, soon, they would seek her in their need. And she would listen to their prayers. She was their Goddess, strict and almighty, just as much above them as the shit they removed. When she and her squad ran them into the hall, they were far ahead of all the other groups.

Madame Kaspersen met them with her kind smile. The four squad leaders placed themselves at attention in front of her. Madame stopped in front of one of them.

– You were the first, 2001. Congratulations!

– Thank you, Madame!

The response was giddy, coarse.

– Everyone is pretty and clean?

– Yes, Madame, the sergeant assured.

Once again the mirage placed itself behind the high dais. Slaves and soldiers listened carefully.

– Welcome, soldiers…

Marches, drills, more drills, more marches. It didn't end just because she had become sergeant. If possible 2001 and her peers were drilled even harder and crueler, now. And in an arena where the spectators sat behind dark nets and cheered, they all fought and died. She recalled vaguely herself standing with raised arms above a dead body. The images flickered and faded, never staying long, never truly going away.

– Kill me, the weakling on the floor had whispered. – You have to do it, in order to survive.

– You're given an order, Lisbeth Kaspersen said. – What do you do?

A male soldier jumped on his feet. She nodded to him.

– We obey! He said promptly. – Without delay or hesitation.

She nodded and he sat back down on the hard floor.

– What do you do without orders?

A female soldier jumped to her feet. The Madame nodded graciously.

– We… don't interpret, but follow the instruction, the last given order.
– What do you do if anyone of lower rank contradicts an order from a higher ranking officer or official?
– We kill him or her, Madame!
Cheers of agreement, loud shouts of support echoed from her fellow soldiers.
– What do you do if a soldier doesn't act enthusiastically on a given order?
– We kill him, Madame, thousand times, submitting him to thousand acts of torment.
Enthusiastic shouts of support echoed from all over the hall. There were no exceptions or omissions.
– Excellent, 2001. Most excellent!
Thus it always had been. Thus it would always be.
2001 and 2010 had the honor of accompanying Madame and her aid, Karlsen at the dinner later that night. Such and honor, such a GREAT honor!
Enthusiastic, the female soldier thought. Long live the instruction. *Obey, serve and please.*
Not think about it. Be it. Be the instruction. Just like 2010 behaved submissive and eager towards Kaspersen, she was towards Karlsen. The instruction said so. The instruction was everything, and it was a Joy to follow it.
She powdered her nose in the bathroom. She brushed herself around the big eyes. The training also dealt with etiquette, with proper conduct.
– We don't follow the training, she mumbled. – We are the training. We do not follow the instruction, we are the instruction. Long live the instruction. Obey, serve and please.
When she helped Karlsen undress, and she undressed in front of him, performing for his pleasure, she felt a flare of anger. Nothing reached the surface. She wanted to tell him, to confess her sin. It was duty, the duty engraved on their mind and soul. She felt a strong urge to tell him everything, but she was so ashamed that she couldn't do it.
When she woke up later in the night, she pushed herself playfully at the warm body.
– Leave me, he rejected her.
It didn't surprise her that he was awake. He didn't sleep much. She slipped quietly out of the bed.
Nothing surprised her, she corrected herself. She obeyed orders. That was all she did, everything they expected of her.
She stood before the mirror. It was a long time since they had first shaved off the long hair. They shaved her bare head once a week.
She found herself in the empty room, on her bed. 2001 slept and dreamed.
The room was different, unreal. She heard the sounds of cars in the distance. Aside from that, it was the pervasive silence she noticed.
– Ah, Miss Vallinger, welcome!
Roar Høyland grabbed her arm and led her elegantly to the bountiful dinner table.
She glanced around her with a confusion she didn't reveal, playing the relaxed female business executive. There was nothing on the surface betraying the anxiety within. She glimpsed herself in the floor to ceiling mirror, the black dress, the thighs exposed in the split, the deep cleavage and the willing smile.
Was that how it had really happened? Had she offered herself to him, allowed him to treat her like… a trophy?
– Where are the other guests? She asked, using the exact inflection of contempt needed

to show him what she thought of him.

– They will be here soon enough, he assured her. – As stated: we need time to discuss the strategy.

Once again he stared at her with the slick, knowing grin she knew so well and feared so much. She feared this was no dream, that he had used his considerable clout to get her back here, that he had made sure he held all the cards this time, that he had b-bought her and that she was his property, that he played this cruel game in an attempt to gain even more pleasure from it, that she was in truth his willing and obedient slave.

– Everything is ready, she shrugged. – Like I've told you, everything will proceed smoothly. Before they leave, they will fall on their knees and beg us to cheat them.

He chuckled. The laughter sounded forced and contrived. She felt a little better.

A servant pulled out a chair for her. She sat down by Roar Høyland's table. The servants served dinner. She digested his food. The servants rushed back and forth, pulled back, hardly even noticeable. It seemed like they weren't there at all, which clearly pleased Høyland to no end. She didn't need to ponder the issue in order to know that this was the impression he wished to impose on her.

He conversed in a witty and entertaining manner, a perfect host. It didn't make her feel any better.

The wind was blowing outside, juxtaposing the ear-shattering, paralyzing silence inside. He raised his glass. She did as well. They had a toast. He drank. She did as well.

– They're late, she remarked.

– They'll be here, he shrugged off her concerns.

She knew that. That shithead didn't need to stress it. She had personally contacted them and sent out the invitations, and they had confirmed their involvement.

He was dangerous, by virtue of his position in society. Aside from that he was nothing.

Her thoughts kept drifting. She could not keep that from happening, keep herself from becoming distracted, anxious and from casting her eyes at the entrance.

– These friends of your…

– Yes?

She deigned herself to look at him again.

– They're making waves.

– Tell me about it, she chuckled, so confident, downright elated.

– Some people view them as a significant threat.

He clucked out loud, evidently seeing himself as the only person in the room.

She didn't speak, deliberately waiting for him to do so.

– Others, on the contrary view them as little more than the irrelevant bugs they are, without any true power, any influence on society. But there are those deeming them to be of some limited value or use.

– What makes you think we want anything to do with you, your kind and your masters? She asked with contempt in her voice.

She had set out to stay calm, to not outright challenge him. He had tricked her into revealing herself. She could not keep herself from breathing faster, from exposing her agitation, her inner turmoil.

And her response didn't sound anything like the rebuffing she would have wanted.

– It isn't like you have any choice, my dear M, he proceeded, sickeningly pleasant. – You wish to survive like all the rest. Our society becomes ever more… polarized. The line between those participating and those not, becomes more and more distinct every day. There used to be certain opportunities to those wishing to stay on the outside or break out, but it becomes increasingly difficult to make it out there, in your tight spaces.

– It is you guys who are living in tight spaces, she countered incensed. – You «thriving» like unmoving statues in your own private hell.

She noticed that she was breathing hard and hated him for it, hated the glowing hatred within she suspected had haunted her from the cradle.

He practically ignored her outburst, and his evident confidence made her hate him even harder.

– What do you think of my dear father in law, btw? He asked casually.

– Quite the nice fellow, she replied and grinned wickedly, – for a would-be tyrant…

It didn't sound convincing, it just didn't. She touched her temples, suddenly dizzy and weak, wondering what was wrong with her. The mere act of changing focus and look closer at him caused her pain.

– I expect you to behave, he stated curtly. – This perplexing anti-authoritative attitude may not be without a certain charm, but tonight it will ruin my plans, and we can't have that, can we?

– Perplexing? She frowned and cursed the audible uncertainty in her voice. – How is that?

– That should be a no-brainer, he replied, his nauseous confidence displayed in full. – You're a skilled woman, not the typical illogical dumb and soft creature. Even if you are a woman, you're clearly one of some limited talent, and not without opportunities. Why on earth do you stay in your job if you dislike it that much?

She fell silent. She had wondered about the same herself.

He used the napkin to clean his lips. Even the way he rose from his chair projected the utmost calm. It was all very civilized.

Pushing a button on the wall activated the concealed stereo. She saw that. The equipment matched the room without even the slightest break in the pattern. Light music filled the over-the-top big living room. She heard far more ominous chords, and feared something was wrong with her. This indecision was impossible to shake off. She wondered where it was coming from, feeling unusually down and timid. Her thoughts remained dark, muddy.

– Dance with me!

He signed for her to join him on the floor, and she did.

They slid back and forth on the parquet. He led. She was led.

– My wife is about to give birth, he enlightened her. – This will be our third child.

– Poor woman!

He looked condescending down on her, ignoring her sarcasm. She wondered when he had grown taller than her.

– My point is that she's late in the eight month of the pregnancy, with a belly so big, so bloated that she's practically inaccessible, unable to perform her marital duties.

His dance partner liberated herself from him and returned with quick steps to the table. She had more wine. It didn't improve upon her lethargy. She decided more wine was out. It would seriously impair her performance when the other dinner guests arrived. The kitchen tempted her with a more downplayed lighting, less garish decor.

She found frantically a glass and filled it up with water. When she devoured the entire glass in one go, she had no recollection of having raised it to her lips. It did no good. She kept the water flowing and cleaned her face in tons of the cold fluid. When she straightened she could not remember having bent down.

The frown cut deep into her brow. She just didn't understand what was going on. Everything felt unreal, as if she wasn't really there, as if she was in truth imprisoned in a tiny dark room, a cell without windows, ceiling, floors and walls. She heard a whistle, the sound of the train approaching, another, completely different whistle completely dominating her life and dreams. She was dreaming, just had to be dreaming.

He closed off the tap water, her tap water. She tried turning. He held her, holding her so hard that it hurt, twisting her arms behind her back. She writhed in his firm grip. He kissed her on the neck. She couldn't quite make herself angry and wondered what was wrong with her.

– So, you want me to be the replacement? No fucking way!

She heard the sound of metal against metal, and felt the cold material against the skin, around her wrists. He had handcuffed her. She did feel shock, but not the raging storm of emotion she had hoped for and expected.

He dragged her back to the living room. She shook her head in distress.

– What are you doing? Let me go!

There was no strength in her voice.

– You should stop with the bullshit, he said irritated. – It's about time you show yourself to be more than a bit reasonable. What you're about to *get,* you've most certainly asked for for months. You've courted a boy, and not had the guts and common sense to do it with a real man. That's so typical of you fucking feminists. You all need a firm hand. It's for your own good.

He sounded as if he actually meant it. She wanted to laugh out aloud, but nothing happened. The shock kept shaking her. It shouldn't have. Nothing worked. An ass like him shouldn't be able to treat her like that, without a strong response from her.

A thought, hard and sore finally dawned on her.

– You put... something in my food or wine?

– Both in your food and wine actually, he replied in a very factual, condescending voice that should have made her simmering with rage. – A new experimental drug making people more pliable. It's for your own good.

– I've heard that my entire life, she mumbled.

– You wonder if I have truly poisoned your food and wine, of course, know that you're a woman, and that women are naturally submissive, and don't need to be drugged in order to behave in the company of their betters.

He opened the door to the bedroom. She writhed in his grip, without coming any closer to freedom.

– Just you keep wriggling, he chuckled. – You won't get free, and as soon as you realize that, you will definitely become more pliable. The cuffs are custom made. A wrestler or weightlifter wouldn't be able to break them.

She twisted her body back and forth. He pulled her close, doing it so hard that he made her gasp in pain.

– Give it a rest, will you? He said with audible irritation in his voice. – You aren't stupid. You've got more brain than that. But I clearly need to teach you a lesson in order for that brain to work better, for you to realize what's best for you.

She kicked him on the leg. It was a hard, brutal kick making him cringe. He didn't change expression. The sight of the bed did something to her. She knocked her head into his face. Blood flowed from the bank manager's nose. His firm grip turned weak and he let go of her altogether. The horror was painted on the blood-stained face. She kicked the same foot again. It broke with a dry crack and he fell, hitting the floor hard. She kicked him in the head. His forehead hit the doorframe. Blood began flowing from a deep gush right by the hairline. She kicked him the belly and in the chest, jumped over his body and kicked him in the back. He lay still. He moaned a little, but the only sound she heard from him was the wheezing breath. She bent down and scratched him with her nails, scratched his face and down the chest. Long claws tore skin and fabric. She kept kicking, kicking, kicking.

She made one final kick in euphoric joy over the fact that it ended the same way as the previous time, like all the previous times. He crouched by her feet, his face swollen and red. She kept kicking him with a snarl around her mouth, screaming in triumph every time a new bone cracked, enjoying every second of it. He had liberated the wild animal in her, torn away all the inhibitions given her by a civilized society. Similar things had happened to her before. It had made her sick then. Now, it strengthened her.

Dizziness overwhelmed her. She fell to her knees. The enormous release of adrenaline leaked from her like the blood from her mouth. It slowly dawned on her that she had bit off a piece of her tongue.

There was a draft. She realized dimly that it came from the door. Dull eyes looked up. The servants stood like glued to the floor right by the entrance to the bigger than big living room. Behind them she glimpsed bewildered dinner guests. She made no attempt at removing the cuffs or move hands or arms from the resting position on her back. The other people, the entrance… so far away. She looked at them from her distant hideout and didn't feel that any of this really concerned her. Strict faces filled with righteous, harmless, but oh so mighty wrath rushed at her on their chubby legs, filled her vision, grabbed her with their fat hooks and dragged her off right to Hell.

She woke abruptly and stared right into the eyes of the soldier on the other bed. His body was coated in sweat, like hers. His eyes stared insane into the night - like hers.

She usually slept in the barracks filled with surveillance cameras. They would quickly spot her unrest and return her to the education facilities. Cold sweat covered her shaking body, and now that fact pleased her. The mere thought made her stronger.

She met the soldier's eyes, a name she could not recall and read understanding, trust.

The morning drills began. Another gray day had started. She studied her subordinates with critical eyes. Her superiors studied her. She portrayed calm, confidence, exposing nothing of her tumultuous insides.

There must be more, 2001 thought feverishly.

++++++++++++++++++++++++++++++++++++

The newly graduated soldiers left the closed-in camp an ice-cold morning for the first time in a very long time. Sharp command shouts sounded from everywhere. Everyone was shaking faced with the changes, the new, unknown surroundings. They focused on the commands, the way they were trained to do. They climbed onboard the train in pairs, doing so with military precision and the gear in one hand, their rifle in the other. They sat down with their backs to the walls in the long transport coach. After an endless wait most of them hardly noticed, the train started moving.

One of the female soldiers looked out between the cracks in the walls without looking out between the cracks in the walls.

Wait, she told herself, like she had done so many times in the camp no one could escape from, the long miles of parallel tracks.

In the camp they had been looked after everywhere. Outside the extensive barbed wire guards patrolled tight like the many wired fences. She had it burned on her retina. The awareness of her bleak reality stayed at the forefront of her consciousness.

And here, they were looked after closer than ever. The constant surveillance never faded.

One day or night it had to. The possibilities of a successful escape had to come. She needed to be patient, that much was clear. And when the time came, the outcome would no longer matter. It would be one of two, and both would be good to her. She clutched her gun. She knew most of them did.

Madame had left the camp and they hadn't seen her after that. It could be days since they had seen her, actually seen her with their eyes, it could be years. They always saw her with their inner eye. She traveled with them, wherever they went. Even though she had left them in the care of others, she never truly left them.

2001 kept having trickles of heat and cold down her back by the mere thought of Lisbeth Kaspersen. She was aware on some level that it was a result of brainwashing, but every time the thought dawned on her, she was struck with awe and an urge to kneel in Madame's presence. Everything else paled in comparison. She clutched her gun, like she knew she was trained to do. The barbed wire blocking both sides of the railway tracks turned blood red in 2001's paralyzed mind.

Their first station pretty much resembled the one they had left. The second, third and perhaps tenth did as well. Nothing or no one seemed different about any of them.

She recalled indistinct images, bloody faces, and loud, hysterical wails and pleading for mercy. One moment it was there, the next it was gone. They were deployed against protesters, striking workers, small and big groups of malcontents. She suspected most of it happened in the east, but could never be certain, certain of herself and the confidence of her thoughts.

They arrived at the city of Gjøvik one early morning. They ran as a tight unit towards Vikodden outside the city, where some of the last recreational areas in the district was vanishing. There were no journalists or TV-crews there. They knew nothing would ever be shown in any news-media, not even on the Internet. Their superior officers had told them that much. The soldiers had beaten protesters with clubs and fists and feet before, but this was different.

– Don't shoot too many, the officers told them. – We need workers, need people to work until they drop, and perhaps even rise from the dead a couple of times before they stay down.

The large group of protesters, *agitators* stood lined up by the forest glen close to where the camping site had once been, right by the giant excavators, machines bigger than the world had ever seen. A grown person hardly reached even halfway up to the center of the wheels of these machines. They were found all around the lake of Mjøsa these days. They ravaged whatever remained of nature wherever they rolled. People had come here because of the water and because of the jobs they had been promised. Huge tent villages had grown up all over the place.

– READY! The lieutenant shouted. – FIRE!

Eager, 2001 thought dully, show eagerness, no hesitation, no reason for suspicion.

She fired and shed no tears, like practically all the soldiers. The agitators fell in heaps of blood and shit. The soldiers kept firing. There were still many people standing. They fell on their knees and begged for mercy.

– CEASE FIRING!

They did and started on the mop-up not long after that. Wounded was shot. The rest of the now very cowed workers were taken away in chains. The soldiers carried off the dead bodies. They changed uniforms later, burned those dirty and stained, and dressed in new, clean attire.

The parade began, and now the media was present in full «force». 2001 knew everything looked impressive. The drill proceeded flawlessly. The lieutenant was very pleased with them. They knew that, felt his praise in every fiber of their being.

They raced across the mountain plains, the three of them, moved across a dusty, windy stretch. They recalled a door slamming in the wind, and a dying tree, three ghosts in a world of shadows.

Tonight, they told each other with dull, indifferent eyes. It must be tonight. 2001 and 2010 passed each other in the refitted railway coach, their home for so long, now. Seats had been removed. Tables and chairs had been placed there instead. They slept on mattresses in the middle coach of the train. The two of them had joint guard duty tonight. They had no idea when that would happen again. Eagerness burned within them both.

She stopped in front of the mirror in her small, private chamber. Privacy was a sergeant's prerogative. She smoothed her uniform. It fit her perfectly. She resembled perfectly the sergeant that had been her sergeant when she had arrived at the boot camp. She had even had his job for a time and done a great job, a damn good job.

There was a knock on the door.

– Enter! 2001 cried.

The door opened. 2013 entered.

2013 was the sergeant's personal servant. She did everything for her, cooking, cleaning and working her ass off day and night long.

– Everything is calm, the aide reported. – Everyone is asleep. The sentries are fully alert. They have nothing to report. Everything is calm.

They could never, would never truly talk, speak about anything substantial. The slightest sign of weakness and one of them would report the other.

– Excellent, you may leave!

The brief conversation ended before it began.

2013 left. The door closed. 2001 stood before the mirror, still indecisive. A hand reached for the electric razor. She shaved meticulously off all the hair on her head, what little there was of it. She had started shaving herself some time ago. She had learned to watch herself in a thousand different ways. It worked. She watched herself every single second of the day, every single shivering eyelash when she was asleep. Everyone was watching everyone else here.

Her world had become a prison and she, like everyone else was her own jailer.

Pain assaulted her, catching her off-guard. The awareness hurt. She quelled unpleasant thoughts with an effort.

Dull fingers slid across the skinhead heated by the glowing knives of the electric razor. The fingers on these hands, able to maim, kill…

The hand moved of its own accord, turning off the lights. It turned completely dark. It was no use. Her shadow didn't disappear. It followed her wherever she fled. She shook, shook hard, and she couldn't make herself stop. A choke escaped her and she pushed the hand hard at the mouth. She fought herself back from the mire of her memories, and it was such a hard, harsh path.

She looked somewhat calm, minutes, hours, years later when she left her quarters and closed and locked the door behind her. Her hands didn't shake. Her mouth didn't choke.

Passion, an emotional storm kept sizzling beneath the calm surface. It comforted her and terrified her. She knew her superiors wouldn't approve.

Everything appeared calm. The hallway seemed haunted to her. It was that quiet. All sounds originated from economical, deliberate movement. The sentries saluted her. She saluted in return. Her walk led her to the kitchen. No one followed her there and she met no one there. She waited ten seconds by the entrance with a hammering heart. 2010 appeared through the opposite door, from his command section of the train. Both moved forward with military precision. They choked on the irony. Two steaming kettles stood on ovens at the center of the room, on each side of the invisible line separating the two sections. They pulled one vial each from their pockets, broke off its point and loaded the content in the kettles. Eyes met eyes. The faces didn't change expression. The two of them turned around and left.

The changing of the guard arrived in the dining hall. They sat down and began devouring their ration with the same mindless efficiency they did everything. There was no sign of intelligence beyond the basics there, no visible change in expression.

They began the night watch right after they had completed their meal. The soldiers they had relieved went to bed. The drug worked quickly. When the two sergeants patrolled the train from first to last coach, everyone rested unconscious on the floor, or on seats. 2001 glanced at her watch. Fifteen minutes had passed. The two sergeants hesitated only briefly, before stepping outside.

The floodlights struck them, hitting them like sledgehammers, casting brightness and shadow everywhere. They sat course directly for the gate, the first hurdle of many they would have to surmount. 2001 saw far ahead with her very active imagination. She didn't have to actively think about it.

The two studying the monitors in the guardroom could see them the moment they stepped outside, like they did every night. There was no more contact between the two and the sergeants than this, a mutual control, a further expansion of the system designed to make them guard each other. Everything was recorded. The guards sat higher up, controlling the vertical and the horizontal.

2001 nodded to herself, pleased with the security, in spite of their current predicament. She couldn't help herself. Fear touched her again, doing so on so many levels. She shook herself to pieces, or so it felt.

She dried her lips. They were moist, so moist that she in yet another weak moment feared the saliva was blood. Insane and shameful images and sensations from her «military career» charged through her. The saliva gathered in the cavity of her mouth, like it had done when she like a shivering imbecile had knelt in awe before Madame

Kaspersen. Her hands rolled into fists and motivated her to keep moving.

The four didn't speak. They never did. If there had ever been words she couldn't recall any. They stood face to face in silence and stared at nothing.

Myriam felt how the cold sweat made her hand slip against the metal of the gun under her coat. All kinds of questions and boundless anxiety flowed through her mind. Uncertainty rocked whatever was left of her self. She knew the silencer would not expose them, that it wouldn't sound any louder than dry twigs breaking in the forest, not even in this quiet, quiet night. The poisoned soldiers would sleep on.

She cast a distrustful glance at the man standing by her side, and he returned a similar stare.

It happened fast, unexpected. She caught a glimpse of a shadow seemingly appearing from nowhere, behind the two behind the fence, glimpsing a blond piece of hair under the black hood. A neck broke, a throat drowned in blood. The two guards suddenly crouched dead or dying on the ground.

2010 and 2001 both drew their guns. 2013 stood still and waited.

The weapons were returned to their place beneath the coats. 2013 opened the gate. They walked through it, hardly even feeling their own legs.

– You will run away tonight, she stated. – I'm joining you.

The voice sounded shockingly clear in their ears.

– You ask yourself if you would have run if I hadn't come, she said softly. – I ask myself similar questions.

They ran off, all three of them, moved on their soles, the base of their soles, like they had been trained to do.

They ran the useless path between the railway tracks. Tall wired fences kept fencing them. There was no light, no darkness. They saw everything with abject clarity, communicating without words. 2001 pulled off the sleeves of her uniform and tied it around hands and wrists. The other two echoed her acts, followed her as she climbed the fence and eventually the barbed wire. All three hesitated, but only for a moment or two.

One hand, then more reached forward. Bodies crawled forward on all fours. The first spike penetrated vulnerable skin. They were unable to keep that from happening, but they braved the pain, ignored it, no matter how much their skin leaked. It felt so inconsequential, really. It hardly affected them at all, except by focusing their effort further.

They stood there, in the open terrain for a very long time, or so it felt, breathing and heaving. What little they had left of strength and will threatened to leave them. They kept moving, crossing endless fields and plains. The low land faded behind them. They devoured the food, the rations they carried with them, resting by day, sleeping a little, running at night. The supreme effort of braving the fences and the barb wire seemed so long ago. They never forgot what they had left behind, the forces lining up against them. In their feverish dreams, they heard a thousand heavy boots stamp the ground.

They glanced at each other in the dark, couldn't see shit in the pitch black night, but they still saw each other clearly, beyond clearly.

– The Storm Child, 2013 said hesitatingly, stubbornly. – He's our link, our common denominator. That has to mean something. It has to!

The others nodded slowly, strangely comforted.

Dawn. They slept.
Twilight. Myriam Vallinger, Roger Norlund and Gerd Ellingsen chased westward, whipping themselves onward, across mountains and plains, desperate and more than half insane. So far ahead, so far to go, towards the sea in the west… and the awaiting Storm.

THE PLANET

Tom Rawlins sat in his armchair, at his office without windows in Marseille. He stared at all the screens simultaneously. They showed nothing but «snow». Not even any of the local video-cameras worked. He could no longer watch the electric storm to the south, but felt it, still saw it in his mind. The very air was shaking. No, that was too simplistic, too limiting. Reality itself was shaking, shaking violently at its core.

– We must leave, now! Ralph shouted. He stood in the doorway and attempted to make an impression on the older man. – The chopper engine is struggling, struggling hard. It might cease working at any time, permanently, and we will remain here, permanently.

Thomas looked good-humored at him. The older man closed his eyes. It had been so long since he had thought of himself as Thomas.

He rose, fought the large body up from the chair. They left the room. Ralph walked ahead, his relief very visible.

– You're too concerned on my behalf sometimes. Thomas shook his head. – Sometimes I fear you're more concerned about me than you are about yourself…

Thomas stopped for a minute, for many years in front of the window. He could study the storm from a somewhat laidback and «safe» distance. It didn't quite reach him.

The basin was boiling already. The enormous, beyond powerful charges lit up the entire northern Mediterranean coastline. Perhaps humanity had seen something similar when Atlantis sank, but not since then.

It didn't rain, not a drop, not anything but saltwater jumping and snarling in a hyper-charged atmosphere. There was no wind anymore, only the intense pressure from the yet distant and sinister flashes felt outside and inside. The city people had finally realized the seriousness of it all and fled mindlessly. No one advanced a centimeter in their four-wheeled coffins. Those fleeing on foot, stamped on those who had fallen. Thomas closed his eyes. It was no use. He saw them just as clear.

Now, when the decision was made, he was suddenly in a hurry. The walk up the stairs suddenly seemed very long and hard. There were only him and Ralph and five others. All the others in his loyal staff had left hours ago.

He stood on the roof. The wind not a wind tore and pulled in him. The chopper, the heavy wreck seemed to have a mind of its own, and wanted to take off and fly off by itself. The pilot had some trouble getting inside. Thomas stood with the guys one second, two seconds and stared at the sea, into the boiling mass.

This, he thought, must be how it is to stare into the sun.

But the sun never was so close that you could reach out your hand and touch it.

– It's like a disco, one of the men said awestruck.

– Like a disco of nature. Thomas laughed aloud.

The particles in the air darkened it in terrifying ways, but that visible terror was practically constantly surpassed by the prolonged, eerie flashes.

In the streets below, as far as they could see, they saw people, saw them run like rats in a ruthless race to escape the flood. Cars had moved a bit a few hours ago. Now, they stood absolutely still, and people left them in droves. The rats ran until cramps left them incapacitated, until the heart stopped and thought itself stopped.

They stepped into the chopper one by one. Time seemed to slow down to a crawl. Rawlins entered the metal bird last. He kept glancing behind him, immensely fascinated by what was happening. He sat down and nodded. Engine RPM speeded up, the rotor spun faster.

The door to the roof opened. An eerie creature stepped through it. Thomas recognized him in an instant, recognized Victor Russel. His clothes were torn, his enormous muscles very visible. He had bruises and lacerations on most parts of the body. The hair danced all over the impressive bundle of flesh. This affected Rawlins more than anything else. Russel had always had well-groomed hair.

Rawlins signed to the pilot. The chopper stopped momentarily its ascent.

– Do you know what? Russel shouted. The look in his eyes seemed even more insane. – My subordinates fled with my chopper. Can you imagine the fear they must have felt in order to do that?

By opposing him, by exposing themselves to his eternal wrath. Rawlins nodded.

– That's some story, he heard himself say. – What's the occasion, aside from that?

– I'm in desperate need of alternative transport, the giant grinned.

– I can't help you. Rawlins shook his head. – This transport is full.

– Throw someone out!

– That's out of the question.

This time Thomas heard his voice as if from far away, as if from ancient times.

– And even if there had been room, I wouldn't have let you onboard, not in a million years.

Russel took one step forward. All the men in the chopper directed their guns at him. Victor Russel stood still. He realized with his ice-cold intellect that even he could not prevail against such a threat.

One single signal from me, Rawlins thought later. Only one....

He had felt that a kind of draw was a good thing. If they fired, there was always the chance that Satan might survive. He had allowed Russel to live, in the certainty that the beyond deadly creature would die in the ruins they left behind. That had been a mistake. Russel didn't die. He was immortal, a banshee that would live and survive when the sun had turned cold in the sky, when the universe itself turned cold. After the Universe had exploded in another Big Bang, Russel would still be there.

The chopper rose from the crumbling buildings. One single human being remained on the roof, a never-resting ghost.

Thomas sat with closed eyes most of the long flight to the city no longer divided by a wall. He never closed them anymore after that.

Lightning hit a building, a giant warehouse. He saw it without seeing it. The entire structure was pulverized. Those surrounding it fell like castles of sand. The sand was pulled into the air and blew away in the wind not a wind.

This later to be revealed as a minor discharge was a forerunner to what was to come, the bigger and far more destructive force. Two, three discharges were similar to the first. Then, the full force reached land, the southern shorelines of Europe. The explosion seemed silent. The first crater formed. Sparks grew to explosive fires, to one single inferno. Its giant footprint grew dramatically, until entire streets and even vast areas were disintegrated in a single monster-like discharge.

Thomas didn't really see all that until later, on long-range scanners utilized by what was basically independent news channels, but in his mind he always mixed what he imagined and what he saw on television many days later. No reporters had words to describe what they saw. He couldn't fault them for that. It resembled an area of the moon far more than bombed-out cities. A few sharp edges remained in what with only goodwill could be called ruins. A few bodies and skeletons were found, but mostly it was just pieces of bones. Marseille and its population were virtually exterminated during the first hours of the new year.

The electric storm had touched Spain and Italy's western coastline. It smothered Europe's southern coastline like a glowing hand, stamping everything to dust, to fine powder. It appeared from nowhere and boiled the rising sea. It dissolved in a moment shorter than the beating of a heart. Wind and ocean were sucked in from all sides and swept away the ashes.

It left nothing else!

+++++++++++++++

It had been almost beautiful, a grand symmetry delivered directly from Heaven. The Spanish army had attacked the Basque Country from the south, the French from the north. The Sun had been frozen in the east, like now. The general squinted his eyes, now, like he had done then, through the dust. And he listened to the sound of the drums.

Rafael Guitierrez stared at the French border. He realized that he had not truly been sleeping lately. Brief and bizarre flashes came to him, his head resting on his desk while the red hot fluid spread on the white blotting paper, flowers with cores like human heads withering and leaving only sand. He had not slept, aside from brief, nightmarish moments… and now… he was awake.

He remembered everything. He recalled every single terrifying detail. It had been a thing of beauty, a work of art awakened to life and honor.

The «Basque problem» had grown huge and menacing the last two decades. With the gradual collapse of Law and Order the damn mountain people had grown distinctly bolder.

But they had gone too far, too fast. A few days before the finalizing of the operation even the French had had enough. They had eagerly joined in. The agreement between the two governments had made the final planning and execution simple.

The houses rested in the morning light. Rafael still praised the propaganda machinery. He couldn't do otherwise, even though he did so with gritting teeth. They had done an excellent job. All the soldiers, all the men and women and children in the two countries had hated the Basques with a vengeance. This hatred that had been nurtured so long had to be given an outlet. It was, right now.

He could imagine in exquisite detail Le Granier at the other side of the border, how she used derogatory language about Spanish people, about their ancestors and low morale, about their strange customs and culture, what dangers they posed to the French way of life. It didn't pose any problem to him. He had made the same speech about others.

Memories returned to him, with mixed, contradictory emotions, of the two armies moving like one, deadly unit. He recalled the Indian wars in the old American west, how the soldiers had enjoyed themselves when they attacked defenseless camps and massacred all tribe members, every single man, woman and child. He recalled a popular expression, one he had even shouted in his blind intoxication:

– THE EGGS BECOME LICE!

Now, with the bitter taste of defeat in his mouth, the memory of victory felt all the more bitter.

He spotted Le Granier's personal pennant on a pole sticking up from the tent behind the borderline. Spain didn't exist any longer. France was blown to pieces from within. This was between him and Le Granier and no one else. There were few or no advanced weapons. Planes couldn't take off because of the close to total lack of fuel. The soldiers carried rifles, pistols, swords and anything else they found useful. If Germany, Great Britain or any of the Scandinavian countries had nurtured thoughts of conquest towards the south now, no one could have stopped them. But they didn't. Then they would have been idiots, and they weren't that, after all. Spain had become one giant desert. France was about to become one. The German army was ten times bigger than the French. The French was that compared to the Spanish.

The army of General Guitierrez was hopelessly outnumbered.

He assumed that the world had not been led by idiots followed by imbeciles, even though he was very tempted to believe that by now. Finally! Tempted beyond belief.

It felt good to lead himself into temptation. Finally!

The French could have invaded Spain a thousand times since the reveille had sounded the first time a few minutes, nights earlier. They didn't bother, of course. The wretched remains of the Spanish army would attack. They wouldn't have any choice. Rafael hadn't drunk anything since the sun had first shown itself in the horizon this morning. He waited, already dry in the throat. Precious supplies waited for them at the other side of the invisible border, enough for them to start the long journey north, the one everyone made these days.

He recalled the attack on the Basque Country with burning clarity. The two perfectly synchronized armies had started off with a good old pincer maneuver. The enemy, military and civilians had been squeezed between them with few real chances of escaping. And the massacre had begun. Hearts and heads had been blown to pieces. *The eggs become lice*. The Basque nation had never truly recovered from it or become a problem for anyone after that. The bloodbath had lasted five hours. Only a few had survived. Everyone located later had been taken care of, both on the battlefield and elsewhere in the subsequent weeks and months. There were presumably people with Basque blood still among the living, but no one bragging about it.

He recalled the burning fires, the heaps of bodies disintegrating in fiery flames, seemingly setting the air itself ablaze. Dry as stored old branches carcasses burned easily these days. Petrol or other combustible fluids were no longer needed in order to start anything. He wondered if he wanted to die. He caught himself in wishing that he had never been born, that his father had never met his mother, that they and a thousand generations before them had never set foot on this earth.

Some people would always slip through nets like those the French had constructed, but it had become exceedingly clear to Guitierrez that they still had satellite surveillance at their disposal. There had been mass desertions. They had been executed en masse, either here or by the French army. There was no mercy for anyone going independent these days.

Guitierrez didn't envy Le Granier. The same mechanisms working against him would shortly, in more than a day or week, less than a year work against her. He still wanted her within firing range. Just one, tiny second would be sufficient. He would die happy then.

He left the tent to make the mandatory speech. He knew it would fill his army with hatred, make their blood boil. They were simple people, and had always preferred to be told what to do, how to act, pretty much like he had.

The cheers rose as he took the stroll across the field. Insane! It took off completely when he took his place behind the dais. Completely insane!

– We are the proud, he shouted. – WE ARE SPAIN'S HOPE! Even if there are only thousand or ten left of us, SPAIN will live on in our hearts. We are many. Perhaps many of us calling ourselves sons and daughters of SPAIN are spread across foreign beaches. Our future may look grim, but that is deception, an illusion. Our SPAIN isn't a rock, a geographical area, but a state of mind. We will continue to make our fatherland proud. We shall gather on a foreign beach and make it *ours*…

It sounded hollow and false to him, but they cheered and screamed. His contempt grew a notch or two more.

A timeless time later his aide handed him the binoculars. He gazed through the morning mist. The sun had already risen above the horizon. The mist stayed red. He shook and kept shaking, wondering if he would ever stop.

Were there hints of unrest in the other camp, small, hardly noticeable signs of imminent collapse? No, not yet, but soon, soon.

An insane laughter erupted from his dry mouth, and when he had first begun, he didn't stop. His people interpreted that as courage and praised him with loud shouts. Every time his thoughts centered on the superior force ahead, discouragement threatened to overwhelm him. The laughter countered that, like an increasingly taller dam with ever bigger cracks below.

They had only water for two more hours. A snowball had a bigger chance of surviving in this hell. This was the day and the hour. You reached a certain point in life, and you knew there were no more choices, nowhere left to go but forward. He had learned that, too early in life - and death.

Trumpets. Someone blew a trumpet, one sounding like hundred. The sound filled every corner in the terrain and pocket of air. That idiot, that insane shit!

Then, the general shrugged. It didn't matter. The laughter kept coming.

The waiting turned unbearable. Just the act of standing still became an ordeal. He had had enough, of everything.

– *Arreté!* Guitierrez howled abruptly. – AAAATTAAACK!

Two moments, three turns on the dusty field and the rolling mass of sweat and shit moved in a direct line forward.

And the river of blood rose yet another level on the shore.

++

Jason Edwards stared at the peaceful, desolate landscape, listening to the sinister silence. He had done so many times before, but now the silence lingered even more in the air. The treacherous peace shook even harder his gut. He wondered how many times he had checked his guns since dawn, convincing himself that everything that could have been done had been done.

They found themselves at the end of the road, it was that simple, so hard, and all kinds of thoughts roamed their minds.

The pipeline burned behind them. Smoke still rose in the air. It tore into throats and weary bodies. Major parts of Norway would get no gas to burn tomorrow. None on the European continent would get a single bubble. Germany would probably declare war on Norway tomorrow, but be helpless to carry out the threat. Nations would go to war for far less these days, using one pretext or another. The desperation and the lack of relations between nations had been visible for a long time.

No one was to blame, really, no nation alone.

Only all of them, Edwards thought and grinned.

It felt good to think it, say it, do it. He lived his dreams. Finally!

– Dreams belong to the night, he stated to no one in particular.

Elin heard him and turned towards him.

– Until the true dawn, she said. – Until the day is anything but fake window dressing.

Hands sought hands in a brief intimacy lasting forever. They checked their weapons again, the assault rifles, machineguns, smaller handguns. Everything was in order.

They wondered how long they had lived like this, with their senses in a state of constant awareness, with their blood boiling in their veins.

Long enough for the mist drifting in from the mainland, the sounds of the thousand feet approaching them to not affect them too much.

– We have lived thousand times during one lifetime, someone said, making everyone nod in solemn agreement.

They were five against a small army. They nodded to themselves.

They wondered how many times they had stood like this, with their backs to the wall, fighting a superior enemy.

– The enemy's power is disintegrating before our very eyes, Jason mused. – All its illusion of power is going away.

– It has been taken away, Elin stated with infinite passion in her voice and stance, – torn from its grip like the castle of sand it was. We, the dreamers in the night did it. We have that honor. Civilization is crumbling. The world, including mankind is waking up from its long slumber.

Finally!

Elite soldiers of what was left of the Norwegian national army advanced against the five on the small hill, the small peninsula. Jason Edwards spotted the soldiers with his inner eye before he spotted them with his two eyes. There was little or no life left in those shells of human beings struggling through the terrain in order to reach them. They would hardly feel anything beyond the pain of the flesh when the bullets hit them, but he and his comrades would. He had no regrets, and he had no obligation to justify that statement to himself or to say it aloud. He felt life, felt the Green Rose in every fiber of his being.

– We show them, he heard Anya say around a campfire far away, – show them that the human spirit is still alive.

They cocked their weapons, fired them, fired grenades and everything at their disposal. The first attack wave appearing from the cover drowned in blood, blood flowing up the hill against its final hurdle. Jason shouted in triumph and froze the red fluid in the enemy's veins to ice.

Kurt Mørch and Anya Kerien stared at each other as they levitated above the abyss. Anya froze like in pain. He saw everything in her closed eyes, in slow and fast motion. She had stood still in meditation, pushed fingers at her temples, forehead and cheeks. Eyes opened. Hands fell down.

Her nod told him everything he needed to know.

She started walking and he followed her.

– Whatever is left of the Taiga in Siberia is melting, she said. In her eyes he spotted thousands of simultaneous events. – People can see it with their own eyes, and if they can't, they can still feel it inside.

He had seen it on satellite images, and nodded. She had no need for that.

Tons of more greenhouse gases were liberated from the once so frozen Earth.

The forest around them breathed and lived, but silence ruled everywhere. On occasion the silence was broken by someone firing a gun or ten. Ahead of them, behind them there was a city. He had forgotten its name.

– I wish I didn't need to do this, she said. – I wish…

– You have to do it, he assured her.

She nodded and led her group further on, into the city state, bypassing snarling and hungry sentries.

Something in the very air kept disrupting whatever peace she had. Since last morning, the entire day she had sensed something that could be described as *rotten*. It wasn't exactly decay, at least not the process of decay prevalent in nature, but something more connected to the city state, with civilization itself. It couldn't really be seen. Only its results could. But she sensed it, as if it was tangible, material, actual matter.

– The world is waking up, she stated passionately, as a response to the others' glances. – It's finally happening, what we've been waiting for so long, what humanity has waited for millennia to begin. What until recently seemed like the dominant force on this planet fights to retain its position. What's more a Machine than a living entity will take painfully long time to destroy completely, and it will keep ruining everything it touches for as long as possible.

– It's a living dead thing, Paul spat.

– I believe that to be a very accurate statement, Anya nodded.

The stench in her nose made her nostrils twitch and turn. She feared she would never get rid of it. Garbage disposal had long since collapsed in this stone desert. Even so, she hardly noticed on a conscious level. The other stench, what couldn't be detected by her nose, was far worse.

She led the small group of people walking through a land of death. Her eyes didn't look at them. There was no need for that. She knew exactly where everyone was, in the space surrounding her. Most of them had trained, fought and killed together for many, many years.

Everyone else still looked to her, her and Kurt. They were the last of the original fifteen. The mere thought made a catching form in her throat. Twenty-five years ago. It felt like yesterday to her.

Paul was the youngest among them, but he had learned early and the hard way how to fight and kill. He had just turned twenty and had learned at a far earlier age compared to his companions, learned the way of the warrior so essential in this age of unparalleled strife.

Drums beat at dawn. She knew that to the others it seemed like the beat came from everywhere simultaneously, from drums without number.

She heard only one.

Bile forced itself up her throat. She couldn't tell whether or not it was due to nausea or rage.

She saw the bloodstained altar well before she spotted it with her eyes between the withered trees. Everything flooded her senses undiluted. The knife the priestess and priest raised in a unison union flashed like lightning in her mind. A boy had been tied to the altar, a flat rock already stained with coagulated blood. The lightning flashing from the knife already penetrated the heaving chest in her overactive imagination.

Many had gathered here this morning, this first light. Anya saw them grow to an irresistible destructive force that would corrupt and destroy the final vestige of mankind.

– The one resting here is a mighty witch, the man and the woman cried in an alluring, to Anya disgusting resonance. – Do not be deceived. This is not a boy, but an infinite source of power, a power soon to be *ours*.

Night and dawn both hummed in the circle surrounding the altar. Tall flames darkened and brightened the open area.

– Gaia, Goddess of the Earth, hear our prayer, accept the sacrifice we humbly offer you…

The woman spoke alone while lifting the twinkling knife above her head.

The sound of the humming grew.

– Gaia, Goddess of the Earth, guard and guide your tribe, make it grow plentiful and strong. Make us your messengers. Grant us the honor of bringing your word to all the corners of the world.

A sigh rose from the gathering. Everyone fell on their knees. Approaching something very similar to trance, they began screaming and howling, and saliva flowed from their mouth and down their unwashed, shaking bodies. It was like a waterfall, like a dam breaking. It felt like that in Anya's head.

– I CAN FEEL HER! SHE'S COMING! YES YES YES. WE CAN ALL FEEL HER.

– YES, YES, YES, rose like a choir from the swaying mass of people. – She's coming, SHE'S COMING!

Anya walked alone, unprotected out on the plaza. Those with her followed four, five steps behind. She reached the circle. The crawling, swaying mass gave way, forming a passage for her.

– Why aren't they shooting? Paul whispered to Celeste. – Why aren't they *doing* anything?

– *Look* at her! Celeste whispered with excitement brightening her eyes.

He did, from behind, from the side, at her front when she stepped up on the altar. He saw Fury drawn on her face.

No, that would be a wrong, insufficient interpretation. Her body, her entire being had become Fury.

The Arena turned quiet as death. The two that only a few seconds earlier had dominated the stage tried speaking, in vain. Anya pulled one knife from each of the man and woman's weak right hands. She killed them both by stabbing them in the heart. They had a heart, coughing and gasping as they fell and died on the flat rock where their intended victim had been restrained.

She turned towards the gathering. They stood around her on all sides, but they felt like she faced them all simultaneously.

– Is *this* what you believe is Gaia's wish? She spat in contempt. – Do you really believe sacrifices, subordination and worship will stay her Wrath? Are you human beings or sheep, when you buy a few, well-placed sweet words from power-hungry tongues? If there are truly gods and goddesses, or anyone like Gaia, do you imagine them looking at this with anything but loathing? I spit on you all!

Everybody looked up, glancing around. A deep chill, a hot gust seemed to cross back and forth on the arena. The flames… they didn't reach for the sky anymore. They looked like they were shrinking, fading away. There was no more fuel left for them to keep burning.

She bent down by the boy, and loosened the ropes binding him, rubbing his head with kind touches. He looked at her in wonder and with growing understanding. She pulled him on his feet and supported him the first few steps off the nightmarish stage. He walked on his own not long afterwards. They left the circle at a different point from where they had entered it. The ambiguous mass split in two here as well.

They found themselves among the trees. Paul caught up with Anya and the boy. She seemed normal again, even ordinary, at least for her, but he stared at her with awe in his eyes. He would never look at her in quite the same way again.

– That was FANTASTIC! He breathed. – I've never seen its like.

– Be prepared, she admonished them. – We don't have much time.

Sobriety dawned on them all.

The potential mob followed them at a distance, hesitant, frightened, ever more enraged. They counted only in the hundreds, only a small part of the worshippers, but more than enough to cause trouble, and sooner or later they would.

Any and Kurt caught each other's eyes across the abyss. They embraced briefly and intensively. There was no significant hesitation there. They had decided upon this among themselves long ego.

She stood before him, ready to leave, with Paul and the boy.

– Is this kid really so important? Kurt asked in a moment of weakness.

– Yes! She replied, confident and certain of her abilities. – Immeasurably important.

The air between them and the city state shook with rage. He nodded to himself.

– We have to say goodbye sooner or later, she said softly. – It would have happened eventually, anyway, one year or hundred from now.

He waved one single time. She held his eyes, before turning, and she and the two accompanying her disappeared into the deep forest.

They would meet again. Paths that cross will cross again.

++

Ross McQuay stood by one of many water plants outside Los Angeles, United States. Dust blew as far as his eyes could see. For well over hundred years, the water had been led from the once so mighty Colorado River to the desert areas in southern California. Instead of flooding the many wet marches and flow down many small rivers from Colorado, it had been led where mankind had directed it. More and more water had been led, and more and more water had been needed. The wet marches ran dry. Colorado itself ran dry.

Now, the desert returned with a vengeance, drier than before, bigger than before.

Ross McQuay drew his gun. There were grains of sand on it, several places on the dark, oily metal. He had never before allowed sand to contaminate his gun.

Without further ado he pushed the barrel into his mouth and pulled the trigger.

++

The heat hovered like a both humid and dry blanket over western Norway for the first three moons of 2015. The drought and the heat hit elsewhere as well, but like the locals put it: the people elsewhere were *used* to it.

Not long after Witchnight, at the start of May, the snow started falling. Two meters fell in only twenty-four hours. All transport ceased and people died howling in the streets and on the roads.

Two days later the storm from the south and west arrived. Warm air returned with the humidity and the wind. People had wished for cooler weather all year and finally had their wish granted. The last two days they had prayed to the Supreme Being for the return of the old weather. They weren't really heard either time.

The heat returned, accompanied by noteworthy friends. Wet clouds were pushed hard at the tall mountains and released almost their entire load in one go. There were heavy showers in the inland, heavy showers by the coastline and basically everywhere. Rivers flooded their shores. Streets and basements were filled with water. The snow and the ice, and not insignificant parts of cities and townships were flushed into the ocean.

People eventually emerged from their hideouts, most of them mostly unscathed. They hardly dared glance at each other, wondering what was going on, knowing beyond knowing in both their hearts and minds. They stumbled around like sleepwalkers in ruined streets, without being able to quite fathom their new reality. The cleaning up started like it always started, but this time the confusion didn't fade from people's eyes.

Those staring at the clouds in the west imagined they could actually see yet another storm form on the assembly line out there, its rage finding easily its echo in the unrest of their minds.

+++++++++++

The woman, the young man and the little boy wandered down the increasingly dusty highway. They walked in worn clothes, but the rags were sewed together and didn't fall off the body.

– Where are we going? The boy asked.

– North, she replied in the same language, with the same accent as he used. – Far, far north. We have quite the stretch to walk, but we're not in a hurry. We will always reach where we're supposed to go.

PART FOUR: BESIEGED CITY

«All things good on this Earth flow into the city, because of the city's greatness».

Quote attributed to Pericles 493 - 429 BC

CHAPTER SIXTEEN

Water from the mountains kept flowing in the streets of Bergen, doing so several days after the melted ice had fallen from the surrounding highland.

People exchanged weary glances and spoke in hushed whispers.

– The weather used to be so predictable, almost boring, an old man choked with a brittle voice, – but is so no longer.

No one commented on his statement. They sat on the sidewalk, outside the small cafeteria without speaking, or speaking much, preferring the silence. They drank their beer with a determined, dull look in their eyes.

Day darkened to twilight. The streetlights blinked off and on for a while, until they stayed on. Steam rose from moist streets. The pervasive heat fooled the air into believing it was locked inside a steaming engine room, a pressure cooker of infinite magnitude. The figure covered by a dark cloak sneaking in and out of the shadows and the mist, was strangely comforted by all the destruction. The twilight failed in hiding the sand on the sidewalk and on the road, the holes in the asphalt and cobblestones, the torn apart signs and poles and broken exhibition windows and exhibitions.

She slipped past the long rows of men and women working to clean the streets. They didn't see her. She was hardly more than a ghost to them.

A gathering of beggars had taken position further down the road. She avoided them, chose another street, but there were almost as many beggars there as well. They clung to her like glue when she attempted to walk past them. She pushed them aside in impatient, brutal strikes. They didn't resist, weak in body and mind after having lost all will and dignity and strength while living months and years on the streets without sufficient nourishment.

She walked alone again. The other people nearby didn't seem more real than all the other ghosts surrounding her. A rat rushed across the street, from one derelict building to another. She hurried along, sweeping her cloak harder around her body. Her head turned often, and wary eyes scanned those walking in the same direction as her. They never did for long, turning either left or right and disappearing into the night, and she relaxed a bit.

A shadow moved ahead of her, way ahead. It was walking, clearly moving its feet, but still seemed to be standing still. The mere sight of it chilled her, chilled her to the bone. It was there, even though she couldn't quite convince herself that it was. She feared it waited for her, but uncertainty haunted her. She turned left, in the opposite direction of where it was heading.

She stepped into a well-lit street. The shadow stepped out of a pub right in front of her. She heard the singing from the tavern, even as it turned both loud and distant in her ears. Even in this strong light the shadow remained a shadow. It stopped right in front of her and she couldn't move.

– You know who I am, Lisbeth, it stated with confidence, with a pleasant, humming voice.

Lisbeth gulped and gulped. She was unable to conceal her fear, only contain it with hateful contempt.

– Who are you? Are you following me? Perhaps you don't know who I am? I can have you arrested before you can blink. I can only snap my fingers and that easy have you in my power.
– I'm not following you, Lisbeth. You're persecuting me. I thought we could have a chat.
All kinds of thoughts regurgitated through Lisbeth's mind and she could not act on any of them.
– I… know who you are, she breathed. – Others may be confused and unable to fathom you and what you're actually talking about, but I'm not. You're nature's fangs and claws and savagery, the red and the green and what idiots call the entire rainbow scale. You're a threat to humanity, a traitor to your species. I've had nightmares about you since I was a little g-girl.
– Your father and mother both have given you those nightmares, Lisbeth, Anya said softly.
– There are tons of vague reports on you in our files, Lisbeth snarled. – Many a weak soul praises you as a goddess.
– What I can do to help you, sweet girl, La Strega said with sadness in her voice, – is to repeat an ancient quote: «There are no gods but man».
They stared at each other, measuring each other. It was no equal fight. Lisbeth lowered her eyes after just a few seconds. She stood there with shivering lips.
The creature glowing in color and shadow turned to leave.
– Wait, don't you dare leave me here like this, damn you!
The eyes of the tall, bright woman turned stealthy, desperate, filled with longing. The shadow creature stopped for a moment.
– You've become the Goddess, now, right, embraced that aspect of yourself? You've got nothing else left. Tell me, how does that feel?
Her voice drowned in a mockery faded before the next heartbeat.
– You will never know!
The Goddess had faded into the darkness and the mist.
Lisbeth stood there alone and cold, abandoned and lost. She hurried on through the night.
Without a single discernible thought in her head, she ran the last stretch to the badly lit house. He stood there waiting for her, on the spot she had chosen. She threw herself into his arms, and they hugged, hugged hard. He was in disguise, but she still recognized every line, every single feature of his face. Both stepped back a little. His eyes swept the surroundings, a reflex he couldn't escape. It didn't make the excited smile, the blush fade from her face. She kissed him on the lips, happily demonstrating her feelings for him.
– There's no need for you to worry. This place is safe. No one followed me. I used two days to check its validity. No one knows we're here and no one will find us in such an unlikely spot.
He nodded, somewhat acknowledging her attention to detail.
They found themselves at the top of the stairs already, at the entrance to the apartment. She opened the door. They walked inside. She locked the door behind them, eager like a child. One single lamp lit itself automatically.
– I love the twilight in here, she said, – I, who have always feared the darkness.

They tumbled down on the carpet. From then on, if not long before, she lost all sense of time and space. She had no idea how they ended up in bed. Eagerness and a wild, aggressive joy dominated her entire being.

The scream and the loud, loud moan turned into one happy choir, a cry rocking their world thrice over.

Thoughts, consideration came later, when they rested in each other's arms and the first stirrings of sleep claimed them.

– We met by chance… right?

She burrowed her nails in his shoulder, her voice fluttering.

– We did, he said, he insisted. – If you believe nothing else… please believe that!

– We just stood there. She shook her head. – Both could have called out and revealed the other, called for backup, drawn our weapons, shot each other to pieces… but we didn't, as if it was preordained.

– We started talking, finding common ground, he offered. – We looked into each other's eyes, and we were lost, just like in a silly romance novel.

– I can't even recall if I recognized you before we ended up in bed, she said frustrated. – We were well disguised at the time.

– When we eventually did recognize each other… it didn't matter, he said softly. – We laughed ourselves silly, and that was that. I didn't shoot you, and you didn't call out to your bodyguards, even though they weren't that far away, and would most certainly have heard you.

– They knew I was with my lover, she snorted. – You aren't the first, so they didn't turn suspicious.

He didn't take offence by her callous tone. She saw that easily when looking into his now very familiar eyes.

Each of them had recognized the other, and they had laughed themselves silly, and eventually made love again.

Their next encounter had been filled with distrust. Both had been reluctant. They had been pretty much convinced that the other wouldn't even show up.

Both did, and now, two months later they had pretty much made it a habit, even though the mood between them grew increasingly anxious, desperate.

They rested tight in bed, hugging the other hard. They felt closer to the other than they had to any other person, ever.

– This is stupid, she mumbled. She raised her mouth and head from the scarred skin on his shoulder. – This is completely ridiculous.

– I agree completely, he responded dryly. – That a rebel leader is fucking a would-be dictator is definitely something out of the ordinary.

– That's the only reason you did it, she said pointedly, – you wanted to get close to the halls of power.

– Of course, he commented, very ironic.

– There can't be any other reason, she spat, while digging her long nails into the skin on his thighs, – no other logical explanation.

He didn't say it, didn't need to say it. She knew what his reply was. He had lived by that philosophy for many years, his entire life, except for a few, short years. He had it far easier than she had, damn him!

The gray light of day seemed to reach them through the small window long before

dawn. Time didn't fly. It flowed on tachyons faster than light.
She clung to him, harder than a castaway to the loose sand of a shore.
++
Erna Jonasen couldn't stop thinking about the snow-free downhill slopes. They kept appearing in her vision and in her mind. She rode the train from Voss to Bergen. It was supposed to take little over an hour, but would take at least two these days, with many involuntary stops. The monotone sound of the wheels turning on the rails echoed in her thoughts as well. The sound rocked her world. Everything did these days.
The giant skiing-towers had been so dominating in the landscape. Now, tall grass and trees slowly immersed them. They were fading. The Earth itself devoured them. The ground swallowed her.
Voss and other communities dependent on winter tourism had become ghost towns. Empty hotel rooms had screamed at inhabitants for years.
Erna shook her head in elevated distress.
The man sitting by her side laughed. She stared hard at him. He didn't take notice.
– It has always bothered me when people laugh without a discernible reason, she stated, told him in no uncertain terms.
He got it. She saw that he did. He clammed up, glancing anxiously at her every other second.
The sound of the train kept echoing in her mind. He didn't laugh anymore.
– I know there are no places to go, she told him. – You're a fool if you don't listen to me.
Or did she? He didn't seem to react this time either.
– I can help you, she insisted, – but I don't know if it will be worth it.
The train stopped at Arna Station, just a stretch of tunnel before Bergen, the end station.
The journey through the dark tunnel seemed to last forever. She glimpsed her face, his face, and countless others in the dark window flashing by. Dizziness assaulted her and she could hardly move.
The train finally pulled to a stop at the end of the railway. She rose, pulling out the small pistol and shot him between the eyes.
– Better safe than sorry, she shrugged.
She put the pistol away again and left the train. No one charged her or made any attempt at arresting her or anything. She continued towards the exit in a relaxed stroll.
– Why isn't anyone doing anything? She heard a curious soul whisper to his companion somewhere ahead. – The woman shoots and kills a person in front of everybody and no one reacts.
Jonasen glanced at the uniformed guards placed in considerable numbers around the station. She speeded up and caught up quickly with the curious man.
– It's because I'm invisible, she enlightened him. – I'm sent here on a mission from the Lord of Heaven, and can't be hurt.
She spotted easily the fear in his eyes.
– You know, she nodded. – Very good! Perhaps there is hope for you. Perhaps you will be saved.
The city council building towered above her almost from the moment she stepped out of the railway station. She looked constantly for hurdles in her path as she approached

the tall concrete structure, but spotted none, not during the short walk and not inside. The man behind the desk to the right recognized her and hailed her with a big grin. She returned his greeting the best she was able. There was hectic activity everywhere. People were rushing back and forth, in and out in a constant flow. No one noticed the invisible woman walking among them. She walked to the guard by the elevator, directed the barrel of her gun at his head and pulled the trigger, and grabbed his machinegun as he fell to the floor. She handled the weapon like a pro as she directed it at the crowd and slaughtered them all in a burst of fire. The elevator doors slid open behind her. She backed inside. The doors closed and the small cage was pulled up by strong wires. She beheld the snow and the athletes racing down the beautiful tracks far below. No other people had followed her up, but a crowd of terrified fools covered in a corner and wished to take the elevator back down. She fired a round or two at them, not really bothering with checking the result. Sometimes she imagined she heard the sound of bodies hitting the floor, but she wasn't confident it was actually happening. There was too much snow on the floor, snow whirling in the air and what could just as well be dust from countless dirty corners and dark places.

She used one clip to blow open the door to the roof, and stepped out on the wild-growing bed of grass and moss. Another frown crossed her confused features. Her memory told her that there had been no growth here once. She smiled when she stopped on the edge and raised her arms to the side, and studied the ants far below.

– I cannot help everyone, she shouted.

And jumped.

+++++++++++

She passed people on her way, *civilians*. The mere word made her frantic, made her glare at them with burning hatred in her eyes.

Enemy! She shouted silently at them. I will crush you, kill you and spread your limbs for the four winds.

The propaganda engraved on her mind stayed active, no matter how much she attempted to reject or deny it.

They didn't notice. Her eyes hid under the wide hood and they weren't sufficiently sensitive on a conscious level to notice the aura of menace surrounding her.

Something, a change in the wind made her ponder, briefly, made her slow down for a moment or two. She heard a thud. Something sounding very much like flesh hit the pavement behind her. She didn't turn and look. It had been a long time since she had done that. She couldn't recall the last time. Detailed memory kept eluding her. The loss of self was so pronounced that she could hardly recall her name, except during the most deep-seated focus. Desperation squeezed her every time she took another step forward. She moved with what she perceived to be an anxious, shivering unrest, but something the untrained eye probably wouldn't notice.

Crowds seethed and boiled around her. She saw straight through what looked like signs of a thriving, dynamic society. Sick, sneaking fear hid behind the happy and excited surface. Myriam saw that without trying.

She spotted glimpses of herself in store windows, diluted, without form. The only thing about it making her somewhat happy was the sight of the thick hair on her head. She didn't shave it off anymore, even though she had to fight off the desire to do it every single morning. That, like so many other sick thoughts and notions, grinded her mind.

She slid through the streets, between the unreal spirits there like a ghost, a shadow, virtually invisible. No one seemed to notice or take notice of her.

Atonal music and wild rhythms flowed back and forth in the boiling pot she moved through. She moved consciously and subconsciously in the direction where it was at its strongest.

Her path brought her close to Bergen's Children Brigade, a hundred year corps tradition in the city, what was basically a training ground for future soldiers. Its drums overpowered all the rest. The close proximity to that almost made her physically ill.

She circled in on her destination, suddenly a bit hesitant. The traveling carnival had been placed pretty much at the center of the city, by the lake. It looked and felt distinctly different to her, compared to all other such she had ever visited. There was a noticeable mood of mystery and imagination attracting her even before she crossed its outer boundaries.

This open space reminded her of an alley, a sizzling spot of chaos in a world of order.

Close by, on her right, there was a true alley, almost empty. Two sentries, clearly not a part of the ordinary police force were hassling a vagrant, a homeless man in rags.

– A dirty shithead like you can't stay here, the female sentry snorted. – This is a decent city. We don't tolerate people like you here.

Her male counterpart kicked the man hard. The woman did as well. Her companion kicked the man again.

The man in rags didn't fall. He quite simply refused to fall. He leaned against the concrete wall, but he stayed on his feet.

Myriam moved forward. They didn't notice her, not until she stood right behind them. She grabbed their necks and smashed their heads at the wall. They fell without a sound.

Her eyes studied them. The training kicked in again. She had been taught to pay attention, to probe her surroundings, and that kept aiding her, far away from the barracks and fellow soldiers.

The two of them wore a uniform, of sorts, and a symbol, a bird in a double circle on their shoulders she didn't recognize.

She spat at them, her lips one single thin line.

– They call themselves Nightravens, Roger said from the left, several steps away, breaking the silence between them. – They're operating in several Norwegian cities.

Myriam knew. She remembered. They had started up in 1994, well before she had arrived here the first time.

– They're a professed «civilian protection group», Gerd said from the right, – supposedly created to aid children walking the city streets at night, but in truth they are just one more fascist organization bent on maintaining order.

– They aren't the true Nightravens, Myriam snarled, – not the Nightravens of the Green Rose, but just one more fake group aiding oppression. That's all that matters.

The vagrant didn't seem to see her at all, even though she stood right in front of him. When she looked into his empty eyes, she realized that there was no one home, that whoever had once lived there had left it long ago. She and her mutual shadow companions left the wreck of a human being, left the alley without exit and continued on their path.

They emerged into the City Park, a somewhat green spot in all the gray, an urban disaster area still not cleaned up after the storm and flood. Broken trees and poles and signs appeared everywhere she looked. Brown slush covered the ground where there was supposed to be green grass. She stepped into the carnival's enclosed area from the west, through one of many small gates not a gate. There were no fences here.

She approached a downtrodden, smaller stage, stopped before she got too close. It was set on ground level, not really there at all, except for the players marking it. A group dressed in common clothes, a mirror image of those watching performed for a fleeting audience. People passed by, walked back and forth in front of the invisible demarcation line. The performers did their thing without microphones or any kind of electronics. Words and moods penetrated ears and minds without distortion.

Myriam and the others didn't see any play as it was commonly understood, hardly even a performance, not in a modern understanding of it. A veil was lifted into the air. It seemed to be happening on one part of the stage, but it became clear that it had happened on a completely different part of it.

– Did you see that? A boy cried excited to his companions. – That was Kurt's Gambit, the same doing-it-with-mirrors thing he did in Gothenburg when they tricked the military units surrounding them.

The events in Gothenburg eighteen years earlier were kept alive in people's minds and hearts. They hadn't forgotten.

– They always do their performance at midnight, she heard another boy, one not yet having reached puberty say. – The stage is dark, and they brighten it with their presence and performance. I feel like anything can happen, really.

– I've heard that the fake Nightravens are out in force tonight, a second boy hissed. – Be ready to blow if they show.

– That's poetry, the first boy whistled.

The youths turned quiet, like everyone else watching becoming mesmerized with the unique performance.

They were many those on the stage, many elves and spirits. No one could state with conviction that there was more than one.

Lights shifted, a reflection from a lamp a mile away. Torches burned with dark fire behind concrete walls, behind thin veils and brightened faces and masks, reaching out to the world Beyond.

DREAMS ON THE CEMETERY
(EXCERPT)

The Gray Fog drifts in from the night. It's nothing natural formed by low clouds, but a soup of poison and despair. The tall tombstones rise around them like monuments of the utmost folly.

THE QUEEN: Never have I heard such noise, such a horrible harmony.

THE KING (entering from the left, accompanied with sweet music): It's the sound of the discontent masses, the many-headed beast not knowing its own good.

The servant enters in silence and obscurity.

THE SERVANT: Everything is ready in the basement, in the basement of basements, Your Highness. Is there anything more I can do for you?

The Stranger enters the room. They don't see him, don't hear him.

THE STRANGER: There is no noise, no discord, only nature's sounds haunting a tortured mind.

THE KING: Come, beloved, let's please our subjects with our presence.
Flames stretch from the hearth. The executioner moves the glowing iron in and out of the darkness, out and in of the unbearable heat. A naked body is stretched out on a torture rack. Poisoned blood and ash flow from open wounds.
THE EXECUTIONER: Confess thy transgression, confess thy travail, and all will be well.
He returns the iron to the hearth, in order to reheat it.
THE STRANGER: A beast I am, and proud of any transgression or travail I may have performed.
A roar of wrath rises from the spectators. The executioner reaches for the iron. The king steps forward and raises his hand, halting the brutal act.
THE KING: Hold for a moment your righteous wrath. No one can say that I am not a just king. Asking my just subjects, what shall happen to this lost lamb?
THE SPECTATORS: BURN THE WITCH, BURN THE WITCH, BURN THE WITCH!
THE KING (giving his consent): So it is in Heaven and on Earth.
The iron is drawn glowing white from the hearth. The executioner does his dance and the iron strikes the unprotected body, the mind laid bare. The king and the queen move behind the executioner in a synchronized, insane dance, pulling everyone's strings.
THE EXECUTIONER: Confess thy transgression, confess thy travail, and all will be well.
THE PRISONER: I CONFESS, I CONFESS, I'm guilty as hell and unworthy of your presence.
Ties are untied, ties remain. Both bow deeply for the regent and his queen.
THE EXECUTIONER/THE WRECK OF A MAN (choiring to the royal couple and the audience): Everything is ready in the basement, in the basement of basements, your grace. Is there anything more I can do for you?
THE KING: Aside from everything, there's nothing right now, dear servant. Feel free to cultivate your own interests, until we call for you anew.
The audience returns to their modest homes, disappointed and filled with misery, mumbling and shouting in unison:
THE AUDIENCE: BURN THE WITCH, BURN THE WITCH, BURN THE WITCH!

Act IV

The king and the queen rest stone cold between tilted tombstones, at the ruin-like cemetery. The meat has turned to rot on their faces and small pieces of their eyes are missing. Lips move, but there's no sound.
THE KING: Where did I go wrong, where is my transgression?
Eyes strive to blink, to close. There are no eyelids.
The servant's skull is only a step away. There's no body.
THE SKULL: Anything for the country, anything for you, dear king. Is there anything more I can do for you?
The Stranger and his followers appear from the ruins.
THE FOLLOWERS: *There's nothing more the king can do for others or for himself. Once*

upon a time, he could. Now, he can only be devoured and no more devour.

She steps forward from the shadows and the ruins. Reflections of flames and sparks dance in her face.

GAIA: We dance towards the fire in shadow and darkness.

The shadows behind her become the Stranger. The shadows behind him become her. It's as if they both grow out of each other's shadows. Reflections of shadows and darkness dance in both faces.

ONE OF THE FOLLOWERS: In a world filled with misery and degradation they rise time and time again from the fire of their own ashes.

THE STRANGER: Yellow am I, said the king, because no other colors there are.

He stands alone on the stage, a stage not a stage, where smoke and mirrors, seemingly frozen solid blink slowly. A distant drum is beating. Flutes play themselves with varying intensity. Somewhere thunders the bass from the center of the earth.

THE STRANGER: The energy of life, the devil-may-care, the savagery, humanity's inner fire is the one force civilization, regimentation's pale society has never been able to tame. Break it in a thousand pieces, in a million grains of dust and it keeps rising anew.

He raises his arms above his head. The whisper sounding like a roar rises from the spectator's throats.

THE STRANGER (with a smile both enigmatic and threatening): We're nomads, troubadours in a brutal reality. We travel through the land and give people fleeting moments of joy, but also show them what they don't want to see. We're the agents of time and change. In a world without dignity, we find ours. In a flash of lightning and thunder, truth is exposed as the lie it is. The sharp blade flashes in silver and red… Time and Space stand still!

ONE END

Myriam rushed on between all the people, knowing without doubt where she was headed. In witnessing a tiny flash of dignity, she found her own.

It was visible in her walk, the way she moved her body, and the fire and devil-may-care in her eyes.

She could smell him, them outside a tent by an old garbage disposal heap. Between ash and age-old stinking trash, she once again sensed the fire.

A tent flap was moving. There were no guards, no one she could see or sense, and if she couldn't, very few others could. The thought brought her even more pride.

Her two fellow travelers approached with her. She was aware of them, as she had been all the time, but now they gained substance, like everything ahead of her.

The tent flap moved. The opening widened in her honor, a clear and present invitation. The very air seemed to be moving, pulling her inside. Before she knew it, she was there, and during a few moments and precious glances, she spotted them all. She heard her heart beat, heard the thunder in her ears and excited mind.

The fire rose from the asphalt, the flames reaching for the high ceiling. The tent seemed filled with smoke. She didn't have any trouble breathing. The smoke mixed with the humidity in the air and transformed into mist. He rose from his spot by the fire and met her halfway. A couple fucked each other senseless somewhere. Both the sound and the imagery of it played in her mindscape, like a dream.

Dreams Belong to the Night. Her lips moved. She repeated it several times, like a mantra. It flowed soundlessly between shivering lips. They embraced, looking at each other across the Abyss of Forever, crossing it with one, single leap.

– I looked for you, he said hoarsely.

– Hush…

She comforted him lightly, effortlessly.

She kissed him on his lips, harder than she had planned, and she tasted his blood, and the boiling of her own.

– Another bitch in constant heat. A female voice with only a little bit wickedness chuckled. – By damn!

– We can look forward to even more pleased roaming cats, a male voice countered.

Myriam giggled and cackled in a single burst of happiness. The happy grin spread all over her face.

So silly, so stupid, so great. She felt, literally felt how the grin transformed her face and body, the first true she could recall ever having. She clung to that, *clung*.

– I haven't forgotten, she insisted, mumbled with her lips close to his ear. – I remember, remember…

She and her two fellow travelers were welcomed into the tribe they had never and ever belonged to.

– It isn't anything you ever forget, he, the man with the very visible beard on his jaw and cheeks, he Damon Terrill said. – One might be fooled into deceiving oneself, into forgetting, but it's just yet another nightmare of the gray light of day.

– Morgana la Fey, she presented herself. – Your eternal servant, Sire.

They pulled back, retreated further into the vast depths and intimacy of the tent. Many surrounded and welcomed the newcomers.

Someone put something she couldn't quite visualize into her open mouth, something she imagined was a tiny, square piece of paper with a purple spot at its center. She more than suspected that it had been the giant, wicked Red Riding Hood that was the culprit. It didn't matter. Myriam had swallowed it, filled with expectation, fear and desire. Time stretched out. It flowed like heat, like warm, warm blood. She had no idea how long time had passed with dance and dirty play until the candles burned and flickered stronger, and the shadows grew longer, longer, longer.

She had feared her nightmare would dominate the trip, the ride, but it didn't, wasn't even present, except like a tiny twirl of hair in her neck.

When it showed itself, it brought no fear, and only little shame.

The hissing fire, the boiling stars, the deep shadows overwhelmed completely the dirty, ugly light that had been her existence for so long.

– LIFE! She gasped. – Life dominates the Universe.

She didn't speak aloud, couldn't do that, only think it, express it inside, at her core, as the crimson flow flushed them all and swept them away.

Everything else was just the deepest shadings of everything and nothing, and everything in-between.

CHAPTER SEVENTEEN

One Sherwood Forest grew around them, so distant, so close, not far from the coastline of the island in the mouth of the sea.

In the opposite direction the city like Nottingham brightened the night sky.

They enjoyed a certain freedom here, in this haven in the House in the Forest. It was far, far enough from the denser populated areas in the southern parts of the island. Trees on almost all sides hid them from curious eyes dwelling in neighborhood houses. It was a haven, even as safety was denied them. They felt a kind of peace, but not even the illusion of safety.

Their unrest was visible here, and wherever they went.

Anya entered the land one day, walking, dressed in rags, with the boy and Paul in tow, wild in the eyes and the spirit.

They all saw it, how she spotted Damon and walked directly to him. The blinding smile couldn't hide the haunting flash at the edge of the eyes. Myriam recognized the signs in her. Even Anya sought Damon, like a parched throat sought an oasis in the desert.

She and the two other wanderers were clearly exhausted, as if they had used up all their strength to get there. Everyone welcomed her, in thousand small and big ways.

She leaned exhausted on Damon, even if the eyes looking at him were as astute as ever.

– We had to get here, she whispered, – had to get here… in time.

He held her, waiting for her to explain further, realizing that that he held her and that she would have fallen if he hadn't, realizing that she had put her head on his shoulder and fallen asleep.

They put her to bed. Claire took a look at her, attempting in vain to appear indifferent.

– She's okay, she said, with relief in her voice. – She's just totally exhausted.

Her relief was echoed throughout the extended tribe.

The man and the boy, not that exhausted, strangely enough fell asleep quickly as well by her side.

Everything, even their very surroundings seemed to have changed with her arrival. The air appeared heavier, similar to that of mirages in desert areas… or something. They could not properly name or describe it.

Everyone caught themselves casting glances at the house where Anya slept.

Most of them stayed up, unable to sleep, to even close their eyes. They kept glancing towards the house where she slept.

Something distracted them, though, distracted them further. It was nothing they could put their finger on at first. They looked at each other and their surroundings without spotting anything substantial.

Then, they grew aware of an eager Vladek standing by the house's left corner and waving to them, clearly wanting them to join him. They quickly did.

He looked at something at the other side of the house. One moment later they all did.

Damon and Kara stood on the cliff to the west, staring out at the sea. A strange, dark glare seethed in the air between them. They held hands, speaking archaic, guttural words, casting spells between them and the world.

Claire watched them, practically in trance. Her eyes seemed to stare at nothing.
Yola shook her. Claire turned her head and focused on the other woman, paralyzing her with the black stare.
– They speak to the Earth, Claire said with the hollow voice. – The Earth responds.
The group stood there and studied the two on the cliff. Time stretched out. Everyone remained there. More joined. Many joined in on the eerie humming rising from Damon and Kara's throat. They stayed there all night, falling asleep on the spot.
Anya gathered them in the wild garden, in the tall grass the next morning, all strangely awake and astute, seeing her in a light of utmost clarity.
– How did it start this system, this world-wide prison, this society working independently of the humans inhabiting it? Was it a chain of coincidences or one single event that started it? My guess would be that it began with a hunter that had a nightmare and woke up as a farmer.
They were listening, far beyond the mere words she spoke, to the nuances and intonations and to the movement of her body, and even imagined they were able to hear her thoughts, what about her that wasn't physical, reminding them about things and thoughts and memories misplaced and only gleaned through dreams.
– Civilization, the horrible nightmare we've suffered for so long is ending, she mused, – and life will return to the planet and human beings will once again become what we're born to be. What and who we've been through all of it and always will be will return to the fore of our consciousness. The Thunder Road is waiting for us out there. It always is.
– What's the Thunder Road? The boy asked with huge, deep eyes.
– It's the human being's path through life and eternity, she replied softly. – What challenges, destroys and strengthens it. The Thunder Road is making a turn, it always is. Burning Ice, Biting Flame... that's how life began, and that's how it will renew itself, no matter where humans are going. The blade will be laid bare, ready to be tempered once more…
She started driving them, drilling them ruthlessly later that same day, quickly imposing herself on their entire existence.
– This is about survival, she instructed them, – about moving wherever you go in the terrain, in nature as a whole or in decaying city streets, about the very state of being itself. You may believe there's no more than one way to move, but that's not true, not true at all, and when we're done, you will know that beyond doubt.
She sent them into the forest, the wilderness in groups, urging them to push themselves ever harder, practically chasing them off.
– You learn now, she told a totally exhausted group after their return, – but while I strive to remove the slag, the everyday garbage of civilization from your system, civilization keeps dumping more into you, and no matter how well prepared we are, reality, when it's hitting us where it hurts the most, will be far worse than we can imagine or train for, here, in relative safety.
Myriam felt her presence, inside, outside, saw it reflected in other eyes, while they chased through the forest and the mountains.
– There are truly lots of wilderness and untouched nature near Bergen, Vladek gasped, – places time has forgotten. I feel like we've explored every single piece of it, but in truth we've hardly started.
They felt power, when standing at the top of Mount Lyderhorn after having run up the

entire, steep trail from the north, looking at the vast expanse on all sides.

They stood there, breathing beyond hard, feeling alive, feeling life burn at their very core, more than equal to the pride in their eyes.

Anya gathered them all in the wild garden one dark and warm night. It marked a distinct departure from what she had been doing to this point and anticipation filled the gathering.

They made five big bonfires, from garbage and debris they had gathered for Midsummer Night, but they had decided to use it early. They expedited everything these days and nights.

Anya dipped sticks in resin she had tapped from pines.

– It contains turpentine, she informed them, continuing on the advanced survival class she was teaching them. – The fire catches on easier and prevails longer, even in the extreme humidity and rain we must expect in this part of the world.

Soon five large fires burned in the secluded garden. The night swallowed tongues of fire and pulled them towards the sky.

– This is a night of celebration and testing, She Who Dances in the Forest cried. – Five chosen will brave the night and the wild in order to bring back our price, our feast. The Dance to Life will bring us sustenance and joy and help us brave the untold future.

Five were brought into the circle between the tall fires. They looked rigid like statues, but only in passing. No statues could have had skin glowing like this, and such hot blood boiling in the veins. Gwen, Yngve, Damon, Myriam and Vladek stood right at the center of the five bonfires, surrounded by them, by the sweltering heat, and sweat flowed from their nude bodies, their body hairs burning off on the most exposed spots. They felt a heat stronger than any flame on every single piece of their skin. Even under their soles they felt it, felt the heat from the ground, from the Earth itself.

Laughing and giggling shadows dancing in life's honor came and grabbed them and led them away from the inferno and into the night. They didn't feel cold, didn't feel any of the considerable temperature difference at all. There was no cold there in the darkness. Eager hands used fingers like brushes and painted colors and patterns on the living canvas before them.

– We paint the shell, Kara hummed, – drawing what's inside to the outside. That's what witches do; painting the fire of mankind.

Anya stood before them, her eyes flashing in wicked joy.

– Our hunters, our shadows in the forest.

The trail, either visible or imagined always felt new and undiscovered.

She had sent them, yet another hunting party testing themselves on their way with kisses and urges and good wishes, and the shadows dancing in life's honor had joined in.

The five slid through the forest, on the forest bed, through the air, felt the bumps and rough edges, catching it almost like patterns of energy, the way she had taught them. This, these skills was physical, but that was far from being all of it. They more than glimpsed the vast, simple truth behind the veil.

– To exercise the body will always be important, they heard Anya's voice, heard she who spoke in the wilderness, – but behind that will always be an underlying texture, a way of life. Humanity belongs in nature and to nature. It's an integrated part of it, not only there for recreation, something we seek in our free time. Nature is our home, the only true home we will ever have.

So much couldn't be conveyed with words. Words would always be inadequate.

There were no walls out here, no tall hurdles.

They reached a small gorge with a small river, large, wet stones, moss and running water. They followed the river upstream. Life always followed the flowing water.

They picked up the tracks of four-legged animals. They didn't stop for a closer look, but kept going at the same, intense speed. There had been a sense, true or false at the start of the hunt that their breath had been labored. It had certainly felt that way. When they started chasing the tracks in earnest, as they disappeared and reappeared and disappeared again they no longer reflected over how easily they all moved. It just happened, without thought or deeper reflection.

Days, years could have passed when Gwen appeared in their vision, and the others stopped behind her. Arrows were drawn, put on the bowstring and the string was drawn and released. All the arrows hit the deer right in the heart or close to it. It made one and a half jump and fell, bleeding out on the ground.

They felt a strange dichotomy or sadness and exhilaration as they walked to the prey and started painting each other on the face and body.

– It's strange, Myriam said softly. – I've killed countless people, but I still feel sorrow at the sight of a dead deer.

– Bleeding heart rubbish, Yngve snorted. – They didn't cure you of that in the military, after all.

– The hunter-gatherers tribal communities both celebrated and honored the death of a beast, Kara stated. – We will do the same, and that, in turn will aid us in the process of learning what we need to learn in order to survive and thrive.

The ambiguity stayed with them, as they made their way back to their tribe.

– We need to learn, and learn fast, Damon said. – Food is already becoming scarce in the world, even more than before.

The food crisis swept the world, and contrary to before also affecting the western lands of plenty.

They felt exhausted long before they closed in on the fields where sheep grassed. In one ruthless, easy maneuver they surrounded a couple of them and slaughtered them outright, using knives, arrows and swords.

Their eyes flashed and twinkled when they wandered into the Sherwood Forest garden after having spent an eternity away from it. Everyone rushed them and used the blood to paint themselves. The sheep and the deer were roasted over the open fire. All kinds of tastes played on their buds.

– The sadness is hypocrisy, and we all know it, Vladek said sarcastically. – We've eaten animals butchered in slaughterhouses since birth. The only difference is that this time we killed it ourselves.

– I know that, intellectually speaking, Kara said. – It still leaves a bad taste in my mouth. It would be great if anyone would explain that one…

– That's easy, Yngve said dryly. – Modern man is a walking contradiction.

– So easy… Gwen twisted her head in irritation, – and so hard.

– Don't despair over the bad taste in your mouth, Anya said. – It will remind you, when the time comes of what's truly important.

They were dancing, dancing together without care or restraint. Feet drummed against soft ground, a weak echo, a pale reflection of daylight.

He still heard the drums on the bus the next day, but had to hold onto it as hard he could for the experience not to fade. The evening and the night before, only a few hours ago had seemed like it would last forever. Now, it only served as a moment's break from the big gray mass surrounding them.

The bus crossed the Askøy Bridge. Damon could see the sea under the bridge. There had been a small islet down there, a short distance from land, with a white house, an old service station, selling petrol to boats. The islet had not moved. One could still see it, an indistinct impression below the ocean surface. The sea reached almost to the roof of the house. He could see the change on both sides of the land in the sound as well, both on the Askøy and Skålevik side. The sound had been visibly expanded since he had left seven years earlier. After the tunnel, on the freeway towards the city, the same «tendency» (the word used by most public officials these days) revealed itself. The walk and bike trail just a few meters lower than the road, was covered by seawater.

The same tendency (Terrill smiled bitterly to himself) repeated itself in central Bergen. The entire road and sidewalk of the old Bryggen were permanently below the waterline, now. «Venice Street» had grown considerably and lived easily up to its nickname.

A considerable stretch out on what had been the harbor, now well into the harbor basin, a tall crane, rusty and covered by moss, towered above the city.

– We got it cheap, Yngve said. – No one else wanted it, and why should they? No one makes tall buildings or large structures anymore.

The enormous redundant tool rose against the western sky. They rowed out there.

The harbor, the city appeared to Damon while he stood with outstretched arms on the crane's arm. The hot wind hit them from the east, all the way from the tropics.

– I've always dreamed of doing this, or something like this, he said, high as a kite. – And, now, when the time has come, I'm nervous like hell.

– That's the point… to a point, Yngve grinned, while he tightened the harness around his friend's ankles.

People rushed to the new Torgallmenningen Beach in order to watch the show.

– Look at them, Yola said in contempt. – They eagerly join the spectacle, but only as spectators, only living through others.

Yngve and the other experienced jumpers calmed the rest down. Damon looked down, and got the dizzy spell almost instantly.

– I've always had a case of vertigo, he admitted, – but that serves me well, now. I need the challenge, need to feel the flapping of my wings, now, more than ever.

He heard them, both faint and loud. The silent roar of the crowd below struck him like a soft wave.

– My advice to you, he shouted with a voice unexpectedly loud and powerful, – is to stop being spectators and start getting a life.

There was no noticeable response from down there, except the crowd's singular hum.

The response came from his siblings, his fellow travelers in the wilderness. Eyes met… had no need to meet, in order to achieve contact. He jumped. A gasp rose from the audience below. He stretched out his body, stretched out his mind, and what was neither. His depths, his core, what reached far beyond the physical body spread all over his self. The ground raced towards him, and he knew he had no chance of avoiding it, if the rope broke.

The movement slowed down, stopped and he was pulled back up, back down, while he was flying just above the ground and the extended seawater, the boiling ocean.

Others followed him in the harness. They stood tight together afterwards. Roger shouted in a seemingly endless outburst of Joy, not caring at all if he drew attention to himself and his runaway status.

They paid attention, even more than usual when they moved through the crowds, through the streets, with impunity.

Roger noticed that Gwen and others scouted their surroundings that much harder.

– We «deserters» aren't really that much more in danger than the rest of you, he said, remarkably relaxed. – Anyone, at any time can be selected for «questioning», and brought in for interrogation.

The others appreciated his candor, his both energetic and phlegmatic devil-may-care attitude.

– We *own* the streets we move through, Gwen said in a sudden burst of inspiration, – even as we know that no one can ever own anything. It's quite something.

She kissed him hard on the lips.

– We feel at home here, too, he mused, – like we can do most places, precisely because we see no value in the fake or real jewelry most people see as so important.

Emotions burned hard and wild within, and empowerment was more, far more than just a word.

Feeling fresh and alive, they felt the contact with themselves even stronger, more powerful. The insignificant surroundings faded away around them. Their uncompromising joy created more fear in the people observing them, and the worst part of it was that none of those people had any idea why.

+++

Emmet led Lisbeth down the dark, dirty hallways. In the light from the soiled windows she glimpsed the long rows of mattresses, blankets and rags, humans reduced to rags.

– W-why did you bring me here? She spat between blue, shivering lips. – What's the p-point? Why expose us to the danger?

– There isn't any considerable increased risk to speak of, he stated with a shrug, and the skewed grin she both loved and despised. – Most of us walk around with the Tuberculosis bacteria in our lungs our entire lives. It can turn active at any time, whatever we do or don't do. I wanted you to see it with your own eyes what you already know, what happens when you give bacteria and viruses such excellent conditions for growth and development as today's society does. Humans live tight together, like sardines in a box. Our immune defense system has been weakened for centuries. «Medicines» and other attacks on the symptoms of a sick society managed to stay the danger for a while, but no more. Most bacteria are immune to all possible and impossible antibiotics, now.

Rows upon rows of dying people, rows upon rows of rooms filed before their eyes. She didn't puke, but it was close.

On another floor patients that had used cell phones and lived close to power lines and similar stared at nothing. Saliva flowed from their slack mouths. In some of them absolutely all lights had been turned off. There was no one home. In other and worse categories there were flashes of intelligence, but mixed with a distress bordering on insanity. There were victims of Creutzfield Jacobs' disease and other illnesses due to consuming the wrong food.

There were many other wards.

– They keep this and similar places a secret, he said. – They've managed to keep the panic from manifesting so far, but most people aren't that stupid. Even if they close their minds to obvious truths, they *know*.

– How did you gain access here? She asked with full blown hatred manifested.

– Wouldn't you love to know…

He grinned, but the grin had a gray, rigid «quality», a sobriety devouring any joy. She was familiar with it, had it the same way herself.

They found themselves in one more bed, one more unfamiliar bed, hanging on to each other for dear life. They kept hanging on hard to each other while making love, feeling that they were never able to hang on hard enough.

They crouched there afterwards, hugging and fondling without break, kissing softly.

The wind picked up again outside. It made the house shake at its foundation. She glanced up anxiously.

– Relax, he said cheerfully. – A little wind has never hurt anyone.

– Oh, you…

She struck him playfully in the ribs.

The wind was blowing all the time these days, with none or few exceptions. Every time it started, it happened suddenly and unexpected. The time difference between a blue and dark sky had shortened dramatically. It did so right now. A few minutes later they heard the rain hammer the windows.

They heard a loud crack from the roof.

– A little wind, he mumbled. – Come; let's get down in the basement.

They dressed in a rush and hurried down the stairs, to the fortified shelter there, one of many he and his fellow warriors in the Green Rose had at their disposal.

He bolted the door just in time. The lights went out the moment he turned towards her, that very moment. She screamed loud and sharp in fright, and jumped into his arms.

In the good old days storms with a hurricane's strength hadn't lasted very long, not its most destructive phase. The 1994 hurricane had only lasted a few minutes, and been a pale copy of what was currently common.

– I watched a satellite feed of «Zephyr» massacring what was left of the American east coast, Emmet said with respect in his voice. – It was the most awesome, horrible event I've ever seen.

– Not now. She kissed his lips to shreds. – Not now!

A few minutes, an eternity had passed. They rested in bed, in each other's arms under the soft blankets. The wind's howl had grown significantly. It kept growing. It was muted, thanks to the insulation in the walls.

– We can only guess how bad it is out there, he said, shaking his head.

They heard a scream from a man passing by outside, a mix between a roar and a banshee howl shaking them to their core. They heard his feet stamp the pavement, the flying bricks striking the walls. The howl stopped abruptly, as if it had been cut by a giant scissor.

After that they didn't hear much, except the wind and the bricks striking walls, and their own low-keyed voices.

Electricity didn't return. They saw nothing, could only feel each other, sense each other's outline in the dark.

They discussed for hours, talking about all kinds of stuff, quarreling, as always, about anything from the origin of the Universe to its end, beyond time and space.

– Valhalla may very well be a real place, she insisted.

– I don't believe that. He shook his head. – I think it's a state of mind, one of courage and warrior spirit confronting a mighty enemy, a fire in the human being making us able to rise from our own ashes, one burning through centuries, millennia, eternity…

– Another fool's view of existence, she sighed, not unkind. – What did your parents have to say about all your crazy ideas?

– Quite a lot, he replied dryly. – I and my parents never agreed much about anything.

– I worshiped daddy, she whispered. – Worshiped him.

The warm body sought his once more. Her shoulders were cold, uncovered as they were. He started rubbing them. It didn't help much, and he felt a strike of panic as he doubled and redoubled his efforts. She whimpered in pain. He stopped stricken. They fell back in the bed, lying still.

The storm continued and showed few or no signs of abating. They slowly, but surely became used to the constant, unrelenting noise. After a while the storm sounded like little more than an insignificant buzz. They finally fell asleep, a restless, slumbering dormancy.

Lisbeth whimpered in her sleep. Emmet noticed somehow, through the haze of his own troubled unrest.

They woke up to the same, ongoing, unrelenting noise.

She yawned deep and hard.

– How long did we sleep? She complained, using her most whiny, childish voice. – I don't feel rested at all.

– I have no idea! She sensed his grin in the dark. – I didn't look at my watch before falling asleep.

He rose from the bed. She heard him roaming the apartment, opening lockers and boxes of canned food.

– Looks like the darkness doesn't keep you from doing anything, she teased him.

– One of the advantages of living with the Sword, he chuckled, teasing back. – I can disassemble and assemble the most complex mechanical constructions during the briefest of intervals.

– I believe you, she said seductively, writhing on the bed, performing for him, knowing he could see her. – I know how handy you can be…

He returned with the canned food. They fed with a hunger easily transcending anything called appetite.

– We should have fed before, she munched. – We need to eat everything. There's no telling how long it will take before our next meal is available. The entire civilization may be gone when we can finally step out of here.

Both froze, stunned that it was she who had actually come out and said it.

– Would that be bad? He inquired, both curious and with evident longing in his voice.

– Not with you.

She caressed his cheek, kissing him softly.

They pictured themselves walking vast distances, first through urban ruins and then through remote wilderness, holding hands, holding on to the other with all their strength.

The roof started cracking at the seams. They looked up in the dark, suddenly out of breath. A few seconds more, and louder cracks made their ears bleed. The building was subjected to an ever worse strain.

– The wind is growing in strength, he cried astonished.

– Maybe not, she said. – The prevailing storm may have weakened the fabric of the construction.

Another loud crack shook their eardrums. She sought closer to him, even closer than before.

The roof began cracking open. The darkness was split by long lines of light flooding them. The insane roar of the storm reached them undiluted.

They grabbed their clothes, in fast, almost subconscious moves and pulled them in a hurry under all the blankets.

The darkness devoured them again, and the light blinded them, in what felt like an eternal cycle.

The roof cracked open. The first board disappeared. More boards and augmentation flew away. Droplets of water sprayed them.

– Saltwater, she cried astonished. – It has become a dry storm, right? This isn't rain. It's coming straight from the ocean.

More boards were shaken loose. The wind pulled at the wet blankets, treating them as if they were feathers. It suddenly became much more powerful. They experienced its full force, heard its loudest sounds.

– You haven't a subsurface chamber at your disposal as well? She shouted to him.

– Sorry, he shouted the few centimeters across the divide of noise. – I never considered it.

They laughed themselves silly.

The bed rose into the air and collided with the nearest wall. They jumped off it and landed on a floor covered with debris. They stared up together, holding on to each other as hard as they possibly could, fearing what would come next.

Then it was as if everything paused above and around them. They looked at each other, and looked up again.

It had turned quiet, at least relatively speaking. The wind had stopped howling. The storm had actually calmed, just as it had been about to jump off the scales.

Their faces showed a strange dichotomy of disappointment and terror, as they braved the hard path of non-existing doors and walls. Numbness and shock supplanted that as they could better study the extent of the destruction.

The buildings still stood, the traffic lights as well, sort of. Most of the buildings lacked glass in the windows. The traffic lights resembled in passing figurative art, formed in nature's own atelier.

– It looks like a war zone, she said, – one even worse than most, one more notch off the scale.

– One is expecting destruction in war, he commented, – not by a little wind. No matter how much and how many times we see demonstrated nature's destructive power, we look at it as a rare occurrence, and never as something hitting us like on an assembly line, like we've witnessed lately.

Everything had been readied, polished to the annual day of celebration, Constitution Day May 17. Right now these thorough preparations and constructions certainly didn't look any different from the rest of the ruins.

They walked through a war zone in a besieged city, where the driving force behind the siege wasn't invading human beings, but an enraged, indifferent nature.

– The cleanup is not going well, she said, quite displeased. – The crews don't seem up to the task at all.

– Just a few years ago, when storms ravaged an area, or a nation, crews from untouched areas were ready to step in and help, he said. – That's not the case anymore. There are hardly any untouched areas, and those few remaining are badly suited to mount a massive aid operation far away.

The two walked around the city without a set direction or goal. Screams reached them from all sides, penetrating deep within them. They had never experienced anything like this, not even close. Through television and the Internet, perhaps, but never straight in the face, on a personal level. And not really now either. The suffering wasn't truly theirs, but those of the countless sore voices surrounding them.

– It looks worse than it is, I guess, she mumbled.

It struck him instantly: he heard relief in her voice.

When he took a second or third glance around, he had to give her right, and disappointment flushed him. Buildings were still standing. Vehicles not gathered in the many heaps of wreckage were still rolling. The infrastructure hadn't been completely destroyed, only taken a tumble, a big tumble.

The truly life-changing event had yet to occur.

+++++++++++++++++++++++++++++++++++++

Thunder and lightning filled the air and rocked the ground. It was always doing that to one degree or another these days and nights.

The rain started pouring, and with the rain the wind began blowing again. The very word «quiet» had become an archaic term,

Hammering sounded near and far. The Children of the Midnight Fire spent the day repairing the House in the Forest, fixing damage surprisingly small. The tight forest surrounding it had acted as a bulwark, protecting it against the most destructive hurricane blasts. There were broken trees in all directions, but the house was still standing.

The damage was negligible, relatively speaking, but enough for rain following the storm to leak through during the evening and the night. The result of the repair work was a patchwork that didn't exactly look good, but kept the water out.

The neighbors and their homes had been far less fortunate. From their relative safety the Children of the Midnight Fire had seen how the two luxurious villas at the mountaintop to the south had been completely destroyed. The roof had gone first. Then the rest had gone, in a series of pulls and pushes. Only the foundation remained.

Other local buildings hadn't fared much better.

People moved to the city or to relatives far away.

– Coastal areas will clearly become uninhabitable for a long time, Claire stated.

– But are the mountains really that much better? Gerd pondered anxiously.

– They're farther away from the coast…

All the members of the tribe moved indoors. All the tents not taken down in time had been ruined. Steam from warm bodies and wet clothes and fabric filled the house, turning it into what resembled an old, smoky cabin. All the windows and doors had been opened wide, a sheer necessity in the lingering, humid heat. There was no electricity anymore. Broken power lines were not repaired. The city and the industry were prioritized. The tribe saved the few candles they had left, burning fat in bowls instead. They didn't really mind the summer twilight. The small indoor fires created a soft, mysterious mood.

Nudity had long since ceased being an issue to them. Seeing a nude body didn't even really excite them anymore, not on its own. It had become a natural, casual part of their lives.

– We've done well, Yngve said, his long hair flowing down his back, – especially after you guys arrived. You learned to survive, to live, and taught us in turn.

They cheered low-keyed, not really raising their voices, happy and content in their skin.

– It helped and helps that all the nearest farmers have fled their land, Vladek chuckled, with a frown, – leaving all the animals behind.

– How can people do something like that? Tamele and everyone wondered. – He would have to know that the animals would suffer and he clearly acted against his own interest.

– People have become so fucked up by civilization that they deny their most fundamental instincts, Kara said sadly, – bury them so deep that they're barely retrievable, and the worst part of it is that they eagerly hunt and hound those few miraculously retaining a sliver of humanity.

– The city is a threat to us, Yola said, – not support, not a good thing at all.

– They might decide to send a squad out here, or quite simply take over, Damon nodded. – They're losing control, and they know it, and thereby become even more desperate. The civil administration is still pretty much intact and set to stay on top. The regional military commanders seem so far to have accepted such a state of affairs, but that may change at any time.

– One big, explosive forge, André said, both humorous and not simultaneously. – It's the same thing that has happened elsewhere, the same, overwhelming signs of a collapsing society humanity has experienced many time before, but with one crucial difference: There's no longer any place left to go.

– The consolation is that this is a big country for the city people to cover. Gwen stretched her body gleefully. – I love the forests and the mountains here. They're more or less pristine, at least compared to most other places.

– There's no lack of herbs either, Claire said. – I've found lots of what we may need. With what we… liberated from the drugstore today, we should face no trouble with that, at least not in the… in the transition, where we'll need it the most.

Her words created gloom, hope and cheerfulness in them mingled together.

– I heard that the visit went well, Dominic said, unable to keep himself from grinning.

– We just walked right in and served ourselves, Claire chuckled almost abashed. – All the most recent and modern security systems are in the banks where the money is. There was only an unarmed guard in the drugstore, no technical security to speak of. We walked in and out effortlessly.

The laughter felt good. It always did.

– People are nuts. Roger shook his head. – They have no awareness of themselves and their surroundings, no sense of priorities.
– But we have, Gwen stated.
When she kissed him on the lips, it was more an expression of unity than pure sexuality.
– It is a strength, this, Yola said, – to be able to laugh, confronted with the worst possibly reality.
The surroundings seemed to dissolve around them. They saw the human beings, not the walls and the trees and the bushes outside, but their senses still felt sharper than any other moment before this.
Their very core loomed there, before them, like a living being.
Slowly but surely they pulled closer together, increasingly feeling the heat from other bodies. Many slept under the same roof in the summer twilight and breathed and lived. When they were turned on, it happened like it often did, in unexpected ways, with few visible signs, not necessarily as a result of someone's obvious or overt acts.
The candles and torches stopped burning eventually, somehow. Fire changed to shadow, to twilight, to fire again, to become both. Contradictions faded away in embers and darkness.
Everyone heard Gwen. She had always been among the most… noisy among them.
But if the house hadn't been so isolated from its more distant surroundings, people passing by wouldn't have had any trouble with hearing the choir of the enormous energy going to waste inside.
While the sea rose and the winds grew in strength.
Anya stayed with them, even when she didn't, also when she the next morning sat with her legs crossed in front of her and her flat hands pushed at her knees, between the ruins of the two houses on the mountain peak.
– We should bring stems when we leave, Claire mused, casting an eye or two at the various fruit trees in the garden. – We may find a place where they might grow.
Gwen didn't speak. She walked and listened to whatever reached her ears through the silent air. Claire looked at her, prompting her to speak.
– The sea strikes the shore, Gwen hummed. – I can hear it as it does.
– I've always heard it, Claire said.
– That comes as no surprise, Gwen said, a little pointed, – Daughter of She Who Dances in the Forest.
– You're jealous of me? Claire said startled. – Of me!
Both looked up at the unmoving figure on the mountain, so far away, so close.
They stopped by the tall plum trees. The plums grew big and juicy. Only a few had fallen down so far, though, and they gathered them all in only two buckets.
André, Myriam, Maxine and Yarath gathered other fruits in large tubs. Maxine whispered something in André's ear. It obviously made him enjoy himself, also made him look quite guilty, for some reason…
– It's not polite to talk about people when you think they can't hear you, Gwen exploded. – And I can understand French.
– We know you can both speak and understand French. Maxine sat down the tub and approached the she wolf.
The other three followed her, to be better safe than sorry, clearly more than a little

worried.
– We heard more than enough of it tonight. You convinced us there, if you hadn't before, of your excellence.
Everyone feared the two would go at each other. There had been a clear and present challenge in Maxine's voice and stance.
– I don't hold myself back, the she wolf stated proudly. – And you were *inspired,* just admit it.
– It was intense beyond words, André concurred willingly, in an attempt to act as mediator. – I don't think I've ever come more times in such a short time.
Maxine looked pretty aggravated. The mood darkened even more.
– Neither have I! She chuckled, unable to keep up the pretense of antagonism, and her face cracked in a big smile.
She pulled Gwen close and gave her a hard kiss on the lips.
– I lost count. I don't think that has ever happened before. We are not worthy, She Wolf.
She made a big mockery of her deep, deep bow.
The hearty laughter began. They embraced and had to support each other in order to not fall.
It took some time before it dawned on them that Claire didn't participate in the fun. She stood with her back to them, facing a tree.
Gwen approached her slowly, not in anything resembling a threatening way, and put a hand on her shoulder.
– It's nothing, Claire choked. – I'm just silly.
– Last night wasn't exactly… successful for you, was it? Gwen strived to keep her voice casual, free of compassion. – You got something from it, right?
One nod, two.
– But even during the most intense moments, when the hot water flowed, you couldn't quite let go, could you?
Another nod, and eyes lowered in shame.
– I want to, want it b-bad, but I just can't.
Everyone could see that Gwen wanted to say «poor little one» or something similar. She was quite transparent. But something akin to compassion won.
– I do envy you, she said. – Of course I do!
– W-what? Claire looked up.
– You're a witch, a sorcerer, a power with a contact with the Earth I can never achieve or hope to achieve.
– What I have isn't much, the still crouching figure mumbled.
– Very funny! Maxine said without malice. – And quite telling. The ancient tales of Greek mythology weren't that far off, it seems.
Claire looked at her in more incomprehension.
– What you have is hidden, Gwen stated. – You must pull it from your insides, open yourself up to it, to its gifts.
– Its gifts? Claire spat and the luring, pointed stare felt like it could kill.
Before crumbling again.
– That's what mom says, but I can't do it. We've made countless attempts. She has tried helping me numerous times, in vain. I'm *no* good!

Gwen looked at her and now her compassion was evident.
– You want to kill Mother, don't you? She said softly. – You *hate* her!
– What...
Gwen slapped her. The very air shivered after the hard slap.
– Admit it! Zeus killed his father, and you wish to walk his path.
– YES, I HATE HER, I WISH TO WREST THE VERY LIFE OUT OF HER, EMPTY HER BODY OF THE JUICE... keeping her going.
Claire Kerien stared in shock at them all.
She fell to her knees. Gwen started rubbing her head.
– She's so great, and I'm so useless, so utterly useless, the girl said, completely relaxed. – I loathe myself, not her. I want to kill myself, not her.
– You've always felt inferior, Gwen continued in her soft voice. – It isn't unheard of in children of noteworthy parents. They overshadow everything you do, and you do anything for them to «acknowledge» you. You've always strived for her acceptance and in order for you to achieve that tall order, in your own mind, you've held yourself to ridiculously high standards.
– But don't despair, Maxine said, eagerly joining the game, – I don't think the problem is as insurmountable as it appears.
– It isn't...?
– Definitely not! You just need a little push... okay, perhaps a harder, pretty brutal push, but we'll fix it, fix you. You see, Mother has been more than a little stupid as well. She might have taught her little witch a thing or two, but she hasn't managed to make herself heard. One can understand and even sympathize with that. She is, after all just one more fucked up child of a fucked up society, and the best one can say about such is that they don't exactly become parents of the year.
All five walked off and started whispering together. They chuckled and laughed and didn't exactly make the kneeling girl feel better.
They returned, Gwen leading them, spurring them on.
– What we'll do for you, She Who Stumbles in the Forest is to put you through an initiation, one that will fill you with magick, and will make your cup run over. We will give the witch her devoirs, and make her acknowledge everything she has denied.
Claire looked straight ahead with distant eyes, not really listening.
– What say you, witch? Maxine snapped.
Claire shook and looked at them and listened somewhat.
– Okay, she shrugged, – if it will make you feel better. But don't tell mom. I will do anything if you don't tell her.
– Of course we'll tell her, Myriam said.
– Her presence is crucial, Maxine said. – You know that, little witch.
Claire looked like she would say something, like she would protest, but stayed silent.
– You see, we have all fucked up pretty bad. I suspect strongly that Mother needs shock therapy just as much as you do. We have, after a while started believing in the myths, believing in the Goddess, and she can certainly not live up to something like that. No one, no human being can! And she suffers because of it, suffers because of her perceived obligations.
– Rise, human being, André bid her. – Take your first step.
She rose, on unsteady feet.

– You guys seem to have given this some thought? She said with uncertainty in her voice and features.
– It suddenly seems like we have, Yarath said boyishly.
That brought a chuckle from everyone present, including Claire. She looked at him, studied him in a way making him blush.
They walked the few steps down the curved road, into the deepest parts of the garden, the few hours to the night and the summer twilight passing so quickly that they could hardly fathom the experience of it.
Drums beat, drums sounded in near and distant ears, and the remaining neighbors felt the unrest grow in body and soul.
Gwen explained the deal in her usual charming and persuasive manner, and made everyone feel the stir of excitement.
– This will be a ceremony used many times. Gerd stated enthusiastically, – in order to serve both the tribe and the individual in question.
It… began. Kara and Damon faced Claire across the garden base. They held hands, turning, standing face to face, no longer looking at Claire, but at each other.
Anya arrived just as the ceremony was about to begin, the «Black Irish» enigmatic gypsy look very much evident, quite contrary to her daughter's more common features and red-brown hair.
– What's going on? She asked, slightly agitated, even more intense then she usually appeared. – I… felt something.
– Be patient, Mighty One, Gwen replied, clearly respectful. – Everything will be clear, in time and night.
Her instincts told her to kneel, faced with Anya's enormous *presence,* but she successfully resisted that, that almost overwhelming urge.
They sensed Anya's reluctant acceptance. It was enough. The ceremony commenced. The very air seemed charged, well before Kara started chanting her spells into the dark night, started speaking an ancient, forgotten tongue long since lost to the conscious human mind.
Everyone felt it, felt how it rose, hard and painful from its slumber. Damon, everyone was mesmerized by the power rising from her form and surrounding them all.
– Now, Child of the Storm, she whispered. – Reach out your arms, reach out yourself. Accept us into your lap.
Damon did as she told him to do, instantly sensing how he liberated himself from her sorcery. She couldn't hold him back. No one could! Darkness descended upon the gathering. Torches flickered. Fire grew and stretched, reaching for the sky above, into the night. Anya shook. The still unnamed boy by her side clutched her hand hard.
The humans in the dark clothes formed a half circle, a half moon. Anya hesitated a bit, before joining it. Gerd and Myriam dressed her in the cape and the hood fast and effective.
Opposite the half circle, at the base of the distant other half moon, Claire stood lonely and abandoned.
Gwen stepped forward. Everyone had trouble recognizing her at first. She seemed like a stranger to them. They had never seen her like this before. They had seen her wild and naked, had seen her dressed and calm. In the dark suit she almost disappeared in the gathering dark, became a part of it.

– We're gathered here to initiate a witch, one that in turn will initiate us, make us aware of what we've forgotten and misplaced.

She spoke with passion and elegance, and with an intensity barring none. Everyone listened and watched. She turned around in a single dramatic move.

– Remove fabric, remove hurdles, you nude witch, you with a burning need to see beyond the veil, to see human fate.

– But you're all dressed, the girl whined.

– Precisely! André pointed out. – Bow to the child's wisdom.

Everyone chuckled, not with malice. She began undressing before he had finished speaking.

She stood before them all, nude, defenseless, with all her defenses up. Two dressed in cape and hood approached her, doing it so fast, so very slow. They pushed her at the stem of the nearest tree. She felt the ragged surface at her skin. Hands were raised up and tied to thick branches.

The drums, their sounds and rhythm turned more pervasive. She could feel it push at her from within.

– It's important that you do everything we tell you to do, Maxine insisted, – not deviating from a single order.

What strange wording. She stood there, tied up, dependent on their mercy. She didn't have any choice but to obey?

Yarath stood before her, nude. She gasped in shock.

– Behold, the male, how he desires you.

Gwen stood behind him, with her hands on his skinny shoulders.

– That can't be r-right? I don't see any sign of it.

Suddenly the She Wolf stood close to the tied up girl, whispering in her ear.

– You still look only for appearances, little girl. Reach out with your senses and touch him. Sense his *savagery,* his bottomless fire.

She stared blindly at him, didn't take her eyes off him, no matter how shy she might be. She studied his body, every single piece of it. His cock didn't twitch or showed any sign of growing. But she could feel the twitching within him, the deeper, beyond all pretenses and paralyzing anxiety. She smelled the hair on his back, the sweat trickling from his skin, smelled her own sweat, her own hairs and hairy depths. She giggled… and shook, and froze… staring straight ahead with wide open eyes.

A loud sound rose from the ground itself. She heard it, sensed the ground shake beneath her feet.

– I can see it, she mumbled, – see what's hidden and misplaced, myself, us, like strands of Night and Fire.

She watched herself through her mother's eyes. She saw them both from above, saw those dancing, dancing to the drums of the night… and saw herself among them, free and wild, the way she had always secretly pictured herself.

Damon stepped forward. Night and Fire glowed in his eyes, weren't merely reflected there.

– Witch, light thy own fire!

His voice sounded more like a series of growls, but she… she understood them.

– My fire, she shouted. – My FIRE!

In one, single powerful move she shook the ropes, pulling them to shreds. The tree creaked, groaning in pain behind her, in front of her. She stopped a few steps from the tree, hardly aware of having taken the steps. She stared incredulous at her hands.

– I've always been strong, she whispered.

And in that very moment… she changed. The Night itself Changed around her. They could all sense the power raging within her.

The power that should have awakened in her early teens erupted into being in a beyond volatile way she would have been unable to comprehend only seconds ago. They could all *see* it. Whipped smoke seemed to whirl around her, dressing her in mist and shadow.

– I can see it, she said with a hollow voice. – Paths that cross will cross again.

The smoke danced around her and the mist and shadow began glowing.

She stood in front of her mother.

– You, she stated, – have been afraid your entire life.

She walked to Damon.

– You don't need to fear anything.

She held Kara's hand.

– You've got nothing to be afraid of.

An arm of smoke reached out to Damon, to Anya, to the boy, to Kara. Fire still danced at the depth of Damon's eyes. Anya became like the trees, like the forest, like the Earth itself. The boy couldn't be seen in the light. Kara became transparent, visible, but transparent, like mercury in a vacuum.

Everything twisted itself, twisted itself right.

And they saw beyond the forest. And they found themselves beyond the Night. And they saw what their friends only glimpsed.

The thunder, always rolling in the eternal night, cracked the air in bright daylight.

CHAPTER EIGHTEEN

Cracked at the center of the city, the stone desert.

Constitution Day finally dawned in Norway May 17, 2015 (western, christian time frame). The large crowd seethed and boiled on the big, open space in central Bergen from early morning. Not many waved flags, but arms and hands moved more than enough. The police and security forces worked constantly to break up fights and unrest, and signs of thereof. Peace and harmony were notoriously absent. André grinned to his closest coconspirators, those who had traveled with him for long years from south to north in Europe. They were all reminded of the… events on Olympia Stadium in Berlin. This was just more bread and circuses brought to its extreme expression. One spark could ignite it all.

Sooner or later it would. They all knew that.

People looked at the world from their hood. They saw no heads, almost no eyes. People looked at the world through the filter covering their eyes. The bright sky didn't look bright at all. The sound of rhythmic drums reached them from all sides.

– The damn corps drums, Yngve mumbled. – Have you guys noticed that it's virtually impossible to avoid keeping in step when you move?

– We've most certainly noticed, Myriam assured him.

She couldn't help it. The images came to her unbidden and unwanted every time she closed her eyes. She forced herself to keep them open, without that doing much good. The taste of the rotting food they had been fed, the luxury food promotion had granted them, the scent of the captain's seed, mixed with that of the dead, rotting bodies, the sense of pleasure when she pulled the trigger and the joy of killing the Enemy… was all there, all the time.

The Nightravens, the officially appointed version that the true Nightravens hated stood on the stage with other branches of the security force and also moved through the crowd in order to seek out the discontent.

– Why are we here? Kara wondered with a twitch in the left part of her mouth.

– We're observers, Myriam enlightened her, – spies on eternity's stage, in order to report home about important events and trends, find out what might be the tiny difference between life and death, freedom and enslavement.

– Should you be here?

– I would go stir crazy sitting on my ass, doing nothing, Myriam said curtly.

The inherent risk of discovery and capture actually felt beneficial, in a backwards kind of way, momentarily soothing the ants crawling through her veins.

– The world has been a powder keg for years, decades and centuries even, Yngve mused. – Now, the explosion has long since begun. As expected it erupted all over the world, one and one place, everywhere simultaneously.

– The world is drowning, Gwen hummed, – in fire and icy water.

They could all sense it, the energy, the total desperation in each and every person present, in the signals the mob emanated, one hiding beneath the not too turbulent surface.

A roar rose from the crowd. The mayor finally appeared on the makeshift stage, doing so after a prolonged delay. There had been some unpleasantness. The considerable detail of guards and supporters had admitted they could not guarantee his safety, but had eventually achieved some sort of control. The applause meeting the rather corpulent, well dressed man was not impressive, though.

He didn't run the city, of course, hardly had control of anything, even less of it than before, but he had become, more than ever the front of those truly in charge.

– FELLOW CITIZENS, he cried forcefully.

The cheering filled the plaza and the streets, as his speech was broadcast through strategically placed speakers.

– We will make it. We will hold out against the rising tide of trouble coming at us from an increasingly troubled world. There once was a thriving industry in this city and the surrounding area. We shall rebuild and surpass it. This, I can assure you isn't an ending, but a new and glorious beginning.

Myriam grinned and froze in the warm sunshine. His assessment was correct to a point, but still far off.

Damn oral wordsmith! She groaned in her hot and dark thoughts.

– We will produce everything we need, the mayor shouted, – right here in our immediate area, and we won't share anything with others, with unworthy souls coming here to steal our gold. We have already secured supplies of oil…

The stench from all the leaks from the enormous tank on the harbor below the Nygård Heights left no doubt what was stored there.

– We will renew our agriculture. There's no lack of land at our disposal around our beautiful city. Nature has been gracious to Bergen and its sons and daughters. We have more than enough production facilities both on land and at sea to feed large parts of the population already.

He took a small, deliberate break before continuing his somewhat energetic speech.

– The world has changed, dear friends, but there's no need for us to change with it, no reason at all to change our celebrated way of life. The only thing we need to adjust is our willingness to share with others, the overblown generosity gaining us nothing. We will grow and survive and *thrive,* good people. The tyranny of generousity will *end.*

The crowd evidently liked what they heard. At least they sent lots of cheers in his direction. Many people stood there with tears in their eyes.

– Let us now sing the Bergen Anthem, he said, equally emotional or seemingly so.

He discarded the national anthem with a shrug, another very popular act, and a very clear signal to whatever remained of the national government.

A considerable majority of the gathering joined in on the singing. The song was repeated, more or less successfully at least three times. The mayor waved to his enthusiastic supporters as he left the stage and they returned loud cheers and thunderous applause and shouted his name for minutes after he had left.

– He has secured his position for a very long time after this, probably for as long as Bergen itself is standing at least. Myriam shook her head in contempt. – His ability to manipulate the mob, an important, even crucial factor in any civilized society is equal to that of the ancient Roman emperors.

She and her compatriots smiled as best they could as they left the sorry assembly.

– The sheep making out the majority of any civilized society has disappointed me long ago, she added.

They stood by the sea, what had once been called Sukkerhusbryggen. Twenty years ago someone had started a major project down here. They had filled the basin with rocks and stuck poles in the ground and covered it all with asphalt, asphalt that now could hardly be glimpsed below the ocean surface.

– I remember reading about this, Yngve mused, doing so with badly concealed irony. – They used a lot of public and private resources to make it happen, instead of using supposedly scarce money on shit like public health services and support for disempowered people.

The towering, discarded oil rigs were impossible not to spot. They dominated the northern sky.

A new tavern, Atlantis North had opened approximately twenty steps from the present shoreline. Myriam shook her head, shook her head yet again.

– There is some sort of irony here, she said. – I don't think they're aware of it, though.

They walked inside. The loud noise and shouts hammered their eardrums. The place was flooded with alcohol, perhaps to an even bigger degree than the night before or the night before that. Myriam grimaced as the stench of the local brew invaded her nostrils. Foreign brands had long since become unavailable, except for those with extensive resources. Local and illegal breweries had become commonplace. An entire industry had developed around them. No one even bothered to hide such activities anymore. Myriam had seen it grow just in the fairly short time since her return.

She sipped the House Special and gritted her teeth. The taste was exactly like she imagined horseshit would taste. She had another sip.

– This is probably not brewed in the basement, Yngve joked. – That's usually far superior to this…

The lights blinked. It returned immediately, but this was a telltale sign. The electricity supply had been fairly good lately. It usually didn't stay off for long, but blinked and shimmered, like it did now.

The five, Myriam, Gwen, Yngve, André and Kara had a toast and drank, and resembled to a point most others surrounding them. Myriam looked at Kara. She didn't have to stress anything.

– There's no immediate danger, Kara said.

She shook her head and there was a twitch in the corner of her mouth.

– There's only the usual, general sense of menace growing every day.

Public officials visited this place often. It was a known in-place for the in-crowd. This could be described as a nice and quiet spot compared to the wild places André and Gwen had visited elsewhere, but the underlying desperation clearly compared with what they remembered from those places. There were lots of talk and lots of shaking and loud voices.

– The possibilities are infinite. A man a few tables away raised his voice more than a few notches. – Infinite!

The humming in the room picked up, but they could still hear him loud and clear.

– I mean… there have been tons of regulations before, and even though they've never stopped us much, they've been damn irritating. Now, we can basically do whatever we wish. There's no lack of cheap labor, and we can squeeze the workers for everything they're worth… before hiring other, well-rested arms and sheep. Factories, health services, restaurants… we can do it all, gentlemen.

A chill more than a cold draft haunted the place. For some reason all the other four looked at Kara then.

She hesitated before speaking, glancing around her with anxious eyes.

– I feel him… the black raven… he's always with us.

Myriam frowned.

– Isn't that redundant? She wondered. – Aren't all ravens black?

There was something deeply disturbing in Kara's eyes making Myriam shudder.

The brief contact seemingly lasting forever was broken and heat once more warmed Myriam's bones.

– I will get us more beer, Gwen said abruptly.

It seemed like she was enjoying herself as she rose and moved across the floor.

– She said beer… right? André burped. – Not dishwater?

They watched her as she approached the bar desk, dressed in a dark and snug hooded dress.

– She's bored to death, Kara grinned darkly, – and feels a strong need for whatever distraction this place can provide.

She passed right by where the two public officials and potential future entrepreneurs sat. Myriam, also distracted from her grim thoughts watched her closely and wondered if she slowed down as she passed behind their backs or if it only seemed like she did.

The mood in the room inadvertently changed. They watched the change unfold, as the sensual beast twisted her body and in downright mysterious ways managed to reach the desk without waiting in line. One look at her sweet smile and all the males stopped in their tracks and allowed her to walk past them. She also managed to avoid the many intended invasive touches. None of those attempting to touch her or touch her much succeeded in their intent. She returned to her four companions with five filled to the brim glasses of beer and didn't spill a single drop.

– Hi, girl, the talkative representative for public management cried out to her.

– Hi, yourself, she replied, and gave everyone a glimpse of her big, sensual lips. – Hi, boy!

She spoke Norwegian with virtually no accent, almost fluently, with only a slight touch of the foreigner.

The guy smiled at first, when she gave him her sweet response. It dropped to horror and shame when she added her condescending snarl and the room exploded in patronizing laughter.

She turned her back to him and he looked at her with a deep, deep frown on his brow.

The five had another toast and drank the ill-smelling dishwater. People stared at the girl with the snug, dark clothing, and also at the other four by her table. Myriam fought in vain in order to keep herself from revealing at least some of her numb fear.

The other four touched her and tried to comfort her the best they could. It worked, sort of, and kept the inner turmoil that made cold sweat soak her forehead from growing to a full-blown anxiety attack.

The five left the room, careful not to rush anything. They sat there and drank some of their beer, but then they left, holding on to their half full glasses, focusing on moving at a slow pace.

The stench of the ocean hit Myriam as they approached the exit, and she felt a little better, a little worse.

– They touched my core, the most valuable in a human being, she gasped, having difficulty breathing, – making me their creature. I can't stop thinking about it, I just can't.

They walked around the corner and stopped there, by the door, and they surrounded her in a warm group hug. She closed her eyes, opening them again almost immediately.

– You're like a wounded beast, warrior, Gwen said softly. – We will keep supporting you in all ways and none. The entire tribe is yours to draw strength from in whatever manner you need.

It didn't really grow colder as the air darkened around them, but only felt that way. That, too, touched their innermost being, something they could not quite acknowledge yet either.

– This makes you stronger, not weaker, Gwen told her in Flemish, a language Myriam hadn't heard for years. – It helps us, not them. But it's eating away at you, and will eventually destroy you, if you can't successfully confront it.

The other three couldn't see Gwen's face beneath the hood in the shadow of the lamp behind her, but they imagined they could glimpse her eyes.

She turned towards them, calling attention to herself in a way that couldn't be denied.

– You've made the same error most of us have done, she told them in English. – You fool yourself into believing we're safe here. You know deep within that we aren't. We're wanderers. This is merely one more transition, one more brief home, another illusion of a safe harbor in our eternal walk.

You know that, she tells me, Myriam thought.

– That sounds so very right, Yngve declared.

She (Gwen) smiled to him, exposing her fangs. He shrunk a bit in his tracks, not feeling fear exactly, but there was a slight sense of discomfort. She turned away from him, quickly loosing interest.

They stood there for a while, listening in on the talk. That was, at least in part why they had come to this tiny, uninspiring spot in a gray, drab city, this place that had been so uninspiring.

– The damn sand is everywhere, a man in a corner deep in the room mumbled.

They shouldn't have any chance of hearing him, but they did.

– What is it with this place? Kara wondered sheepishly. – We can hear what's far away, but not those closest to us.

– I've heard many tales about places such as these, Myriam mused. – By sitting or standing at a particular spot in a given room one can hear gossip and crucial conversation taking place across the room or even on another floor. Rumors fly about several brokers having «earned» loads of cash that way.

– It *is* strange, the mumbling man's buddy nodded. – There have been lots of rain and Bergen has practically been swept clean lately. I don't think it has been cleaner since Adam didn't wear pants.

Gwen grinned. She found the last part extremely funny.

They looked some more at her, and she eagerly humored them.

– I've felt like I've been sleeping for so long, she whispered. – I'm slowly, painfully waking up. We're all waking up from civilization's deep and dreamless, restless sleep.

– It isn't just the sand, the man sitting in the deep corner of the smoke-filled room said. – Have you heard the old vagrant walking aimlessly on Torgallmenningen every

day and scream about the souls of the dead? He's absolutely right, you know.
His buddy looked at him with anxious eyes.
– Hey, perhaps you should take it a little easy.
The other jumped on his feet. Everyone sitting close by jumped in their seat.
– I CAN HEAR THE SOULS OF THE DEAD WHISPER TO ME
The man left the place in a fast, an uncannily fast pace. His eyes brightened in an insane glow. He was sweating hard and those eyes, those insane eyes almost popped out of their sockets. Many people saw it and started talking about it in hushed voices, unable to put the sight out of their never resting minds.
– The grains of sand rub against each other, Kara mumbled. – I can hear them move. I can hear their whisper.
She looked just as bad as the man that had just left, perhaps even a notch worse. Myriam shook her head. She couldn't shake off the sense of dread. It stuck to her like mud… or sand.
The mood in the room had fallen to dismal levels and it stayed that way. Myriam knew why. Most of those present had come here to drink themselves to oblivion and now that option had been denied them. The world's stark reality had returned with a bang.
– Cheers! Gwen grinned wolfishly.
The others returned her cheer more out of duty to their friend than any true desire to drink more. There was no real ding when the glasses met and parted, only the usual dull sound. The obvious lack of quality in the glass prevented that. The dishwater slid down their throat, debasing their lives.
Gwen leaned forward. They spotted a sudden eagerness, even desperation there.
– Pull yourself together, damn you, she said, raising her voice to a higher level.
She turned to Myriam.
– Don't hold back your rage, damn it! She swore. – Embrace it!
Myriam felt something then, a rush, a rise from what she desperately hoped was her deep self.
– You're absolutely correct, of course, she nodded. – Rage is one of several emotions frowned at in today's society. By embracing it, we embrace ourselves, our true self and take one more step on the path we need to walk in order to become a true human being.
The impertinent girl should not enjoy the last word, damn her!
Then something softened in Myriam's face and the hard knot within did as well.
She grabbed the girl and pulled her over the table and gave her a hard hug, a jubilant embrace.
All the five stared stunned at each other. Suddenly it seemed like everyone else around them faded away and they were alone in the suddenly so misty, dank room. They heard the distinct, unmistakably howl of… of a *wolf.*
– I knew we were on the right trek, Gwen whispered in exalted happiness. – I just knew!
It turned darker outside, also today, in the height of summer. Very few waved flags or even celebrated Constitution Day, as had been the unavoidable custom in bygone years. Local patriotism wasn't supplanting nationalism. It had already done so. The Bergen Anthem was sung several times during the evening. The national anthem was generally avoided.

– Time for tonight's fifth pee…

Gwen stretched and crouched in the chair before rising, more than a little unsteady. There had been quite a few trips to the bar and back tonight. She looked into Myriam's hazy eyes, and quelled the notion of both disgust and compassion at its infancy.

The restroom was just as noisy as the rest of the building. People seemed to be everywhere. There were long queues in front of all the locked cubicles. More or less painted dolls pushed and spoke aloud to each other in their strong effort to not lose their spot in each queue. Several of them had actually peed on themselves, but they refused to let go of their hard earned position. The pee flowed down thighs and down on the floor. They stared at everyone with hateful eyes.

Gwen moved straight to the nearest sink and sat down on it as the most natural act in the world. Her almost cracked bladder relieved itself fast and easy, and it was such a great feeling, almost just as great as watching the stunned and shocked and envious stares the chicks sent her. She slipped back down on the floor, straightened her dress and left the overcrowded restroom that brought no rest. Several chicks rushed to the sinks. Howls and wild screams filled the stinking room. She had already forgotten about them when she returned to the hallway.

The hallway seemed strangely empty and quiet, as if it was actually waiting for her.

The well dressed businessman and city council member grabbed her arm and held on. He was a brick of muscles and energy. She stopped resisting.

– You will come with me! He stated brusquely.

– Okay, since you ask so nicely. I'm just gonna inform my friends.

– Absolutely not!

He let go of her, eying her zealously. She shrugged and nodded, giving him a sweet smile. He directed her outside, into the backyard.

– I have an apartment nearby, a place where we won't be bothered.

– I can imagine…

She nodded and grew and thrived on the flash of irritation very visible in his sticky and wet eyes.

They walked through the older part of the city. She hardly registered it in her conscious mind. Her attention sought completely different places. She allowed herself to be distracted, her mind to drift.

He didn't touch her and hardly spoke. She shrugged.

– What is it? He suddenly asked. – What's wrong?

– It's nothing much, she replied. – I'm just silly. This is the first time I've been without my pack for years, and I feel lonely.

– Your… pack? He said casually.

– My wolf pack, she grinned, hiding her sudden sense of vulnerability. – We roam the mountains and forests together, looking for prey.

They walked on in relative silence and she preferred that.

– Do you mind if I ask you a question? He eventually said.

– Ask away.

She turned her face, exposing herself to him.

– The sun is down. Why does a pretty girl like you keep hiding her face?

He didn't mention the scar. He didn't have to. His loaded tone of voice said it all.

– I love covering myself.

She turned her face away from him again.

He turned left by a worn block of flats, and she followed him. The yard had been cleaned and brushed, one of the first places in the city that had been. There were still dry grains of sand rubbing against each other, or she imagined there was. She heard them whisper, heard them sing. There were no other humans here.

– I know who you are, she stated. – I've seen photos of you in the papers, in spite of me not reading papers.

– I'm hard to avoid. He chuckled and shook his head. – You're a strange cutie.

They walked into the smaller, modern building with eight flats.

Seven flats, she thought when they reached the top of the building, and he locked them in, and she realized that one luxurious apartment covered the entire floor.

There were no windows here, no windows at all. It was the very image of «discreet».

Her eyes kept moving under the hood, kept checking out the place, in ways she had trained on since childhood, not really visible to others. Her head hardly moved at all.

– So, what do you think?

He was fishing for compliments. He was one of those people that needed others to attest to their perceived success in life.

– It's pretty much like I suspected.

She grinned, standing with her back to him, confident that he stood there with his mouth wide open. She opened the fridge and grabbed one of the many Cola cans there. When she opened it, the sticky fluid decorated furniture and carpets.

– Look at me! He said with a commanding voice, one expecting to be obeyed.

She obeyed, while slurping the chilled, sickeningly sweet soft drink. Her face appeared under the hood, the smooth black hair again.

– Remove your rags, he growled, in her eyes making a ridiculous attempt at growling.

She teased him with her smile and didn't move.

– You first…

A second or two passed before he responded. He shrugged.

– Okay, I'm a fairly liberated guy. It isn't a problem, the way I see it.

He removed his tie first, in a manner more than suggesting practiced ease. She didn't take her eyes off him. He felt a sense of unpleasantness. She saw it in his anxious glance, the rounding of his shoulders and general body language. He unbuttoned his shirt and removed it, kicked off his shoes, pulled the pants and underwear down his thighs and looked away for a moment in order to avoid the sticky stare. She stepped close to him in a single move, twisted her body in midair and kicked him hard in the belly. He gasped and fell on his knees. She struck him on the side of the jaw. His head was pushed hard to the side and blood flowed from his mouth. He fell on the side. His head hit the floor hard and he stayed still. She grabbed his wrists and pulled the big body to the bed, pulled it up on it with swift, effective show of strength. Her breath was labored, but she handled him without considerable trouble.

She pulled electric wires from the sockets, tore them off lamps and used them to tie him up. He tried moving, struggling. She responded with a brutal thrust in his belly. He gasped and turned limp. She stretched him out in an x-shape on the bed, tying his ankles and wrists to the bed's legs. He gasped and kept gasping, attempting in vain to give voice to his thoughts. She tore off two long pieces of the sheet and put one in his mouth, gagging him. She tied the other tight around his head, making the gag stay in place. He had to breathe through his nose. His chest heaved in an ongoing battle of his lungs to receive sufficient amounts of air. She checked his bonds, nodding pleased to herself, giving him a wicked grin. She rushed to the kitchen and pulled the stove into the living room, making sure he knew what she was doing. He did. He was looking at her with bulging eyes. They were practically popping out of his skull. Sweat drenched his skin and hair, filling his eyes. She filled a big kettle with water, putting big kitchen knives and other big hunting knives she picked from the wall into the slowly boiling water. He kept striving to breathe properly through his increasingly snotty nostrils. It was like she never took her eyes off the sweating man.

– I feel it, she whispered, – feel it in every nerve. Do you?

She turned her attention westward, turning her back to him, not really looking at the nondescript wall at all, but something completely different, almost forgetting about the man stretched out on the bed, still never truly taking her eyes off him.

Dark energy sizzled in the air. She felt and even saw it as she looked west and stretched out her arms.

– I can *see* you, she whispered, – see you stand on your mountain and stretch your wings. The fire in your hands burns me. You're growing. Your power is growing.

She saw! She flew on the wings of the raven, to the mountain peak.

He sat on a rock in the west, at the top of the Lyderhorn Mountain, between the island and the city, a spot with a magnificent view on all sides. Looking west he could see far out, at sea. Looking down and west, south and east the suburbs brightened the dark earth. Looking north, across the sound Askøy's southern point was also brightened by the electric light of thousands of homes. But this place, this peak, a considerable walk from any house was surrounded by comforting darkness.

With the powerful binoculars he could spot people miles away. The movement stopped for a moment while sweeping central Bergen.

The wind blew away from him. He could still smell Yola approach him from behind.

– You're thinking about Irena again!

He didn't nod, but still agreed.

– She trained hard, he said slowly, as if the words forced themselves from his throat, – to become one of the truly dangerous fighters among us, clearly feeling she needed to.

– Perhaps she trained too hard? Yola offered.

– Perhaps, he acknowledged, – but that had nothing to do with how she died. She was good, good at the skill of survival, but that didn't help her in the end. Skill, in itself isn't sufficient. Luck is needed as well, and luck always runs out. You don't even need to be particularly unlucky to end up in a hopeless situation. One can hide at the most remote location, and still be a victim of circumstances. The odds for any given individual of surviving the upcoming disaster are statistically insignificant…

– So, what you're saying is that the usefulness of the cautious path is considerably exaggerated? She mused cheerfully. – Haven't we realized that long ago?

She slipped close to him. He could sense every single move she made, every hint of curves on her body.

He raised the torch above his head. It had been about to go out. Now, it flared anew. He pushed it into the heap of dry branches and paper. It ignited in a burst of fire. For a moment, two the flames surrounded him, before pulling back. He hardly felt their power.

Something waited for him out there and kept doing so, no matter where he settled down. He looked towards the east, towards the mountains. The wolves howled at him, greeted and challenged him. He felt their power.

The wolves' howls echoed between the walls. Gwen responded with a howl equally fierce.

The man on the bed shook his head. He started tearing at the wires binding him. She allowed it, allowed him to exhaust himself. She waited until he was so weakened that he could hardly move… and then she struck him hard in the belly. Air left him, blood left him through his nose and mouth. He started gurgling.

– Samhain, ruler of the condemned, she whispered. – I bring you a gift. I bring you life!

She grabbed a torn wire, one still stuck in the socket at the other end, and pushed the exposed, unshielded wire at his thigh. Electricity poured into him. He screamed in shock and pain and exhausted himself further in a hopeless attempt at pulling away.

But he was stuck, there on the butcher's bench.

Kara gasped, and shook in the chair, making the others notice.

Damon straightened. Yola froze while studying him.

– Your face… it is as if the fire's light doesn't… reach it.

– That sounds strange to me, he said. – I feel like my entire face is burning.

The fire rose, rose again and again, gaining further strength every time. They stood close to the cairn and immersed themselves in its power, in the wilderness beyond the bright, so very pale city lights. The city seemed to fade away, disappear.

Yola stared straight ahead, her eyes catching movement.

– G-Gwen? She stuttered.

– You do see her! Damon stated pleased.

He seemed to crouch just a bit, as if in pain.

– You haven't frightened me in years, Damon, she shuddered. – I guess you were overdue.

Her knees shook and she almost fell when she attempted to go to him.

Gwen once again pushed the electric wire against the man's thigh. He didn't shake very hard this time. Tears flowed from his eyes. The gag drowned in blood. Loud, frightened chokes made the large body shake harder.

– You poor boy, she said compassionately and rubbed him on the forehead. – Such a helpless prey face to face with the predator.

The kettle boiled and spat water. She pulled one of the kitchen knives from it.

– Your thigh is probably numb by now. I could have started on the other, but I don't think there's a need for that, is there?

He shook his head, shook his head, shook his head.

She started cutting patterns into his belly skin, humming happily.

– You will tell me everything you know, everything you possibly know about the workings and goings of the city. You know a lot, I know that. I'm confident you even know far more than you believe you know.

He nodded in dull compliance, his eyes covered by a cloud of pain and fear. Loud and quiet whimpers kept rising from his sore throat every time she cut another figure in his skin.

She pulled out the gag. He started coughing. She held his head up and to the side.

Slime and blood flowed from his mouth. She held his head, and rubbed and petted it.
– This isn't dangerous, she hummed. – It won't kill you. Relax, relax…
The hypnotic voice made him relax, his body turning limp to an even bigger degree. The troubled mind was brought to a deep, deep waken sleep. He started talking, and didn't stop. She asked questions now and then, but it wasn't really necessary.
– That's a good boy, she whispered, – such a very, very good dog.
He crouched there, after what felt like an eternity, but that probably was just a few minutes.
She pulled another knife from the boiling kettle and began cutting the healthy thigh. He didn't scream anymore, but voiced his complaints in low, involuntary whimpers.
– You can no longer recall who you are. She nodded. – I know. You believe that your old life is only a fever dream and you're correct. Your mind is just a dark cloud. Everything turns dark. This is your life, now, this eternal darkness. And it happened so fast and easy, didn't it? The shock is still there, but fading, fading. Just a little longer and you will be ready.
She straightened, towering above her prey.
– SAMHAIN, she cried, – accept this sacrifice, this wretched man. Come and DANCE with me the Dance of Life.
A tiny spark was lit in the man's eyes, while he kept shaking his head in incredulity. She pulled the hunting knife from the kettle. In one simple, effortless move she pulled the plug from the outlet. The water in the kettle kept boiling. She stabbed him in the belly. Blood squirted between the blade and the edges of the wound. She let go of the knife. It was stuck in the flesh. It moved as the belly moved.
– It isn't dangerous, she whispered into his ear, bending over him. – Feel your heart? It beats fast and hard.
It kept beating, like a sledgehammer with a noise overwhelming everything and everyone.
– This won't kill you, she spat with the deep chill in her voice. – You will have more than enough time to tell me everything I wish to know. You don't think you know more, that I've taken everything from you, but you're mistaken. There's still juice left in you, lots of blood to drink.
– Come to me! Damon bid Yola.
She did, fading into his lap.
– I'm coming! Kara shouted, making everyone in the room stare at her.
She remained totally oblivious to their presence.
Gwen was dancing, to a music she only sensed, one growing stronger and louder by the second.
Damon felt pain, something glowing and devouring him, spreading from his chest and to the body at large and to the very air surrounding him and the mountain itself. He watched Anya. She sat on another mountain top, deep in a valley. Her eyes burned him. Life's fire burned him.
Gwen pulled out the knife. Blood flowed from the ugly wound. The man on the bed started talking, talking, talking. She kissed the blade, the blood-stained blade.
– The blade is consecrated, now, polished and hardened in blood and fire.
She made a fast move, slicing the throat of the living corpse below. Words drowned in blood, in death.

– You and yours have ruined so much, she whispered, – ruined for so long everything making life worth living. You have partied and thrived on a heap of suffering and desolation. Nevermore!

She stood there with her head tilted, as if she was listening, before rushing to the stereo and turning on the music, music filled with rhythm and heathen chords. The dance began. The music flowing from the speakers was incidental, anyway. This came from within. She turned around in a whirl, as her dance grew wilder and wilder.

On Lyderhorn the mountain Damon Terrill and Yolanda Durant circled each other in their dance. He had reached out a hand with a teasing smile. She remembered, remembered the first time after she had met him, how wild and crazy she had felt. He remembered himself. Finally, after hours and days of dancing Gwen collapsed on the floor, completely exhausted. Demon and Yola were still dancing. They always would!

Gwen rose, pulling off the wet and blood-stained clothing. She took a relaxed stroll to the bathroom and had a shower under the boiling waterfall. It ended slowly, after an eternity bathing in the pleasant water. She dried herself thoroughly, taking her time with that as well. She tied her hair into a ponytail and took a peek at the wardrobe.

It didn't surprise her to find lots of women's clothing. She picked a passable set, not exactly fitting her taste. She disconnected the fire alarm, grabbed a bottle of oil from the kitchen and decorated carpets, furniture and walls with it. She lit it. The fire spread fast, almost too fast. She retreated to the hallway. The flames chased her almost all the way to the street. At the mountaintop two figures danced in and out of the bonfire with equal ease, while the flames reached higher and higher and the fire burned ever stronger in the ever harder blowing wind.

+++++++++++++++++++

Electricity finally returned to the northern parts of the island. They sat in the living room in the summer twilight when the light started blinking on and off and on again, and eventually stayed on. Two minutes later it still was.

They sat there, glancing at each other, uncomfortable in the glaring artificial light. Renate rose.

– Where are you going?

Damon wondered. They were playing chess. She beat him soundly.

– I'll be right back.

The smile in the dark face flashed white.

She rushed to the fuse box in the hallway, removing the main fuse. The twilight returned. Smiles returned to the darkened faces.

Later that night they roasted another sheep in the wild garden.

– One of the things there seems to be no lack of on this twilight road to a new world… is sheep, Claire giggled.

Everyone chuckled. The dark laughter spread among them like waves.

– Some become wild sheep again, Roger said, a bit more somber, – but most can't help themselves and keep grassing old fields.

– No matter, André said pleased, – there aren't many things that can compare to a campfire and roasted meat. I say that, I that have always been a city rat.

– Have been, Yola pointed out.

Damon sat on his hind legs. The visions kept coming in an uneven flow, but more… relaxed now. He could almost separate them from each other, almost understand them.

He walked the streets of Bergen, knowing this would have to be the next day. It was the next day, but he had visions of himself sitting by the campfire yesterday.

It had turned quiet around the campfire, inside the house and in the surrounding area. Almost everyone had fallen asleep. Some still fooled around, enjoying each other's company and bodies. Gerd giggled positioned between Vladek and Yngve. Damon heard it from Myriam's position. He had heard her wake up, wet with sweat and with a hammering heart a few minutes earlier.

She sat on the roof, by the pipe and stared at the sea in the west. He joined her, jumped up there, striving a bit to balance on half broken roof tiles, striving to see where he was going while looking at the world through her eyes.

– I can handle this, she said, rejecting his help, his compassion. – The waken dreams are far worse. I cannot wake up from those.

– Come and join us in bed, he insisted.

He put a hand on her arm, his own arm.

– No! She hissed. Then calmer, but just as decisive: – No! I'm not good company for anyone right now.

He fell silent. Gerd and Roger had been through pretty much the same, but didn't feel that hard, think that deep.

– You will never walk around like a living dead, he assured her. – They tried that with you and failed miserably.

She didn't reply, but pulled away from him in bitterness and shame.

He felt that, that, too tear him apart while walking through the streets the next day.

A man, a vagrant sat by the entrance of a store and hollered at his own and the world's insanity.

– I… HEAR them everywhere, he shouted enraged. – I hear them on the bus, at work and while sitting on the toilet bowl shitting.

Damon walked on. He didn't turn around.

– I heard them in the Sahara sands, and I hear them now.

Damon didn't stop. He had to make an effort to not turn around and stare into the man's bottomless pit resembling eyes, and not fade away by the mere sight of the pale skin seemingly drawn right on the bones.

– Can… you… hear… them? The hiss only resembling a voice whispered. – I know you can. I've always heard them. I heard them in distant deserts, and I hear them now. They're always there, with us, no matter where we go.

He cackled and laughed, bowing while sitting to those passing by.

– You notice the sand. Of course you do. Everyone does. You hear it speak and know at your core that it isn't a million grains of sand rubbing against each other, but the SOULS OF THE DEAD speaking to your Self, to the place where everything is FAKE AND ROTTEN.

He laughed loud as thunder and the laughter was a horse gasping in death throes and bathing in rotten blood, flesh and guts.

– The condemned walk the Earth and they are Death, death, death.

Terrill sat down on a bench, his body drenched in sweat, and it didn't stop, but kept flowing. He could no longer hear the man, but only the eternal echo, saw only the sick grin in the dried face.

When he walked full speed back in his own tracks and returned to the store entrance,

the man was gone.
+++++++++++++
They had spent weeks, months in order to become familiar with the mountains and trails, with the various paths leading to the far mountains in the east. There had been swarms with military units there, but now those units pulled down to the lowland, to the various cities. News about that happening reached them with increasing frequency.
The soldiers either joined with the local government… or eradicated it. Unrest grew steadily in Norway, like it did all over the planet.
The Children of the Midnight Fire sat in their Sherwood Forest, memorizing maps and trails and travel descriptions, drawing maps of soil and air in their mind.
– There's an intersection in the Trengereid Turns, André mumbled, – where we may choose between going straight east or north east. Circumstances may arise making it impossible for us to choose, but we must be prepared, prepared for anything.
– I can see the pattern, Dominic said astonished. – The invisible labyrinth is there. It is!
– I can as well, Gerd said. – We've been sitting here for days and nights without end, and it feels like a veil has been brushed aside. I can *see* it, like invisible trails, an infinite number of them forming in the air.
– I can see the Crossroads, Kara shouted into the night. – All roads lead there and from there.
Some of them frowned in temporary confusion, as if catching themselves, considering their own statements.
And the bonfires formed in the air itself, and the entire tribe danced between the fires, between the stars.
– This is how school should have been, Gwen chuckled, – how all learning should be.
– The place beneath the mountains is called Eidfjord? Vladek said loud and clear. – But it doesn't really matter, does it? The road up is called… is called… is a narrow valley with many steep turns…
– … MÅBUDALEN!
– Bravo! Myriam applauded fiercely.
– You even got the pronunciation right.
Yngve said and shook his head in mock disgust.
Vladek sat by the campfire, sweating like he imagined pigs would sweat. The dark approached him, entered him. He had experienced it all as if he really had traveled through the area and hadn't found his way. Everything he had learned about spatial orientation through the years had seemed to be lost, and he was lost as well… until everything returned in a rush of emotion and rational thought.
– So, what do you remember about the other places? Anya asked lightly.
– We will pass through many small cities, villages, he replied with large, wide-open, closed eyes. – The biggest is called Voss.
He started listing names, places and directions, appearing to them more like a walking encyclopedia than a human being.
– The road up there also has many steep turns, he said, – but is more visible. The village in the valley is called Aurland. It's practically abandoned already, partly covered by water.
They looked stunned at him. Tears and laughter formed, as they fiercely embraced

him.
Smoke rose from valleys and waterfalls. Eagles floated on warm air. They drove down a remote road, leaving a remote beach, a crossroad, a place where many roads met. Dust flowed from the worn tires. The van was the only visible vehicle for miles. The road seemed to fade and disappear as they drove from the suburb Åsane and to central Bergen. Damon hadn't been here for years, and the landscape and everything seemed totally changed. This was a wasteland without illusions.
A car, a police car approached them from behind. It had appeared, hardly noticeable from a side road. The driver clearly had long practice when it came to sneaking up on prey.
The eight in the van glanced at each other. Stefan, the driver rocked so hard to the music that the big wreck practically rocked with him.
– Turn off the music, Damon said. – We're about to instigate a somewhat intelligent conversation.
Maxine laughed short and sharp. She was looking forward to this.
They all were.
Stefan turned on the direction light and drove to the side of the road and stopped just beneath a road bridge. The police car stopped right behind them. There were two officers in it, a man and a woman. They stepped outside the same moment the eight surrounded it. A nervous frown appeared on both set of brows.
– Hello, June and Ulf, Claire said, speaking rather bad Norwegian, still easily making herself understood. – Welcome to us.
The two of them glanced uncertain at each other, suddenly rocked from the confidence they had felt only seconds ago.
– Nice to meet you, Gwen said.
– A pleasure! William greeted them.
The two glanced at the revolvers they carried on their hips, before relenting, hardly even considering that option.
– You're Terrill! The man said stunned.
– Terrill junior, the woman said patronizing, – not yet wanted by the law.
– Call me Damon, the young, intense man told them lightly. – June, Ulf, allow me to express my delight of having met you on this bright, fine day…
A sense of complete bafflement entered the two.
– How do you know our names? The woman practically exploded. – If you think we're unbalanced by this pathetic attempt at getting at us, you should reconsider.
– But you are, June, Gwen pointed out. – Don't lie to yourself.
– Why did you stop us? The man asked, almost stuttering.
The laughter greeting his words felt even more off.
– But we haven't stopped you, Damon said. – You stopped us!
He put an arm around the other's shoulder and led him and his fellow officer to the van.
– And truth to tell, you made quite the bust…
Exotic scents from the bus tore at nostrils, more so as they walked inside. The two cops started running seriously scared.
– It is like you surmised, Damon confirmed. – We're running our own, small smuggler operation here, combining the profitable with pure necessities, so to speak.

The crates in the back of the van seemed newer, not so dusty, but even they had that indefinite sense of age.

None of the crates had covers. Ulf and June exchanged glances, while already wet skin became soaked in sweat.

The sight of the shiny swords blinded them. In the other crates there was important merchandize as well, but for some reason their attention was always drawn to the shiny blades.

– Guns will soon be nothing but expensive rubble, Maxine Leary said in English. – The production of bullets will probably continue on isolated places for a few years, but then it will end. A well made sword, on the other hand will be useful for centuries.

– You've cruised on a high note for a while terrorizing smugglers believing the myth of an almighty police force, Gwen informed them. – You've been damn lucky, avoiding the hard, cruel version transcending your cruelty and brutality in all and every way. You're actually quite the nice guys, so nice that you haven't even killed those you've stopped, but just roughed them up a little and confiscated the goods.

– We won't kill you either, Maxine said sweetly. – There's no place you can hide from us, though. Travel to the far corners of the world and we will be there. We will cut the throat of your small children first, Ulf. We will do so while you and your wife watch. Then, we will torture your wife before we start on you, keeping it up until you, in a distant future, will die with one, long shriek of pain. We will take your brother and sister first, June. Then, we will start on you, cut off limb by limb, until we, in an act of mercy, will allow you to die. All this and more we will do, if you rat on us, if you do anything, voluntary or not harming us, in any way.

Both fell on their knees. They couldn't stay on their feet. The beasts towered above them. They believed them, believed everything they had been told. Tears flooded their eyes, like with small children. Fear paralyzed them, and would stay forever a part of their self. All the midnight's children smiled.

The two never quite left this place. They left the van, walked the few steps to the patrol car and drove off. The car faded away in the dust and the haze, but they remained… forever.

CHAPTER NINETEEN

Myriam was sweating. She stood still, while the others moved, but droplets of ice and fire formed on exposed skin and burned her.

The women and the men moved in front of her in military drills and her vision turned hazy. In the flashes of waken night terrors she was pulled back to another time, one she desperately tried to forget.

Whirling swords and wands moved in the air, somewhat deliberate.

The warriors moved across the wild growing lawn, a lawn no longer, moved between the trees.

A simple, almost invisible sign from her and the movement stopped. Everyone on the field stood still and looked attentive at her.

– The good soldier I was would have wished to turn you into more such, she cried, – but you will become something far superior to that: You will become *warriors!*

She walked among them, hardly standing still for a moment, making it hard for them to focus on her, to actually know her exact position.

– I teach you to use all kinds of close combat weapons, she said aloud. – The difference between a sword, a wand and a knife isn't really that big. The balance is different, but the most important is this: They're an expansion of the body and the mind, and only a short such, not like the more far-reaching weapons at all. One would think that is a disadvantage, but it isn't. With a sword, a wand or a knife everything within your reach is yours to control. Everything is an extension of the body, of the mind and spirit. One can't sit on a safe spot and fell the prey, but have to get up and close, get very, very personal.

She talked for a long time, and they paid attention, very attentive, not distracted from her beyond passionate voice for a single moment.

– I learned «Martial Arts» from I was very young, learned the moves, the concentration exercises and what my sensei perceived as the spiritual part. But he wouldn't or couldn't teach me the most important: he didn't teach me to kill, to channel an ever growing murder impulse. He made the same mistake many are doing: he left out what is perceived as «negative» emotions in the training and even attempted to exorcise it from my consciousness, as he believed he had exorcised it from his own, as he, according to himself had achieved inner harmony. As you know I was punished for that ridiculous assumption many years later. The rage, the hatred might be briefly shelved, but can never be removed. Suddenly, when one expects it the least it returns, like a storm, an explosion, inevitable, lethal…

She moved the sword. In spite of her doing it slower than she normally would, it seemed practically invisible in her hands.

– This is a Katana, a Japanese «samurai» sword. It's light, easily maneuverable. It can be just as deadly in a woman's hand, as in any man's. Its strength is mostly in the sword, not in the arm. The weak part is for attack. A strike is focused at its point, a dynamic movement that can cut through concrete, steel and flesh easily…

The blade sliced a branch. It was as if she hardly moved her hand, or exerted herself at all.

– Now, while you're learning, I want you go deep within yourself. Even as you slice and stab your imaginary enemy, I want you to analyze the process, learn to keep two and even three lines of thought in the upper part of your consciousness. I was lucky. I learned self-awareness, learned to draw on the murder impulse in spite of myself. The most dangerous to a human's development of self is to blindly echo others' thoughts and acts. When you train with a sword, when you strive to glimpse the sharp blade in red and fire, you can't run from yourself…

– … That's really everything, all of the timeless knowledge I have to teach you…

Her current students stared at her. She more than sensed their admiration, when she demonstrated her skill. Her teacher had always been quite proud of her, even if she never had been very impressed with herself. She recalled that with shame and regret.

She called them forward one by one. Claire embittered. Vladek even more so. André more or less indifferent. Ralph eager to find a new teacher. Maxine slid forward like a cat, displaying herself to the teacher. Myriam suspected she still wanted the cheers she had lost in Marseille, and pondered if that would be a concern.

– I can't help you with the Abyss within, she stated. – You have to deal with that one yourselves.

Anya was that spiritual leader, even though she still resisted such a role for herself.

She spoke now and then, interrupting, adding to Myriam's words. They gathered before Anya, their priestess in their mind.

– I'm the carrier of knowledge, she had told them. – Judith chose me for that. She made me realize that I had chosen myself.

Judith, the first Silverhair, Myriam thought.

– I resisted the thought at first, Anya continued, – because I, in that very moment realized the hard truth. I would live and they would die. We went to war against civilization itself, and we won. Victory is ours! We're nature's vengeance against a totally destructive society. We are those walking in the shadows, now, and forever.

Myriam held up the wand, the sword.

– These are mere tools, she cried, in a moment of inspiration, – nothing but an outer manifestation of the power resting deep within each and every one of us, what those in charge have always feared, a Power beyond all manifestations.

Another signal. Maxine attacked her. She was discarded fast and without mercy, was struck to the ground in a supreme, effortless move.

Maxine Leary, born in the land of France, later a nomad of Europe rose, pretty much unscathed.

– I will learn everything you can teach me… and more.

Gwen attacked. The result was pretty much the same.

The she wolf rose and dried blood from her lips. Myriam questioned her own motives, wondering whether or not she had deliberately given the other woman a distinct wound. Gwen licked the blood and grinned, her long, sharp fangs exposed.

– You should follow your own advice, Gwen told her.

Suddenly Myriam wished she had struck the other that much harder…

They all came at her. No one prevailed, not even Damon and Anya. Everyone attacked her, time and time again, and had their asses kicked, having her teaching knocked into them in a way that she never had. Her sensei had been kind, considerate. He had taught her the techniques, taught her the moves. He had not taught her survival.

They eventually had enough. They had been unevenly distributed all over the terrain, their breathing labored, their faces bloody and maimed. All the fire seemed to have left them. Myriam walked to Gwen.

– You're just a lazy bitch, aren't you? She teased softly the other woman.

Gwen stared at her with hatred and spite.

– I enjoy spending time on my back on the ground.

– Get your ass up, Myriam snarled, – before I kick you senseless.

She turned halfway around.

– That's a message to you all, she cried.

Gwen fought herself up. Her eyes were hazy and she was visibly dizzy. Myriam grabbed her jaw and squeezed.

– You're just an ant beneath my heel. I could have killed you, and you couldn't have lifted a finger in order to keep that from happening.

Gwen struck with the wand, fast and unexpected. Myriam couldn't avoid it completely. Blood filled her mouth.

She quite simply pushed the other woman back and Gwen fell, but jumped back up instantly, snarling in wrath.

– An amazing change! Myriam grinned. – Most excellent!

She tasted the blood, pondering pleased the rush it gave her when it further stirred the flowing through her veins, when they came at her again, when she struck them to the ground once more.

This was different. She kept pushing them, far beyond what they had previously believed was the limit of their endurance. They had practiced, trained earlier, but that had been random, born of the moment's need. Now, she hammered it systematically into them with a tool hotter than glowing iron.

They trained with bow and arrow. Arrows struck targets, trees, movable targets.

– Draw the bow all the way, Myriam instructed Yola, – or the arrow won't be fast enough.

– It's hard, Yola complained. – My hand and arm hurt.

– Don't be such a spoiled child, Myriam chastised her. – Ignore the pain, use your entire strength.

Yola, gritting her teeth, did as she was told. She released the arrow and hit the tree at the other side of the wild garden. She looked stunned at her teacher, her eyes filled with happiness and gratitude.

– LISTEN UP! Myriam cried to them all.

They looked very attentive at her.

– You find it hard to hit the target, to let go of the arrow, because you fear you will miss. What you don't realize is that the arrow has either hit or missed the target the moment it leaves the string.

– Zen, Yngve commented dryly.

She placed herself behind him, suddenly, startling.

– Now, she commanded, – Empty your mind. Draw the bow, release the arrow and make your inner life real.

He was sweating, his head filled with distractions. The sound of his beating heart hammered in his ears. He was breathing, focusing on breathing. He practically observed it while it happened. The loud sound of his breathing faded. Thoughts faded one by one. They were switched off, like light in many rooms, until there were hardly any lights left in the entire house. He visualized the arrow, the target, forgot the target, became the bow, became the target, and suddenly he knew he would hit the target, achieve his meaningless objective. The arrow raced through the air, and he knew it was a hit before he heard the distant, very close sound of the metal point penetrating the little wooden box tied to the tree.

Hearing returned. Sight returned. The cheering and the howling of the wind mixed, becoming indistinguishable.

They sat on the ground with their legs crossed in front of them. She sat in front of them.

– Breathe, she told them. – Breathe deeply. Don't ignore the pain. Embrace it! Touch it, feel it inside.

They sat there, battered, exhausted, and they felt it coming.

Anya suddenly released a loud wail. Her eyes had been closed. Now, she stared straight ahead with wide, remote eyes. Myriam was over her immediately.

– You've never truly gone deep within yourself, have you? She spoke with a distorted voice she hardly recognized. – It's about time that you do that, and embrace what you find, and stop fearing yourself.

Anya focused on the fury above. A lone tear slipped down her cheek.

– You have no idea what you're asking, she choked, – what's waiting in there.

Myriam slapped her. A gasp rose from the gathering. Myriam gave her another slap, and another. Myriam was shocked, frightened over her own actions, but that something deep within made her keep it up.

– You're… our shaman, she said imperiously, – our window to eternity. You've chosen that, chosen your path. You've repeatedly told us your power is weak, that you in another reality would have been far more powerful, but that's just the mouse in you talking, the part of you wishing you were like all others. But you're not, *Strega*. You're even more special than the rest of us, and from now on you will do your utmost to live up to it, to your great and wretched potential.

– YES! Anya shouted. – YOU'RE RIGHT! I should do it, should have done it a long time ago, but I've been so afraid, so very afraid…

She embraced Myriam's legs, like a little girl seeking comfort.

The two of them stood frozen like that for a long time.

– It's alright, Myriam said, while petting her head. – It's okay. Fear is quite common. You're not alone there, either. Now, I want you to embrace it, making that, too a part of yourself. Keep your eyes open. See everything you can see.

Anya let go of her, nodded, sniffed and nodded again. She sat back down, shifting back and forth a little, until she felt somewhat comfortable, and pushed at each other each pair of thumb and index finger. Her breathing frequency slowed down again. Eyes turned distant. They had watched her sitting on hills and mountaintops, but they understood, sensed that something was added, now. Something happened, strange, unexplainable. It pushed at their boundaries, penetrating them, as if they were nothing. The sight of her burned into them, burned something far more fundamental than a retina, filling them to the brim. She gasped, and they gasped as well.

Myriam pulled back, attempting to remain untouched, but failed completely. It was impossible for her to stop breathing, to feel each breath like a fire. She gasped, and couldn't stop gasping.

She knew, now, why she had always seen fear in her teacher's eyes.

Drums near and close hammered them all, as they crawled from the deep well. It was like floating, like flying. The evening stretched out, like time itself, while the shadows stretched and grew.

Reality… dissolved. Glass broke somewhere, or so they imagined. It melted like ice, and water covered the floor and the yard. The house itself seemed to melt into basic ingredients like soil and water. Someone played music somewhere, a drum or a set of strings. They no longer knew the difference. The world transformed around them. Eternity passed and passed again. Anya was the only fixed figure in an ever-changing landscape.

She sat there with wide open eyes and stared at the movements in the shadows. They heard steps. They saw nothing. Something… touched them. The dreams assaulted them while they were wide awake and aware.

They sat there and had a conversation, unending and beyond deep. Sometimes they spoke simultaneously and other times they didn't. Everyone heard everything, every word spoken.

– I saw a wolf stand before me, Gwen said with dreamy eyes. – He pushed his snout at mine.

– I smelled the putrid stench of a large animal, Vladek breathed. – It lifted me up with its trunk, and I breathed on my tiny shell where it hung suspended in eternity.

– The Long Walk continues, Anya stated with a sleepy voice. – There are breaks, but there's no end to it.

They heard the sound of something resembling metal against rock. It sounded very much like that. Eyes opened slowly… and re-experienced the world.

Damon grabbed the big, heavy sword and liberated it from its sheath. Fire flashed in its blade. Night had fallen. Night had fallen again.

– We've been down all of us lately, he said with a distinctly sore voice. – It's inevitable like a poisonous wind in the society constantly brushing at our feathers. We needed this, need this ritual of life and dreaming giving meaning to the meaningless.

Metal will always follow humanity, he thought.

He felt the heavy sword in his hand, the gravity of the gun push at his skin.

– We haven't been very mainstream lately, but kept to the edge of society. We have still adapted too much, way too much.

His words fell into flesh, into mind, blowing open blocked paths, liberating pain and joy and everything in-between.

He held out the sword, its flat side. Claire kissed that first, then her own. André followed her. Everyone did, one by one. The catching in his throat grew.

– I can see the black hole and nothing more, Kara complained.

He shrugged.

– We can all feel the coming Storm. What form it takes is ultimately unimportant. You don't need a weatherman to see where the wind blows, not a crystal ball in order to see the obvious.

Anya rushed to him with a haunted expression in her face, in her entire attitude. She grabbed the sword with both hands and kissed it, practically embraced it. When she let go, she was bleeding hard from her palms. She kept staring at him.

– We should do something about that, he said uncertain.

– No! She shook her head. – I'm perfectly okay. I've never felt better.

She rubbed his face, painted with the blood on his body and eventually licking what remained off her hands. He felt her touch long after it had ended.

Without another word, looking straight ahead with empty eyes, she faded away in the dark.

The scenery changed. The council hall seethed and burned with voices and sweat and unrest.

It didn't resemble even remotely the dull council meetings held here only a few years earlier. Spit, blood and fire underscored every address, every single move. «Everyone» was present; the mayor with his Guard, Frank Moldhaug with worshipers and many others. Tore Fosse occupied his part of the hall, enjoying the company of his close relations and clan, with his son in law Roar Høyland surrounded by four gigantic bodyguards. Leif Indrehus with daughter. The up and coming Ingrid Tofte, with her fiancée Frode Tlam. Fredrik Holm and Anita Holt. Lisbeth Kaspersen sat close to the mayor with her aide Captain Karlsen, their company of soldiers and a man no one recognized. Among the spectators, from the city and the area's more informal centers of power, there were also quite a few people eager to voice their opinion. Everyone was present. The hall was packed. All windows and doors had been opened wide. A wall that had been blown up by a malcontent citizen a few days ago had not been repaired. The sun shone from a blue sky. No one inside seemed to notice the gathering wind outside. It bent trees and shook the roof tiles, but didn't reach the humans inside.

Anya pushed deep into the night and the wilderness, following the same trails where she had sent others. She removed all her clothes, everything distracting her from her surroundings. Trees and bushes whirled around her. Rush in a swamp whispered her name. She recalled having done something similar before, also in a forest glen outside a house in England, but she had never done anything like *this* before. A door had been kicked open to her depths, and she kept it open. The animals whispered her name. The forest, the enormous forest seemed filled with animals. Time passed, days and nights passed, while she walked and was lost within the ancient forest. Mists of time and shadow rose up around her and thickened in her chosen direction. She sat on a vast plain, by a pond, by a mountain, with her siblings gathered around her, and a hole appeared in the air, in reality itself. It called her. The mole on her leg hurt, a pain spreading to her entire body. It was like being born. She saw herds of wild animals on the plain below, saw the very planet stretch out before her. The stone deserts were flooded and covered with green and brown. The gray returned to the stone and the mountains where it belonged. There was resistance, in more places than one, within, without. She pushed beyond it. Her core, everything she was, slipped into all that, the green and the brown and true gray. She rose out of the forest, and saw the house and those awaiting her arrival. She saw, for the very first time the plains, the endless forests and the mountains rise above the stars themselves.

She returned to the wild garden as the sun broke the horizon in the northeast. The brightest days of the year approached. She hadn't been gone long. It just felt that way, both to her and to her fellow tribe members that saw her walk out of the forest. She seemed ghostly to them, transparent and distant. It didn't seem like she saw them at all. They spoke to her, but she didn't respond. She walked to the small mound south of the house where they sometimes had made a campfire, and sat straight down in the ashes. Her hands dipped into it and started painting her skin with it. Soon, all of her, every piece of her skin and hair resembled ash. She appeared to them like one of those burned bodies after an explosion, but she was alive, so very much alive.

The mayor knocked the big club at the table in front of him. It turned quiet, in a way. The humming of people and wind didn't go away.

The mayor rose, imposing his ostentatious shape on the gathering.

– We live in a besieged city, ladies and gentlemen, he rumbled. – There are no armies at our gates, but a treacherous nature threatening our very existence. Nature has always threatened mankind. There's nothing new here. Our situation is a bit more complex these days, that's all.

The applause started on a low note, but grew slowly in strength.

– You can say one thing about bad weather: It doesn't last forever. We just need to keep our cool, and everything will be okay.

A loud bark of incredulous laughter interrupted him. A deep frown appeared on his brow.

– They say the… *bad weather* will last a thousand, even ten-thousand years, the laughing man, Emmet Terrill said.

It took a few seconds for the mayor to recover, but he kept going, sticking to his gums, his plan.

– Hundred years ago there were factories all over the city, he cried. – It was only when we allowed strangers from out of town to come and take over, everything went to hell.

The applause grew overwhelming. He raised his hands above his head to each and every part of the room. He even nodded to those standing outside following the séance on big screens. Everything had been planned and executed carefully.

Terrill pictured one of those old TV-comedies where it had been revealed that the audience had applauded because they had machineguns directed at them. The very thought made it hard for him to control himself, to keep himself from collapsing in a loud, mocking laughter. For some reason the very thought appeared to him as extremely funny.

– An excellent idea! The unknown man sitting close to Lisbeth and the captain rose. – One that the central government will look at with favor.

It turned even quieter. Terrill gave that some thought, wondering how anything could be quieter than quiet.

The mayor smiled generously to the man. His canine teeth suddenly became extremely well exposed.

– It's nice that the… *central government* looks with favor at our decision.

The central government operated out of Trondheim, these days so very far away.

The man kept his well-crafted mask, ignoring the crowd's mocking laughter.

– The government encourages local rule, he stated, and sat back down.

The laughter turned even louder.

Anya pulled back a little. Myriam looked at her with curious eyes.

– I know him, the witch said in Italian, before continuing in Gaelic, which Myriam didn't understand. – I know him from somewhere.

Myriam looked casually at the man in the chair, a tall, skinny middle aged man with gray stain at his temples. He seemed completely ordinary to her. She could not quite understand how he could make such an impression on Anya.

He clearly did. Her… fear was tangible, impossible to misinterpret.

That fear brought Myriam's own. Her attention was drawn to Lisbeth. She couldn't tell whether or not she wanted to kneel before what she saw as a giant, towering figure, a great Goddess, or kill her. The vomit rose in her throat.

– She won't recognize you, Anya told her, comforted her. – You're just one of thousands she has «treated» with her kindness.

Myriam knew her friend was correct, knew it on an intellectual level, but the cold sweat kept flowing from her skin and made the stench rip into her nostrils.

The mayor kept going. His beguiling smile made his words sound more benevolent than it was. His approach spoke to all segments of the population, or most segments.

– Today, we free ourselves from our chains, he shouted. – From this moment on we rule ourselves.

The tall, skinny man rose abruptly.

– I must protest, he said with a striking, squealing voice. – The proposals haven't been formally presented to the delegates in advance the way protocol demands.

The mayor responded with an overbearing smile.

– I should point out that the representatives for the central government are here as observers only and should be a little more humble.

– What do you mean?

– You know very well what I mean!

And just like that was one of the mightiest unknown men in Earth's recent history discarded. A man thriving on secrecy was destroyed by the daylight he loved so much.

He sat back down, a shrunken, small man.

Terrill stepped forward. Suddenly everyone could see him.

– I would like to say something.

He didn't laugh anymore. It hadn't really been funny, anyway.

The tall, skinny guy rose again and pointed with a shaken finger at the dark man.

– That's Emmet Terrill!

Everyone gasped stunned. The heavily armed guard froze.

The mayor held up a hand, stopping any action that might have been taken in its tracks.

– So what? He shrugged. – What does it concern us? What does it concern *Bergen?*

– You can't be serious, the tall, skinny man whimpered. – You can't!

The mayor ignored him. If there had ever been doubt about whether or not the central government had retained any power, any power at all in Bergen and the region, that doubt had been removed.

The mayor nodded to Terrill, visibly pleased with himself.

Terrill spoke. He spoke quiet and insistent, a far cry from the mayor's bluster.

– First of all, you have my adamant support in your desire for more power to local government. Even if it is only a small step on its way towards the necessary total dissolution, it's one in the right direction. Your plans for a new, grand industrial development are very backward, though. You say nothing about the need to prepare for the upcoming, inevitable disaster. There's no action taken at this late stage that can guarantee people's survival, but the chances would have increased significantly if a controlled evacuation and a long row of smaller, necessary preparations had been made.

It should have happened long ago, but it's still not too late.
Short, and straight to the point. People stared at each other. The room turned really, really quiet.

– Believe me, the mayor conceded. – We will return to issues like environmental protection, but like you say yourself, such acts demand thorough preparation.

Terrill smiled, or rather gritted his teeth. It wasn't a very pleasant smile, and even the most ignorant saw that.

– C'mon, mayor, a man cried impatiently from the gallery, – let's get on with the voting, or we will be late for dinner.

The loud, mocking laughter more than suggested that this was pretty much the current mood and inclination among the majority of the gathering.

Myriam didn't remember much from the «debate». Only a few ridiculous anecdotes stuck in her mind.

– The garbage is a problem, a delegate complained. – It smells bad and makes people unnecessary cranky.

– I put it to you, Terrill yet again broke through the noise, – how can people be «unnecessary cranky»?

It was like he hadn't spoken. Only a few nervous, very nervous people expressed any kind of support.

– It's all just a matter of priorities, the mayor said, very, very smug. – People's priorities have been more than a little off lately, but we will fix that, fix that, too. Soon, everything will run smoothly.

He was paying attention to people's concerns. At least he fooled them into believing that he was. He allowed them to state their concerns, and with his winning personality and calm exterior, he calmed their fears, telling them everything they needed to hear.

Once again he stopped what could have ended up as unrest and protest and even a riot in its inception. Emmet didn't visibly shake his head. He had seen this happen too many times for that, seen a fast tongue smooth rough edges and justified grievances in a given population or crowd. Suddenly he met Lisbeth's eyes, and he realized that he stood there with his hands rolled into fists. She looked at him with eyes so naked that it hurt. He hurt as well, hurt inside, where everything hurt so much worse than on the outside. He had believed he had put stuff like that behind him years ago. Fortunately he hadn't.

The voting was a farce, of course, a masquerade, a well-directed show where everything was decided in advance. The expanded Bergen city council voted in favor of «loosening its ties to Norway's central government and create a new, local government», mirroring what had been pretty much happening all over the planet recently.

The mayor didn't care much for Emmet's grin, and that at least pleased Emmet, shaking up even more his shaken core.

– You made it this time, Emmet called to him on his way out, – but only because people still cling to the lost past. When they no longer do that, and very soon now, they won't, you will have no more leeway, no more room to maneuver and play your games.

The mayor waited until everyone had left the room. Then he finally dried the sweat off his forehead, attempting in vain to rub the acid sweat from his eyes. It didn't do any good, but still gave him some degree of satisfaction.

A prevailing anxiety grabbed the citizens the next few days. No one would quite believe that the central government would send its few remaining soldiers to the city, but no one was willing to bet on it either.

The night had a nice, backward quality. Emmet visibly shook again.

– I can hear the owl howl, he said with distant eyes.

– What? Lisbeth held around him, warming him with a desperation chilling them both, both thunderstruck and incredulous. – An owl doesn't howl, my love. It hoots.

– I haven't heard it in twenty years, he mumbled.

– I've never heard it, she said with very distant eyes.

– You do hear it, he insisted. – Everyone does! You don't even have to listen, but if you do, you become conscious of the process.

He gave her a hug, one more intense embrace.

– Listen! He whispered.

They stood on a balcony turned towards the ocean. The moderate ocean waves reached the second floor.

– The city is under siege, she said, – not by any human army, but by nature, invading us on all sides. That idiot oaf of a mayor was certainly right about that.

– It's returning to us, he nodded, deliberately misunderstanding her, – where it belongs. We're returning to it, where we belong.

He held her hard and she listened, listened hard.

– I hear something! She mumbled. – I hear something!

A chill passed down her spine, and her body shook.

A bigger wave hit the balcony, hit them, as they stood there in tight embrace. He wanted to pull back, pull her with him, but she resisted. A new wave made water rain on them. She stood there rigid and still. He lowered, in quiet despair his head until it rested on her shoulder. A hand rolled slowly into a fist.

The silence ruled the night. At a popular disco no one heard the sound of the music. The volume was raised a notch or ten, but the speakers were unable to overwhelm the piercing scream of birds, of the night's silence and roar.

Trude Indrehus rushed to the toilet. She puked on the middle of the floor, not reaching a bowl in time.

– A bad mix, she explained to the others in the room, red with embarrassment and shame.

They shrugged. Vomit had long since penetrated every crack and corner of the room. It had been washed and rinsed countless times, in vain. The stench remained. She felt a deep and paralyzing fear in her bones as she stumbled to the nearest mirror. The pretty face didn't seem that changed, slightly swollen because of the puking, but nothing dramatic. She bowed down and flushed her face in the sink, straightening again, staring into the mirror. Nothing, there was nothing there, nothing her eyes could see.

The change was deeper than that.

She heard the snarls and spiteful words, as she returned to the dance hall.

– Look at that, she heard a voice. – The high and mighty Turid Indrehus has finally gone off her rocker.

The wicked laughter echoed in her ears.

She heard worse things than that, but it still failed to impress her. She watched people, watched everybody, their altered behavior, their display of an anxiety, a desperation making itself known in thousand big and small ways, in the too wild laughter and dance, their beyond exaggerated motion.

Someone put another drink in her hands. She drank it half empty without any conscious contemplation. Someone grabbed her and dragged her out on the dance floor. She was dancing, watching herself dance, watching herself as she rushed towards the toilet and puked on the floor, imagining she was levitating outside herself, no longer herself.

A girl sat in a corner, with remote, feverish eyes. She wasn't there anymore. She was gone. Every shred of reason had fled.

The streets of Bergen filled up, packed in the middle of the night. Youths and others flowing like a single mass from the pubs and discos mixed with those crouching on the ground, rags of people that had lost all hope.

Turid didn't really become drunk, never quite losing control of herself. Everything just dissolved within her, in the horrible endless void she had become.

One of her friends glanced at her. Turid pretended she didn't catch the inquiring stare.

She floated through the city with a vacant stare in her eyes.

A young girl and boy sat on the sidewalk. They begged everyone rushing past them for small change, but they sat still and didn't speak a single word, didn't meet the eyes of those looking away, anyway.

The friend looked closer at Turid once again, and this time Turid had the choice between her and the beggars. She chose the least unappetizing alternative.

– I've watched you the entire evening, the woman said in a confidential tone of voice. – You need something… need something *special.*

Turid felt a flash of curiosity, wondering if the other would offer her drugs.

A jacket flap was pulled aside, and the friend revealed a wet cotton ball. Turid felt how her blood rose to her head. In a flash she was overwhelmed by a vision. A bunch of youths sat in a smoke-filled room with half closed eyes. Some had the cotton balls in their armpits, others in… more intimate parts of the body.

– No detours, she heard the whisper in her ear. – No pale imitations.

The new fad had started around the turn of the century. Cotton balls was dipped in alcohol and placed either in the armpits, in the intestinal orifice or even in the… cunt. The alcohol was drawn directly into the veins and the intoxication was abrupt and intense, intense beyond words. Turid had never tried it out, but had observed how it worked on others.

– We're such frail beings, she mumbled. – Civilization is just an apple we may peel at any time.

– What did you say just now?

– Nothing. She shook her head. – Nothing important! Forget it!

She half closed her eyes, with sweat trickling from the forehead, her hair drowning in fat. Her friend pushed the cotton ball into her hand. She smelled the strong stench of liquor.

She opened her blouse and pushed the hand holding the wet ball into the armpit.

– That's potentially lethal, a boy said with excitement in his voice. – The alcohol goes straight into the bloodstream. Nothing is filtrated.

The impact was almost immediate, or seemed to be. She saw herself lean against a wall, saw herself slide down that wall and sit down with her friends on the wet cobblestone, saw them all sit there with the remote expression in their eyes suggesting that they were using heroin or something. It failed to shock her or rock her world in any way. The mood was light and bright, and became even more so as the long, long seconds passed.

I'm floating, floating, falling, falling…

She sat down like the girl in the room, taking her place, becoming her.

Everything vanished. Everything floated away.

– And when the apple is peeled, it will rot on the vine, everything not already rotten.

She couldn't tell if she was actually speaking aloud. None of the others reacted, but she saw them move their mouths without her hearing anything.

The large, open space seemed more like a sardine box to her. If she squinted her eyes just a little, she saw the cover fall on them, squeezing them all. She giggled. She chuckled and cackled.

Someone had lit a fire, at the biiig, open space in central Bergen.

– The wandering gypsy really exists, a boy insisted. – I've seen her, at least once, probably more.

– Probably? Someone teased him.

– Yes, she isn't necessarily the same every time you see her, he said with dreaming eyes, – but you recognize her when you see her. You smell pine needles and wet dirt.

– Get out of here. One of the girls stuck an elbow in his ribs. – That's just an urban legend.

– That it is, another nodded. – If you hear it enough times, you start believing it. You see a badly dressed gypsy walk through a dark alley and your imagination starts working overtime. It's just one more badly dressed gypsy.

– Gaia! The boy insisted. – Her name is Gaia.

More loud laughter.

– I heard about one Gaia, the girl enjoying sticking elbows in people's ribs said. – It's said that a number of her worshipers wanted to sacrifice a boy to her, a boy filled with *power.*

She rolled her eyes.

– The high priest was about to stick his knife in the boy. After a long, exhausting ritual everything is finally ready to roll. The blood is about to flow from the skinny body and paint the holy rock red. But then Gaia intervenes and stops the entire ceremony from completion. She grabs the kid and quite simply walks away. The worshipers left behind stand paralyzed for minutes… before going completely nuts. They attack each other and kill wantonly everything in their path. Some claim that the Goddess cursed them. Others say that they grew so disappointed because the goddess disappointed them that they had to have an outlet for their grievances, and they were the only people left in the area. They had killed and eaten all the others.

– What an absolutely horrible story, the cheerful boy shivered. – It isn't strange that people start seeing ghosts in bright daylight.

He spoke with an indistinct drawl. They all did, or seemed to do. The air itself seemed to be filled with waves, with voices and shrieks and wails.

The ground shook beneath them, one more of the recent small, but noticeable earthquakes.

Anya entered the large, open space. Some claimed she appeared from the alley dressed in rags. Others said she arrived from nowhere, dressed in gypsy party clothes. Their perception of her shifted from angle to angle, from person to person.

Both her face and the skin elsewhere on her body was torn and stained with blood. Even her eyes were bleeding. People screamed. The crowd split in two long rows, making way for her. She started dancing, started swaying. She Who Danced in the Forest and the Darkness, the wild beast was dancing Kacha, danced it in a way none of those present had ever seen. They danced with her. Everyone danced with her, whether or not they moved. They had no choice. They moved and forgot who they had been.

They glimpsed shadows in the shadows, shapes dissolving the buildings and concrete surrounding them.

– I'm the wolf sniffing you, she shouted. – I'm the bee stinging you, the moss warming you. I'm you killing or being killed.

They crouched completely exhausted on the concrete, the soft moss. Anya, wild and crazy sat down in their midst. They stared at her. She looked completely normal, ordinary.

A big and tall man approached them and spoke with a harsh voice.

– This is an illegal gathering. You don't have permission to gather here.

– You're not a uniform anymore, Anton, she said softly. – You never were!

He pulled back, clearly scared or shocked or both, moving so fast that it seemed like he was fleeing.

Everything turned quiet while the subterranean choir rose up and overwhelmed them, making them all listen.

– We've ruined everything, an older man sniffed.

– No! She shook her head. – You made a damn good attempt, but «failed», and now everything will be better.

They had a conversation, a completely normal conversation.

She raised a hand and suddenly she looked far from normal. The fire rose, far into the night. People started screaming and some of them fled the fastest they were able, but a considerable number stayed, both stubborn and fascinated beyond words.

– Humanity returns to nature, returns home, she told them. – Magick returns to human life.

People looked around, and they saw nothing but forest wherever they turned. Forest surrounded them on all sides. They imagined that they had glimpsed trees during the dance, but now they saw nothing but trees. And between and beyond the trees they glimpsed all their hopes and dreams.

She moved among them like a shadow, completely intangible, but they could feel her like a shadow, like a fist in the face.

– You shouldn't be anxious. Anxiety is something tearing at your soul, and there's rarely any validity for it. Can all your worries add a single moment to your life? The dangers won't lessen with your worry, but rather grow. Fear is natural. Excessive, ongoing anxiety won't do anything for you, except gain you early furrows.

A girl cried out in distress.

– What does it MATTER? We're lost, no matter what we do or don't do. Who are you preaching to us?

– I'm a human being, Gunda, just like the rest of you. I'm not preaching. Why should I? You're human beings, and you're alive. You don't need anyone to tell you how to live your lives.

She paused and moved her feet a little. Everyone heard her sandals touch the

cobblestones.
– And now you will soon, very soon have to make your own decisions, whether you want to or not…
The wind blew in the treetops. The stem groaned in the storm.
– Our life is already over and done, a boy said in deep, deep despair.
– You think life was so much worse, before civilization? She shook her head. – I guess it is to be expected. It's the way you're taught to think, or not think.
The young boy was behind her. He was always there, following her everywhere. They hadn't noticed him, but now, suddenly they did.
– Life before was not a picnic, but was overall much better, she stated firmly. – While today's fading society amplifies all our bad sides, the life of a nomadic hunter/gatherer amplifies all the best in us. If you grab life by the tail and hold on, you will have a chance, both at survival and at a life. You may even thrive. Please try thriving, try tasting its pleasures, and you'll find what is misplaced, what you've been missing your entire existence.
– BULLSHIT!
A man exploded in rage. He rose and attacked her with all his stored aggression.
She kicked him back down, making him hit the ground like an empty sack.
– Aggression is good, she remarked, – but not if you use it as an outlet for your bias and ignorance. Life will never be easy or completely fair, but the fundamental imbalance so prevalent on Earth for so long is correcting itself. Humanity will once again live with nature, not against it. The chances of surviving the upcoming calamity is ridiculously low, even statistically irrelevant, but those of us surviving, by skill and circumstances will enjoy a far better life.
– A daily struggle, filled with dangers.
– Do you have to express yourself using clichés and established «truths», Jack? She gave him a teasing smile. – Before civilization only two hours «work» on average each day was required in order to survive, to put food on the table, a far lower number than today's beyond work-intensive slavery. The more advanced technology, the more we're required to work, to slave for a master, but now humanity's path to freedom, our way *home* has started.
They wanted to tear her apart. They wanted to kneel before her. She didn't allow them to do either.
She stood before them, surrounding them, instead of the other way around, removing all smothering blankets from their self, a person, an individual, an independent force frightening them out of their wits. They felt curiosity and life itself burn within.
The wandering gypsy continued her long walk. They saw the dark shadow on her skin crystal clear, saw the black hair blow in the wind.
It was quiet. There was no wind.
She faded away before their eyes. The boy wandered in her shadow, and they wandered with him.
– I know her, another older man cried. – I saw her dance Kacha in Marseille. I saw her dance in London when I was a boy. She's riding with the Nightravens.
No one had any doubt which version of the Nightravens he meant.
They heard the boy speak.
– Will they make it? He asked.

– They have a better chance, now, she replied, – at least some of them have.

Everything shifted, blurring around the edges.

The beach stretched on forever. Sand had supplanted trees, bushes, grass, asphalt and buildings. Some shapes might be mistaken for the tall structures of old, but were probably only waves of sand, as if it moved in an infinite desert. He glimpsed an island far out, at the distant sea, one half hidden in mist, the island in the stream, where all secrets hid.

Asphalt and concrete and glass and plastic faded, turning into sand. Distinct gray snakes in the landscape were supplanted by a shimmering cover soon to be impossible to separate from the terrain surrounding it. He saw everything, through dry and wet eyes. Everything raced towards him at an insane speed. He saw everything incessantly slow, as if he experienced a thousand years in a decade and not during a second. Time rubbed him gently on the cheek, haunting him with its sharp blade.

He saw the eagles rise and didn't see them stop. He saw the wolf race through the dark forest.

Yola kissed him hard, passionate. It should have worked on him, hell, it should have set him on fire, but he felt only a remote, detached interest. She snarled and slapped him. He saw her vanish behind the cliff.

The city stretched out below him, in gray and shit. Its lights were not very bright or powerful, not even in the night. It was fading before his eyes.

But the image of it didn't fade. He could still see it, even when he turned his back to its dull and hostile lights, even when he was sleeping and dreaming.

Even when he raced through the tight forest, when he flew above the highest mountain.

CHAPTER TWENTY

Emmet felt an icy gust from the alley behind him, through the open door to the room inside. He looked at the mountains and saw a dark, dark shadow.

He smelled the dust on the wall, the scent of oil on the road he walked. Emmet sees her face, Lisbeth's face.

– What is it? She asks.

He turns towards her and grabs her collar.

– Don't ask silly questions, he gasps. – You feel it, too, don't deny it.

– I'm not… Deny what? What do you mean? Emmet, are you okay?

He walked down Strandgaten, walked down it alone, a long, long endless walk. He, Emmet Dalton Terrill did his desert walk among the derelict buildings for hours, eventually finding himself in front of a computer. Text and images turned indistinct in his vision. The Internet still worked, to a point. Many links led nowhere, but one could still find old links if one knew the correct address. No search engines worked, but the web did, like it had in its humble start, like a personal exchange of information between individuals, perhaps a little more advanced. It was the technological final event horizon before the vast and dark deep. A female danced in the forest, and he heard ever stronger her song. Walls turned to trees, the keyboard to branches stabbing his fingers. The messages usually covered one of two subjects; reports about disasters or calls for help, heartbreaking calls for help, filled with rage and despair and pure desperation.

In vain.

In bygone years there had always existed bodies of aid, various organizations that could step in and help in any given disaster area. Now, there were hardly anything but disaster areas, and no aid organizations left. People asking for help hadn't realized that, or wanted to realize that. They had clearly lost touch with reality.

A guy had been very creative in his desperation.

«I have an atomic bomb mounted on a long distance missile at my disposal. If you don't show up soon, I will not hesitate to fire it».

Lisbeth, Damon's face floated in his inner vision and without any discernible reason they mixed and turned virtually identical.

A man entered the room, hesitating, almost scared. Emmet knew him or knew of him, having met him off and on through the years.

– How does it look?

– It doesn't! Emmet said, somewhat pleasant.

It seemed like the guy appreciated the somewhat kind response. He stepped the few, necessary steps into the room and closed the door behind him.

The hours slipped away. After just a few minutes, it seemed like they had known each other for years. The smoke drifted close to the ceiling. The sweet stench infected the entire room, their clothes and skin. The man giggled and kept giggling, unable to stop.

It turned quiet. Emmet lay on his back and looked at the patterns in the ceiling.

– I always believed that the choice was between a good and a bad mood in life. I realized only recently that we, in that particular regard don't really have a choice.

There was more hysterical giggling.

It turned even quieter. None of them spoke for several minutes.
– Have you checked www.weather.info recently? The man asked casually.
It took a few more minutes until Emmet managed to rise and stumble the short, vast stretch to the old, dusty computer countless universes away. He bent forward. It still had a constant connection. He didn't have to dial up, to do anything but writing the web address. That hadn't changed, not yet.
It was slow, very slow. Most of the pages had been made for far faster connection than what was now available. It helped that almost no one used the machines anymore, though. The images, the text appeared slowly. He sat there for a long time, before turning around.
– Can this be right? He asked stunned.
The other man had quietly and without calling attention to himself left the room. Emmet couldn't decide if the departure was recent or just after Emmet had sat down. He never saw him again.
This changed *everything*. He roamed lockers and storage rooms for a printer and finally found one, and even cartridges of ink made for that particular model. He spent just as much time in front of the computer in order to make the connection between the two machines work properly.
There was a lot about the weather on this particular site, but that was everything these days, wasn't it? It was also about other related info, about worse things. A satellite image showed a giant dark cloud approaching the British Isles, a storm center bigger.... bigger than Europe. He couldn't quite handle it. It didn't register in his conscious mind. He put several photos together and drew, fairly unnecessary a line. The storm was definitely on its way to Scandinavia, on its way everywhere, but Scandinavia would be next after Western Europe. He sat there wondering, his mind working overtime, wondering if such forces could make the planet itself... crack.
The other, worse info he refused to acknowledge just then. He wasn't that different from most people staring at insanity incarnated.
He once again wandered aimlessly through the streets, unable to tell how many times he had done so. Clouds, fake like God, were dancing on glass and steel walls. Someone pumped air into an enormous plastic man. It rose slowly, painfully. He carried the papers in heavy plastic bags with fortified handles, a science developed for notorious shoppers. It did the job. He stopped abruptly and started pulling the papers out of the bags, throwing them around like money, and share them with everyone passing by.
– You're free! He shouted. – You can do what you want!
No one interfered or even spoke to him. Some of them cast a fleeting glance at him, a painful peek times thousand reflected in windows and streets before hurrying on. They left him in peace, leaving themselves in pieces.
– You can read, I presume, he raged against them. – This isn't that hard to comprehend, is it?
He was being ironic, even sarcastic. Sore, angry eyes stared holes in him.
People read. At least a few of them did, and eventually a few became many. They spread the word, and against their will they opened those sore eyes.
– There's not really anything new here, Lisbeth told him later that night.
– Everyone reading it clearly disagrees with you, he said, still eager, still driven. – It made them both scared and pissed. Their rage overpowered the apathy, a miracle in

itself.
– I love the fire in your eyes, she whispered.
Even later that night a big crowd of enraged people gathered outside the mayor's home. Three rows of soldiers guarded each of the four walls. People threw rocks. One hit a window, but didn't break it. Another, bigger hit the same window not long after that. It broke in a thousand pieces.
The mayor emerged through a fortified door, surrounded by even more guards. He signed for the soldiers to calm down. The agitated crowd lowered the volume of their shouting a bit, just a bit.
The mayor felt, almost in a physical way the chill from the oozing torches, the frenetic mob.
Emmet and Lisbeth stood in the shadows, under a tree by a ruined streetlight. She looked closer at him. He shook his head.
– So, the mayor cried, – what can I do for you guys?
– You LIED to us! One cried.
– A level 100 - HUNDRED - hurricane is coming our way, another chimed in. – What do you intend to DO about it?
– Good people, good people, the mayor responded. – This is nothing new. We've known for a long time that hard times are coming. At the meeting tomorrow, we'll introduce new, extensive measures against everything threatening us, against wind, the common cold and anything revealing itself the next thousand years.
The voice of twisted reason spoke to them, twisting their minds even further.
– It's imperative these days to keep our cool, to not exaggerate an already grave situation, he shouted. – We achieve nothing by resorting to panic. Go home, now and come to the meeting tomorrow.
People mumbled among themselves, discussing lively between themselves, before leaving, before going home, still unable to act on obvious, unavoidable facts.
Lisbeth looked stunned, virtually shocked at Emmet.
– They're desperate, he shrugged, doing so deliberately, – desperate in their desire for the world to never change.
One single man turned and raised a finger to the mayor.
– This time we expect more than words.
– Tomorrow, the mayor repeated. – It's late. We should all get some sleep.
It was a joke, one that actually made people laugh. Those not laughing stared hard at those doing so, but they didn't do anything or raise their voices.
– I knew early on where this was headed, he said. – I have long experience with situations like this.
She saw that the fire was burning even stronger in his eyes and shuddered.
– Come, he said and grabbed her hand, – we're not safe here!
She started laughing. She shook with laughter, while tears flowed down her cheeks.
Waves struck the shore, the walls and houses. Someone sang somewhere, so beautiful that all tears ceased, and they stood there and listened in awe. A geyser erupted from the frothing sea. There were no words, only sounds penetrating deep into the soul. There was song, there was joy.
A car stopped right in front of them. A door opened. They jumped inside. The car drove on.

Smoke drifted in the enclosed room. Lisbeth was very aware of the curious stares. Did she only imagine that none of them was vicious? She recognized a slew of those present. The majority of them had figured prominently on international wanted posters. It caused astonishingly few reactions in her. She wondered if the past could truly… be the past.

They sat there and checked their guns, as they had done so many times before this.

The metal flashed in the red light from the candles. The heat spread in the room, into her.

– You have powerful forces at your disposal, she told him. – So have I. If we join forces, we have more than enough power to add to our influence in this city.

He had given her his irritating smile and grabbed her hands.

– I think you truly mean that, he said solemnly. – I, we will consider your offer carefully, but I should tell you that I probably will never be desperate enough to join party politics…

They were back at the well guarded hotel room. Her aide, Captain Karlsen stared at her.

– The situation is quickly becoming complex and untenable here. It might turn explosive at any time. We should pull out before the match is struck.

– Not yet! She stated, gritting her teeth. – Not yet!

A man left the hotel. He walked without escort, like he always did. No one had spotted him when he arrived, and no one noticed when he left. He wore a hat, but aside from that he wore prosaic, common clothes.

He observed everything happening around him. No one saw his eyes below the brim, but he missed nothing. The face remained impassive, a mask not revealing anything beneath it.

His walk seemed casual, as if he didn't have a destination in mind, but to those with experience with such things, he clearly moved with purpose.

His movement turned seemingly even more casual after a while. He even started turning his head. Even amateurs in tailing, in silent following would have realized that he knew someone was tailing him. A few minutes more passed, and he actually started staring. He knew someone was following him, but didn't spot any, couldn't be positive, not with all his experience in the game.

He clutched the gun in his hand, but before he managed to pull the trigger, he felt a sharp pain in his wrist. The small knife penetrated tender flesh. He wished to pull it out, wished desperately to do so, but he couldn't move, not a finger. He stared hard at a given point in the alley. Nothing moved there. He couldn't see anything, no matter how hard he tried.

There, in what was clearly a very deliberate move, he saw something, saw her.

– You're not wearing a coat anymore, Melvin? The shape in the shadows said softly.

He drew breath fast and painful, abruptly drawn many years back, to a ramshackle tavern in Liberty City, Copenhagen and also to the black hair and golden earrings he had spotted from the South African embassy.

– I've been looking for you for a long time. Thank you for coming to me.

He had spotted several of the members of the Green Rose in glimpses in the course of years, but never her, not as anything but a shadow he had never been certain truly existed, except in a thousand worrisome nightmares.

– I knew you would!

She stepped out of the shadows, and for the very first time he could see her clearly. The panic almost made him flee for his life, but instead the sight of her paralyzed him completely.

– You've done so many bad things, Melvin. Perhaps I should have put a stop to you earlier, but now your time is up.

She stepped forward. He didn't see her movement, only the fact that she was moving. Pain cut through his flesh. His feet failed him and he collapsed. He crouched on the wet cobblestones. The heat leaked from the many wounds. He wished to shout his protest at the sky, but she didn't even grant him that. He didn't see her leave. She didn't even allow that. She refused herself the pleasure of seeing him die.

Her heart hammered with joy as she left the place, the joy of the hunter having caught the prey, the triumph of the human being having vanquished an irreversible enemy. She juggled the knives while she walked down the street. People saw her, noticed her. She didn't care, not anymore, revealing herself to them, challenging them with a snarl.

– Come to me! She shouted. – Embrace me, embrace yourself!

The artificial ground below her feet would, not so long ago have blocked her power, her contact with the Earth. It no longer did. She felt the soundless cheer rise from her very body, the arms she stretched above her head. The people watching her saw the knives fall from her hands, but they never saw them hit the ground, never heard the sound of metal against cobblestone. The next moment the knives returned to her hands, as if they had never left.

– DREAMS BELONG TO THE NIGHT! She shouted, and the ground and the buildings and the very city shook under the onslaught of her power.

Lisbeth heard her. She heard her so well that she imagined that the other woman stood right in front of her.

Strega's passion flooded Damon, where he stood by the broadcast tower at the top of the mountain. It mixed with his own and liberated it through a thousand small pinpricks no longer pinpricks, but wide open doors.

Lisbeth couldn't imagine how she was able to locate Emmet, but she was. He stood on the northern wall of the ancient fortress staring at the ocean below. The sun was rising in the northeast. She couldn't feel its heat.

He stood there with binoculars, as if attempting, attempting hard to see what was coming, whatever it might be. It did him no good, of course. It wouldn't come from the north.

All bad things came from the south and west.

– Have you slept? She asked.

– No!

He shook his head without turning.

– Neither have I. I haven't even been close. It's impossible for me to close my eyes. Everything reaches me undistorted.

She embraced him from behind.

– There's a dead body in the yard. He's bluish and swollen all over. I could see every detail, every little blemish. I can hear people whisper anxiously to each other at the other side of the town. I can feel the wheels in the machinery rust. All new buildings, big or small are rusty from the moment they're constructed. Civilization has always been in a constant state of repair, or rather disrepair, and now no one is repairing anything. Everything is collapsing.

The last sentence she stated with a kind of cheerful anxiety. He turned and kissed her. It felt very bitter, very tender.

They glanced down. From their vantage point the distance to the surface was still considerable, even though it didn't feel like that. Several minutes of staring didn't convince them otherwise.

– I've always suffered from hydrophobia, he admitted. – It has never disappeared completely, not even after many years of swimming.

He frowned, as if something… touched him.

– I've never found out why.

They walked hand in hand towards the town. She read something in his eyes. There was a distinct movement behind the cornea. She had become skilled at reading him eventually, at reading whatever she was able to read. Aside from that she understood nothing.

He once more put the binoculars in front of his eyes, directing it at the body crouching fifteen, twenty steps to the right.

– The wind is blowing away from us, she hissed relieved beyond words.

A man seemed to sit by the wall, a pale, skinny body. They were unable to tell whether or not he was actually breathing, if a spark of life still remained. Emmet and Lisbeth both easily noticed the black swellings and several other details.

– We might be infected already, he shrugged, – also by other, seemingly well people, but there's no reason to not take simple precautions.

– So, the reports are true? She asked, totally unnecessary.

– They're more understated than the opposite, he pondered.

Images of Stockholm filled with soldiers flashed before their eyes, soldiers eventually firing at each other, paranoid and frightened out of their wits. Close up satellite photos had made it all even more gruesome. The last visuals from the extreme surveillance regime that had ruled the final years of civilization had brought the stark truth to everyone.

– Humanity has never, even during the best of circumstances found an effective way of fighting this, he stated.

She nodded with cold sweat covering all exposed skin.

He offered her the binoculars, but she declined.

– I don't need to see the details, she mumbled.

Yersina Pestis - The Black Death - had returned from its long exile.

They walked on. She imagined she felt some kind of constriction in her throat, but couldn't say for certain.

She stopped him, pulled him around, forcing herself to meet his eyes, as she heard the first loud cries from the nearby crowd.

– Don't go, she said. – Please don't! I've done horrible things. Kill me! You achieve far more by doing that than by staring into hundreds of rifle muzzles.

He kissed her hard, squeezing her body in such a brutal manner that she could hardly breathe. She expected, at any moment to feel the pain of him stabbing her, of the knife penetrating her heart.

It never happened. He smiled his teasing smile, turned, and left the place, left her. She heard him talk, at some point, unable to tell exactly when.

– Don't use me as an excuse. If you slip back to your old life, you've got no one but yourself to blame.

She set off in the opposite direction, fleeing as fast as she could.

A man, a vagrant, a naked skull sat on a corner and howled. He seemed totally insane, beyond terrifying.

– You think it's just the grains of sand rubbing against each other, but that's just something you tell yourself in a desperate, pathetic attempt at achieving some kind of peace. YOU KNOW! You know that the sound you hear is in truth the souls of the dead whispering, whispering all manners of horrible secrets in your ear.

– ... *whisper,* he whispered, long after she could no longer see him.

The roar once more rose from the city's big square, Torgallmenningen, a real roar this time, not just its pretense, not just loud voices. There was only some limited cheering when the mayor appeared on the stage almost completely surrounded by bodyguards. Almost all pretenses had vanished in the rising and ongoing heat.

People were dancing. Others sold sausages and souvenirs. Many evidently had lots of fun. An unreal mood ruled the gathering.

– We will put forward lots of suggestions for your approval today, the mayor shouted.

He cut to the chase so fast and in such a way that they looked stunned and speechless at the stage and each other.

– There's a need, in my opinion for drastic measures in order to save our celebrated way of life. I've personally led meetings with associates and specialists the last few days, and I can tell you with unequivocal certainty that this will demand great sacrifices of us all.

The ants flowed to the city, to the center of power, to those sending the commands running their lives. The many that had recently seen through the deception, the angry and the lost also showed up. They all came, in order to visit the ant hill one last time.

The mood was fairly relaxed, at least in parts of the crowd the first few minutes of the gathering.

– Where's Johansen? One asked. – He usually stays close to his lord and master.

– That asshole should return to the shithole he came from, just like the damn gooks and blacks and other Muslims, one in the other's company foamed.

– But he's born Norwegian and white? Another frowned, clearly a little put off.

– He's from Trondheim and speaks like a duck, the foamer foamed on. – He's from far away and isn't one of us!

The statement was echoed eagerly by others nearby.

Others again became visibly angered and distressed by the statement and the support it enjoyed.

– Local patriotism rears its ugly head again, one said in contempt.

The mood grew further agitated. Unrest kept spreading.

Bits and pieces of words and sentences, screams and howls of pain reached Kara in the alley. She stood there alone, shaking in terror.

– We will close off both passage ways between Askøy and the mainland, the mayor shouted. – We will empty the inner basin of water and liberate lots of unused land for agriculture and real estate. Professor Hansen will explain it in greater detail.

A fairly big man with glasses stepped forward.

– It sounds implausible, even impossible, he began, – but we are in truth only talking about a considerable task of engineering, not a…
– As they say, the mayor interrupted, – the impossible only takes a little longer.
The professor started explaining it in almost intimate detail. Most people didn't understand squat when it came to all the technical stuff, which was probably the intent.
– We will hollow the mountains, the mayor kept going. – We will build windmills…
– FINALLY! One from the crowd spat.
– More like chasing windmills, another cackled, cackled loud, very loud.
The mayor turned a deep shade of red, but kept his cool.
– We have the resources, he shouted even a tad louder. – It's about time we liberated ourselves from our limitations, from the paralysis that has dominated our society the last twenty years. It won't be easy. I would lie if I said it would be. But when have people in this city been afraid of stepping up?
That brought cheers, but strangely little of it, really. The discontent and fear didn't fade. The first cracks in the man's facade began showing.
Another «expert» stepped forward. He read from a manuscript, and it didn't sound like he was at all deviating from it. His voice didn't sound good. He looked quite pale, even quite dead. They imagined that a walking dead man stood there and talked to them.
– There are lots of minerals and materials left in the ground in this area, he read. – For various reasons they weren't excavated in the previous century, but they're there, ready for us to find and use.
– We will turn every rock, one of the mayor's supporters on the stage added. – We have immense resources at our disposal.
– So, environmental protection is out, huh? The man not chasing windmills said aloud. – Isn't that as backward as it can be, considering today's situation, the stark, immediate danger created specifically by such attitudes of denial and destruction of nature?
The caustic irony cut through the crowd and made the stage floor shake, shake hard.
– I wouldn't buy the old, hysterical prophecies if I was you, the mayor rolled on like a tank.
– So, you haven't truly changed your opinion, have you? The same man said with biting sarcasm. – You just pretended you had. Thanks for the clarification…
Angry voices grew louder, much louder.
– What about the coming storm? What about all the prevailing illness? What about all the poison we will be exposed to at the factories?
Angry voices rose from the crowd. Others hushed them or attempted to hush them up, in vain. The unrest persisted. The rage that had gathered momentum for centuries was about to explode. Finally!
Kara stood and shook her head in a constant, repetitive movement.
– There is something here, she frowned. – Something…
No one heard her. Not even those standing close by did.
– I'm not saying that there aren't problems, the mayor shouted. – I'm not saying that at all. Isn't that what I've repeated endlessly during our meetings? Haven't I reiterated our plight in detail, point to point?
He started feeling the pressure. It started showing in his face and eyes, his entire pose.
– But you still persist in keeping the immediate real and present dangers hidden.

A voice amplified by speakers seemed to appear from nowhere. Everyone heard it.

– Who said that? The mayor scowled, staring everywhere with a savage expression in his eyes.

No one revealed themselves. The voice could have come from anywhere at the plaza.

Everything turned silent all of a sudden. Everyone listened hard.

– We will expand the city, the mayor tried again, sounding pompous and frantic and downright desperate, – doing so where there are water, mountains and even within the mountains. We will become a standard to uphold for everybody in the twenty-first century.

– Why should we follow the Christian western time frame anymore? A woman cried. – Isn't it time we put such silly stuff behind us?

The loud whistling grew even louder, and would have been heard even without the relative silence.

– So, how do you intend to handle the impending Storm?

The man on the stage dried the sweat from his brow, attempting in his desperation to pull at his clothes, to find room between the soaking wet fabric and his skin. He looked at his accomplices with an empty stare.

One slowly being filled with fervor, even rage. He rushed forward, grabbed the microphone and stamped his feet on the wooden floor stage.

– I've served this city and you my entire life, he shouted with savage eyes. – Have I ever lied to you?

He stared at the sea of people, while moving his eyes back and forth, like a bull just before it attacked.

The crowd didn't fall silent, but the noise didn't further add to itself either. The mayor sensed, like the sly political animal he was one final opportunity.

He straightened, pulling himself up by the hair, like many of his townsmen had done so many times, both before and during his reign.

– I can't promise you anything but blood, sweat and tears… he began.

The laughter rose from somewhere. No one could tell whether or not it flowed through speakers. It rose from the opposite side of the plaza. Many recognized Emmet Terrill.

– Congratulations, sir, even today, on the edge of the abyss, you're a great snake-oil salesman.

They imagined they could see him, somewhere, hidden among the masses, but couldn't say for certain.

– Does anyone really need to point out to you what is a given, that your dear mayor has indeed lied to you and done so numerous times, that he has hardly done anything but lied to you, through a long life of deception and maneuvering behind the scene, that he continues doing it now, with humanity at the edge of the abyss? Study this man carefully. Did you truly elect him, or did he fool you into believing you did?

– I can't promise you anything but blood, sweat and tears, the mayor repeated meekly.

During one single moment he seemed to have been deprived of the final shred of authority, his tiniest remains of dignity. Everything exploded, several minutes before the actual explosion.

– The time has finally come to let go of the old, Emmet shouted with a powerful voice, – to discard old, established truths, and the «new» that are only more of the same.

Today's society, locally, nationally and globally rotting on the vine has always been and will always be fundamentally wrong. Civilization itself is a dead end. We've walked on a high wire blindfolded long enough. It's my conviction that we must become a tribe again, not in size, but in preference, many tribes, one tribe spread across the Earth, an Earth once again scarcely populated. When we once again, far into the future rise like Phoenix from the ashes, we'll be changed, transformed. We will once again be human beings, not the pale version of it we are now. Brothers, sisters, I salute you. May we all eventually meet again, where the Thunder Road turns.

– OVER THERE, the mayor howled. – FIRE! FIRE!

Some trigger-happy people did. The roar of rage rose from the crowd as the first bullets hit flesh. The fat man on the stage gasped as other bullets struck him. One bullet hit the microphone and there was a crack like thunder. The cauldron began boiling in earnest. One, two, ten figures ran in all directions simultaneously. Smoke rose from their flesh. The first strokes of panic struck people as the truth dawned on them. Everyone crashed into each other in a desperate attempt at avoiding those with smoking skin. One man howled:

– STREPTOCOCCI DEATH!

Total insanity erupted.

Each of the smoking figures crashed into a cluster of people, spreading the deadly decease all over the plaza. A moment later the second wave of those contracting it collapsed in heaps of flesh and bone. Many more started on «The Final Run». Close and distant observers could practically see in their open, open eyes how the virus set their limbs on fire, how flesh started boiling on exposed skin. Clothes and skin turned into one burning mass. There was no fire, only ashes, but that blackened substance still burned.

Suddenly bullets rained from all sides. The air turned red. Boiling blood landed on naked skin and more blood started boiling. More flesh was torn apart.

Everything happened so fast. Before anyone had really realized what was happening, the entire plaza had been transformed into an inferno of blood, decease and death. Twisted faces and bodies seemed to be everywhere, brief, nightmarish flashes impossible to avoid. A woman attempted to climb a wall and managed to reach fairly high, but not high enough to avoid the blood splashing her leg. She screamed in fear and pain and fell back into what seemed to be an endless firestorm of smoke and death.

Very few of those present at the plaza escaped. Many were shot the moment they appeared from the seething mass. All the entrance points were eventually closed off, and no one was allowed beyond them. The utter and total chaos faded only slowly, so slow that it seemed to those still watching that it never would.

The Streptococci Death wildfire finally burned itself out, as was its want. It always erupted in a horrendous display of violence, inevitably fading because there was no more flesh to feed its appetites.

The surprisingly high number of survivors formed heaps of flesh miraculously whole. People in containment suits moved in and swept the area. They found those still breathing and led them away in chains. The bowed and broken prisoners didn't resist the brutal treatment in any visible way.

Others poured gasoline on the heaps of dust and clothes and set them on fire. Everyone watching from a perceived safe distance imagined they heard muffled screams.

Lisbeth sat and bit her nails in front of a computer screen. She imagined she glimpsed *his* face somewhere in the many grueling pictures.

But she had no chance in hell of confirming that to herself.

– That idiot! She mumbled, gritting her teeth. – That damn idiot!

In the gray, foul weather Torgallmenningen was chemically cleaned of whatever bodies and remains were left. The cleanup kept going for days, day and night.

The survivors were transported to an islet outside of the city, one with a derelict building that had previously served as an infamous prison and also equally infamous orphanage. The creatures chained there in the yard resembled scarecrows more than people.

Lisbeth sat in the assembly hall with Captain Karlsen by her side. The third representative for the «central government» had long since left the city or so most people assumed. No one Lisbeth had spoken to had seen him since his rather poor performance at the previous official city council meeting. No one had seen him leave the city either. She knew, or felt strongly she knew what had happened to him, but she didn't want to think about that, about that either.

It didn't exactly take much imagination or rational thought to know what fate awaited the people on the islet. The soldiers stood with loaded guns in front of the broadcast cameras. They awaited orders.

– This is completely unnecessary, she tested the waters, – and not the least unproductive. I can fix it during just a few weeks.

– I do have respect for your work, Dr. Kaspersen. A grim and abrupt man interrupted her. – It isn't without its uses, but is ultimately worthless. Too many soldiers become deserters for it to be of true value.

– The program has been ruined by short-sighted and frightened men, she burned at him. – With free hands I can…

The order was given. Hails of bullets hit the walking dead on the desolate yard.

– But… Lisbeth rose. – But…

She held back, held herself back, and took a good, hard look at the unmoving faces around the table. They stared at her with what was clearly a savage glee. She froze and stood there like a statue, unmoving on her base.

Captain Karlsen grabbed her shoulder and half led, half pulled her away, out of the room, out of the building, away from everything.

The wind was blowing around her, tearing at her brittle surface. In every single pair of eyes she met, she read accusation and burning hatred. They wanted to tear her to pieces. She wanted to do it to them, doing so piece by piece and stamp on what was left. She had never before felt such powerful emotions. The numbness paralyzed her to the point that she was unable to feel the wind.

– We have no authority here anymore, he insisted, fairly unnecessary. – Let's get away before they realize that, before that self-evident fact dawns on them.

She shook her head. She nodded. Both acts were a form of denial. The wind created by the chopper rotor blew hair in her eyes. She stepped into the comforting darkness. The wind ceased. The loud sound when the door closed thundered in her ears. The chopper took off. She cast one single glance back. The mountains shrunk as the chopper rose above them. They turned insignificant in her vision. Bergen vanished below her, until the city was nothing but a gray, dirty spot on the map.

CHAPTER TWENTY-ONE

Kara stood there before them, once again seemingly a tiny and timid girl, like she obviously felt herself to be.

– I was almost caught up in it, she whispered. – I fell when I panic-stricken ran the wrong way. Pure luck!

In her eyes, in her mirrors to the soul they saw it all, saw the flames rising from rotting corpses, smoke turning all visuals to mist, except the inner, razor-sharp vision dominating through fear and danger.

– I saw the light fade from their eyes, saw emptiness take its place, saw everything disappear until there was nothing left.

A man had fallen on her. She had scratched him bloody on his face and chest. Her claws had torn his clothes as if they were paper. She had leaned against the brick wall by the theater and watched the security forces take aim. She had rolled herself sideways in an insane movement, staying on her feet until she reached the end of the wall and fled from there the fastest she was able.

Damon left them without a word and rushed down into the basement. He sat down in front of the monitor, grabbed the keyboard and started reading. He hadn't downloaded news for a while, hadn't bothered with it. Disasters, cries for help, threats, intolerance… everything just blurred to him. He rose, sat down again and sat still for a long while. He rose, grabbed the monitor and pulled it back in one, brutal move, pulled it free from everything binding it. The rest of the equipment fell to the floor. It sparked and burned and died. He carried everything down the hill, out on the cliff and threw it in the ocean. He had to do three tours, and between them he ravaged completely the small basement room, with a rage that showed no sign of receding.

A while later he sat in the living room, fairly relaxed.

Slowly, methodically he shaved off all his hair.

– Such a waste! Yola, visibly pale attempted to joke about it.

He recalled easily that particular comment while charging through town a few days later, while racing through the mountains many days later. Most of the recent events had faded against the backdrop of the red mist, but he recalled her words and her face. He imagined that no time at all had passed. The people seemed like… no, not like shadows… like… shapes around him. Even the two not far behind him did that.

– So strange, Myriam said, shaking her head. – Nothing surrounding us seemed real. I'm confident that if we should look behind the facade, we will be able to confirm what we have always known, that it's just cardboard, nothing but props.

– That's because it *is* an illusion. Even his own voice sounded distant, seemingly reaching him from far away. – Not in the sense that it doesn't exist, but in its significance.

They wandered through a kind of eternal twilight, a night where the pale neon lights couldn't quite penetrate the shadows surrounding them. Damon could feel them, now, almost see them, like something tangible in his surroundings.

He had allowed Myriam and André to join him tonight, allowed it with a kind of double indifference. They were concerned. He didn't believe it was due to his recent

bout of rage, not exactly.
– So, how does it feel? André wondered cautiously.
Damon looked calmly at him.
– The hair, I mean?
– Ah, the hair, Damon nodded, as if it just now dawned on him.
He smiled.
– Liberating, very liberating!
The city… moved around them in a way it had never done before. The city, so long dead and still, woke up with its people.
The restlessness was almost visible in every big or small movement they noticed.
– CURFEW IN AN HOUR, the slightly electronic voice declared through the many speakers placed all over the inner part of town.
The recent… unrest had been met by clubs and guns and a massive show of force from the security forces. Cowed people returned to their daily chores. The mood in Bergen this late evening could be interpreted as… relaxed. The dust had settled and so had the people breathing it.
– It seems so… peaceful, Myriam mused.
– The peace of the grave, André stated.
Many raging people had found their grave lately.
A bunch of younger boys and girls enjoyed the evening and its pervasive heat. Damon stared at them. They froze, stopping briefly, before hurrying on.
He kept walking. The other two followed him. All three did as they always did: observing and digesting the impressions created by their surroundings, a cautious approach that had helped them recognize dangers before they arose, helped them survive.
Life consisted of images, sensations, bits of information put together.
The danger had become consistent now, reminding Damon and André of Berlin, but worse.
– Look at that, boys, Myriam mused. – Everything has become so much more *active,* now, hasn't it? One can spot it in the streets, in people, at how they move according to each other, in conscious and subconscious patterns. Everything is rising towards the surface. The Chaos has become obvious. The skin of the apple, the thin skin of civilization is already gone. It probably doesn't come as a surprise to you, but…
Nature pulsed in the streets, as if it had always been there… and it had. Myriam danced in front of Damon, flirting with him, while speaking from her depths.
– … I like it…
A man walked back and forth on the sidewalk, from one corner to another. And he didn't walk past the corners, but turned and walked back in his tracks. A woman with a baby stroller appeared from one of the corners. The man continued his repetitive, monotone dance from corner to corner. The calm, the traitorous calm kept dominating the scene.
– Speed up! André said.
The other two had already done that the moment before he spoke.
None of them could later point at what had made them react and do that. The scenery looked very similar to one a peaceful Sunday afternoon, but it didn't truly matter. The unrest hid beneath the surface and they had taught themselves to recognize that.

The woman with the baby stroller stopped for a moment. She stood there unmoving, not doing anything but studying the scenery in front of her, looking very serene and relaxed. The pacing man stopped a little bit and glanced around him with suspicion in his staring eyes. The woman pulled a machinegun from the stroller and pulled the trigger without hesitation. She fired in a wide dispersal. People scattered in panic, but didn't get away. They were hit by a rain of bullets. The woman fired short bursts. She never lost control of her weapon. People crawled off in desperation, hardly raising their head from the ground. She went for them and shot them in the back. Damon, Myriam and André reached the corner just in time and were fairly safe while bullets flew everywhere, hitting the ground, walls and traffic signs.

The police arrived eventually, rushed in from all sides with cars and uniformed officers in body armor. More bullets raced through the air. The woman and people caught in the crossfire were hit numerous times. They bled from countless wounds. The man kept walking back and forth. He seemed completely unaffected by it all. Several officers screamed to him, but he didn't react. No bullets hit him. He continued his desert walk without interruptions.

The three left the place in a rush.

– I want very much to go back there and say BOO! Myriam said and giggled like a young girl. – But that is an impulse I can resist…

The three kept their calm. Most others rushed off with pale faces and empty stares.

The sound of bullets and even its echo turned distant in their ears. People kept shaking while they stumbled off.

Two girls sat down on a bench, quiet at first, before starting a brief, philosophical conversation concerning the issue at hand.

– What… was that about?

– I have no idea! The other replied. – It could have been anything.

They turned quiet again, looking bewildered at each other.

Damon, pondering his action for just a moment walked to them.

– Do you think she knew why herself? He inquired.

They froze. The sun suddenly seemed cold and distant, like a moon compared to what stood in front of them.

– He asked you a question, girls, Myriam said.

She seemed to suddenly appear behind the bench. They had not seen her move.

– We don't want any trouble, one of them whimpered.

– But safety is nothing but a myth, superstition, she pointed out to them. – You're alive, and therefore in trouble.

One of the girls froze even more. Her eyes turned distant.

– I think she stopped knowing anything long ago, she said sleepy, trance-like.

– That's more like it, Myriam said pleased. – You show potential.

Damon looked good-humored at her.

– On your feet, girls! Myriam commanded. – Let me have a look at you!

They obeyed and practically stood at attention.

– Ah, you know how to stand. I guess you've learned it through watching movies or perhaps through the recent pervasive military presence in town?

The two girls nodded, staying wide-eyed and anxious.

– You learn proper behavior at school these days, right? They no longer accept

unhealthy display of independence anymore, do they?
The two girls frowned, but kept nodding.
– You look quite fit, Myriam nodded to herself.
They looked confused at her.
She studied them, assessed them, the strength of their body and attitude.
– I think I can do something with these two, she said to the two accompanying her. – There might not be sufficient time, but…
– You must be kidding me!
André shook his head.
– You will come with us!
She told the two girls in quite a decisive manner.
– Tonight? But we can't…
– Not only for tonight, Damon told them, – but forever, and you will probably live longer.
– But I *can't,* one of them said with a childish voice. – I'm getting married tomorrow.
Myriam slapped her. She choked and jumped in her tracks. Tears jumped from the wide eyes.
– Stupid cow, the grown woman shouted. – It isn't surprising that you, a born slave do exactly like you're told. No one has given you the opportunity to think for yourself.
They faced her confused and down, while they kept choking.
– What do you WANT with us? The girl standing closest to her whispered.
– I want you to choose your names.
– My name is…
– No!
Myriam Christine Vallinger told them.
– Not the name others have given you. It's time for you to stand up for yourselves, now, and no longer accept the direction of others. I want you to choose a name symbolizing your departure from your old and trite existence, with the enslavement others have chosen for you.
The two stood there with lowered eyes, ashamed and fearful.
– They will slow us down, André said with contempt. – They will put the tribe in jeopardy.
Damon and Myriam nodded. The game was over and done. The three walked off, already far away.
– Betty!
Myriam turned her head, slowing down a bit.
– I'm Betty, one of the girls said. – I've always liked that name.
She still looked down, but had a stubborn look in her eyes.
– I'm Tove, the other whispered. – Only Tove.
In one spur of the moment decision they had changed their lives.
Myriam walked back to them, and grabbed their shoulders. She saw stubbornness and life, desperation and longing, and suddenly felt much better.
– You will never see your families again, she said lightly – Welcome Home!
– We're in good shape, Tove said fierily. – We can run for hours. We won't slow you down! I swear we won't!
– What if we slow you down? Betty said anxiously, more to herself than to them. –

Goddess, we're not ready!

They stared miserable and ashamed at Myriam. She waited a few heartbeats before replying.

– No one is ready! She stated.

They had been on their way to Nygård Heights, the Nygård Park forever, or so it felt.

The lights in the park were out, like they had been for a long time. There wasn't a single functional bulb anywhere. Twilight, the twilight summer dominated everywhere.

– This is our destination tonight. Myriam taught the girls and strived to recall Damon's words, Anya's words. – It isn't exactly a place, but more a state of mind. Listen to my words, but be aware that they're just words. You won't truly learn, understand anything until you understand it within, live it and dream it, until you're awake every single second of the day and night, until you live the life of a nomad.

She once again felt the burning cold within and wondered if she had truly known this truth herself… until this very moment.

Youth who had come to the city to study had lived on the Heights, close to the faculties. No one came to Bergen from other cities to study anymore. Ghosts and hardly anything but ghosts lived here, now. Here as well. Damon didn't close his eyes. He couldn't recall how long he had kept them open.

– The trees are moving, Tove said. – They're moving all the time.

– In a world of death all life suffers, Damon told them what they already knew.

– I won't be going back, Betty stated, strangely calm. – It's still not too late to do that. The city is still here. The houses are here. People live the same places. I can go home. It's just a few minutes since we sat on the bench. But I know with absolute certainty that I'll never see my mother and father and siblings again. It's crazy, isn't it? You shanghai us, drag us with you to Goddess knows where… and we join you… on a journey to nowhere.

– Myriam is correct, Damon said dryly. – You do show potential…

She glanced shyly at him, at the young man of the same age as herself, staring at the revolver in the holster concealed inside his jacket. The silhouette of the sword on his back concealed under the big jacket seemed to flash in her eyes.

She giggled a bit and he knew why. She had attended bible school when she was younger and knew that the Nightravens had a tradition of recruiting fallen Christians. The story of Janni, Jannicke Martens had been banned bed literature and discourse for many of her old friends from they were very young.

The two groups moved in conjunction with each other. Those studying them carefully could see that easily, at least if they had some basic experience with such stuff. There were quite a few groups and people in the park, but these two approached each other cautiously, slowly, inevitably.

Damon walked in front. André and Myriam walked half a step behind him, Betty and Tove a couple of steps behind them again. The group formed a half moon. It felt very familiar to the three in front.

Damon studied the four approaching them and excluded, like he had done for a while everything else.

They approached with fast steps, clearly aware of Damon and his reputation. They looked even more over-the-top hostile than they would usually do.

– I desire one single delivery. He went straight to the matter at hand. – Tonight!

– Tonight? Are you nuts, man?

The leader stopped the objections from one of his henchmen with a very telling move of his hand.

– We can do that, he said lightly, – can do tonight. Will that be all?

– That will be all, Damon Aleister Terrill confirmed.

With the brief conversation and the deal made, the four pulled back the same way they had come.

Damon sat down on a bench. He looked completely relaxed.

They spent some time there. Everything seemed quiet, peaceful. They spoke with each other in low voices. Tove danced around the bench with half closed eyes, more liberated for every new circling she completed.

– I'm free, she hummed. – I can do what I want!

A man passed them. He cast dark, suspicious glances at them.

– You're free, she shouted at him. – You can do what you want!

He rushed past them. They saw a very distinct fear in his eyes.

Betty looked shyly at Damon.

– You're the new urban scarecrow, she said cheerfully. – We were cautioned against you during our entire adolescence. The witchnights quickly gained a legendary status.

– I'm very happy to hear that, he said dryly.

– What was it about, the meeting with the four scoundrels? A smile formed easily on her lips. – You know what I mean.

– The four represent one of the biggest arms dealers in the district, he enlightened her. – It's big business, for as long as it lasts. There's no lack of customers. And what we needed could not be procured at short notice through our own, more limited network.

She nodded awestruck.

– You're exactly like I assumed, she breathed. – And far more!

The conversation ended before it had truly begun. He remained intense, but also obviously distracted. They noticed. All of them noticed.

He looked at all the four people gathered in front of him with his steady, penetrating stare. They could not help but being affected by it.

– There haven't been public executions in Norway for almost seventy years, he stated. – They will use it to scare people even more than usual, and they can't be allowed to, not anymore.

Damon looked at them, looked away from them. The two newest recruits frowned, striving to understand what he was getting at. His two longtime companions didn't.

– You should go back, he said to the air. – It's just as well. I don't need any help for what I'm about to do. There's no reason for you to accompany me.

Myriam stepped close to him with fingers stretched like claws.

– Don't talk like we aren't here, she said with a low, but enraged voice. – We will always be here. I will always be here. I will go with you. You may reject the others, but not me.

They didn't see him rise. He sat on the bench. Suddenly, he stood straight at full length. Betty gasped in terror.

Damon grabbed Myriam like she had grabbed him. André stared stricken at the two standing there wrestling. They didn't touch physically, but wrestled with the will. She didn't give an inch. He stared at her with his black eyes, for the first time without filter. She moaned. He held her eyes in an iron grip. They weren't black. How could she ever have believed that? But filled with shadows, terrifying shapes living, dying and resurrecting themselves during fleeting moments. Saliva flowed from her slack mouth.

– You guys return to the others, Damon told André. – Tell them that there's something we must do, and that we will be back.

André nodded, suddenly very relieved that it wasn't this version of this man he had first met in Marseille, happy that he had been allowed to gradually get to know him.

– C'mon, girls, he said lightly, – let's go.

There was some resistance in them, but they did follow him, as he led them out of the park, away from the two standing by the worn bench.

The three faded away to Myriam long before they were physically gone. She watched them walk on the shingle road until they disappeared beyond a turn. Then she turned towards Damon. She sat down when he did and they waited somewhat patiently, not speaking much, but touching and fondling, giving each other the occasional comfort.

The four they were waiting for appeared from the same direction their friends had vanished. They had no trouble carrying their load. There wasn't that much of it and that heavy. This meeting didn't last much longer than the last. There was exchange of cargo and funds, and a few awkward words, no more.

The four had left again. Myriam and Damon sat on the bench and checked the equipment. It didn't take long or expose them too much. They didn't talk much, not beyond the rudimentary level needed. They communicated without words, often without eye-contact even, way more and better than they had previously done. Body language and distinct sound of breathing said more than a thousand words. He lived with her, like a volcano or an iceberg. She couldn't get rid of him even if she wanted to, and she didn't.

– Everything goes up in flames, she said excited. – It finally does. I've wanted to see the world burn for a long time and now it does.

Lips burned when they touched, when they met and parted.

They rose, doing the last checkup of the gear.

– I like your new hairdo, she said. – Your hair is finally shorter than mine again.

He didn't voice a reply, but she still felt his response. Even that small thing rocked her.

It turned dark, as dark as it could be an evening in late May this far north. Only the lights from the close, distant city could be glimpsed at the edge of the eyes. They looked at each other. They didn't have to, but they did anyway.

– I can see them, he stated.

– Who?

She asked, filled to the brim with curiosity, with the need to know him even better.

– Spirits, he replied, – both the living and the dead. I can't see them with my normal vision, but if I squint my eyes just a little, change my angle just a bit, I can glimpse them. Sometimes I can even see their faces. The air is filled with souls.

He took a noticeable break, pondering his words as he spoke.

– And «behind» them I can glimpse even more. These shapes are mere mirror images of their physical shell, not the true entities. Beyond is their true form, their Shadow, something far more than we can usually perceive. Do you know that in Voodoo the word for «shadow» and «soul» is the same?

She shook her head, beyond fascinated.

– This… he pushed a hand at his chest, – is just a temporary form and even though mighty in its own right, it's like nothing compared to the Shadow casting our shadow. There are stories about people encountering their Shadow, their «doppelganger» and falling apart completely. I think there is something to those stories. Many can't face something like that, a reality like that, can't face themselves and keep any kind of equilibrium. Some people are convinced they meet God or Satan. Such reactions are the perfect self delusion. They get, through both desire and coincidence a chance to grow, but choose instead to devolve. I think they sigh exasperated at themselves, these creatures when they leave their shells and consciousness expands and they have no choice but to face the truth we all know.

She shook where she stood in front of him.

– Have you, have you…

– Met him, It? No, not as I'm aware of, not face to face, but I've glimpsed It, in dreams, visions and in times of extreme duress. I will meet It, like we all will, one way or another.

Behind half closed eyelids, he glimpsed the Shadow, a vast entity roaming time and space.

– You have nightmares sometimes, she said softly. – You wake up sweaty and anxious, but you can never recall what it was about.

– One day I will!

The wide coats hid the weapons, hid everything they desired. They didn't deviate from the crowd in this. Everyone dressed in wide coats these days and nights. The summer night, the long twilight surrounded them and they it. They crossed the Heights again, and descended down the streets to the city on the other side. There were lots of people outside tonight and it had the council's blessing. The curfew was temporarily suspended.

– The curfew is suspended, she remarked, – but they still announce it.

– They're some piece of work, he acknowledged.

Thousands gathered on Torgallmenningen, attending the council-sponsored «truth and reconciliation meeting», eager to contribute to yet another deception. The contempt both of them felt festered in their core, and their rage grew to an explosive level, and that made them feel a certain sickening gratitude.

The exception on the ban on public gatherings had been given for Torgallmenningen alone, but those in charge had decided to be generous tonight.

The police and the army, practically the same these days had been given strict orders to remain invisible, orders effectively restricting them to stay in the headquarters and the new and shiny additions to it. Not even provocateurs were allowed.

It didn't really matter that much. They were stationed only fifty meters away and could effortlessly be dispatched to the plaza.

Damon and Myriam moved at the edge of it all, but close enough for them to feel yet another wave of rage rise within. They welcomed it. The mind cleared. The body readied itself without conscious thought.

– I can feel the city's fear, she marveled. – Cities have a twisted form of consciousness, you know, and now it's looking at us with fear and loathing in its dusty eyes.

Her words echoed within him and found support.

– We're on the same page, he nodded.

He grabbed her and held her, and she looked mesmerized at him.

– When we get going, I want you to let yourself go completely.

He spoke to her with a raised fist. She had never seen him raise his fist before.

– Everything will be decided in seconds. We are going to get out of this alive, do you hear me?

She nodded with numb lips, a numbness spreading fast to her entire face.

They moved forward in what felt like an eerie, non-synchronized beat. All their hesitation, the last thread holding them back dissolved in the hot cauldron that had formed them.

There was one, long street from the Heights to the administration area, and they followed it all the way. The city council building was on the right up the street. They walked past it. The walk, filled with sweat and rapid heartbeat didn't take that long. Both felt quite relaxed in their rage. It didn't unbalance them.

They encountered a few cops on patrol. Damon waved cheerfully to them. Myriam gave him a look, but didn't actually reproach him. She wasn't afraid. They had put fear behind them.

They passed the old fire station, also on the right, the modern shopping mall on the left. Spots of red paint were missing on the right, spots of green on the left. The large building housing a bank and a grocery store was straight ahead, and to the right of that… was the police headquarters.

Steady hands assembled the final pieces of the weapons, an act at least partly concealed by the wide coats. He looked at the wall clock, and as he did that, he began hearing the music, a low roar of rhythm and chords growing by the second. They pulled their bazookas from the coat and turned off the safety in one, fluent movement. Each of the bazookas contained four grenades, compressed destructive power. They fired one each at the new and shiny police building ahead. Tongues of flames erupted from the back of the pipes. The grenades raced through air comprised of smoke and sparks, chasing their prey vigorously. The two children of the midnight fire spotted a few uniformed people inside before the explosion, before everything dissolved in a glowing inferno of fire and destruction. The outer shell of the grenades exploded first, but inside it there was another, smaller grenade with even greater destructive power. The first explosion shook the building. The next touched every single part of the building's concrete, steel, glass and plastic. To those watching it appeared as if the solid construct blew itself up. It dissolved to dust and a gray and red mist flowed in an endless stream from the point of impact.

– The arms industry hasn't suffered from the general industrial decline lately, Myriam chuckled wickedly.

Myriam fired once against the bank. It exploded and collapsed with a tearing sound. Damon fired at the closest shopping mall. The grenade struck the center of the building and a considerable part of the debris flowed through an entire block and reached the plaza and the council-sponsored «truth and reconciliation meeting» came to an abrupt end. People howled in desperation and insane panic when pieces of concrete and glass rained down on them. People fled in all directions. Some fell and was stamped on by those right behind them. Others were pushed down by people running faster than them. A somewhat peaceful moment had turned into a stampede from one moment to another.

The two turned as one and fired at the city council building. It broke in two, nothing but a dry match of concrete and glass. It fell and hit the street by the water, landing on many of those fleeing from the panic. The two last grenades were directed at buildings at the north of the plaza, and pieces fell on more fleeing people.

The smoke drifted past and around the two. She looked at the bald head covered by dust and blood and dirt. It didn't turn quiet around them, on the contrary, but they felt like it did. Someone fired at them. She felt a pull and a lock of hair fell to the ground. They pulled their guns and fired with both hands. Four already half dead soldiers fell in a rain of bullets. The two placed their guns back inside the jacket and started walking. Panic reigned around them. They started running, setting course south through the fairly peaceful Marken, not looking any more suspicious than any other panic-filled city dweller in the stampede of feet and twisted features. She looked into his eyes. They ran, ran so hard that the lungs felt like they would explode. They reached the railway station and the bus station not long after that. It didn't feel like a long time at all, but they still ran for days during that short run.

They slowed down, stopped briefly outside the bus station and looked, melted into each other's eyes. Both saw a deep well, a universe of creativity and life.

He reached out a hand to her. She hesitated, wondering what he had in mind.

There and then he started dancing, in the midst of panic, of danger. She joined him. And she saw something, a shadow grow from his flesh, something much bigger than the body. In the mirror image of a window… she saw herself.

No one had time for them. They danced without major disruptions. When the dance ended and they walked hand in hand up to the parking garage, they didn't quite relax and kept going through various escape routes in their heads, knowing from experience that a fairly peaceful scene could change to unrest and danger at any time. They walked with a crowd sharing their objective: to get out of town as soon as possible.

Nothing happened! No one shouted in alarm and pointed at them.

No one cared about them any longer.

THE PLANET

The last great ships sailed on Earth's seas that year.

The fuel sources dried out or were quite simply not excavated anymore. There was a lack of resources needed to utilize the few resources left.

One of the last in ordinary traffic, Princess Ragnhild sailed from Hirtshals in Denmark to Horten in Norway. It had fallen on hard times, becoming more or less a ghost ship and resembling pretty much many derelict buildings on land all over the world, but it could still sail.

Magnus Breen, standing by the rail and puking his guts out still managed something resembling laughter at least. He had been ill on most of the voyage. It had started right outside overcrowded Danish beaches and just taken a turn for the worse since then.

With his worn face he almost looked like an adult. Just the light, ongoing shadow on his upper lip exposed his age. He had become downright skinny in the months since he had been separated from his tribe. Nightmarish images and sensations from Copenhagen kept haunting him even in bright daylight.

He dried the vomit off his mouth and face and finally managed to somewhat raise his head. Skagerrak, the sound between Norway and Denmark was big, far bigger than he had imagined by looking at a map. He couldn't see land anywhere.

For some reason that struck him as extremely funny. The insane laughter made the others, his numerous fellow passengers, freeze and shake. The wild man in their midst stood out, both by physical appearance and implied inclination.

The ship crawled with ghosts. He decided that in one of his less insane moments. In the saloon he heard the roulette wheel spin, saw the cards turn, the aces, the deuces in an endless spin.

Then there was the living ghosts traveling with him. He had never spent much time with ghosts before. His fellow tribe members had always appeared like complete, powerful human beings to him. He understood better, now, the worry he had spotted in his mother's eyes, why she had insisted he and the others should leave with the Storm Child. She had feared he hadn't had sufficient experience to venture into the world alone.

The hallways, once the foster child of luxury had now degenerated into something resembling more the thick line at the center of the cow privies he had seen as a child. It seemed like someone had eaten of the carpets. The walls had holes and several of the cabins lacked doors.

There were four beds in each cabin, but he was left alone. No one dared sharing a cabin with him. He fell down on the bed and fell asleep, even as he writhed and turned a thousand times and hardly did anything but slumber. And when he woke up in the dark, dank room, after having suffered through a nightmare lasting a thousand years, Blanche, as usual, sat on the edge of the bed. But not Blanche as he preferred remembering her, but like he had seen her for the last time, crucified on rusty sewer pipes. And the insane, pleased grin frozen on her lips scared him just as much every time. He jumped from the bed, fled from the cabin and rushed barefoot into the hallway, the cow trail of a corridor, fleeing head over heels from the banshee that had come to take him to the underworld and the asshole ruling there.

She belonged to *him*. She had done so while she was still breathing and still did.

He stopped. He slowed down first, slowed down to the point of finally standing still. His head turned. He turned and forced himself to walk back. It took time. He had ran long and hard. When he finally pulled himself together and turned around, he almost found himself at the opposite end of the ship. He could enjoy more of its favors, far more than desired. People crouched on the floor and puked their guts out. He walked through a pyramid filled with pale skin and bloodstained eyes, and felt fresh as a hen fleeing from the henhouse. Every time another breaker wave struck the metal down there, there were those gasping in despair and desperation, and releasing a bit more of whatever slime remained in their stomach. No one corrected the skewed paintings and photographs on the walls. The walls themselves seemed skewed. People grew even more unhinged by the minute. He shook his head good-humored.

This wasn't a passenger liner anymore, but nothing but a rusty wreck that, for some unfathomable purpose sailed between two set points, an empty ghost ship sailing south, one even more a ghost ship on its way back north.

The dark still lingered in the air in his cabin. The sour stench of the vomit in the bucket blocked his pipes and kept him from breathing. Blanche remained on the bed, looking just as bad, as if she had rotted in the grave for months (and she had). His shoes remained where he had placed them, by the wall by the pillow. He grabbed them, more than a bit distracted, never taking his eyes off the ghoul, not even for a moment.

– I know you don't like seeing me like this, Magnus, she said with a hint of sympathy in the rusty voice.

The shivers ravaging his body and mind became something lasting, something he would never get rid of.

Blanche looked up and turned her head.

– But, as you may realize, I don't feel much like cheering right now.

The darkness, the shadow lingered in the air like something physical, tangible, and perhaps it was.

– No, one might claim quite empathically that I don't feel very good right now, and not that I have reason to feel good either.

He caught sight of a dark shape crouching behind her, something that had to crouch in order to fit within the confines of the cabin. No, what a ridiculous notion! How could anything that large find room in such a limited space?

He sensed it beyond the senses, an infinite creature roaming space and time with impunity.

Blanche rose and stood before him. She grabbed his jaw with a soft touch, a wet, slimy hand, a sympathetic expression in her face. Even more worms crawled through her bright, beautiful (greasy, dirty) hair.

– He will come for you, Magnus. He will come for you all.

She faded away before his eyes.

And left him alone.

He stood there, and kept standing there, unable to tell for how long. The air in the cabin didn't improve, he knew that, but suddenly and painfully he caught its complete fragrant and fullness. The oxygen reached his lungs without obstruction. He sat down on the bed and put on his shoes. A few minutes, hours later he found himself on deck and realized that he hadn't tied his laces. He sat right down on the wet deck and did so, as an afterthought. After sitting there for a while, he returned to his cabin and undressed. He hung his clothes to dry and went back to bed. He slept.

Magnus Breen stands by the rail with many other hopefuls, desperate people seeing Norway's shores for the first time. It's raining. He's laughing some more and the others place themselves at a somewhat safe distance. He's laughing even harder.

People whispered among themselves, exchanging the persistent rumors, ugly, ongoing rumors about how Norway treated their new citizens. He had heard them whisper all the way from Hirtshals, when everyone had been registered and received wristbands. Most rejected all the wild stories, of course, because they had to, in order to keep a semblance of hope alive. He had given a false name, without placing much hope in that. He stood out like an ugly wart wherever he walked. Nothing he did would make a difference. Not the coloring of hair or anything. Even if he constantly crouched while walking, and wore baggy clothes and a cloak the big and muscular body would have exposed itself. He could just as well have worn a tattoo on his forehead.

In a dark alley in Copenhagen he had met a man, an old man, experienced in the game. He easily recalled a refugee's first lesson: «Never stand out or call attention to yourself. Anonymity is crucial in order to succeed».

He sniffed in the air, breathing the fresh ocean air, laughing a bit more and shaking his head. He acknowledged that anonymity would never be one of his strong suits.

The sound turned narrow on both sides. The harbor was somewhere ahead, not far away. He looked with regret at the bag he carried on his shoulder. He shook his head good-humored, dropped the bag on the deck and jumped up on the rail, balancing easily on the metal bar. People stared at him with wide eyes, even more than before.

– LISTEN UP! He shouted.

The small talk ended. The whisper ended. He had their full attention.

– You know the stories about what happens to everyone going to Norway these days? Well, everyone I've spoken with in Norway about it can confirm they're true. A monster with a stinking gap awaits us at the harbor.

He jumped and dived at the surface far below, neither knowing nor caring about how many was following him. The water struck him as he cut into the dark deep. It hurt, but he had learned to handle pain. The force of the dive pushed him far away below the surface, away from the ship and the deadly propellers. He kept swimming with long, strong strokes. Not many would have managed to stay under for so long, but he was something else. He had always known he was. The emaciation had not lessened his strength or endurance, not significantly. He swam without straining himself along the seabed, the dead seabed stretching far ahead. Tons of garbage, cars, trucks, boats, cardboard, baby strollers, iron beds, traffic signs, computers, monitors, bikes, guitars… decorated the underwater landscape, but no life. Chemicals, yellow, green, brown and inedible, in heaps of powder were visible everywhere, a result of centuries of massive pollution and lacking waste management. He felt death nip his skin.

Blanche appeared a stretch ahead of him. He felt the chill she emanated, but the shock had at this point become something distant, insignificant.

– That's correct, Magnus, child of the Green Rose. Your journey through the Kingdom of Death has just begun. I can assure you that it will be long and hard.

It didn't surprise him that he could hear her as if they were above the water. Very little surprised him these days.

Just a few strokes from land he still felt like air was unnecessary, but then the need manifested, abruptly and painfully. He couldn't say for sure if he would have been able to hold out a single moment longer. Just sheer willpower had brought him this far.

The big body crouched on the shore and heaved for breath. His body stank like a sewer. It had been a long time since he had felt so good.

The soil was dry, but the hard ground still made it hard to climb up the small rise. He dug his fingers into the soil and pulled himself up to higher ground. Not long after that he found himself in a fairly normal street, with normal houses, but he didn't see a single human being there.

Everything had become remote, abandoned.

He started running, slowly at first, then faster and increasing the speed at he ran. He sat course towards what he believed was the edge of the city. There were sounds, sounds of activity. He removed himself from them with every step, every new touch of the ground.

This couldn't really be said to be a city anymore. It resembled one. Most of the old trappings remained. But the tiresome buzz, the overwhelming noise was gone. Green growth had started appearing everywhere. Asphalt and concrete were slowly supplanted with soil, with life. Houses were devoured by the invading forest. Inside a ruin new, powerful growth had pushed its way through the floor.

But his first, optimistic assessment failed quickly. The forest wasn't that big. Most of the old forest had been removed and only stumps remained. Small trees were on their way up, but it would take years, even decades for them to become another forest. He kept running.

He reached another area of old trees. Every single tree flashed in his mind as he rushed past it. Something jarred at the edge of his vision. Suddenly, he was blinking and unable to stop. He found himself on the ground, looking at the world through a persistent haze. When he finally managed to raise his head and look up, he only managed to do so with the strongest of efforts. Several indistinct figures approached him. He noticed the small arrows sticking out of his thigh.

– Didn't I tell you? The woman's voice sounded very familiar, even though he heard it through a buzz growing to a waterfall. – Five hunting parties and he still reached all the way here.

The others responded. He knew that, but heard only the woman's voice.

– You see, I knew you would get here. I waited for you, dear Magnus.

Everything faded to black, but he still heard her voice and her laughter.

– Look at him! He's still moving and would have been wringing our necks by now, if we had been stupid enough to go near him. He's just a boy, and he would have made mashed potatoes of us all.

After that nothing much made sense for a while. At least it didn't seem very sensible to him.

There had been those on the boat staring at him, but almost everyone did. He suddenly realized that it was those not staring that were truly strange, out of place. He imagined that he could feel his jaw hit the ground, but he couldn't say for certain. They might be carrying him, but it was just as likely that they threw him into a cell or a cage. He seemed to recall bars. There was no air. No matter how much he gasped for air, nothing reached his sore lungs. He remembered puking. The stench of vomit stuck in his nostrils like glue.

– Wo sind mir? A voice wailed. – WAS IST MIT UNS PASSIERT?

Magnus opened his eyes, forcing them up. He glanced around him, scouting the room subconsciously, automatically. He needed to squint his eyes just to see a couple of meters, but the room wasn't much bigger than that, anyway. It was constantly shaking. They had thrown him into the back of a truck. At least twenty people that he could see had been chained together. He looked down on his own big hands. He hardly felt the heavy chains, but he had no trouble seeing them.

They had thrown him into the arrival section of the ferry terminal with all the others, the more or less frightened travelers. He had fought them tooth and nail, in spite of the chains, and they had beaten him until he crouched half unconscious on the floor, the once so soft carpet that undoubtedly had seen better days.

At least that was what he believed had happened. It had had a dreamlike quality, a touch of insanity, even to him.

The others had protested very loud. They had been chained and beaten as well. The rest had been driven off like cattle.

A worn middle-aged man held up a piece of paper, squeezed it in his shaking hand.

– I have a passport, he shouted. – Don't you want to see my passport?

And a while later, with uneven and even breaks.

– DON'T YOU WANT TO SEE MY PASSPORT?

No explanation was ever given. The guards hardly spoke, except through curses and snarls. Virtually all the communication was done with strikes and kicks. Magnus had eventually seen the futility in letting himself be hammered half to death, and had walked «voluntarily» into one of the dank trucks. He couldn't tell how long he had been sitting there. His sense of time had disappeared as early as on the boat or even before that. He only knew when he was hungry and when he needed to shit. Somehow, he managed to keep himself from shitting in his pants. It was possible to maneuver in the sardine box. He took two steps away from his spot. Those he stamped on whimpered when his heavy body and boots descended on them, but those he peed on and shit on didn't protest in any way. When the food was brought no one dared challenge his right to be first in line. He didn't even sit close to the exit, but just stamped on everybody when he smelled food. The others started carrying the food to him, in the hope that he would share with them. He could just sit there and wait for the good stuff to be brought to him.

He didn't know where the meat came from. He didn't care.

There was a window in the truck. The man who had fought and won that spot willingly stepped aside every time Magnus Breen wanted to take a peek.

The man with the passport had stopped moaning his eternal litany. Magnus didn't quite know whether or not the man resided in this truck or another, but he had heard his voice well not that long ago.

– You keep wondering, don't you?

A man close to him shook his head. Magnus gave him a stare and the man by his side didn't open his yap anymore on this trip.

Magnus Breen nodded to himself. He had always wondered about things. His mother and Anya, and the rest had taught him that, taught him to wonder. They had done their best to rid him of whatever naiveté he possessed, but had also stressed the importance of keeping a crucial part of it. He was a child, like all people, and that part of him had to remain, like it had in Judith, and Sivert and Kimberly and many of the others.

He sat for a while with his head between his knees and listened, not closing his eyes, but mostly using his ears. He had learned to listen at an early age, learned so much.

Blanche stared at him with her burning, staring eyes. In those eyes he could study the Universe, if only he dared. She stood between two people on the floor, except that there was no available space there.

– Take comfort in the fact that it will be much worse, she teased him.

He didn't reply, had never enjoyed speaking to empty air.

– I'm leaving, now, she said with regret. – You won't see me again. From now on you must manage on your own. Remember what I told you.

She faded away. The final moment before she vanished completely he imagined that he had seen her change, to the face from his fever vision.

He missed her terribly. The sense of being abandoned cut into him like a widening wound.

– «He will come for you», she had said. – «He will come for you all».

After a few minutes the inactivity grew unbearable. He walked to the window again and pulled everyone away before they had a change to step aside.

The truck shook constantly on the bumpy road. He felt some modest pleasure over the fact that it hadn't been repaired for years. He saw the sand blow in the wind, flow like a gray blanket above land and road. His fellow passengers crouched in misery. He laughed at them. They were prisoners on their way to an unknown and beyond unpleasant destination and they worried about a little sand, about stuff like that?

He caught himself. They probably didn't know what he knew, that the soil in western Norway and increasingly in the mountains was more fertile than ever.

He had no idea how long he had been awake. He felt a thorough, manifested exhaustion, not the one forcing him to sleep, but another, far more fundamental fatigue. His vision almost failed him. Empty blocks of flats towered along the highway, like props in an unreal western. Everyone knew the buildings were made of cardboard, but everyone held on to the illusion. Not even the truck seemed real. He couldn't recall the last time anything had felt real to him.

The trucks eventually stopped, but their cargo didn't. The powerful lights blinded the prisoners when the cattle door opened. They were chased like beasts to the slaughter. Magnus instantly corrected himself. They had been fed. He knew they hadn't been brought here to die, at least not until they had been useful for a while.

He kept wondering, scouting his surroundings, pondering their situation, wondering what awaited them at the end of the line. He tried to think, to analyze, in vain. Fingers dug into his face. It didn't work. Illumination eluded him.

There were no civilians anywhere, only ragged soldiers and other uniformed people. The arrivals from the ferry were marched from the truck to a train, a cargo coach without windows, but with plenty of holes in the walls. The railway station was a dusty landmark and hardly even that.

The door to the cargo coach closed and locked with a crack. He felt closed off from everything, from the generous nature he dimly recalled. Everything here was dead.

Except him.

The stench of burned coal ripped into his nostrils. This was an old steam locomotive, a historical treasure once more brought to life by circumstances. He imagined the sight of the stoker loading chunks of coal into the inferno he could never quite escape from.

The holes in the wall were mostly small. He could only glimpse the outside through them. The rails turned and the rusty metal screamed. He heard the sand rub against the wheels. Progress was slow. Sometimes the train didn't seem to be moving at all.

The stench of vomit mixed with that of burned coal. People couldn't keep the rotten food down. Everything mixed into nothing. The boy stared with longing at the distant mountains, reaching out to them with his mind. That mind could fly part of the distance, but the body could not follow.

He sat on his spot, brooding. No one bothered him. No one dared. The pressure within grew. The pain and misery fed him far better than the food did. He saw the fear of those surrounding him, heard their whisper.

– You wish to get out of this room, away from me, he said aloud. – You're more afraid of me than the dire situation where we find ourselves. Know that I spit on you, you daring to call yourself human beings.

Nothing more was said. There was no more talk.

He believed he had slept, but couldn't say for certain, when he sensed a draft in the air. His eyes swept the room. He turned his head several times, but saw no bigger hole in the walls. They hadn't stopped, hadn't slowed down. He lost interest. His head fell between the knees again. He was resting, but did not truly sleep, not deeper than he could wake up merely by opening his eyes.

It was raining. At least that was the thought that first struck him when he heard the sound of something resembling droplets hit the outside wall. But when he saw the dust pulled through the holes and people began coughing hard, he realized it was sand, grains of sand striking the coach. It stopped after a while, and a relative silence entered their existence anew. People seemed to finally have realized their dire circumstances. They kept their mouth shut. He closed and opened his eyes, rubbing his tongue against the palate in order to make the saliva flow.

– Are we dreaming? A thin voice asked.

A small boy looked up at him. It dawned on Magnus that the tiny creature was talking to him.

– Is this a nightmare? The boy asked.

Magnus shook his head, not so much denying it, but more because he shared the boy's desire to get an answer to that crucial question.

– The train goes round and round, a voice squeaked, – and we're not going anywhere.

He couldn't decide whether or not it belonged to a man or a woman, human being or an animal.

– This eternal daylight... another picked up the pace, – ... is this Hell, or a place where the sun never sets?

– Shut the fuck up! Another barked from the other side of the room.

The silence returned quickly. They didn't have the necessary energy to keep it going.

Magnus looked outside again, seeing no signs that the sun would ever set.

– The sun must be on its way down, logically speaking, one claimed. – I mean, it's always on its way down, even when it's on its way up...

They heard a crack and a scream of pain, and that was it.

Someone whispered here and there, but didn't raise their voices. Magnus had learned to read lips, but still appreciated the somewhat lasting silence. His eyes closed again. An ironic smile formed around his mouth.

They were finally fed, given food and water. The train didn't stop. A solid steel door they hadn't noticed earlier opened, and a large table was rolled in. People were brushed off like dust. The food and plastic bottles with water were thrown on the floor. The table was pulled back out. The door closed.

The food might not be too bad, but Magnus couldn't decide one way or another. He fed like a machine, without really tasting anything, wondering in a detached way if the guards had put anesthetics in the food or in the water or both. He didn't notice anything, but the others turned even calmer, like domestic animals after being fed.

Time stretched out. He lost any sense of time and place. The train moved on.

When he once more looked up, there was still bright day. This time, when he felt the draft in the air he didn't doubt that it was something significant. The train hadn't slowed down, but something happened or was about to happen. The boy, the small boy that had spoken to him earlier stood by a hole. His features told better than words in a book that something was going on. Magnus stood up. His back hurt, but the pain didn't stop him, didn't slow him down the slightest. The train slowed down. This time he didn't imagine it. He joined the boy by the hole, looked outside and froze.

He didn't know exactly what he had expected at arrival, if he had indeed expected anything, but whatever speculations he had done couldn't even begin to compare with this.

The cattle door opened wide. The light reached them undiluted and blinded them. They were kicked and struck and pushed outside. The air stank of acid. Throats burned and many crouched. Magnus had known some bad air quality in his short life, but nothing compared to this.

The condemned stood huddled together on a platform by something resembling a Disney version of a classic Norwegian railway station, but Magnus's entire attention was locked on the structure towering above them. Magnus, son of Lene looked at an enormous steel construct encircled by thick pipes filling everyone's vision, and they weren't even that close to it. They were still a long road off from the «city gate», several hundred meters away.

The noise hammered them and made them deaf, blind and numb. Large and horrible construction machines worked ceaselessly to raise further the structure already blocking the very sun from the sky. The crowd of refugees was brought into the fairly big hall, one way too small to house all of them. They were lined up towards a passage, a gate with many soldiers waiting for them. Even in here they heard the numbing noise of the machines.

Some had to be pushed forward. Others were eager to clear up «the misunderstanding». He heard them shout to be heard, when they finally seemed to face what they felt had to be the immigration officer, how they had been misplaced, how they could contribute, as doctors, engineers, teachers and so on. The contemptuous laughter made them shrink in their tracks.

Everyone was chained and headphones were placed on their heads. The noise faded away and the Voice began speaking to them. It made them shake their heads in distress after just a few seconds. No one could tear off the headphones. They were well secured and everyone's hands had been chained behind their back. Some attempted to rub themselves against each other in a desperate effort to get rid of the incessant Voice. They were beaten so brutally that it discouraged the rest from repeating their mistake. Through the Voice they were promised eternal servitude and hardship, and nothing more. Breathing masks were placed over their mouth and nose. Magnus looked for the woman he connected with the Voice, but didn't see her. He felt fairly relaxed, removed from what was happening. He suspected that his eyes looked just as distant as all the rest gathered here.

The walk to their final destination proceeded at a quick pace. Dolls moved like this, with shaky, monotone steps. The short chain between the ankles allowed them to walk, but just with small steps. Those attempting to do more stumbled and fell, and were beaten soundly.

He turned his head, not looking behind him, but turning his attention towards what he couldn't even be certain existed: the mountains in the west.

– Are we dreaming? The same thin, boyish voice asked. – Is this a nightmare or is it truly happening?

The big boy, the much bigger boy shook his head, while they were driven forward, like cattle, like sheep, like ants, first into the deep shadow of the construct, then beneath it,

into the belly of the beast.
– I've never been able to tell.
++++++++++++++++++++++
Somewhere by the coastline, in southern Norway.
Waves struck the rough-edged landscape.
Two muscular men dressed in black suits studied the large, steady racer boat braving the insanely high waves. They waited inside, protected by the fortified walls and glass. The house was well above current ocean levels, but the waves still struck the windows.
The two exchanged glances. A slight anxiety rocked their carefully crafted calm.
– Time to get going, one of them said.
– The moment is long overdue, the other nodded.
They took the elevator down in the basement. The engine operated like well-oiled machinery, virtually silent. They hesitated a bit when the door slid open and revealed the overbuild quay, a place not quite protected from nature's rage. A thousand small droplets from the sea struck them.
The boat approached, emerging from high waves to waves not quite that high, those reaching into the boathouse. The boat didn't stop but hit one of the walls and instantly burst into flames. A few seconds passed. The two men exchanged glances again. More seconds passed. A giant of a human being appeared by the rail and jumped casually down on the quay. Long, fair hair blew in the wind. He was impeccably attired. They watched him straightening his tie, before he, with regret tore it off.
– Is everything ready? He inquired.
– Very much so, Mr. Russel. Welcome to Norway!
– Thank you, Victor Russel, said cheerfully. – I've wanted to come here for a long time, but the opportunity never seemed to present itself… until now. But now, gentlemen, the mother of all opportunities is here.
He started walking and the other two followed him. There was a loud explosion. More smoke and flames rose from the boat. Russel showed no sign of having noticed. Flames began licking the wall of the boathouse. The two in the reception committee exchanged more glances. Fear and expectation warred for dominance in the unmoving faces.
– Everything is ready, one of them repeated with a coarse voice. – We have…
He held back. They followed Russel out of the house and up the hill. After just a few seconds they had all become soaking wet. They followed him without thought, without considering alternatives. He seemed to know exactly where he was headed. The three men, so large compared to other humans drowned in the storm and the violent nature surrounding them. The house behind them had become completely submerged in fire. Soon, in just a few, short years no more than traces of it, of the ruin it was fast becoming would remain.

PART FIVE:
THE TWILIGHT STORM

«We had scarcely sat down to rest when darkness fell, not the dark of a moonless or cloudy night, but as if the lamp had been put out in a closed room.

You could hear the shrieks of women, the wailing of infants, and the shouting of men; some were calling their parents, others their children or their wives, trying to recognize them by their voices. People bewailed their own fate or that of their relatives, and there were some who prayed for death in their terror of dying. Many besought the aid of the gods, but still more imagined there were no gods left, and that the universe was plunged into eternal darkness forevermore».

Pliny the younger - eyewitness to the obliteration of Pompeii

CHAPTER TWENTY-TWO

It had just been raining, a violent shower making water flow in the streets. But it hadn't cooled down the air, like it would have done in bygone years. The hot moisture had only grown more pronounced. Clothes and hair were constantly soaked in sweat. To walk felt like moving under water. Even walking around practically nude felt like having a constant layer of humidity covering the skin.

Fog drifted in from the sea. Steam rose from broken pipes. The harbor drowned in water from the sea. Houses drowned. The ground floor was abandoned. Streets still above sea level were empty of people. Only a few people dared going out this evening. Bright summer nights tempted few, if anyone at all. People didn't come here anymore. Some had moved, but most stayed in their dank houses, shaking in the hot summer night. Not even the bright morning made them go outside. Empty stomachs, empty minds screamed with hunger.

Garbage floated in the streets and the stench invaded every house, every single home within the city's closed-in system. No one had made any effort at removing it in a long, long time.

It started off as a sound, one so integrated in their collective consciousness that they hardly needed their ears to hear it. They closed all windows, but it was no use. The sound couldn't be removed from their troubled thoughts.

The marching started early in the morning. Even most of the soldiers stayed inside during curfew, but at dawn they filled the streets. They marched in their worn uniforms. They, too, screamed with hunger, hungering for anything filling their belly and mind. Older children, boys and girls from the junior troops walked first, playing marches, striking the drums with empty, dull eyes. Water penetrated everything, and the Storm approached, like a phantom menace at the edge of the eyes. Heavy military boots splashed through the water flooding the streets.

People rushing to their jobs, passing the burned out ruin of a police headquarters cast stolen glances at it. Those not having a job, those having nothing to distract them from the ruthless reality stayed in their humid prisons resembling apartments. The attack on the headquarters had been mentioned in established media, and the ruins, the bloodstained ruins had been photographed and documented, but that was also the final event even resembling real news that was shown. All the remaining channels showed entertainment 24/7, interrupted once each hour by strict men and women preaching Law and Order, conveying strict guidelines for «correct behavior». Damon and the wolf clan didn't see much to it, since they mostly stayed away from bigger population centers and popular entertainment, but what they did see more than reminded them of Marseille, Prague and Berlin.

– There's still the absolute chaos in there, Vladek reported. – No one is certain who is in charge, if anyone is anymore, but they've started registering people and raiding islands like Sotra and Osterøy, even inland areas like Øystese and Norheimsund. They will come here, soon.

They sat around the campfire, like they did ever more often.

– Whether or not they will have time enough… Damon looked at them all, – … our time here is done, like we've known for quite some time that it would be.

They glanced stealthily at him, at his new look, at how the invisible aura around his body seemed to pulse and glow.

– So very true! Anya stated. – Our future isn't here, but *in there,* the last and final hiding place, where we no longer have to hide.

– Everything is ready, André shrugged. – There's no excuse to delay our flight any longer.

– We know that most military units have left the mountains, Myriam stressed. – They've relocated to the various city states and declared their loyalty to their residing rulers. There's no way of telling how many who are left. It will be hard enough just to get away from Fortress Bergen. We should have left long ago, but the inland has crawled with soldiers. We now know that not that many remain. Our odds aren't like we would have wished...

– They rarely are, Dominic said cheerfully.

– ... but we *are* well prepared. Together and as individuals we will once and for all *claim* our humanity.

– And we will KEEP claiming it, Anya shouted, – beyond all ashes.

They shouted and cried and responded in earnest to her. Their loud shouts filled the night.

++++

They crossed the Askøy Bridge on their way to town with three buses late the next evening, further delayed. One of the engines hadn't started, and they wished to start out with three transport vehicles. They worked with a fervor surpassing even their most passionate moments. The buses were basically for them, for transport of people. They didn't bring more than they could carry.

Sunlight bathed the inside of the buses. The sky was blue, except for the pitch black cloud in the southwest, there wasn't a single cloud in the sky.

Their eyes kept glancing at that cloud. It pulled them in, like a giant vacuum cleaner.

The wind was blowing, blowing hard. The queue moved slowly across the bridge, and the giant human construct whimpered and complained to the point of resembling a living being.

Damon blinked. The surroundings turned gray and wet, and he saw the storm unfold. He blinked again and it faded. His reality returned to the present.

Everyone looked at the Sotra Bridge further out in the sound. It was obviously in far greater trouble, swaying violently from side to side, practically jumping up and down.

– The wind is far stronger out there, Yngve mumbled. – We should be safe, though.

He smiled ironically at the second part of his own statement.

They heard the Sotra Bridge groan in pain, saw its thick iron cable moorings give.

They found themselves at the top of the bridge bow, at the point where the road bent downward. Everyone watched as the Sotra Bridge collapsed, saw in unexplainable detail how cars and people fell into the frothing sea. Small, distant explosions filled ears and eyes, and the drive across the bridge seemed indefinite, never ending.

They finally reached the other side, driving into the tunnel, the dark, dark tunnel. Its lights had failed long ago. In spite of the bus headlights, it seemed like they drove through a vast, total darkness. They reached its end after something they feared was an eternity. The blinding light at the other side and subsequent tears filled their eyes.

On the right side of the road the sea had long since flooded the biker trail. It had been a nice beach ride once. Now, it was just another sea bed.

Everyone exchanged glances, unable to meet each other's flickering eyes.

They drove into another tunnel. Everything looked worse, even worse here. They saw traces of fires and wrecks. Not all the wrecks had been removed either. It looked like a disaster area, an endless stretch of calamity incarnated. The bright summer evening between the tunnels appeared downright unreal to them. In the darkness, in the shadows they saw so much better how the world worked. They all saw the light play in Kara's deep, deep eyes, saw her windows to the soul twinkle and burn.

– It… begins, she said with pain in her voice.

Suddenly, something changed. The wind was no longer blowing. Even if all the windows and doors were wide open, they could hardly register a single breath of air. In a matter of seconds the air pressure had changed to become very, very sultry and imposing.

The ground, the road outside glistened with humidity, appearing to be flooded with water. The sky kept its deep blue color. The sun kept burning the ground, making the wet ground seem even more of a mirage. One was tempted to believe that someone had stood there with a giant bucket of water and emptied its content over the soaking wet landscape.

The enormous black cloud, still far away filled the sky in the southwest. To them it resembled a bloodhound on the prowl, one that that would inevitably catch them in its already bloodied jaws.

A final message had reached them on the shortwave frequency from the now distant city of Stavanger ten minutes earlier. It had been disrupted in mid-sentence.

Most of the night sky still kept its light blue color above them, but they knew one of the year's brightest nights would soon become the darkest. They imagined they could see the beyond vast black cloud from above, see how it covered most of Europe, how Great Britain could no longer be seen because of the black monster covering the island. The very planet itself seemed to be shaking itself apart.

– We're not moving!

Maxine stamped the floor hard.

The queue moved like a snail in front of them. It lasted all the way to the central parts of town. Progress was slow, but noticeable. It was still faster than to walk or run. They reached the spot where the old toll booths had stood. Some vehicles left the main road and took the detour around Laksevåg, even if it was clear that that wouldn't help them.

They moved through another tunnel, another modern ongoing disaster area. Something was happening. They all felt it, in smaller and bigger ways.

– Do you hear… the fizz? Claire asked.

Anya nodded, with a shadow of a smile and of unrest.

– What fizz? Ralph asked irritated.

Claire wanted to say something, but found no words, and faded into her own mind.

Everyone sensed it in their depths. They had been drilled in empathy, in opening themselves to their instincts for so very long, now, and did not have the option of not sensing it. They looked with disapproval at Ralph.

– The roar, Claire shouted. – THE ROAR!

They seemed to be racing out of the tunnel on the city side of it. The rain splashed the windshield and all other sides of the buses. It had been quiet when they drove into the tunnel. Now, small and big vehicles shook in the powerful gusts. A big, gray blanket covered both the sky and the earth. There wasn't a single blue spot left up there. They felt the bridge shake before they reached it. It rocked and shook and groaned at is joints.

– That was like fuck, André mumbled.

There was a loud crack from somewhere, a sharp, singing sound, as if from a string breaking.

– No, *that* was like fuck, Yola grinned, suddenly very pale.

They looked anxiously around them. As they reached the bridge, they heard the sound again.

– It isn't the bridge, Dominic stated, both with certainty and doubt in his voice.

He rushed to one of the windows, but couldn't see much through the thick film of water.

The bridge still stood. None of its wires or joints had cracked. But the sound had been of a wire, a steel wire cracking. Damon frowned. He tore open a window and instantly turned soaking wet. He stared north, at all the oil exploration platforms lined up at Laksevåg. The sight echoed within him. He remembered. Almost everyone realized what was happening. Paolo had already left the lane, crossing over to the empty, ongoing, opposite lanes. Part of the middle of the road blocking was long since gone. He crashed into a piece still there and demolished it completely. The two other busses followed suit. All the Nightravens stared stunned at the incredible sight of the oil exploration platforms rocking and dancing towards them. They were still fairly far away, but raced towards the bridge at an ever higher speed. In 1994 one single platform had been stopped by a sandbank. Now the sea had risen too much for that to happen.

The bus started sliding, doing so abruptly, without visible, discernible cause.

– SATANA! Paolo cursed in Italian.

He barely managed to retake control. The busses rocked and danced and balanced on a knife's edge in the Storm. More cars broke the line, but most remained, their drivers dancing the death dance with a passive, empty stare. Sirens approached from the Laksevåg side and from the city side both.

– Drive on, Damon ordered casually.

Paolo had already pushed the pedal as far as it went.

– The sounds weren't from the first moorings breaking, Myriam said, – but the last.

That was a very accurate statement. The first platforms had already been on their way before they reached the bridge. Now the one in front towered above the bridge like an angel of death. The Nightravens could see it wings.

The armored bus hit the closest police car and pushed it back at the rest. The loud whining of tires overwhelmed momentarily the sound of the Storm. The other police cars tried turning around in order to pursue them. Several of them turned over. The wind grabbed one and pushed it through the rail and into the empty air. The first platform hit the bridge. Everything shook violently. Paolo finally and irrevocably lost control of the bus. It fell over on the side. The metal screeched while it slid on the asphalt. The force of its movement pushed it on, towards the tunnel a while ahead. It raced past the bus shed with the other two on its tails. Thunder cracked and lightning flared in the air. Damon blinked, wondering if it was in truth thunder and lightning. With all the noise and the sparks flying around, he couldn't say for certain. The second platform in the queue hit the first. The middle part of the bridge vanished. Many cars, including the police vehicles vanished with it. The screams rose from the dead and dying, and those watching. During a fairly short time span everything had been transformed from a slow pace, from relative calm to a total, encompassing chaos. Damon and the others strived to find anything to grab hold of. They did and held on to it with all their strength. Everything seemed strangely calm within the buses. They looked at the twisted features of other drivers. Sparks kept up until they reached the water that had flooded the tunnel weeks ago, and slid on on its surface. Water flooded the buses. The front vehicle hit the tunnel wall right by the entrance, not very hard. The long slide had slowed them down considerably. They were still pushed forward, at chairs, walls and windows. The other buses hit the first.

They stopped. The buses stopped. They stopped. The buses sank twenty, thirty centimeters before it hit the bottom and stayed there. The water surrounded them, but not very dangerous, more like a valve on heated thoughts.

The silence dominated for a moment, until the roar of the storm reached them anew.

Damon looked up, attempting to shake off the dizziness. The door had been torn open, almost like an invitation. He wondered if he was looking at the tunnel ceiling, or straight into an unfathomable abyss. He turned his head. The windshield had been broken. The way out was clear.

– UP! He shouted. – OUT!

Everyone from the tree buses made it. Some rubbed their head, some walked on unsteady feet, but they could walk. They were bleeding from small wounds, but all seemed healthy. He felt an enormous sense of relief.

They rushed towards each other, hugging each other, while involuntarily glancing back at the bridge. It collapsed completely that very second. A cluster of oil exploration rigs floated through the rift without any sort of obstruction.

Everything had happened so fast, so unimaginable fast.

Damon looked around. He was already to his knees in water, a few steps into the tunnel, where the road tilted downwards. He stared at the queue on the side road leading to the central parts of the city. The queue had stopped moving completely. That was just not an option anymore, in any way. The use of machines had become obsolete, a total bust. He felt both joy and a cold chill. It was happening.

It was happening!

His fellow tribe members gathered around him. Everyone had become soaking wet.

– We knew this could happen, he said, – even that it was likely to happen. There may be no other option than to walk all the way to the distant mountains. Let's do it!

– The path through the city would have been the shortest, with all things being equal. André shook his head. – Would have been.

They ran up the hill, to the Heights. The wind hadn't reached the same level as it had on the bridge here yet. It still tore at them, tore them bit by bit to pieces. Through the portal, the short passage to the former University area a violent suction made several of them lose their balance. The others helped them up, pulling them onward. People ran back and forth around them, without quite knowing which direction to run. Lightning started filling the sky. Lightning and thunder reached them simultaneously. There was more than one crack and flash. Heaven and earth cracked in countless small pieces.

– Hell! Yngve shouted. – Blackest Hell!

One tree broke and shot into the air, like it was being fired from a gun. It landed twenty meters away and smashed an entire wall of windows. An ear-shattering crack made everyone fall to the ground. They stayed down, anxiously wondering what would happen next.

– THE OIL TANK, a man running past them shouted. – A lightning strike BLEW IT APART!

Myriam smiled relieved, giving the others encouraging waves. They jumped on their feet and ran on. Thick, black smoke rose into the air northwest of them. A giant campfire burned and warmed everyone. The flames mixed with the lightning, the electrical storm in the air, a mighty, compelling disco of nature. Several people in the crowd froze and stared at it with empty eyes. Several shots were fired. Some people directed their guns at themselves. The lightning started hitting buildings. Terrible, powerful discharges blew them to pieces. The tribe, the two, three, four half moons reached the central parts of the stone desert at the other side of the Heights, after something resembling an eternity rushing through the storm of fire and electricity and a wind penetrating everything.

The wind no longer came from any specific direction. It was just as strong no matter which direction they turned. There was no shelter anywhere. They could run from the flames, but not the fire, not the wind and the rain and the lightning. Garbage floated in the air like it was lighter than air. It stayed afloat, not even coming close to the ground.

All over the city and everywhere close to it, people left their homes and started on their long walk. Some did it with some sort of plan in mind. Others just did it. The soldiers began firing. Some of them cried out and reminded people of the curfew, but most of them just started firing. The air was filled with the sound of people firing weapons. People were hit. People returned the fire, catching the uniformed men and women in a massive crossfire. The soldiers were massacred. They stopped firing. Flickering eyes glanced at the sky and the ongoing calamity, and the soldiers joined in on the running, the leaving of the city. People cheered and shot the fleeing uniformed dolls in the back.

Most of those running didn't manage to run very far before they had to slow down. Ever more flickering glances looked back, and they started running again.

After a while people fired at the soldiers, armed or unarmed the moment they spotted them, but eventually they grew tired of it and stopped.

Scores of casually gathered groups fought themselves through the city. Just the feat of standing upright demanded an inhuman effort. With each new step forward the wind threatened to unbalance their footing.

Damon shook his head.

– We have no choice, he shouted. – We must seek shelter!

They looked around them, studying hard all the nearby brick buildings. Damon, after seconds of indecision pulled out a gun and started firing at the nearest candidate. The bullets struck the wall inside, through the open door and windows without glass. There were no screams, no reaction or response. All drew their weapons and advanced cautiously towards the seemingly empty room. The first of them reached it. There were no other people inside.

A few of them chuckled in relief. They crouched there, in the humid twilight, constantly on guard, looking for possible approaching threats.

A car flew by outside. It crashed into a tree and broke it in two.

– This is supposed to be the weaker front of the storm?
No one could tell who had spoken. The voice was so coarse that it had become unrecognizable.
Maxine looked at her right wrist, at the watch that was no longer there, a habit she never seemed to break.
They huddled there, a timeless time. The stem of a tree broke without anything crashing into it, broke like a dry twig. The howling wind never seemed to leave their ears.
Kara frowned. She rose and walked forward. Maxine attempted to grab her and hold her back, but Kara was too quick. She walked to the doorway.
– Do you guys hear that?
They realized that they had no trouble hearing her, and that they hardly heard anything else. It had turned quiet outside. Kara knew before she reached the threshold. The others followed her. Everyone joined her in streets where there was no longer any wind to speak of. They glanced uncertain at each other.
– How long were we in there? Maxine asked.
– Ten, fifteen minutes tops. Vladek shook his head. – The storm lasted longer than other storms of this type, but…
They got the implicit of his words, and didn't join in on the general celebration.
People hugged each other and cheered, and were once again ready to rebuild their lives following the old, destructive pattern.
– It's not over, Damon cried out to them, not to his tribe.
They stopped and stared at him as if they didn't see him, anxious and angry.
– Do you truly believe this is what we saw on the satellite images, or that it is sufficient to explain the giant black cloud? He spoke with venom in his voice. – Are you truly so lacking in basic rational thinking?
They stared at the wild beast in their midst and didn't dare doing what they wanted to do. They wanted to tear him to pieces, but only stood there and glared at the ground.
A man stepped outside what was clearly his house and stopped on its stairs. Sea water reached him to his legs. He didn't seem to notice that his feet had become wet.
– It's only natural variations, he choked, – nothing but NATURAL VARIATIONS
A man stepped closer to Damon. He looked fairly bright and rational.
– I've heard things making it all even worse, he stated, glancing nervously at everyone, as if he feared they would attack him like wild animals at any moment.
– Please, speak, Anya encouraged him.
– I heard that the West Antarctic Ice Sheet has broken off from the mainland, *completely* broken off. That alone is sufficient to raise sea levels with at least six meters, right?
– Is that recent? Myriam asked him.
– It's hard to tell these days, he replied. – I think they've set the news on repeat. There was a lot of other news as well, none of them good.
– It's only natural variations, the man on the stairs shouted, – nothing but NATURAL VARIATIONS
Damon nodded and turned towards the crowd again.
– I think it's wise to view this little storm as a precursor to what's coming, he said ironically, – «sent» to test your defenses, if you wish. Perhaps that will make it easier for

you to comprehend what we're facing.

He drew breath before continuing.

– I'll tell you what we're facing, what we must challenge and embrace the coming days, weeks, moons, years is untamed nature, like our ancestors did every second of the day ten thousand years ago.

A man crouched on the other side of the street. An iron pole had penetrated his body. He was fading as they watched.

– I'M DYING! The man wailed.

– Then die, Terrill told him. – Why make such fuzz about it?

He kept going, speaking to everyone present.

– Gaia's rage has been gaining strength for untold seasons. Now, the dam is breaking and the water is flooding. Nature has taken everything we've thrown at it, and now it's fed up, now retribution is coming.

He stood there with a raised fist, suffering and passionate, a human being no longer holding any emotion or nuances of emotion back.

The man with the pole through his body exhaled one final time and died.

People pulled back, removing themselves from what was burning in front of them, doing it in order to keep themselves from getting burned.

The nightravens faced each other, looking around them at the devastation in savage joy.

– We're all still alive, Myriam said stunned, – with only a few bruises to show for it. It's almost too much of good luck. It won't last!

They started laughing in pure happiness, feeling the joy of breathing, of living.

While they left the stone desert, what to a growing degree resembled a ghost town, they felt the fire within grow even stronger, more powerful. They passed the ruined shopping mall that once had been the city's main post office, the fallen city hall, the ruin of a police station. They walked through streets that had become beaches, seeking higher ground in order to avoid the worst of the rising sea. The sea rise had clearly become an observable process. Second by second, minute by minute they imagined that they could actually see it happening. They walked through what had been Øvregaten (upper street) that for practical purposes had been rechristened New Beach Street. They kept to the upper parts of town, as they left it behind forever.

Time folded and refolded upon itself. The date showed May twenty-fifth, 2015 (western, christian time frame), and humanity's time had finally come.

++

The rain fell hard from the sky and all loud voices were softened by the sound of the water flowing everywhere. Screams from despairing and desperate people sounded more like wails or even whispers from throats too dry to elicit sound. Some people crouched by the roadside, hardly moving at all. They had lost everything in their possession and didn't have breath left to give voice to their horror. Some of them did move, waving their arms and screamed loud enough to attract attention. They were given a few brutal, indifferent kicks, beaten into submission by people passing by. Some of them were robbed of their clothes, of whatever scarce possessions they had left. No one made any attempt at aiding them, aiding destitute and lonely people robbed by groups of scavengers roaming the roads. There were those walking to them, giving them pale comfort afterwards, but only half-hearted, an imagined memory from a former life.

A family stumbled on. The father and the mother carried one child each. The other children followed with frozen features and empty stares.

Smoke drifted in the air, a mist in the body, mind and soul.

Several buildings were on fire. The heavy showers didn't seem to affect that at all.

Some people were kneeling and praying. Others shouted at the heavens while continuing their stumble.

– HELP US, GOD! PLEASE, HELP US! YOUR HUMBLE SERVANTS CALL UPON YOU.

Some people were just screaming. Suffering lingered in the air like an explosion lasting forever.

The nightravens shook their heads in dismay and kept moving on.

No one could tell how long they had walked, how long they had moved, existed in this gray mass. The rain had started small, almost cautious, and once more there had been cheers of relief among the easily swayed parts of the refugees. It felt so long ago, now. One could recognize, if one made an effort the stretch north of the city, the blocks of flats reaching into the gray mist. No one knew when the day had started, if it had started. The darkness had fallen when the night had seemed to be ending. Watches had stopped working. Nothing electric worked anymore, nothing artificially electric. They heard the sound of thunder, still distant, and if they looked south they could still spot a few lightning bolts, but they were gray, inverted, without potency. A rope hit a flag pole in a constant, repetitive motion and added to the horror of the ghostly surroundings. The rain fell straight down. There was no wind… but everything still moved. The thud of the rope hitting the flag pole sounded strangely sharp, in spite of the humidity in the air muting everything else.

All people moved in the same direction. The broad highway pointed north, not into the country, but it led to another road that did. The entire wide road was covered by both wrecks and cars probably still in good working condition. Anya turned and looked back. There was nothing there, except more wrecks, more people walking their long road.

The Nightravens were running, walking and running again. They already felt exhausted, but kept at it, filled with an energy most of the others stumbling around clearly didn't possess. They passed the cluster of urban shopping malls that had been such an important part of most people's former life.

– Each afternoon people visited these monsters, Yngve noted. – Each afternoon they fooled themselves into buying lots of stuff they didn't really need.

– And what they did need was choking them with poison, Gwen snorted.

They ended that conversation early, turning their back to it, like everything else except what was ahead.

Gwen brightened, her face visibly changing.

– It's happening, she stated excitedly. – It's all really happening!

They continued their long walk. The monuments of the past were far behind and they always would be.

Anya looked behind her several times. The others saw her exhibiting small signs of worry, saw those signs grow, until she eventually stopped and turned around. Everyone stopped, also quite a few people not members of the tribe.

Damon saw it. He saw Styx, the river of knowledge, death and life crawl towards them, saw it flooding the horizon.

– We can't postpone it any longer, she said. – We must seek higher ground.

Damon scouted the hillside to the right, the only one available to them.

She turned towards them, and gasps of terror and astonishment echoed in the crowd. In her eyes danced a greenish, mystical fire. It wasn't something they imagined, but something that was actually happening. Her very face seemed to have changed. They couldn't quite tell what that change was, but they saw a different or a changed face. She was changed! The costume was gone, of course, in the hard rain and circumstances, but that had always been only the physical surface she revealed to the world, not her inner being, what she now revealed to everyone.

They departed from the highway with large jumps, pouring energy into their muscles, because they had to. Everything turned indistinct around them. They didn't feel the fatigue anymore. They imagined they heard the loud roar right behind them, knowing it to be a false impression. Whatever they heard, they didn't hear with their ears.

There were still trees, even wild trees left in the valley. They raced towards them, passing houses, houses mostly empty, but also some where people crouched and hid, closing the lid of their coffins. Finally, after something resembling years, the ravens of the night reached the forest. They kept running up the hillside, leaving behind the final asphalt-covered road.

Loud, desperate screams, whimpering howls that would make any voice crack reached their ears.

– How far away? André wondered stricken.

– Central Bergen, probably farther.

– The Earth itself is screaming, Claire said in pain, in relief.

They heard, heard what they had heard for weeks and months, but now it turned real to them.

– I can see the skeletons rot, Damon mumbled.

He glanced at the others. Had he said anything?

They found a natural hole in the ground, a… hollow, not too deep, a somewhat protected spot in the terrain. There were several trees there, a sufficient number. They tied each other to them, hard, painful. Attempts at smile, laughter faded quickly. Damon, Anya and Myriam tied themselves to the thick stem pushing at their back. Everyone stood there and waited for the inevitable. They glanced at each other with eyes filled with anxiety and longing, their attention slowly drawn to the horizon in the southwest.

It… was coming. At first they couldn't quite connect to it, to what they saw. Their brain strived to properly interpret the visuals.

They saw it, at full force, a wave, a wall of water hundred meters tall, the precursor to the Storm, the first tiny sign of what was coming. When they had convinced themselves that it was close, it was in truth still far away. They saw how it consumed everything in its path. Trees were razed off hilltops. The wave roared so loud that its voice cracked their eardrums. Cars flew through the air. Straw huts reaching for the sky collapsed like houses of cards. All talk faded and only action remained. The wave ravaged the lower areas in their vision. During just a few, brutal seconds the valley was reduced to the primitive, natural landscape it had once been. Damon observed how everyone drew breath, how they did everything they were supposed to do. He, himself drew breath and closed his mouth… just in time.

The water flooded them. It hammered them, pushing air from their lungs. They wanted to draw breath, wanted it desperately. They held that instinct at bay, until they almost blacked out. Even long after they no longer had any air left to lose, they kept holding back. They caught brief glimpses of each other during the ruthless onslaught, ghostly shapes growing and fading in and out of reality. Damon heard screams, heard ropes break.

Steam rose in the air. They imagined it like a wall. The water pulled back, almost like a waterfall, until it no longer did anything but washing their shoes and ankles.

Anya stood frozen with her back to the tree, her eyes wide and terrified. The rope had fallen to the ground at her feet. Before he had managed to free himself she threw herself at him, clinging to him, beside herself with fear and shame.

– Sorry, she sniffed. – Sorry!

– Don't be silly! Ha said. – Why apologize? You've got just as much right to be scared as the rest of us. You're not a goddess!

– Heh, heh! She pulled back and laughed a little. – You're really funny. That's also how I remember you.

The last comment was more than a little cryptic, but not compared to much of the other stuff she spoke about, and he let it go, giving her time to calm down.

– You're different, but the same! She stated.

The valley was different, but the same. Death had ravaged it. Life had ravaged it. They stared breathless at the incredible sight. All signs of civilization hadn't vanished, but there weren't much left. They stared at each other. Everyone had made it - again. Some of them coughed hard and gasped for air, but they were alive.

We're alive! Damon thought.

The wind started blowing. The gusts came and went, but seemed to be doubled in intensity every time. The wind had already grabbed them. It became just as much a constant in their lives as the rain.

– We've seen once again what we already knew, he said. – This is no place for us, for anyone who want to stay alive more than hours, a few days tops.

The mountains, suddenly so far ahead haunted their dreams. It had taken them only hours to drive there. Now, it felt like years away.

He stared at Anya. She nodded. He sensed a rock-hard determination in her.

The image of Anya faded away, never vanishing completely. It burned within him, boiling the chill away, doing so as he step by step made contact with the rocky ground. They ran through the heavy showers. There was no cold. The greenhouse-like heat kept that away, and the sweat warmed them and kept the rain from completely penetrating their clothes. The dryness in the mouth was kept away by the simple act of opening the mouth and drinking the rain. They had long since passed the moment when they were supposed to be exhausted. The transformed, totally unknown landscape seemed infinite. They felt with some confidence that they moved north and east, on their chosen path, imagined that they recognized certain familiar landmarks, glimpsing the remains of the old asphalt road here and there, but uncertainty kept haunting them. They found the tunnels after sometimes having searched for hours. The names, the blue signs with white letters were still there.

The dark landscape inside the manmade passages had practically been stuffed with wrecks. The dead still sat in their seats. It seemed more than probable that they had died ignorant. The water still flowed from the cars. Everything seemed insane beyond words.

The Nightravens clutched each other, held and rubbed those closest to them. The need for human contact burned within them.

The giant wave had made significant cuts in the crowds walking with the Nightravens. There were no bodies outside the tunnels. The water had washed away most of the dead. Those heading east had been reduced to about one third of their numbers. They were still too many too count. Numbers had become something surreal, abstract.

People stumbled forward, taking one more step in front of the other. The wind kept gaining strength. Lightning struck the mountaintops almost constantly, now. The earth and the sky had become one, singular mass. The Nightravens stayed close together, switched on running the gauntlet on the edge of the pack.

The rain didn't even resemble rain anymore, but sharp knives cutting and molesting everything.

They reached the crossroads, the major intersection where the tunnel further on led to Highway 16, leading east. The road to the opening had been completely disintegrated. The opening was still there. The wind hammered them. Everything kept hammering the small group.

The black hole towered above them. When they stepped into it, it seemed like they stood still, as if the hole swallowed them whole and they didn't move. The wind picked up even more, because of the suction created by the tunnel. This dark passage stretched on further than any other they had passed through. They couldn't run. Wrecks, sharp objects and bodies appeared or could appear at any time. They used one of their flashlights. Dead faces grinned at them. A man had been impaled on a bumper, and they caught themselves in wondering how that could have happened. His face retained the rigid mask of panic. It had frozen in the moment of death to this caricature of an expression.

An entire world awaited them, welcomed them in there. The wind struck them, tore at them. A car rocked upon another's roof. It kept rocking up there, threatening to fall at any time. A body hung from an open door. The safety belt had tied itself around the man's neck and strangled him. The dead swung back and forth, while his face glowed at them with its insane grin. Some people had died in a rain of bullets. Other bodies didn't have a scratch on them, but they were just as dead. Damon glimpsed shadows everywhere. He almost fired at them.

– I can see them, Kara whispered, – see the shadows, practically see what has happened here.

He could as well. It played and replayed in his inner vision.

– Several of us do, Anya said. – You shouldn't be afraid. The only thing making these shadows stand out is that they're more visible in their intensity. They're everywhere, really. Our surroundings are and will always be filled with spirits, both dead and alive.

– You guys are nuts.

André shook his head.

– You've seen so much and still you reject it, its undeniable truth? Anya shook her head in sadness.

Damon saw the dead, but also the shadows of his tribe. He saw them flash and fade in an endless flow of movement. He saw the shadow of his arm reach beyond the confines

of its flesh.
– We are on our way home! He whispered with happy conviction.
They didn't see the light at the end of the tunnel, but a glowing shadow. Thunder shook the ground, a deep rumble making the mountain itself rumble. They rushed out of the darkness into a different kind of darkness. Some of them glanced up, and their expression made everyone do so. They saw the dark cloud directly above. It covered only one third of the sky, but it still looked beyond menacing, like an eye staring at them.
– My God!
Dominic crossed himself and looked embarrassed at the others. No one noticed.
What they had seen on the satellite photos could in no way compare to this, how it looked in real life. Only the cloud's outer circle resembled an ordinary storm, with lightning and the violent shaking of the air. Its inner, deeper parts resembled in their minds how they had imagined a black hole. They stared into it, and imagined they were staring at Eternity.
– We can't stay here, Damon said, – can't stay out here.
They turned their heads and looked behind them, before returning in haste to the tunnel.
It took a while, but they finally found a spot fairly free of wrecks and stinking fumes. They crouched close to each other and remained like that, frozen in place, their eyes the only part of them moving. Looking out wasn't exactly hard. Sometimes they did, sometimes they didn't. The constant warm wind created favorable conditions. They didn't have to light a fire in order to dry their clothes. No one was freezing in their nudity. All the bodies stayed warm, warm in the cauldron of flesh and feverish minds. Everyone had become moving embers heating each other.
A wall of water raced past the tunnel outside. They saw nothing of the nature outside anymore, only the eternal wall of rain. They fed, consumed the food they had brought that wasn't smoked, that wouldn't stay fresh for very long. They felt hunger gnaw at their innards, their consummate feverish minds. The physical hunger made them search the empty and filled cars for smoked and salted food and they found far more than they could eat and carry. They had to pull themselves together to not eat too much.
– It's wise not to eat too much, Tove nodded. – It is to our advantage that we can acknowledge that, think and analyze even in the face of desperation.
– You're correct, Anya remarked, – but what is too much? We know that other animals can stuff themselves to the point of not having to eat for weeks. Lions can, and snakes as well. What is our limit? During our last age as hunter/gatherers we could practically hibernate in caves, at least partly living off the fat we gained during the summer and autumn. As with so many things we need to find our limits anew, trying and failing until we get it somewhat right.
– Don't you know such things?
– I'm no nutrition expert, Gerd, she said dryly.
– And let's not forget that an expert was hardly an expert in any area, Betty grinned.
They laughed a lot about that, in the minutes and years following that moment. It became their little private joke.
Betty and Tove had both handled the extreme hardship well, their hard exercise the last few years paying off. They also fit well in with the rest of the Riders of the Thunder Road in other, more fundamental ways. Betty blushed when Anya looked at her with

what she interpreted as approval.

Anya rose. Without the use of her hands she slipped in one single movement into an upright position. The hot wind was blowing in a constant flow from behind, from the front and from the sides. A flow of water, the biggest to this point washed her feet. The stench of the salt water ripped into their nostrils.

– We can't stay here, Anya said. – We're «safe» for the time being, but we can't stay.

Damon nodded. They all did. Visions, distinct and indistinct of the now so distant mountains shifted in and out of their consciousness.

They looked at the tunnel opening. They saw nothing there but the eternal wall of water. There were no landmarks, nothing solid to point at, only the sea floating by.

The cracks of thunder hammering them turned into one, ongoing stream of sound and sensations. Night and day became one. Anya and the tunnel wall became interchangeable. She walked around the campfire in uneven, broken circles.

– I'm the Carrier of Knowledge, she stated, obviously ironic and self-conscious, but not without a certain pride. – I carry many stories, many cheers around the table of life. Wrap the dark blanket well around your body and listen up.

They did, reaching wide and far. They looked both good-humored and passionate at the dancing shadow in their midst.

A group of people drove on a road, a well-lit road, with lamps and painted lines, but for every meter it still turned darker and darker, until they could no longer see it from the vehicle. They stopped it and walked outside, kept walking on the darkened road. The walk turned more difficult for each new step. Every time they lifted a foot, it seemed like they were moving through thick quicksand. The heart broke every time they put one foot in front of the other. But outside the road there was nothing, not even darkness, so they kept walking.

After a long, long time they were unable to measure, they arrived at a forest, a very dark and threatening forest. They wished to go back, but when they attempted to turn around, the road was no longer there. There was nothing except the Forest.

So, they took the crucial step forward, into the moist, dark place filled with trees, a forest without form, exit and entrance. They had never come here from the outside, never stepped into it, but always wandered here, through the invisible labyrinth.

There was nothing there, not even darkness, only an endless, eternal Nothing. They kept walking. They couldn't tell why. But they kept looking, for something they knew they would never find.

– And then, Anya ended her story, while the fire danced across her face, – they arrived somewhere. They had never experienced a place before, or they had forgotten that they had, so they didn't know what it was, but what they felt was that both eternity and infinity opened up to them, and in that very moment… they were born. In that very moment they emerged from their mother's womb.

Everyone stared startled at the sorcerer and at each other, and a huge smile transformed their faces, transformed their entire being. They stared stunned at each other while they realized what they had always known.

The rain whipped their faces. The four winds tore at every piece of their body. There was no longer any heaven, any earth, only the never ending flow of water. They had dressed in protective clothing from top to bottom, with solid, protective goggles covering their eyes. Only the mouth, only sore lips stuck out from the face mask. Their time in the «cozy» cave already felt like a distant past. The Long Walk continued. They hadn't spotted other faces, heard other voices in a very long time. The wanderers learned to recognize each other solely by the language of the deaf, the hand signals and body language. The pain in their collective memory softened, but the wound stayed open. They imagined that they were crossing a bridge, while on a bridge farther away the moorings started breaking. They heard the sound as if it originated from a spot close by. The lot of them reached the other side and believed they had reached safety at the other side of the boiling sound. Damon kept recalling Dominic's open mouth, glimpsing his face beneath the mask, as it had been during less desperate days. He watched with blind eyes as the torn wire pushed through his friend's chest. He re-experienced the moment when the ruined human body was pulled into the air and faded away in the mist and watery wasteland everywhere around them. He felt death touch him.

Dizziness threatened to overwhelm him, but he moved on. He kept putting one foot in front of the other.

There were fewer people around him. He registered that in his numbness. The storm continued unabated. It seemed to last forever, and if it weakened in any significant way, they couldn't detect it or decide whether or not it had. They glimpsed an islet somewhere in the fjord, one surrounded by mist. Sometimes they feared that the wind would tear the air from their lungs, and they pushed a flat hand at their mouth in a desperate, useless attempt at keeping that from happening. Other times they just crouched together in a hollow, clutching each other hard, before once again stumbling on. They had to take frequent breaks, often exhausted after only a few minutes of intense struggle. There were occasions when the storm seemed to lighten up, and an easier path revealed itself, but it hardly brought any relief.

It went on and on. They were half convinced, *convinced* that it would never end.

They slowly turned deaf in the eternal noise, slowly blind in the infinite, gray stretch, in the repetitive lightning. Then, at uneven intervals there was a brighter flash, a reminder that there was greater danger beyond their immediate proximity.

They made several attempts at walking higher up, to get away from the sea and the fjord, the risk of frequent floods, but the strength of the wind increased just a few meters up. Damon waved them all back down, shouting and gesticulating in order to be certain that everyone followed him. He was never quite positive that they had. Those disappearing didn't necessarily die. As far as he knew, they might only… disappear, fade away like ghosts.

He kept seeing shadows, and they didn't appear indistinct, without shapes, like everything else in the torn apart landscape. They turned ever more distinct.

They finally reached the major crossroads they had sought, by the Trengereid Turns. The path they most of all wished to go, went over Gullbotnen, went straight east and into the country. But the wind stayed just as bad. It hadn't calmed, as they had imagined or hoped for, and it started grabbing them, becoming irresistible just a few steps up the hillside. They had to turn back again, and set course northeast, towards Voss.

The first tunnel towered above them almost instantaneously. Then, there were more, more, more in a long, long row. Once, at the entrance of one the wind caught Maxine and pushed her through the air. They imagined they could hear her scream of pain when she hit the wall. Everyone rushed to her to help, but she rose on her own, on shaky legs. The arm hung down, at an impossible angle. Gwen, examining it signaled that it wasn't broken, but only sprained. The shoulder was dislocated. Gwen pulled hard. Maxine froze and opened her mouth, and this time they knew they heard her scream. Gwen grinned viciously. Maxine gave her the evil eye, seemingly not that grateful for being able to move her arm again.

They noticed that the terrain tilted downwards and each time they excited a new tunnel they came closer to the sea, the boiling sea again. They kept finding food in the wrecks, by many of the rotting bodies, but ever smaller amounts of it, and ever less that hadn't become inedible.

It turned quieter, in a way, perhaps because the roar in their ears became permanent, a filter against the eternal roar. But it didn't bring silence, didn't bring peace, but an ever stronger unexplainable unrest. Something seemed to be crawling beneath the skin, behind the eyes. The why of it finally dawned on them after the road made a turn, when they noticed the sand flooding the path in front of them.

They spotted fresh tracks in the sand, in the sand and the soil generously sharing the road ahead.

– The wind has calmed, André stated, – or the tracks wouldn't be there.

Uncertain smiles mixed with the unrest not leaving them.

They had reached a somewhat calm pocket between the mountains.

Damon studied the tracks. He didn't say anything but frowned, frowned visibly.

– You have so big feet, auntie, Gwen said and giggled nervously.

Damon rose and straightened. He didn't really have to look closer at the tracks.

Willy's eyes froze over, and also Anya's and Yola's. The why of it slowly dawned on several of the others.

– Be ready for anything! Damon stressed to them all.

He stated the obvious, the necessity they had had hammered into themselves time and time again. That told them everything they needed to know and made them nervous to the point of being downright shitty. They woke up from the numbness, from the paralysis they had experienced in the unending gray landscape.

Myriam studied the mountainsides through the powerful army binoculars, studied them piece by piece, area, by area, squinting her eyes in order to see better through the mist of water everywhere.

– We're very exposed here, she mumbled, – but we will always be, everywhere. We may relax. If anyone wanted to shoot us they would have done so already.

That brought more nervous laughter, more calm.

They walked like on needles around the turn, ready to explode in action. Nothing happened and they relaxed again. The next moment they saw or believed they saw movement, and everyone tensed once more. That rollercoaster of relaxation and calm stayed with them, time and time again. They had learned to focus by relaxing, to go from one extreme to the next.

It kept raining just as hard, straight down, now, a waterfall seemingly moving with them. Sight turned lousy no more than ten steps ahead.

They didn't follow the tracks, but the road, because they had to. Fear and uncertainty had settled in their bones. They walked on.

It didn't take long until monotony returned, until timelessness haunted them anew.

After a while they knew just as little of how long they had walked through the silence of the rain, as they knew how long they had fought themselves forward through tunnels and wind. Night and day remained one, indistinguishable impression. The separation of the earth and the sky could be glimpsed somewhere ahead, somewhere behind, but only as yet one more possible mirage in the wilderness.

The sky above them, the air surrounding them stayed the same, shimmering darkness. The twilight storm had finally come to Earth.

– I'm a raven flying through the mountains, Gwen sang, – a wolf chasing through the forest.

She kept humming, and they sensed the life and sensuality in her voice and moves. The scar didn't really dominate her face anymore, or they paid less attention to it.

They walked past a few houses, a dispersed settlement reduced to smithereens, to ruins, only sensing more up ahead. The houses seemed just as much like ghosts as the people. They appeared to be dissolved, far more a part of the landscape than actual buildings.

It was then that the Nightravens, the wanderers of the twilight storm heard something not far ahead, a chord, a disharmony in the ether both foreign and familiar.

– A choir? Vladek said incredulous.

– A choir, Damon confirmed curtly.

– It reminds me of my Catholic whims as a boy, Vladek recalled.

– This is far worse. This isn't a whim.

They passed another turn, a heap of soil, dispersed parts of ruins and garbage.

The storm had only passed through here, but still left unparalleled destruction in its wake.

They caught sight of the group of people almost instantly. Everyone sat out in the open. The Children of the Midnight Fire stuck their hands inside their jackets and found the guns that could withstand water. They could have drawn them fast as lightning if the need had been there.

– It *is* fucking Dung Heap, Vladek whistled.

A visible anxiety accompanied his words, one shared among those among them aware of what those condescending words signified.

A giant of a man towered above the biggest group of miserable individuals. Damon recognized him the moment Vladek did, confirming to himself what he had suspected since he spotted the footprints. He and the others had met Frank Moldhaug in the Norwegian mountains an eternity ago. Moldhaug was probably taller than even Victor Russel, but didn't possess the uncompromising savagery. Good ol' Frank was very calculating in everything he did and said.

Damon saw that easily as he studied the man, as he took his measure, and found his initial impression to be more than true.

The Nightravens sat down a considerable distance away from the other crowds, especially from those singing psalms. The people in the ruins slowly woke up, once again becoming aware of their surroundings. The Children of the Midnight Fire devoured more of their meager rations.

– Have days or mere hours passed since we started walking? Kara wondered.

– What does it matter? Paolo shrugged.

Gwen pushed herself at him, smiling enticingly. He pushed back.

All those gathered at the calm at the center of the Storm looked up a few times. It felt just as eerie every time. The air whirled and boiled in a forge hotter than any unnatural fire. Damon reached out a hand, and it was as if he could touch the Storm, partake in its fury.

Frank Moldhaug's preaching reached them, penetrating their defenses like dull blades. They made a considerable effort at ignoring it, in vain.

Damon heard Anya breathe beneath the mask, heard the blood boil in her veins and her heart beating faster. She began unwrapping the headscarf, the Arabian piece of clothing. Those watching her when she rose stared. The green fire once again danced in her eyes, permanently, Damon assumed.

The twilight, the gray rain didn't weaken in any way the power in them, in her. An enormous determination and will power were inherent in every move she made. She stared good-humored at Claire. Claire returned the stare with stubborn defiance.

– I can feel the rage, she said aloud, – feel the fear and the joy. My friends, we will soon be home.

Damon also rose. He kept his mask on. All of them rose. With the life and the shadow and the rainbow at the point, they started moving. They walked past smaller and bigger groups at the small place, the brief stop on the Thunder Road. People stared at them in fear and curiosity. Damon saw himself and the other riders on the storm through their eyes, saw the mirages not walking, but floating on air.

The sand floated in the air. There was no humidity there what so ever. Damon felt the desert and perspired hard in its close proximity.

When they sat down close to Moldhaug and his followers everyone there shifted uneasily on their spot.

The big man seemingly kept up his monotone monologue, quickly regaining the attention of his flock.

– Behold the two-legged hyena, Gwen said aloud and pointedly. – A scavenger for sure. One not necessarily lacking claws, but one preferring not to use them. One wandering aimlessly for an eternity in search of what is rotten, what is dead. Nature needs those, too, but only the real thing, not the pretender.

Moldhaug didn't turn his head, but if one looked closely, one could easily spot the rounding in the transition between his neck and shoulders.

– We're being TESTED! He shouted. – We were being punished for our weakness, but now the Kingdom of God is close. We're the Chosen. We will build the new land, rebuild Norway…

At the end of the last sentence he had finally gained everyone's attention. He smiled blissfully.

– The Lord be PRAISED, he spat. – By his decree and aid we shall cleanse this land, removing everyone coming here to steal its riches.

Maxine, and also Renate, Razim, Jaiwad, Yarath and others froze. They stared at the preacher with burning anger and were about to stand up, to *approach* the man… when Damon with an almost invisible sign stopped them in their tracks.

Damon sat there five, ten seconds without speaking.

– Are you a messenger? He asked.

Moldhaug didn't reply, but stopped hesitant for a moment, before setting out to continue his speech.

– Are you God's messenger? Terrill shouted loud and clear.

Moldhaug turned towards him with a heartwarming, sickeningly confident smile on his lips.

– You speak true! He replied. – I'm the Lord's emissary on Earth, sent here to strike down the heathens.

– Are you absolutely certain? Damon wondered.

– Absolutely certain… what do you mean?

The first visible uncertainty, the first crack in his armor revealed itself.

– It's a fair question, isn't it? The man with the mask rose abruptly.

The massive figure covered by a hood and dressed in thick clothing focused its entire attention on Moldhaug.

– Listen, my friend…

– And what's this bullshit that no one but christians can inherit the land? You may not know this, but the christians invaded this land with massive brutality and deception a thousand years ago. I'd say that a thousand years of occupation is enough, wouldn't you agree?

There was no response, except the puzzled frown.

– While you're at it, you may give me your definition of a Norwegian, except for the religion thing? Is it one that is born here? One with a particular skin color? Or one which ancestors have spent a certain amount of generations here?

Everything turned very quiet. Damon had seemed withdrawn, even meek at first. The last few words hadn't exactly been screamed either, but had been accompanied by a silent roar echoing between the mountains.

Moldhaug stared at him, with a smile still in place. He nodded. His muscles bulged under the worn and dirty clothes. He recognized a challenge when he saw one. Everyone present did. Their ancient Memory made a somersault in the depths of their minds and emerged into the twilight storm constantly blasting them.

– Good people. He turned towards his congregation with raised hands and open palms. – As you can plainly see, the ungodliness is even closer than we suspected. We must all stand firmly against it. We must, with our faith and strength of belief…

Damon shot him. The big man shook and there was incredulity in his eyes. Damon fired again, and kept firing. The man was pushed backwards. As incredible as it seemed, he didn't fall until the fourth bullet hit the shaking figure. Frank Moldhaug crouched on the ground and died. No one present could take their eyes off the incredible sight. They had read about it, heard about people being shot and killed, and even watched it on television, but never experienced it close up like this. The signal from Damon made the Nightravens stay back. He walked right in between the followers of the late Frank Moldhaug. One more realization hit them. What shocked them the most wasn't the killing itself, but the casual way it had been implemented.

The wolf placed himself in their midst, and it seemed like the Storm itself had stepped down from the sky above. It had, and he had brought it, or it had brought him.

His eyes stared at them, even when he stood with his back turned. His entire being stared at them.

– Get on with it! He shouted and threw the gun on the ground in front of the scared congregation. – Shoot me!

Gwen shifted position anxiously. Anya stopped her from acting with a glance.

– I can assure you that the gun will work, he told them. – The shells are water proof and if there is water in the gun, you may only point the barrel at the ground and empty it of water.

No one moved. He turned his back to them, slowly. No one moved.

– I thoughts so, he said with contempt in his voice. – You're just one more group of mindless followers listening to every power hungry asshole coming your way. Well, listen to this particular asshole, now.

He was breathing, breathing all the time. They felt the pressure of his breath.

– Factors like religion, need for power, alienation and hierarchy ruined the old world, he shouted, penetrating their ears, the shroud covering their mind. – They will never be allowed to ruin the new, never to dominate anywhere. Worship is hereby banned. Laws are rescinded. Permanent structures are rescinded. Only one law is from now on valid: the law of nature, of life, of true humanity. Break this one law, and you will perish.

Damon Terrill stood in a straight, half bent forward position, with a fist raised to his face. The air cracked and sparked around him. They could actually see it, see it with their eyes just as easily as they did with other known and unknown senses.

He spoke to them all, all life's driftwood reaching the shore of life.

– We're children of the storm, the riders of the Thunder Road. We're the power of life moving in the shadow of death, related souls, survivors of holocaust, children of the Abyss. Now, in this age, in the eternal age of man, we need the rage, the drive within. Now, it has its legitimacy. Happiness is no longer cut in a thousand pieces and reduced to nothing in a joyless, beyond destructive society. We have all awakened from the long sleep. Don't fall asleep again. Then people will come for you. I will come for you. There are very few duties in this new, old world, not more than one, really: to become truly independent people, individuals thinking and acting and *breathing* independence, beings striving to grow, to be born, not only passively accepting variety, but *encouraging* it. That's my demands, now, and forever.

It turned quiet once more, quiet in the storm and the relentless rain falling from the sky.

They stayed in the valley for a while, feeding, resting.

The reaction hit them eventually, long delayed after their long trek through the rain and the wind, like a hammer in the face. Tears flowed, even in sufficient quantities to be noticed in the rain. They heard their own chokes muted against the sound of the flowing water.

– It's pretty funny, Kara said aloud, strangely calm after a while. – We made every effort to grow familiar with the tourist trails and the old mountain tracks, but it hasn't helped us much so far.

– So far, Myriam corrected her.

– It still helped us, André pointed out. – We learned the road of roads, gained knowledge of the eternal labyrinth and our place in it.

– Damn, Andy, Yola joked, – you've become such an excellent poet.

They sat there. Claire started rocking back and forth, and after a while they rocked with her. She started humming, and they hummed with her.

It turned quiet. Only the eternal night was heard above the muted roar.

They started crying once again, like a repetition of the first time, almost like it was the first time, as if time repeated itself. They once more fought themselves up on their feet. With that act, almost as if it was ordained, the new, returning gusts of wind started.

Gwen dried her tears, dried the water, a hopeless task, of course. She looked ashamed at the ground, staring hard and unbowed at them all.
Other groups started moving, some independent of them, others following in their tracks. The followers sought close to Damon and Anya.
Anya stopped. They stopped as well. She stopped them.
– I can't fill the emptiness in you, she told them. – Neither can the Child of the Storm. Only you can do that.
She started walking again. They stood still. When they started moving again, they stayed back, keeping their distance to the two far in front.
The valley ended. They reached another fjord. The foam at the top of the waves reached all the way to the shore. André tasted the water.
– Still salt, he reported, shaking his head. – Damn!
The world stretched out an endless distance before them. The wind picked up, growing from one moment to the next into yet another storm. They had to take more frequent breaks. Even after several minutes' rest the heart hammered in their chest. The first started collapsing of exhaustion. A man died standing on his feet. Eyes turned wide and still. No more than a rag hit the ground. Some in the long row of wanderers rushed forward in order to clean the body of clothes and whatever «valuables» they could find. The Nightravens stared at them and felt disgust, both directed at the people and themselves, because they wanted to do the same. Both their emotions and common sense told them it would be a smart move.
Then they shrugged and moved on, fighting themselves another step, another mile, another inch forward.
Damon and Willy carried one slack body each and wondered quietly how long they could keep it up, how long it would take before others would have to carry them.
All time… faded. All steps vanished beneath their feet, becoming impossible to count.
The road made a turn and ran even closer to the shore. Tall geysers rising as waves hit land and water rained down on the small groups of people. One of them cried out, his voice aloud and clear, not drowning in the roar of the storm.
– I'm coming! He shouted. – FATHER AND MOTHER, I'M COMING HOME!
He dived into the inferno making the expression «frothing sea» totally insufficient, vanishing from their sight in an instant.
Yngve puked his guts out. He hadn't traveled through Europe and witnessed the events that had hardened his companions. They hadn't known him for more than a few months. In those months rested the vast sea. He crouched, but managed to stay on his feet, and kept putting one foot in front of the other. When they looked at him, knowing how bad they felt, they wondered how he felt.
– It never stops, never stops, Claire mumbled time and time again, supporting herself on Damon, holding on to him for dear life.
He fell and she fell, and those he carried fell hard.
Rest. Night. Eternal twilight. Night in their minds. Day in their minds. They woke to another morning more or less resembling the one before, awoke just as dead tired as they had been when they had fallen asleep.
They slumbered while moving on.
The dream visions began, completely uncontrollable. The wheel of life turned. At almost all stops there were skulls grinning at those turning the wheel, those daring to

approach its deadly, burning hot horizon.

They fed while walking, now. They couldn't stomach even the thought of stopping, of standing up one more time, rising from the dead yet again.

But they did, time and time again.

The cramps in the stomach, of hunger, of starvation screaming in body and mind in equal measure made sparks flow in their vision. Everything turned indistinct, distinct, and he imagined he glimpsed Blanche somewhere ahead, and the soreness within turned into something solid, tangible, a festering wound making him push on, making him keep putting one foot in front of the other.

The long row of people stumbled on on the narrow trail of gray increasingly covered by sand and dirt… and water and wine and blood.

They couldn't hear the roar above the eternal roar. The wind gained strength anew, and the wind grew to a storm. Damon heard loud and penetrating warning cries, but they didn't quite register in his conscious mind, anywhere that mattered.

He turned slowly and looked dully behind him. A wall of water raced through the fjord, a wave that had to be much bigger further out. It rose and fell like a rollercoaster, a river flowing through the very air. They watched as it fell one final time…

… until it rose like a waterfall flowing upwards right at them, at Damon. He threw himself on the ground, but didn't quite make it before the flood, the waterfall hit him, hit them, and threw him, threw them far, far away on its path to nowhere.

CHAPTER TWENTY-THREE

Blanche stood in front of him, just as distinct as everyone else standing there.

– He's coming for you, she said, – coming for you all. In the new world it's either him or you.

He heard her just as well as any nearby voice, better, a pure instrument in a choir of hoarse whispers.

The coughing assaulted him abruptly. It burned deep in his throat, deep in his cave when all the water, all the slag flowed from his throat, out of the mouth. The salt, the acid, the fire burned and warmed.

– I can see The Nine Worlds, he mumbled. – I see them becoming one.

People crouched on the ground around him, spread out and in clusters. He knew some of them, while others were totally unfamiliar to him. Some bodies had turned rigid. They had been dead for a considerable time. Others fought themselves on their feet. Others writhed and shook in cramps, pain and suffering.

– I can see the Thunder Road, the human being's path through life, what challenges, destroys and strengthens it.

He looked at Blanche. She had turned transparent, and while he watched, she faded away, and the air was once again only air.

The journey continued. They fought themselves on their feet and continued their walk.

– I caught a glimpse of Myriam and André, someone said to him. He was unable to tell whom. – I'm confident they survived.

He didn't see Anya anywhere either, but knew she was here, somewhere.

Damon glanced around, without glancing around. There were many, way too many he wished to search for. He knew it would be useless. There were no places where he could search, too many, way too many.

He looked west, north, south… and east. The Storm was everywhere, now. There was no place where the Storm paused.

Whatever glimpse of calm there might be, it vanished like dew on a grain of sand in the transition from night to morning.

The gray night, the gray day kept surrounding them, weigh heavily on them. The wind constantly threatened to unbalance them, to pull them to the ground, into a hole they would never re-emerge from. All places looked the same. There was no break in the conformity, in the cold and the heat. Everything looked the same.

He saw himself walk the same damn road time and time again. Immediately after a certain hard trek had been completed, they started on another, were returned to start. He saw them fade on the hilltop and be moved back to its base. Occasionally, he feared the very worst: that it wasn't his imagination playing tricks on him, but that they all existed only as ghosts, revenants in the eternal event horizon.

A woman had an enormous belly. Everyone saw it as a miracle that she hadn't given birth already. Two big men pulled her on a travois. They looked like they could keep it up for a considerable time, but it clearly strained them. Each new step strained them.

The long row of hardened wanderers, survivors of untold horrors and disasters moved through a landscape where nothing seemed solid or could be taken for granted. On ground level, where they stumbled, there was only water, an eternal shower making it hard to breathe. They glanced up now and then, and glimpsed the mountaintops high above. The wind was blowing up there. Soil, rocks and everything there might be of materials were torn from the solid foundation and moved in circles, like in a centrifuge making it seem like all of it was floating, as if there was no gravity anymore.

– Can you feel the wind? A guy by his side wondered.

Damon shook his head, misunderstanding on purpose.

– I can feel it, the man said, – feel it in my bones. It approaches me on its elephant feet.

Damon shook his head again, dismissing the rather disturbed man.

The very mixed crowd moved on. Its members didn't stop, didn't dare stop, fearing they would never be able to keep moving, that the big keys on their backs would stop turning.

Soil and rocks, dark and menacing danced between the mountains. Damon squinted his eyes and studied the spectacle. His eyes had sort of gotten used to the eternal water by now. He imagined that the enormous mass up there… stared at him, that it changed into a human form with eyes burning with hatred. A chill trickled down his spine. He realized startled that several rocks had broken free of the main mass and that they were falling… falling on a trajectory clearly directing them towards the human beings on the ground.

The rocks were falling like rain. A giant hit the ground only ten steps ahead of those in front. Rocks not bigger than shingle hit some people and they could do nothing to shield themselves. A man stumbled on with a large wound on his forehead. He kept himself on his feet and stumbled on. The hard rain stopped as fast as it had begun. The human beings slowed down, slowed down so much that they almost stopped.

– No one was hit or at least not seriously wounded, the man dragging the travois cried. – It's a miracle, a…

The woman screamed, a horrible, prolonged howl. Both men let go of the handles and rushed to her. The bulky body twitched and twisted. The scream went on and on. They stared at her, stared perplexed at each other. There was no wound, no blood. The woman's face contracted and didn't resemble a human face at all. Her eyes rolled in the socket. Damon noted without trying that there was no one home there anymore.

Then she *screamed*. Everyone present shook. Suddenly, there was blood everywhere. She seemed to crack, to break into pieces before their eyes.

The shriek was cut off, like a wire. All life left the demonic creature and she laid still.

Everyone stared and kept staring. They couldn't take their eyes off the hideous sight, the bloody bundle of what had once been a human being.

They couldn't say how they managed to keep going, but they did. When they looked down on their feet, they saw how they were moving. When they listened they heard that their heart was still beating. They left her where she had died. No one touched her. Soon, she became only one more distant memory of what had been.

– No one was hit, one of the men mumbled.

He repeated it many times to himself as they slowly made their way towards the Norwegian highlands.

– I'm positive! He mumbled. – I'm damned certain of it!

They heard him long afterwards, also when he no longer walked with them.
«No one was hit».
The words seemed to echo in their ears, among them, like a curse.
Damon looked up with burning eyes, with eyes burning straight through the rain and mist. The mountaintops had been scratched clean. He could no longer see any free-floating soil or rock up there either. Everything had fallen down or perhaps just vanished into a black hole. It was gone!
The terrain began tilting, so much that they noticed. The road made a left turn.
They had walked for hours, for hours since the last time they had considered stopping, since they had thought at all, period.
The road made a turn. Everything pulled to a halt. Terrill stopped.
Existence… shifted. His vision (his inner vision?) revealed a changing landscape. He saw a desolate, broad trail in a dry, torn terrain. The trail continued straight forward, seemingly forever, but somewhere ahead, far into the mist and twilight, he imagined that it made a turn.
A characteristic, familiar scent reached his nostrils. It was well known, but brought no particular reaction. They understood the significance intellectually, but the acknowledgement brought no emotional response.
The scent…
One rushed down to the water. Damon couldn't tell whether or not it was a woman or a man, was unable to identify the person, the movement, the voice. Everything was anonymized in this hellish remoteness. The creature raced down to the river so fast that the sand was whirling in the air. Terrill blinked. A desert of dust surrounded him. He blinked. The mirage faded. He was once more surrounded by a desert of gray and water.
A hand was stuck into the water. A hand was led to the mouth, a thirsty mouth tasting the life-giving fluid.
– It's freshwater.
The stench of salt, the heavy, sickening stench of salt was gone.
– Are you certain? Another seemingly unknown voice asked.
– Positive! There isn't even the implication of salt anymore.
Terrill attempted to picture the map, the terrain as it had been, in another life. He had been driving a car here, an eternity ago.
That experience was no longer useful, for anything.
The discovery of the water didn't really bring that much joy. There had been no lack of water. The mouth turned up would sate the thirst, even though it took some work compared to a running river.
They gained altitude and closed in on their goal, whatever that was.
The wind returned with a vengeance shaking and striking beaten bodies and minds. The Storm kept pace with them. It always would!
Hours, years later he felt worse, felt completely exhausted mentally and physically. The lake stretched out on his right. The road, the snake of a road was still there on the left side of the lake, of Vossevangen, even if most of it had been taken by a landslide. They had to crawl across swamps of soaked soil and mud. Many remained there, became a part of the mud forever. They reached what they felt was safe ground, but that was treacherous and vile. Many fought in vain to thread the surface. Many dropped below, unresisting and drained of their final portion of willpower. There was no fight left in

them. They were never seen again.

Voss the city, a few buildings and collapsed hotels reached sixty meters above sea level on whatever remained of official maps. It looked like just one more disaster area.

Everything vanished in a vortex to Damon. One blink and hours, more hours had vanished from his consciousness.

He sat there, between tents and fires with some from the wolf pack and some from Moldhaug's group, and other lone wolves seeking kindred company. He glimpsed military uniforms and men and women with guns. The sight should have worried him, he knew that. But right now he couldn't be bothered to care.

Many voices, none of them Rawlins' roamed his dull mind. They were all totally incomprehensible.

Slowly, painfully awareness returned to his hard tested being. Exhaustion haunted him, stuck in every single piece of flesh and spirit he possessed. Every time he closed his eyes, there were sparks on the dark wall. Each time he opened them he hardly saw anything but indistinct spots resembling something physical, something real. He preferred sitting there with half closed eyes, in order to both see and don't see.

The church stood not far away, practically undamaged at the center of what had been described as «a vital community». The large stone construction had stood against the recent brutal rigors of nature, while most of the modern business buildings surrounding it hadn't.

Slowly, painfully his senses and his ability to use them returned. It wasn't necessarily a good thing.

Some of the beaten up, downtrodden people stared at the church as if it was the only thing keeping them from drowning. The thought made his innards twist and burn.

A machine roared and made noise somewhere. He couldn't see it, but the sound surrounded him, paralyzing not only his hearing, but all his senses, the balance system in his inner ears, and worse. He was reminded of a science fiction story which name he couldn't recall. The authorities had enslaved a group of telepaths, mutants, using them to enslave the population, to darken, control thoughts and weakening people's will to resist. The old world had been like that, of course. Everything the various private and public governments did, they did with that in mind. It had been like that for a very long time.

They found themselves at a military camp, a military camp now, if it hadn't been one before. There were heavily armed soldiers in all directions, not that many, but more than enough. One single soldier could guard several hundred of the collapsed wrecks having hit the ground at this particular ruin of a city. There were no visible fences. There was no use for any. Most people just sat there, apathetic, and completely receptive for whatever was coming.

The stench of food tore at their nostrils.

He looked up and couldn't deny the sense of joy and gratitude flowing through him.

– SOUP! One cried. – They serve soup.

– How much? A woman with a baby in her arms asked, not tempted by the hope in other eyes.

– Several large KETTLES, the man running past them shouted, – more than sufficient for everyone.

And hope was lit in her eyes as well.

A loud, electronic voice coming from several speakers simultaneously made the air shake.

– STAY WHERE YOU ARE. WE HAVE MORE THAN ENOUGH FOOD FOR EVERYONE. WE WILL SERVE SOUP SHORTLY. YOU HAVE MADE IT, PEOPLE. YOU HAVE SURVIVED.

Damon stared at the church, speculating about its fate, wondering how long it would stand, if it would do so even covered with water, a thought strangely pleasing, in a backwards kind of way.

Time… faded, slipping through his fingers like nothing, like empty air. Right now, that frustrated him. So many other things faded with it, in the vortex of the world, where he sat at the center of its ruins, an event that didn't touch him at all. This was far into the country, but in spite of that the storm had left this village of small, solid houses in ruins.

A man not far away attempted to talk. He managed after several unsuccessful tryouts.

– There's an old saying that you should be careful with what you wish for, he choked.

He sat still, sobbing quietly.

Terrill was reminded of a young man on a motorbike long ago and smiled ironically.

Guards in worn uniforms brought paper spoons and deep paper plates when the stomachs of those waiting for soup had stopped rumbling.

– Hold on to this, they told each and every one in the long row. – You won't be given more than one set.

People looked grateful at them, as if they had just brought tasty, hot soup.

Time passed… or not. Damon, knowing that sat there without moving for an eternity. He just didn't know how many centuries had passed while he sat there and rotted, decaying like an unprotected dead body in the ground.

The rain fell hard. There was no day or night, only twilight. He observed while a long row of new, downtrodden people joined those already waiting there.

– The odds of us reaching this spot is just… enormous, a woman mused. – We have challenged the odds time and time again and emerged from life's pitch black soup as a somewhat thinking, living human being. The dice will soon be cast again. The wheel of life will keep turning.

Damon nodded to himself. The stench of the burning wheel kept returning to him, no matter how many times he managed to let go of it. Something resembling anxiety cleared his vision.

There had been no signal telling them to rise. They didn't see the jeep approach, didn't hear the sound of it, but the stench of the soup tore at their nostrils, and would have transformed them to a howling mob if they hadn't been totally exhausted. They stumbled forward the last few steps to the target, collected the food they so desperately needed, and stumbled on in order to find their spot in the open dining hall presented to them.

Everyone pulled close to each other. The place was packed or seemed to be. So many had survived, only a handful out of thousands, a miracle for sure. They clung to each other, desperate to feel the heat of another human being in a world of frost.

Terrill sat there, sweating. The steaming food was enough to make it happen. He heard many slurps around him. He dried his forehead with the dirty sleeve of his jacket. The smoke and the extreme humidity assaulted him. He waited. The coughing came as if preordained. It made him shake hard. His throat suddenly felt hard and painful. He was coughing hard, like it would never stop. In the long silence afterwards he feared, like he always did that it would return and *never stop*.

He found the small bottle and drank the brew of Coltsfoot «and other weird stuff» that Claire had prepared for him. It still seemed to be steaming, as if it had heated itself the entire time it had rested in the pocket of his jacket. It did serve its purpose. He noticed it immediately, the moment it slid down his throat, how it alleviated the pain and his sore throat. The fear of another assault lessened.

She had glanced shyly at him when she handed him the bottle, yet again apologizing for existing.

He heard the voice from what seemed like far away:

– The soup is poisoned. Tell the one by your side.

The other side, he presumed, since the man sat on his left side.

Nothing more than that, no explanation, no confirmation.

The man didn't eat anything. Damon stared at him, but the man pretended he didn't know he was there.

The first taste of the tasteless dishwater already warmed the insides of Damon's mouth.

– The soup is poisoned, he told the woman on his right. – Tell the one by your side.

He heard it be repeated like an echo down the line, in the cluster of downtrodden people. No one cried out. No one turned loud and alerted guards. A few kept eating with empty eyes, but most did as he did: lowered the paper plate between the legs and let the content flow down on the ground.

Damon Terrill stood up. Others did the same. Several of those eating with desperate pleasure looked like they would cry out and alert the guards. Just the beyond sinister stare he sent them kept them from doing so.

– Look at you, a woman snarled with bitterness and horror painted in her features, – a beast in human form.

– My friends and siblings would have been proud of such a designation. So am I!

He smiled brightly to her.

– You, a pathetic sheep will soon be captured or dead, but we will live!

She shrunk in her tracks, more dead than alive already, unable to grasp the horrible reality she had succumbed to.

He left her. The completely exhausted body started moving, removing itself from the hellish place. He saw no soldiers. It was a large camp. They quite simply didn't have the resources to guard everybody, and they were lazy, and didn't see the point of trying, of guarding what they saw as sheep.

They don't realize, don't realize that the world has changed either, he thought.

– They don't realize that the world has changed.

He said it aloud, said it again, even louder. Those around him, those behind him raised their heads. His vision sparked, turning red and pale of starvation, of many things. His surroundings slowly turned clear.

They started running. He couldn't tell whether or not he or any of the others had started it. They could no longer see the camp, even if they heard the large engine at the center of town and several of the vehicles. The loud sounds stayed distant. Fear kept striking them. They knew the hunt could start at any time. In more ways than one, it already had. He looked without, within, checked up on himself. The flaps on his coat struck his legs. He felt the sword's heaviness on his back. He still retained all the weapons in his possession.

Food, they needed food, nourishment. The will could keep the body going for a long time, long beyond exhaustion and early death, but only to a certain point. Beyond that point and the body would collapse like a rusty bucket.

He stopped. He hadn't realized that he had until he discovered that the others stood still. The closest man looked attentive at him.

– There is something… He shook his head. – I smell something.

He stood with his head tilted. Something touched him.

– Something stinks, the man confirmed, wonder still present in his voice, in him.

Damon had felt this smell before. He had never liked it much. Something so natural and disgust rose in him. Evidently, he wasn't that much different from the other civilized animals disliking natural processes.

– It's the smell of rotting meat, he stated curtly.

Several gasps echoed in the terrain. More of them followed when he directed his walk in a particular direction.

– Hey, shouldn't we go the other way?

They were all following him up the hill, down the hill. They didn't stop at the top of the hill, no matter how hard they desired it.

Then, there, they saw it.

In a shallow hole in the terrain they were all confronting their worst nightmares. They believed they had seen it all. Everyone had been gravely mistaken. A few steps in front of them heaps of bodies decorated the landscape. The vocal chords tightened the throat of the living. Their feet couldn't make a turn. They just kept walking forward while they squeezed their nostrils shut.

– They've been shot, one cried out.

Some of the dead had thrown up. The unmistakably sight of undigested soup made the living nod to each other with eyes filled with frost and understanding.

– There are mostly men and older women here.

What that implied didn't evade them either.

– Those assholes! A woman shouted. – Those damn assholes!

Not all the dead had had soup.

They saw that best when looking at two young women. None of them had been shot, but they had possibly, probably died an even more violent death than the rest here. Damon stared blindly at her. He knew, had known the young, unmoving body on the ground. He saw that she had fought, fought hard. The body was beaten up, her neck broken. He swallowed in joy, in sorrow.

– Good for you! He said quietly.

– The assholes have glorified the use and discard philosophy, the closest man said hoarsely. – Everything they can't use, they get rid of.

– They were shot here, brought here and shot.

– Why not use knives? One wondered. – They must have insane amounts of ammunition in their possession.

– They're frightened, cowardly assholes, Damon swore. – They don't want to be close to their victims when they execute them, not even when the victims crouch sedated and helpless on the ground.

He faced the others, now, without them being able to say when and how it had happened.
– I hope you realize that the dead here are the lucky ones, he said with a hard-edged, penetrating voice.
Those standing around him nodded with a grave expression on their faces. They understood, deep in their own skin.
– We do, one said curtly. – We will never forget!
– We won't! Damon stated. – Our children and grandchildren and their grandchildren's children ad infinitum won't!
He remained. The others wished to leave this wretched place, but he remained there in his thoughts as well. He would make certain they would always remember.
Some of the bodies had started decomposing. In this heat and this extreme humidity, it happened fast. The stench this close was pervasive, overwhelming.
He looked into the future, doing so easily, without more than a slight concentration on his part.
A man, a storyteller stood in a circle around a campfire.
– *… and the Storm Child arrived at the Valley of Bones, and he took a final, decisive step towards his destiny…*
And the Storm Child, abruptly, finally conscious of his own significance looked closer at the steaming bodies.
– They're separated by heaps, he said slowly. – Those in the most recent heap are still warm.
– That's correct. But what…
The man fell silent. Damon didn't have to watch him in order to see the shock on his face.
Joy flowed through him. He had been traveling for so long. All his paths had led him here.
He didn't say anything more, just started on his deed, his meal.
There was a roar in his ears when he bent down by the young girl, the one he once had known. He started coughing. In the smoke and the humidity he coughed one single time. He deliberately started on her first. The knife slipped into his hand from the sheath… and he stabbed what had once been a human being, a person. The others hesitated five, ten seconds before they as one person practically assaulted all the fresh bodies, all the fresh meat.
– Avoid the brain and the spine, he cautioned them, – if you wish to live longer than twenty years or so.
It surprised him how long this had roamed the back of his head, how long he had been carrying it around, refusing to acknowledge it, acknowledge numerous thoughts and emotions.
He fed slowly, only one piece at the time.
– Raw meat has a… great taste, doesn't it? The same man said. – I wonder if it was only circumstances making humanity turn to cooked meat twenty thousand years ago.
The visions kept coming, unwanted… so very wanted. He felt the energy, the embrace of life itself, felt it strengthen him. Pain cut through him and made him gasp. He felt Death as something tangible, physically, eternally walking by his side. The smile was no smile, but a grin, a skull slowly being painted by skin, blood and life. He straightened.

His fingers sparked. His eyes flashed.

There was pain, but it didn't weaken, but strengthened him. Strength came to him. Power came to him. He felt it in his limbs, at his core and outer nail. A fire spread from his chest and to every single piece of his body, well outside his body, to the air surrounding it.

And they all felt it.

And Damon spread his wings.

The others saw it. There was nothing specific they could point at and say that this had changed, perhaps except his eyes. Life was something indistinct, ephemeral sometimes, something that could change a human being from a walking shell to a creature filled with life and lust for life.

You could see it in a person. It would make a person of forty look younger than a twenty-year-old. It was true. The human will was independent of physical realities.

Anya had never looked old and Claire never would either.

He saw them cross the hill ahead, in front of his entire tribe, all the remaining Shadowwalkers. Just two minutes ago he would be unsure whether or not they were dead or alive, but now life breathed within him.

Someone rushed at him, while others just smiled hard enough to make the body glow.

A big, delightful beast jumped him and hugged him.

– We feared we had lost you. Mmmm!

Yola kissed him passionately.

– I feared you were gone, he said with a shaky voice. – I was prepared to move on, to start over.

– You won't get rid of us, Storm Child, André told him. – Not that easily!

When Damon returned Yola's kisses, when he enjoyed the entire lovely body, she howled in joy.

– We caught eyes of the soldiers and the barracks from far away and managed to avoid them, she said. – We took the long way around. They're pretty cocky. I think they just expect people to stumble mindlessly into the village.

He stepped back a bit, away from her a bit, looking good-humored at them all, without shame. Finally!

The hunger revealed itself as desperate longing in their eyes, their presence as well. He waved them with him to the heap of slowly-cooling bodies.

– Don't eat the brain and the spine, he repeated. – We should use all parts of a body in one way or another, though, not just the meat.

– We must remember everything we've forgotten, Anya stated.

They bent down and started feeding. Some threw up, but they just kept feeding.

– Feed, he bid them, Claire said, – and they did.

Some of the old, grumpy Claire showed herself then. No one scolded her for it.

– Our stomachs are filled, Vladek said, – just like during an ordinary meal, and this is such, isn't it?

No one contradicted him.

The hand grabbing the meaty thigh was steady. The blade cutting a big piece of it didn't shake. He put the meat in his mouth and started chewing, very determined.

Damon stopped for a moment and surveyed his tribe.

– You belong to me, he stated, – like I belong to you, like no one belongs to anyone.

He stood still, turned away for a moment, before turning back, turning his full attention on them… before puking. The load flowed from his mouth like a beam. He crouched with sweat pouring from every piece of his body. Comforting hands, soft lips touched his pale and wet skin. He bent down instantly and cut another piece off the nearest body, resumed feeding without hesitation.

– I kept some of it, he said. – We will keep more and more of it, as we keep feeding, as nourishment fills us to the brim. We've been without food for so long, but a human being can keep going for weeks without feeding. It's the powerful energy discharge the last few days that has led to the faster depletion. But we will get used to that, used to that, too, and adapt to a life of scarcity, of true abundance.

He paused, knowing it had an effect on them, on him.

– The soldiers will come here, he said harshly and filled with contempt and passion. – They will come to rid themselves of more perceived enemies, and those they see as useless. Men refusing to submit. Old men. Women refusing to submit. Women too old, or «ugly» or what the hell the soldiers use to justify themselves. They will come, and we will wait for them and butcher them to the last man and woman. If anyone attacks you, kill them. If anyone flees, kill them. If anyone falls on their knees and begs for mercy, chop their head off.

He could have said more, about how he was confident that virtually anyone present would survive the coming battle, how he, a very long time ago in France had seen them in a vision, seen them dance around a bonfire, seen them bathe in a dark water and seen the fire cutting open the sky above the dark mountains, but he didn't. He held back the potentially good news. Whether he had dreamed true or not, there was no need for them. The people gathered before him knew the score. They felt fear, but it wouldn't keep them from doing exactly what he had just told them to do.

They stayed on the spot the next day and night, and the next following those, scouting for the vehicles they knew would come. They were eating normally, strengthening themselves, preparing themselves. Early the third morning they saw and heard the Nothing, the walking dead rolling on the ruined road.

– They're testing prospective soldiers and discarding those not acceptable as part of their clan, driving those not even acceptable as slaves up here.

Myriam spoke fast and with burning eyes, revealing how personal she felt this was to her. The bloodthirst revealed itself in every move she made.

– This is a ritual to them, Anya said. – Having completed the initiation, in all its horror, there's no turning back. They've become an integrated part of the clan, the cult.

They hid and observed the vehicles and soldiers as both man and machine became more and more noisy. They studied the open trucks and jeeps. There were many soldiers, but even a higher number of their victims. Some were bound, others slumbering, already half dead.

– We can't save most of the prisoners, Myriam snarled. – We can only *avenge* them.

The hard and cruel reality dominating the world once again revealed itself to the Children of the Midnight Fire, making them even more determined to see this through, see this through as well. Wrath and despair warred within them, and there was no winner.

The procession left the vehicles twenty meters or so away and marched in step the last stretch to their destination. Damon saw that they were hardly marching out of step at all, except when they beat up on their defenseless victims. Strikes and kicks moved them forward. Empty eyes saw nothing, cared for nothing. Prisoners, soldiers were all empty inside. Damon was shaken by yet another chill.

An officer held a short speech. He blessed the soldiers, and their «holy calling».

– Norway is for Norwegians, he thundered. – Those with another skin color or culture will either bow down in the dust before us, become our humble servants, or be exterminated. Blessed be you, our soldiers, our protectors. You're the very best of the remaining, true Norwegians.

He drew his gun. The soldiers raised their rifles. They stood about ten meters from the prisoners, those half standing, half crouching close to one of the heaps of bodies. One took a step forward. The guns were fired in that very instant. Everybody fell. A few kept moving. The soldiers kept firing. They stepped closer and fired time and time again.

Those in hiding waited, waited with a painful focus for the right moment. They held themselves back, doing a horrible measure of odds in their heads.

– THE LORD IS GREAT, the priest/officer shouted. – LONG LIVE HIS SERVANTS!

– LIVE! All the soldiers choired in unison agreement.

Then they emptied their guns in the shaking figures on the ground.

Myriam killed the leader, firing her gun a tiny moment before her fellow tribe members. His head exploded like an empty eggshell. They rushed forward while firing. Thunder filled the valley.

– Kill them all! Myriam shouted. – Attack without break. Attack until everyone is dead.

Many of the soldiers were hit by several bullets. Not everyone died instantly, but a considerable number fell during the first salvo. Those left strived like sleepwalkers to reload their weapons. Just a few managed to do so. There were also those among them who hadn't emptied their guns completely.

Here, on an insignificant field, in an insignificant part of the world was one of the last regular battles fought and lost and won. Mars, the war god, the agriculture war god was given one final injection of power, before expiring in rage and wrath on the heather.

The soldiers managed to fire one more or less coordinated salvo at the attackers, before the new barbarians, the wild hordes were right there, in their midst.

Myriam emptied one gun, drew another, emptied that, and drew one more. Then she drew her sword. A soldier fired at her, but missed, and in one powerful swing of the sword, she chopped his head off.

The bloodlust filled her, filled them all. She glimpsed her own twisted expression as a mirror image of the others. This wasn't like pulling a trigger and watch a living target fall. This was close-up and personal. The bloodlust kept filling her, making her fight far beyond exhaustion, beyond any rational thought. She saw her brothers and sisters fight and die and live, and she fought on, with no thought beyond the burning bloodlust. She had never felt anything similar and ecstasy grabbed her, and she hardly recalled anything but enemies falling and dying.

A bullet hit André's foot and he fell. Anya screamed aloud. She killed the soldier who had fired the bullet with a knife deep in his heart. The berserker rage that had hidden beneath the surface of them all for so long exploded in a beyond violent eruption. The soldiers kept firing, but for every male or female attacker falling, another, even more savage, more dangerous appeared behind them. André grabbed hold of two guns. He held one in each hand and fired from his position on the ground. A uniformed man stood with a grenade in his hand, but uncertainty riled him. Friends and foes were everywhere and he had nowhere to throw it. The indecision cost him his life. The grenade exploded in his hand and blew him and those closest to him to pieces. Myriam got hit in the shoulder and was pushed half around. She lost the sword. Her arm had become useless and hung straight down. The soldier who had shot her took aim again. He fired just as she kicked his hand and broke it like a dry twig. She grabbed his hair with her left hand, pulled down the head and broke the skull on her knee.

– HA! Her shout was both triumphant and free of anger.

She saw a sister die by her side, felt it as it happened. Grief mixed with rage in an even more explosive mix, an endless flow she could draw strength from, a waterfall that would never stop falling. She saw Damon kill, saw him fall on their enemies like a demon from the most remote corners of the abyss. A savage laughter rose from her throat, her open mouth filled with blood. He pushed his sword through two people simultaneously. He pulled it back out. Both fell dead to the ground. The faint light in their eyes faded to the nothing it had been for so long. Myriam cackled. She cackled all the time while she killed and kept killing, an unstoppable predator on the prowl.

Slowly, only painfully slow the murderous rage faded. The enemy had been defeated, had been *vanquished*. No soldiers remained standing. Most of them had suffered a brutal death. The crimson mist rose from the battlefield. It dawned on Myriam Vallinger that it was no longer raining. Nothing muted the sounds rising from the wounded, from the uniformed men and women crying for mercy. The mist faded from her thought. The berserker returned to her murky self, ready to erupt whenever it was necessary. She felt calm, collected, almost relaxed. With the sword in her left hand she wandered this final battlefield and killed off the still breathing soldiers one by one.

One young boy managed to spit a few words of hatred before she ended him.

– You're Angels of Death, he gasped. – Sent straight from Hell.

– Thank you for those kind words, she said. – We appreciate it. Know that we will pursue you, pursue you all far beyond the threshold of death and to the very gates of eternity.

He believed her. The nameless fear overwhelmed him completely before he died, and she couldn't say it didn't please her. She smiled and stabbed him a single time in the heart before moving on. The wounded attempted to crawl away when she came for them. She smiled. Damon smiled. They crawled to Anya like those drowning would to the shore. She granted them a blinding smile… before her sword penetrated their heart, before her savage snarl returned them to the nothing they had come from.

The frightened choir rose from the twilight.

The dead rested in heaps. The crimson tide floated away, floated in the very air, in the heavy mists of the Twilight Storm.

– It's no longer raining. The wind is no longer blowing.

Vladek lifted his head and lowered his sword.

He was covered in blood. They all were. Gwen tasted it with one hand, while she used the other to draw circles on his face. His face mask had been more or less torn off.

– We've won, Anya said. – What began so very long ago has finally been completed.

They felt an enormous relief, because they took her words literally and knew what she was talking about. Everyone looked back, at the past, Willy and Anya especially, one last time, before once and for all directing all their attention forward.

– We're alive, Damon enlightened them. – We will keep living. I've seen us, far into the Norwegian highlands at the top of Torch Mountain.

Torch Mountain... they tasted the name in their mouth and their mind and vision.

Now, when he finally told them the truth, they knew what he was talking about, knew it beyond doubt.

He had been reborn. He remained the same.

– I can see us, he said with a remote look in his eyes, – like strands of night and fire.

Everyone nodded eagerly to themselves, to the others.

– Pack your lunch, Myriam joked. – We're leaving!

The others glanced, somewhat uneasily at all the bloody corpses, but didn't really hesitate to her bidding.

Myriam and Damon walked down the hill while the others started cutting the already mauled carcasses. The two walked to the vehicles. The others studied them, hardly taking their eyes off them.

Damon opened the fuel tank on one of the jeeps and as light as thought he turned it over. The petrol started flowing. He started some of the vehicles, those farther away, gathering them all in one place. He opened the fuel tank and turned more of them over. The petrol started flowing like a river. Terrill struck two rocks hard at each other. Two times sufficed and sparks flew, and the river that had been the black gold erupted in an inferno. The river of fire flowed upwards until it reached the technological wonders and everything exploded in a prolonged burst of pyrotechnic violence that could be seen all the way to Voss, all the way to Antarctica, where the steam and mist and heat rose from the once so cold continent.

They all packed as much meat as they could carry. Some of them stumbled a bit the first few steps, but as soon as they learned to balance the added load in the rucksacks they were okay.

The nomadic tribe once again started walking, continued their wandering. Their Journey was not yet done. They had realized a long time ago that it never would be. Their Journey would never end.

André couldn't walk, and they made a travois to him, one they took turns pulling. Wounds were tended. A haze covered Myriam's eyes, but she could walk. She and the other wounded didn't carry anything. Her arm hung weak and useless in the sling. Anya made her magick, and strengthened them. It was as if her hands were glowing, just as much as her eyes.

– We crushed civilization under our heels, she said forcefully. – We're the returned power, among the many giving voice to nature, to the earth itself, giving it consciousness, giving direction to its rage and bounty. From now on humanity's fate, no matter what it might be is our own.

She pushed a hand into her bag, where she, among other things carried her snakes (the tribe shivered). She pulled up an amulet in a chain. Strange words flowed from her mouth, perhaps Gaelic, perhaps an older, forgotten language. She hung it around her neck. The amulet glowed in shimmering green. They knew it wasn't an emerald. The glow was different.

Then, for the first time in a long while they heard the howl of the wolf, first only one single, distant howl, then as a choir rising from the valley they had just left.

– Feed, brothers and sisters, Gwen called out. – Live!

She threw her head back and howled. It couldn't be distinguished from that of the wolves in any way the others could discern.

The reply filled the air and made them hot and cold simultaneously.

They pulled higher up in the terrain, no longer feeling even remotely safe on the road.

Energy filled them, pushing them forward. They scouted behind them and to both sides, in order to see if anyone was chasing them, but no one did.

– There aren't that many of them left, André said darkly, – not even many enough to continue their extensive recruitment policy.

His words were met with hearty laughter, not that brittle or shaky.

– Those few left are only one of many rivaling groups in the new, twilight world, Myriam said. – They're done!

– I'm confident there will be no lack of other lunatics around, Damon said.

They nodded, knowing it would be wise to expect the worst. That cautious mindset had been beaten into them since early childhood.

Dragging André's travois didn't slow them down much. They seemed to be filled with energy, and the extra load felt completely insignificant.

Muscles and limbs remained sore. But they fed regularly and they grew stronger, not weaker. Life burned in every single cell of their body. When they sat down and fed a time without time later, the feeding still made them slightly drowsy, but not more than they were supposed to be. They lit a small campfire and joined around it. They smoked the meat they didn't devour, knowing beyond knowing that it would take weeks to empty their… their supplies.

They sought close to each other, so close that they could swear they could catch each other's thoughts, not just the heat of the bodies.

Myriam leaned on a rock with half closed eyes, eyes far clearer than her open eyes had been just a few days ago.

– I know where my teacher went wrong, now, she said with peace on her mind. – He was wrong about many things, but most of all, like many others in the belief that emotion is something separate from the body, that it can and should be removed from the Whole. Nothing can be removed, subtracted, without harming, diminishing everything we are, everything we might become. Emotion sharpens our focus, isn't dulling it, like we, like we all were fooled into believing.

She fell asleep. She didn't snore, but she slept tight. They all did, for the first time in a long time. Some of the guards did as well, long before they were supposed to wake up their replacements.

Damon sat there for a while, blocking the lure of sleep. Everything swarmed in his head, but it didn't feel unpleasant anymore. He probed himself for regret, disgust, but found only acceptance and… and peace. And even that didn't bother him. The puking was an expected reflex of their wretched upbringing, but it hadn't stopped them from continuing the relentless feeding.

The battle replayed itself in his mind. Super sharp images and distinct sensations rivaled for his attention. He remembered the battle, remembered every single little detail. He could recreate it in his thoughts like a chess player could recall the moves on the board, like a poker player could evoke the cards, the hands, the betting, the game.

The wolves stayed close to them, like shadows in the misty terrain. They prowled their surroundings and more howls filled the valley and feverish minds.

– Come, Maxine said huskily. – The bed is so soft. I don't miss the unnatural bed of civilization at all.

He went to her, to all the other soft-limbed creatures calling to him, embracing him. There was some brief, passionate, soft interaction, as natural as everything else. They, he fell asleep fast.

He slept… and was dreaming. The bonfires reached for the sky. The male wolf pushed his snout forward and sniffed his groin. The she wolf performed for him, horny and greedy. Anya stood at the center of a huge herd of animals. She stood far away, but he had no trouble spotting her, seeing her close up. He would always see her.

Damon Terrill sat on a hill. The old, «freeze-dried» man, the walking dead he had faced in the Berlin catacombs stood above him with a sword in his hand. The man laughed and cackled triumphant, but Damon saw straight through his falsehood.

– You're hardly more than a ghost, a scarecrow, the Storm Child mocked him, – a specter desperately clinging to the mistakes of a past long gone.

The man with the parched skin snarled and attacked. Damon sat there calm and centered. The sword flashed and penetrated him. He remained calm. It didn't hurt, didn't harm. He was bleeding from a wound, but that had been there a good while and closed while he looked at it. The man *screamed,* a scream resembling that of an exhausted car engine on its last leg. The parched skin fell off the skeleton in bits and pieces, and the skeleton itself dissolved and floated away like a fresh spring.

The ongoing unrest didn't leave Damon, but he felt peace, as much as he would ever do.

He stood on a tall mountaintop and surveyed enormous, eternally green plains below.

The ground was shaking. Dust floated in the air. A close rumble reached his ears. He frowned. It felt so real, almost as if…

Vladek shook him awake. He woke up immediately, ready for what was coming. Vladek seemed both shameful and excited, but it didn't really worry Damon that much.

– I… fell asleep, Vladek said, both with shame and a strange wonder.

– I did, as well, Yola said. – I guess we were entitled. We were dog-tired, worn down, and it worked out this time, but it must never happen again.

Everyone woke up. The low, but intense voices were more than sufficient for that to happen. They had become light sleepers.

– I woke up when the ground started shaking, Vladek said, and now wonder dominated his voice. – I nearly panicked, but then I saw them, looked straight at them.

They followed him up the hill. They were all following him. Everyone stopped there and stared.

Dust whirled in the air. In the horizon, the eastern horizon they imagined they could spot a brighter sky. They stared at hundreds of feet stamping on the field down there. The ground wasn't really shaking, not so much that they should notice. With their old lack of awareness, their old dull senses, they would probably not have noticed anything at all, but now the movement of the animals echoed within them like… like thunder.

– Reindeer? Yngve exclaimed incredulous.

– Reindeer, Kara confirmed, – and deer and fallow deer and several other species I don't even recognize.

– I'm reasonably certain that I can see Llama, Willy mused. – I have no idea where they're all coming from.
He paused a little, while the others looked at him.
– A South American animal, he grinned, – not an Asian holy man…
– Farmers have imported tons of foreign animals to the country the last fifty years, in order to add to their income. Damon shook his head cheerfully. – I think they even tried camels…
– And ostriches, Gerd added.
Damon sniffed in the air. The wind blew towards them, towards the humans, the predators. Everyone glanced at each other.
– We do need more meat, Anya said. – We always will! Leaner times may always be around the corner.
– We used to kill by proxy all the time before, Gwen said with a silent, savage snarl. – Now, we once again need to do it close-up and personal, a much more pure form of killing.
Yngve studied the animals through the binoculars for a while.
– Will they try to run away at all? He wondered.
– It's impossible to tell. Maxine shook her head. – I hope so, or they won't last long. My suggestion is that we take for granted that they will. Perhaps not the Reindeer and the domestic animals, but the rest.
– They will flee, Anya said with a low and intense voice. She stared at them with her three green eyes. – We will make sure they do, make sure they will spread to the four corners of the world. We are hunters! We will always find them.
They nodded in understanding.
The hillside pretty much became their home, at least their brief home that day. They prepared as thorough as they could, taking more baby steps on their path.
– No pregnant females, Anya cautioned them.
They nodded in acknowledgement, understanding.
– How do we spot them? Renate wondered. – I mean, in the cases where it isn't obvious.
– Do your best! Anya replied. – We will learn eventually.
They approached the game down there with utmost caution. There were no voices, only signs and silent communication. They chose their bows, leaving the handguns behind. Damon stepped on a branch on the ground. He managed to stop himself from putting all his weight on his foot, keeping the branch from breaking.
So clumsy, he thought. Hopefully, we can look back at this and laugh about it a year from now.
He knew they would get that chance. They were learning. It was the chosen task of human beings to learn.
– It's the chosen task of human beings to learn, he told the tall and big and supple girl and other children around her, told them in a whirl of water and wind, – learn to develop our ability to survive and grow independently of others, learn to learn for its own sake.
The reindeer clearly hadn't had people around them for years and was just as nervous as most of the others animals. The hunters left all limiting thoughts on the hilltop and charged silently forward.

The adult male deer was easy to spot. They selected a few animals as candidates for the killings, slowly isolating them as best they could from their herd, going after them with everything they had of instinct, skill and bloodthirst.

– We have no spears, Myriam told the other wounded on the hilltop. – They would be better than bows and arrows on this particular hunt and they would be easier to reuse. We screwed up there and must take steps to correct our mistake.

They pointed at the heart to the left of the reindeer's belly and missed more than they hit. Bucks fell and died on the wet ground. The animals started pulling away, running off, including some wounded. They would die far from here and suffer long before they died, but there was nothing the nascent hunters could do about that. A few was caught with lassos and chopped to death. Vladek hit one buck right in the heart and shouted in triumph. Dust whirled up and the hunters could only glimpse each other in the inferno of screams and blood. It ended quickly. They held back deliberately. The few animals they had killed were more than sufficient, for now. It would be a heavy load as it was.

Dust fell slowly to the ground. The hunters stood there breathing, breathing hard. They stared at each other with wide open eyes, with savage joy. Their clothes, soaked in blood should feel heavy. They felt light, very light.

Loud cries rose from the pack as they walked to the cadavers, as they pulled the arrows from steaming carcasses, as they grabbed their trophies. In the midst of joy, they found, to their sadness a female with a big belly. They imprinted the sight in their mind, swearing never to forget and to learn from the experience. They rubbed and touched each other in the expectation of what was waiting. Gwen's eyes twinkled when she danced and turned her body slowly and lustful and performed for males which blood was boiling just as much as hers.

– It's exactly like I imagined it would be, she said aloud… – just a thousand times better.

The intoxication faded slowly, but never completely. It remained a fire burning with a weaker flame.

The job with flaying and carving the animals felt far harder than the actual hunt. The hunt had been a physical ordeal, even during the brief time it had lasted, but this was worse, was hard work they weren't physically and mentally prepared for.

Some of them had to sit down, only half conscious, double vision and sudden fatigue assaulting them.

They sat there, fighting to get their bearing.

– Mountain climbers, Roger said, feeling like he was still breathing hard an hour later. – There's no trouble as long as they climb slow and steady, without panic or anger, but if they slip and have to act in order to not fall, the adrenaline is flooding their system and they're exhausted in seconds.

– Indigenous tribes and hunter-gatherer nomads hunted for days without rest, or much rest, Maxine breathed.

– Like we eventually will do, Josh stated with conviction in his voice.

The pride and determination in his voice warmed them all.

– There's just so much *waste* we must get rid of within ourselves.

Claire shook her head.

– And we're doing that, Myriam insisted. – We show other people with our actions, our very existence that the human spirit is still alive.

– Your words are so damn uplifting, Roger said, clearly deeply affected. – Thank you! Thank you so much!

He grabbed her hands and held on to them, only slowly letting go.

– I should thank you, Myriam said and smiled with feverish eyes. – I used to see myself as a victim of circumstances. I don't do that anymore.

It was notable. When Roger let go of her hands, they just fell down. Suddenly she looked visibly weak. Claire looked closer at her with a worried expression in the big eyes. Everyone did.

Anya had already knelt down by Myriam's side. Myriam attempted to keep her away, in vain of course. Strega anxiously unwrapped the bandage. The fever burned in Myriam's eyes. She had clearly fallen ill. The inflamed wound hammered at Anya's sensitive fingers.

– I can smell the stench. Claire pushed a hand at her mouth and choked. – Damn!

The skin had turned red, but also started changing to a darker, sinister hue. It was swelling, so fast that they could almost see it as it happened.

– It wasn't supposed to happen, Anya shook her head. – The wound was clean.

She rushed over to everyone else that had been hit by enemy bullets. Claire was right behind her. Maxine the nurse helped out as well. Not all the wounds were infected, but their worst suspicion was confirmed.

– Those damn inhuman demons, Claire choked. – They dipped their bullets in shit and banshees know what.

– Pull yourself together, Anya snapped quietly. – We can do this, but not if we behave like children scrubbing our knees.

The daughter blinked and straightened. She nodded and nodded again, as she returned to the stunned crowd of healthy tribe members.

– We need to find lots of plants, she informed them.

Damon smiled to her, and she blushed deeply.

Anya grabbed Myriam's shoulder and cut the throbbing abscess. Myriam bit her lower lip and didn't utter a single sound. Pus flowed from the wound. Anya squeezed out all of it. Myriam screamed and fell backwards. Anya applied herbs, wrapping a new bandage around the wound.

Steam rose from kettles heated with fire. Mother and daughter and Maxine made lots of medicine, adding to their already considerable arsenal.

– It isn't even close to sufficient, Anya said to Damon with visible concern in her face, audible concern in her voice. – This area is far from ideal when it comes to gathering what we need. I'm afraid we need to use of our reserves.

He found the large, waterproof bag filled with modern antibiotics and held it up, showing without showing that he agreed with her.

– Let's hope it works, that most of it works.

Anya gave some of them her brew and others the modern day, accepted medicine in a random pattern, carefully noting who got what.

Myriam drank the brew. She fought herself up in a sitting position and held the cup with shaking hands, before falling back down on the soft bed they had made for her.

– Thank you, Strega, she said.

They saw it, saw how the fever clouded her eyes. They watched helplessly while she fell into fever fantasies. She started mumbling, clearly out of it. Several of the others also fell victim to the fever. Anya, Claire and others of the tribe helping them worked tirelessly to wet their forehead and to keep the fever down. Others started exploring the area, looking for a good spot for defense, if it should come to that. There was no way they could move on right now, not for days. The rage, the dark rage settled deep in their core.

Myriam's eyes cleared briefly. They gathered encouraged around her.

– This isn't a big deal, she stated firmly. – It's just something we must deal with, like everything else in our new life. Remember that joy will always be with us, along with the bad.

The fever returned, and so did her delusions. She screamed in fear, looking at them like she didn't recognize them. They had to hold her down when it was at its worst.

She and the others fighting the infection finally fell into an unrest resembling sleep. Claire and half of those helping Anya had also taken a break in order to get some much needed rest. Josh and team took their place.

Some time later, when sleep had finally claimed them Myriam woke them up with a loud scream and a crystal clear voice.

– I CAN SEE IT!

Maxine and Yngve grabbed her and held her again.

– I CAN SEE ALL THE EAGLES FLY!

Claire was awake and prepared. She had taken over the command from a still exhausted Anya. She rubbed Myriam's forehead, speaking to her in a low and soft voice.

– I can see it, too. I didn't think I could.

Myriam blinked slowly with swollen eyelids. Her surroundings faded and faded again. She struggled to speak more, but failed. Time faded and faded again.

Anya and Damon stood on another hill where the wind was blowing, engaging in a quiet conversation.

– I think they will be okay, she said with a shaking voice. – I was seriously afraid for them for a while.

– *You* were seriously afraid? He joked, shaking his head.

She had more on her mind. He saw that easily, without trying. She noticed that he noticed and nodded in acknowledgement.

– I'm also thinking about the soldiers, she said with a chill in her voice. – How they had allowed their hatred to completely overtake them, had thrown all humanity away, how they had died even if they were talking and breathing.

– Don't be concerned with that either, Damon insisted. – Myriam said it like it is. Joy will always be with us, side by side with the horrible and dangerous life gives us.

She turned towards him with her direct, staring look, with the shadow of a smile.

– The Storm Child, she stated, reaching out with a feather-light hand touching his face.

A new day dawned and the night fell. Some of the antibiotics didn't work, but Anya recognized the signs of that fast, and changed tactics. Most recovered quickly and those that didn't, did so in an extra day or two. Anya walked among the no longer ill tribe members. She recognized their looks, the doglike admiration she didn't much care for.

Perhaps I should have allowed someone to die, she thought unmotivated, stunned by her own dark notions.

She stood with Damon, Myriam, Claire and Kara on the windy hill.

– It's time! She stated firmly.

Myriam nodded pale and drawn. Claire looked like she would say something, but stayed quiet. No one spoke.

They left what had been their home for such a short time. It became just rock and soil again. Just. The rock and the soil changed beneath their feet, remaining what it had always been.

Everyone aided the wounded. It felt harder at first, but quickly turned easier. Both the wounded and the healthy grew stronger every day.

They looked forward to what was coming, they dreaded it. Somewhere ahead waited what they had been waiting for, for a long time. Anya walked at Damon's side in front of the procession. Her eyes, her very body was glowing in desire when she directed her attention at the tall, dark man, the very grown twenty-one-year-old boy. He feared he would drown in her eyes, in her vast lap.

– Have no fear, She Who Danced in the Forest whispered. – You're ready, now. I'm ready, now.

They crossed the remains of trails, and made half-hearted attempts at following them, but relented quickly.

– We will follow our own trails from now on, anyway.

Anya smiled to Damon in unconcealed lust.

– I would swear she's in heat, Yola whispered to Maxine. – An extreme version of it.

A moment later, they felt Anya's presence, her all-encompassing heat.

The land turned indistinct around them. The humans turned distinct in the twilight land. They slipped into it, becoming one with it. The night finally arrived.

The fire reached high up, splitting the night sky, making it seem even darker. Anya was dancing. She stood still. She was dancing, circling the fire, the dancing, whispering fire. The others sat around it, around the center fire and between that and the outer five, well within the pentacle she drew on the ground using her hands and feet, her bare feet. Her shoes burned in the center bonfire, dissolving like sand, like ashes. She started removing her clothes. Fabric by fabric fell off her. The supple young body looked even lighter, moving like it flowed above the ground instead of stepping on it. Damon stared at her. She was well over fifty years old. He didn't know exactly how old she was, but her age showed no more on her than it had on Victor Russell. Big, firm breasts danced on her front. Hips wriggled from side to side. Muscles moved beneath the firm and generous thighs. The males felt how they hardened below. The females started swaying like she was swaying. The «Black Irish» remained a Black Irish, but grew to become far more this night. Horny moans and grunts rose from dry throats. Everyone stared blindly at She Who Dances in the Forest and the Darkness. Just in the deep wells of her eyes, they could glimpse her age, her true age far beyond this one. The long hair didn't cover her, but flowed up and down and in all directions in the wild rhythm and dance. Only when the violent moves finally ceased the raven hair slowly fell in place, even as it kept flowing around her like a dark fire. She finally turned, turned towards them all, and they could all see her, see both her front and back.

The burning desire would usually be followed by instant action, but now they just sat there and enjoyed it, in expectation of what would follow.

She walked to Damon and put her hand on his forehead.

– You will sleep. The voice was deep, hoarse and seemingly rusty. – You will dream, and you will be transformed. You will all sleep. You will all dream and be transformed.

The flames reached even higher. She stood before Claire, as she grabbed her necklace and removed it.

– Rise! She bid her.

Claire rose hesitatingly, but eventually stood straight.

– You're the carrier of knowledge, Anya told her.

– No, don't ask that of me, Claire protested weakly. – Ask me anything, but not that.

– You're the carrier of knowledge, Anya repeated, – not because you're my daughter, but because you're best suited for the task. You will carry our story beyond time, until you pass it on to another.

Claire accepted the small pouch and hung the greenish amulet around her neck. The slow smile brightened her face.

– Out here, she said softly to them all, – beyond all borders, where heaven and hell are one, you can't hide from yourself, and you don't want to.

She reached her hands above her head and cheered quietly, a sore, happy sound echoing between the mountains.

They saw each other clearly, while running within the circle so fast that they couldn't possibly touch the ground.

But they did.

The broken wheel burned and warmed them, and there was no distinction between those two extremes.

The woman and the boy crossed the plains. They had walked forever. They still did. Everyone walked with them, walked through forests and mountains, sailed the seas. They lived and died and lived again. And even the mountains grew old. And even the stars stopped burning, while the snake devoured its own tail.

– Time is not a river, Anya stated later, much later, – but a flood flowing all fields and plains.

They squinted their eyes, attempting to focus at one specific point, any specific point. And then she stood before them, and they saw her unexplainably clear. They sat in a half moon, in an unbroken, broken circle and stared at the woman standing there with the boy by her side. Claire stood between the odd couple and the half moon. Anya pulled a snake from her bag. Claire sat down on her hinges, placing many small cups around her. She mixed ingredients in a bowl and shared it among the cups, doing so hesitatingly at first, but then with a growing confidence revealing her experience.

– It turns and bends like the Thunder Road in its desolate landscape. What is first may be last, and what is last may be first. Action can follow as a logical consequence of an event, just as much as the other way around. We have sat like we do now many times, both before and after this. We're the Riders of the Twilight Storm, its Agents of Change and thus we will stay and live forever. Time bites its tail, and we're there. We're the snake coiling on the dusty road, the boat riding down the raging river. We aren't passengers, but a part of the boat, a part of the mighty river, of the riverbank, of the fields it's flooding, the bird surveying it all, the one rising above the tallest mountains. We're the ant contemplating the Universe and the Universe contemplating the ant. There's nothing that should make us underestimate ourselves, overestimate ourselves…

Claire hesitated a few more moments, before stepping forward with a cup in each hand. Anya held the snake's head above the cups. Drop by drop the poison hit the fluid, the steaming fluid. Anya accepted one of the cups, the boy the other. They drank everything in a single attempt.

Anya filled more cups with poison from the snake's mouth. Claire brought one to Damon and one to Myriam. They drank. When one snake was empty, she pulled another from her bag. Everyone drank one by one. Everyone felt how the brew burned as it flowed down their throat, how the stomach twisted itself into knots and the heat spread from there to their bodies. It resembled a bit the effects of spiced food mixed with wine, but far more potent.

– I'm not feeling anything, Kara said, shaking her head. – Ten minutes have passed, and my thoughts are just as clear.

– It will come like a flowing river, the boy hummed.

They stared at him, attempting to recall if they had heard him speak before, ever.

– Until the waterfall is getting close, Claire said. – Then you hear the roar. Then, you experience fully the boiling water.

Anya swayed towards Damon, slipped close to him and started undressing him. He began helping out. Everyone removed their clothes, removing everything that had weighed so heavily on them for so long.

They were standing on the shore of the water, right where the river reached it, flowed its last stretch, washing their clothes, doing it with slow, thorough moves. White foam floated on the surface. They started washing themselves, washing each other. Arousal grew slowly. The clothes were hung to dry near the fires. The steam from the water and the humidity rising from the circle, from the pentacle mixed with the pervasive heat between the fires, between those calling themselves the Children of the Midnight Fire.

– I'm so clear-headed, Kara mumbled, – so extremely lucid that I feel like I can catch every single thought.

Everything turned indistinct, so very distinct, practically crystal clear.

The water circled round and round. Terrill stood by the riverside and looked into the water mirror. Things moved down there, moved within him. He caught a glimpse of Renate's dark brown skin. There was a breath of wind, and he turned around, and there she was, right by his side.

– I can see it, she whispered. – I feared I had imagined it, imagined all of it at the time, but now I know I didn't.

The drum was beating. The heartbeats of the gods hammered them all. They heard sounds of feet, of paws hitting the forest bed, the hollow of the field where they had gathered, where they danced and lived. On one side was the mountain, on the other the lake. Between those two extremes humanity and the dancing fire burned. The fire coated in flesh saw trees appear in the middle of the day, saw countless animals emerge from nowhere. The entire plain crawled with animals and everyone gathered around and between the bonfires felt a catching in the throat. They pulled in between the fires and felt the flames warm them from all sides. The Storm Child sat with his back to a tree. The wolf wriggled towards Damon and sniffed him out. Damon returned the favor. In a flash, in several flashes he saw Gwen roll on the ground. The wolves sniffed their flesh when they slept, moving with them in their circle dance. Damon reached the arms above his head and let them fall slowly down his sides. He reached out with his mind and his body followed. He flapped his wings and rose from the ground, into the twilight darkness.

Giants, dragons, beasts and men crossed the land and the ground shook beneath their feet. This was The Other World (there was only one world), where life and death, dream and reality and the colors of the rainbow were one, the same they had always known and walked.

The fire flickered, burning in the wind.

Vladek sat there. He held his hand half raised, staring at them, staring at a point far beyond them.

– I feel like I'm cracking up, he said to himself, to anyone listening, – but I'm not, of course. It's just the old ways of thinking haunting me. I am, in truth opening up to everything around me.

The crazy, uninhibited laughter echoed between the mountains. The fire, the ice whispered to them, to the mountains and forests and humans and all living things.

– This is so amazing! He shouted. – It exceeds everything I could ever imagine. Everything *is* connected. Through a thousand angles we experience ourselves… in a world on the edge of what we know, but not outside it. I'm flying, flying, and juMPing and danCIng across the endless plains. Everything is awaiting us out there. We're awaiting ourselves.

Myriam stood straight and did some yoga, or yoga-like movements. It didn't end well. She fell and hit the ground, but it didn't seem to faze her at all.

– Everything comes together. Everything is falling apart.

The loud giggle shook the night.

She sang and she expressed herself through the song and speech became a barrier.

– The song expresses what we can neither express nor deny.

She couldn't stop laughing.

She danced completely uninhibited, jumping higher each time her feet touched the ground. Then… it was as if she stayed in the air. Then, with one more heartbeat, it was as if she changed. She could sort of trace the progression, the transformation. Then, it was complete. She had become a giant fire-spitting dragon making the air shiver with the flapping of her wings, the earth shake under her feet. She towered above the mountains. A mountain was just a rock, a lake only a pond.

The fire-spitting dragons flew across the sky, between the stars. The big bird floated down the mountainsides, until it met the air pressure from the valley and rose anew.

Damon Terrill stood by the shore of the dark water. Renate slipped close to him while laughing throatily. She started kissing and biting him. After a while she pulled away and let him see, unabated, without holding herself back. She jumped into the dark water. He heard the laughter from out there somewhere and jumped after her. When he caught up with her, he didn't just find her, but also Yola and Maxine. He stared back at the river bank, watching the tired, wild bodies dance with a vigor not even comparing with anything they had experienced before. The three females surrounded him on all sides. Renate pushed her butt at his groin. The water suddenly felt infinitely warm. Abruptly, even unexpected he found himself inside of her, pumping violently back and forth while she was held steady and floating by the two other females. It happened fast and completely uncontrollable. He emptied himself in her. She released a prolonged, loud moan before she stretched out and floated in the water, while breathing and breathing and floating away with a big smile on her lips.

The water was filled with warm, warm bodies. The land where the fire burned was

covered by a sea of skin and twisting limbs.
Everyone flowed from body to body, from mouth to mouth, from groin to groin. No one could say whether or not they were in the water or on land. The experience was the same. They just enjoyed each other's bodies, enjoyed each other without ulterior motives, without reservations. Myriam approached through the water with powerful thrusts and she shared Damon, shared Yngve, shared Vladek as well. André sat supported by a rock. The she wolf rode him. Sweat flowed down the supple body. She gasped and kept gasping. Then she turned rigid and collapsed on the body below.
– Don't fear, dearest, she whispered and gave him a wet kiss, – there's nothing wrong with you… with your kick. I felt it to the very bottom, far deeper than ever before. We're more, so much More!
She crawled on, slipping down on the ground between Vladek and Damon. In her violent impatience, her eternal hunger, she began writhing, performing for them. Damon grabbed her, pulled her up on all fours and took her from behind. She took Vladek in her warm mouth and pulled and pushed her lips back and forth over his hard limb, while Damon pushed and pulled her back and forth from behind.
– I've lost count, Josh marveled. – It's the truth. I've actually lost count!
Talk like that belonged to the past, to a past fading more and more from their mind with each passing hour, but right now and precisely because of that, it didn't matter.
Claire performed like a belly-dancer for a pack of males having a hard time keeping themselves in check. She seemed to be growing, expanding before their very eyes. They stared awestruck at her, in ever stronger need. Her body wriggled and small and bigger snakes hissing and spitting twined themselves around the female body.
– I feel such a desperate need in you, she said softly. – It's okay. I feel the same way myself.
She walked to Jaiwad and pushed him down on his back, and sat herself on him, with her feet on both sides of his excited body. The snakes kept twining around her body.
– I feel such… gratitude towards you all, he gasped. – You haven't just accepted me without reservations, but also shown me that there's a completely different life available to me, compared to how I visualized it in the close confines of my family and clam.
– Your family and your former view on life stink. She smiled ironically. – Your religion was just as bad as all other religions. But like you have realized, you aren't that religion, as little as that religion is you.
She sensed his anger then, when the still present vestiges of his old life revisited him. She didn't back down, but met his eyes without fear and submission. He felt her sting, and then… she felt his, and a big, pleased smile transformed her face.
Willy found himself surrounded by nymphs and felt no fear. Their expectations, demands didn't hold him back anymore. Nothing did! When he jumped on top of Yola and she howled in delight, he shouted just as loud in return.
It ruined the silence for a moment, nothing more than a brief delay in the whirlwind. Between desire and ecstasy they all felt the cold wind.
– O'Child of the Storm.
Everyone ceased their activities momentarily, the chill trickling down their backs in delight and fear.
– O'CHILD OF THE STORM
It originated from the dark, from somewhere out there on the dark water.

She slipped out of the shadows and they, everyone present glimpsed Anya's glowing eyes and face.

– Come to me, Damon! She called him. – Come to me… *now!*

He rose, liberating himself from Yola and Maxine and other hungry females. They stared at him with disappointment, with their hungry and distant eyes, with their eternally burning and devouring desire. The males stared as well, in envy and fear.

And he walked into the water. And he slipped into the shadows, fading from their vision.

– You will grant me a gift, she whispered within the large cave, far out on the big water, – and I will grant you one, one for the road, the long, long walk.

– Everything is changing already, he said, – making quantum leaps into a distant future.

– It has been changing for a long time. Even language, its basic expression is changing. We've changed for a long time, preparing ourselves for our new and fuller lives.

The voice reached him from behind.

– Come with me to the deep, Damon. Join me at the core of mankind, of all life.

She stood right in front of him. A light concentration and he spotted her. She flared in all the colors of the rainbow. He saw a completely ordinary woman with a body writhing in desire.

He dived below the surface. His feet rose in the water and pushed him deep under. He saw her stand on the bottom. He joined her there. There was such a pressure in his groin. She chuckled.

– You're so sweet, so dangerous, so irresistible, my Damon.

They swam ashore on an island at the middle of the lake, on the water that had grown to a sea. The island was like a cork at the mouth of the fjord, hidden in the mist everyone had to pass through on their way out, on their way in.

She pushed herself at him the moment they reached land, kissed him with hot lips. They stretched out in the sand, just as dry, as if they had never taken that swim, the long swim through the water. And then he mounted the warm, warm body and emptied himself in her before they had even started, and it just continued. He moved up and down, in and out in an endless stream, gasping for air, getting more of it than he had ever had. She moaned and the Earth shook. Sweat soaked them, mixing, rising like steam in the air. The hair, the hair suddenly long again fell down in his face, but she could still see his eyes.

In the days, years they spent on the island covered in mist, they were also talking, exchanging thoughts in often exhaustive ways. It was as if they never got fed up with talking, as if they feared they would never do enough of it.

– I'm a wanderer, she pondered. – I've always been wandering. I still am. You're the one wandering in twilight, flapping your wings in the night, the bird flying in darkness. A very long time has passed since we last remembered who we are.

She rocked up and down on him, turning a bit, drowning him in her warm water. Her tongue tasted like strawberries. He could hardly believe it.

– But… It will take a very long time before we forget again. Brahma sleeps for eight billion years and hardly closes an eye the next eight.

– Poor guy…

He felt a playful hand below, one grabbing his cock. She stared straight at him, without pretence of modesty. Her eyes, her entire shape told him she wanted more, wanted to fuck him again and again. He had emptied himself so many times, also in her, since she had called out to him. He was spent and didn't really feel ready for more. Then, she bent down and surrounded his cock with her lips, with her greedy lips. He gasped. His cock rose hard and sore. Suddenly, he once more felt his desire spread to his entire body, to the forest, to the mountains.

– You're such an amazing human beast…

She sat on him again. Her hip muscles contracted and she was back on rocking on him. The sweet mouth opened in a loud, pleased sigh. He sat up and pushed her back, turning her around, putting her down on her belly, climbing on top of her. He pushed and pulled within her from behind. She sat on him. Her hips seemed to rock up and down of their own volition. She bit him in the shoulder and sucked his blood. They touched each other, touched everywhere, or so it felt. There was no distinction between mind and body, spirit and flesh (burning, burning flesh). She stood on all fours while he once again emptied himself in her warm, warm hole. They shook, shook even harder during that final, *explosive* release.

Thought slowly returned. The burning passion remained. There was no shame, no sense of shame holding them back. They shook the ground, making the air shiver with the flapping of their wings.

Loud drums kept echoing in their ears. The giant worm slithered across the Earth. It was long and thick and the mountains shook when it passed them. The rivers and hazy air shivered in its presence. The trees didn't break when it slid through the forest, but their branches whispered and howled in ears and land alike.

They rested in the thick and pleasant heather, completely spent, enjoying each other's closeness. The birds sang to them. The animals called their name. Her sleepy and content voice spoke in his ear.

– Kali Yuga - the Machine Age has ended in glory and exalted happiness. Now, the true age of man has returned.

– Anya Kerien has wandered for a long time, he stated. – She's wandering still. Anya Kerien hasn't always been her name. She has had many.

– The Storm also has had many names, she said. – He has ravaged the world since the wind was given a name.

– We all have!

They looked startled at each other. None of them had spoken. The voice came from the left. They turned and froze, the chill trickling down their spine.

Blanche sat there, on a rock turned to glass.

– «I've become Death, the destroyer of worlds», she said with a voice chilling beyond chilling.

Until she faded, until the sight of her burned into their memory.

– You recognized her, Anya said with a hollow voice. – That's why you felt both repulsed by her and drawn to her.

And then, for the first time, he understood fully what she meant.

She took two steps forward and kissed him on the lips.

He felt the breasts' rounding against his chest, how the broad hips embraced his own. Her thoughts touched his… and they… Danced. And the Dance was not merely physical, but by the mind and spirit as well. He felt the legs, legs, legs move above the ground. He had never felt lighter. It was as if he didn't touch the ground except during a few, fleeting moments. He had never felt heavier. It was as if the Earth was shaking every time he took a step.

– I never thought I could do this.

He laughed and kept laughing. A choir of laughter rose from them, and it spread in the between worlds, between the world.

And he saw himself walk across the Earth, a giant taller than the mountains.

All worlds, all realities opened up to him.

He saw Jonas Bergli arrive in New York City in 1931, experienced how the shadows danced and shifted around him. He saw several versions of Jonas Bergli walk side by side in a hue of blue dancing and sparking. They all looked completely identical… until that very moment. Then they changed, becoming distinct, different from each other. Destiny, an endless chain of coincidences had chosen the seemingly insignificant man to play an incredibly important role in the scheme of things, in the web of life.

A man calling himself Henry Ronald waved his sword at the gates of life and death, at the end of time.

Somewhere, sometime Jeremy Zahn took his first, hesitant step on his eternal path.

Damon wandered with Carla Wolf through time, through Space. Carla Wolf had always been wandering. She was wandering still.

He stared at Anya.

In her dark cave Ethel Warren sat and viewed all times, all places.

Nicholas Wharton, an intense, obsessed creature without eyes, flesh and blood stumbled back and forth between his machines. He didn't live in the here and now, but in the past and an undefined point in a distant future.

Janet Kathryn Caldwell died for the first time.

Lucinda Patterson made her initial, ill-advised moves.

Chloe Webster reached out and touched the ether and changed in beyond fundamental ways, becoming a creature beyond anything anyone could imagine.

The Phoenix rose from all fires, all ashes.

The storyteller sat by the campfire and spoke to anyone interested in hearing his tales.

The music fell silent, retreating to the background, where it always *was*.

He didn't blink. The images, the dream visions, mirages from times that never were faded, but never faded away completely.

She returned his stare.

– Time is up. I must take my leave.

The voice was no more than a whisper in the twilight where everything thrived and lived.

She seemed far away already.

Somewhere in the distance a haze began rising from the ground. It was as if the haze opened, forming a passage in the very air.

– Wait…

He held out a hand, slightly desperate.

– We will always meet again, Damon Terrill… where the Thunder Road makes a turn.

She had used his name, the one he was using now. He belonged here. Now! She didn't. Not now!

The dancer retreated one step, pulling away from him. He wished to follow her on her

path, but stood still, and she faded away in the darkness.
Her smile followed him deep into sleep.

THE PLANET

The group of elite soldiers arrived at the place where the skeletons and ordinary clothes and military uniforms were stabled in heaps. An armed patrol jumped off the jeeps before they slowed down and started sweeping the area.

Ten minutes, with surveys and security sweeps in the nearby hills passed before they were somewhat content. They signaled to the far bigger group of soldiers waiting further down in the valley, and that group started driving up the hill.

A man standing in a jeep jumped easy-going off as the vehicle pulled to a stop. He was never close to losing his balance. It didn't take more than five seconds before he was surrounded by his closest people, his personal security detail. They never moved far from his person.

He lit an enormous cigar and stopped in front of one of the biggest heaps of steaming remains of people.

– I never cared much for these bastards, he snapped. – Such damn racists are a disgrace to their profession. Let's spend a few moments enjoying the fact that they've been wiped off the surface of the Earth.

Everyone removed their caps with a big grin.

The captain nodded to the woman in the nearest jeep.

– Let's also take the opportunity to enjoy the King of kings.

– There can never be enough such opportunities, sir, the lieutenant nodded, in something resembling the conduct of an American Navy Seal in a movie. She pushed a button.

The voice of Elvis Presley flowed from the speakers. All the soldiers stood at attention.

They did so during the entire tune. The lieutenant briefly touched her nose, or was about to before catching herself.

Her nose was itching, but she suffered in silence.

The music faded. Silence once again fell in this valley of death.

– So moving. The captain shook his head. – I feel it in my very bones!

– Heartbreak Hotel is no doubt one of his best, the lieutenant added.

– So true, so true…

The captain stood there for a while. No one interrupted his line of thoughts. Not when he picked up the remains of a uniform, not when he looked down at the burned-out vehicles. They remained silent when he kicked a half-digested bone in his path.

– How many would you say there was, lieutenant?

– Considerably fewer than the rac… the soldiers, sir. They butchered them with a rare savagery and skill, sir.

The captain shook his head. He did so several times.

– We can't let… can't let a threat like that run wild, can we, lieutenant?

– Definitely not, captain!

– We can't have loose cannons on deck.

He hesitated a bit before continuing.

– It just won't do. Norway won't survive with loose cannons on deck.

He turned around, scratching his back before turning even more.

– I wouldn't be surprised if those anarchist savages look at us right now, he mumbled.

He led on back to the vehicles.

– SADDLE UP! He shouted.

++++++++++++++++++++++++

The stone city rose above the steaming water, the now so stinking lake. Smoke flowed from the concrete and all the pipes. Lifelessness ruled, to such a degree that one would be tempted to believe that there was no life at all here.

The enormous construct could be seen from far away. It practically touched the clouds as it dominated the desert that once had been one of the most fertile areas in Northern Europe. The sun boiled the land from early morning to late evening. The soil became holes in the ground and the holes turned to sand. The sand penetrated every single spot of the construct.

Lisbeth stood behind the thick glass at the top of the pyramid. She stared at the mountains. The evening haze covered them, making them practically indistinct. She walked a few steps and looked north. The mountains there were just as hidden, just as inaccessible.

It had become a kind of ritual to her, this. Every night she looked in all the four directions of the sky.

She placed herself at the eastern window. The yellow, ruined landscape faded slowly to red by the sun's dying rays. When she looked south, there was nothing there, really. Once upon the time the river had flowed from the inland sea. Now, it flowed to the structure, but no longer. She stood at the top of the Pyramid, her creation, her Domain, surveying the world, the only world there was.

The Machine pulsed and lived beneath her. She felt its power. There were no audible abnormalities, no suspicious noise. The machine worked like clockwork, and she was pleased.

She wore simple, but well designed clothing. No one needed to cover themselves as long as they were within the stone desert's fortified gates. Everyone here was protected from the deadly sun rays.

She smiled at the dying sun above the western mountain range.

Magnus didn't know how long he had been there, forcibly resting on his back, chained on the cold flat rock. They gave him regular or irregular meals. Half nude servants, boys and girls fed him. He had given up talking to them. They never replied to him. They never spoke. Someone had trained them well, with a thoroughness making repeated chills pass down his spine, even here, in the hot, dry chamber.

He fell into slumber, there on the slab. Time and the room itself dissolved around him. Everything did! The fever visions assaulted him and he screamed and writhed in his chains, in his bottomless rage. He shook the chains, shook them for days without number, until he collapsed on the slab, completely exhausted.

He slept and was dreaming, horrible nightmares that would have driven ordinary people insane. He laughed aloud, but there was no sound.

The beast slumbered. The man did as well. Sometimes he was searching for thoughts in his own mind, but found none. The beast, the human being just lay still and waited for the inevitable.

– Hello, Magnus!

Magnus woke up. He opened his eyes.

– Hello, Magnus, Lisbeth Kaspersen greeted him. - Welcome to Heaven!

The chill surrounded him, like a draft, like arthritis. Behind her stood five of the young girls that had fed him, five of the Goddess's high priestesses, with her hairdo, her clothes, eager to do her bidding. He saw the worship in their eyes and realized stunned that it was directed at him.

– They do worship you, Magnus, Lisbeth said throatily. – And why shouldn't they? You're so precious…

– What the fuck are you…

She slapped him lightly on a cheek. Then she did it one more time, and one more after that again.

It didn't really hurt, even if the callous, patronizing way she treated him did hurt, most of all inside.

– Hush… She placed the tip of an index finger on his lips. – You're just a whippersnapper, a young boy. You shouldn't behave like that in the company of those older and more experienced.

He stared at her with spontaneous anger, but when he met those big eyes he saw nothing there, nowhere to focus his eyes, making him wonder if there was anything left there at all.

She covered his eyes with a hand.

– Relax, young god, she whispered. – Others might rightfully fear the Goddess, but not you. The Goddess has decided to honor you.

She removed the hand and brought to his closer attention one of the five girls. She… was she *undressing?*

When he once again directed his attention at Lisbeth Kaspersen she seemed pretty normal. The insanity more than implied only a few seconds earlier had left her, or at least retreated into her depths.

– They say that men can't be raped by women, Magnus. I've pondered that issue at length and have concluded that it is hard, but that it is doable… if you take your time doing it.

She signed to the girl and the creature covered in red hair and filled with need climbed on top of the big male.

– No matter, it's just a distraction, a secondary consideration. We just need your seed, not your submission.

He shook the chains. Lisbeth chuckled. The huge, glassy eyes stared feverishly at him.

– You will give us your seed, young god. You will do so many times!

The young redhead that hardly seemed to be anything but desire, breasts and hips and thighs writhed on top of him, enticing him to no end, no matter how hard he fought against it.

– Don't do it, he shouted. – Get the hell off me!

She didn't seem to hear him or notice that he did everything in his power to throw her off. He felt humidity on his thigh and realized it came from her. She grabbed his cock with an exalted expression, grabbed it with both hands and started playing with it. He gritted his teeth, but it started twitching almost immediately. While he stared in embarrassment and despair it grew big and sore. The redhead gasped and the four other priestesses echoed that. Everyone stared at Lisbeth and she acknowledged their prayer by nodding.

– The young god is ready, Mary. Grant him your gift, your sacrifice.

With eagerness, expectation and devotion Mary sat down on him, pushed him unresistingly into her. Her mouth opened wide and she started rocking up and down, up and down. And then… he pushed helplessly back. Lisbeth chuckled pleased once more.

– The young god is happy, is so much looking forward to everything.

He screamed in rage, in despair.

– Don't be so hard on yourself. We're all slaves of our desires.

He emptied himself so hard in Mary that he almost threw her off himself and down on the floor. She fell on him and lavished the sweaty body with kisses.

Black eyes stared at the ceiling. He felt withered, littered, just like Lisbeth had wanted.

– Your turn to be honored, Ani. Don't shame your clan. Enjoy god's gift.

– I'm looking forward to it, Goddess, the girl said. – I receive with enthusiasm and humility the gift of the gods.

She undressed. A simple shift of her body and the robe fell off her and down on the rock floor. She climbed on top of the man on the rock and instantly started playing with his spent limb. Magnus focused hard on not feeling it, but it was hopeless, of course. Hardly more than half a minute later he was ready, and Ani could receive the gift of the gods.

He was left completely exhausted. Time just floated away. He had no idea how long time had passed, how long he had enjoyed their company, how many times he had granted them the «gift». He fell asleep eventually. Being asleep and awake blurred to such a degree that if it was possible to distinguish between the states of being, it became ever harder.

The Goddess and her priestesses visited him often. They fed him and fucked him. They fed off his juice, squeezed him dry like they would a sponge.

One day Lisbeth displayed one of the girls like a trophy.

– June had a notable morning sickness today, and not long afterwards the happy circumstances were confirmed.

The Goddess's skin had a glow he couldn't recall seeing on her before. He stared at her with his burning eyes. She didn't seem to care. She undressed with slow, determined moves. It took longer time than with the others. She had more clothes to remove, but not long afterwards she stood nude before him.

– I see that those big, ugly muscles of yours have started withering. She rubbed him on the chest, squeezing the slack skin on his belly. – You shouldn't mind, though. It won't affect your performance. It doesn't. You become ever more attentive and attentive of our needs, dear, dear Magnus.

His cock rose to its full size and strength. She laughed triumphantly and expectantly.

She took her time, very patient and cunning, until she climbed on top of him and then, so unlike her, lacking in ceremony, she sat down on him and started rocking.

– Fabulous beast, she gasped. – Useful beast.

Her face seemed blown and dissolved when he stared up at it.

He couldn't recall whether or not he or she came then. He recalled a number of orgasms, also hers, but not the first. For some reason he didn't recall that. The next time he saw her somewhat clear, she stood before him and rubbed her belly, smiling in something approaching ecstasy. And while he watched her, her belly seemed to be growing. He recalled meals. Long after he remembered exactly what he had eaten and even the order of the meals. He remembered that he suffered loneliness in the dark and missed her company.

– I can recall you screaming to me, she said.

He didn't see her. She could have been standing right there, close to him, as far as he knew, without him being able to see her.

– You shouted your wrath at me, howled at me like a wolf, accusing me of being insane.

She spoke softly, in a completely different tone than the hysterical, religious chanting she used when the priestesses were present.

– I replied that yes, I'm insane. Finally, I am, too. I've waited so long for that. You have no idea of how long, my love.

He believed she had left the room, left him, but she hadn't.

– I can't kiss you, dear wolf. If I had, you would have taken me in your big gap and torn me apart.

He had attempted to bite her once, but hadn't been fast enough, had only caught a piece of her dress. It felt like it had happened such a long time ago.

– It's no big deal. You've gotten too much soft hair on that strong jaw of yours, anyway. It's tickling me and distracts me from what's important.

Did she imply that she had kissed him not that long ago?

He wanted to snarl at her, but there was no sound, none that he could hear.

Her pregnancy and that of the other females, all the other females became very distinct to him. It worked like a watch to him, a timepiece telling him the correct time, information he didn't want.

June stretched out on a bed, one rolled in for the occasion. She was breathing in and out, in and out. The pace speeded up, until the sound of breathing overwhelmed everything else. He felt really bad. His muscles seemed like they weren't there. The weakness hammered at him with every move he attempted to make. He had moved constantly in the time since he had been chained in an attempt to keep at least some of his musculature. He knew it was a hopeless measure, but he kept doing it for minutes, hours, days, weeks, months…

He drowned in Lisbeth's eyes. She was so sneaky, had approached him and seduced him with such a cruel cunning that he had trouble distinguishing between fantasy and reality.

But that wasn't anything new to him… right?

He heard the scream of an infant. June and several of the others sat there and nursed babies. Lisbeth screamed, a penetrating wail in his sore ears. The infant screamed. Lisbeth stood before him with it in her arms. It nursed on an exposed breast.

– Poor Magnus. She rubbed him on the head. – So down, so weakened. People have asked me about you. They would want you to join the gladiator fights. But I've told them like I've told you that you're mine, only mine. No one but I and my selected few will ever enjoy your power, the one flowing in a steady stream out of you. There is still juice left in you, and I suspect that will be the case for a very long time, but you aren't much to speak of aside from that anymore. I, your Goddess suck up all your power, as is my right. Everything you are, everything you might become belongs to me. To me!

She didn't raise her voice. It kept staying in the soft range he recalled from what had to be the last year. An entire year had passed. In his growing despair he felt how the catching in his throat grew. She studied him with the twinkling eyes. Her desire and possessive stare were glowing indistinguishable from each other.

He knew she would come to him again soon. She hadn't been with him in a while, not since the last weeks of her pregnancy.

She came now, an eager ball of hair, skin, passion and hatred. He saw her bend forward, felt her kiss, felt her kiss him bloody, how he returned the kiss, biting her lips to shreds, bit her entire infected head off. But she didn't kiss him, never kissed him, just sat there and rocked on him, scratching and cutting into him. He emptied himself in her in an insane scream of wrath.

She slipped off him. He imagined that he felt a taint of anxiety behind the content facade.

– You're a wild animal, she mumbled, she snarled.

She slapped him. She slapped him again, before waving to her subjects and they all left the room, left him.

It turned very quiet. He couldn't say for how long, before he started pulling the chains, the thick, unbreakable chains.

Everything turned indistinct, so horribly distinct. He imagined how Lisbeth Kaspersen returned to her bedroom, how she threw herself on the bed, sobbing loud and quiet.

The stone desert moved beneath him. He sensed its pulse, its oily veins of death and depravity.

He grew weak with rage. It filled him to its last thread, every last piece of skin, of thought. He pulled the chains. He pulled them long after all his muscles had turned weak and useless. With a mighty ROAR

He broke them in pieces.

They fell on the floor, striking the walls around him, making the walls shake.

He rose, brushing off dust and pieces of plaster and traces of blood.

Later he would never understand how he got away, how he could move at all, how he could move practically undetected through the Pyramid, how he became a shadow floating away in the nothing. He explained it to himself with the fact that the place was guarded against outer enemies, not those wishing to leave. No one wished to leave, according to them.

They believed that. This had already become a very conform place.

He reached the bedroom. The tiny creature slept in the cradle. There was no one on the bed. He picked up the small human being, packed it in soft fabric and rushed out of there on silent feet. The nameless shadow, a shape without eyes, flesh and blood slipped through endless identical hallways like a ghost, until he finally found an exit and three sentries. He hardly touched them when he killed them. Fingers formed like claws cut into their chest and pulled out their hearts.

He ran away, a transparent creature wrapped in the sand and the steam rising from the lake hidden by the monstrous construct, the last of the world's seventh wonders. There had been many of them, many ruining everything making life worth living.

The desert sand devoured him. The night met him with its soft fabric.

The heat surrounded him like a warm blanket.

Magnus Breen, with the small bundle in his arms vanished into the darkness and the shadow. Magnus, son of Lene, son of Rolf, grandson of Judith, grandson of Olav, grandson of Victor released his boundless rage on the world.

The Living Planet

The West Antarctic Ice Sheet broke off from the main, inland ice. It happened suddenly, without any forewarning, except the numerous scientific reports that had been published about the subject. The enormous mass of ice resting mostly on land slid into the ocean, hitting it with beyond dramatic consequences.

The sea level actually fell close to the sheet, but rose far away, to a far higher level than most had expected, at least temporarily, and this was easily observed from various satellite observations. The earth's rotation axis started what would become a shift of about 500 meters.

Global average sea level rose with six meters in just a few hours, adding to what was already in the system.

A tsunami spread from that central point and across the planet causing untold disasters far away.

A few weeks passed. The big change touched all areas, the smallest pieces of the globe. All the ice hadn't melted yet, but the melting grew exponentially and so fast that the change was practically visible from one day to another. The remains of the West Antarctic Ice Sheet had melted, had vanished. Freshwater flowed into the ocean from what had once been the 4.8 kilometers thick inland ice sheet. Steam thick like mist rose from the seething and boiling land. An entire continent changed from being covered by ice to become green and fertile.

There was no ice left in the Arctic. Nothing but ocean awaited those sailing there. Greenland lived up to its name for the first time in ages.

The deserts spread in dramatic ways. The process that had started in small areas of Sudan, China and the south western United States thousands of years ago, had gone haywire in just a century. From Tierra del Fuego in the south to Canada in the north, from Africa's south point to far north in Europe, from Australia to what had been the Siberian tundra, the ground cracked and turned to sand. The sand penetrated everything, everywhere.

In areas of extreme heat roads and parking lots became rivers and seas of tar. People and animals drowned in such rivers and seas.

In South America, hordes of twilight storm people sought to the Titicaca Lake, the world's deepest lake, the only remaining major source of freshwater on the continent. Or they sought to Antarctica, a continent now submerged in humidity and eternal mist, a fairytale world, the new and fertile land, where few humans had ever walked. Australia, the small part staying above the ocean was just steaming away, until no more than a dry, dead cliff remained. Dead carcasses of animals and people were rotting all over the scorched Earth. The pale-skinned people that had briefly lived there the last few centuries, wishing to be left alone finally got their wish. The ocean around the dead cliff was fertilized with life and the few ocean animals that had survived the temperature increase had a feast.

To the northern Europeans, the forgotten land in the south gained a mythic quality. They called it the same that the ancient North African nomadic tribes had called the southern land: *Sahara* - The Wasteland.

In what had been called the United States of America there were only a few habitable areas left. The Great Lakes dried up. The few survivors headed northwest, to the somewhat still fertile western coast, and the far north, all the way to the former polar sea, to its now so bountiful coast, eventually covered by a hot, humid forest. The Bush family and their peers were cursed up and down the generations. The name itself became a four letter word, one used for describing only the worst kind of madman or inhuman creature.

Vast lands all over the world vanished into the ocean. Just the meter that had been inherent in the system in 1990, the one the authorities had done their utmost to hide, had led to a dramatic increase in coastal erosion. Now, when the sea level had passed a ten meter relative rise in just twenty-five years, local and global maps would have to be redrawn… if anyone had been interested and capable of doing it.

And the ice kept melting. And the sea kept rising.

Most coastal cities were crushed by the extreme storms unleashed on an assembly line. The sea rose and covered the rest, covered the ruins, humanity's hubris. The roads faded away quickly. What the storms didn't destroy or the sea drowned was covered by sand and green, wild-growing plants. Nothing kept the process of life back anymore. Nature recaptured what humanity had spent the last ten thousand years taking. Streets were slowly but surely overgrown. The nomads walking on a very big Earth witnessed great changes each time they passed a given area, one once covered by concrete. In fertile areas the growth also covered the tall buildings. Soon, in just a generation or three, there would hardly be a trace of the immense structures that had dominated people's lives for so long. Their very existence would fade into myths and legends.

Life's diversity returned slowly, painfully to the ocean and the land. It had suffered hard during the hardship of civilization. Recovery would take time, but without humanity's crushing hand, the ecological systems corrected themselves. The fish shoals grew big and numerous again. «The greedy whale», an expression used by a loyal mainstream newspaper, grew in numbers. Predators and prey spread and multiplied in all ecosystems. Except for humans. They went from dominance to insignificance with a snap of fingers. And they grew powerful and great once more precisely because of that.

The human beings learned to hunt again, learned to live again. It required patience and sufferance by those who had grown up in a time where true independence wasn't appreciated, but they learned, learned the hard way, and to their children and grandchildren it wasn't hard at all. Those born into cruel and bountiful nature learned to know its wiles. Only tiny leftovers of civilization continued to bother humanity and life on Earth a bit longer, until those faded away as well, into the insignificance it had come from.

The censorship on knowledge vanished. The human animal no longer sailed only a single wave, but all of them, on all the vast oceans.

There were still books. Those remaining were highly treasured, as stories of what had been. But it became ever harder to distinguish between fact and fiction as the generations lived, died and lived again. The oral tradition finally had its renaissance. Stories were told around the campfire. Those sitting around it could see it and themselves. If they turned their head, they saw straight into darkness. Beyond the campfires, there was nothing, nothing but ghosts and shadows, like it had always been and always would be.

– Horrible structures reached for the sky, the old woman, old man, young woman, young man told those gathered around the campfire. – The air, soil and water, and even the fire were filled with poison… and no places were the poison worse than in human hearts.

He, she paused, before continuing.

– The Storm Child… He - Who - Came - With - the Storm… was born, returned to the world in such a place. He was born into the Twilight Storm and survived its rage. Its rage was his, and his was its. He gathered his tribe, and they walked his path, walked their own. Humanity's fate, whatever it might be, is once again our own.

The storyteller began relaying details. He knew he didn't quite tell the story the same way as a colleague of him in a tribe he had encountered a few years earlier did. There were notable differences in both detail and execution.

It was one of his favorite stories, also because it was among those his tribe more than any wished to hear.

– What happened to him? A boy asked.

– He lived with his tribe for many years until he left them and wandered into the wilderness. It is said that he's wandering still, that he will meet again his tribe in a distant time and place… where the Thunder Road makes a turn.

Voices faded. The fire shrunk. The small group of Wanderers and Nomads slept… and dreamed.

The wind blew between the mountains. In the mountain mist, where there was still an icecap on the tall mountain peak giants walked. In Asgard, in the world between the stars lived, died and lived the fire-spitting dragons. The sleepers around the campfire shivered in joy. People walking in the wilderness knew well that dreams were gates to other worlds.

The Tree of Life, withering not that long ago grew and reached out anew, grew from the mountain with the icecap and reached into the world, the new and exciting world. Yggdrasil spread its branches and buried Nidhogg, the dreadful serpent where it belonged… as nothing more than a wrinkle in one of its tiny roots.

++

The sound of a hammer against a rock was heard somewhere at dawn, a bright morning followed by the growing day.

A Nightraven sits somewhere where a railroad and a road vanish into the ocean, engraving words in stone, the epitaph of civilization:

And on the pedestal
These words appear:

My name is Ozymandias,
Kings of kings: look on
My works, ye mighty,
And despair!
Nothing beside remains
Round the decay of
That colossal wreck,
Boundless and bare
The lone and level
Sand stretch
Far away

Percy Bysshe Shelley

CHAPTER TWENTY-FOUR

When they woke up the next morning, the two were gone, as if they, Anya and the boy had never been there, had never walked with them since the day long ago they had joined the tribe. But the others understood, sensing immediately that it was just their own insecurity and fear speaking to them and twisting their vision. She remained in their midst and would walk with them far beyond the forever gates at the end of time itself.

Damon rose. His hair had become *short* again. Claire stood a few steps away, turned towards him. She met his eyes calmly and measured. The final remains of her old, destructive insecurity had gone during the night. Her earrings shone in the rust and blood, prompted by the light of the rising sun. She didn't wear a headgear. She had tied her hair into a ponytail, sometimes blowing horizontally in the wind, sometimes coiling around her body. She carried the pouch like she had always carried it. She resembled Anya in many ways, but was herself.

– Greetings, forest dancer, Damon said, slightly ironic.

– Greetings, Terrill, she responded.

People woke up. The broad smile, the deep satisfaction revealed itself in eyes, body and every single move. Even when they pulled on the clothes fully covering them, and they suffered even more in the choking heat, they kept the wild mood, the devil-may-care attitude.

They stood there in silence. Everyone studied the valley, the humidity turning to haze, the haze turning to mist. They stood there for a long time.

– Are you aware of something in particular? I know you are!

Kara took a few steps forward and turned towards them, bewitching and more herself than they had ever beheld her, more confident, more certain of herself and her power.

– This is a sight that in the old days, ten days ago they would have said called on heathendom and prehistoric times.

– A great sight indeed, Yngve said with tears in his eyes.

– A great sight, Kara nodded. – And no longer «necessary». We're there, now, where we've always wanted to be every time we've seen anything like this, every time we've stared into the Night and seen the Fire.

The laughter came easy, effortlessly to them, dissolving some of the catching in their throat.

They fed. By every piece of nourishment they devoured, one more crack of wonder, of Joy revealed itself beneath their mask.

– It's beyond strange how good the food tastes, Yngve shook his head, – how it's actually possible to distinguish between the various parts of the animal.

– Like Kara points out, it isn't just the food, Gwen pointed out. – We experience everything so much better, in more powerful ways. All senses are like… one big, so beyond how we used to perceive things, that merely saying it feels hopelessly inadequate.

She had learned to speak fairly normal, but in every shade, every move she was far wilder than the woman Damon and the others had met in the Alps.

She resembled a wolf, now. She had embraced that aspect of herself, no longer just playing at it.

They had all changed, in a day or in a night, changed yet again.

The majority, but not all was still spent after last night. The sound of eager mating pleased everyone present. Their experience of total, utter freedom was confirmed. They didn't apologize for their desires anymore. Whatever remaining sense of shame engraved by civilization had vanished during the night.

And so much had been added.

Everyone glanced around some time or another, in the hope of seeing the woman and the boy in their midst, of glimpsing them as they wandered the remote road.

And they did, every time they looked.

Damon rose. He had embraced all aspects of himself. The black eyes were pools of boiling oil. The air itself moved around him. They saw his shadow now. Even in direct sunlight, his body stayed in the darkness. When they saw him in silhouette against the sun's disk, it was as if the entire disk… vanished. He was like a hill when the sun fell behind it, but a hill containing all the world's secrets.

They broke camp fast, with a joy touched by sadness.

– It already feels like we've always been doing this, Roger remarked pensively and pleased. – I feel like I can hardly recall my life ten days ago, far less thirty.

– Thus is the Traveler, Jaiwad said. – Today means everything, yesterday only a memory.

They fitted on their body their rucksacks and weapons, their few possessions, everything they owned in this world, what they were able to carry, what would help them survive and thrive the next days, weeks, months, years. They moved further down the valley, then up, then down, an endless, slow-moving rollercoaster.

The days passed like that, while they walked ever further east.

Myriam was exercising. She was exercising hard. Everyone saw, with their increased awareness that her shoulder remained stiff. But she worked past the pain, ignored it to a point where they grew worried for her.

Everyone was exercising. André limped around on his healthy foot. He could even walk on the injured now and then.

Kara came to Damon at dusk. He had been expecting her.

– It has become something tangible, she stated very pushy, almost aggressively so. – No longer just an ephemeral glance on the edge of the vision, but something tangible I can touch and move.

– I know, he confirmed. – I have it the same way. It's like an ocean has turned dry from one moment to the next and I can suddenly see the bottom.

– The eyes are burning, she whispered. – All the senses are aflame. I can understand why Strega backed away from it for as long as she did.

– She had to get rid of her baggage of insecurity and self-denial, he said. – We all had, have to do that. And now, whatever happens, we're Free.

She nodded and nodded again.

– Chief, she said, very formal, waiting for his response.

– I'm not Chief, he stated, shaking his head decisively.

– I'm the tribal witch, now, she declared. – The new Strega isn't as powerful as the one that left us. She's a healer and not much more than that.

– That isn't entirely correct, he remarked. – But no matter… isn't it enough?
She didn't speak.
He stayed quiet a bit, too, before speaking.
– You're one of several witches. There is room for more, more than one, more than two. It is like you said: you're complementing each other.
– Yes, He Who Came with the Storm.
She curtseyed and pulled away from him, with him being unable to decide whether or not she was being ironic.
He sat there for a while, shaking his head both good-humored and anxious. He didn't miss the point that she insisted on calling him by one title or another.
They approached the inner mountains, the large plains, as they walked on with the sun in their back. It wasn't hard to spot the road down there, both under and over the rising water. It splashed ever higher on land. The sky stayed blue, but the air also stayed… restless, almost like a living being.
They definitely remained antsy, agitated, on guard. «Expect the unexpected» had become their most important tenet, and they stuck to it.
Roger woke up Damon in the twilight's twilight. Clouds once more covered the sky, but it never really turned dark in the summer half of the year in this country. Roger didn't speak. Neither did Damon. The others still woke up, as if they more than sensed the unrest hiding in Roger's eyes.
– I hope I'm wrong, he said, – but I imagine we have a bunch of very eager soldiers on our heels. They're still fairly far behind, but gaining on us.
The two of them hid behind a rock. Damon used the binoculars to scout the terrain. Along a straight line through the air covering several mountain peaks, he spotted them, saw them guard their vehicles.
– They're not that many…
He knew it was an ill-informed statement the moment he spoke.
– I believe most of them have left the vehicles and started chasing us on foot, Roger whispered. – I haven't seen anything proving that, but if I'm right, they're closer, much closer.
Damon nodded. The camp where the vehicles were parked looked like a more or less temporary stationary camp, and the soldiers there were way too few in numbers compared to those raiding the country before Ragnarok. They didn't seem like the sorry remains of what had once been a larger army either, but exactly like they looked like: a group that had been ordered to stay behind and guard valuable equipment.
– We're leaving, he said back in the camp, fairly unnecessary.
Everyone had already packed and was ready to leave. They looked good-humored at him. He smiled and shook his head.
They all looked at André on the travois then.
– I can walk, he insisted.
– No, you can't! Damon stated firmly. – William!
William nodded eagerly and bent down and grabbed André, putting him on his shoulder.
Yola carried the travois. It was a light load compared to what she already carried.
They made their way in the pre-dawn landscape, feeding as they walked, once again feeling the power in their legs.

– Hopefully, they won't realize we have wounded people, Damon said, knowing once again he spoke against his better judgment.

They already knew, if they had any ability to interpret tracks of walking people. Damon didn't say more. There was no need for that. He saw the awareness of it in all the eyes of his fellow tribe members. Sometimes, he would have preferred that they weren't so clear-sighted.

But not often.

The legions of death were marching. The legions of death advanced. The army of decay pushed forward. Like it had done on the Konya plains in what had been Turkey at the beginning of civilization, like it had done by the rivers Euphrates and Tigris in old Persia, in the land that had been called Egypt, in the Roman Empire, in Europe, Asia, America, Africa and Australia. It had been all-present. Now, it had been crushed to dust and only its pale remains were still marching.

The captain ran in front of his soldiers. He ran behind them, firing up with strikes, kicks and swearing those even indicating that they were falling behind. The soldiers ran mechanically, without thoughts, with empty stares and expressions, doing what they had been taught, obeying the commands beaten into them.

The evening arrived. They didn't really notice the changes in light and temperature. They registered the actual stop, the sign that they could finally rest.

They fed while the captain, very agile and energetic walked back and forth between them. Some cast him ugly stares, but they didn't dare voice anything even resembling a murmur.

The lieutenant spotted the tracker as he returned from his mission. She met him by the entrance to the smaller gathering of tents.

– They still have one wounded, the tracker reported. – They dragged him for a while on a travois or something, but now they carry him.

– How can you tell? The lieutenant asked distrustful.

– That's as certain as Elvis, lieutenant. The one carrying him leaves far deeper tracks.

The lieutenant reported back to the captain.

– So, the bird's wings are still curtailed, the captain chuckled. – That's excellent!

They settled for a cold camp and cold, half decayed meat. Elvis was played on an old, portable cassette player. The soldiers rocked up and down and joined in the singing with empty eyes.

– Too bad we can't listen to the King on a better player, a soldier said unusually astute. – This… doesn't sound like it should, like it… *deserves.*

– The King has always been played on such players, the lieutenant explained curtly, patiently, as if to a child. – There hasn't been and never will be a need for fancy equipment while listening to the King.

There were murmurs or agreement. Elvis was great. Elvis was the greatest. Not the most derelict cassette player could diminish the greatness of hearing Elvis. His voice cut through all noise.

– Traditions, the captain grunted. – It's important to retain traditions.

– Traditions are what we live and die for, the lieutenant declared.

– LIVE AND DIE FOR, the soldiers echoed.

The soldiers sat there and exchanged words until they were called to the tents

substituting for barracks.
– I've always been excited about Elvis, one stated. – All his songs are classics, so superior compared to the other, mediocre stuff. Nothing can compare with Elvis and the songs he wrote.
– The songs are such beyond great compositions. Another added his voice with empty eyes. – And he composed all his stuff himself, a rare thing at the time.
One wearing a leather cap shook his head in wonder. The cap almost fell off.
– My favorite is no doubt Love Me Tender.
– Mine is Love Me Do, the astute soldier stated firmly.
– That isn't the King, you idiot. An idiot by the name of Lennon or something did that one.
– What are you saying, pebble head? You dare insulting the King?
– You are the one insulting him by being Elvis illiterate, another cried out in an attempt at appearing knowledgeable.
– You are mistaken! Another shouted.
Others nodded in solemn agreement. A moment or two later all the soldiers faced each other with weapons in hands.
– SOLDIERS!
The authority in the captain's voice made them all freeze, listen attentively to the voice of reason.
They stood at attention, awaiting the captain's word.
– We have a mission, ladies and gentlemen.
Loud words of agreement accompanied his statement.
– It pleases me to tell you that we're closing in on the enemy…
As if on command, a pale light was lit in their eyes.
– We will catch up with them and kill them. I know I can trust you in this, like with all things, you proud SOLDIERS in the Royal Norwegian army.
– YES, CAPTAIN!
He held back a bit, allowing it to register in their dull minds.
– It's just a matter of time before we catch up with them… and exterminate them. ELVIS LONG LIVE!
– ELVIS LONG LIVE! A united choir replied.

The small group struggled up the mountain, like they had struggled up countless others. Damon relieved William of his burden before the big man began stumbling. He put André on his own shoulder.
– We take turns, he said. – I'll make sure to tell you when I grow tired.
They chased along a cliff. They saw the fjord far below, saw the ocean reaching ever farther into the massive mass of land. They no longer saw the cliff. It wasn't there anymore, except like a distant memory in their feverish thoughts. The past reached into an eternal darkness behind them, even as it threatened to catch up with them all like a wandering, vengeful soul.
Damon Terrill, the Storm Child saw Death, saw it dance, saw it chase them, saw it dance in their midst. He dried the cold sweat off his forehead, doing so time and time again. Yola and Josh added to his effort with cold hands and wet cloths.
The landscape was a natural rollercoaster, rising and falling constantly. Flat land

appeared rare or not at all. They couldn't make a single break. Even when they sat down to rest, they didn't.

Myriam placed herself before Damon, a considerable distance away. She spoke to him. He could read her language, the language her body spoke, in its tiny nuances and movements. Knowledge, instincts age-old and incredibly valuable rose slowly to the surface. They hardly needed words anymore, except as a way of treasuring old habits.

He rose and walked to her, where she stood straight and aware behind a large rock, one having fallen from the mountain long ago, an excellent hideout from those hunting them.

– I can see them Myriam said.

She handed him the binoculars.

He started scanning the terrain in the direction she had indicated. At first he didn't see anything, anything but trees and haze and soil and the sea boiling in the fjord.

There was lots of movement, the nature moving, nothing but distractions right now. He saw them, the women and men in shiny uniforms. The lenses brought them so close that he could spot the white in their eyes, their pale, distant look. He froze and embraced the frost, this frost as well.

– Up! He told the others.

– You can't stand steady on your feet, Yola pointed out.

He lifted up André and put him on the shoulder. The others rose. Their desperate walk continued.

Sun rose. Sun fell. And he didn't notice. He studied Willy as the big boy fought himself forward on the verge of exhaustion. They had taken turns at carrying André many times by now. They couldn't say how many. Others had also pitched in, two and two.

They pushed themselves close together on a small mountain ledge, invisible to those chasing them.

– They're better trained than we are, Myriam said, – or at least their training and the tactical support available to them make them more effective in the field. They would have caught up with us, even if we didn't have to drag André with us.

Very brutal and straight to the point. Very characteristic for her.

Damon and Willy carried André together. They struggled a bit with balance and stuff, but it relieved the pain in their legs, the ever stronger pain in limbs and muscles.

Damon didn't see the sun in the morning. They used it as their guiding star on their way east, but it hid behind the mountains. During most of the day they had it above, on their right, very visible, and in spite of the clothes protecting them against its deadly rays, they imagined that the side of their face turned towards it always burned and swelled. They were sweating profusely and drank a lot of fluid. It was as if they could never get enough. They feared they didn't have enough of it, that the endless supply wasn't enough. They chuckled. The brittle sound hardly reached their ears.

The road stretched an eternity in front of them.

The soldiers moved forward in a rigid, soft movement. They rested when they were ordered to do so and marched when they were ordered to do so. They did slip, stumble and fall occasionally. They jumped back on their feet and continued moving forward with the same, mechanical movements.

One just collapsed and lay still. Another kicked his unmoving ass. There was no life left there. The army moved on.
The tent village grew from nothing at dusk. It was always the same. No matter where they camped, independently of the terrain, there was no deviation from the norm. It grew at dusk. It fell at dawn. The soldiers stayed the same. The length of their hair, the expression, every single move could not be distinguished from the rest.
The captain stood at the entrance of his private tent. He and the lieutenant had one each.
– A campfire, captain? The lieutenant inquired.
– A large campfire, lieutenant, the captain confirmed. – I want our prey to see it. I want it to burn their black souls.
The campfire grew, its flames stretching and twisting in the night. The captain stared at it.
– Does it burn, lieutenant?
– It burns like hell, captain, the lieutenant confirmed.
– I'm confident that you're correct, lieutenant, the captain nodded.
The lieutenant stood there and looked uneasily at him. She had taught herself the art of reading her superior's mood with millimeter precision.
– I just think there are way too many shadows around the campfire, that's all, the captain mumbled.
The lieutenant turned towards a group of soldiers.
– FIND MORE DRY WOOD, she shouted. – Get your ass in gear!
The campfire burned tall and burned everyone even remotely close to it. They writhed covered by sweat and moaned in their sleep. The man that these days only answered to the name «captain» awoke abruptly and sat up in his tent. He looked at his watch, at all the dancing shadows on the tenth walls.
The watch showed a few minutes past midnight. According to it, he had only slept a few minutes. He shook his head in distress.
The captain and the lieutenant faced the early dawn together, studying the rhythm of the soldiers packing the tents and equipment.
– Have I showed you my watch, lieutenant?
The words came abruptly, unexpected, definitely unexpected. The lieutenant stared for a moment at the man before the professional mask once more proved ascendant. What was wrong with the fucker?
– No, you haven't, captain.
– I bought it five years ago, while good watches were still available. The advertising claimed that the batteries will last for centuries. I bought three.
He paused, frowning.
– A good watch is important.
The tracker returned from his morning reconnaissance just before they marched off.
– They hide well in the terrain, he reported, – but I catch sight of them now and then, and they can't hide their tracks.
– Good, good, the captain nodded, clearly distracted.
The lieutenant cast a fearful glance at her God and master, before signing for the day's march to begin.
The captain noticed the lieutenant's hesitation. He noticed everything. He heard low-

keyed conversation between the soldiers, whispering and sounds growing in strength and extent as the day passed. The captain waited.

The fire burned the next evening. The captain waited. A considerable number of soldiers had been sent to find and fetch dry wood. The fire burned skin, burned hair, boiling the air itself in its wrath.

The captain stood outside his tenth. The lieutenant arrived with a private in tow.

– Greetings, captain!

Both the lieutenant and the private saluted the superior officer and stood at attention.

– At ease! The captain said graciously.

– This loyal soldier brings you important news, captain.

The captain turned his full attention on the anxious youth.

– So, what do you have to report, son?

The man hesitated and kept hesitating before he finally committed to the course of action.

– There is talk… open doubt expressed about the captain's… qualifications, about the value of continuing something being seen as… an insane venture, a hunt for ghosts and shadows.

Time passed and passed again, until the captain finally nodded.

– It was the right thing you did, obeying the chain of command, son: The captain nodded. – The chain of command must always be observed, or we're nothing but a bunch of uncivilized barbarians without any true purpose in life.

The storm around the campfire calmed to a breeze when the captain approached and placed himself in their midst. He went straight to the point, took the initiative in a move that certainly would have made all old soldiers proud.

– For your information, the supreme command has asked us to…

– The supreme command no longer exists, the soldier not knowing the difference between Elvis and the Beatles spat.

The captain drew the gun and shot him down, shot him several times. The soldier dropped to the ground with an astonished expression on his face. Blood soiled his uniform. The captain kept firing until the man stayed still and dead, until his gun was empty.

– If you want to throw dirt on the King, it is your own business, the good captain mumbled, – but when you criticize the supreme command, I have legal right to exterminate you from the face of the earth.

The shadows gathered ever tighter around the huddling soldiers.

In spite of what Damon had said, he eventually stumbled and fell, with André falling on top of him.

– Leave me, André said quietly.

– Just wait a minute, Damon breathed, – just wait a minute…

– Leave me, damn you! André snarled. – Get the fuck up!

Everyone stopped. Damon rose slowly. He dried himself around his mouth, dried off the bitter bile. He had to do it several times. Claire knelt down by their wounded friend. She surveyed the foot once again, doing so with a rigid expression in her face.

– It needs at least a week's rest, she said. – We need a miracle. I'm sorry.

– What is there to be sorry about? Terrill spoke casual, low-keyed.

He was unable to keep up the pretence of indifference.
– We should have speeded up earlier, he choked.
– And missed the great, mindless fucking? André joked. – Don't be silly!
And adding, like an afterthought:
– Not to speak of the fact that we would have surely starved to death...
The entire tribe gathered in a circle around him.
– You're so funny, so damn funny!
Yola chuckled, a choking sound resembling sobbing.
– We're struggling, André stated, very determined, thorough. – We might have been able to make considerations before, but no longer. You've done everything you possibly can for me. It's time for you to fully consider the means needed for your own survival.
No one spoke. Everyone had a strong urge to do so, but no one did. The wounded man on the ground, the brother they had learned to know the last few years changed on the spot, becoming everything he could have been.
– We don't have a prayer against them in open battle. They're way too many for that. So what remains is guerilla warfare. It's obvious. We should have realized it far sooner.
He spoke with a quiet conviction. Damon wished he could have contradicted him, but he couldn't.
– Small assaults, Vladek said. – Many tiny stings making them bleed to death.
– Desperate measures, Damon stated. – Doing everything possible in order to improve our odds.
They saw his wheels turn, very aware of what he was considering, what course of action he was fast deciding.
– I will be the first sting, André said. – They will easily spot bigger groups in hiding, but not a single person. I'll hand them a great demoralizing defeat and the brainwashed assholes will collapse like the houses of cards they are. I can walk and even run if I need to. I'm fully capable of engaging them for a while. The reason I haven't been walking is that we've been worried I eventually wouldn't be able to walk. That isn't a consideration anymore.
There was a kind of relaxed, dry humor to his words. They weren't amused.
– What the fuck are you saying?
Yola dried her tears. It was no use. They kept coming.
She turned abruptly to Damon, not requiring an answer or any sort of consent.
– I want to fight with him.
Damon wanted to say «no way» and he wanted to nod. He couldn't do either.
– I will as well, Ralph said.
– I agree that they should, André said and added: – before others yap absurdities...
He was laughing. Several others were as well. A very accentuated and sore laughter.
– It is an advantage, Damon, Terrill, the Storm Child acknowledged, – that the initial hail of bullets comes from several angles simultaneously. I give you my blessing. The two of you fire one, extensive salvo. Then you withdraw and leave André, leave as fast as your feet can carry you. Is that *understood?*
– Understood! Yola said and Ralph nodded. – Thank you, Storm Child.
Both acknowledged his words, his command, and straightened inevitably.
– I saw an excellent spot just a few minutes ago, André remarked, almost completely relaxed. – This isn't just a good opportunity to execute our plan. It's an *excellent* moment

to do so.
He rose, standing on shaky legs. The pain cut into his features, but it didn't keep him from moving.
– Until we meet again, he greeted them.
– Until we meet again, Damon greeted him in return.
The three ran off, retreating the same way they had come from.
Damon stood like frozen a few seconds before he turned towards the tribe. The determination, grief and rage shadowed his eyes. The shadow danced and burned as something they could touch, like a rock, a lump of ice, a handful of soil, a fire burning them.
– Enough! He stated.
Death was close, so close that he could reach out a hand and touch it. But he reached out even harder. He needed it to be even closer.
He looked to the east, at Aurland in Sogn, a totally changed landscape compared to how he had experienced it as a boy. But not compared to how it had been earlier this year. Much of what had once been land had already become sea then.
Such a short stretch, no more than a tiny walk down and up a mountain, and they would have reached their goal, their illusory goal.
– Expensive tunnels are being filled with water, Roger mumbled, – filled to the ceiling. Soon everything here will be gone, here as well.
– Our situation has not changed, will not change, Myriam pointed out.
She was smiling. The smile wasn't pleasant. It still made their insides shake and burn so pleasantly.
– WARRIORS! She shouted in an obvious imitation of a military commander. – It's time to use what we have learned… *everything we have learned.*
Her voice, her very being slowly turned serious, turned intense.
They split into groups, squads, those who had trained the most together.
– Death is coming.
Claire shivered and burned.
– «I've never heard so musical a discord, such sweet thunder».
The voice seemed to come from nowhere. Damon shook, as he led a group through the valley of death, towards the mountain of torches. He visualized André, Ralph and Yola as they cut at the heart of the Gray Fog. He recalled vividly the Gray Fog.
He spotted the tracker. He saw the three letting him past them. The uniformed man seemed very, almost supremely confident, so used to the hunted fleeing from the army he served.
Kara and Yngve walked one way, Josh and Claire another. Damon kept charging forward, right at the tracker. The five didn't speak, but communicated on a much deeper level, moved according to each other in a way that would have scared them shitless only a short while ago. Josh and Claire attacked the lone man where the road made a turn. Claire struck him at the side of the neck, paralyzing him. Josh stuck him with a needle and he turned limp. He was conscious, but helpless in their grip.
– What amazing efficiency, Kara marvel with excited eyes. – I'm in awe!
– Anya trained us since our earliest childhood, Josh remarked. – She knew what would come.
– She always told us that we were brother and sister in eternity, Claire said, revealing

a sore subtext in her voice, – that it would come a time when we would do everything together, that we needed to become a unit, one breathing and moving as one when necessary.

– Accept my humble apology, Strega. Kara took Claire's hands. – I, in my foolishness underestimated you. You truly moved like a snake at your prey. I was practically stunned when I saw your eyes fixed on the prey.

– Thank you, Kara, Claire grinned, feeling strong, alive, – you say the nicest things.

– We must all dig deep within ourselves. Damon spoke harshly to them the truth they all knew.

– You would have wanted to avoid this? Kara said softly to him.

– Not anymore, he replied casually.

The chill trickled down everyone's spine. They felt the heat glow within, sensing it as a deep, deep part of the human beings they had become.

They dragged the prey with them, led the half drugged man far away. He stumbled on as they pushed and pulled him. He opened his mouth to breathe, to speak. Kara struck him in the balls.

– You shall not speak, she whispered. – You shall only do.

She allowed her words to sink in, before continuing.

– You're such a perfect victim to us, you see. You're everything we despise.

He was sweating, sweating hard. She dug her claws deeper. The pain was written in his face. He blinked.

Damon blinked. Through André's eyes he saw the armies of death whirl dust into the air from the wet soil less than hundred meters away.

André blinked. He felt Yola and Ralph around him. Yola he knew. He suddenly realized that he had always known her. He had never known Ralph, but now he did, his insecurity, his burning desire to survive, to live. The three of them had never hunted as a unit before, not like anything but an exercise, a casual thing in Askøy's forests and Bergen surrounding areas. But now they moved like one person, like one body with several heads, with one head, one mind, before parting once more. They had already parted before they split and slipped away from each other. Yola sent him one final look of regret and emotional heat.

The armies of death were marching, looking neither left nor right. It sent out its scouts to look for whatever enemies there were, but blind and deaf as they were, they found nothing. André saw them. He moved like one with the terrain, with the Earth itself, and was like invisible to them, to mere eyes and ears. He chose a hiding place he long since had chosen and put all his guns, the rifle, the grenade launcher, the bazooka on the ground, easily accessible. He kept the sword on his body. He hardly felt the pain in his foot anymore, not as anything but a faint irritation.

The soldiers lifted a foot, lowering it back down. Lifted it, put it down. He stared into their eyes, their emptiness, their weakness, their strength. He found his savagery, his strength. He saw the savagery in Yola's eyes when she fucked, saw the death in her life. He shook his head. He had never been much of a philosopher.

He saw… did he see Blanche among the soldiers? He shook his head again. It cleared. The vision of Blanche faded away.

Damon drew a single circle in the soil, in the moss. It seemed like soil and plants turned black when the knife touched it all. Claire and Josh held the tracker.

– Look at me, Kara bid him, looking far older than her nineteen years.

He focused his hazy eyes on her. She grabbed his uniform jacket and with a single pull, with swelling muscles, she had torn it apart, exposed his chest. She drew her knife and held it up for him to see. He started shaking his head. She slapped him, once, twice, more, until his head hung down and the jaw touched his chest. She started drawing symbols on his chest. They resembled runes, but were more elaborate. She kept drawing, half knowing, half guessing their meaning. It was working. She knew it did, feeling it in her bones.

– Don't worry, she mumbled, she comforted him. – The symbols don't mean anything. They mean everything. They prepare you, prepare us. You're a human being. You're life, you're death. The life you have discarded is infinitely valuable.

He stared at her with infinite fear in his eyes.

The drums, the silent drums reached his mind, and they were practically able to observe as it somehow rekindled his rage, the hate that had always been there.

– I'm just a tracker, he cried.

– And you believe that frees you of responsibility? Damon spat, spittle flowing from his mouth. Suddenly he was the one standing right in front of the man. – Are you a total idiot or what?

Kara stood farther away, at the spot where Damon had stood, making the man baffled and scared and stunned. Panic, and pure, undiminished hatred, the fear haunting him his entire life filled him.

– You're just a filthy rebel, the man that was «just a tracker» shouted. – I curse you. I curse all your descendants!

– No, I'm the one doing the cursing, Damon said with a crushing blow.

Fear supplanted once more the rage. Everyone saw it.

Damon struck out with a fist, striking deep into the man's abdomen. Blood flowed from a wide open mouth.

The man saw what was coming. He knew that neither rhetoric nor anything else could save him, and he crumbled completely, and began moaning in desperate, helpless despair.

– No, no, no… No, no, no, no, no, no, no…

– You aren't that tough now, are you, when you're not dishing out hurt to others.

Damon grabbed an arm and twisted it around. Everyone heard it break. The man's initially loud shout turned into an even louder wail. Damon did the other arm and the legs the same way. He broke them and then twisted them around. WHAT AM I HEARING? The captain howled from the edges of the world. He seemed to actually hear and feel the pain of his most loyal man. The man, the heap on the ground stopped whining after a while. Then, as Damon started kicking him, he started howling in boundless horror.

– WHAT THE HELL IS GOING ON? The captain wailed like a ghost. – WHERE IS ELVIS? WHERE THE HELL IS ELVIS?

The wreck of a human being crouched on the ground.

– You're still awake? Damon kicked him again and again. – Very good! You know I will haunt you forever if you faint, don't you, you worthless shit?

The wreck of a human being on the ground nodded, nodded, nodded. Tears drowned the swollen face.

– *Very* good! You are indeed worthless, not good for anything. You will stay awake just for a little while longer, and it will be over. Do you hear me, you mindless asshole?

The wreck of a human being nodded and nodded and nodded.

The armies of death reached a turn. André fired the bazooka. Yola and Ralph fired a moment later, a double echo of the first. The grenades exploded in the midst of the cluster of soldiers, of flesh and blood and guts and cut-off limbs.

Far away, so close that André could see it in his feverish mind, Damon drew the sword and raised it above his head. It pointed down, at the shaking life form below.

André fired. Yola and Ralph fired. Hands and arms and shoulders were numb already. The body was filled with an energy penetrating everything. Yola and Ralph pulled back from their positions. They glimpsed the scouts in the terrain and knew they would encounter them eventually. André sprinted off, switching position, throwing himself behind another cover and fired. He fired and kept firing. A scout appeared right in front of Yola. She fired several bullets in her chest. Yola heard shots from elsewhere, but they didn't really concern her. She and Ralph ran in a straight, crooked line off the battlefield, what had become one from one moment to the next. The soldiers, the army slowly gathered their wits. The training hammered into them through a thousand hours, thousand eternities of brainwashing ascended. They focused on the attackers, on where the firing was concentrated. Orders were shouted. The soldiers advanced, one, two falling for each step forward. Yola had one final glimpse of André down there. Soldiers surrounded him. Everything happened so fast. The bodies had fallen in heaps around him. One man, she thought. One man did this. André was hit. He kept firing, kept fighting. He threw away empty guns, picking up new as the need arose. He pulled the trigger and kept pulling the trigger, alternately with his left and right hand and eventually, at the end simultaneously.

The very moment André was filled with bullets Damon penetrated the wreck by his feet with the blade. The body shook one single time and stopped moving.

A draft pulled in from all sides struck him. He shouted in pain and triumph.

Heat and cold and everything else struck him. Josh, Claire, Kara and Yngve standing around him felt the power erupting from his being. He felt their heat, pulling it into himself, releasing it again. He saw it, saw the characteristic shadow hovering in the air, recognizing his own face in its dark features.

Then… it *happened!* A sound rose from his throat and he crouched. A film of sweat covered his skin. He stood there heaving with an open mouth.

– Are you alright? Josh asked anxiously.

– He's more than «alright», Kara snarled in contempt. – He's merely taking one more step towards the being he's born to become.

– It hurts, Damon acknowledged, – but it's supposed to. Birth is pain, is release. Being born hurts!

Something was born. It pushed at him from within and made flesh and spirit bleed. He was screaming, and the scream echoed between the mountains, spreading like ripples in the water, something without eyes, flesh and blood, pulsing like a sun, something alive, something growing, living and dying in a never ending cycle.

He felt like he was floating, as if he was rising, and then he experienced himself outside the body, almost removed from it. Where he floated above it, without substance, without form he was able to see himself far below, and he was growing, growing taller than the mountains. Everything faded around him, everything he had known. He no longer saw his body or his friends anymore. There were only the mountains, and then it wasn't even them. He wondered alone through the void forever. But everything he had known was still there, right around him. A light concentration brought it back. He focused on direction, form and time, and found himself between the tents, between the soldiers, their flesh and thoughts, and the Shadow he had become snarled in wrath.

They noticed his presence, even though there was nothing solid, tangible they could point at and say categorically that it was There, and without being able to tell why, they grew sore afraid. What they could neither see nor fathom scared them far more than the physical enemy lurking in the mountainside.

– Anya was right, he, being both here and there told Kara, with a voice sounding like an echo in an empty room. – The Power isn't the same here. Another place, on another Earth, a parallel reality all the dead seething and boiling in me would have given me enormous power. It will grow instead of diminish, but now there are merely nails stuck in the surface, not penetrating very deep below, not quite reaching the infinite awaiting me.

She stared awestruck, fearful at him.

– I HEAR SINGING, a soldier shouted in abject fright. – I CAN HEAR ITS SONG AND IT'S SUCH A HORROR TO BEHOLD!

The smoke, the haze lingered on the battlefield.

– MARTCH ON! The captain commanded. – FULL ALERT, LADIES AND GENTLEMEN, MY PRECIOUS ELVIS'S. THE HUNT IS ON!

The haze faded into red as the soldiers added to their efforts. They fired while running, fired at nothing, at the air screaming back at them, and a pained expression grew in their ragged features. They moved through the terrain as if it was completely alien to them. There was just nothing there being familiar or even known. They chased on, exerting themselves beyond the ability to breathe. Finally, they stopped. They rushed around a turn and *froze*, unable to keep moving, unable to take their eyes off the terrifying sight facing them.

Exactly on the spot where the many tracks split into many smaller, a tree blocked their path. On that tree a piece of meat hardly even resembling a human being stared blindly at nothing. Sticks had been stuck into the tracker's eyes. Poles stuck deep in the tree penetrated his chest and thighs. Blood still flowed into the ground, nourishing the tree and it pulsed in an eerie light and grew as they watched.

The captain stopped. Everyone did. He stood there shaking his head, shaking, shaking, shaking.

– What animals can do a thing like that to another human being? He exclaimed, unable to say more.

He was shaking all over his body. They could see it, how his brittle grip on reality finally flew out of the window and faded away in the air like steam.

– Make camp, he, the dog on two legs barked. – Full alert. They're here, ladies and gentlemen. The hunt is done.

The appearance of confidence in his voice impressed them, or at least comforted them, like it had so many times before, in many a bad moment.

He was bleeding from a scratch on the forehead. The medic rushed forward with bandages, but didn't dare get close, not yet.

– Make camp! Organize squads. We're at *war,* soldiers! This is the Mother of all Wars. This is the war that will end all wars. We're privileged, soldiers.

They worked like sleepwalkers, slowly getting on with it, setting out into the unknown, searching through the terrain piece by piece, returning unsuccessful.

Everyone sat there in the light created by the dancing flames. Tall fires burned during the bright day. Darkness enveloped them like clouds.

– I don't see them. The lieutenant searched the mountains and mountain slopes with her binoculars. – I should be able to.

– Set up double sets of guards, the captain barked. – Set up triple sets!

He placed himself before them, a mighty statue surveying its children.

– SOLDIERS! He began. – We're chasing an enemy well versed in using the terrain to their advantage. We're fighting cowards that will fall facing our superior firepower, our skills and superior morality. This is the test. It's even better, sexier than I imagined. Through our enemies' bloody carcasses we find our validation.

He took a break, while the ashes of his look burned them.

– And more than anything… REMEMBER ALAMO!

– You're bleeding, Yola told Damon, not really worried, but enjoying fussing over him.

– It isn't that bad, he replied, not quite present, still up there, down there. – I think one of the bad guys shot off my earlobe.

She grabbed his hands, squeezing hard the burning skin, kissing it, burning her wet lips.

They moved. All moved around him. He moved around everything.

– We've thrown away everything except small food rations and weapons, he said. – This will be settled quickly. We've created ourselves, become weapons, two-edged swords laid bare and tempered in eternal fire, creatures with many masks, and thus we will live and grow forever.

The groups reunited and parted again, spreading fast as lightning through the battlefield.

The doll still hung on the tree. The captain sat and stared at it. He wished to take it down, wished to let it be. He shook his head.

– What WAS THAT?

He cried suddenly.

– What, captain?

The lieutenant asked the question with a touch of uncertainty in the thin voice.

I saw a shadow move at the edge of the eye. I saw it!

– … a shadow

a soldier whispered.

– What the hell are you saying, soldier? The captain grunted uncannily calm and relaxed. – There are no shadows here. Look around, we've got many fires. The many sources of light cancel the shadows, GOD DAMN IT

Everyone looked anxiously at him. The soldier nodded vigorously.

– It's true what you say, captain, he assured the obviously unstable man, attempting in vain to appear convincing.

There, by the tent. The captain turned around in a whirl of motion. Sweat, more sweat broke on his forehead, adding to the thick layer that was already there, what had long since appeared because of the many tall fires.

The soldiers… stared at him, didn't they, those servile fuckers.
Loud cracks echoed between the mountains. They heard a few short bursts, before silence once more grew ascendant.
The soldiers stared at him. He returned the stare.
The radio cracked, too, suddenly buzzing with activity.
Everyone stared at it.
– YES? He barked.
– We're closing in on a group, captain. At least we think we do. Tracks part and join in an endless cycle up here, but we're getting close. There was a brief exchange of fire. We returned their fire and they ended their attack.
– Those cowards, the captain mumbled. – Cowards, cowards, cowards…
The nightravens met on a mountain ledge, in a cluster of trees close to the divide.
– They're catching up with us, Vladek breathed in front of Damon. – I don't know how long we can keep them away. We didn't wish to lead them here, but we had to warn you. It's a big group, bigger than all of us combined.
– Gathering! Damon declared calmly.
Yngve stared at the mountains.
– We need to get higher up, he said, – gain altitude on them.
But in order to do that they had to cross the valley, the final short and long field.
They ran across the field, ran like the wind, like statues that could hardly stand on their feet.
Damon grabbed the radio he had taken from the tracker. He whispered into its microphone.
The thick smoke lingered in the air. He had never before experienced such thick smoke, but he breathed it like it was air. There was no indication of any coughing, nothing even remotely close to it.
– We're in pursuit of the enemy, captain, the squad leader shouted. – I REPEAT, WE'RE UNDER HEAVY FIRE. WE ARE CLOSE. CONFRONTATION IS IMMINENT!
A loud and violent salvo thundered from every angle.
Myriam and five others hid above the advancing soldiers. They fired, retreated and fired again, delaying the armies of death.
– Damn! She mumbled.
She had been hit again, in the same arm. It hung down, weak and useless. She fired with one hand.
– Get ready to march, the captain commanded.
The Storm Child appeared in their midst. The voice spoke from open air.
– We're like the wind, like the night, like the fire. How can you imagine that you can beat us?
The soldiers glanced around them, desperately attempting to catch the origin of the voice. Then they started shaking, and they couldn't stop.
– S-SPIRITS, a soldier screamed, raising his gun.
The captain slapped him.
– Stop that bullshit. The voice came from the radio, of course. They're fucking with us.
– No, captain another soldier insisted. – The radio is there.
He pointed with a shaking finger.

– And the voice came from…
– … everywhere.
– S-spirits, the stuttering soldier repeated.
He pulled away from the captain with two fast steps, suddenly out of reach of his steel fists. The captain shot him. The soldier fell. In the fall, in death he pulled the trigger of his gun. Several soldiers were hit and fell.
Another soldier started screaming, a piercing wail penetrating everybody's thick hide. The captain struck him down, looking at his men and women with insane eyes.
– SOLDIERS, he shouted with spittle flowing from his mouth, – AT ATTENTION! IGNORE THE VOICES, THE WHISPERS, THE SHADOWS, THE HORRIBLE, HORRIBLE
A gun pointed at his head. A bullet blew away most of his brain. The proud captain fell like a sack of flour.
A woman stood above him with a gun in her hand.
– I've always liked the Beatles the most, the lieutenant mumbled. – And let's not forget that Elvis stole many of his songs from black artists.
She just managed to complete the sentence before she was hit by many bullets, from many angles. Many of the bullets went straight through her and hit soldiers on the other side.
– What the fuck is the MATTER with you? A soldier chuckled and shouted while he fired and kept firing at a cluster of soldiers in front of him. – Why are you FIRING? The enemy isn't here, but over there.
He pulled the trigger and more, many more soldiers fell. He laughed and kept laughing wickedly.
– BEATLES, he shouted in joy. – BEATLES BEATLES BEATLES
The soldiers in pursuit of the enemy froze. Feet drumming at the ground suddenly seemed glued to it. They stared behind them, at where the many bonfires burned, staring at each other as if they couldn't quite believe their eyes.
After a prolonged period of silence, the squad leader said with a shaky voice.
– Beatles?
– That's just as good as anything else, sergeant, the closest soldier shrugged.
Damon stopped for a moment. He turned his head and looked at the bloodied battlefield and mountainsides where soldiers lay in heaps. He saw his own, irrational hope mirrored in the others' eyes. He raised a hand. Everyone stopped.
Myriam and her squad appeared from the dark. Vladek shook his head while laughing hysterically.
The Children of the Midnight Fire met at the base of the eastern mountains, where the road with the many turns started rising. They looked uncertain, incredulous at each other, as if they couldn't quite believe their good fortune. It dawned on them slowly, the certainty that they would survive, survive and thrive and Live.
They looked behind them one last time.
For some reason they focused on a single house, the last house, more floating on the surface than standing on the shaky sandbank. It was derelict beyond belief, its walls crumbling as they watched. A flock of birds had made it their nest, crowding the roof, proudly proclaiming their domain.
The surviving uniformed puppets, at the heights and the many campfires stood and

stared at each other with blind eyes. They stood completely still. It looked like they would keep doing so, until wild animals would come and devour whatever remained.
The remains of the armies of death, the scarecrows hung where they had stopped, on invisible gallows.
All of them were easy to spot, where they stood frozen, in silhouette against the rust of dawn, on the living Earth.

CHAPTER TWENTY-FIVE

They spotted more of the soldiers from their ever higher position in the terrain. Many of the uniformed wrecks had sat down on the ground. Several of them had thrown away their weapons. Those not sitting stood still, like statues slowly crumbing. They died there and then, without visible wounds
– Keep an eye on them, Damon commanded. – Don't let them out of your sight, not for a moment.
But after a while they did, allowing themselves to relax.
The Forgotten Valley disappeared behind them. The armies of death faded from their vision, from their immediate memory, delegated to the nightmares of a long forgotten past.
Life finally resumed.
The females stared at him. The three of them had approached him without him noticing. The lusty bitches.
– My bleeding didn't come yesterday, or the day before yesterday, or the day before that, for that matter.
Myriam smiled brightly to him. He attempted to focus on the sight of the fresh blood on her white bandage, but what he saw of red was the dance in the depth of her eyes.
Time passed. Damon waited with infinite patience, fully aware that everyone had heard Myriam's statement.
– I puked my guts out today. Gwen enlightened him, as she rushed to his side. – It was the most extreme morning sickness I've ever felt.
– You've never felt morning sickness before, Yola pointed out.
– Neither have you!
The laughter came easy and they smiled half embarrassed, half challenging to each other. It felt good to be alive. They felt the beyond potent joy of living on in every erg of their being.
The road stretched an eternity before them.
– Everything is just ashes, Maxine said. – Everything is ruins.
– Good riddance! Damon spat with a huge, pleased grin.
New life was coming, while the old faded. It felt good, felt great beyond great.
The final ash died down there. The flames rose from the ruined tents.
– The new barbarians have finally come home, Claire said. – There's reason for celebration. Humanity has returned from its long exile.

She quietly approached him. He looked at her. She reddened.
– You haven't used your medicine since Voss, she said.
– No! He shook his head.
– And you haven't been coughing, not the slightest. And there have been many times where you would have… before.
– The air and the smoke slip like velvet through my throat, he said cheerfully, pensively.
His smile, their smile wasn't that exactly, not like their former, limited perception of it, but something that didn't just transform their faces, but their entire being.
Roger Norlund walked with light steps up the steep mountainside. He didn't have to turn in order to look behind, not raise his eyes in order to look ahead.
Claire treated Yarath's wounded arm as they walked, as they moved.
– It doesn't look that bad, she remarked, – but heavy lifting is out for a while, understand.
– As you wish, Stumbles, Yarath said.
– Stumbles? Claire inquired nonplussed.
– It's your name, your name shortened, isn't it? It's certainly better and more practical than to call you She Who Stumbles in the Forest.
Claire chuckled. She had long since grown comfortable with her old insecurities.
Heimdal's Bugle was still blowing. It would keep doing so for a long, long time.
They pulled further up the steep terrain, instinctively, before once again glancing back down at the road and landscape covered by seawater far below, the gray belt, all the houses now only habitable to fishes, an invisible ghost from a bygone era.
Damon Terrill, walking in front looked behind him. The tribe he led consisted of many colors, many origins, a fact pleasing him immensely. He knew it made life more interesting and also improved their chances for survival.
He looked up. Somewhere up there, beyond all the tunnels and turns the land would start leveling. Far below, in the valley they could still glimpse the smoke from the dying campfires, the red haze in the air. The warriors of the Twilight Storm walked forward with light steps as they once and for all left the past behind.
The plains up there stretched like infinity before them. They knew that up here they were only one group of many…
And that pleased them as well.
People, human beings of all races and cultures strived, lived and died in the land the ancient Germans had called Norwegir - the road north.

Author's word - 2016

This is coming full circle for me.

This, my second longest novel was originally completed in 2002, and it was ready for publication not long afterwards. I was very pleased with that version and still am for that matter.

But I still know that I am taking it many steps beyond that as I translate and expand upon it. The narrative flow is much better. Fourteen years have passed, and I have learned even more and experienced so much more, and I can add bits and pieces from my later experiences as I go, and also change the overall story slightly, moving it towards something that is even closer to my original vision.

It is the same story, but this is a different book, really.

Looking at it, it's amazing everything I see now that I didn't see then.

This is one of my third generation novels, unlike the fourth generation I'm currently writing.

A lot of new knowledge has also been added about the human created climate change, even though I'm also pretty pleased about how the first version was in predicting the future. I and other people and scientists were right and those taking the cautious approach in their predictions were wrong: Reality, what is actually happening is far worse than those early official predictions.

The story of the novel culminates in 2015, but that's mostly due to its connection with Dreams Belong to the Night and its internal timeline. The story should be seen to take place «a few years from now».

Most of what is described in the book has already happened in real life, though. Only the last few, decisive events have yet to occur.

Dreams Belong to the Night was never meant to be the end of it. «Dreams» is about people challenging tyranny head on. This one is about them vanquishing it.

I made a thorough study of Bergen before and during the writing of the story, studying old and new maps and noticing how far each spot was above the current sea level, stuff like that and more. It's amazing to make such a study of a city I've known since birth, and realize that there was a lot I didn't know. My recent photo walkabouts also added to that.

One curious fact is that the length of chapters varies dramatically. Usually, in other books they're close to the same length.

I took the cover photograph for the book in 1987 and instantly knew its distant future value, and it was indeed one of several images in my head when I started formulating the story in the early nineties . I've had it as my desktop background for almost two decades.

At least three of my poems, The Twilight Storm, Caravan and Ragnarok also served as templates for the writing.

I had originally planned two more books in the series. Then I decided I would never do them, that I would give my other books and projects priority instead, but while redoing this one, the desire to do the rest of the story has re-emerged. Sigh...

Excitement grew as I approached the ending of this book.

This is not a warning. It's a celebration. Civilization is collapsing and the characters, the author and the aware readers are all doing the happy dance. It's cold, hard reality, not a fairytale, but still an optimistic story, exactly because humanity says a roaring NO to what has oppressed us all for so long.

This story clearly differs significantly from other collapse stories. There's nothing of the usual praise for what is Going Away, but on the contrary a pure joy of what is returning to human life.

«In the embers of the century, we are drawn to a glow. We crave the white heat of technology, while our hearts are growing cold». Tilda Swinton - Visions of heaven and hell - UK Channel Four 1994

Völuspá - the poetic Edda - two interpretations:

I recall of giants from primordial times.
Those who gave me birth in former days:
Nine worlds I can reckon, nine huge expanses,
And the glorious tree of the world, deep under the ground

I tell of giants from times forgotten.
Those who fed me in former days:
Nine worlds I can reckon, nine roots of the tree.
The wonderful ash, way under the ground

WHY PARTICIPATE IN THE RUIN OF CREATION WHEN YOU CAN PARTICIPATE IN THE CREATION OF RUINS?

Earth First slogan

They say that those living by the sword will die by the sword, and there is something to that, inevitably, since the chances of dying early are certainly increasing. I'm certainly not romanticizing anything here.

But those same people don't say much about what will happen to people not living by the sword, not wielding a sharp blade when it's called for, when it's desperately needed.

Today, today, it's desperately needed, not by the meek soldier, the eager puppet of tyranny, but by the true warrior, by those using any available and unavailable weapon or given method in order to end tyranny, by those hungering for freedom beyond words, beyond reason, by those eager to see all tyrannies crumble to dust, by those burning by a desire to see the entire, irredeemable current human society be washed away, until only its ashes remain.

Passion, one almost consuming you, one mostly lacking in those seeking peace no matter the price, is burning in those living and dying by the sword...

Peace is for the grave, a pipe and wrong dream, and will only rarely touch the warrior in twilight.

Somewhere, somewhen a hand shaking in fire is picking up the bloodstained blade.

Amos Keppler
April 1, 1994 - August 22, 2002
215. night 12057
In the second year in the time of the Twilight Storm

Revision of story and English translation
December 29, 2010 - June 20, 2016
181. night 12071
In the sixteenth year in the time of the Twilight Storm

Printed version ready August 15, 2016
Final proofreading complete November 17, 2016

Appendix 1
TUMOR (CANCER CELL)

The Tumor, civilization itself, isn't just making our physical self sick, it's also destroying our spirit, the Fire inside.

10.000 years ago, a moron - or a group of morons - decided to go to war against the Planet. This unacceptable situation has continued until this day.

10.000 years ago, we humans were hunter/gatherers and nomads. We moved our camp and often sought new grounds. It was a necessity, but it also gave us variety and spice in our lives. Travels were encouraged. Diversity was a preferred way of living. Then... something happened. Maybe it happened overnight or it evolved over a longer period of time. Who can tell? The final(?) result was that we got stuck in permanent residences.

There were about five million human individuals at the time. That's too much. There wasn't enough game for the human beast anymore. Of course, the «chosen» solution made some sense there and then when they couldn't, as we can today, look at the terrible consequences.

I don't know where the first city was located. Nobody knows. One of the first is called Catal Hoyuk; and was built on the plains of Konya in present-day Turkey. It precedes the communities in Eufrat and Tigris, Mesopotamia, with several thousand years. It was indeed the cradle of civilization.

It is unimportant. The important thing is the result, the result we keep struggling with today.

There have been some archeological digs inside and close to Catal Hoyuk. The most important about them is the evolving of the exposed gravesites. In archeology gravesites are seen as very important indications on how people lived. In the oldest graves there are no significant differences in how the dead was buried. But after 500 years or so, there was a major change. A few people are buried with an increasing number of distinctions. More weapons, finer clothes, more women etc. We see a distinct difference between chiefs and other tribe members. Women were increasingly seen as a commodity, not as an equal partner.

The Disease started with a few scattered settlements. We lost the Freedom. We lost our minds, we lost our spirit. Not with the use of the first fence, but with the first wall. There are people today claiming that agriculture is capable of feeding more people with less energy. More and more people are fortunately beginning to disagree with them. What is becoming more and more evident is that while most people today are working eight hours a day on average to survive, many hunter tribe members, don't need more than two hours a day on the average. «Pure» agriculture communities are somewhat in-between. Another lie of civilization exposed.

But even if the claim about feeding was true... There are those who claim this to be beneficial, but I reject such a foolish notion. We can't look at life from the isolated and narrow perspective of the twentieth century. I *refuse* to do that.

Agriculture made us resident, it made us stuck. And «able» to stay resident, we built cities. To stay resident in the cities we expanded the agriculture. To expand the agriculture we expanded the cities...

We became *dependent* on our environment instead of being an integral part of it. Crafts, specialization developed, and as a result the hierarchy appeared. From the top gods, priests, kings, aristocrats, craftsmen, workers, thralls, slaves. People began to toil under the gods, under the burden. They begged for more rain, less rain, more crops, etc. They begged. And they began to fear the generous and merciless nature. And it became more distant century by century. Priests interpreted increasingly the will of the gods.

«In the beginning the fear created the gods».
(*Genesis 6:6.6*)

In this first era of The City, it had clear advantages over the surroundings when it came to survival, and not the least, propagation. More children was born, more children grew up. More and more tools were made. The City grew ever bigger.

Until it grew too big. And all the crops, all the grain, the nearby fields could give, were no longer enough. Families and groups began to move out and away from the city. Those without major means, the lowest of rank within and without families. Or a high ranking official sent out to clear new land. «Catal Hoyuk's» influence spread across The Earth. The first city or the first cities may have created ten copies of itself during this first, critical cycle. Or maybe just two or three. Anyway, it was enough. The original ruled the outgrowths. A while. It did not last long, before the rivaling did start. Quarrels about land, about influence, about Power... The overgrown tribes started their first, destructive wars. Better weapons were developed. The group/tribe who made and/or possessed weapons that killed the highest number of enemies most efficiently won the war, and expanded its influence over land and people. The losers, if they survived, were made slaves or they escaped far away and built their own cities, their own kingdoms. Determined to once upon a time make their own tribe bigger, deadlier and more powerful than the Enemy Mine they had run away from. New land was «cleared» and less untouched Earth remained.

The hunt for new land has continued to this day, when there is no more land left.

A malignant tumor will always attempt to recreate itself. It represents a system *other* than the established organism and will ever seek to undermine it. But it's not a life form in a traditional sense. It doesn't compete with other species about survival in a given environment, but instead it degenerates and eventually destroys its natural environment, what it needs to survive. Once it has established itself within an organism it spreads like wildfire and destroys everything in its way. These scenarios are however far from being totally comparable, because a fire can be seen as nature's way of clearing way for new life. Cancer only leaves unfruitful ashes. It breaks down, destroys the host organism. And by this its own chance for life. It probably doesn't know why, doesn't know how. It just happens. And it expires in a despairing, intelligible death rattle. The reason why it behaves as such an utterly and complete idiot is hidden in its remote and forgotten past. It cannot halt its disastrous journey. It doesn't know how.

We can see it all of us. Easily. Easiest from the air, of course. The Tumors strangle the landscape, like a gray, poisonous mass. Between each tumor we can see the interconnected lines, lines of Stone Desert stretching in every direction and the moving coffins transporting corrupted material between the hungry pits.

Call our societies anthills. It's not (unfortunately) an altogether wrong comparison. We obey commands from central command systems. We obey eagerly and with a certain twisted ingenuity. Their purpose is ours. And their purpose is total insanity. We know this inside, and we know it well, but we do nothing about it. Nothing that has much purpose. Of course, there is nothing inherently wrong with anthills or with ants for that matter... *but we're not ants!* If there is a leader ant sitting somewhere, hiding in plain sight, then the person concerned is obviously totally nuts, completely off its guard. And we follow its orders, until death and destruction, all our days.

Yes, people, we have most certainly made our bed.

It's about time now, to behave like the sophisticated, intelligent species we claim we are. We know what we are not. We are not sheep that without a single independent thought let ourselves be driven off the cliff. In the midnight fire we know what we are. We are, quite simply, human. We should begin to behave like human beings again. Soon. If not, there will very soon be only an anthill left. An anthill...

Or a cancer cell tumor.

Appendix 2
THE CAVES OF DOOM

Civilization has spawned its final knights...

Bill Joy, the Sun System's co-founder and one of the IT-pioneers, is very worried. About the future, about mankind's place in it. Some years ago he wrote an article in the magazine Wired, entitled «Why the future doesn't need us.» In the article he is stating three areas of scientific development in the 21st century, Nanotechnology (smart, microscopic machines), Genetic Engineering and Robotics (GNR), that single-handedly or in unison may spell the end of the human species.

He's just worried, of course, nothing more. He doesn't really believe it will happen, just that it might, if we're not careful. The good scientist isn't really probing very deep in the matter. The article is more of a discussion of possible consequences, an illumination of problem areas to be solved, than an attack on technology, civilization itself.

This article isn't so much about Joy really, as much as his «opposite number» Hans Moravec. Moravec is the true techno guru. He isn't only stating that the transformation from human to cyborg or even machine is inevitable, but also desirable. Humans are obsolete, he says, in the brave new world...

Nanotechnology, Genetic Engineering and Robotics (GNR) has one thing in common, not possible for other, previous human suicidal creations like the atomic bomb: They can easily replicate themselves in vast numbers. Beyond a certain point, of no return, they can breed completely independently of human «aid». This is in fact, the very foundation of the three of them, the center point of their intended «benefits»; that they can create completely independent self-sufficient systems. It's one step further, perhaps the final step in our tailspin suicidal run. One thing is what individuals can do with the technology. Another far more grave aspect is what society itself can do with it. It doesn't really have to spiral out of control, as such. As all technology it will immerse itself into the world, and it will conquer it, but on a scale never before seen. There are a lot of possible, probable scenarios, where the inventions completely overtake their inventors.

We have the doomsday, terminator scenario, of course, just as probable as the others, where a conscious, self-aware mechanical entity or a host of entities see humanity as their enemy and decide to exterminate it.

But this isn't really the most likely scenario. The most likely is, in short, what happens today, a humanity slowly, inevitably undermining its own footing, making itself obsolete. Every possible nightmare, imagined by science-fiction writers, is finally possible.

I, myself, find more and more common characteristics with Holocaust, the German genocide of Jews during World War 2, and current human society. It was a slow process really. First the Jews were terrorized, than collected, than skipped on trains, gathered in camps, made to build the camps, digging trenches, later to be revealed to be graves, to be instrumental in their own extermination. The difference is, of course, that no one is doing it to us. There's no outside force engineering our genocide. We are doing it... to ourselves.

Moravec is «right».

Moravec and people like him, (who among other things, want to freeze their own brain upon death), aren't really the world's decision-makers. They're just enjoying excellent working conditions in this modern world of ours. Like Doctor Mengele, the infamous death-camp scientist, they're merely taking advantage of the situation as it presents itself and is able and willing to excel in it. In many ways, they're the ultimate sycophants. In a world of followers, they're an expression of the sheep-mentality so prevalent among the present day humanity.

There aren't really any decision-makers...

There is one knight in each of the three Caves of Doom, waiting to save us, save us from Nature, save us from everything from the common cold to a bleeding finger. Three more knights in a long row, but these three may very likely be the ultimate culprits. Yes, the noble knights are always at hand... Our only hope is that the dragons can slay them, slay them all, before it's too late.

Throughout the «rise» of civilization, bad as that has been, there have always existed possibilities for saying «no», (even if the dynamics of such an act more are suggesting a return to the wilderness through a *temporary* doomsday scenario) and return our birthright of the Wild to ourselves. That possibility, and even the possibility of Life at all, is approaching a point of No Return.

The Final Surrender, Submission (to The Machine) is at hand. As it stands humanity has set itself up nicely, «to go silently into the night». Go, not with a cry, but with a whimper.

Appendix 3
Brink - The Sixth Great Mass Extinction Event is here and it's us

When is a given species in most danger? At the top of its dominion of a given ecosystem.

Humanity currently dominates, with a few exceptions, directly of indirectly virtually all ecosystems on this planet.

Once again, we get to know for ourselves the obvious truth that civilization is organized insanity. This isn't a matter of doing some limited «conservation» or fixing a few problems concerning release of pollution like climate gases or poisonous chemicals. It's about human society, about civilization itself. What has been more than obvious for a long time has recently become even more so: It must go!

Rachel Carson with her book Silent Spring made a splash with its stark warnings about human produced chemicals more than fifty years ago, but it didn't really make an impact, not even approaching one necessary in order to deal with the issue at hand.

The dire warnings about global warming have been with us for at least twenty-five years now, but even though we talk a little about it, there is no real impact on our society. Even if virtually all solutions currently on the public table are implemented it will do us little good.

Nuclear power plants continue to bombard all life on the planet with the deadliest poison in existence.

We are screwing with life and nature on all levels. Frankenstein products, like genetic modified organisms, are numerous and pervasive, their proponents wealthy and influential, with all mainstream politicians in their pockets.

And now, these days we get the beyond dire warnings of the final nail in our coffin, the facts about what we have wrought.

There has been some limited debate whether or not the Sixth Great Mass Extinction is on its way or already is here. Now, more and more reports make it clear that the latter is true. The report, led by the universities of Stanford, Princeton and Berkeley in the United States confirms and exceeds the findings in earlier studies. Vertebrates are disappearing at a rate at least 114 times normal. The species going extinct in the last century would have normally taken thousands of years to do so, and would probably not have without humanity's pervasive dominion. The total loss of biodiversity is a reality and is fast approaching an irreversible state that will take nature millions of years to recover from.

The culprit is human civilization, is practically everything we, humanity are currently doing and humanity is also one of the species that will go early, in about hundred years or so. «Conservation» is a joke and has always been. We save one or two tigers, for instance while the species are heading for extinction, and we do nothing about the actual cause. And as stated; this isn't about a few species, but about all of them, except perhaps cockroaches and similar.

If we manage to kill off the cockroach, one of the most adaptive creatures on Earth, there is really no hope for us.

We are destroying the foundation of our own survival. Urban «development», destruction of ever more wilderness, habitats and the ever-stronger level of pollution and chemicals soaking ecosystems are choking all life. We seek cheaper and «cleaner» energy, but don't realize that it's the use of energy that must go way down, not the access to energy that must go way up.

To make it totally clear: the extinction isn't due to a few limited factors, but to the beyond excessive presence of humans on the planet and our equally excessive capacity and penchant for destruction. Our tools become ever more «improved and effective». A small group of humans can remove a given large forest or destroy huge chunks of wilderness with a snap of fingers, and that has happened countless times. Such groups are numerous and widespread, are everywhere, really. Advanced technology can not help us. Advanced technology is a huge part of what got us into this mess and a major part of the vast wrongness surrounding us. The claim that what is causing the problem can help solving it is definitely yet another proof of the ongoing insanity. The massive priorities of our totally unsustainable society are pushing all other life forms out. The depopulation of all life, along with all the other factors threatens our own survival in countless and massive ways. «Our way of life» is horrendously wrong. We have long since become like a cosmic disaster, a force of unparalleled horror and devastation in this world.

To repeat: all current human activity is grossly unsustainable. Civilization itself must go if we want to survive as a species.

You think this is pessimistic and/or drastic? Then, quite frankly you are just one more dangerous idiot refusing to acknowledge reality.

One more concern, among many is that even if humanity returns to being hunter/gatherers, like we should, there won't be enough left of nature and wildlife, making our changes of surviving even slimmer. The longer we wait, the less likely our survival.

Human society is going in the wrong direction, in all areas, going from bad to worse to horrible with practically everything we do, with every new act and «invention», bringing us ever closer to the brink.

We don't need more capitalism, more inequality, more injustice, more «free trade», more technology, more destruction of lives and nature, but that's where we are heading. We are headed for a totally unprecedented destruction, a tailspin collective suicide run of our own making. We are fading, heading for death with a pitiful whimper, and we're taking life on Earth with us.

Chemical Cocktail

Supplement: Stolen future, past, present,
all of the above.

It is said in an ironic tone of voice by some enlightened, cynical scientists, that today we live inside a giant, manmade laboratory. Live through a giant, mindless experiment. A lot of ingredients are recklessly thrown in and we don't dare imagine the result. Most of these ingredients are poisons, used in some misunderstood notion, in order to protect humanity from the harsh environment Nature offers.

Some years ago there were several works published where the writers were very aware of this and similar subjects. Including articles published in Nature and a book aptly entitled Our Stolen Future. Complementing former published books on the subject, among them a book even more aptly called Silent Spring, written in the early sixties. There was some initial uproar as some attention was paid to the presented information, but typically, as always, the public interest quickly faded.

The articles, books and studies dealt with the effect long term influence of environmental estrogens have on human flesh and also, ultimately, on human behavior.

Basically, it goes like this:

We start life as female. All of us. Then the natural influx of testosterone in male fetuses changes them in the way predetermined by the genetic code. This development is blocked and sometimes reversed by influence of a special kind of pollutants ever more often called environmental estrogens. It may cause children «meant to be» male to be born female. A simple chromosome screening determines that the child who looks like and is a girl in all outward ways, is «supposed to be» male. In others, not so extreme cases, it causes changes in the hormone release and early changes in the brain, making us more docile, less wild. More likely to accept what's being done to us. In fact if I were most people I would have questioned every, single decision I've ever made, especially those concerning obedience toward authorities. I'm not suggesting that all sheep mentality has a chemical cause, far from it, only that it contributes to it.

Females, by the way, are not much better off, if at all. One of the more pronounced effects of the unnatural, chemical society we're born into, is an enormous increase in cancer cases. Especially brain tumors among children seem to have exploded in recent years.

Besides, there are chemicals making females grow male organs, among them a compound of ship paint.

It has always been claimed and assumed by those in power that environmental estrogens are a much weaker agent than those naturally produced by the body. This is true, as far as it goes.

One type of «environmental» estrogen is exactly as weak and inactive as was supposed. The dramatic change comes into effect when there is present a mix of agents, a chemical «cocktail» of estrogenic and other pollutants. When two or more in itself «weaker» chemicals are influencing an individual, their sum of the parts is far more potent and far more dangerous than each single ingredient should indicate. And as usual humanity as a whole remains clueless.

Dreams Belong to the Night

New, emerging urban rebel guerilla groups, freedom fighters, called terrorists by enraged authorities are overwhelming Europe.

What is, in truth terrorism? Who does it to whom?
How much can a human being take of bondage, injustice, degradation and destruction of spirit... before being fed up?

Present day society is a wound not closing.
In a modern world society destroying everything making life worth living there are those, who, through coincidence and fate, have decided not to take it anymore.
And as they are making that decision, together and as individuals, they are also starting on a journey, a journey back to humanity's roots.
Judith, Sivert, Kim, Willhelm, Anya and many more.
A handful of people against an entire world.

This is their story...

ISBN 978-82-91693-11-8